BORN TO FIGHT

ISBN: 9798665729589

Published July 12, 2020

by BookBreeze.com LLC

Written by: Jay J. Falconer

CHAPTER 1

Jack Bunker leaned his head back against the padded headrest of the Amtrak train as it chugged its way higher through Rocky Mountain countryside.

He kept his eyes turned to the right and focused on the colorful tapestry rolling past the passenger window, knowing all the while that a pair of piercing blue eyes was locked onto his face by the fidgeting young boy sitting across from him.

The stare-down began an hour ago, when an attractive soccer mom and her redheaded son decided to share the adjoining seat in the sightseeing car.

Bunker didn't blame the kid. Curiosity was part of a young person's nature, especially when confronted with a tall stranger wearing playing-card-sized bandages across both sides of his neck.

Fortunately, Bunker's long-sleeve t-shirt covered up his chest, back, and arms, keeping his self-indulgent political statements hidden from the rest of the planet.

If Bunker had to guess, he'd estimate the inquisitive boy was around ten years old. The freckles across his cheeks and nose may have been thin, but his weight was a tad thick.

"Excuse me, Mister. What does that mean?" the kid asked, pointing at the three tattooed letters on Bunker's knuckles. "What's B-T-F?"

The kid's mother—a pretty, voluptuous blonde woman in her late 20s—didn't interject or stop the intrusion, so Bunker decided to answer the lad.

"It means Born To Fight. Something my dad used to say to me when I was about your age."

"Did it hurt when your dad put those letters on your hand?"

"No, son. I had those letters tattooed on when I joined the Marines. I did it to honor my father's memory after he passed away."

"I think I want some letters, too," the boy said, swinging his eyes up to his mother, who was seated next to him.

She didn't answer her son, seemingly more interested in the iPad sitting on her lap. Ever since she'd sat down, her cell phone never seemed to stop chiming from yet another text message.

Working her technology was keeping her too busy to notice his obvious cover-up with the bandages, or her son's questions.

Yet, she wasn't the only one who was distracted. Most of the other rail riders had their eyes focused on the countryside streaming past the windows at a steep incline, or had their heads buried in their portable tech, too.

Bunker wondered what the rest of the passengers would think if they knew who they were traveling with. It had been two months of off-the-radar wandering since he'd left behind his past and went in search of a new life. So far, he hadn't found what he was looking for, but at least his jet-black hair had made a full comeback, resuming its sweeping fullness.

He'd almost forgotten what it was like to have something to comb after running bald for what seemed like forever. He planned to keep it simple by slicking it straight back, at least for now.

Next up, he needed to find a new, stress-free life that would match his simple hairstyle. He wasn't sure where he was going when he'd got on this train, but he figured he'd know it once he arrived.

When you start a fresh journey into the unknown, it helps to allow random luck to select your path. If not, then you run the risk of letting old habits and burnt-in thought patterns influence the decision-making process. When that happens, it increases the chances of falling right back into the same swirl of discontent from which you are trying to escape.

At least, that's what he hoped for himself by letting fate guide him to this place and time. His decision to find a new life started with an off-the-books name change and the selling of his most prized asset for cash, clothes, and a few supplies, most of which were stuffed into an army surplus duffel bag stowed in the overhead bin. He'd gone minimalist by shedding most of what made him, him. At least the old him. Hopefully, this reboot would change everything.

He had been walking the back roads mostly, though he'd caught a few rides from generous strangers who'd stopped to see if he needed any help. He didn't have his thumb out hitchhiking, nor was he asking for help. They just stopped on their own to make sure he was okay, and that surprised him. And gave him hope for the cesspool known as society.

Two months of mostly anonymous travels had taught him a few things already. One of which was that when you immerse yourself in the reality of rural, off-the-radar living, you can actually feel the difference in the atmosphere around you. Not just with the crystal clean air entering your lungs, but in the way the air cradles your soul, allowing you to absorb a more casual, free lifestyle through the pores in your skin.

"Excuse me, sir," the slender yet curvy woman with the plunging neckline said, finally speaking up after leaning forward and touching his forearm from across the gap between the seats.

He kept his eyes in check, even though her abundance of cleavage was screaming at him to look down.

"Yes," he said, giving her a thin smile and a quick nod. He didn't want to have a conversation with anyone at the moment, but if he was going to become a new and improved version of himself, then it was time to engage the rest of civilization. Like any normal person would.

"Do you happen to know when we're supposed to pull into the Denver station?" she asked.

"I'm guessing about two hours, give or take. Gonna take a while to climb some of these hills. They're pretty steep. You can really hear the engine chugging now."

"Two hours? I don't think my bladder is going to hold out that long."

He wondered why she didn't know the schedule already. Unless she relocated from another seat on the train, he assumed she'd just gotten on the train at the previous stop. Maybe she was in a hurry when she purchased the ticket and didn't have a chance to memorize the stops. "You do realize there's a head at the rear of the car, right? No reason to hold it."

"Yeah, I know. But have you seen it? It's a unisex bathroom and it's disgusting. No offense, but you men can't seem to ever hit what you aim at. Especially my ex-husband. He was the worst. I swear he did it on purpose, just to push my buttons."

Bunker nodded. She was right. Most of the men on the planet were pigs, and on so many levels. The least of which was spraying the seat when taking a leak.

If she only knew the kind of men Bunker used to run with, then she'd truly understand what constituted an asshole and a disgusting bathroom. The shitter at his last job was biblical. Talk about ripe.

When a series of memory flashes from his past decided to dance front and center in his mind, he couldn't help but offer up a smirk.

The woman's eyes lit up with energy after she leaned her head back. "Just once, I'd like to walk into a shared bathroom and not have to bring a stack of wipes and can of Lysol with me. I mean seriously, is that too much to ask?"

He wanted to verbally agree with her, but before he could think of something clever to say, the overhead lights in the car blinked out and the train began to slow. The only light in the train car was the sunlight beaming in through the windows.

"That's weird," she said, flashing a look of confusion. The woman fiddled with the iPad screen, then checked her cell phone. "How could both of them be dead?"

"Mine too, Mommy," the boy added, holding up his videogame unit in front of her eyes.

When the kid turned it around, Jack realized it wasn't a game after all. It was an educational system with a blank screen in the center and a series of raised, multiple choice buttons across the bottom. The stamped metal nameplate at the top said *Frankie's Science Lab.*

Bunker turned his eyes from the kid's device and ran a quick visual survey of the passengers with electronics in his vicinity. Each of them looked to be either confused or concerned.

He heard a smattering of "what the hell?", "stupid battery", and "this cell phone never works right" comments, plus a few other, more colorful phrases that the young boy across from him should not have heard.

The locomotive continued to slow until it came to a complete stop, thanks to the steep incline and the pull of gravity.

"You've got to be kidding me," a portly man with a bad comb-over job said from Bunker's left, throwing up his hands in disgust. His wrinkled pinstripe suit and loose-fitting tie screamed businessman heading home to Denver. "My wife is going to be pissed. She hates it when I make her wait at the terminal."

"I wonder if they stopped for something on the tracks, sis," an elderly woman said. She was sitting with a woman who looked like her twin. Both of them were in their 80s and sporting scarves, sweaters, saggy skin, and liver-spotted cheeks.

The woman's sister spun her head and said, "I don't think so, Dolores. Why would the power be out?"

"Don't you remember, Dottie? That's what happened last year on our Alaskan cruise when the engines quit."

"Yes, I remember. Their generators went down when the engine stopped."

Bunker stood up in a flash and stepped into the center aisle. Something was nagging at him to head to the engine room and see what was happening.

"Where are you going?" the blonde woman asked, still seated.

He wasn't sure why she was asking since it wasn't any of her business, but he decided not to be rude. "I gotta go check on something."

"Can I go with him, Mommy?"

"No, Jeffrey. Little boys don't go off with men they don't know. Remember what I told you about stranger danger?"

"Yeah, but I wanna go see, Mom."

"No honey, it's best if you stay here with me. Where it's safe."

"Geez, ever since you kicked Dad out, I never get to do anything fun."

Bunker was about to turn for the exit, but something caught his eye outside. High in the sky and banking left was a commercial airliner. He could see the entire spread of its mighty wingspan, soaring like a metal eagle in search of prey.

It was moving slower than expected and dropping in altitude. The turn looked to be controlled, but the speed of its descent was much too fast. The hairs on the back of his neck started to tingle. Something was wrong. He could feel it.

He checked, but didn't see any sign of smoke trailing behind it. Nor was there any indication of a mid-air collision in the sky around it.

While the stark white plane continued its steep turn, he ran a quick trajectory check of its course. A second later he realized it was headed straight for them, on an apparent intercept vector with the train.

"Get down!" he shouted to the passengers in the car. "Get down, now!"

Heads turned and a few people flinched, but nobody took his advice.

Bunker pointed out the window. "There's a plane headed right for us!"

The blonde and the friendly boy he was sitting with whipped their heads around and looked out the window. The woman screamed but never took her eyes from airplane headed right for them.

Bunker grabbed her with one hand and the kid with the other, pulling them both to the deck. He covered their bodies and then looked around at the other passengers.

Many of them were now on the floor as well, covering their heads with their hands. A few were still in their seats, their minds unable to reconcile what their eyes were reporting. Some passengers were screaming hysterically, while others looked frozen in time and unable to move.

He waited for the roar of the jetliner's engines to reach his ears, but it never came. Instead, a massive explosion rang out as the floor beneath them began to shake violently. It felt like an earthquake and the ground tremors were intensifying.

The thunderous sound of twisting metal dwarfed the passengers' cries and screams, leading him to believe a massive fireball was headed their way next. Soon they'd all be sprayed with jet fuel, burning alive in a metal coffin built for fifty.

When the windows shattered, he sucked in a breath and held it, figuring he'd just taken his last breath.

CHAPTER 2

When the deafening noise and bone-rattling vibrations stopped, Bunker let out the breath he'd been holding.

Somehow, he was still alive. So, too, were the mother and son cowering beneath him. He could feel the pounding of their heartbeats and heaving of their chests against his skin.

The train car was all quiet and so was the countryside, even with the windows blown out. It was as if the entire planet was in shock and rendered mute. Even the ear-splitting screams and desperate cries for God's help had vanished, replaced with stunned silence.

He raised his head and looked around. There was glass everywhere as the wind whistled through the passenger car. But the train was still upright and on its wheels. Everyone looked to be alive and there wasn't any blood that he could see. A miracle, to be sure.

"Are we dead?" the blonde woman asked, uncoiling her arms from around her son.

"Unbelievably . . . no," Bunker answered before rolling his two-hundred-plus pounds off of his seatmates. "Are you two okay?"

They both nodded, but their teary faces told a different story. All four eyes were wide and showing an excess of white, looking like Jesus himself had just paid them a visit and touched their souls.

"How are we still alive?" Blondie asked.

"I don't know. I was sure that plane was headed straight at us."

"It sounded like it crashed right outside," she added. "I thought we were all going to die."

"Maybe the pilot turned at the last second when he saw us," the boy interjected, pushing the words through his trembling lips. "I've read about pilots doing that to try to save people on the ground."

"Maybe," Bunker said, crawling to his feet. "I'll go check."

He made his way down the aisle, turning sideways and pushing past a half-dozen passengers who were standing and milling about.

Some of them looked lost and confused, while others were pawing at their cell phones with wobbly hands and pale faces, trying to get the screens to come on. There were plenty of tears visible and a few hugs being exchanged, but nobody was actively crying.

He slid the door open at the end of the car and stepped outside, making his way down a set of metal steps. Three steps later, his feet found the gravel base surrounding the train tracks below.

The hairs on the back of his neck began to tingle as if he'd just felt a chill, even though the sun was in the throes of a midday burn.

He changed his focus and scanned the length of the train cars ahead. All of them seemed to be intact. However, behind a thick stand of trees on the left was a huge plume of black smoke furling into the nearly cloudless sky.

There weren't any flames that he could see, or heat for that matter. But he could definitely smell the fire thanks to the stiff breeze smacking him in the face.

Based on the rising speed of the smoke twisting in the wind, he knew it was close. He took a step forward but was knocked off stride when someone bumped into him from behind. It was the plus-sized businessman with the bad comb-over job. He'd taken position on Bunker's immediate right.

The man's eyes locked onto the winding smoke trail. "That's gotta suck." His voice had no emotion fueling his words. He smirked, looking slightly amused. "Talk about your community barbeque."

Bunker couldn't believe the man's indifference to the horrible deaths of what he assumed were hundreds of passengers aboard the downed airliner. He decided to move three steps away for some much-needed airspace from the sweaty man, who reeked of cigarettes and cheeseburgers, even with the breeze ruffling the tail of his untucked long-sleeve shirt.

The familiar scent of vanilla made it to Jack's nostrils, making him think the forty-year-old, oversized chunk next to him must've come from a strip club somewhere. All that was missing was a sprinkle of glitter transfer and a red splotch of lipstick on the man's neck.

"I wonder how many were onboard?" the man asked. Then he let out a short chuckle and cocked his head. "Their attorneys are going to have a field day. I wish I had a piece of all those billable hours. I know my firm could use it."

Bunker ignored the lawyer and stepped around him. He took off for the locomotive with a quick, churning step as he worked his way along the procession of train cars. The tracks were elevated on a steep embankment, giving him a high angle view of the foliage below.

When he arrived at the engine, he found two men standing on the tracks in front of the engine. They were close together and slightly turned, looking at an angle to the left.

Both men wore similar business-style clothing, including black shoes and pants, colored dress shirts and ties, and black vests. Each man was clearly in his middle years, with wrinkles, trim waists, and broad shoulders.

The man with a thick mustache had an iconic black hat in his hand, holding it over his heart as it flapped in the wind. Bunker could see the Amtrak logo printed on the front, just above the narrowing brim. The words above the logo said *Amtrak Conductor*. Jack assumed the other man was the engineer.

When some loose rock crunched under Bunker's feet, the two railroad employees spun their heads and looked at him.

"What happened?" Bunker asked, hoping he didn't startle the men.

The engineer, who was still wearing his cap, pointed at the trees to the left and spoke next. The slope of his eyes and shape of his face signaled he was of Asian descent. "Just missed us. I don't know how or why, but thank God it did."

Jack took a quick inspection of the scene, recording all the facts his eyes were reporting in mere seconds.

The plane hit the tracks ahead first, taking out a long section of the iron rails and wooden railroad ties underneath. A huge section of the embankment was missing, too, leaving behind an open crater that wouldn't be fixed anytime soon.

To the left, a path of destruction had been cut through the forest, angling down and into a vast canyon below. Some of the trees looked charred, but they weren't on fire. He didn't understand how, but it didn't change the facts.

He walked ahead a few yards and followed the trail of smoke into the valley beyond. There was a river cutting through the center of the canyon. The whitecaps of its rapids were clearly evident, indicating it was a fast-moving current.

Just on the other side of the water were chunks of the plane—at least fifteen—each of them burning. The jagged sections had been ripped apart and spread out in directions leading away from the river. Some of the trees around the mangled wreckage were on fire, too, sending intense columns of flames up from their trunks.

The conductor showed up at his side. "Do you think anyone is still alive?"

"I don't see how," Bunker said.

"Someone should go down there and check."

Bunker shook his head. "Not without climbing gear and a full rescue team. That's too steep a drop. Besides, I doubt anyone could've survived that crash. It was too violent. No, I'm afraid they're all gone."

"That fire doesn't look good, either," the conductor said, sounding concerned.

"It'll head away from us."

"How could you possibly know that?"

Bunker pointed at the raging water below. "I doubt it's gonna cross that massive river, plus the wind is blowing away. I'm not sure, but I think that's the Mighty Colorado."

"Actually, it's the Arkansas River."

Bunker nodded, then turned and went back to where the engineer was still standing, his mouth agape. The conductor joined him.

Bunker swung his arm, pointing at the airplane's flight path. He decided to channel something Jeffrey said a few minutes earlier. "It looks like the pilot banked right at the last second when he saw our train sitting here, helpless."

The engineer shook his head, his eyes locking onto Bunker's. "I don't think that's what happened. It looked like the pilot had a dead stick to me. I think it's more likely that a gust of wind caught the wings and changed its trajectory. That's why it missed us."

"All those poor people," the conductor muttered.

Bunker looked at the engineer. "I take it the train stopped because you lost power?"

"Yeah. The engines quit when our systems suddenly failed across the board."

"They're controlled by a computer system, right?" Bunker asked in a leading manner.

The man nodded. "Corporate is going to be pissed. They just spent a bundle upgrading everything a few months ago. We finally had the latest and greatest, and now this. Shit, you know they're gonna blame us. We're responsible for everything that happens to this train."

"I wouldn't worry about it. Not anymore."

"Why?"

"Same thing happened to all the passenger cell phones and tablets."

"What does that have to do with our engines failing?" the engineer asked, his partner remaining silent.

"Well, it's pretty obvious all of this is connected."

"How do you figure that?"

"Just look at the facts . . . A commercial jet suddenly falls out of the sky and crashes right in front of us. And it happens at precisely the same moment your state-of-the-art locomotive fails. Then, let's factor in all of the passenger electronics failing, too. I seriously doubt any of this is just coincidence."

"Okay, I'll give you that. What do you think it is?"

Bunker took a deep breath and pinched his eyebrows. His mind churned through dozens of facts he'd read about. One answer came to mind. He craned his neck to look up. "I think we're looking at an EMP."

"EMP? As in electromagnetic pulse?"

"Yep. High altitude, I suspect."

"Aren't those caused by nukes?"

"That's one way. But I don't think one went off."

"Why not?"

"If I remember right, EMPs only work in direct line of sight so we should've seen a mushroom cloud in order to be affected here. Since we didn't and none of us have been incinerated by a nuclear blast, it must be something else."

"Some kind of new device?"

"That's what I'm thinking. Probably in space."

"Do you think it's our technology, or someone else's?"

"Could be either. But unless this was just an accident, then it's probably one of our enemies. The US has plenty of them who'd like nothing more than to take out all our electronics and send us back to the Stone Age."

"What about a solar flare?"

"Maybe. But I think we'd see some indication of all that energy hitting our atmosphere. I'm guessing it would be one hell of a light show."

"Makes sense."

"If I'm right about this, then the electrical grid is probably down, too. So I wouldn't worry about your corporate office. I'm sure they have their hands full at the moment with more than just your train."

The engineer nodded, but didn't respond this time.

The conductor finally joined in. "Did you notice the plane? It was all white with no markings. Even the windows were painted white. I haven't seen one of those since my younger days, when I was stationed at the Tonopah Test Range."

"Isn't that in Nevada?" the other man asked.

"Yeah, not far from Area 51," the conductor said with inflection in his voice, then hesitated. "But I thought they only flew FLUFs."

"FLUFs?" Bunker asked.

"Fat Little Ugly Fuckers, otherwise known as a 737-200. Janet Airlines' aircraft of choice. At least it used to be. What almost hit us was larger and a lot newer. 737NG if I'm not mistaken."

Bunker shrugged.

"It's a 737-800. Seems odd that they'd be flying here in Colorado," the conductor said, turning to face the engineer. "That's what? 900 miles out of their way?"

"Yep, due west. But don't forget, Cheyenne Mountain isn't far," the engineer answered in a matter-of-fact way, while Bunker stood silently and listened to their discussion.

"You mean NORAD?" the other man asked.

"The very same. Maybe the crew of Janet was on their way for some meet-and-greet with the military when the EMP took them out."

"And us along with it."

"You know, it's possible they were delivering some new technology they just developed to NORAD."

"Could the plane have been targeted?"

"The timing does seem a little too perfect. Someone may have wanted to stop that delivery."

"My God. Then this wasn't some accident."

"Definitely not."

"I wonder if the EMP was supposed to make the plane crash into NORAD? Sort of like 9/11, except this time using super high tech instead of onboard hijackers."

Bunker needed to change the discussion to something a little more constructive. These men obviously loved to speculate on conspiracy theories. Probably did so to help pass the time while they traveled across the country for hours on end.

"Hey guys, I hate to interrupt but you have a train full of passengers to take care of right now."

The conductor turned his head to Bunker. "Right. Right. Sorry."

"Do you have an emergency plan in place for complete engine failure?"

"Oh yeah. We have plans for every conceivable emergency."

"Can you get it? We should look it over."

"I would if I could, but it's not printed anymore. It's all on computer. When they did the new upgrades, the old paper manuals went away. The bean counters are always looking for ways to save costs."

"Seriously? That doesn't make any sense. Once they're printed, they're printed. The cost is over with."

"Not with how often the government changes the safety rules and regs. We used to get an all new set of manuals every six months, with revisions and inserts being released every week. Now it's all electronic. And since the computers are down—"

"You've got nothing," Bunker said, finishing the man's sentence.

CHAPTER 3

Bunker retraced his steps, passing a number of passengers he recognized from his train car. They were outside and walking along the tracks to the front of the train where he'd just been. It was obvious their curiosity about the plane crash was pulling them forward. He could see it in their eyes as he zigzagged his way through them. He went inside the sightseeing car and found his original seat.

"Well?" the blonde mom asked, while cradling her son in her lap. "What did you find out?"

"Somehow the plane missed us. It went down a steep cliff and broke apart at the bottom of a canyon by the river. It doesn't look good."

"So I was right?" Jeffrey asked in an excited voice. "The pilot turned when he saw us?"

"Maybe. I'm not sure. There's a lot of wind out there, too. It could have caught the wings and made the plane turn. But it really doesn't matter, sport. It missed us and that's all that matters right now."

The woman cleared her throat, sounding a little choked up. "So, what about, uh, you know, survivors?"

"Nope. Not a chance," he said, keeping with her obvious desire not to reveal too much in front of her son. Bunker grabbed at his duffel in the overhead bin. He pulled it down and slung it over his right shoulder.

"You're leaving us?" she asked him with a frightened look on her face.

He nodded, though he wasn't sure why he felt compelled to respond. "Time to vacate."

She hesitated for a second, then her eyes lit up. "Is there a fire?"

"Yes, but it's not coming this way."

"Then what is it?"

He lowered his voice, not wanting the nearby passengers to hear him. "I don't think this is a simple power outage. There's more at play here. If I'm right, then staying with the train is a mistake. It won't be long before the rest of the passengers come to the same conclusion and start a panic."

"What about the Amtrak people? I'm sure they have emergency plans for this sort of thing."

"You'd think so, but no."

"Then my son and I should leave, too, right?"

"Yep, I'd suggest grabbing your gear and bugging out."

The woman's eyebrows pinched and so did her nose. She hesitated for a full breath, then slid over on the seat with her son in her lap. When her feet hit the floor, she let her boy slide off her legs before she stood up and pointed. "Can you hand me the blue backpack and the one next to it?"

"Sure," he said, snatching both of the bags and giving them to her.

"Lead the way, kind sir," she said in a matter-of-fact way.

"I'm sorry, what was that?"

"We're coming with you."

"Uh. . . no. I don't think that's a good idea."

"Why?"

"Because I always travel alone."

"Not today you don't."

"But—"

She interrupted him by holding her hand up like a stop sign. "This isn't open for discussion."

Bunker thought about continuing the debate with her, but the determined look on her face told him it would be a waste of time. Time he didn't think he had.

He sighed. "Fine. It's a free country. Do what you want. But the minute you slow me down, you're on your own. Both of you. Understood?"

"So much for chivalry," she said with a sweeping roll of her eyes.

"Hey Miss, nobody's holding a gun to your head. You can go wherever you want, but if you decide to tag along, then you do so under my rules. I make the decisions, understood?"

"Sure, fine, whatever. Oh, and by the way, my name is Stephanie King. Not Miss. Not Steph. It's Stephanie. And this is my son, Jeffrey," she said with a firmness to her words. She held out her hand in a friendly manner.

He wrapped his palm around hers and gave it a firm but quick shake. "Bunker. Nice to meet you. Now let's jet."

"Is there first name? Or are you one of *those* guys who only goes by his last name? Some kind of uber-cool, macho thing."

"It's Jack. But I prefer to be called Bunker."

"Okay then, Mr. Jack Bunker," she said, extending an open palm in the direction of the exit. "Lead the way."

Right then, Bunker knew she was going to be a handful. She may have agreed to follow his rules, but he figured her compliance would only last as long as it suited her. He was starting to understand why she and her old man didn't get along.

"Wait, what about me?" Jeffrey asked, holding out his hand.

Bunker took the tiny boy's palm in his and gave it a gentle shake. He didn't know what to say to the wide-eyed kid, so he kept his mouth shut.

"Now we're not strangers anymore," Jeffrey said, his face beaming a full smile.

"Where to first?" Stephanie asked after wrapping her arms around Jeffrey and pulling him in close to her.

Bunker leaned in and put his lips next to her ear for an even quieter whisper. "Dining car. Need to stock up on some supplies before they're all gone. Once the rest of these people realize help isn't coming, it's going to be a free-for-all. Let's grab what we can and get the hell out of here."

* * *

Ten minutes later . . .

Stephanie kept Jeffrey in front of her as she followed the gruff man and his drab-green duffel bag out of the dining car and down the set of aluminum steps. Her backpack was now twice as heavy thanks to the three bottles of water Bunker had stuffed inside.

She didn't like the fact he put the heaviest stuff in her pack, while filling his with mostly candy bars and other snacks. At least the man was gracious enough to pay for everything like a gentleman should.

Not much had gone right since the recent divorce from her high school sweetheart, but she was thankful for her sneakers. If she'd worn heels today like normal, her feet never would've made it through the upcoming hike. She wasn't sure where the three of them were going, but it was obvious it was going to be a long walk.

"Which way?" she asked, keeping a close eye on the muscular man with the tattooed fingers and bandages on his neck.

"South, to a small town we passed a half hour ago. I think the sign said Clearwater."

"Are we going back home, Mommy?" Jeffrey asked.

Stephanie kept her eyes on Bunker, never looking down at her son. "Why downhill and not up? Shouldn't we be heading to Denver?"

"My rules. My decisions. Remember?"

"Yeah, I remember. But it doesn't mean I'm not going to ask any questions. Maybe you forgot, but I've got a son to protect and we don't exactly know you."

Bunker didn't respond. He only stood there blinking rapidly with that deadpan look of his. Granted, he was a nice-looking man, but Bunker's stare made her stomach uneasy.

She continued, "Well, Mr. Bunker, you might as well get used to it right now, I'm gonna ask questions. And I'm gonna need answers. I don't think that's too much to ask, do you?"

His shoulders slumped and he shook his head. "No, I guess not. Just try to keep it down to a minimum, okay? Otherwise we're just wasting time."

"Agreed. So why south?"

"Well, Ms. Stephanie, for three reasons. First, we don't know how far we are from Denver. It could be a couple of days' walk, or maybe longer. But we do know how long it's been since we passed the last town. In survival situations, accurate information is key to making good decisions. Decisions that just might save your life. The worst thing you can do is make risky assumptions when your life is on the line."

"Sounds like you've done this before."

"More or less. Plus the tracks ahead are out. We'd have to find another way around the canyon before we could even think about heading up to Denver. That means miles and miles of additional hiking."

"You said there were three reasons."

"The third reason is in your pack."

"The water bottles?"

"Yep."

She put her hands on her hips and pushed out her jaw. Her hands tugged at the uncomfortable straps of her backpack, wanting to drive home her next point. "Thank you for that, by the way. Such a gentleman."

He smiled, showing a set of uneven teeth, one of which was gold. "Look, somebody had to carry it, and your pack was the lightest. So you got the honor."

"Lucky me."

"Hey, I try."

"Not hard enough, I'm sure. So what about the water bottles?"

"Since we can only carry a limited amount of water, we need to take the path of least resistance. We'll burn far fewer calories and drink only a fraction of the water if we go downhill to Clearwater instead of hiking around the canyon on uneven ground and then heading uphill to Denver."

"Okay, that makes sense. But there's a flaw in your logic."

"Oh really? What's that?"

"My son and I weren't going to Clearwater."

"How's that a flaw?"

"Well, first of all, we were on our way to Denver, not Clearwater. And second, there's someone in Denver waiting for us—Jeffrey's grandmother. He hasn't seen her since last Christmas. Neither have I. And right now, we need her support, with the recent divorce and all."

"I can appreciate that, but I'm not headed to Denver. Not anymore."

"So this is all about you?"

"Hey, you're the one who wanted to tag along, remember? Like I said before, nobody's holding a gun here."

"Well then, maybe we should go to Denver on our own."

"You can if you want to, but I'd advise against it."

"Why?" she said with attitude.

"A heavily populated city is the last place you want to be when the shit hits the fan."

Her hands reacted instantly, covering Jeffrey's ears. "Hey, watch the language. Young ears around."

"Right, sorry," Bunker said with a stammer.

She let go of her grip on Jeffrey's ears. "I take it you're expecting trouble?"

"Yeah, you could say that. Big-time trouble. If I'm right about what's happening, everything is about to crumble. Trust me, I've seen the underbelly of society firsthand and when it gets desperate, things turn ugly fast."

"Desperate? Because of the train stopping and the plane crash?"

"Bingo. There's only one thing that I can think of that can take down planes and trains, plus fry cell phones and computers."

"You're talking about an EMP, aren't you?"

Bunker's eyes flared and his posture straightened a bit. "You know what that is?"

"Yeah, it's called reading. It's the thing you do to better yourself in your spare time. What? Did you think I was just another dumb blonde?"

"No, no, not at all," he said, stuttering like an idiot. "Just never met a chick who knew anything about science."

She didn't appreciate the chick reference or the blanket statement about women not knowing anything about science. "Well, I do. Some of us actually have a brain and we try to use it whenever we can. Can't say the same for men. Most of you wander around like rutting cavemen, letting little Willie do all the thinking for ya. Like my ex. That SOB."

"Damn, girl. Such hostility. Sounds like someone really did a number on ya."

"If ripping out my heart and throwing it down the garbage disposal is called doing a number on someone, then yeah, he did. Can we move on now? Don't we have somewhere to be? Like Clearwater?"

"So we're in agreement? We head south."

"Yeah. Your rules. Your decisions. But you better be right, Mr. Caveman, because all our lives are depending on it."

"Lucky me," he said, using the same tone and inflections in his voice that she'd used earlier when uttering the same two words.

"Cute," she said with a leer, watching the man open his bag and take out a long-bladed knife. It was wrapped in a leather sheath that carried the initials JT near the top. Bunker attached the sheath to his beltline on the right side.

"What's that for?" she asked, seeing the tip of the blade hanging down to the middle of his thigh.

"Hunting, among other things."

"What do you hunt with that? Elephants?"

"If needed, yes," he said. "Anything else?"

There was one other thing—the letters on the knife's sheath. They were JT and not JB, as she would have expected. She pointed at the knife. "What about those initials? They're obviously not yours."

"Belonged to a man long since forgotten," he answered, spinning and heading away from her.

"Did he give it to you?" she asked.

Bunker didn't answer and just kept walking away.

Stephanie thought about asking if he'd stolen the knife, but decided against it. She needed to be careful what she said and how she said it, at least until she knew a lot more about this new traveling companion. For her sake and her son's.

Right now Jeffrey was a mostly happy ten-year-old whose birthday was coming up soon. However, like most children his age, he was a sponge and listening to everything being said around him.

Confrontation and overly negative conversations would only confuse him. Emotionally and mentally.

If she didn't want her only child to turn out like his a-hole of a father, she needed to take the high road and keep the conversations with Bunker cordial and clean. Otherwise, her impressionable little man might start to absorb all of this and grow up to be a rude, arrogant piece of navel lint, like her ex—a wealthy man who treated women like secondhand citizens.

Stephanie brought her focus down to Jeffrey, standing next to her. He was tugging at her hand to follow Bunker down the tracks, so she let Jeffrey lead the way.

CHAPTER 4

Forty minutes later Bunker stopped walking next to a railroad control signal and turned to his left, looking down the slope of the raised embankment holding up the tracks. At the bottom was a worn trail running from left to right. It appeared to branch off, cutting a path into the nearby forest.

Stephanie and the kid caught up to him and stood on his left. "Something wrong?" she asked.

"Looks like an old logging road down there."

"Is that a good thing or bad?"

"Logging trails typically lead to larger roads, and that means civilization is not far off. I figured we had to be getting close."

"Wait, you want us to go down there?"

"Absolutely," he said, resting his hand on top of the control signal post. "This is the best place I've seen to work our way down."

Jeffrey stuck his arm out and pointed, aiming it at the base of the trees on the left. "Look Mommy, a rabbit."

She put her hands on his shoulders. "Yes, honey. A rabbit. But Mommy's a little busy right now. Mr. Bunker and I are talking, so I need you to please be quiet until we're done. Can you do that?"

Jeffrey nodded, bringing his arm down next to his side.

Stephanie looked at Bunker, flaring one of her eyebrows. "Did you bring a rope?"

He hesitated, calculating the distance and trajectory. "No, but we shouldn't need one."

"Are you serious?"

"Yeah, shouldn't be too hard. We'll just daisy-chain our way lower. Jeffrey first, then you and then me."

"I'm sorry, what?"

"Did you ever play Barrel of Monkeys when you were a kid?"

She nodded. "Once or twice."

"So you understand then?"

"I'm pretty sure you're talking about locking arms and working our way down. But I still don't like the idea."

"Trust me, it'll work as long I'm the anchor. My strength and weight will be key until we get to the bottom."

She looked down the slope and hesitated before shaking her head twice. Then she looked up at him. "I don't know. That's a long way down. I think we need at least one more person."

He put a hand on her shoulder without thinking, planning to explain.

She pulled away and shot him a piercing look of concern.

"Sorry," he told her, realizing his touch was unwarranted. "Didn't mean anything by it."

"Well, Mr. Bunker. Personal space exists for a reason. I suggest you remember that."

"Like I said, sorry. My mistake."

"Okay then. You were saying?"

"I was saying that my daisy-chain idea will work. I know it seems like a long way down, but it looks worse than it really is. As long as we use overlapping hand grips and keep our footing, everything should be fine."

"What about our luggage?"

"Simple," he said, taking the bag off his shoulder and tossing it end over end. The duffle landed with a thud at the bottom, nearly standing straight up before it finally toppled over a second later. His hands latched onto her backpack, hanging on straps over her shoulders. "Your turn."

"Wait, let me do it," she said, sliding out of the straps until the bag was in her hands.

He let go of the straps. "I take it there's something breakable inside?"

"No, not really. Just don't like strange men touching my things, that's all. Personal space, remember," she said with attitude, before tossing the pack over the edge.

Her aim was spot-on, sending the backpack on top of his. He didn't know if she meant to do that or not, but it was a soft landing nonetheless.

"You better be right about this," she said, repositioning her son in front of her. She took her son's hand, overlapping her palm and fingers around his wrist and vice versa.

"Jeffrey, I need you to listen carefully to Mommy. Mr. Bunker and I are going to lower you down little by little, so don't be scared. Everything's going to be okay, honey. I promise. Just hang on tight and don't let go until your feet are at the bottom. Do you understand what Mommy's telling you?"

Jeffrey nodded, letting a mile-wide smile grow on his face. "Cool! We're gonna play Mountaineer. Just like on the huge dirt pile across the street from *Daytimers*."

"Yes, sweetheart. Mountaineer."

Bunker wasn't sure what the term *Daytimers* meant, but figured it was either the kid's school name or possibly the name of his daycare.

When Bunker brought his hands to the front of his waistline and undid the clasp on his belt, Stephanie shot him a concerned look, staring at his hands.

"Relax, it's not what you think," he told her in a steady voice, pulling the leather from his belt loops. His fingers brought the two ends of the belt together, then reengaged the clasp. He wrapped the buckle in his palm then tossed the looping end over the top of the control signal and pulled it tight.

The look on Stephanie's face vanished. "Oh, I see what you're gonna do."

"Like I said, I got it covered," Bunker said. "But I need your son's too."

She didn't hesitate. "Jeffrey, take off your belt and give it to Mr. Bunker."

The kid did as he was told and Bunker quickly looped the two belts together. He extended his hand toward her, palm up. "May I?"

She nodded and held out her hand in response.

He used an overlapping grip on Stephanie's palm and wrist, then set his feet before she began to lower her son over the graveled edge.

Jeffrey sent Bunker a playful smile as he slid down and out of view, with his feet turned sideways and spread out. At that same moment, Bunker felt the mother's grip double on his wrist.

When Stephanie began her descent down the embankment, the tug on Bunker's arm instantly doubled. He inched his feet closer to the edge, needing to maintain his pace with her.

She was already skittish enough with him and the current situation, so he had to keep his movements smooth and his feet secure. Any sudden jolt or momentary slippage might make her overreact and let go unintentionally, sending the two of them tumbling to the bottom.

When Bunker's lead foot passed the threshold and worked its way lower, the rope he'd made out of their belts finally pulled tight. He'd looped it around his hand a few times before they started this process, planning to release more of the slack when the time came.

He could see clear down to the forest from his position. Jeffrey was three quarters of the way to the bottom and looking up. His face was covered with excitement and his eyes looked electrified.

"You all right down there, sport?" Bunker shouted, continuing to lower both of them with the remaining slack in the makeshift rope.

"Almost there," the boy said, looking up. "You guys are supposed to let me go now so I can slide the rest of the way."

Stephanie flashed a look at Bunker, asking for his approval with her eyes.

"He'll be okay. Kids don't break that easy. Besides, he's probably done this a bunch of times on that dirt pile."

"You sure?" she asked.

"Well, he's your kid. So you need to make the final decision. But I think he'll be okay."

Bunker could see a fleshy bulge race down her throat while she was looking up at him. She gave him a tentative nod, then brought her head down and gazed at her son. "Okay, on the count of three I'm going to let go. You ready?"

"Yeah, Mom, do it already."

When her count reached three, her hand released, sending her son sliding down on his backside through the mixture of gravel and dirt.

Jeffrey held his hands high and let out a cheerful squeal, as if he was flying down the waterslide at his favorite theme park.

When the kid's feet hit the forest floor, his knees bent as they cradled the landing and kept him upright. He spun around and waved his arms at his mother.

"I'm okay, Mom. Now it's your turn. Just let go and keep your hands up. It's really fun."

"Mommy's going to take the slow way down, sweetheart. And so is Mr. Bunker," she said in a nervous voice, looking up at Bunker as he continued to ease her down a few inches at a time.

Once the rope slack had been exhausted, he let go of the tether and tested his footing. Without Jeffrey on the line, the pull on Bunker's right arm had been cut drastically, giving his shoulder and arm muscles a much-needed break.

The weight drop also told him he should be able to anchor Stephanie on his own as they worked the rest of the way down. With the exception of her full chest, Stephanie's physique was ultra thin and she probably only weighed double what her son did. That meant a third of the weight had just vanished when the boy freestyled it to the bottom.

Bunker noticed Stephanie was looking up at him, so he brought his free hand up to show it to her. Sure, it was mean, but he couldn't resist, wanting to razz her a little.

Her eyes flared and her face flushed red. "What are you doing? Are you crazy?"

He smiled, knowing his ploy worked. "Just take it slow. I gotcha."

She froze for a few seconds before nodding and turning her eyes lower.

A few minutes later, Bunker's feet landed next to hers and Jeffrey's. "Like I said, piece of cake."

"That wasn't funny," she snapped, pulling her wrist free from his grip.

"Yeah. It was," he said, not able to hold back a chuckle.

"You scared the crap out of me."

He nodded, still laughing. "The look on your face was priceless."

"I could've been killed."

"Not likely. It wasn't that far of a drop. Besides, I had it covered. You were never in any danger."

"But still," she said, sneering at him before bending down to give her son a hug. "I'm just glad you're safe, sweetheart."

"Mommy, can we climb back up and do it again? That was really awesome!" Jeffrey said with eyes wide.

Bunker laughed again, watching the reaction on her face. It looked like she was doing all she could not to snap at the kid. Obviously, she wasn't an outdoors type and probably not into *mountaineering,* as Jeffrey had called it.

Bunker patted the boy on the back. "As much as I'm sure your mother would love to do that again, we really need to get moving."

A pouty look sprang up on Jeffrey's face. "Please, Mr. Bunker. Can we do it again? Just one more time. Please."

Bunker let out a long slow breath before he answered. "How about I make you a deal? If we come back this way later, we'll stop and play Mountaineer all you want. But right now I need to get you and your mom back to town so you have a place to stay for the night."

CHAPTER 5

Sheriff Augustus Apollo put on his wire-rimmed glasses and adjusted his sagging duty belt before walking into the bathroom connected to his office. He stood in front of the sink and checked his appearance in the mirror.

The middle-aged reflection staring back was shrouded in a medieval glow thanks to the flame from a stubby candle sitting on the marble countertop.

"You ready for this, Gus?" he asked himself before running two fingers through his thinning hair. The strands fell into place from right to left, covering up his ever-expanding bald spot.

Even though he never wanted this new job, he still needed to look his best before taking on his first official crisis as the chief lawman of Clearwater, Colorado.

The muffled voices beyond his office door had grown in volume over the past several minutes. Tensions were mounting and so was the fever of the crowd in the reception area outside.

Gus couldn't put it off much longer. It was time to face what was sure to be a barrage of questions. Some of them would be aimed at the power outage, but others would be about him and his obvious lack of experience. His ten years in the Sheriff's Reserve Unit wasn't much of a resume, especially since that stint took place in Clearwater, where nothing ever happened.

Before Gus accepted this appointment, Mayor Buckley had assured him that heading a small-town sheriff's office would be a cakewalk. History had proven that violent crimes and serious emergencies were rare commodities, and had done so for as long as he could remember.

Even if something unexpected did pop up, Mayor Buckley advised him to call the County Sheriff's Department or the State Troopers for help. But that conversation was three weeks ago. Long before what had happened today.

Now the town was facing a sweeping power outage and most of the electronics in town had been fried. Communications were down, and so was his ability to call in backup.

The tuck of Gus' shirt was off a bit thanks to the heft around his middle. He adjusted it, straightening the wrinkles out and tightening the fit under the belt.

The new diet wasn't working very well, but he wasn't quite ready to give up on it. Truth was, it wasn't the diet's fault, or the fault of old Doc Marino for insisting on it after the mandatory physical Mayor Buckley forced him to take prior to being sworn in as town sheriff.

The additional weight gain was due to the endless string of hot fudge sundaes and servings of hot cherry pie a la mode that seemed to find their way into his belly each night after work. Well, that and the fact his new mountain bike and helmet were still virgins and sitting in the corner of his office behind him.

His late-night bingeing wasn't because he had a runaway sweet tooth or some kind of sugar craving. No, it was because of the new waitress in town. She was a real looker and he simply couldn't help himself when his shift ended.

Gus' feet seemed to have a mind of their own, taking him to Billy Jack's Cafe and forcing him to go inside and sit at the front service counter. The draw to the middle stool was undeniable, and so was his attraction to the new, friendly waitress who worked that section each night.

So far their interactions had been sparse and limited to typical server-patron style banter. He wanted to ask her out, but the platinum blonde in her late forties, Allison Rainey, hadn't given him any indication she was interested. But he was still hopeful, nonetheless.

Allison, like him, had a few miles on her, but her depth of spirit, beaming smile, and cheerful personality had already captured his heart. So had her perfect backside, catching his eye whenever she turned and walked away. He couldn't help but stare and wonder what her curves would feel like in his hands.

He wasn't sure if the spark he felt would ever lead anywhere, but maybe something might happen down the road. His plan was to remain patient and keep smiling at her. Eventually she might look past his obvious physical flaws and get to know the real him.

A knock came at the door. "Chief? We really need you out here," said Daisy Clark, his deputy and former beauty queen of the Miss Sunflower Festival ten years prior. "Chief?"

"Be right out, Daisy," Gus yelled after turning his neck to aim his voice out of the bathroom and at the office door.

He brought his attention back to the mirror. His sausage fingers were busy tacking on the newly-minted nameplate above the front pocket of his official uniform. Brown and tan weren't exactly his colors, but he really didn't have a say in the matter.

The placard's reflection showed the letters in his last name backwards, much like his life felt at the moment. Everything he knew had been twisted around and intensified, just like the knot raging in his stomach. He knew the pain wasn't going to disappear until he went out there and did what he needed to do.

He sucked in a full rush of air and let it out slowly through his lips. "It's now or never. You've got this, old man."

Gus figured if he nodded with confidence while making strong eye contact and listening to the citizens' questions, he could fake it until his brain came up with some poignant words to offer his fellow Clearwater residents.

It wasn't like he was completely inexperienced with small town politics or the basics of law enforcement, but this whole *protect and serve* mantra was going to be something new and challenging. Especially on a full-time basis.

In effect, the Mayor had *drafted* him into service, something Gus never saw coming. Maybe the term *drafted* wasn't the right word to use—*railroaded* might be a better choice.

He rolled his eyes, knowing that when a master chef, like Mayor Seth Buckley, seasoned the guilt ever so perfectly, an honorable person had little chance to resist. Or say no.

His time on this Earth had taught him a great many things about people and their tendencies. He knew what was coming. No matter how well he handled this new job, or even the next ten minutes, many of the residents would always see him as the middle-aged town planner and not the new sheriff. Respect and trust were going to be hard-earned and he accepted that as he turned and headed for the office door.

Gus knew from all his readings that sometimes a turn of events is so profound that it actually changes a person's DNA, almost like a cascading chain reaction at the cellular level, transforming a man into something else. The question was, what would that something be?

Usually the triggering event came in the form of some horrific personal tragedy, but maybe, just maybe, the crisis waiting for him outside would elevate him into a better man—a man filled with confidence and leadership skills. Not a loner who preferred a good book and a glass of wine, rather than the close proximity of the public and all their paranoia.

When his hand landed on the doorknob and his fingers began to turn it, he realized his future and that of the four hundred-plus residents in town were now on a high-speed collision course.

CHAPTER 6

Stephanie King kept pace with Bunker's steps as she watched her son run ahead to pick up a three-foot-long tree branch. Jeffrey started using it as a walking stick, acting like he'd done this hiking thing a million times before.

She brought her eyes to the tall man next to her, unable to keep from staring at the bandages on his neck. They stuck out like a ketchup stain on a white shirt, drawing her eyes every chance they got.

"Can I ask you a personal question?" she asked Bunker as her feet took her forward on the dirt path.

"Yeah, sure."

"What's the deal with those bandages? At first I thought you cut yourself shaving, but that's not likely. Not on both sides of your neck, unless you really suck at it. So I'm guessing it's some kind of skin condition. Or maybe you had recent surgery or something along those lines. Am I close?"

"Sort of," Bunker said, never taking his eyes from the road ahead. His face was stiff and focused, but the sudden redness in his cheeks told her that the question resonated with him.

Her voice stammered a bit. "Hey, I don't want to butt in and all that, but I'm kind of curious. I think it would help if we got to know each other a bit more. Don't you think?"

"Normally, yes. But some things are a little too painful to share with just anybody. You know how people are. They talk. They gossip. They pass judgment. Then the rumors start, taking on a life of their own. Long before anybody ever gets a chance to know the person they're gossiping about."

"I get it. People have been judging me all my life," she said, putting her hands under her ample breasts and pushing them up. "Especially when you're born with these. I can't help it that I'm prettier than most women. I mean, come on, really? Trashing someone just because they have a nice figure. God, I hate people who judge."

She waited for a reaction from him, but none came. "But I know what you mean, Bunker. You don't have to tell me if you don't want to."

"Well, that's not what I meant exactly. I don't mind you asking, but right now doesn't feel like the right time to me. We need to focus on getting back to town."

"Understood, loud and clear. We all have our secrets."

"Yes, we do, and I appreciate you respecting my privacy. For now, let me just say that these bandages are connected to the man I used to be. A past I'm trying to forget."

"Yeah, I hear ya. My past isn't something I want to remember, either. Well, my recent past, that is."

"Everyone has baggage these days."

"Me more than most. My entire life seems like a string of bad decisions. Except for Jeffrey, of course."

"I understand. Sometimes you get to a point when you just have to say *no more* and walk away. That's what I'm trying to do—start over. You know, a clean slate. I hope that makes sense."

She smiled, feeling a connection starting to form with the ruggedly handsome man. "It does," she said, lowering her voice so Jeffrey wouldn't hear. "Sounds like you and I are not all that different. Nothing on this planet is ever easy, especially after a seriously nasty divorce from the town slut. And when I say slut, I mean a total man-whore. But sometimes a girl just has to rise above all the drama and change everything, including her address. That's why Jeffrey and I were on our way to Denver—to go live with my mother and her four brothers. My family has a big ranch up there. Jeffrey thinks we were just going for a visit, so please don't say anything."

"I won't. But he's a smart boy. He would have figured it out soon enough."

"Yeah, he would have. But I wanted to get a little distance from my ex first."

"I can appreciate that."

"Like you, I got to that point where I decided to leave everything behind and get as far away from Clearwater as possible, but still not leave the state. You know, shared custody rules and all."

"I didn't realize that's why you needed to be in Denver. I'm sorry. I never should've made you turn around and head back to your past. But there's really not much of a choice at the moment."

"It's not a huge deal, really. It was my decision for us to tag along with you, remember?"

He nodded.

She continued, "I probably need to grow a pair anyway. Besides, it's not like everybody in town hates me. Just some of the people who consider themselves better than everyone else. Like my ex and his family of mouth-breathers."

"Yeah, I know the type. Thinking they are above the law and the rules don't apply to them."

"Exactly. But you know what? After everything that's been said and done through this whole mess, the thing that probably pisses them all off the most is that I didn't give back his name. I mean, it's not like King is a famous name or anything. But it's way better than my maiden name, Radiwanski. Nobody could ever say it right. Or God forbid, spell it."

"I can see why you stayed with King. That's a mouthful."

A minute later, they rounded the corner and found Jeffrey waiting for them a short distance away. He was bobbing on his heels with an anxious look on his face.

"Do you have to go potty?" she asked her son.

"No, Mom. Look!" he said, pointing to his left.

After a few more steps, Stephanie could see her son standing next to a long stretch of pavement. Her chest filled with excitement. "Oh, the highway! It's about time."

"Probably isn't far now," Bunker said, stopping and putting his duffel bag on the ground after they made it to the hardtop. "We should probably take a break and rest for a minute. Can you turn around so I can get the bottles from your pack?"

Jeffrey grabbed her hand and tugged at it repeatedly.

She looked down at him. "What?"

Jeffrey whirled and aimed his arm down the two-lane highway. "Look, Mom!"

She brought her eyes up while Bunker continued to dig inside her backpack. It took a second for her vision to focus a few hundred yards down the road. But when she did, her mouth dropped open.

"What is that?" she asked, seeing something scattered across the roadway. Everywhere she looked, there were small black mounds.

"They're birds, Mom. Dead birds. Lots of them. I ran back here to tell you."

CHAPTER 7

"Now folks, I need you all to please remain calm. I can't answer all of you at once," Sheriff Gus Apollo said to the two dozen citizens crowding in and around the reception desk.

Some of them he knew; others were strangers who did not visit town very often. Regardless, his heart was pounding under the pressure of a platoon of eyes burning a hole into his face.

Officer Daisy Clark was standing next to him, blowing her whistle in short, powerful bursts. She may have been short in stature, but she could fire that whistle like a champ.

Gus put his hand on Daisy's arm, lightly persuading her to remove the whistle from her mouth. She dropped her arm, then looked at him.

"That's not helping, Daisy."

She nodded. "Sorry, Sheriff. I got a little caught up in the moment."

"It's understandable. Just let me handle it from here."

"You need to send out a search party, Gus," one of the younger men wearing a military style crew cut said. "My twin daughters are out there."

"They should've been back by now," a redheaded woman said as tears streamed down her face. "Something terrible must have happened. You need to do something, Sheriff."

Gus nodded, making eye contact with several of the citizens. "Yes, we will. But first we all need to take a minute and catch our breath. There's no reason to jump to conclusions here. They may have been running late and stopped somewhere to rest or use the bathroom. There's no reason to think the worst. We don't know anything at this point."

"Exactly. We don't know anything and neither do you," an unidentified male voice said from the back.

"Why are you just standing there?" the older woman added, slapping her hand on the countertop. "My grandson is probably scared to death right now."

"Look everyone, this is the first I've heard of the missing kids. You gotta give me a minute here."

"What about the miners trapped in the shaft?" a slender man with curly blonde hair said. "We can't leave my men down there. The backup batteries won't last forever."

Gus recognized him. It was William King, son of silver tycoon Henry King. Their family owned the Silver King Mine and had done so for three generations. Rumor had it he and his wife, Stephanie, had just concluded their contentious divorce.

"We'll get to them, Bill. But we need to prioritize."

"Yeah, the Sheriff's right. Our kids come first, Bill," the man with the flattop said.

"That's not how I see it, Stan," King said, shaking his finger at the square-jawed kid in his mid-twenties. "They have families, too."

"Ah, that's a bunch of bull. You just don't want to take the chance that your silver goes missing," Stan said with a bite to his words.

"You got it all wrong. This isn't about money," King fired back, his face flushing.

"Oh yes, it is. That's all your family cares about. Trust me, my wife told me all about your underhanded dealings after she quit your compliance division."

Gus wasn't sure how to calm the escalating tensions in the room, including his own. Everyone was stressed, and he couldn't blame them.

He looked at Daisy, and she back at him. Her eyes told him she was anxiously waiting for orders. "We'll figure this out, Daisy. One step at a time."

"We need the Mayor on this. Where is he?" the grandmother in the front row said, wiping the tears from her cheeks. She looked around. So did Gus. But there was no sign of Mayor Buckley.

Gus kept his cool, even though the 60-year-old's lack of faith in his ability was obvious and not helping his confidence. "I'm sure he'll be here any minute. Now, can any of you tell me where they were headed?"

"They went on a hike to spot birds for their nature class. Somewhere down by Clayton's Ravine, I think. Not far from the old Gypsum mine on County Road C," one of the other parents in the back said.

"Who's driving?" Gus asked. "Does anyone know?"

"Richard Wilhelm," the man with the short-cropped hair said.

"Wait, isn't he the biology teacher?"

"Yeah, that's the point. With all the recent budget cuts, he's pulling double duty. He's all by himself with our kids."

"What happened to Joe Kassel?"

"They let him go a couple of weeks ago. Wilhelm was the only one left with a commercial license, so the principal kinda volunteered him for the job."

"Yeah, and he's no spring chicken, either," the redheaded woman added. "He's older than me."

"Martha's right. I heard he's got some kind of heart condition," another man yelled from the back of the room.

Gus brought his head around but couldn't identify who made the last comment.

"My God, what if he keeled over or something? Our kids might be stranded and all alone somewhere!" Martha added.

"I told the principal she never should've fired the only *real* bus driver we had. Especially now that we're stuck with the year-round school sessions. But she never listens to what any of us have to say," Stan with the short-cropped haircut said to the redheaded woman. "This is all her fault. That penny-pinching bitch!"

"Easy now, everyone. What did I say about overreacting?" Gus snapped, holding up his hands like a preacher.

"If you had kids out there, Sheriff, you'd be doing something by now," a different woman's voice said from the right.

* * *

Bunker stopped running and stood next to Stephanie and her son on the highway. As far as he could see, the road ahead was covered with dead birds. It looked like the pavement had a bad case of chickenpox—though the pox was black instead of red.

"Crows?" Stephanie asked.

"No, these are much bigger. Ravens, I think," he said, bending down on one knee to get a closer look at one of the carcasses. He reached out with his hand, planning to grab the bird by its feet and turn it over.

"Wait! Don't touch it!" Stephanie snapped. "It's probably got some kind of horrible disease."

Bunker realized she was right and pulled his hand back in a lurch. He took a few seconds to study more of the birds with his eyes. It looked like each of their necks had been mangled, just like the raven in front of him. "I think their necks are broken."

"From the impact with the road?" she asked.

"I don't think so, unless they were all dive-bombing the asphalt for some reason."

"Maybe their radar got all messed up," Jeffrey said. "My science lab game taught me that birds have a compass inside of them. It lets them find their way back home when they go on really long trips."

"Yes, I think you're right. I do remember reading something about birds using the Earth's magnetic field for navigation," Bunker said, nodding slowly. "When the EMP went off, it must have disrupted the magnetic lines in the area."

"That's a chilling thought," Stephanie said, looking around the area. "What now?"

"We find our way around the carcasses and keep going."

CHAPTER 8

Sheriff Gus Apollo moved aside to let Mayor Buckley take center position in front of the crowd. Daisy moved a step back as the reception area quieted down to less than a whisper.

"Status report?" the Mayor asked in a raspy, authoritative voice.

"We've got some miners trapped, plus an overdue school bus."

"Any reports of damage? Fires? Looting?"

"So far, all quiet. People are behaving. I think the worst is behind us in that respect."

"Let's hope you're right," the Mayor said with a hint of cynicism in his voice.

"Is there a problem I should know about, sir?"

The Mayor put a firm hand on Gus's shoulder, turning and leading him away from the eavesdropping crowd.

Daisy joined them by taking position across from Gus, with her back to his office door.

The volume of Buckley's voice dropped in half when he asked, "Do we have any Geiger counters?"

"Geiger counters? Are you serious?" Gus fired back.

"Deadly serious. We both know there's only a handful of things that can knock out the power and the electronics across a wide area. And each of those things takes us down a very dark path. Literally."

Gus glanced at Daisy and shot her a look of bewilderment, then brought his focus back to the Mayor. "If we have any, I haven't seen them. But then again, I haven't exactly had a chance to inventory our equipment and supplies since I took over this position. With that said, I can't imagine something like that would just be lying around here somewhere. It's not like they're needed very often. If ever."

The Mayor hesitated before he spoke again, looking like he was searching for just the right words. "Well, you *were* the town planner at one point in time. And a successful architect before that. Am I right?"

"Yes sir, on both counts. But what's my job history got to do with Geiger counters?"

"I'm guessing that somewhere along the way you've designed a bomb shelter or two. Assuming I'm correct, which I usually am, then maybe one of your clients might have what we need. Correct me if I'm wrong, but wouldn't the first thing you'd need to stock in a fallout shelter be a radiation detector?"

Before Gus could answer, one of the female residents shouted from behind them, "Excuse me, Mr. Mayor. I'm pretty sure my neighbor has a bomb shelter. It was a while ago, but I remember all the equipment in his yard, digging up everything. That conspiracy nut is always working on something."

Buckley appeared shocked that someone overheard their guarded conversation. He brought his head around and so did Gus, both men looking to identify the woman who just interrupted their conversation.

"Which neighbor was it, Mrs. Rainey?" the Mayor asked.

"Frank Tuttle. His place is opposite mine at the end of Old Mill Road."

"That's across the old Henley Bridge, isn't it?"

"Yeah, we're the only two homes out there," she answered. "Oh, and by the way, when are you planning to fix up the bridge? A bunch of the support beams are starting to rot. It's the only way in or out, so if it falls, we'll be stranded out there."

"Yes, Ms. Rainey. I'm well aware. Let me assure you the town council is working on it. But I don't have a repair date for you as yet. We're facing a bit of a funding problem at the moment."

Daisy cleared her throat. "Tuttle's a bit trigger-happy, Mayor, but I've managed to build a good rapport with him over the years. I should probably be the one to go out there and see if he'll let me rummage through his stuff. He's not going to like it, but I'm sure I can smooth it over."

While the Mayor and Daisy continued their conversation, Gus ran through the facts he'd just learned about some of the residents standing in his office.

He needed to begin memorizing information about every resident, even those who rarely came into town. Otherwise, he'd never become an effective small-town Sheriff.

The old redheaded woman's name was Martha Rainey. The same last name as the new waitress in town. Her mother? If he was right, that's where Allison might be staying.

Assuming he was correct, then the old woman's grandson was Allison's boy. A boy who was missing while on a school outing.

A tingle washed over Gus when he realized that the boy would be his way into Allison's good graces, as long as her son came home in one piece. Then she'd have to notice him and possibly show some interest.

He ran the idea through his head one more time and came up with the same answer. A slight grin found its way to his lips—*maybe this Sheriff gig wasn't all bad.*

The Mayor, Daisy, and Gus turned away from the crowd once again, huddling a little closer this time.

Gus made sure to keep his voice low when he spoke. "Assuming Daisy is able to find a Geiger counter at Tuttle's place, then I'd suggest we take readings every hour over the next few days just to be sure radiation doesn't find its way here."

"Excellent idea," the Mayor said.

"I'll head over there now," Daisy said, turning to walk away.

Gus stopped her with an arm grab. "Take the mountain bike in my office. God knows I'm never gonna use it."

"Are you sure, Chief?" she asked.

"Positive. Someone might as well get some use out of it."

"On it, boss," she said, heading through the door and disappearing to the right. A few seconds later, she reappeared with an unstrapped helmet on her head, pushing his bike by the handlebars. She made her way through the buzzing crowd and out of the Sheriff's office.

Gus needed to cover one more topic with the Mayor while he had the man's attention. "Other than electricity, the next biggest problem is going to be transportation. Whatever just happened took out the vehicles, so it looks like we're on foot for the foreseeable future."

"What we need are more bicycles," the Mayor added while rubbing his chin with two fingers.

"Ye Old Bike Shop on E Street has loads of them, sir."

"That's all well and good, but what we need are riders. Like my grandson, Rusty. He's a freak on that racing bike of his, and I doubt there's anyone faster. You should see his thighs now. They're like tree trunks."

"Is he still planning on trying out for the Olympics?"

"Yeah, but he's a long shot to make it. If nothing else, at least it gives him a goal to shoot for. And we all know how important that is for a young person. But he's very reliable and can gather radiation readings from multiple places in town. I'm sure he's gonna want to help."

"Thank you, Mayor. We're going to need all the help we can get. We'll probably need him to ferry communications from place to place, too."

"Comms . . . right," the Mayor said, nodding slowly. His eyes were thin and pinched, indicating he was deep in thought about something. "He's got a few friends he trains with, too. I'll see if Rusty can get some of them to help around town."

Gus snickered, not realizing he did it loud enough for anyone else to hear.

"Something funny, Sheriff?"

He wanted to keep his amusement to himself, but couldn't now. Not unless he wanted to offend his boss. Gus cleared his throat and stammered a bit before his mind found the words he wanted to say.

"It's funny how the tables can turn almost instantly. A few days ago, no one would've seen this coming, after all the complaints about the bicyclers clogging up the streets in town. Kinda poetic, don't you think? Now they may end up being our lifeline for communications."

The Mayor squinted a bit. "Yes, yes, it is. But history has proven time and again that desperation can yield a change in mindset. That's how a society evolves. Why should this situation be any different?"

"Roger that, sir. Everyone's gonna need to change their entire way of thinking now. At least until this crisis is over. Whatever *this* turns out to be," Gus said, keeping the rest of his thoughts about the power outage to himself.

"Agreed," the Mayor answered.

Gus was almost positive an EMP caused the grid and electronics failures, but wasn't sure if it was the right time or place to bring it up, even after the Mayor had hinted at the very same cause a few minutes ago. He decided to move on to another topic.

"What about the riding stables?" Gus asked in a leading manner. "Bicycles are great for young people who are in shape, but what about for the rest of us? Altitude and steep hills are not something we old dogs can handle anymore."

The Mayor nodded, obviously understanding what he was hinting at. "Excellent idea. We go old school. Franklin's not going to like it, but we'll need to commandeer some of his horses. I doubt his tourist season is gonna continue now, with what's happening outside."

"Exactly what I was thinking, sir."

The Mayor nodded once, then slapped Gus on the back in a friendly manner. "I knew you'd find your sea legs and grow into this job, Gus. Only a matter of time. All you needed was a little incentive to grab the bull by the horns and run with it."

Gus couldn't hold back a smile when his heart filled with a swell of pride. The Mayor was right. The badge was starting to feel like it may have found a home on his chest. For now, anyway.

He was on a good roll, but he knew it was going to take more than a couple of clever ideas to solidify him as a respected sheriff. But it was a good start.

Emboldened by his momentum, Gus decided to throw out another idea. "We should probably think about activating the reserve unit, assuming we can track the team down. I'm not sure if they're back yet from their annual fishing trip to Canada. I think they were supposed to arrive today."

"Excellent idea. However, if you can't find them, I authorize you to start deputizing the men you need. The time to act is now."

"Absolutely. As soon as I can, I'll send search and rescue teams out for the missing school bus and to help King with the miners."

"Just make sure you're very clear with the new men that this is a *temporary* assignment, nothing more. The town budget can't afford to carry any more full-time salaries."

"I'll get right on it, sir. Is there anything else?"

The Mayor nodded. "Where are we on the backup generators?"

"The one for this building is toast. I tried to get it started earlier, but I think the electric start is out. Something tells me the rest of its electronics are fried as well. Just like what we're seeing all across town with nearly everything."

"Nearly?"

"The town hall's genny is still working, albeit barely. Someone forgot to change the fuel and it degraded. I had the mechanic, Burt Lowenstein, take a quick look at it for us. He said he replaced the fuel and was able to get it started. It's not running great and needs a complete overhaul, but Burt won't do it unless he gets paid for his time. Oh, and he wants overtime."

"That sounds about right," Buckley said in a sarcastic voice. "Am I correct to assume it doesn't have any electronics in it?"

"I really don't know, sir. But it may not have mattered. With all the copper thefts a few years back, the town had secured it inside a metal cage to protect it. That cage might have shielded it from whatever took out the rest of our electronics."

"Just dumb luck. But we'll take it."

"Couldn't agree more, sir. Dumb luck is better than no luck at all."

"That much is true. Something tells me this is going to get a lot worse before it gets better."

CHAPTER 9

Bunker felt a soft tug on his left elbow. And, like the other four yanks on his shirt in the past few minutes, it meant the inquisitive kid had yet another question.

"Mr. Bunker, does your grandmother live in Denver, too? Is that why you were on the train like us?"

Stephanie snapped at her son, "I think that's enough questions for a while, Jeffrey. Let the man be."

Bunker flashed a quick hand signal at her, wanting to stop her from dressing down her son any more. "Nah, it's all good. I know he's just curious. I would be, too, given the circumstances."

Her frown evaporated and was replaced with a casual smile. "You should see him at home. He never stops. After a while, I find myself just tuning him out. I know that sounds horrible, but it's better than yelling at him to be quiet all the time."

"I understand. I'm the last person to judge anyone, on anything. Especially on how to raise kids," he said, pausing for a few moments. "People have been judging me my whole life, so I refuse to go there. We all know kids are going to be kids and ask a ton of questions. That's how they learn. I figure it's best to just roll with it and not get impatient or short with them. I don't care for most people on this rock, but for whatever reason, I always seem to get along great with kids. And cats, too, as crazy as that sounds."

She took in a sudden breath and held it, looking as though he'd just shocked her for some reason. A few heartbeats later, she let it go and gave him a head nod.

Bunker sent a thin grin at Stephanie, then turned his attention to Jeffrey, who was still hovering at his side and looking up with his clear blue eyes. He felt like a giant next to the boy. "I wasn't going anywhere in particular. I just bought a monthly ticket and thought I would take a journey to see where I ended up."

"You mean like a walkabout? You know, from the movie *Crocodile Dundee*."

Bunker laughed. "Sure, a walkabout. But on a train."

"But why? I don't understand."

"That's a good question, Champ. Like most everything else in life, it's complicated. When you're older, you'll know what that phrase means. For now, let me say this . . . sometimes a man just needs to make changes and the best way to do that is to go somewhere he's never been before.

For me, that was a one-way ticket heading north. That's when I met you and your mom," he said, winking at the kid.

Jeffrey opened his mouth and looked like he was about to respond, but didn't. Instead, his feet stopped and his face froze.

Bunker stopped walking as well, wondering what was wrong.

Stephanie must have realized that something was afoot because she swung her head around and discontinued her trek alongside her son.

"What's wrong, sweetheart?" she asked.

Jeffrey turned his head a few degrees to the left. "Listen. Do you hear that?"

Bunker turned his ear and held his breath for a few seconds, but he didn't hear anything. He wasn't surprised since his hearing wasn't the best. Putting in all those road miles on his last job had taken a percentage of his hearing away. Mostly on his left side—15%, according to the physician's assistant at the walk-in clinic in South LA.

Jeffrey's face lit up with intensity. "I hear crying. From a kid, I think."

Bunker flashed a look at Stephanie, hoping to glean a response from her. But she only shrugged.

Jeffrey spoke again. "I think it's a girl but I'm not totally sure. But she sounds really scared. She keeps saying *help me*, *help me* over and over again."

Bunker's heart tightened when he heard those words. He knelt down on one knee. "Which way? Show me."

Jeffrey pointed at a thick bank of oak trees. They were covered with a crop of starter growth around the bases of their trunks. "Over there. We need to help her!"

Bunker stood up. "We will, but you need to stay here with your mom until I see what's going on."

Stephanie swooped in and wrapped her arms around her son.

Jeffrey's eyes grew large. "Why do we have to stay here, Mom? Why can't we go help?"

"Because it might be a trap, honey. We need to let Mr. Bunker check it out for us. Just to be safe."

Bunker gave her a tight look with his eyes, then took off running in the direction Jeffrey had indicated. When he made it to the edge of the pavement, a loose crush of dirt found the soles of his shoes.

But that wasn't all: the cries for help had finally landed on his ears. However, there wasn't just one desperate plea coming from the forest. There were several. All of them kids by the sound of it.

An eight-foot-wide section of the foliage to the left of the trees looked like it had been plowed through by something heavy. Some of the stalks were broken near their midpoint and leaning forward, plus he could make out two equally spaced depressions running with the destruction path. The grooves in the dirt contained a familiar pattern: tire tracks.

There weren't any skid marks on the pavement, so it didn't appear the driver had a chance to apply the brakes. If Bunker was right, it meant the vehicle veered off the road and probably did so at high speed.

Given the depth and width of the tracks, he figured it was a heavy truck or possibly a cargo van. Something large enough to lay down a wide trail in the dirt.

Bunker continued his sprint until he entered thick underbrush. His feet slowed when he was forced to use his hands to separate and deflect the taller stalks of bushes so they wouldn't keep smashing into his chest and face.

The volume and quantity of the cries increased proportionately with each step. He couldn't tell how many kids were calling out for help, but there were many.

When the thick undergrowth finally gave way to a clearing, he stopped running and found himself standing in front of an oddly shaped boulder.

At that instant, he understood why there were so many kids crying for help. Forty feet ahead was a full-sized, modern school bus laying on its left side. The front half of the transport was hanging over the edge of a drop-off that marked the entrance to a valley ahead.

The bus' back end was in the air, leaving only its midpoint in contact with the ground— like a cantilever on a fulcrum. The bus looked like a yellow teeter-totter with the number 37 stenciled on the back.

His mind studied the scene and digested the facts in an instant. The path of the tire tracks told him the bus was traveling into the forest on its wheels until it reached this clearing, where it ran into one of the granite boulders in the area.

The vehicle's right front tire tore up the leading edge of the sloping, angled rock, creating the necessary angular momentum to send the bus off balance and careening onto its left side. Its forward inertia continued, plowing through the dirt and scrub brush like a derailed locomotive, until it stopped just short of the abyss.

As dire as the situation was for the teetering bus, the kids were lucky. Had the heavy transport hit one of the other taller, more prominent rocks, it would have stopped instantly, causing a powerful front-end accident.

From his position, he couldn't determine the depth of the crevasse beyond the bus, but given that he couldn't see the tops of any trees ahead, it must have been a steep cliff. However, it didn't change the fact that these kids were in trouble. Serious trouble.

"Mister! Mister! Please help us! Please!" a young boy's muffled voice said as a chorus of thumps rang out the back of the school bus.

Bunker brought his focus to the rear door and made eye contact with a round face wearing thick spectacles. The kid was staring back at him through the glass. Three more faces appeared alongside the boy, all of them crying for help while beating on the door frame and its glass.

"Hang on, I'm coming!" Bunker yelled, running forward.

"Help us! Please, you have to help us! Please, Mister! Please!" said one of the girls with a tearful, petrified face.

Bunker approached the back of the bus and jumped to grab the elevated door latch. His hand found its mark, allowing him to use his weight and strength to pull the rear of the vehicle down without much trouble.

Once the sideways transport was level and on the ground, he kept his weight pressing on the door handle to keep the bus from tipping back up.

He tried to turn the handle and open the door to free the kids, but it wouldn't spin. He wasn't sure if it was locked or if the door had suffered damage during the accident.

Bunker was about to start yanking on the door to force it open, but his brain stopped him. A sudden and terrible thought flashed in his mind about the vehicle's precarious position and its weight distribution.

If he freed any of the children, it would cause a decrease in weight at the rear and might send the front of the bus over the edge.

"Come on! Hurry up!" the round-faced boy said, resuming his pounding on the inside of the door.

Bunker shook his head, making close eye contact with the kids pleading with him. "Hang on. Let me think about this."

"Please! Help us!" the pig-tailed girl next to the boy cried. "You can't leave us in here!"

"I won't, but I need all of you to hold very still."

"Get us out, please!" the girl screamed as more and more kids squeezed in next to her.

Bunker was about to tell her to remain calm but stopped when he heard the smash of glass breaking above him. He looked up just in time to see a backpack tumble into his vision and land at his feet.

A pair of hands appeared along the top edge of the bus before a head came into view. It belonged to a long-haired boy with dark, deep-set eyes and a pointed nose. He spun his legs around and was about to shimmy down.

"Wait! Don't!" Bunker yelled.

"Why?" the boy asked from above, craning his neck to look down.

Bunker didn't want to scare the kids by relaying too much information about their dangerous predicament, but he didn't have time to mince words. "I need you to go back inside the bus and stay with the others so it doesn't—"

"No way I'm going back in there," the tall, lanky kid interrupted, jumping to the ground on his feet. "Later, dude," he said after a confident flip of his hair, grabbing his backpack and running off through the forest.

Now that some of the counterweight had been removed, he couldn't let go of the door handle. Otherwise, the rear end of the bus surely would rise up again, this time sending the vehicle tumbling to the bottom of the ravine. It was precisely balanced before his arrival, but now that the boy had taken off, Bunker was the only thing keeping the vehicle from falling over the cliff.

"What about us?" the little girl asked. "Can't we get out, too?"

"No! All of you need to stay where you are. I'll get you out, but none of you can move until I say so. Do you understand? Nobody moves from the back of the bus until I tell you it's okay."

Bunker waited for an answer, but none came. All he heard were the sobs of the children as they froze in place with their faces glued to the inside of the glass.

"Oh my God!" Stephanie said from behind Bunker. "The children! Don't let go, Bunker!"

"I'm trying not to, but I need some help here."

"What can I do?" she said, coming to a stop next to him.

"Well, for starters, you can climb up. We need to add more weight in the back to keep this thing stable. But whatever you do, stay to the rear. Maybe we can get a few of the kids out in exchange for your weight."

"Are you serious? You want me to get on top?"

"Yes, but stay to the rear."

She shook her head vehemently. "I don't think I can do that. I'm terrified of heights. And death, too."

"You have to. These kids' lives depend on it."

Stephanie's head wasn't shaking anymore, but the look of fright on her face was still in full bloom. "How many kids are there?"

Bunker moved his head from side to side, peering inside the glass to get a count. The throng of kids was thick and he couldn't see past the first few layers of pre-adolescents.

"I count at least twenty, but there's probably a lot more that I can't see from here. Especially if the bus was full."

Bunker adjusted his grip on the door latch to relieve some of the finger pressure on his right hand. He stuck out his backside and bent forward. "Here, Steph, get on my back and climb up. Maybe your weight and mine is enough to get the kids out. Most of them, anyway."

She shook her head again. "Not if there are like sixty kids in there with backpacks and stuff. That's too much weight for the two of us to counterbalance when they get off. Look at me. Do I look fat to you?"

Jeffrey was next to his mother when he spoke up. "What about rocks, Mom? We could pile a bunch of them in the back. Wouldn't that work?"

Bunker liked that idea. The kid was sharp. Sharper than he was, obviously. "Good idea, sport. You and your mother start bringing me rocks."

Jeffrey pointed to the left. "Mom, there's a bunch over there. I saw them on the way in."

Stephanie grabbed her son by the hand and the two of them took off in the direction Jeffrey had pointed.

The kids in the bus were still crying but at least they were staying together like Bunker told them to do. He assumed hysteria hadn't started because he was close by and the kids could see him on the other side of the glass.

"The glass," he mumbled, feeling a new idea burrow into his mind—an idea he should've thought of before now. *Break the glass to get them out.* His brain was obviously not functioning at full speed under all the stress.

He figured once they had enough rocks on the bus, he could let go and then use one of the stones to shatter the glass and free the kids. Most of them should be able to fit through the broken window without issue. He didn't need to force open the door like he first thought.

However, should his plan with the rocks fail, he'd need to calm his heart and keep his focus sharp. He'd only have seconds to save as many of the children as he could. That meant he'd probably have to choose who lived and who died, and do so in an instant.

Save the girls first, he told himself quietly to prepare for what might come next.

He turned his eyes away from the kids, not wanting to remember their faces in case he couldn't save them all. It was a heartless thing to do, but he couldn't let his emotions enter the equation. Not now. Not until this was over. Emotion might make him hesitate and that would cost lives. He needed to keep his heart cold until the rescue mission was complete.

Stephanie appeared from the forest first, carrying a rock about the size of a small toaster. "Is this one big enough?"

"Yeah, but we're going to need a lot more of those. You need to try to bring two at a time or this is gonna take forever."

"Is this one okay?" Jeffrey asked after he appeared from the woods. The stone in his tiny hands wasn't much bigger than the size of his own shoe.

"Just keep them coming as fast as you can," Bunker said, stopping himself from rolling his eyes. He didn't want to curb the boy's enthusiasm.

In reality, he knew the size of the rocks didn't matter. It was the quantity. Every bit of weight would help as long as the children didn't move or panic.

When Stephanie arrived, she was out of breath, and that surprised him. He thought she was in better shape based on her skinny frame and curvy figure. That meant her thin profile was not from endless hours of cardio. Probably a rigorous diet, or she was just blessed with good family genes.

"Here you go," she said, trying to hand it to him.

"Just put it on the ground and keep getting more. Once we have enough, you and I will change places so I can carry them up on top of the bus."

She stared at him with eyes wide and her mouth agape.

"It'll be okay, Steph. I need you to trust me on this."

She nodded, though she didn't seem convinced.

"Now keep the rocks coming," he told her.

CHAPTER 10

Deputy Daisy Clark leaned to the right on the Sheriff's mountain bike as she centered her path across the wooden planks of the Old Henley Bridge. The back tire fishtailed a bit when she glanced down at the Arkansas River, sending a charge of adrenaline into her muscles. Once across the expanse, she made a hard right to turn east, passing a hand-carved wooden signpost that read *OLD MILL ROAD*.

Her destination was Frank Tuttle's place at the far end of the dirt road in front of her. His home sat on the north side of the street, across the road from the Rainey homestead, which Daisy would first pass on the right.

She glanced behind her to check for approaching cars. The road was empty, allowing her to safely cross to the left and continue her mad peddling, pumping her thighs with force.

Before she could take another breath, it hit her—there wouldn't be any cars or trucks—not modern ones anyway. Not with the widespread electronic failures after the grid went down.

She scoffed at her own stupidity, realizing it was going to be difficult to break free of habits associated with normal life. A life inundated with modern conveniences, all powered by integrated electronics and abundant electricity.

It meant her regular Saturday night Netflix movie marathons were going to be a thing of the past, at least until this event was over—whatever this event turned out to be.

She had her suspicions as to the cause and figured the Sheriff and Mayor did, too, based on their generalized statements. Only a herd of mindless sheep, whose collective heads were buried in denial, would think everything was okay or going to be okay.

But in the end, it wasn't up to her to speculate. Or raise concerns. Nor could she take the chance of speaking out of turn and causing a town-wide panic over what might turn out to be nothing.

God knows, she wanted it to be nothing, but her gut was telling her that this was more than nothing.

The thickening tensions in town seemed to support her uneasiness. Everywhere she looked, she could see it on the townspeople's faces. A blanket of fear had quickly taken over, creeping from person to person like some kind of airborne pathogen hell-bent on destroying the masses. She couldn't believe how quickly the mood in town had changed—all of it happening in a matter of hours.

Think positive. Everything's going to be okay. Just do your job, she thought to herself as dirt and pebbles continued to fly up from the back tire and land on her back.

The trail of dust behind her was growing with each push of her thigh muscles, hanging in the air like wayward smoke from a raging forest fire. It hadn't rained in almost two weeks, stressing the health of the forest and making the road dustier and harder than it would normally be this time of the year.

The ruts, dips, and bumps were many, jarring her body with every jolt in terrain. Her biggest concern was the sharp rocks that seemed to be growing up through the dirt like an infestation of weeds.

If one of them hit her front tire straight on, it might pop the tube and send her flying. She needed to be extra careful since her standard issue two-way radio was useless. There weren't many people around to help on this road to nowhere.

Mrs. Rainey owned one of the two homesteads on this side of the river, but the woman was back in town and probably still pestering the Sheriff about her overdue grandkid.

That left only Frank Tuttle, and he was most certainly home. He always was, never seeming to leave his property. For anything. At least not since his wife passed.

Daisy stopped pedaling to catch her breath, while the bike coasted the remaining twenty feet or so to Tuttle's front gate. When she arrived, she used the foot brake to send the back wheel into a full skid, then put her other foot down to keep from falling over when the bike's momentum came to an abrupt stop.

The dust cloud she'd made floated on past, almost as if it had just staged a mutiny and decided to set out on its own mission in the high country of Colorado.

She kept her butt on the seat and waited for Frank Tuttle, who was somewhere beyond the gate with a pair of binoculars, studying her from afar. He was a bit jumpy, and the last thing she wanted to do was alarm the gray-haired man. Doing so would be a sure-fire recipe for getting shot.

"Wait for a sign," she mumbled, holding up her hands to show him she'd come in peace.

His rectangular, thousand-square-foot home was set back about two hundred feet and running parallel with the road. The singlewide mobile home had been permanently mounted to the mountain terrain through the use of a brick foundation a few decades before.

Yet, it still looked out of place for the area, especially since it was sitting across the street from a modern site-built home—Martha Rainey's place, an all-brick, two-story ranch style home with a green and white color scheme that gave it a true country feel. So did her upscale wooden shutters, impressive redwood deck and covered patio across the entire front, and the three towering chimneys rising up from the roofline.

Tuttle's shack was just the opposite—a run-down aluminum firetrap, featuring cheap horizontal blinds across the windows and only space heaters to keep its sole occupant warm in the winter.

Frank Tuttle was cheap. She knew it and the rest of the people in town knew it, yet he'd spent some serious money on the four-story pole barn in the back. It was easily the biggest structure on the property and built to span the ages. It rose up like a redneck skyscraper on the left of the house, just beyond the end of the dirt driveway that stretched out before her. The barn's tall double doors were looking straight at her, begging her to come inside for an inspection.

A pump house and ground-mounted solar panel array, both of which were inside their own giant wire cages, stood to the right of the main residence. She knew from her years of visiting as a teen that countless acres of grazing pasture and miles of cattle fencing were beyond the water and power facilities.

The four mini-blinds across the front of the home were shut, and there were no vehicles in the driveway. Even though no signs of life were present, she knew Tuttle was there—watching her.

The seven piles of river rock in the driveway were new since the last time she'd paid him a visit. It was a couple of years ago when she'd stopped by to check on Tuttle after the poorly-attended funeral for his late wife, Helen.

The ten-foot-tall rock mounds seemed to be spaced randomly, like an obstacle course. She figured Tuttle had left them untouched after the dump truck driver backed up and dropped them wherever he pleased.

All but one of the piles had a smattering of loose stones around their bases. But the fallen rocks weren't the only items needing Tuttle's attention. She counted at least a dozen unruly bushes whose branches were sticking up and out in random directions.

There were also clumps of weeds growing everywhere; some of them were green, while others had turned a light brown. The two-week drought had obviously started to take a toll on his front yard, if you could call it that.

To her right were three old Ford pickups. The paint across their rounded hoods had peeled away long ago, and the rusting side panels looked like they were barely holding together. She wasn't sure what year they were made, but it was long before she was born.

Daisy didn't understand the need for the hillbilly yard art, but Tuttle was obviously fond of it. Just past the trucks were dozens of rusting gas station and roadway signs sticking up at odd angles, plus a couple of ancient safes sitting in the weeds with their doors open.

The oddest item in his yard was the red Honda lawnmower. It looked relatively new and didn't seem to match the rest of the man's antique clutter.

She knew from her younger days that Tuttle cut the massive pastures out back with his tractor, so why have a Honda mower? There wasn't any grass to cut out front, so why purchase something he didn't need? The man hated to crack open his dust-filled wallet, so if he spent money on purchasing the unit, he must have had a good reason. That was assuming the man hadn't gone completely nuts, which was a distinct possibility.

It was time to make contact, she decided, taking in a deep breath to charge her vocal cords.

"Frank? It's me, Daisy. Daisy Clark. Can you come out and talk to me? It's urgent."

An instant later, she heard a response. "Since when, Daisy, did you join the Sheriff's Department?" a man's voice called out.

She recognized the ragged nature of the voice, though she couldn't determine its location. "Yeah, Frank, about six months ago. I'm a deputy now."

"I see that. Kinda hard to miss the badge and the gun. Why you here?"

"The Sheriff sent me to—"

"—arrest me?"

"No, Frank. Nothing like that. I swear."

"Then you must be here to take my land and my guns."

Daisy shook her head, keeping her hands up high. She still couldn't track down his position. He was in front of her somewhere, but his voice didn't seem to be attached to a body. "Why would you think that?"

"Because that's what the law does. Takes stuff from the people. Hard-working people like me. Then they give it to those who never earned it. Look, I haven't done anything wrong and I pay my taxes, so you got no right to be here. I just wanna be left alone."

"I know all that, Frank. Nobody doubts you're a law-abiding citizen. That's not why I'm here. The Sheriff and I need your help with something. I don't know if you know, but there's a serious emergency in town."

"Yeah? What kind of emergency?"

"There's a problem with the power—"

"No! You can't have my generator. Or my solar panels. They're mine, I tell ya. Mine. So are my Faraday cages. I told every last one of you this would happen. But noooo . . . nobody listens to an old man like me. You should've gotten off the grid and protected yourself like I did. Them damn power lines. They killed my Helen with that woman cancer. Ate her down to the bone. It got so bad, I could almost pick her up from the sheet with one hand. But they ain't gonna kill me. No way. No how. Not with my Faraday cages. They are the key, Daisy. The key to everything. You all should've been building 'em like I said."

Daisy took a deep breath, trying to remain calm as Tuttle continued.

"So you turn that pretty little ass of yours around right now and go back the way you came. You can't have any of my stuff. I'm not kidding, Daisy. Do it now before I empty both barrels at ya. Just because you were friends with my daughter doesn't mean I won't shoot you."

"Frank, you're not listening to me."

"I've read the Constitution and I know I'm well within my rights to defend myself and my property from all threats, foreign and domestic. And that includes that new Sheriff of yours. Make sure you tell him I said to stay the hell away from this property. None of you got any right to be here. Not without one of them warrants. And an army to back it up."

Daisy heard the distinctive ratcheting sound of two shotgun hammers being pulled back, one after the other. "Easy now, Frank. Let's not do anything rash."

"I'm gonna count to three."

"Wait, let me prove it to you," she said, bringing her left hand down slowly and unhooking the clasp on her duty belt. She took off the belt and held it out to the side with its holster and her Glock semi-auto handgun nestled inside.

She knew disarming herself while facing an armed threat went against all her training, but she was friends with this man. At least, she used to be. Tuttle wasn't going to shoot unless he had a good reason to pull the trigger.

"Look, I've taken off my gun," she said, leaning over to the left. "And now I'm putting it on the ground."

He didn't respond.

She sat upright and took off her badge and tossed it next to the holster in the dirt. "See, no more badge, either. Right now, I'm not a deputy. I'm just a defenseless girl who needs the help of a patriotic friend. A friend who's known her a long time."

"What about the other one?" he said in a sharper tone than before. "Cops always have one of them backup pieces. Let me see it."

"You will. It's on my ankle. But first I need to get off this bike. Can I do that?"

"Yep. But no sudden moves. Don't make me blast a hole in ya."

Daisy slid off the bicycle, then bent down and pulled up her right pant leg. She hesitated for a few seconds to give Tuttle a chance to see the holstered Ruger LCP .380.

"All right, now remove it," Tuttle said.

She latched onto the gun's stock and pulled it free with only the tips of two fingers. She held it out to the side as if it were a dead fish before putting it on top of one of the wraps of her duty belt.

Someone else might have simply tossed it to the ground instead, but she didn't want her backup gun sitting in the dirt. She'd just cleaned and oiled it after her last trip to the range and didn't want the internal mechanisms to be compromised.

"Now, back up ten feet," he said. "Leave the holster and guns where they are."

She did as he instructed, walking backwards with the bicycle's handlebars in her hands. "Okay. I've done as you've asked. Now, will you come out and talk with me? It's super urgent."

One of the piles of rock in the middle of Tuttle's driveway began to move, but not like Daisy expected. Stones weren't falling to the ground from gravity. No, this was something else—a hatch opening along the front—a hatch covered in stationary rock. It rose up like the rear door to a minivan.

Someone stepped out with a shotgun pointed at Daisy. She assumed it was Tuttle, but she couldn't be sure. The person was dressed in full camouflage, including pants, shirt, boots, gloves, and a balaclava covering their head and face.

"Frank? Is that you?"

The person holding the gun lowered their weapon for a moment to rip off the mask off with one tug from the bottom.

It was Frank Tuttle, all right.

His hair was much longer and a few shades grayer than the last time she'd seen him. His face seemed ten years older, too. Paranoia and stress must have been getting to him.

"You got two minutes, so make it quick," he said, sounding like he was chewing on something. He opened the front gate and walked through, never taking the gun sights off her as he approached.

Daisy ignored the gun and kept her eyes locked on his. "Mrs. Rainey told the Sheriff a little while ago that you have a bomb shelter on your property."

Tuttle shook his head and snorted an angry breath. "That nosey bitch. She really needs to mind her own business. You know, one of these days, some of them fleabags of hers might just turn up dead. You know, from mysterious causes."

"Let's keep it civil, Frank. She's just trying to help everyone."

"How is that, exactly?"

"We're hoping you might have a Geiger counter we could borrow."

"I knew it! Someone nuked us!" he snarled after spitting out a patch of chewing tobacco. "Must be them damn Russians."

He held the shotgun in one hand while pulling out a white handkerchief from his front pocket with the other. He covered his nose and mouth with the cloth, giving her a clear view of its surplus of yellow stains. "Or is it that cocksucker, Castro? He's plumb crazy enough to do it. They all are. Even that rag-head . . . old what's his name. The one who took all them hostages in the embassy."

"That was way back in the 80s, Frank. I'm pretty sure he's not in power anymore."

"You sure about that?"

"Positive. Reagan got them released, remember? Way back in the 1980s."

"Well, someone else then. The name don't matter. They all the same. Always wanting to kill us. I'll bet you didn't know that the first thing they do when they capture you is take your children and wrap them up with them turbans around they heads. Then they brainwash your kids and burn your Bibles before cutting off the heads of the parents. Heathens, I say. Every last one of them."

She didn't know how to respond, so she didn't.

He continued with eyes wide. "How close did they drop the nuke? Denver? Kansas City? LA? Is the radiation cloud on its way here? How long do we have?"

"Let's not go there, Frank. We don't know if it was a bomb or not. The Sheriff just wants to check the radiation levels. It's his job to keep everyone safe, including you."

"Well, I don't need anyone's help, thank you very much."

A vision of four men in white coats appeared in her mind. The short video clip showed a team of doctors dragging him out his front door in a straitjacket, while stuffing Valium down his throat.

She flushed the image from her thoughts and brought her attention back to the armed man. "Do you have one or not? I'm kinda pressed for time here, Frank."

He nodded. "Got me two of 'em. One primary and one backup. You gotta have backups, Daisy. For everything. Only a fool don't have backups."

"Do they still work?"

"You're damn straight they do. I test them every month on the third and the twenty-second, exactly at 10:24 AM. Just like the handwritten notes in the manual says. But it's gonna cost ya. Big time."

"Okay, how much?" she asked, wondering where this crazy old fart was going with his request. He better not ask her to take off her clothes or something else even more sick and twisted. His living alone in a homemade fortress with only his demons to talk to had obviously eroded some of his mental foundation.

Tuttle took the hanky from his mouth, then rubbed his chin with it for a few seconds before speaking in a calmer tone. "Three dollars. Cash. And none of that Mexican peso crap. I only accept American. You got it? I don't do Jap, neither."

She held back a laugh, wanting to play along. He was finally settling down a bit and she needed to complete this mission and get back to town. "Okay, three bucks. But you gotta put the shotgun down. We're both friends here."

Tuttle didn't answer, only staring at her with his cloudy, brown eyes. The swatches of wrinkles around his eyes were heavy and distinct, compressing and releasing each time he blinked.

His weathered face showed the cumulative effects of an old man's tormented life—a life capped by the slow, methodical death of the only woman he ever loved. Daisy felt sorry for him. He'd been through hell with his wife's painful end, only to be left with a lonely shadow existence.

"Come on, Frank. You know me. You know I'm not a threat. Your daughter and I were best friends growing up. I was over here all the time, at least until Misty ran off with that skinny artist from overseas who blew into town right after high school. Can't remember his name, though."

"Cowie."

"Yes, that's it. Angus Cowie," she said after testing Frank's memory with the carefully worded question.

His mouth turned south. "Always ragging on our country about this and that. What a pompous ass. I never liked him. Not one bit, I tell ya."

"That makes two of us," she said, seeing his eye soften and his chin release its clench. She was getting through to him. "Look, I've done everything you've asked me to do. Now I need you trust me. Please, Frank. Put . . . down . . . the . . . gun."

His whole body relaxed as he lowered the barrel and tucked the stock under his arm.

She gave him a friendly smile. "That's better. Now, where is it? I need to get back to the Sheriff."

"Let me see it," he said in a more serious tone as all the expression ran from his face.

"See what?"

He held out his hand, palm up. "The cash. I don't offer credit, missy. Cash up front or the deal's off."

She smiled, then took out a money clip from her pocket. Her hands unrolled the small wrap of bills and shuffled through them until she found three one dollar bills. She pulled them free and gave them to him in a clump.

He took turns holding each one up to the sun for a moment before stuffing them into his pocket.

"Follow me," he said when he was done, spinning his boots in the dirt and walking toward the pole barn.

She followed behind him as he sauntered around the rock piles and through the weeds on his way to the massive structure. The man's movement left a trail of stench she had to walk though—a strong combination of cigar smoke and body odor.

Daisy couldn't imagine how bad it smelled inside his singlewide home. The sun's relentless baking of a tin can like that would etch the smell into the walls and floor permanently.

Fifty feet later, Daisy could see behind the house. Tuttle had built an impressive chicken coop beneath one of the majestic oak trees. Next to it was a two-story pigeon house about the size of a Jeep. Neither of the two wooden structures existed when she last visited, and both of them were full of animals and surrounded by dense wire cages.

When they reached the pole barn entrance, Tuttle unlocked three padlocks with a set of keys from his pocket. He slid the double doors open from the middle, then went inside and disappeared into the darkness.

She waited in silence for him to turn on a flashlight.

"Well, you coming in or what?" he asked from inside the void.

Daisy didn't like the idea of following a creepy old man into a dark building, but she didn't want to raise the man's suspicions. Not after spending the time to get him to trust her. She stepped inside.

He closed the doors behind her, then flipped on a light switch, igniting a series of overhead lights high above in the rafters. Since the power was out in the area, Tuttle obviously had backup power. She didn't hear a generator puttering in the background, so that meant battery backup. She should have expected that, given his solar panels, Faraday cages, and reputation as a prepper.

The barn was filled with stacks and stacks of provisions and supplies—an impressive sight. Everywhere she looked, it was more of the same.

All of the columns were sitting on raised platforms, like heavy, reinforced pallets, and wrapped with several layers of shrink wrap. Each stack went from the floor up to the ceiling, some four stories away. Wal-Mart had nothing on this man.

"Holy cow, Frank. Did you buy all this stuff?"

"Yeah, you know what they say . . . you can never have enough ammo. Or supplies," he answered, wearing a slight grin. He was obviously proud of his inventory.

"Well, I don't think they were talking about you. You certainly have enough. How did you stack all of this crap up?"

"A series of chain hoists," he said, pointing at the ceiling at the far end of the center aisle. "And my forklift parked around back. I keep everything out of sight from that witch across the street. I swear, she sits around all day just waiting for me to do something."

"Is that why you parked the old trucks and put the signs out front? To piss her off?"

"Yeah, 'cuz it seems like every time I look over there, she's out on her front porch, staring at me from that there rocking chair of hers. My plan is to stack up so much stuff that she stops looking over here. Until then, I have to work mostly at night just to have a little privacy."

"Night work, huh?" she said, letting her eyes take a quick inventory of what was around her.

"Well, when the moon's not out. Truth is, it's not easy living alone, but it's even harder when you're living across the street from a crazy person."

He should talk, she thought quietly.

"But I make do as best I can," he added. "It just ain't the same since my Helen passed."

"You probably don't know this, but she was one of my favorite people in the whole world. She always had a smile on her face and made me feel welcome every time I came over."

"Yeah, she did that with everyone. She had a big heart."

"Yes, she did. When I used to hang out here with Misty, I could see how much she loved her family, Frank. I think everyone in town knew that, too."

He nodded. "Helen was the best."

Daisy walked down the center aisle and took in the size and scope of his inventory. Tuttle even had four pallets of disposable diapers. "This is totally unbelievable. How could you afford all this? It had to cost a fortune."

"Helen's parents. They were loaded when they passed."

"Helen helped you do all this?"

"Yep. That woman was freakishly strong for her size."

"Like I said, she loved you very much," Daisy added, wondering if she'd have the same selfless dedication to back her husband like Helen did with Frank. After all, spending all their money on doomsday preparations took a special kind of love—and madness.

However, to test herself like that, Daisy would have to get married first. Which, of course, would never happen unless she found a man she could stand to be around for more than a few days.

Not likely, she thought. She hadn't managed to scrounge up a real date in over a year. Though it wasn't all her fault. The town gene pool was pretty slim when it came to eligible men.

It wasn't like she was overly picky, but they needed to at least bathe regularly and have all their teeth. Oh, and not be married, like the last man she'd been with. She'd let her guard down for only a moment and somehow he found the crack in her armor and worked his way into her life.

She hated herself for getting involved with him and broke it off soon after it started, but the damage was already done. You can't undo the heartache you cause to someone you know. Not in a small town, where everyone knows everything about everyone.

"Over here," Tuttle said, leading her with an outstretched hand.

They worked their way back through a maze of stacks on the right, eventually passing a series of heavy-duty metal filing cabinets sitting side by side. All of them were six feet tall, with double swing doors that met in the middle.

Every seam in the metal frames appeared to have been taped shut with wide strips of metal-reinforced tape. On the front of each was a handwritten cardboard sign that read KEEP SEALED UNTIL TEOTWAWKI.

She quietly mouthed out the words from the acronym's letters: *THE END OF THE WORLD AS WE KNOW IT.*

Tuttle kept walking past the line of doomsday cabinets and eventually stopped in front of what appeared to be a trap door built into the floor. He pointed. "It's down there."

"You built a fallout shelter inside your barn?" she asked as another round of acrid BO and cigar smoke invaded her nostrils. She wanted to gag, but managed to hold it back.

"Yeah, this one. Can't build them all outside. That's too predictable. Gotta keep 'em guessing and you gotta have options. Options is the key since you never know what's coming your way or what you're gonna need. Gotta prep for everything. Got to have backups."

"You have more than one?"

His eyes pinched and he straightened his posture, but didn't respond.

Daisy got the sense Tuttle just realized he'd shared too much information. She needed to redirect his focus elsewhere before he got upset and refused to cooperate any further.

She nodded and then pointed at the floor hatch. "Okay then, let's get to it."

"You wait here. Nobody goes down there except me."

"No problem, Frank. Whatever you want. But please hurry."

CHAPTER 11

Sheriff Gus Apollo stood in front of the six men he'd just drafted for temporary assignment as Clearwater Deputy Sheriffs. None of them were over thirty but they were in good shape. Well, except for the two on the left.

One of the questionable selections was tall and grossly underweight, while the other was short and must have weighed three hundred pounds. Maybe more. Gus wasn't exactly *rockin' a killer bod* as Daisy would say, but compared to this kid, he felt like an underwear model.

The odd pair reminded him of Laurel and Hardy, from the black and white TV days. Even though their shows were first broadcast well before his time, Gus had fond memories of the reruns.

When his Reserve Unit rolled into town after their annual fishing trip to Canada, he planned to say goodbye to these six recruits. Until then, they'd have to do. None of them were trained or ready, but they should be able to help if he kept them on a short leash.

For privacy, Gus closed the door to his office before giving each man a Deputy Sheriff's star. He motioned for them to pin it on. "Left side pocket, gentlemen," he said, waiting until they were done sticking the tin to their chests.

"To save time, I'm gonna shortcut the swearing-in ceremony and offer a revised oath of duty. I'll recite it from start to finish and then have you all agree to it in unison when I'm done. Understood?"

Each of the men nodded.

"Excellent," he said in a firm tone. "If you can all follow orders that well from here on out, this new partnership might have a chance to work. Are you ready, men?"

A collective though disjointed set of affirming answers came from the group. "Yes . . . Yes, Sheriff . . . Ready . . . Roger that, sir."

"Raise your left hand and put your right hand over your heart."

Gus waited until everyone was in oath-taking position, then pulled out a note card from his front pocket and looked at the words inscribed on it. The Mayor's handwriting was excellent and easy to read.

"I, Sheriff Augustus Apollo, do hereby deputize each of you under the rights granted to me by the esteemed Mayor and the proud citizens of Clearwater, Colorado."

Some of the men puffed out their chests and stood a little more erect than before.

"Do each of you swear your solemn oath to support and defend the Constitution of the United States, the Constitution of the State of Colorado, and the laws of the city of Clearwater? Will each of you faithfully discharge any and all duties that I or the Mayor assign to you in accordance with the policies and procedures of this Sheriff's Office, and do so until such time as your temporary duty ends or is revoked? If you agree, then step forward and answer with *Yes, Sheriff.*"

Each man in the group took a single step forward and answered as instructed.

"Therefore, by the power vested in me, I hereby grant each of you legal standing as Deputy Sheriff of Clearwater, Colorado."

There was a long pause in the room.

"That's it?" one of the younger men asked after making eye contact with the man standing next to him. Gus remembered his first name as Wayne, but his last name eluded his memory.

"That's it, Wayne. You're now on the team. So are the rest of you. Welcome aboard."

The tallest and most muscular of the group stepped forward. "Orders, sir?"

"I need you to break into teams of two. Team One will head out to the Silver King Mine and assist Mr. King with the recovery of his men trapped in the mineshaft. Who wants this assignment?"

Sheriff Apollo waited, but nobody spoke up. "Okay, since none of you want to volunteer, we'll do this another way," he said before pointing at the closest man on the right. "You and Wayne, head out there. From now on, you're Team One."

The two men nodded.

Gus waited for them to turn and leave, but they stood there, looking confused. "On your way, boys. Time to get cracking."

"On foot?"

"Yeah, we really don't have a choice now, do we? Mr. King will guide you. He's waiting outside my office."

They nodded and left the office, failing to close the door behind them.

He pointed at the skinniest and the fattest of the two. They were standing together on the left. "You guys are Team Two and assigned to crowd control."

"Crowd control? Really? That's all?" the skinny man said.

"Watch the square and try to keep everyone calm. I'm not sure how long this outage will last, but there's bound to be some stressful moments around here."

"Do we get guns?" the shorter member of Team Two asked. Gus remembered his name as Albert from their brief introduction outside. This man's excess poundage was only outdone by the pimples across his nose and neck. There was probably more acne hiding along his chin, but the thick stubble across his rounded chin and plump cheeks covered up some serious acreage on his face.

"No, you don't get guns. Not until I've had a chance to train you on proper handling techniques and certified your ability at the range."

"Come on, Sheriff, I know how to shoot. I've mastered all fifty-five levels in Call of Duty, Black Ops 3," Albert said, reaching for the holster on the side of Gus' waistline.

Gus blocked Albert's attempt with his hand. "Let me say this one more time. *No guns!* Now, you two get outside and stand watch before I change my mind and revoke your deputyship. If anything pops up, notify me immediately. You're my eyes and ears out there."

They nodded before leaving the room single file. Albert was the second of the two and sauntered with his shoulders slumped and head hanging low. It bobbed from side to side on his neck thanks to his rocking, peg-legged walking stride. Gus figured if the kid lost a hundred pounds, his knee-locked stride would be a lot smoother. Possibly even non-existent.

The sheriff addressed the remaining two men. "Team Three, you're on search and rescue."

"Who are we looking for, boss?"

"A group of kids who haven't returned from their field trip. When Deputy Clark returns from her field assignment, I want the three of you to ride out to Atwater's place and borrow some of his horses."

"Ride, Sheriff? Before we have the horses?"

"Wrong kind of ride," Gus said. "Grab a couple of bikes from Ye Old Bike Shop and head out there. Exchange them for the horses we're commandeering, then assist Deputy Clark in search and rescue efforts out by Clayton Ravine on County Road C. You guys can ride a bike, can't you?"

"Yes, sir. Spent most of my high school years riding to and from school every day on those uncomfortable seats," the blonde man with the stout chest and wide shoulders answered.

Gus knew him as Dick Dickens, the former starting offensive guard for the high school football team a few years back. The brute would've finally earned All-State honors if it weren't for his Achilles' tendon snapping in the second game of his senior season. Gus decided to address the young man using his nickname. "Must have been a darn big seat, Dicky."

"That it was, Sheriff. We grow 'em big in Colorado."

"That we do," Gus said as a smile hit his lips. He glanced down at Dicky's right leg, then brought his eyes back up. "Looks like your foot is all healed up."

"Rehab took forever. But for the most part, I'm as good as new."

Gus looked at the other guy. "And you?"

"Yeah, I can ride. It's been a while, but I'm sure it'll come back to me."

"Fair enough. Now get out there, men, and make me proud. Daisy—I mean Deputy Clark—should be back any minute."

"Yes, Sheriff," Dicky answered, leading his partner out of the office.

CHAPTER 12

Stephanie King doubled her grip on the door latch of the toppled bus as she kept a close eye on the kids inside. They were packed in like gophers, sitting only inches from her on the other side of the glass.

"How are the kids holding up?" Bunker asked from five feet away.

"They're okay, for now. I think watching you haul the rocks up on top is keeping them preoccupied. But we need to get this done before they lose interest."

"Working as fast as I can," he told her, loading another round of rocks inside the back of his tucked shirt.

"That's gotta hurt," she said, seeing splotches of blood dotting the cloth covering his back. Each time he dropped another rock inside the collar of his shirt, the stones clanked together at the bottom and sent the bulge of material wider along the man's slender waistline.

"Ah, this doesn't hurt. I've felt worse, trust me," he said, climbing up the yellow metal wall. He planted his knees on top of the sideways bus after pulling himself up. He stood up and with a quick yank, he untucked his shirt and let the rocks fall like he'd done the previous six trips, then dropped back down to the ground.

"How will you know when we have enough weight up there?" she asked, looking at the remaining stones she and Jeffrey had brought from a nearby creek bed. Thanks to the recent drought, they didn't have to wade through any water, so collecting the stones was simple.

Bunker pointed at the pile. "When all of those are up there," he said, swinging his index finger from low to high. "I don't want to take any chances."

"I hope we brought enough," she added, wondering if his shirt could stand up to the stress of the remaining sharp edges and weight—a cotton t-shirt wasn't exactly the strongest material.

Jeffrey interrupted. "It should be enough, Mom. Since the bus was balancing on its own before, all we need is the same amount of weight as all the kids inside. Plus a little bit extra just to be sure."

"How do you know all of this, angel?" she asked, figuring Bunker must have told him when she wasn't paying attention.

"*Frankie's Science Lab*, Mom. Remember?"

"Oh yeah, right," she answered, remembering how hard it was to track down that educational game in Denver at Christmas. Hardly anyone stocked the slow-selling item, but she finally found one in a rundown secondhand toy store on the west side of town.

Until then, she thought her trip to visit her mom and take her shopping for the holidays was a complete bust. But the effort was worth it. Jeffrey loved that game, spending hours upon hours interacting with it to answer questions. And now, it appeared he actually learned something useful along the way.

Bunker spent the next handful of minutes transporting the rest of the counterbalance material to the top of the school bus. After the final load was delivered and stacked, he stood atop his perch and looked down at Stephanie. "Moment of truth."

"Would it make sense for you to stay up there while I get the kids out? You'd add more weight," she said, not knowing where the idea came from. She'd just put herself square in the middle of what must come next, heaping all the responsibility upon her thin shoulders.

"Yeah, it would. But that means you're gonna have to get the kids out and do so in a hurry. Do you think you're up to it?"

She took a deep breath and let it out before answering. Her brain was telling her to say no, but her heart had other plans. "Yeah, I think so."

"Are you sure? Because if we don't have enough weight up here, then the bus will . . . well, you know. If that happens, you'll have to make a snap decision on who you will sa—"

She didn't need to hear any more of his explanation, and neither did her son. Or the trapped kids who were listening with curious ears. "I got it. You don't have to spell it out for me."

Stephanie turned her neck to look at Jeffrey, standing behind her. She wanted to wrap him in a tight hug and give him a series of tender kisses across his forehead while she had the chance, but she couldn't. Not now. Not with her hands pressing down on the door latch. She couldn't take the chance that Bunker's plan with the rocks was wrong.

"Jeffrey, honey, I need you to go stand over by the big boulders."

"No, Mom," he answered in his most boyish voice.

"Yes. Go. Like I said."

"But I should stay and help you."

"This isn't open for debate, young man. Over by the boulders, now! I'm not going to say it again."

"Okay, fine," he said, turning and walking away, stomping his feet with force.

"You're gonna need this," Bunker told her from above. He dropped a rock the size of a softball. It landed near her feet.

She spread her legs out and bent forward, trying to reach the stone with her right hand. It wasn't easy to do and keep her left hand on the door latch.

"Hang on a sec," Bunker said.

Stephanie froze, her fingertips only a few inches from the rock.

"You can let go of the handle now. I'm pretty sure things are stable," he said in a confident tone.

She wasn't sure she heard him correctly. "I'm sorry, what?"

"Try letting go."

"Really?"

"Yes."

"Okay," she said, pulling her hand back from the rock and bringing her legs together again. When she straightened her back, she made eye contact with the kids inside. They must have known what was about to happen because all of their little eyes were now wide. "It'll be okay, kids. I promise."

Some of them nodded, but Stephanie could see their fear building. She eased her hand off the door latch but decided to keep it close just in case she needed to grab it again.

The bus didn't move.

"Like I said. Stable," Bunker quipped. "You really need to think about trusting me."

"I do. Mostly," she answered, picking up the rock in one hand. She held it in her palm, bouncing it gently to get a feel for its weight. "What about the glass breaking? Some of the kids might get hurt."

"Right. I forgot about that," Bunker said, hesitating for a three-count. "I think I have an idea."

Stephanie watched him turn away from her and pull the bottom of his t-shirt up and over his head. She expected to only see bloody scrapes and cuts across the white of his back, but that's not what she saw.

The man's sculptured back and powerful shoulders were covered in a tapestry of colorful tattoos. The ink featured numerous symbols, shapes, and animals, plus some numbers scattered about.

A beautiful red, white, and blue eagle with its wings raised at a ninety-degree angle took up a good portion of his back. The wingspan stretched from one shoulder blade to the other and was easily the biggest piece of artwork.

The smallest item was a bloody upside-down peace symbol over his left kidney area. Next to it were the crosshairs of a target, and farther to the right was a red spider's web drawn over an all-black skull with fiery red eyes.

Above the prominent eagle were the numbers 14-88 written in black ink and underlined in drops of red blood. Below the black skull was the number 666, also in red.

Other than the devil's number, she didn't know what the rest of it meant, but the colors and symbols seemed to be everywhere—at least where there wasn't a raised scar in the way.

The artwork looked to wrap around the side of the man's impressively slender waist. She figured there was more across his front, but since he was facing away from her, she couldn't see any of it.

The same was true for the hard-to-identify ink on his arms. Most of it looked faded and old, like he'd started his self-expression on his forearms first.

When Bunker spun his head and glanced over his shoulder at her, she moved her eyes away. She didn't want him to catch her staring at his tattoos. He'd obviously covered them up for a reason. Otherwise, who would decide to wear a long-sleeve t-shirt in the middle of the summer?

She wondered if the bandages along his neck were hiding more of the same. Made sense, she thought. He couldn't cover them up with his shirt when he was out in public, so maybe the bandages were his attempt to protect his secrets.

"It's okay," Bunker said. "You can look. I don't mind. But let me say this . . . what you are seeing isn't what you think. At least, not anymore. I'm no longer *that* guy,"

"You don't have to explain," Stephanie said, figuring she was either looking at jailhouse or gang tattoos. Probably both. "It's really none of my business anyway. And besides, we both agreed not to judge each other, remember?"

"True, but I'm sure you wanna know what kind of man you're traveling with."

She had questions, sure. But in truth, she really didn't want to know what kind of man he was. Not after seeing all the disturbing artwork.

Sometimes, too much information is a bad thing. She'd learned the hard way that there are times when it's better not to know the answers since you can't unlearn what, in the end, turns out to be something you really didn't want to know in the first place. If his secrets turned out to be something horrible, she could never go back.

Sort of like when she decided to follow her ex-husband one night and caught him cheating on her. Once she knew it to be true, she couldn't pry it out of her head. Up until that moment, she could live in peaceful ignorance by convincing herself he wasn't being a total douchebag.

Right now, she didn't know anything for sure about Bunker, and that was enough to keep her sanity in check and her denial in place. She needed to count on this man to keep them all safe, and adding a pile of worry about his past wasn't going to help her get through the day.

She shook her head. "Like I said, it's your business. Not mine. Let's just get the kids out, okay? They're the only thing I care about at the moment."

"Agreed," he said, kneeling down in a crouched position, still facing away from her.

She took a quick step back and watched him wad up his shirt and toss it inside the bus through what she assumed was an open window.

Bunker pointed and spoke to one of the kids inside the bus. "You—what's your name?"

A deep voice said, "Tommy."

"Tommy, you look like the tallest, so I need you to hold my shirt over the glass on the door when Stephanie breaks it. Keep your hands high and turn your head away, okay? Can you do that?"

"Uh-huh."

"Just don't let any of the other kids move any closer to the front of the bus. Everyone needs to stay in the back. Okay? It'll be a tight fit for all of you, but you can do it."

Stephanie returned to her position at the back door. Bunker's shirt was now hanging on the inside of the glass like he'd instructed the kid to do.

"Go ahead. Do it," Bunker told her. "Then work the rock around the frame to clear all the sharp edges so the kids can crawl out safely."

She swung the rock at the glass, but it slipped out of her hand before impact. It flew through the glass and wrapped itself inside the cotton of Bunker's shirt before landing inside.

Her trembling hand went inside the window. "Here, give it back to me," she told Tommy. "But be careful."

The boy gave her the wad of cloth and stone. She unwrapped it, then tossed the shirt up to Bunker, who was now sitting along the edge of the bus with his knees in front of his chest. She could see small portions of tattoos along his side, but not enough to make out what they were. "Here, you need to cover up so the kids don't see."

She was tempted to look away as he began to put the shirt on, but didn't. Bunker slipped the garment over his head and pulled it down before uncoiling his legs from in front of his chest. His movements looked awkward and clumsy, indicating he didn't want her to see whatever was drawn on his chest.

It was time to clear the shards from the window frame as Bunker suggested. Stephanie ran the rock around the edges, keeping her fingers away from anything sharp. When she was done, she tossed the stone away.

Inside, two of the kids had their backpacks on. It gave her an idea. She pointed at the boy on the left—a blonde-haired lad with dimples on his cherub cheeks and a line of freckles painted across his cute, turned-up nose that came to a rounded point. "I need your backpack, honey. Can you give it to me?"

The boy nodded, then slipped out of the straps and gave it to her. She positioned it just inside the door, on what was now the floor.

Her plan was to pile the backpacks on the floor to protect the kids from the broken glass and to create a soft staging area for them to use when they crawled out.

"Give me the rest of your backpacks," she commanded, taking them from the kids and putting them in place.

"Let's go. One at a time. Crawl on top of the packs so you don't cut yourself," she said, taking the hand of a girl with pigtails.

Stephanie's hands supported the child as she worked her petite frame across the backpack and out of the door's missing window.

When the girl was safely outside, Stephanie pointed for her to go stand by her son, then reached inside the vehicle for another child's hand.

Stephanie continued the process, helping more of the children escape. Each time another pair of tiny feet found freedom, she knew the bus might give way and tumble to the bottom of the ravine.

Like her heart rate, the chances of tragedy were rising with each child she rescued. But she wasn't about to stop. She could feel the burn of Jeffrey's watchful eyes pressing on her from behind.

Her son was probably more scared than she was, and that made her want to stop what she was doing and go comfort him. But she couldn't. Lives were at stake and she had to work faster.

Child after child climbed out, each time using the makeshift step she'd built from the backpacks as a handhold and kneeling point.

Her conviction seemed to grow stronger with each young person she saved, adding to the weight of her responsibility.

No way any of these precious kids are dying today. Not on my watch.

Her heartbeat continued to escalate, stiffening her chin and her resolve. The unsteadiness was gone from her hands and replaced by added strength, allowing her to work faster.

She was doing it—saving these kids from certain death. Never in a million years would she have imagined herself in this position and having the guts to see it through.

CHAPTER 13

Sheriff Gus Apollo stood next to Mayor Buckley while his boss ran his finger down another page in the dusty binder containing the town's Official Emergency Plan.

Buckley's hand stopped a second later, indicating his skimming had turned into reading. "When was this thing written?" he asked a few seconds later, moving his hand to the upper right corner of the paper and flipping through two more pages.

"In the seventies, I believe. Obviously, long before word processors and laser printers were invented. Based on the typeset and ink, I'm guessing it was typed on an old IBM Selectric. I used to rock that thing back in the day."

"Seventies, huh? That sounds about right. There's all this talk about the USSR and Czechoslovakia. Country names that don't even exist anymore."

"Then it's probably not going to be very helpful," Gus said, hearing a commotion behind him. He spun in time to see one of his newly-minted Deputies coming through the thinning crowd in the reception area of the Sheriff's Office.

It was Deputy Albert and he was holding onto an eight-inch, bronze-colored handle belonging to a yellow metal box. Its distinctive block shape and bright color told Gus what it was: a vintage Geiger counter.

Albert held it up, sending the flab on the underside of his arm into a full wiggle. "Here you go, Sheriff. That smoking hot Daisy chick dropped this off a minute ago before she took off with those jocks you assigned to Team Three."

Gus ignored the digs and sexual references as he took the unit from his underling and held it up for closer inspection. The nameplate told him it was an Anton CDV0700 Model 5, and it looked to be in great shape. There were no scratches anywhere on the paint and the glass covering the meter was clean and intact.

Albert held up his other hand. "You might need this, too."

A black headset with a dangling cord came at Gus from Albert's position, catching him off guard.

Albert cleared his throat. "This plugs in the jack labeled *Phone*."

Gus took the item and inserted the connector as Albert had suggested. Then he slipped the headset on and positioned the single speaker over his ear.

"The black knob turns it on," Albert said. "The x10 setting is what you should use."

Gus got the feeling that Albert had tried the device before bringing it inside. "Does the battery still work?"

"Ten-four. Pretty damn surprising if you ask me, considering how old that thing is. I think Moses must have used it last. You know, before loading the animals and all."

"That was Noah and the Ark," the Mayor said, with frustration growing on his face. "Moses parted the Red Sea, you dum—"

It looked like Albert was going to respond to the Mayor's forthcoming insult, so Gus decided to jump in and run interference. He brought the unit up to block Albert's view of Buckley. It seemed to keep the overweight kid from speaking.

Gus spoke an instant later. "Yep. This thing is almost as old as me, and that's saying something. But you know what they say . . . they don't build 'em like this anymore. Thanks for bringing it in, Albert. You may return to your post."

"Yeah, okay," he said before looking at the Mayor and letting a lingering sneer hang in the air. "I'll be outside in case anyone needs me," he said before turning and waddling away.

The Mayor looked at Gus and gave him a raised eyebrow and a quick smirk.

Gus let out a genuine smile as he focused on the device in his hands. He turned the unit on, ratcheting the black control knob to the setting of x10.

He could hear the subtle, high-pitched whine of the Geiger's power systems ramping up inside the earpiece. A few moments later, a sparse, random crackle began to take over.

Gus moved the device from side to side in front of him, listening for any drastic changes in tone and intensity through the headset. There were none.

"I think we're okay," he told his boss.

"That's one piece of good news," the Mayor said. "We'll see what my grandson comes up with when you send him out into the field. Assuming he can follow instructions properly."

"Shouldn't be a problem, sir. It's pretty simple to operate. Won't take but a couple of minutes to show him what to do."

CHAPTER 14

Bunker stood with the tips of his shoes hanging over the edge of the bus, looking down at Stephanie. The slender woman's hands moved with precision and speed as she rescued two more kids through the shattered glass of the rear door.

A few of the children had cuts, bruises, and some blood on their cheeks and foreheads, but so far none of their injuries looked serious.

Shock and fear are the biggest worries now, Bunker thought. *These kids are going to need some serious counseling when this is over.*

Stephanie's right arm went into the bus again. "Okay, come on, sweetheart. Just give me your hand. I've gotcha, I promise," she said with a breathy voice.

A few seconds later, Bunker could see a patch of curly brown hair and a blue and white pullover shirt coming out of the opening below. They belonged to a stocky boy who was now free and running toward his classmates, who'd formed a half circle twenty feet behind Stephanie.

She looked up at Bunker and nodded, showing a face full of disbelief. "The kids are out. We got 'em, Bunker. All of them."

"No, you did, Steph. Nice work," he said, waiting for her to scoot away from the bus.

But she didn't. She sighed instead, then leaned a bit forward and peered into the bus. "Now we just need to figure out how to get the you-know-what out. If we even can."

Bunker knew what she was referring to—the driver's corpse—and agreed with her decision not to use the words 'dead body' in front of the kids.

He'd been thinking about how to recover the driver and wasn't sure if they could do it safely. If anyone went inside the bus and moved forward, there was a good chance the shift in weight would send the bus over the cliff. There was no way to know how much counterbalance the rocks on top were providing, so going inside was a blind gamble.

When he tossed his shirt down to Tommy earlier, he got a good view of the driver. The man's neck was twisted back and to the left, sitting on his left shoulder at a grotesque angle.

As far as Bunker was concerned, dragging his body out now wasn't worth the risk. That left only one choice—jumping off the bus and letting it plunge into the ravine. Law enforcement could recover his body later.

He figured Stephanie wouldn't want the kids to see their bus driver disappear over the edge. She'd probably want to gather up the children and escort them to the road. He was about to suggest that very idea, but held his tongue when one of the kids blurted out an unexpected question. It was the boy in the pullover who'd been rescued last.

"What about Megan?" the kid asked, his voice crackling with pubescent tones.

"Who?" Bunker answered, feeling the sting of the question rattle his bones.

"Megan. She was goofing around on the back of the seat when we crashed. I think she got hurt pretty bad when she went flying. We heard her crying for a while after it first happened, but now I think she's asleep or something."

"Where is she?" Bunker asked, feeling a sharp pressure squeezing the blood out of his heart.

"In the front somewhere. By our driver, Mr. Wilhelm. He has a pacemaker, but I think he's dead."

When Bunker was taking off his shirt earlier, he was so focused on the kids in the last few rows of the bus that he never thought to check the front for any more children. If the boy's recap of the accident was correct, then the injured girl was probably unconscious and near the dead man in the driver's seat.

"We can't leave her in there, Bunker," Stephanie said, her face now devoid of color. "We have to get her out."

"You're right, but if she's in the front, how are we going to get to her? This thing's probably going to go you-know-where if someone walks to the front," he said, shooting a head nod in her direction to divert her attention from his eyes.

She must have understood because she swung her head around and looked at the kids. The throng of grade-schoolers was closing in around her.

Stephanie stood up and held out her arms to corral the unruly flock of sheep. "Kids, you need to stay back. Jeffrey, you too."

"But we want to help, Mom. To get the girl out."

"It's not safe, son. Not for any of you. I need you to take the other children away from here," she said, pointing at the line of trees behind them. "Go up on the road and wait for us. Can you do that, honey? Please?"

"But Mom," he said in a long, drawn-out tone. The other kids were nodding and mumbling supportive phrases to Jeffrey.

"No, sweetheart. You need to take everyone back up to the road. Right now. Okay? It's very important."

Jeffrey stood motionless, looking unsure as his eyes drifted away.

"Baby, look at me," she snapped.

Jeffrey did as he was told, but didn't speak.

"Go . . . Now . . . Show them the way up to the pavement. I need you to be strong and make sure everyone is safe. Mr. Bunker and I will handle this. I promise, everything is going to be okay."

Her son nodded, then began to lead the kids away from the bus like she wanted.

Right then, a soft cry came from inside the bus. Then a girl's voice spoke up. "Daddy?"

"Wait!" Bunker said.

"What is it?" Stephanie asked.

"Listen!" he said in an excited whisper.

The girl called out again for her father, over and over, crying in between the words.

Stephanie ran to the back door of the bus. "Megan? Honey? Can you hear me?"

"Yes. Who's out there?"

"My name is Stephanie and I'm here to help you. Where are you, sweetheart?"

"By Mr. Wilhelm. Behind his seat."

"Can you make your way to the back of the bus?"

"No. My leg hurts really bad. I can't move it."

"It'll be okay, honey."

"Who's on top of the bus? I hear someone."

"That's my good friend, Jack Bunker. He's here to help, too. We're going to get you out of there."

"Are you coming to get me?"

"Yes, Megan. Just stay where you are and don't move until we tell you. Okay?"

The girl answered with a yes.

Right then a new idea tore into Bunker's mind. "Hey, Steph?"

She looked up.

He made a sweeping finger motion at the kids, who were still standing behind her. "Their belts. I need them."

"Why?"

"Remember how I got us down from the tracks?"

"Oh yeah. Right," she said, turning her focus to Jeffrey. "Have all your friends take off their belts and leave them here."

Her son nodded, then collected the belts from the kids who were wearing them. Some weren't very long, but a few were, giving Bunker hope that his plan just might work.

Bunker watched Jeffrey pile them up by his mother's feet, counting at least twenty. The boy made eye contact with him. "That's all of them, Mr. Bunker."

"Good work, now get everyone to safety like your mother said."

"Will Megan be okay? She sounds really scared," Jeffrey asked his mother.

"We'll get her out, I promise. But you need to go take care of all your new friends. Up on the road, now."

Jeffrey nodded.

One by one, the group filtered out of the clearing and into the brush, where the incline to the road was waiting for them.

After the last one disappeared, Stephanie looked at Bunker. "For a moment there, I thought he wasn't going to listen to me."

"He's a good kid. So are the rest. They only wanted to help the girl, and that says a lot."

"Thanks for saying that. As a mom, I try to teach him to always do the right thing, but sometimes, I'm not sure I'm getting through. It's tough with his asshole of a father always getting in the way. Plus, all the influence of social media and video games. Kids these days are hit from all sides with way too much information. And way too much opinion. It makes being a parent just that much harder. Sometimes, I want to scream."

"From what I can see, you did good," Bunker told her in a firm tone. "But I have to ask, you said the phrase *new friends* a little bit ago. Doesn't Jeffrey know these kids from school? It's a small town, after all."

"We've always home-schooled him. It's what his father wanted."

"You taught him?"

"No. We hired a full time, live-in tutor. Cute girl. She was great until the divorce. Then she took sides. Since I wasn't the one paying her, you know how that turned out. I'm pretty sure she was another notch on his conquest belt, too, though I could never prove it. And to think I trusted that girl."

"It happens."

"I mean, I get that he has all the money and power, but until recently, I never realized how many ways a man like him has to screw a woman. God, it never ends. Every time I turn around, it seems like he's doing it to me again."

There was a long, awkward pause.

"Wait, that didn't come out right," she said, looking embarrassed.

He laughed, feeling his face flush. "I know what you meant. But we should really be focusing on Megan right now."

"Yeah, I agree," she said, clearing her throat and taking a deep breath. "As far as I see, there's only one way to do it . . . rescue Megan, I mean."

He nodded. "One of us is gonna have to go inside and get her."

"Yep, one of us," she said while staring into the back of the bus.

"And by that, I mean me. That's why I wanted the belts. But I need you up here for counterweight."

"Wouldn't it be the same if I just got in the back? Not on top?"

"Up here is better. I think we'll get a little more leverage that way."

"Really? I don't see how. The back is the back, right?"

"I don't know, maybe. But either way, up here is where you need to be. It's safer for you."

She looked up and nodded, not giving him any more grief about climbing up. Her hands and feet worked quickly, bringing her to Bunker's position.

He grabbed her by the shoulders and was about to explain the plan, then realized he'd just violated her personal space rule—again. He pulled his hands away in a lurch. "Sorry, I keep forgetting."

She grabbed his hands and squeezed them. Her eyes were tight and fierce. "Focus, Bunker . . . Megan, remember? The little girl who needs our help."

"Right, right," he stammered, unwrapping his fingers from hers. He pointed at the edge. "You sit there with your legs hanging over the back, while I go inside. But I need you to promise me something."

"Sure, what?"

He lowered his voice, not wanting Megan to hear. "If you feel the bus start to go, you jump off."

She looked at the edge, then back at him. "You really think that's gonna be necessary? I mean, we have all these rocks. And me."

"Well, if I were still a betting man, I'd say it's three to one against. Maybe higher."

She blinked at him and didn't respond.

"So, promise me . . . You'll jump off the very second you feel this thing start to move. Our number one priority has to be your son and the rest of the kids up there. Someone has to get them back to town."

She nodded, but kept silent.

"I need you to say it."

She gulped, then whispered, "Okay. I promise. I'll jump off if I need to."

CHAPTER 15

Albert walked past his newly-assigned partner on Team Two and put his wide backside against the rectangular base of the memorial statue in the center of the town square.

The towering bronze-colored structure was a likeness of Cyrus Clearwater, the town patriarch. The shadows being cast by the monument's raised arms were long and pointing east, reminding him of a time not that long ago when he was sitting below the Great Sphinx of Giza in Egypt.

Cyrus' left hand was holding a huge spade-shaped shovel. In his right was a massive groundbreaking pick, both representative of the endless hours of hard work put in by the town founder and his family to forge a life in this lush but unforgiving wilderness.

At least that was the story Albert had been told by one of his grade-school teachers. He couldn't remember the old broad's real name, but her saggy cheeks and the huge mole on her forehead were legendary. The kids called her Cyclops, that much he remembered. Not that any of it mattered. The tale of Cyrus Clearwater was ancient history to him.

The man died way back in the dark ages—something like 1938, if he remembered correctly. Colon cancer was his downfall, he thought. Or maybe it was a brutal bear attack. He couldn't be sure. Either way, the man got his ass handed to him and Albert couldn't care less.

He turned to his teammate standing to the right and put out his hand. "My name's Albert."

"Dustin Brown," the short-haired man answered, shaking hands with a doubly firm grip.

Albert couldn't believe the size of Dustin's hand. It was both long and wide, reminiscent of what he would expect from a burly, 6'5" lumberjack.

Dustin was tall, but not that tall, and he certainly wasn't burly. He was maybe a buck-forty in weight, with a good portion of that in his massive, hooked nose. The dude's deep-set eyes and stork-like physique made him look like something only the casting directors in Hollywood could conjure up for some movie shot in the starving deserts of Ethiopia.

"Why'd you join this detail?" Albert asked, pulling his hand free from the grip and wondering if the underweight pencil standing across from him would snap under the first sign of pressure.

"Seemed like the right thing to do when Sheriff Apollo asked me. For some reason, I just couldn't say no. What about you?"

"Always wanted to wear a badge. And maybe I'll get to fire off a few rounds now and then."

"I'm sorry, what was that? Did you say you wanted to shoot somebody?"

"Chill out. I never said that. But they must have a stockpile of weapons and a shooting range we get to use. Right?"

"Honestly, that never crossed my mind."

"Oh, really?" Albert said, sizing up the guy's answer. It didn't sound legit. He decided to probe a little more, hoping to free the truth.

"Don't you want to test your skills and see if you measure up? I mean, what red-blooded American male doesn't want to send some rounds downrange? They might even have some Tannerite we get to use."

"Tannerite?"

"It's a binary explosive," Albert said, letting a smile grow on his lips. "It's normally used for exploding targets. However, if you mix up a big batch of that stuff and shoot it with a high-powered rifle, it'll send a garbage can into orbit. Been there, done that, if you know what I mean."

Dustin didn't respond, so Albert decided to continue. "Well, actually, it was thirty pounds and my dad's old, broken-down Ford Bronco. You should have seen it. It was epic. Looked like something out of Afghanistan when it was over."

"So that's the reason you accepted this job? To blow stuff up?"

"Yeah, sure. Part of it. But really, it's all about the respect. You know, people doing what I say, when I say it. I finally have a chance to show all these assholes who the real Albert is."

"Okay, I can see that," Dustin said, nodding slowly. "But remember, we're *only* deputies. Temporary ones, at that. The Sheriff and Mayor are the men calling the shots."

"When they're around, yes," Albert said, pointing at the badge on his chest. "But when they're not, this little piece of tin takes over and so does the man wearing it."

"Wow, and I thought I had issues."

Albert ignored the insult, deciding to drive home his point to his new partner. "I'm sick and tired of people judging me because of my weight. That's why I took a sabbatical from this shit-stain of a town when I had the chance. Just 'cause I'm heavy doesn't mean I'm not a real person. Or that I'm stupid or something. It never ends. It's just like with my hair. I can't help the fact that it's super curly. It came that way."

"You could cut it, though. Wearing it long like that must get hot in the summer. I'm guessing the Sheriff Department's Rules and Regs call for high and tight, or something along those lines."

"I used to keep it short, but with my round face, it gave the cretins in school more ammo to cut me down. So after high school, I went with the long, scraggly look to portray a different persona. Hopefully backing a few of them the fuck off in the process. Being me in public is exhausting."

"I get that. People have been doing that to me, too. When you're the skinniest kid in school, it isn't exactly a recipe to make friends. Usually it just gets you a serious beat-down at lunch hour. But what really sucks is that it didn't stop after graduation. I thought once we all got older, the slams and insults would've stopped. But they didn't. Seems like every time I turn around, someone's calling me stork or Starvin' Marvin or something along those lines."

Albert held back a laugh, even though those nicknames fit Dustin perfectly. He didn't want to insult the man or sound like a total hypocrite. "Yeah, I feel your pain. I may be slow of foot, but I can be agile when I want to be."

"Adrenaline can do that."

"You got that right, brother. We all know that mass times acceleration equals force, and trust me, there's a lot of force in this body."

"You think we're gonna need it? Force, I mean."

"No doubt. There's no telling what's gonna happen now that society is tumbling into chaos, right before our very eyes."

Dustin turned his head, then his shoulders toward the activity in the center of town. Albert's eyes focused on the same.

On the left was Charmer's Market and Feed Store. On the right was a seven-pump gas station called Billy's Pump and Munch. Both were packed with people milling about.

"Stupid morons," Albert said, pointing at the grocery store. "I wonder how many of them are expecting to pay with their debit cards? Not going to work, dumbasses. Neither are the cash registers. Or freezers. Or anything else."

Dustin chuckled, then nodded in the direction of the closest gas pump. "Almost as bad as the idiots standing in that line to get fuel for their gas cans. Pumps don't work without electricity, people," he said, shaking his head. He looked at Albert. "And they call us stupid."

Albert laughed. "Gonna be some generators running dry tonight."

Right then, he realized Dustin wasn't a total goof after all. They certainly shared the same sense of humor, so far at least. Even so, he wasn't quite ready to label Dustin a *cool dude*, but he was considering it.

During his stints in LA and then the Big Apple, Albert had met a slew of candidates who turned out to be nothing more than Neanderthals who could spell. Well, sort of—their names at least, but getting the cement heads to follow orders was always problematic. Was it any wonder the fat stacks of cash always seemed to elude them?

Stupidity is an endless commodity was his favorite saying. If he hadn't shown up when he did in LA, the crew would've eventually perished, along with their inventory.

"Look at them," Dustin said, chuckling.

"Maybe we should go over there and explain it to them."

Dustin smirked. "Nah, why bother? It's not our job. I say we let 'em figure it out on their own. Besides, watching those morons gives us something to do. It's almost like we have our very own reality TV channel, right here in the center of Clearwater."

"Oh, shit!" Albert said, seeing two of the men near the front of the line put down their five-gallon gas cans and start throwing punches at each other.

"What should we do?"

"You go inform the Sheriff."

"What about you?"

Albert looked at the gas station, then back at Dustin, feeling his blood pressure rising by the second. "Time to start earning my deputy pay."

"Are you sure? Those guys are pretty big."

"Yeah. Go. I got this."

Dustin took off running for the Sheriff's Office, looking like an uncoordinated giraffe crossing the square. Jogging clearly wasn't his thing.

Albert sucked in a breath and put on his warrior face, then charged across the street. He wasn't sure what he was going to do, but it was time to see if his new gig would change people's perception about him. His old persona, at least. The new Albert needed to stay locked away and out of sight until the time was right.

When he arrived, he wedged his shoulders in between the two combatants, both of whom were at least six inches taller than him. He turned sideways and put a raised forearm on each man's chest, shoving them apart.

"What's going on here?" Albert asked, his voice choppy and out of breath.

"You need to leave, Albert. This doesn't concern you," the bronze-skinned man said, his voice deep and his chin stiff.

Albert recognized him as town mechanic and former high school acquaintance, Burt Lowenstein. A man whose fingernails were always dirty and so were his coveralls. His BO was legendary, even before he became a professional wrench.

"Well, actually it does," Albert said, pointing to his chest. "You see this badge? It says Deputy Sheriff. I know you flunked English and all, but those words mean I own your ass and you need to do what I say, Burt."

"Yeah, right. So what genius decided to give a tub like you a badge?"

"Sheriff Apollo. And just so you know, my partner just went to get him. He'll be here any second."

Burt looked around, then brought his eyes back to Albert. "No, I don't think so," he said, pressing the tip of his index finger into Albert's chest, once for each word. "It's just you and me, fat ass. Just like old times."

Albert knocked his hand away and refrained from retaliating. He didn't want to give away his recently acquired skills. He puffed out his heaving chest. "Raising a hand to an Officer of the Law is a felony, Burt. You need to stand down, right now, before I have no choice but to arrest you."

"Officer of the Law? Oh really, now?" he said, laughing. He brought his face in close and changed his tone to one of anger. "That's not gonna happen, Albert. Ever. Do you remember what happened senior year after you turned my ass in for that chemistry experiment you did for me?"

"Yeah, I remember. They expelled you. Should've paid me the two hundred. I warned you."

"No, not that. I'm talking about what happened a week later in the parking lot of Seven-Eleven. When me and my boys paid you a little visit."

"Yeah, that was like ten years ago. A lot's changed since then."

"Just in case you forgot, you cried like a little bitch after it was done."

A series of flashbacks entered Albert's mind, all of them filled with fists, pain, and blood. "I'm not that guy anymore. Besides, it was four on one. Not exactly a fair fight."

Burt ran his eyes up and down Albert's physique. "Well, it's just you and me now, jumbo," he said, ramming his finger into Albert's chest again, this time with double the force.

"I'm outta here," the man behind Albert said.

"You just gonna let him leave, *Officer*?" Burt asked with attitude after leaning to the right to look past Albert.

The boiling in Albert's chest wanted him to lash out physically at Burt, but he quashed the idea. He swallowed hard, then licked his lips to make sure his words came out crisp and firm. "He's of no consequence here. I figure you started this and he's just an innocent bystander. Probably just protecting himself against you, like the rest of us have been doing all our lives."

Burt looked down at his feet and shook his head before bringing his eyes back up. A sly smile appeared on his lips as he held his arms in front of his waist. He brought his filthy wrists together, side by side. "Okay then, arrest me."

Albert had two ideas roaring in his brain. The first was tied to the man he used to be before he left this town, and the other was bubbling up from the new and improved version of himself.

One plan would result in pain for himself and the other was targeted for Burt—the overconfident and unsuspecting Neanderthal standing within easy striking distance.

Albert decided to keep his secrets a secret. He grabbed the man's wrists with both hands. As expected, Burt reacted in an instant and grabbed Albert's right thumb, bending it back with extreme force.

The pain was intense, sending Albert down to the pavement on one knee. "Eeeooww," he said, bending his elbow and swinging his body around to keep Burt from breaking his thumb.

Before Albert could take another breath and plead for him to stop, a rush of wind whistled in from the right. A moment later, a black nightstick came into view and landed on the side of Burt's head.

The brute went down hard, landing awkwardly with his arms and legs sprawled like a dead body. He was out cold.

Albert looked up through the glare of the setting sun to see who was wielding the nightstick. It was Sheriff Apollo. Next to him was Dustin Brown, whose eyes were as big as pears.

"I thought I told you to just observe and report back?" Apollo asked, moving a step over to block the sun, his eyes tight and energized.

Albert sucked in a few breaths and let them out before answering. He needed to let the pain in his hand ease a bit. "You know how Burt is, Sheriff. Someone needed to step in and keep the peace."

"By getting your thumb broken?"

"Well, that wasn't my plan originally. And, just for the record, I don't think it's broken," he said, flexing his thumb gingerly.

Albert could feel the eyes of everyone around him, silently judging and mocking the person kneeling before them. It was difficult not to speak up and expose the onlookers to the real story about the fat man with the badge. But he chose to keep his cool and stay in character.

"What were you thinking?" Apollo asked with a sharp tongue. "You don't have any training for this."

"I was thinking I needed to do my job. I thought he'd respect the badge."

"Burt? Come on, that guy doesn't respect anything."

"I know. I went to high school with him."

"Then you should have known this would happen."

Albert did know and he expected it. But he didn't want the Sheriff or anyone else to know it was all just a ruse and he let Burt manhandle him. He stood up, then shrugged. "Just trying to do my best."

"Next time, just wait for backup."

"But what if you're not around? Or that delicious POA, Daisy?"

"Get one of the other teams to help you. They're more . . . physically able."

Albert nodded, though he didn't want to. He had much more to say in his defense, but decided to keep his mouth shut.

With the grid and electronics down, he was sure the current situation was going to last for a while. If he was right, he needed time to reestablish his tradecraft and start recruiting. All of that would be much easier if everyone's attention was focused elsewhere. After all, it's much easier to hide in plain sight when the entire town thinks you're a fat, lazy, incompetent human being.

Oh, how he couldn't wait to show them all how wrong they were.

CHAPTER 16

Bunker felt a twinge in his back when he returned to the clearing with an awkward eighty-pound load in his arms.

Stephanie's eyes locked onto the boulder he was carrying. "I thought you went to find a splint for Megan's leg?"

"I did. But then I saw this just sitting there, begging me to use it. I couldn't resist."

"Seriously? Now? We need to get Megan out of there."

"We will, but a little more weight in the back can't hurt. If we're wrong, we won't get a second chance at this," he said, continuing his trek to Stephanie. "How's she doing?"

"Scared, but I've been talking to her so she knows we're still here. But her cries for her daddy are killing me inside."

"I know, but we're almost ready," he told her when he arrived with the heavy stone.

The rock was narrower than the frame around the missing window of the rear door to the bus, allowing him to easily slip it inside and let it drop. It landed on the stack of backpacks and rolled to the floor with a loud thud.

"Please, Stephanie. Hurry. It hurts so bad," the girl cried out.

"My friend, Jack, will be there soon. Just hang on, baby."

Bunker pulled a two-foot-long stick he'd found in the forest from inside the tuck on the back of his pants. It was about an inch in diameter and almost perfectly straight.

He bent down and, with his free hand, picked up the wad of belts he'd lashed together. Earlier, he'd looped the ends through the buckles and connected them all to each other to form a makeshift rope.

"Do you think it's long enough?" she asked.

"It should be, if I can get close enough."

"Let's hope so."

"Wish me luck," he whispered to Stephanie.

"Believe me, I've already said my prayers. Twice. Now it's up to you."

He bent forward and climbed in, wedging his torso in and through the missing glass. He used the wrap of belts to support his left hand as his legs came in next, then he slid the stick in carefully.

"Stephanie? Is that you?" Megan asked, stopping her crying for a few seconds.

"No, honey. It's my friend, Jack Bunker. He's coming to rescue you."

"Yes, I'm in the back right now, Megan. I'm working my way to you. So just hold on," Bunker said.

"Okay, but please hurry. I'm really scared."

"I will, I promise."

The bus' stability was solid, as expected. With Stephanie and the pile of stones on top, plus his weight and the extra mass of the rock he'd just brought in, there was more than enough counterbalance to keep the bus from falling—for now anyway. But he knew the physics at play would change as soon as he moved forward, and that was the deadly, unknown part of the equation.

Bunker walked across the inside of the windows on the left side of the bus, using the seat backs on his right as a stabilizing brace. He did his best to keep his movements even and slow, knowing that if the bus was going to start moving, he needed to be able to feel it or hear it so he could react.

This rescue would've been a lot easier if the bus was still upright and on its wheels, not laying on its side. Moving down the center aisle would have been smoother and faster, versus having to walk across rows of sideways windows and frames.

He continued his journey, passing row after row, each time stopping to see if there was any movement before continuing. He was five rows deep when the metal frame under his feet began to wobble, telling him the bus was jostling a bit.

"Whoa! Whoa! Whoa!" Stephanie yelled, pounding on the top of the bus.

"I feel it," he shouted back, putting his arms out for balance.

"I think that's about as far as you can go," she said.

"Hang on. I might be able to get a little bit closer. Just be ready up there."

"Okay, but be careful. I've got a bad feeling about this."

He took a shorter step this time, gently moving his shoe forward. There was a sound of creaking, but the angle of the vehicle didn't change.

When he shifted his weight from his back foot to his front, the rear end of bus lifted off the ground about an inch, letting in a stream of light from underneath. He thought it was stabilizing, but then the bus lurched forward, sliding several inches.

"Stop! Bunker! Stop!" Stephanie screamed. "The bus is going to fall!"

Bunker quickly backed up a step, realizing some of the dirt ledge had given way. It took a few more steps in reverse before the rear of the bus was touching the ground once again.

He ran it through his head, thinking about the weight of the rocks on top and the counterbalance mechanics. When the bus slid forward, the fulcrum point changed, making the situation even more dangerous and unpredictable. The weight of Stephanie and the rocks were less effective now.

Megan's crying was louder than before. The vehicle's sudden movement had obviously scared her.

"Megan? Can you hear me?" he called out, hoping his voice would trump the sound of her weeping.

"Yeah," she said, lessening her cries.

"Can you put your hand out for me? I need to see exactly where you are."

"Okay," she said, stopping her crying altogether. "I'll knock for you."

A petite, dark-skinned fist came into view for Bunker, pushing past the seats and rapping on the metal to the left. Her knuckles were hitting what used to be the underside of the top of the bus.

"Okay, I got ya. Now, there's something else you gotta do for me," he said, unwrapping the clutch of belts from his hand.

"What?"

He looped and tied the end of the last belt around the stick he'd brought in. "I'm going to throw you something you need to use for your leg."

"What is it?"

"A small branch from a tree."

"What's it for?"

"To help keep your leg straight, so it doesn't hurt when you move it. It's called a splint."

"Okay."

"Here it comes," Bunker said as he swung his hand back and brought it forward quickly. He let go of the branch and the attached strings of belts, sending the stick whirling sideways like a helicopter blade.

Unfortunately, his aim was off. One of the ends hit a seat back, then ricocheted left and crashed into the metal top of the bus. It landed about two rows short of the girl's position.

"Did you throw it? I don't see it," Megan said.

"Hang on. I missed. Let me try again."

He pulled on the belts and brought the makeshift splint back to his hands. Once again, he launched the stick, only this time he tossed it with an overhand motion, as if he was throwing a hatchet at a stump. It somersaulted through the air, hit the mesh guard behind the driver's seat with a ping, and dropped down. A perfect shot.

"Okay, sweetheart. It's right there. Now unhook the stick from the belts."

A pair of tiny black hands grabbed it a second later. He watched her delicate fingers fiddle with the looping tie he'd used to secure the end of the belts to the wood.

She worked it free in a few seconds. "I got it."

"Good. Now I need you to put it alongside your injured leg. Be sure to put the middle of the splint right next to where your leg hurts the most. We need some of the stick to be above the pain and some of it below. Do you understand?"

"Yeah," she said, turning quiet for a bit before speaking again. "It doesn't work."

"What do ya mean?"

"My leg looks funny and I can't put the stick next to it. I think it's too long."

He sighed, realizing what the problem was and what she needed to do next. "Can you straighten your leg? It's really important so the splint can work."

"I'll try." A few seconds later, she cried out in pain, sending a chill down his spine. "I can't, Jack," she said, sobbing. "It hurts really bad when I move it."

"You gotta try, Megan."

"No. No. No. It hurts," she said, sobbing through the words.

He couldn't let her give up. "You can do this, sweetheart. But you need to be really brave and straighten your leg so you can put the splint on. Then I can get you out of here."

"It hurts too much. I can't. I just can't."

His head slumped. If she couldn't put her leg in a splint, his only choice would be to drag her out with force. But with an unstable leg, the pain would be excruciating and he doubted she'd be able to hang on to the belts.

The girl was crying heavily now. He wasn't sure what to do, but he wasn't about to give up.

"Megan?" he asked with a louder voice, needing to get her attention so he could calm her down. "I need you to listen to me."

Her crying slowed before she spoke again. "Please, Jack. Come and get me. I just wanna go home to my dad."

CHAPTER 17

Stephanie couldn't stop the tears when she heard the little girl's desperate pleas for help. Bunker was trying his best, but it was becoming clear this crisis wasn't going to end well. For any of them.

Images of her son flashed in her mind, initially filling her heart with joy. Then the pain came crashing in when she imagined Jeffrey in Megan's place.

Every parent knows when their children leave the house, there's never a guarantee they'll return home safe. Not in today's world. Not with danger and evil lurking around every corner, just waiting for an opportunity to strike.

She wondered where this girl's parents were. What they were doing? Could they somehow sense she was in danger?

Her mind flashed back to Jeffrey again, thinking about her son being trapped inside a bus with an injured leg. If the roles were reversed with Megan's parents, would they do everything they could to help save a little boy they didn't know?

Deep down, she knew they would. There's a bond that all loving parents share and it stems from the primal need to protect their offspring at all costs.

But not just your own kids—everyone's, and it stems from more than just instinct or love, or from some unwritten social contract. It's part of our genetic code and was installed in our DNA back when humans first roamed the Earth.

"Bunker?" Stephanie called out, hearing a break in the conversation inside the bus. "Can you come out here for a minute? It's important."

"I'll be right back, Megan," Bunker said.

"No. Please, Jack. Don't go. Don't leave me here," Megan said in an emotionally charged voice.

"I'm not leaving you, Megan. I'm just gonna talk with Stephanie for a minute. I'll be right back. I promise."

"Okay," she answered in a sweet voice.

Bunker appeared a few seconds later, standing with his hands on his hips in the dirt below. He looked up. "What's up?"

"You're wasting your breath. Megan's not going to be able to splint her own leg. Heck, I don't think I could do it. So we need a new plan."

"I know. I'm working on it."

"Well, work faster," she said, thinking about Jeffrey and the other kids waiting up on the road by themselves.

"I'm afraid we only have one choice," he said.

"What?"

"Pull her out as is."

"With a broken leg?"

He shrugged. "It's not a great plan. But I'm out of ideas."

"It's too bad we don't have some way to pull this bus away from the cliff. Then you could go inside and get her, like she wants."

"Well, that's not gonna happen. Not unless we had a heavy duty block and tackle rig, or a tow truck."

"What about that tree back there?" she asked, pointing. "Could you use the belts like a long rope?"

"It's too far, Steph. Plus we don't have the pulleys."

She wasn't sure where the ideas were coming from, but her brain was formulating them as fast as she could utter the words. "What about anchoring the bumper to the tree? It might help hold the bus long enough for you to get her out."

"I thought of that, but the belts are too short. That's at least a hundred feet away."

She pointed to the right. "That tree's a lot closer."

"Yeah, but it's at the wrong angle. The bus would swing sideways and out of control before I got close to her. Once that happened, there'd be no way to stop it from dropping."

She nodded, letting her eyes wander across the clearing and blur together. When her peripheral vision took over, her brain saw an imaginary shape—the letter S—and it was coming from the boulders in the clearing. Their placement, size, and shape formed the letter from left to right, like the S was lying sideways in the dirt. An idea roared in her thoughts.

"Hey, what about these rocks? Couldn't we just run the belts around this first one," she said, aiming her finger at the huge rock on the left, then tracing a path to the right, "then take it up and loop it around these others before tying it to the closer tree?"

His face lit up with excitement. "Yes, I see where you're going with this. We use the rocks like a pulley system."

"That's exactly what I was thinking."

Bunker stood motionless with his eyes pinched and jaw slightly ajar for a three-count. Then he nodded. "They're all pretty good size and probably wouldn't move much, if any. With the belts looped around them, it would give us a considerable mechanical advantage."

"Enough to keep the bus stable?"

"Maybe. But it's still one hell of a gamble. There's no way to know how strong the belts are, or how well they'll hold up around all those rough edges."

"I gotta believe it's better than trying to drag a little girl out with a bad leg."

"Can't argue with that. But I'll have to move quickly."

"Then all we need are the belts," she said, wanting to kick him into gear.

He turned in a flash and went inside the bus. When he returned, his hands worked quickly to find the end of the belt string before tying it to the lower edge of the bumper. He followed the path Stephanie had suggested, looping the belts around the rocks in a snake-like pattern.

Ten feet from the tree, the length of belts ran out. "Are you kidding me?" she asked in a sarcastic tone.

"I thought it was long enough, too."

"Maybe we need to wrap it fewer times around the rocks?"

"No, I have a better idea," he said, taking his knife from its sheath. He grabbed hold of his blue jeans below his left thigh, then pulled the material away from his body as he stuck the tip of the knife inside and began to slice around his knee in a circular pattern.

When Bunker was done, the denim fell to the ground around his foot, revealing the whitest calf she'd ever seen. No tattoos either, like she expected. His skin was pristine and devoid of any more of the curious artwork.

Bunker shook the piece loose from his foot and then cut off the bottom of the material on his other leg, leaving him with an uneven pair of ragged jean shorts.

"What are you doing?" she asked him as he scooped up the cutoffs and quickly sliced them lengthwise into equal segments of cloth, about one inch wide.

"Making more rope," he said, braiding a few strands together. When he was done weaving all the strips, he tied the braided sections to each other to make a new length of rope several yards long. "That should do it," he said, coiling the jean rope on the ground like a rattlesnake waiting to strike. "Now I just need to strengthen it."

"How?" she asked, seeing him move around to the front of the coil and turn away from her, the rope lying at his feet.

Bunker's hands went to the front of his jeans and a few seconds later, she saw a heavy stream of pee hit the rope on the ground.

"Now that's just wrong," she said with attitude.

"It's stronger when it's wet," he said, spraying his urine around in a circle like he was trying to write his name in the snow.

Bunker finished pissing, zipped up, and then took the wet material and attached it with a thick knot to the end of the belts. He stretched it out and carried it to the tree on the right, then looped the excess pee-infused cloth around the trunk a few times before tying it.

"I hope it holds," Stephanie said.

"Me, too," he answered, wiping his hands on his shorts. He walked back to the rear of the bus.

"What about her leg? You still planning to use the splint?"

He nodded. "It needs to be stabilized first. I'll use the stick that's still up there."

"How you gonna secure it?"

"I'll tear some strips from my shirt," he said, reaching down to pull his t-shirt up and over his head.

"Wait," Stephanie said, not wanting the frightened girl to see his tattoos. She removed her shirt and tossed it to him, leaving her in only a bra. "Use mine."

He gave her a sidelong look after catching the garment in his left hand, but didn't say anything.

"It's better this way. First impressions and all," she added, hoping he'd understand her reasoning without her having to say the actual words.

"Right. Right," he said, climbing into the bus.

"What took you so long?" Megan said to Bunker. Her voice sounded stronger than before, but still unsteady and full of emotion.

"Had to set everything up, but I'm back now."

"I wanna go home, Jack."

"Just hang on. I'm coming to get you."

CHAPTER 18

Bunker took another step, leaning his left elbow against the metal top of the bus, with Stephanie's shirt in his opposite hand. So far, the bus felt stable beneath his feet. However, he'd just passed the middle row and knew the stakes would rise with each step forward.

If the ground gave way under the bus like before, another shift forward would happen. Even with the rock formation being used as pulleys, he wasn't sure the belts would hold. If they snapped, the massive weight of the vehicle would take its occupants to the bottom of the canyon.

"I'm almost there, Megan," he said, after two more rows were behind him. The girl didn't answer. He stopped and listened, but couldn't hear her crying anymore. "Megan? Can you hear me?"

She still didn't respond. He didn't know if she was ignoring him, in shock, unconscious, or worse.

He resumed his march to the front, picking up his pace.

"Whoa!" Stephanie yelled a second later when the back end of the bus started to lift up a few inches. "We've got movement here."

"Yeah, I feel it," he shouted back to her, stopping his feet. "How do the belts look? Are they holding?"

"So far. But they're totally stretched tight and the tree is bending a little. I don't know about this."

"I'll take it slow," he said to the shirtless woman on top. "If that tree bends any more, you need to tell me."

"Okay, will do. But something tells me you'll know it before I do."

Bunker realized she was correct. If the bus leaned forward any more, the position of the belts around the rocks would change, causing them to rub against the porous surface. If that happened, they might snap in half, or work themselves up and off the boulders altogether.

He moved again, reducing his pace to about half what it was before. After each step, he stopped each time to check the angle of the vehicle. There was a small amount of vertical sway vibrating through his feet—like a soft shudder—but the tilt wasn't getting any worse.

When he finally made it to the mesh screen behind the driver, he leaned around the seat back and saw Megan for the first time.

The tiny girl was lying on her left side and curled loosely into the fetal position, with her head resting on an outstretched arm. Her feet were facing away from him, and the makeshift splint was only a few inches in front of her knees.

Looking straight down, Bunker could see that her eyes were closed. Her petite, turned-up nose seemed to flare its nostrils each time she took a breath, so he knew she was still alive. She must have fallen asleep—probably a good thing given the stress of the moment.

The dark-skinned tone of her upward facing cheek had a noticeable sheen to it that accented her extra-long eyelashes. If he didn't know any different, he'd think she was a pre-teen ebony model who'd spent all day in the makeup chair before a photo shoot.

Her black hair had been braided evenly into a series of cornrows that came together in a tight bun near the crown of her head. He guessed she was about ten years old, though there wasn't much to the girl.

The waistline of her blue jean shorts was very small, and so too was the thickness of her wrists and arms. She looked underweight, but he wasn't sure if that was normal or not for a girl her age. He was no expert when it came to kids.

Megan's casual red top looked new and matched her red-colored studded earrings, but her outfit was going to need a good cleaning to remove the obvious dirt when she got home.

He visually studied the condition of her legs to see if he could determine which one of them was broken. Both were bent and stacked on top of each other, but neither had blood showing or any bones sticking out through the skin.

There was one difference, however.

The knee on top was noticeably swollen and much larger than the other. Her free hand was loosely wrapped around it, indicating she'd been hanging on to it before she fell asleep.

Maybe the girl had twisted her knee and didn't break her leg after all. If that was true, he'd need to use the stick as a two-sided brace and not a lengthwise splint.

Bunker knelt down and shook her shoulder gently. "Megan, it's your new friend, Jack. You need to wake up now so I can take you home."

She didn't respond. He tried again and again, but she never opened her eyes. Either this girl could sleep through a hurricane or she'd passed out. If the latter, then it was probably from the pain or a concussion. Either way, his task was the same.

He grabbed the stick and put its midpoint under his own knee, pulling up on the two ends with force. It snapped in half like he'd hoped.

The girl's injured knee was still bent when he slid the first half of the broken branch under it. To stabilize her leg, he decided to angle the brace diagonally to connect the inside of her thigh to the upper part of her calf.

He positioned the remaining piece of the brace on the other side of her knee so it would match the angle, then tied it with four strips of cloth he cut from Stephanie's shirt. With the brace now in place, Megan's knee should stay bent while he carried her outside.

Bunker put his knife away and got to his feet. He bent over and scooped his arms under her legs and head to pick her up. The moment he straightened up his back, the bus moved again, this time the back end lifting up a good six inches.

Stephanie shrieked.

The change in angle was unexpected and knocked him off balance. He took a quick step back to keep himself from falling over, but the sudden shift in weight from the two of them caused the bus to move yet again. Now the rear was at least a foot off the ground, he estimated, possibly more. And it was bouncing and swaying.

"No! No! No!" Stephanie said from her position on top of the bus.

Those sudden, panicked words caused the video player in the back of Bunker's mind to flash a short clip of the belts outside, working themselves up the rocks. Then the vision changed, showing him what would happen if the ground under the bus gave way again. He didn't hesitate, leaning forward to begin his trek to the rear door, planning to retrace his steps from earlier.

With the steeper incline ahead of him and an injured girl draped in his arms, it was much more difficult to keep his balance than before. He soon discovered that he needed to wedge his right shoulder against the side of the bus before stepping forward with his left foot. Otherwise, he would fall to the side.

Once his foot was firmly planted, he bent his right knee and pushed hard with his thigh to shift his weight to his front leg. Then he brought his back leg forward to even out his footing.

Since he couldn't use his hands to brace himself, this deliberate wedge-step-push process was his only choice to keep from falling and causing more unwanted movement of the bus. It was an awkward traveling motion that slowed his speed considerably, but he was making progress. Two rows were behind him now.

"How's it going in there?" Stephanie called out, hesitating only briefly before she spoke again. "Bunker? You still with me?"

"Yeah, working my way out now," he said with diminished breath after another strenuous step. The bobbing motion of the bus seemed to be getting worse with each step. "This ain't exactly easy in here."

He expected Stephanie to respond to his last comment, but instead she screamed, "Over here! I need help!" It caught him by surprise.

Bunker kept marching forward, while listening to what was happening outside.

A new female's voice spoke up. "Quick, get some ropes on that bumper."

"You got it, ma'am," a man's deep voice answered.

Bunker's heart lit up when he heard the new voices, adding strength to his legs.

"Kids, stay back," Stephanie said. "Don't get in their way."

"Mom? Is Megan okay?" Jeffrey said.

"We're working on it. Now, all of you, back up to the road."

"But we wanna see," a young girl's voice said in response.

"No. That's not a good idea. I need all of you to go. Now. Back to the road. Right this second."

Bunker passed another row, stopping for a quick second to take in an extra breath. As he did, the motion of the bus quieted down considerably. The newcomers and their rope must have been helping.

He continued, passing row after row until he could see around the last row of the transport and through the back door.

A pretty brunette woman in a uniform was standing there with an outstretched arm. The badge on her chest was facing Bunker—a deputy's badge.

Three horses stood behind her, about twenty feet away. Each of them had a rope running from their saddle to the bus. He figured they were tied to the bumper and helping to stabilize the situation.

A tall, well-built man was positioned between the two horses on the left. He was struggling to control them, with his hands on their bridles. Another guy was in charge of the remaining horse on the right. Bunker could see badges on both of their chests, even though they were in street clothes.

"Here, give me your hand," the female cop said, shaking her fingers at him.

"Nah, it's easier if I do it," he said, stepping past the last row of seats.

The cop's other arm came inside the door when he arrived with Megan. "I'll take it from here."

Bunker nodded. "Just watch her knee. It's hurt pretty bad."

He waited until the woman's arms were under Megan before letting go. "I tried to wake her, but she's out cold. Might have hit her head in the accident."

"Could be a concussion. We need to get her back to town right away so Doc Marino can get a look at her," the cop said, easing the girl through the open frame in the door.

"Oh, thank God!" Stephanie said from above as the cop carried Megan away from the bus.

Bunker slid himself out. When his feet found the dirt outside, he felt an enormous pressure vanish from his chest.

He spun and craned his neck to look up, making eye contact with Stephanie, who was on her knees.

She smiled, showing all of her teeth. "For a minute there, I thought I might never see you again."

"Me, too. It was touch and go there for a bit, but we did it."

"No, you did it, Jack. You."

He couldn't take all the credit. "With a little help from some new friends," he said, pointing at her and then the horses and their crew. "They just showed up? Out of the blue?"

"Uh-huh. God was definitely looking out for us today. All of us."

He wasn't sure how to respond, so he decided to change the subject. "The kids okay?"

"Yeah, I sent them back up to the road. They led the deputies down here," she said, spinning onto her stomach before climbing down from the elevated position. A second later, her arms were wrapped around him and squeezing tight.

"That has to be the bravest thing I've ever seen," she whispered in his ear before kissing him softly on the cheek. She let go and backed away.

"I don't know about that."

"It was, trust me. Not many men would've done what you just did. That was amazing."

He blushed, then felt a twinge of dizziness when a wave of tingles raced across his face and neck. He wobbled a bit on his feet, feeling the trees start to move and close in around him.

Stephanie grabbed him by the arm and led him to one of the smaller rocks in the clearing. "Here, sit down a minute. You don't look so good."

He planted his butt on the rock and ran his hands across his head and down the back of his neck. "I'm okay. I think I'm just coming down from the adrenalin rush. It was pretty intense in there."

"Let me get you some water," Stephanie said before walking away with purpose in her step.

CHAPTER 19

Sheriff Gus Apollo tore across the town square and pushed into the horde of citizens gathered in front of Charmer's Market and Feed Store. The moon was full, showering the faces of the night crowd with a medieval glow while he used his hands and elbows as pry-bars to advance.

Some high-pitched, excited young voices were chanting *"fight, fight, fight"*, bringing back vivid, painful memories from his schoolyard past.

He could almost feel the warmth of the springtime sun from long ago as he lay helpless in the grass, while the oldest of the King brothers pounded at his chin. The same brother who was close to finishing his ten-year stint in jail for selling meth and would soon be released.

The chant was coming from somewhere ahead of him, leading him to believe a group of kids were watching the scuffle in the front.

"Sheriff's Office, coming through," he yelled as each new layer of people presented itself. Some of the citizens heard him and moved apart; others didn't. He pushed onward regardless. Neither the dense bodies nor the rowdiness of the crowd was going to stop him from doing his job.

When he arrived at the front, he was standing only a few feet from the store's front door. It had been propped open with a three-foot-tall ashcan filled with cigarette butts, one of which was still smoldering with red lipstick on it.

Inside the market, two women were rolling around on the decorative concrete floor in a tangle of arms and legs. The one on top had long, platinum blonde hair that hung to the middle of her back. The woman on the bottom had shoulder-length hair—mostly gray—except for a patch of pure white strands above the ears.

The blonde had her hands up and was blocking wild punches from the skinny female on the bottom—though the term *punches* might not have been the best description. They looked more like wild, roundabout slaps, some of them landing on their intended target, while others only caught air.

A broomstick with a patch of blood on the handle sat on the floor next to the combatants. An open, liter-sized bottle of Pepsi was on its side nearby, soda spilling out in spurts from the end.

One of the wire-framed potato chip stands to Apollo's right had been knocked over, sending at least a dozen bags of chips sprawling to the floor. It looked like some of them had been trampled on, spraying the contents like potato spores. A few of the chips had made their way into the mouths of onlookers, who were munching them like popcorn at the movies.

The stand of produce beyond the bags had also been toppled, showering the store with green apples and broccoli clumps. He also saw a few squashed tomatoes sitting in their own red juices.

His new deputy, Albert, was stationary on the left with his arms folded and resting on top of his generous midsection. He looked dumbfounded as the scuffle between the two women continued.

Next to him was the other member of Team Two—Dustin Brown. The pencil-thin, goofy-looking young man who stood more like a hunched-over stork than a peace officer.

If Apollo had his pick, he'd rather have the athletic members of Team Three watching his back instead of these two. Their size and strength would have come in handy if this crowd decided to turn violent.

Just behind the deputies was a ring of people, some of them wearing store-issued aprons and name tags, while others looked to be customers who'd stopped their evening shopping spree to watch the middle-aged bantam-weight fight.

With the power out, Apollo couldn't make out the faces of the women beating on each other. The only source of light was from a series of gas-powered lanterns burning nearby, making the shadows in the vicinity dance with every flicker. The moonlight outside was also present, but its effect was limited to the area just inside the door.

The woman on her back had a store apron on, but the rest of her was a mess of tangled hair, grunts, screeches, and hand slaps.

Right then, he heard the powerful smack of several blows landing on skin, mostly on the cheeks of the female fighting from the bottom. Gus needed to end this altercation before someone got seriously hurt.

"All right, break it up!" he shouted, wrapping his arms around the waist of the female on top. He pulled back with force, prying her up and away from the other.

The woman on the floor rolled to her side and got up in a staggering motion, then swiped her hair out of the way to reveal her face. She took a breath and charged the other woman.

Apollo let go of his prisoner and jumped between the women to stop round two of this bout from starting. He put his hands out, landing them as stiff arms on the women's chests. "I said, that's enough! It's over!"

He finally got a good look at the store employee in the brawl. It was Grace Charmer, the owner and manager. Her cheeks were covered with a string of lengthy red marks—just short of being scratches. "Grace? What's going on here?"

She pointed at the other woman, then at the half-empty bottle of soda lying on the floor. "Miss bad dye-job over there was trying to steal from me. So I whacked her over the head with my broomstick. Then she jumped me."

Apollo turned his eyes to Grace's sparring partner. Blood was trickling down from a small gash above the woman's left eyebrow.

When his eyes landed on the other person's face, he couldn't believe it. It was Allison Rainey, the waitress he'd been wanting to ask out on a date.

He brought his hand up to his mouth and cleared his throat to cover up his look of shock. "You're the last person I expected to be in the middle of a fight, Allison."

"Hello to you, too, Sheriff."

"Why were you stealing Pepsi from Grace?"

"I wasn't stealing. I was thirsty, so I opened the bottle and took a sip. Is there some law against drinking soda while you're waiting in line to pay for it?"

"That's not what happened, Sheriff," Grace said, raising her voice and wagging her index finger at the other woman. "She was on her way to the door and was gonna walk right out. I had to stop her."

Allison threw up her arms and began waving them as she spoke. "I was heading to the back of the line, you stupid bitch. There's like a hundred people in here. Maybe if you knew how to run a business, you'd have more registers open so customers wouldn't have to wait around all night to pay."

Grace put her hands on her hips. "Okay, if what you say is true, then tell me this . . . Why did you run? Only guilty people run."

"Because I saw a crazy woman coming at me with a broom! You'd run, too, if you were in my shoes."

The sheriff looked at Grace, pinching his eyebrows. "I thought you said she jumped you?"

"She did. After I hit her with the broom."

"Of course I did! I had to defend myself," Allison snarled, pointing at the cut above her eye. "Look at what she did to me, Sheriff. And for no good reason. She's dangerous and should be locked up. We can't have people running around town and committing attempted murder with a deadly weapon!"

"Deadly weapon? Are you crazy? It was just a broom."

"Still, you could've killed me with it, if I hadn't fought back."

"I wasn't going to kill you. I was just protecting my store from a *thief*. I had every right to stop you before you ran outside."

"Don't believe her, Sheriff. You need to arrest her right now, before someone gets killed by this *witch* and her *broom*," Allison said, with disdain dripping from her lips in the form of spittle.

Apollo looked at Albert and Dustin. "What did you guys see?"

Albert responded, "Pretty much what they just said. Next thing I know, they're pulling hair and trying to punch each other."

"Why didn't you stop it?"

"Us?"

"Yeah, that's your job. To keep the peace. That's why I sent you here. To make sure everyone behaved in an orderly, efficient manner."

"I thought we were only supposed to observe and report. Not get involved after what happened to me at the gas station earlier."

Apollo shook his head, realizing these two deputies were going to need a lot of training just to perform the basics of their new assignment. It didn't take a brain surgeon to know when to step in and stop two older women from trying to beat the snot out of each other. "Can you at least tell me if there was theft involved?"

Albert shrugged. "No way to know for sure. She could've been headed for the back of the line or the door. But she was definitely drinking the item before paying. That much I'm sure of. Oh, and the gray-haired lady definitely hit the other one first. The rest of it was just an old, wrinkly blur."

"What about you?" the sheriff asked the other deputy. "Anything to add, Dustin?"

The string bean shook his head and swallowed his lower lip for a few seconds before answering. "Nah, that's basically what happened. I was thinking about going to get ya, but then you just showed up on your own. I thought, cool. I can just watch. You know, catfight and all."

"So, Sheriff . . . are you going to arrest her or not?" Grace asked. "We can't just let people steal."

"I told you, I wasn't stealing," Allison shot back at Grace.

"I'd prefer not to arrest anyone," Apollo said, making eye contact with both of them. "As far as I'm concerned, this was just a big misunderstanding. What I'd like to see happen is for both of you to apologize to each other and then shake hands. Can you do that? Or do I need to throw both of you in jail?"

Grace folded her arms over her chest and let her head sink.

Allison put her hands on her hips and tilted her head a few degrees to one side. Her lips were pinched.

"Come on, ladies. I've got more important things to do right now than referee the two of you. I'm not going to ask again. Shake hands and apologize or I'm locking you both up. Your choice."

Grace nodded, though tentatively.

Allison did the same.

"Sorry I hit you with the broom. I shouldn't have done that," Grace said, putting her hand out for a shake.

"I shouldn't have jumped on you like that. I'm sorry, too," Allison answered, taking Grace's hand in hers. The two ladies shook, then turned and walked away from each other.

"Nice work, Sheriff," Dustin said.

"All in a day's work," Apollo said. "But next time you see a couple of women start to go at it, jump in and stop it. Just be gentle. Understand?"

"Got it, chief," Dustin answered.

Apollo looked at Albert and waited for him to respond.

"Yeah, okay. Next time. Though to be perfectly honest, I kinda wanted to see the rest of the fight. I've heard that sometimes clothes get torn off."

Apollo rolled his eyes and turned for the door.

Just then, someone outside yelled, "Oh my God!" It was a woman's voice, and her sudden outburst caused the rest of the crowd to turn in unison and face the center of the square.

A collective gasp rose up from the throng of onlookers, as if it had been scripted for a Hollywood movie. A split second later, most of them took off in a slow jog in the direction they were looking.

"Good God, what now?" Apollo said, turning to Albert and Dustin. Their eyes were glued on the ruckus beyond the door. "You two, stay here."

"But it looks like the action's out there," Albert said.

"Hey, there's the Mayor," Dustin added, tapping Albert on the shoulder, then pointing his bony hand outside.

Apollo whirled his head around and spotted Mayor Buckley, trotting alongside the citizens in his sport coat.

Apollo looked back at Dustin. Then Albert. "Wait here till I get back. That's an order," he said with a clenched jaw before breaking into a full sprint to catch up to the Mayor.

CHAPTER 20

Five minutes earlier . . .

Bunker adjusted the position of the tiny black girl lying in his arms as they headed farther into the town of Clearwater. The makeshift knee brace he'd attached to Megan's leg seemed to be doing its job. As long as he kept her ride smooth, she didn't scream in pain.

The streets were littered with abandoned cars and trucks, many of them sitting with their hoods open, and he knew why. When the EMP hit, it fried their electronics and killed their engines, just like with the Amtrak train. The drivers must have gotten out and lifted the hoods to see what was wrong.

He wondered how long it took before they all realized some catastrophic event had just taken place. Sure, cars break down all the time, but never this many all at once. They had to realize something unusual had happened.

He peered down at the injured girl in his arms when she fidgeted. The only light source was the moon, but he could still see her innocent eyes looking back at his. "We're almost there, Megan. I'm sure your dad is going to be very happy to see you."

"Jack? Can I ask you something?" she asked in a tender, sweet voice.

"Sure. Anything."

"Do you like horses?"

"Sure. I like horses. Why?"

"Because I want you to meet my horse when we get home. His name is Star. He's really beautiful and gentle. You're gonna love him."

Jack didn't want to tell her no, or that he planned to skip town the first chance he got. So he chose something more neutral and noncommittal.

"I'm sure he's a wonderful horse," he said, seeing Megan's eyes close right before her breathing turned deep and full. She was out again, like she'd done several times since he rescued her.

When they'd first left the scene of the accident, he and Deputy Clark tried putting Megan in a saddle, but her knee couldn't take the long, uneven strides, or the effects of gravity.

The girl cried in pain after every step, forcing Bunker to pull her off the animal and carry her to town in his arms. Megan didn't weigh much, but after several miles, even his stout biceps were starting to feel the strain.

Bunker turned his head for a moment, checking on the kids following behind. So far, they'd been pretty well behaved. He brought his eyes forward. "Looks like you were right," he said to Stephanie.

"About what?"

"The kids walking."

"I'm glad you agree. Though I could've used your support earlier when I was trying to convince Daisy we didn't want to try alternating who rode and who walked. That plan never would've worked. You can't play favorites. Not with a bunch of hungry, tired kids."

"I figured you two had it handled. That's why I stayed out of it. You know, go along to get along."

"Coward," she said, wearing a smile.

Bunker had another question to ask, but wasn't sure if he should. Something had been nagging at him ever since they'd rescued Megan from the bus. He thought about it for a few more strides, then decided to let the words fly. "So what's the deal with you two?"

The smile vanished from her lips. "What do you mean? With Daisy?"

"Yeah. The tension is so thick, I can taste it."

"There's some history."

"I gathered that."

"It's too bad because we used to be good friends. But after what she did, I can't stand to look at her anymore."

He could hear the emotional pain in her words. "That's why she seems to cave into whatever you suggest. I was wondering."

"Yeah, she owes me. Big time."

"What happened?"

"I really don't want to go into it right now," she answered, shooting a look down at Jeffrey then at Bunker.

He understood. She didn't want her son to hear the details. "Gotcha. Forget I asked."

Stephanie had also persuaded Daisy earlier to leave the bus driver's body behind until someone could return and retrieve him from the bus. She didn't want the kids seeing the dead body of their teacher flopping around on a horse.

If the rumor was true about the driver having a pacemaker, then it seemed logical to assume the device failed when the EMP blasted the area. Assuming Bunker's theory was correct, then the bus accident was random and uncontrolled. The kids got lucky. The bus could have easily plowed into a tree or hit one of the unmovable boulders in the clearing, sending more of the kids flying than just Megan. The injury toll would have been much worse. Some may have been fatal.

Stephanie let go of Jeffrey's hand for a moment to adjust the oversized coat she was wearing. One of the male deputies had given up his jacket so she could cover up her bra and stay warm.

If Bunker had to do it over again, he never would have used her shirt as lashing material for Megan's knee brace. Instead, he could have cut strips of material from one of the seats in the bus.

Jeffrey hadn't been talking much during the trek back to town. For most of the day, the kid had been a non-stop question machine, giggling occasionally for no apparent reason. Bunker figured the boy was tired and running on fumes.

When you're exhausted, the first thing to go is your willingness to engage in excess conversation. *Cranky Mute* was term Bunker's mother used to throw at him when he was little.

On the right, Deputy Daisy had her hands full with two redheaded girls, both literally and figuratively. The twins, Barb and Beth, loved to swing their arms and were chatterboxes, yanking on Daisy like a pull toy. The deputy seemed to enjoy it. She played along with their frivolity, never complaining once.

Barb was a little heavier than Beth, making it easy to keep them straight since her face was rounder. The key to telling them apart would be to look at them together, then he could compare their plumpness.

The rest of the kids were behind Bunker and walking in a loose herd of pattering feet. At the rear of the slow-moving mass were the two male deputies who'd showed up in the clearing with Daisy.

They were on foot, herding the kids like cattle while leading the horses loaded with packs. They seemed content to just do their jobs and take orders from Daisy. And from Stephanie. But that wasn't the only thing Bunker found odd about the law enforcement trio. Only Daisy was dressed in uniform. The other two were in street clothes. He wasn't sure why, but figured it had something to do with a sudden rescue mission on horseback.

When they turned the next corner and passed a bicycle shop, his jaw dropped open. The massive town square was dead ahead, but so, too, were dozens of people facing away from him. There was a buzz of conversation going on.

"Something's happening inside Charmer's Market," Daisy said.

"Grace's place," Stephanie added. "I hope something hasn't happened to her."

"I take it you know her?" Bunker asked.

"Yeah, nice lady. She lost her husband a while back in a freak tractor accident and was forced to step in and run his store. I remember the first couple of weeks. She was in way over her head and completely lost. I felt so sorry for her."

Before Bunker could take another step, one of the men in the crowd noticed their approach and pointed his finger at them. The man leaned to the left and must have said something to the others nearby because more of them turned around and stared.

"Oh my God!" a woman's voice called out from the crowd.

With that, the rest of the crowd turned around and gasped. A second later, they started jogging—toward Bunker and his group.

"Should I be worried?" he asked Daisy. "They're not going to like some strange man carrying one of their daughters back to town."

"No. I got this. They know me," she said, increasing her pace with the two girls. She raced ahead to intercept the flood of townspeople.

"Mom!" one of the boys behind Bunker said before taking off in a full gallop.

"Dad!" another said, following the first boy.

More and more of the kids ran forward, sprinting to their respective family members. Hugs and kisses ensued, showering the children with love and affection.

"There's the Sheriff," Stephanie said a few seconds later, pointing at a burly man wearing a uniform. He was in the middle of the pack and not very tall.

"And the Mayor," Stephanie added. "He's the taller one in the sport coat."

Jack didn't like the idea of getting cozy with all these strangers. Especially those in charge of an entire town, or those who happened to be wearing a badge.

Luckily, Deputy Daisy hadn't asked a lot of questions during their hike back to town, so he didn't have to evade or lie to her. But the Sheriff would certainly want to know more. A lot more.

Bunker's fingerprints were in the system and he couldn't take the chance someone would run a check and discover his past, if the power was ever restored.

He looked at Stephanie. "Just so you know, once we get Megan back to her father, I'm gonna head out."

"You're leaving?" Jeffrey asked, breaking his long silence.

"Why?" Stephanie asked. "We just got here."

"I'm not all that comfortable in large groups. It's best if I get on my way as soon as this is over. Besides, the last thing this town needs is another mouth to feed. With the power out, things are going to get dicey."

"Is it because of what I saw under your shirt?" she asked.

"Partly."

"But you said you weren't that man anymore."

"I'm not. But a man's past follows him wherever he goes. No matter how hard he tries, he can't outrun it. It's always there, stalking him."

She rolled her eyes. "Not exactly sure what that means, but whatever."

"Look, I know you have a million questions and frankly, I don't blame you. But let's face it; I don't exactly blend in. Or fit in, for that matter. I'm a complete stranger to these people. An outsider. So trust me when I say my presence here would only add more risk to what's already a risky situation."

"Please, Mr. Bunker, don't leave. Please," Jeffrey pleaded.

"I have to, sport. It's for the best."

She shrugged. "Fine. If you wanna leave, then leave. It's a free country. All I can say is I'm not surprised. You can never count on men to step up when you really need them."

"I understand why you say that, but you really don't know me. There's more to this than you realize. I'm just looking out for you and your son."

"Hey, we all have a past," she said like a talk show host, tilting her head back and forth.

"That's true. But not like mine."

"Then explain it to me."

"I can't."

"Why not?"

"Because I'm afraid you'll hate me. So let's just leave things as they are," he said as residents of Clearwater began to surround the four of them.

"Like I said, whatever," she said, changing her voice to a whisper before she spoke again. "The dude in the cowboy hat is Megan's father, Franklin Atwater. He runs the horseback riding club just outside of town."

A tall, trim black man with broad shoulders and a full beard stepped forward. He was in full Western gear, including flannel shirt, jeans, and a bronze belt buckle. His boots were polished and so was the silver bolo tie around his neck.

"My goodness, what happened to her?" Franklin asked, looking at Bunker first, then Stephanie. "Is she okay?"

Stephanie took the lead and answered. "We think she was sitting up on the seat when the bus crashed. I'm afraid she took quite a tumble."

"You two found her?" Franklin asked.

Stephanie nodded. "Her and the rest of the kids."

"Where's Wilhelm?" Franklin asked.

"He didn't make it," she answered in a somber tone.

A long pause fell over the group.

"Don't forget, I helped, too!" Jeffrey said, breaking the silence.

"I'll bet you did," Franklin said, smiling at the boy and patting him on the head.

"Yes, he was very brave," Stephanie said, bending down to wrap her arms around her son's shoulders. She finished her squeeze, then stood up to face Franklin. "You should know that the bus was hanging over a cliff when my new friend here, Mr. Jack Bunker, crawled in and risked his own life to save your daughter."

Franklin looked stunned for a moment, then returned to reality. "Thank you, thank you," he said, holding out his arms to receive his daughter. "I don't know how I'm ever going to repay you."

Bunker gave Megan to him, letting her slide gingerly from his grasp. "Careful with her knee. I'd suggest keeping it supported and not moving it around too much. It's pretty swollen."

"I see that," the father said before kissing his daughter softly on the cheek. "Megan, sweetheart. Wake up. It's Daddy. I'm here now, darling. Everything is going to be okay."

Megan's eyes remained closed and there was no reaction to his gentle words.

Franklin shot a look of confusion at Bunker, but didn't say anything. He didn't have to. His eyes said it all.

Bunker could see his pain. "She's been in and out since the crash. We think she might've hit her head, too. But since there's no apparent bruising or blood, we really don't know much for sure. You need to get her medical attention right away."

When Franklin's face turned from confusion to concern, Bunker continued, hoping to alleviate some of the man's dread. "When she's awake, she seems coherent and in reasonably good spirits. So hopefully it's nothing serious. It could just be exhaustion. After all, your daughter's been through a lot today. But a doctor really needs to examine her, just to be sure."

"I'll make sure she gets everything she needs. I can't thank you enough. All of you, for bringing my little girl home to me."

"It's our pleasure, Franklin," Stephanie said, putting a hand on Bunker's shoulder.

Franklin turned and headed east, across the square.

Bunker waited until Stephanie looked at him, letting his courage rise before he had to speak again. "Hey, it's about that time."

"Please don't go," she said, pleading with watery eyes.

"I don't have a choice. It's been great getting to know you and your son. He's a good boy, and you should be proud of him."

Jeffrey wrapped his arms around Bunker's bare legs and squeezed them tight.

Before Bunker could pry the kid loose, a swarm of children from the bus and their parents surrounded him, led by the Sheriff and Daisy. The Mayor remained behind, chatting with some of the other parents and kids.

The lawman came forward and put out his hand. "I'm Sheriff Gus Apollo."

Bunker gripped it with force and shook it twice, looking the man in the eye. "Jack Bunker." He needed to size up the new acquaintance and see if he could detect the sheriff's intentions.

"My deputy tells me all these kids are safe because of you," Apollo said. He turned his gaze at Stephanie and then Jeffrey. "And you two, as well."

"We were just doing what anyone else would do, Sheriff," Bunker answered, as Jeffrey let go of his legs and stood by his mother.

"Well, I'm not so sure about that. Risking your life for total strangers is not something you see every day. Not in today's world of never getting involved."

Apollo turned sideways and held out an open hand. "These parents have something they'd like to say to you. Both of you."

A second later, a dozen hands came at Bunker and Stephanie, along with a barrage of appreciative phrases, including "God bless you," "We owe you," and of course, "Thank you."

Bunker gripped each of their palms and gave them a quick shake. Some of the moms exchanged their handshakes for a firm hug, wrapping their trembling arms around Jack's neck, then Stephanie's.

Just when Bunker thought it was almost over, some of the little ones they'd saved decided to tackle Bunker's legs with a group hug.

He wasn't sure what to do with everyone watching, so he just stood there in the limelight, offering up a forced grin as he waited for the hug-fest to end.

Stephanie bent down and greeted the children who came her way with an emotional hug for each.

Bunker watched her with the little ones and wished he was as comfortable around emotional kids. Her motherly instinct was impressive and genuine.

When it was over and the children returned to their parents, he announced to everyone, "Thank you, folks. But I really need to be going."

"Oh no, you're not," Deputy Daisy said, latching onto his arm. "We've got some celebrating to do."

"That's right," one of the male parents said. "There needs to be a hero's party."

"No, that's really not necessary," Bunker said.

"Yes. Yes, it is. It's the least we can do," one of the soccer moms said, grabbing his left hand and leading him forward. "Do you have a place to stay, Mr. Bunker? We have plenty of room in our house."

The twin girls Daisy had been walking with grabbed his other hand, pulling his arm free from Daisy's grip. "Please, Mr. Bunker. Stay at our house. Please."

Bunker looked at Stephanie, who was grinning from ear to ear. It was clear she was getting a kick out of all the attention he was getting.

"Welcome to my hometown," Stephanie quipped. "Where no one ever leaves. Including me, apparently."

He sighed, knowing it was going to be impossible to say no. He felt like a carnival freak who'd been imprisoned behind viewing glass with everyone huddling around and staring at him. The word uncomfortable didn't begin to cover it.

"Just roll with it," Stephanie said, winking. "You really don't have a choice."

He nodded. She was right. He didn't have a choice. Not without raising suspicions. But it wasn't all bad. Even though he'd never admit it, it felt amazing being appreciated by a bunch of strangers for once, instead of being feared when he rolled into a new town.

A genuine grin grew on his lips.

Maybe, just maybe, the new life he'd been looking for had just found him.

CHAPTER 21

Jack Bunker kept an eye on the whirl of activity in the town square of Clearwater, Colorado as he slumped down in the back seat of an abandoned car.

Everywhere he looked, he saw more townspeople cruising by. Most of them had a candle or a gas lantern in their hands. A few flashlights were providing light, too, but after the sweeping failure that had crippled the power grid, the rest of the mountain community was relying on the only other source of light: the moon.

When the area around the car was clear, he unbuttoned his makeshift shorts and slid them off. It was time to replace them with long pants to hide his embarrassingly white legs and provide some warmth. A second later, his feet were inside and after a quick pull up, he was dressed in a full-length pair of jeans for the first time since he'd cut the bottoms off the other pair to help save the kids on the overturned bus.

He fastened the lone button and yanked the zipper up to complete his cover-up, before stuffing the cutoffs into his duffle, where they'd probably remain until he got settled somewhere.

Bunker got out of the vehicle and went back to his previous spot: fifteen feet in front of the entrance door to the small-town clinic, where his new friend, Stephanie King, was waiting.

"That's better. I thought I was going to need my sunglasses. Talk about a pair of supernovas," Stephanie said when he arrived, her smile full.

"Yeah, I've never liked my legs much," Bunker said, wanting to change the subject. He looked around for her son. "Where's Jeffrey?"

She pointed at the ice cream parlor across the way. "They're giving cones away before it all melts. Doesn't look like the power's coming on anytime soon."

"Probably not," he answered, watching the adolescent step up to the takeout window of the confectionery store and take hold of a vanilla cone wrapped in a white napkin.

The ten-year-old backed away from the purveyor and stood with the twin redheads he'd just met from the school bus accident. The girls were about half done with their melting treats, but Jeffrey looked determined to catch up.

Bunker smiled when he saw the spread of creamy white across Jeffrey's pale skin and freckles. "Looks like he missed. Must be out of practice."

Stephanie laughed. "Oh, I seriously doubt that. That boy has ice cream all the time. In fact, if I let him, he'd have it for breakfast, lunch, and dinner, seven days a week. No, he's just being silly for the girls. I never should've told him that the way to a girl's heart is to make her laugh."

Bunker nodded, thinking of his first crush in school. "Ah, I remember those days well. Life was so simple back then."

"Yep. Just school, homework, and ice cream. Doesn't take much to entertain that boy. As long as he has his science game to play with, he's good for hours."

Jeffrey's enthrallment with the educational device, *Frankie's Science Lab,* was obvious when the three of them first met on the Amtrak train. But now that the EMP blast had taken it out, along with the rest of the electronics, the boy would surely miss it.

Bunker couldn't hold back a laugh as Jeffrey continued his antics for the girls. "Well, I don't know, Steph. Judging by the way he's interacting with those girls, he might be changing his focus to something other than science. Something a little more interactive and tactile, if you know what I mean."

"Oh, good God. Not yet. He's only ten."

"Kids start early these days. Not like when we were their age. I don't know about you, but I didn't know crap."

"Me either. But with social media, they're exposed to way too much at too young an age."

"At least with the grid down, you don't have to worry about that for a while."

"One good thing at least."

Even though Bunker had just arrived in this small town, its residents had been exceptionally kind and welcoming. Of course, showing up with fifty of their kids he'd just rescued from a bus hanging off a cliff didn't hurt. It was certainly a memorable first impression, and a positive one at that.

Good impressions were not what usually happened when he arrived in a new town, at least not while on assignment for his former boss.

Actually, now that he thought about it, his last two jobs yielded the same results—the locals loathing his arrival, but doing so for two completely different reasons.

He figured as long as he kept his body art hidden from public view, his new-found reputation and cover ID would remain intact. The blowtorch had eradicated the ink on the sides of his neck, but burning the rest of it off his body wasn't going to be an option—not just due to the excruciating pain and lengthy healing process, but because it was nearly everywhere, covering his arms, chest, and back.

He could accept living with a pair of disfiguring two-inch scars on his neck, but he wasn't willing to cover himself with dozens of scars, even to hide all his sins.

Before the blowtorch decision, he considered checking into a tattoo removal center to see what they could do. However, that would've created a paper trail and raised too many questions, risking his former employer, Connor Watts, learning of his location.

Jack knew the rule like everyone else who'd joined the group: nobody walks away and lives to tell about it. Yet, despite his boss' ruthless reputation, that's exactly what he'd done.

If he continued to wear long-sleeve shirts, the truth about his past would stay hidden. So far, his plan seemed to be working. As long as he stayed in character and didn't get noticed, there was little chance anyone would track him down under his new name. Especially now that the grid and communications were down.

At this point, only Stephanie King had caught a glimpse of the artwork on his back. She may have noticed some of the ink on his forearms, too, when he was shirtless and turned away earlier that day. However, with the Internet offline, she wouldn't be able to look up the meaning of the numbers and symbols.

He figured he was safe—for now, anyway. The most condemning tattoos were on his chest, and those he could never let her see—or anyone else in town, for that matter. If word ever got back to Watts, he and his loyal men would come gunning for him and anyone else who got in their way.

Bunker felt a tap on his outside shoulder. He turned. It was one of the kids from the bus.

"What's up, Tommy?" he asked the boy.

"My dad told me to give you this," the tall, lanky kid said, his eyes blinking rapidly. He held up his hand and gave Bunker a lunch-sized brown paper sack.

Bunker hoped it wasn't money or some other gift he couldn't accept. "What is it?"

"Open it," Tommy said, bobbing on his heels. "Dad said to tell you to share it with Stephanie, before it goes bad."

Bunker opened the bag. Inside was a pile of thinly sliced roast beef. No bun, lettuce, or anything else. Just a big batch of Arby's-style meat.

Tommy continued, "Charmer's is selling their meat super cheap before it goes bad. Dad made me promise not to eat any of it on my way over here."

"Where is your dad?"

Tommy turned and pointed to a round, stocky man who was about the same height as the kid. Their resemblance to each other was uncanny: same curly hair, wide nose, and chipmunk cheeks. No doubt they were related.

Bunker raised his hand and sent a single head nod as a thank you.

Tommy's father gave him a thumbs-up signal, then turned his attention to the elderly woman standing next to him.

Bunker put his hand inside the sack and pulled out a clutch of roast beef. He held it up. There were almost no strands of fat in the beef. "Ah, the good stuff," he said.

Tommy licked his lips.

Bunker took a wad of slices and split them equally between Stephanie and the delivery boy. Both of them devoured the food like a couple of starving T-Rexes. He gave them another round of slices before putting some into his own mouth.

The flavor exploded on his tongue. "Damn, this is good. I forgot how hungry I was."

"Me too," Stephanie answered, her mouth full. She smiled at Tommy and the kid grinned back, both of them working their teeth to grind down the food.

"Is all their meat this lean?" Bunker asked her before cramming another handful into his mouth.

"Yep. Charmer's get their beef from a cattle ranch outside town. Doesn't get any fresher than that."

Charmer's Market and Feed Store was on the left side of Clearwater's central square. From what he'd been told, Charmer's was the only true mercantile in the area, not counting the postage stamp of an ice cream shop on the adjacent corner and the newly-built convenience store and bait shop across the street. The long line of shoppers snaking its way across the grassy square from Charmer's seemed to confirm that fact.

'The Event' earlier that day had sent everyone scrambling. The grid had failed across the area, plus all the electronics seemed to be fried. He expected as much, given what he'd seen that day during his train ride.

A sudden flashback tore into his mind, replaying the important events of the day: meeting Steph and her son in the Sightseeing Car, the locomotive stalling in the mountains, and then the falling aircraft narrowly missing the front of the train.

It still seemed like an impossibility: the airliner getting caught in a wicked updraft, sending it to the side at the last second. When he saw the wide swath of tracks missing, he knew how lucky they all were.

He could still smell the smoke in his nostrils from the fiery crash that took the unmarked, all-white plane deep inside the canyon along the river. If not for a miracle gust of wind, that brutal end would have been his destiny, too.

Bunker figured the unusual combination of failures meant only one thing—a high-altitude EMP blast. Nothing else seemed to fit the facts he'd gathered thus far. No mushroom clouds. No signs of radiation poisoning. No widespread destruction. Yet the power was out and electronics were useless.

It all fit the pattern. However, without more information, Bunker couldn't be sure of any of it. Nor could the Mayor or Sheriff, who were huddled with a pack of citizens ten yards away.

Bunker wasn't a technical expert by any stretch, but he'd read his share of technical magazines and science fiction novels during his free time since high school. That same span of fourteen years had also included two stints of employment, both of which made his skin crawl upon reflection.

He wasn't proud of all he'd done for brother and country; however, if it weren't for all the bad decisions he'd made, he never would've been here, in Clearwater, at this exact point in time. Without him, the busload of kids he'd rescued would've met their deaths at the bottom of Clayton's Ravine. It was the first truly heroic thing he'd done in a long time.

For the moment, he didn't hate himself, and that was a positive first step. His personal ledger of good deeds versus evil acts was still horribly out of balance, but saving dozens of kids had to count for something. If not, then he was doomed to spend the rest of eternity in the flames of hell.

His eyes wandered across the square and landed on a busy seven-pump gas station called *Billy's Pump and Munch*. Bunker pointed at the establishment's sign and smirked. "Gotta love that name."

Stephanie rolled her eyes. "I don't think the town council was too fond of it at first, but when Billy Jack explained how much cash he was going to dump into downtown, they approved his plans in a heartbeat. Funny how that works."

"Money talks."

"Yeah, even from a long-haired hillbilly like him. Though I think he should've spent some of that money on some new teeth. I've seen hockey players who look better."

Bunker laughed, appreciating her humor.

She continued, "When he decided to add a bait shop and convenience store, Grace Charmer wasn't too happy about it. Not that I could blame her, especially when it happened right after her husband died."

"Judging by the line in front of her store, it hasn't hurt her business too much."

"That's what the town's planning commission kept telling her, but she still flipped out. Not too surprising if you know her."

"She's the one who attacked the customer with the broom earlier, right?"

"Yeah, for stealing soda, apparently. From what the Sheriff said, I guess it was one hell of a catfight."

Tensions were understandably high but the citizenry seemed to be handling the day fairly well, probably due to small-town values where everyone was a neighbor and friend. At least on some level.

There was certainly more of the community he hadn't seen, so it was possible for looting and altercations to be breaking out all across the area and he'd never know about it. But something in his gut told him that wasn't the case. Not here. Not in this quaint little community—a destination where summer tourists flocked when the sun started its boil atop the arid deserts of Arizona and New Mexico.

Bunker was thankful he wasn't in his brutal hometown of South LA, where there'd certainly be widespread trouble escalating by the minute. If the EMP blast had affected life in southern California like it had here, the City of Angels was probably tearing itself apart by now.

Bunker knew as well as anyone that mixing a major catastrophe with millions of desperate people usually results in lawlessness and anarchy. Especially when the citizens are already living on the edge and angry about their meager existence.

Bunker kept an eye on the ongoing conversation between the Mayor, Sheriff, and eleven of the townspeople. It looked intense based on the animated facial expressions. He tried to read some of their lips between the arm waving and finger pointing, but couldn't make out what they were saying.

Occasionally a phrase or two would land on his eardrums, but he hadn't heard enough to determine if the group was chatting about him or his mysterious background.

He was about to make a joke to Stephanie about the free floorshow, but held his tongue when the group seemed to reach an agreement. Smiles erupted on the faces of the citizens, then handshaking ensued before they split up into small groups and headed off in different directions.

"Here they come," Stephanie said, referring to Sheriff Apollo and Mayor Buckley. She took the empty food sack from Bunker and crumpled it in her hand. "Do you want me to run interference?"

"Let's see what they want first," he answered, checking the bandages on his neck. They were still secure and covering up the wounds he'd given himself before he set off on his 'walkabout'—a term Jeffrey had coined to describe Bunker's one-way train ride to nowhere.

"Mr. Bunker," the Sheriff said, "I'd like you to formally meet our esteemed mayor, Mr. Seth Buckley."

"Damn fine to meet you, sir," Bunker said, putting his hand out for the customary shake.

The Mayor grabbed his hand, wrapping his oversized grip around Bunker's palm like a suffocating octopus. "Likewise. Jack, isn't it?"

"Yes, Jack Francis Bunker is my full name, sir. But you can call me Bunker or Bunk, like everyone else, if it's easier."

Stephanie giggled. "Francis? Seriously?"

Bunker shrugged, shooting her an embarrassed look. He wasn't sure why his lips decided to reveal his middle name, but they did. Usually he was in full control of himself, but for some reason, his skills were slipping, mainly around Stephanie.

He decided to disguise his overshare with some friendly banter. "It's not like we get to pick our own names, now do we?"

"No doubt," she quipped, still laughing.

Mayor Buckley cleared his throat, catching everyone's attention. He looked at Bunker. "Sorry I didn't get a chance to introduce myself earlier, when you brought the kids back to their parents."

"That was some kind of rescue," Sheriff Apollo added.

"Glad to help. But I wasn't alone. We all pulled together," Bunker answered.

"Like family," Stephanie added, shaking the Mayor's hand as well. She was still smiling, but at least she wasn't laughing at Bunker anymore.

"Well, hello Ms. King. Back already, I see," the Mayor said, offering up a crooked smile.

"You knew I was gone?"

"Of course. It's my job to know. Besides, news travels fast in a small town."

"Then you must know about the divorce, too."

"Yes, I'm sorry things didn't work out between you and Bill. But these things happen. I always thought you two looked good together."

"I'm guessing he knows I took off for Denver," she said in a dejected voice.

"Probably. But at least you're back."

"Well, I wasn't planning to be, Mayor. At least, not this soon. But what's a mother to do? When your train stops in the middle of nowhere and a plane almost crashes into it, you gotta make a choice."

The Mayor nodded, his eyebrows pinched. "Deputy Clark briefed us about everything a few minutes ago. That must have been terrifying."

"It was. But Jack here kept me and my son safe. Like he did for all those kids."

"Is that how you two met?" Buckley asked, pointing at Bunker, then at Stephanie.

She nodded. "We were sitting across from each other in the viewing car when the engines went out. I kinda forced myself on him and luckily, he let us tag along. Though I'm pretty sure he hated the idea."

"I can understand that," Buckley said. "I've known you since you were knee-high to a grasshopper. You're not used to hearing the word no."

"That I can believe," Bunker said, flaring a snide look at her. "She's an acquired taste, that's for sure."

"Hey, watch it, buddy," she said, slapping his shoulder with a quick swipe of her hand.

Bunker laughed. "But in all seriousness, it's a good thing she did, otherwise there's no telling what might've happened to the kids. It was a team effort out there. Rescuing Megan wouldn't have happened without her help—and, of course, Jeffrey's."

"Speaking of which, how's that brilliant young man of yours doing?" Buckley asked Stephanie.

She pointed past the Mayor, aiming her finger at the ice cream parlor. Her son was still out front, making a mess of the treat. "He's right there, if you want to say hello."

Mayor Buckley twisted his neck and took a look, then brought his attention back to Stephanie. It looked like he was about to say something when out of nowhere, Deputy Clark showed up, gasping for breath.

"Sheriff, you need to come with me," Daisy said in an eager tone, stopping the friendly banter of the group.

"What's wrong?" Apollo asked.

"We're picking up a signal."

"How? Nothing's working."

"I found a hand crank radio in the supply cabinet. It looks ancient but I was able to get it working. Somebody's transmitting."

"Emergency services?" Mayor Buckley asked.

"Not sure. Whoever it is, they're using Morse code."

"I can help you with that," Bunker added.

Stephanie shot him a surprised look but didn't say anything.

"You a military man?" the Sheriff asked him.

"In my younger days."

"Come on, before it stops," the Deputy said, waiving for Bunker to follow her.

Bunker gave the straps of his upright duffle bag to Stephanie. "Watch my stuff for me, okay?"

She took them, but kept quiet.

Bunker started behind Daisy, then stopped and whirled around to check on Stephanie. She looked both concerned and confused. He knew why and didn't want her to worry about him taking off once he was out of sight. "If you see Megan before I get back, give her a hug for me."

Stephanie nodded, though she didn't look convinced. She gave him a tentative hand wave, like she was saying goodbye forever.

CHAPTER 22

Jack Bunker adjusted his butt in the chair behind one of the desks in the Sheriff's office. Next to him was Deputy Daisy. She, too, was sitting in a metal swivel chair as they listened to the dots and dashes arrive across the weak radio signal. Sheriff Apollo and Mayor Buckley had crowded in behind them with their arms folded.

"Keep cranking it," the Sheriff said to Daisy. "Don't let the power run low."

Behind the men in charge were a few townspeople Bunker didn't know: three males and two females. So far, none of them had said a word.

Bunker jotted down the Morse code message on a yellow pad, using line breaks when he heard extended pauses in the communication. After the ninth line of the message, the broadcast stopped, sending only static across the airwaves. He waited another thirty seconds to see if the message continued. When it didn't, Bunker put the pencil down. "I guess that's it."

"What does it say?" Daisy asked.

"Not much. Just a series of numbers."

She leaned in close. "What kind of numbers?"

He ran the tip of his finger under the first line to reinforce his explanation. "Whole numbers in groups of five." He tilted the pad up for the Mayor to see.

Bunker decided to call out some of the numbers so everyone could hear, even the citizens in the back. "The first set is 32, 71, 117, 161, 10. The second is 39, 83, 104, 82, 11."

"What do you think they mean?" Daisy asked.

He brought the pad down. "Beats me. Maybe if I'd caught the first part of the transmission, we'd know what these are for. Without a frame of reference, they could be lottery numbers for all we know."

Daisy gave him a look of amusement. "Well, I'm pretty sure they're not. I've been playing the lottery most of my life and I don't ever remember seeing a number over a hundred. Winning is almost impossible anyway, so having over a hundred balls in the hopper would raise the odds to astronomical."

"You're right," Bunker said. "Nobody would ever play."

"Let me take a look," Sheriff Apollo said, extending his hand.

Bunker gave him the pad of paper.

Apollo studied it, his eyes scanning down the page one line at a time. "This one," he said, tilting the pad and pointing to the second string of numbers, starting with 39 and 83. "I think I know what this is. Back in the day, I used to do pro bono work for the Colorado Historical Society, helping them conduct architectural surveys for protected lands and other culturally significant areas. All the surveys included specific sets of GPS coordinates, so I knew the exact boundaries of the land in question. Seems to me a lot of my work involved sites that started with 39 and something in the 80s."

"Latitude?" Bunker asked.

"Yes, and 104 for the starting longitude. But GPS is usually four numbers, not five, when it's written in shorthand like this."

Mayor Buckley grabbed the list from Apollo. "Do you have a map around here? We need to see if these line up to something."

"I'll get the area maps," Daisy said, standing up from the chair in a flash. "They have coordinates along the side." She returned a few seconds later and gave the thick book to Apollo.

He opened it and fanned through the colorful pages until he found the section for Colorado. He ran a finger down the two sides of the map until he found the numbers on the list. He brought his fingers together until they met at the intersecting point. "Yep, Colorado Springs, all right."

"But what's the eleven on the end for?" Daisy asked.

"Maybe it's the local time?" Bunker answered.

"Time for what?" she asked.

"Detonation?" he said in a leading manner.

Her face pinched for a second, then released as her eyes went wide. "Oh my God."

"Check the rest of them," Mayor Buckley ordered, giving the list to the Sheriff.

"Looks like the first set is for San Diego," Apollo said after flipping forward in the book and tracking the numbers down.

"Not far from my hometown," Bunker muttered without thinking. He hadn't planned to reveal that information to anyone but Stephanie. But now that it was out there, he needed to play along with his own mistake. Otherwise, it might raise suspicions. "Gonna be chaos in the streets."

"You're from San Diego?" Daisy asked. "I love San Diego, especially the Gas Lamp District."

"Actually, I'm from LA. But San Diego is nice. Been there a few times."

"Well," Apollo said after checking more coordinates, "looks like the others are for Pensacola, Virginia Beach, Huntsville, Tacoma, Anchorage, Charleston, and Las Cruces."

"If the part of the message we missed contained more numbers—" Daisy said, stopping in mid-sentence.

"Then a bunch of other cities are without power," Bunker said, "and tech."

"If we're right, then these were planned detonations," Buckley added. "Not some random accident."

"Detonations? Did someone nuke us?" one of the male civilians asked from the back of the group.

"I don't think so," the Sheriff answered. "We haven't seen any signs of a mushroom cloud or radiation. No, this was probably something else."

Bunker agreed with Apollo. "Since EMPs only work in direct line of sight, it must've been somewhere overhead to affect all of us here. Otherwise, the height of the mountains would've protected your electronics from a surface blast. Since we're all still alive and not suffering from radiation poisoning, this must be some kind of new EMP device. I don't know what else it could be."

"Who would do this to us?" the same man in the back asked.

"Could be anyone. Seems like everyone hates us these days," an unidentified woman's voice added.

"Well, not just anyone," Bunker said, letting his mind churn through the possibilities. "It'd have to be a country who's technologically advanced. Someone with the capability and the guts to plan something like this."

Apollo nodded. "Damn smart, if you think about it. They didn't want to run the risk of contaminating the atmosphere, or themselves, with a series of nukes. Radiation would drift everywhere in the high-altitude winds."

"Yes, high altitude. That's where the blast must have been in order to affect us here," Buckley said, regurgitating what Bunker had just shared.

"Long-range missiles from Russia or China could probably deploy what we're talking about here," Bunker said.

"How? Don't we have defense systems and radar to stop something like this?" Daisy asked.

"Yeah, we do. But what if the attackers launched a cyber attack at the same time?" Apollo asked. "Remember, NORAD's not far from here, in Colorado Springs."

"Then they must have blinded us so we couldn't react," she said, nodding.

"Exactly," Apollo answered.

Daisy exhaled slowly. "Probably targeted the grid computers as well. You know, to make sure their plan worked. With all the cyber attacks we hear about on the news, there's no telling how many systems they've hacked."

Bunker agreed, connecting a few more ideas in his thoughts. "Let's face it, our government always seems to be distracted with endless bickering between the parties and dealing with scandals and cover-ups. It left the door open for our adversaries to plan and execute this while we weren't paying attention. There are some really smart people out there, and I don't think it would take much to plant a bunch of sleeper programs in our critical computer systems. Then, when they were ready, unleash hell to take us down. Like today."

"The NSA was doing the exact same thing to other countries. Remember the Snowden leaks about sleeper programs?" Daisy said.

"Then the whole country is without power," the male voice in the back said.

"What if those coordinates are not for detonation, but for destination?" Buckley asked, his voice sounding more authoritative than before.

"You mean invasion?" Apollo asked him.

CHAPTER 23

Bunker saw the look on the Mayor's face change to one of deep concern. Then his head sank. After a short pause, the well-dressed man brought his eyes up to the Sheriff. "What if the last numbers in those strings don't represent the time? What if they are military division numbers?"

"Whole divisions?"

"Yes, one assigned for each location."

"How many troops are in a division?" Daisy asked Bunker in a casual whisper.

"About 10,000. Sometimes 15."

Her face ran white and she sucked in her lower lip.

Apollo's eyes drifted away from the Mayor for a few seconds, then he scratched his chin and said to Bunker, "They *would* need GPS coordinates to find their way across a foreign country. So maybe." He flashed a look at Bunker to indicate he was waiting for another take on the idea.

Bunker took a moment to sift through what he'd learned during his stint in the military. He knew the Mayor's idea about division assignment had merit, but it didn't seem to fit what his gut was telling him about the last digit in the string of numbers. He didn't want to be rude, so he decided to spin his answer softly.

"Since we didn't hear the entire broadcast, anything is possible at this point. Could be about detonation or destination. But either way, before someone puts boots on the ground, they'd want to take out the enemy's ability to communicate. Then focus on their transportation systems so they can't resupply. I can't think of a better way to accomplish those two objectives. It's brilliant, actually, using a combination of cyber attacks and EMPs."

"Maybe all these years of cyber attacks were just tests to get everything set up. You know, to study our weaknesses," Daisy said, looking at Bunker. "Then plant those sleeper programs you mentioned to wake up and take out our networks."

"Christ, we're sitting ducks," the man in the back said, his tone depressed and angry.

Bunker shook his head. "I doubt small cities like this will be of much interest. If they're planning a ground action, they'll most likely start with the major cities first."

"Good luck with that in Texas and Arizona. Everyone's got guns down there," a woman's voice from the back said. "And plenty of ammo. You should see the stockpile my cousin Rocket and his neighbors, Dennis and Kathy, have in Northern Arizona. They could start World War III. All three former Marines, if I remember right."

The Dogs of War, Bunker thought to himself, studying the looks on everyone's faces. Panic was imminent. "That's exactly why I think they'll stay out of the rural areas and focus on the larger cities. It's easier to occupy and control a population when it's densely packed together."

"He's right," the man in the back shouted.

Bunker continued. "That way, you know where everyone is and can deploy your limited resources more effectively. In the rural areas, your enemy is spread out and hiding in the mountains and the deserts. That's one of the reasons Russia had such a hard time when they invaded Afghanistan back in late '79."

"Not to mention the fanatical religious aspect," Apollo added.

"But why Pensacola and Virginia Beach? Or Huntsville, Alabama, for Christ's sake? Those aren't exactly big cities," the same man in the back asked.

"Yeah, if Bunker's right, who in their right mind would invade small towns like that?" Daisy asked, looking up at the Mayor.

"Maybe I was wrong," Buckley said, sounding disappointed in himself. "If those coordinates weren't for destinations, then they were just detonation points. To get this whole thing started."

Daisy shook her head. "But still, why target those specific towns? Why not New York, Phoenix, or LA? Not Pensacola and the others. EMPs would do a lot more damage."

An idea broke loose in Bunker's thoughts. "Military bases. Those cities all have strategic value. Think about it: NORAD in Colorado Springs, the Naval Air Station in Pensacola, and the list goes on. Daisy's right. They wanted to blind us so we couldn't react. What better way to do that than to target our most important installations first?"

"To get this whole thing started," the Mayor said again, sounding as though he was pandering for approval.

Daisy nodded. "Take out the bases first, then move to the big cities."

A frantic woman's voice from the back spoke next. "Come on, guys, we can't just sit here and do nothing. The invasion could be happening right now. The borders along Mexico and Canada aren't exactly secure. Wouldn't take much to march across right now, while we're all trying to figure out what's going on."

"Yeah, we have to get prepared! Immediately!" the man in the back snapped.

"Easy now, folks," the Mayor said, glancing around the room. "Let's not get ahead of ourselves. This is all just conjecture. All we have so far is part of a cryptic message."

"Come on, Mayor. You heard the evidence. We're fucked!" the man snarled. "We gotta do something, right now!"

The Sheriff held out his arms and faced the citizens as well. "The Mayor's right. Everyone stay calm. We really don't know anything at this point."

Bunker stood up to face the group, taking position next to the Sheriff. "I'd suggest we send out small reconnaissance teams to gather intel. One team in each direction. Let's see what's going on out there and what we might be up against."

"Excellent idea, Mr. Bunker," the Mayor said, patting him on the back.

"We're gonna need more horses then," Daisy added. "I'm pretty sure Franklin is still at the clinic with his daughter. When we're done here, I'll go have a talk with him. Need to see how Megan's doing, too."

"I have some old dirt bikes you can use," the man in the back said. "I'm sure they still work. No electronics in them bad boys."

"No, we stick to horses and bicycles for now. Motorcycles will only put a drain on the town's fuel supply and we can't afford that. Not when we don't know if we'll ever see another tanker truck. No, we need to start conserving everything. And I mean everything," the Mayor said with conviction.

Bunker didn't agree entirely. "With all due respect, Mr. Mayor, it wouldn't hurt to make sure those rides are still in working order, just in case we need them down the road."

"Good point," Buckley answered after a short pause. "Until our teams report back, we should make contingency plans for everything."

The Sheriff flipped the atlas pages showing the state of Colorado. "If we *are* being invaded, then they'll have a lot of troops and equipment to move. I'm guessing they'll want to stick to the interstates."

Bunker was surprised the Sheriff came up with the idea so quickly. "Yes, interstates would offer the most efficient travel and the best sightlines. Whoever we're up against won't want to get bogged down on back roads or in mountain passes. Too much chance of an ambush."

Apollo's index finger traveled up the paper and found Clearwater, tracing across the roads as he spoke. "We should send the North Team up Interstate 25, toward Denver."

"What about possible radiation?" Daisy asked.

"If Mr. Bunker is correct, there won't be any."

"That's a pretty big if," she said, locking eyes with Bunker. "No offense."

"None taken," Bunker answered before Apollo spoke next.

"It's a risk our teams are gonna have to take. We only have one Geiger counter, and the town needs it."

"Agreed," the Mayor said. "This is strictly a volunteer mission. We make sure everyone knows the risks and what's at stake before we let them accept any assignment. What about the other directions?"

Apollo changed the location of his finger on the map. "The West Team should take highway 50 up to I-70. South Team will take I-25 to Santa Fe and if needed, head down to Albuquerque. East Team should take 50 east to 385 and then up to I-70. That'll give us eyes on all the major roadways in the area. If there's an invasion rolling in, we'll know about it soon enough."

"How are the teams going to report back? The radios aren't working," Daisy asked.

"Other than smoke signals, I'm open to suggestions," Apollo answered.

Daisy let out a short laugh before her face turned serious again. "Earlier, when I was out at Frank Tuttle's place to borrow the Geiger, I noticed he had Faraday cages around all kinds of stuff—even his pigeon house and chicken coop. Though I'm not sure why."

"Because he's nuts," the woman in the back snapped. "You can't trust anything that man says. He's insane."

"You were saying?" the Mayor asked Daisy after rolling his eyes.

The deputy let out a thin smile. "His pole barn was crammed full of all kinds of supplies and gear, so I gotta believe he has some communications gear hidden away somewhere. If he does, then it's probably stored inside one of the cages—"

"—and still working," Apollo said, completing her sentence.

"Then you need to go back out there," the Mayor said. "ASAP."

"I figured as much," she answered. "But he's not going to let it go for nothing."

"What do you mean?" the Mayor asked.

"I had to pay him three bucks for the Geiger."

"He wants money?"

"Yeah. Otherwise, he's not going to part with any of it. He's been stockpiling for years and thinks the end of the world is coming. That's why he got off the grid in the first place."

"But this is a town emergency. Didn't you explain it to him?"

"Yes, I did, sir. But he doesn't care about us. Only himself. Besides, legally, we can't just make him give up his possessions, right?"

"The hell we can't," the Mayor snapped, before shooting a sharp look at the Sheriff.

Apollo shook his head. "Legally, I don't think so. He's done nothing wrong, sir. Word has it he's dug in deep and well-armed. I don't think showing up in force and making demands will go over well."

Daisy nodded. "He's wound pretty tight after living out there all alone. Without Helen around to keep him balanced, I'm afraid he's a ticking time bomb. Speaking of which, he might even have the place wired with explosives. Wouldn't put it past him."

"She's right," Apollo said. "It's best if we keep the channels open with diplomacy."

"You mean pay him. With money we can't afford," the Mayor said.

"And put up with his idiosyncrasies," Apollo added.

Mayor Buckley threw up his hands and huffed, then paced the room a few times before speaking again. "Fine. We buy what we need from the man. I'll authorize a cash withdrawal from the town treasury. But let me be perfectly clear about one thing. If he resists, then we take what we need. We're not going to play games with this man."

"I think that'll work," Apollo said.

The Mayor put a hand on Bunker's back. "Since you seem to have the most tactical training around here, I'd like you to head out to Tuttle's place with Daisy."

"As backup?" she asked the Mayor.

"For a full assessment. Grab whatever you think we can use. Just don't overpay."

"You got it, sir," she said.

"Can the town count on your help, Mr. Bunker?" the Mayor asked.

"Sure, whatever you need," Bunker said, wondering if he should use the chance to disappear. He'd have his own horse and it wouldn't take much to give the deputy the slip.

Daisy's eyes lit up. "I only saw a small portion of his inventory, but it looked like he has a little bit of everything. There's no telling what we'll find once we start digging around."

Bunker appreciated the Mayor's trust in him, but he didn't want to head out with Daisy until after he got something important off his chest. He wasn't sure how'd they react, but he needed to come clean about it.

He caught Apollo's attention with his eyes, then whispered, "Before I go, Sheriff, can I speak to you and the Mayor somewhere in private? There's one more thing we need to discuss."

CHAPTER 24

Bunker waited until Buckley and Apollo were inside the Sheriff's private office before he shut the door. The rest of the group was still outside in the work area, huddled around the hand-crank radio, chatting away.

"Okay, what is it?" the Mayor asked. "We're a little pressed for time here, Mr. Bunker."

"Well, sir, there's something I think the two of you should know. But before I tell you what it is, let me say that I'm pretty sure you're not going to like what I have to say. In fact, it'll probably change your view of me completely. So I ask that you please don't judge until you hear me out."

"Come on, man. Out with it."

Bunker took a deep breath and swallowed hard. Every fiber in his being was screaming at him to keep his mouth shut, but something else was pushing him forward. He had to get the words out while he had the chance.

"After the jet barely missed us, I went to the front of the train to see what was going on. I ran into the Amtrak conductor and his engineer, who were standing out front. We started talking about the plane crash and trying to figure out what happened, when one of them said he used to work at Area 51—"

"Seriously? Area 51? That's what this is about?" the Mayor snapped, throwing his hands up in disgust.

"No wonder you didn't want to say anything in front of the others," the Sheriff said, looking frustrated. "Dreamland?"

"Yeah, I know it's a little out there, but I still think you need to hear what these men had to say. I didn't want to bring this up with the civilians around, because I know they'd start to question their leadership if they heard the words Area 51. And that wouldn't do anyone any good. May I continue, sir?"

"Fine. You got two minutes. Make it quick," Buckley said. "But so help me God, if this has anything to do with Little Green Men—"

"No sir, it doesn't. It has to do with the secret airline that Area 51 uses for staff and equipment. It's called Janet Airlines. Have you heard of it?"

Apollo nodded. "Yeah, everyone around here knows about it. Groom Lake is due west from here. They fly into Colorado Springs all the time."

"To meet with the brass at NORAD," Bunker said, wanting to show he was on the same page as the two leaders of Clearwater.

"That's the rumor. But what does Janet Airlines have to do what's happening outside?" the Sheriff asked, pointing at the office door.

"The commercial plane that crashed was all white and had no markings on it."

"All white?"

"Yes, even the windows were painted white. Apparently it was from Area 51."

Buckley looked stunned. So did Apollo. Neither of them said anything.

"The Amtrak engineer wondered if the EMP was targeting the Area 51 flight specifically, possibly to stop top secret technology from being delivered to NORAD. Now, I know what you're thinking. I thought the same thing at first. But after the Morse code message and the coordinates we've just decoded, I'm not so sure. Maybe the engineer wasn't some conspiracy theory nut after all. Maybe he was on to something."

Buckley nodded, but still didn't answer.

Bunker looked at Apollo, wanting to gauge the Sheriff's interest as he laid out the rest of his argument. "At this point, you have to ask yourself, what are the odds of a top secret flight being overhead and on its way to NORAD at the exact same time an EMP hits? And then there's the apparent cyber attack that blinded our defense systems so our military couldn't track the inbound missile and stop it. Assuming, of course, that's what delivered the EMP."

"I see your point," the Sheriff said. "It does all seem a little suspicious."

The Mayor paced to the far wall and back, running his hands through his hair several times. "So let me extrapolate a bit here . . . what you're suggesting is that top secret technology was being delivered to various bases around the country when the EMP strike was launched. Apparently, to stop the Area 51 deliveries before they could be deployed."

"Yes sir. It does seem to support the facts we know so far," Bunker answered.

"To what end?"

"I have no idea, Mr. Mayor. But if the engineer was right, whatever tech was being delivered to NORAD was important enough for a foreign adversary to stop. And, by doing so, expose their new technology."

The room was quiet for a full minute before the Mayor spoke to Bunker. "What's your gut tell you about the engineer's claim that he used to work at Area 51?"

"Seemed credible. He knew a lot of details about the base and the type of aircraft they usually fly. In fact, he mentioned that the downed plane was a much newer model. Apparently, Groom Lake upgraded its fleet recently."

Buckley sighed. "Then we could be caught in the middle of something much bigger than any of us realizes."

"Which is why I wanted to speak to you in private. I know this is all just a guess, but we can't ignore everything we've learned so far. But it sure seems connected somehow. Almost like Clearwater is near ground zero."

"If so, then this is not simply a prelude to an invasion by Russia or China," Apollo said. "This is part of some master plan."

"Okay then, let's assume some of these theories are correct," the Mayor said, raising his eyebrows. "What does it mean for us? Does it change what we have to do to defend ourselves and ride this out?"

Bunker shook his head, taking a moment to choose his words carefully. "No sir. It doesn't. At least not yet. But the two of you need to factor in the possibility of Area 51's involvement. It may change what you have to do, depending on what you learn after the reconnaissance teams are sent out."

"Agreed," Buckley said, looking focused and determined. "One thing we know for sure, whoever is behind this has the burning desire to see our country fall."

CHAPTER 25

"I'll catch up to you in a minute," Bunker told Deputy Daisy, turning and walking across the town square to talk with Stephanie King.

"What's going on with the radio signal? Is everything okay?" Stephanie asked when he arrived.

"That's what I want to talk to you about. Something's come up."

Jeffrey stood silently next to her, his tiny hands wrapped around the top of Bunker's duffle bag. The kid was smiling and nodding with pride, making Bunker think Stephanie had put him in charge of the oversized pack.

Stephanie leaned to the left and looked past Bunker, her eyes thinning into a long stare. "Let me guess: it's got something to do with her, doesn't it?"

Bunker turned and followed Stephanie's gaze, finding it trained on Daisy, who was looking back at him.

Daisy's head dropped immediately. She began fidgeting with something along the far side of the duty belt wrapped around her waist.

Stephanie scoffed. "I get that some men are attracted to the whole chick in a uniform thing, but I just don't understand what my ex-husband ever saw in her. I mean, seriously. Look at her. She obviously eats a lot of carbs."

Bunker didn't agree. Daisy was in excellent shape, though not as ultra-thin and voluptuous as Stephanie. The two women were polar opposites in every respect, but he didn't want to get in the middle of their apparent history.

He decided to redirect the focus of the conversation. "The Mayor asked me to help retrieve some items from a homestead outside town," Bunker said before locking eyes with Jeffrey. "So it looks like you'll need to watch my pack a little while longer. Can you do that for me, sport?"

"Uh-huh. It's really not that heavy," Jeffrey said, pulling the straps up and over his shoulder. The kid grunted as he lifted it off the grass. "See, I can carry it."

Stephanie worked the wraps free from her son and put the bag on the ground with a thud. The fire in her eyes was apparent when she looked up at Bunker. "Asked you to help? Why? He barely knows you. Why can't someone else do it? Why does it have to be you?"

Bunker shrugged. "Apparently he trusts me, thanks in part to you putting in a good word for me."

"I doubt my recommendation had anything to do with it. It's more like he trusts you because you brought the kids back safe and sound. Like the Pied Piper, except without the flute."

When Bunker's mind conjured up a vision of the legendary character wearing his long robe and floppy hat, he couldn't hold back a short chuckle. "He wants me to evaluate some of the items we need. Tactically speaking."

"I'm guessing you didn't tell him about your past."

"You know I'd never do that. I just helped them decode the transmission and then we tossed around some ideas."

"What did it say, exactly? The transmission, I mean."

He hesitated, wondering if he should release the information. The Mayor didn't deem the Morse code signal or their discussions classified, so he figured it was safe to tell her. Some of it, at least. Not all. He was pressed for time and Stephanie was already on edge, so he decided to keep some of the aspects a secret. He didn't need her causing a scene.

"It contained a series of GPS coordinates that correspond to cities across the US. It's possible Clearwater wasn't the only town affected by what happened today."

She stood there, silent, with her eyes blinking.

He'd expected her to connect the dots about what the GPS coordinates meant, so when she didn't react, he decided to continue. "The Mayor's planning to send out teams to see what's going on out there and report back. We need more information."

"Are you part of those teams?"

"I haven't decided. Right now, I'm gonna go do a little recon and see if I can score some items to help the Sheriff and his staff."

Stephanie leaned to the side again, sending a nasty look across the square. "You and Daisy? Together? That's why she's waiting for you, right?"

"Yes. The Sheriff doesn't want her to go alone."

"I thought you said the Mayor was sending you out there, not the Sheriff."

"He is. Both of them are. Like I said, we tossed around some ideas after I decoded the radio signal. I'm to go with her and see if we can locate some communication gear that works. If we're successful, it'll help the scout teams report back on what they learn out there. Communications are going to be key moving forward."

She bit her lower lip and nodded slowly. "Whose place are you going to?"

"A guy by the name of Frank Tuttle."

"That nut job? What could he possibly have?"

"Apparently, he's been stocking up for the end of the world. Daisy went out there earlier and got a look at some of his inventory. We think there's a lot more we can use."

Stephanie pointed at the front door to the clinic. "What about Megan? She should be getting released soon. Don't you want to see how she's doing?"

"Yeah, of course I do. But I need to go do this. It's in everyone's best interest, including you and Jeffrey."

"Sounds like you've already made up your mind."

"Look, I'll be back as soon as I can. I'll come find you and Jeffrey. Just let the Sheriff's office know where you are."

She folded her arms and stood with more weight on one leg than the other. He couldn't tell if she was pissed or finally coming around to his way of thinking. Either way, he needed to get moving.

He put his hand on Jeffrey's head. "When I return, I wanna hear all about how you did with those cute little redheads."

Jeffrey's face turned a deep shade of red, then he grinned. "Okay. But hurry back."

CHAPTER 26

Stephanie King bent down and gave her son a tight hug as they watched their new friend and local hero, Jack Francis Bunker, head off with the meddling female deputy—the same brunette who always seemed to be around when something went wrong in her life.

Everyone has an albatross in their life, yanking them back a few steps just when they think they're making progress. Some call it bad luck or a dark moon rising. Others call it their inner demon.

But Stephanie's cross to bear was an unstoppable force who went by the name of Daisy Clark—a natural beauty whose life seemed to run on autopilot.

People like Daisy seemed to breeze through life with a perpetual smile on their lips, as fortune always found them around the next corner. Others struggled just to make it through another day, trying not to grab a machine gun and take out their frustrations on the rest of the planet.

Stephanie knew the casting of those two roles all too well, always feeling like the understudy.

Even so, the sweet young boy who was wrapped in her arms made the torment of life worth it. When he giggled like little boys do, it melted her heart and she knew she was exactly where she was meant to be.

Her son was the one advantage she had over her nemesis, even if Jeffrey was tethered to a 6' 4" pile of curly blond baggage who went by the name of William H. King. Her ex. The town man-whore. Another one of those people who found success and happiness with everything he touched—just not with her, apparently.

"Don't worry, sweetheart. Mr. Bunker said he's coming back," she told Jeffrey as her mind played out a dozen scenarios of how the next few weeks would unfold.

Her precious little boy's silence was deafening and ripping at the petals of her heart. She knew exactly what Jeffrey was thinking and feeling about Bunker at the moment, because she was thinking and feeling it, too.

Their stressful day together had been filled with a series of heart-pounding moments, each strengthening an invisible bond between the three of them. She couldn't explain how it got there or why it existed, but it was there nonetheless.

She'd read somewhere that tragedy can bring people together and do so in ways nobody could've predicted. She never believed in that kind of fantasy before, but today's events were proof that it did happen. Even though she knew nothing about the troubled, mysterious man, his soul had touched hers. And her son's.

Her friends from high school would have called her naive or totally nuts for trusting some guy she just met on a train. But somehow she knew that she could, even without a shred of proof. Sure, it was strange, twisted logic but sometimes you can truly know a person before you really know anything about them.

Today's events had taught her a new, important lesson: how people handle themselves in an emergency reveals who they really are, even without knowing any of the facts from their past.

Her mother had always told her that your past makes you who you are. Up until today, she always accepted that adage. But now, she didn't think that old saying was entirely correct. She had a new way of looking at it.

Your past herds you along its own path, pushing you toward the person you truly want to be, whether you're ready for it or not.

The draw to Bunker was there and she couldn't deny it, even though she wasn't looking for any of it. Just yesterday, she swore to give up men entirely and vowed to never get involved again.

The pain she'd endured was just too much to ever trust another man. Her heart had been broken into a million pieces and she didn't think she'd ever feel normal again. Or feel anything other than hatred for those who peed standing up. But then Bunker came along.

Some of her girlfriends gauged the value of their lives by the men they were with, like it was some kind of contest. Some even judged their success as women by the mere fact that they had a man in their bed—any man—vowing to never be alone at any cost.

She never understood their unwavering need to be in a relationship. It was almost as if being alone was some kind of social taboo. Or the kiss of death as a woman in this world.

Stephanie never wanted to be that shallow or transparent, but it was hard not to cave to peer pressure. She'd heard the whispers echoing around town about her tantrums and her series of relationship failures, ever since grade school.

And now, after the most painful and disruptive period in her life, she'd met this mysterious soul, Jack Bunker—a man who was destined to generate an endless storm of whispers. Whispers that would follow her everywhere she went.

Her heart skipped a few beats, knowing fate had stepped in and dealt her another wickedly sinful hand of cards.

"Who's that guy with Daisy?" a familiar male voice said behind her.

Jeffrey spun around in her arms. "Daddy!" he said, prying himself loose from her grip. The boy leapt into his father's arms, wrapping his hands around the man's slender neck.

"How's my little chief doing? Did you miss me?" William King said into Jeffrey's ear, shooting Stephanie a judgmental, penetrating look. "I heard something happened today on the train. Are you okay, son?"

"Yeah, Daddy. It was really scary. First, the train stopped moving, then this really big airplane almost crashed into us. But our new friend, Jack, got us out of there. Then we found this huge bus in the forest with all these kids. They were hanging off a cliff but Mommy and Mr. Bunker got them all out. And I helped."

"Sounds like you're a little hero today. Your father is very proud of you," William told his son, standing the boy on the ground. He looked at Jeffrey's shirt and pointed at the fresh stain. "What's this?"

"Ice cream. It was really good. They were giving it away before it melted."

William smiled, though it looked forced.

Stephanie knew that look. Her ex was deep in thought and about to impose his will, again.

William took out his wallet and handed Jeffrey a five-dollar bill. "Here, son. Go get yourself another treat while Mommy and I have a little talk."

"No, he's had more than enough sweets for today," Stephanie snapped.

William ignored her response, turning Jeffrey by the shoulders and aiming him toward the ice cream parlor. "It's okay, son. Heroes deserve two treats when they help save lives like you did today."

"But Daaaad, they're free today. We don't have to pay."

"I know, Jeffrey, but remember what I've taught you. A real man always pays his own way in this world. He never takes charity from anyone. Charity is for lazy people who don't want to work for what they have. And the men in the King family are never lazy. So take this money and go pay your way. Enjoy your ice cream while I speak to your mom in private."

Jeffrey nodded, then took the greenback in his hand. He took off running for another round of ice cream.

"Why do you always do that?" she asked in a firm tone.

"Do what? Buy my only son some ice cream?"

"No, always go against my wishes and spoil him like that. I know what you're trying to do, but it won't work. The judge gave me primary custody, despite all your lawyer's dirty tactics. Little boys belong with their mothers, and the judge agreed with me."

"So who was that man with Daisy? Was it this Jack Bunker asshole I've been hearing about?"

"Yes, and he's no asshole. In fact, he's the bravest man I've ever met. He risked his life for a bunch of complete strangers. Something I know you'd never do because there's no profit in it."

He hesitated, looking like he was holding back a torrent of rage. "Word has it you two hooked up on the train. It's been what, seventy-two hours since the ink dried on our divorce decree? And you're already spreading your legs?"

"It wasn't like that at all. I'm not like you. I don't just hook up with anyone. That's your deal, remember?"

"I'm betting if my lawyer went back to the judge and explained how you were running away without permission and shacking up with some complete stranger on a train, and doing so in front of my son, there'd be some quick changes to the custody terms. I'm pretty sure they call that child endangerment. Shame on you, Steph."

"You can't do that! That's a complete lie!"

"Watch me," he said, looking away for a moment, then bringing his hateful eyes back to her. "When you decided to file for divorce, I told you to watch your step and never cross me. I own this town, just like my father before me."

"It never ends with you, thinking you're all that. Just because your family owns the silver mine doesn't mean you control the courts."

"I don't need to. Not when you're tramping around like some bitch in heat. All I need to do is put doubt in the judge's mind and I guarantee you, he'll see things my way. Slutting around on that train just gave me all the ammo I need."

She raised her hand to slap him, but someone grabbed it from behind and held it.

"Easy now, Stephanie," a man's steady voice said.

She turned and saw Franklin Atwater's fingers wrapped around her wrist. His daughter, Megan, was with him and walking with crutches, her knee in a shiny metal brace.

"What's going on here?" the tall black man asked, looking extra handsome in his fitted cowboy shirt.

"Mind your own business, Atwater. This doesn't concern you," William said, flaring his eyes and pushing out his chin.

"I think today, I'll make it my business," Franklin said, letting go of Stephanie's hand and turning his attention to her. "Are you okay?"

"Yeah, well, sort of," she said, pointing a nervous hand at her ex-husband. "I just can't stand to look at him anymore. Every word out of his mouth is a lie. It never stops. I'm tired of everyone taking his side all the time."

Atwater looked down at his daughter. "Megan, sweetheart, why don't you go talk to Jeffrey for a minute? Looks like he might need some help with his ice cream."

"Yes, Daddy," she answered, hobbling away.

Atwater waited a handful of seconds before he turned and looked at William and then at Stephanie. He held out his hands, pointing at both of them. "Maybe both of you need to take a step back. Think about what's happening here and how it looks to the little one in your life. I get that you two have some troubled history and things are a little heated right now, but it really doesn't have to be like this. Don't you think there are more important things to consider? Like Jeffrey's future? I hope you both realize that everything you say and do to each other affects your son. There will be scars from all of this. Is that really what you want?"

William's tense look hadn't changed, still burning a hole into Stephanie's face. "Ah, come on, Franklin. She's an emotional mess. Everyone knows it. She's always going ballistic over the littlest things. All I did was buy my son some ice cream and she gets all physical about it. I mean, look at Jeffrey. He's happy. That's how kids are supposed to be."

Stephanie couldn't believe the gall of her ex. "See, that's exactly what I'm talking about, Franklin. That's a complete lie. That's not why I wanted to slap him just now. He threatened to—"

Franklin interrupted her before she could finish the explanation, looking frustrated and upset. "The whys and whats don't really matter at this point."

"But wait, you don't understand," she said, trying to make him listen.

Franklin shook his head. "You two are divorced now. It's time to act like grownups and stop hurting each other. Couples always know exactly which buttons to push, but this kind of behavior has to stop. For Jeffrey's sake."

Before she could raise another appeal to the towering cowboy, a heavyset man with a deputy star hanging from his plus-sized shirt appeared out of nowhere and stood behind her former spouse.

The unidentified deputy was accompanied by another man, this one taller and as skinny as a light post. He, too, was wearing a deputy's badge on the loose-fitting shirt covering his obviously concave chest.

The words *Blimp and Wimp* burned into her thoughts when she saw the two of them together. Both men had their arms folded across their chests.

"Is there a problem here?" the fat deputy said, his voice ringing a familiar tone from her past.

"Do we need to call the Sheriff?" the skinny one said a split second later.

Stephanie took a long, hard look at the heavy guy, letting the contours of his round face, curly black hair, raging acne, and full, ragged beard soak in. She recognized him. "Albert? Is that you?"

Jay J. Falconer

"Hey Steph. Long time no see," he answered. "I wasn't sure for a minute that you'd remember me."

"Who is this clown?" William asked, stepping to the side as if he wanted to keep a safe distance from the sudden wave of law enforcement.

"I'm Albert Mortenson. The new deputy sheriff in town. I went to high school with your wife."

"Ex-wife," William said, looking smug and condescending, like the complete jerk he was. "Crazy ex-wife, to be exact."

Stephanie took a step forward, feeling an overwhelming desire to strike him dead. Whatever was controlling her heart right now was powerful and all-consuming.

Franklin grabbed her by the elbows just as Albert stepped between the former spouses. The other rail-thin deputy remained silent and still, looking as though he'd rather be somewhere else at the moment.

"See what I mean? Look at her. She wants to kill me right now," William said with a crooked grin on his face. "And for what?"

"You're such an ass," she snapped, struggling against the grip on her arms.

Atwater spun her away and ushered her toward the ice cream joint. "Let's go see how our kids are doing."

She took a series of deep, choppy breaths, trying to regain control of her temper. It wasn't easy, but the fury finally bled off.

"You can't react that way. Especially in public," Franklin said.

"I know. I know. But when Bill's around, something just takes over and I wanna scream at him until I can't scream any more. I don't know how to explain it, but it's there and I totally see red."

"Like I said before, you both know how to push each other's buttons. It's called marriage. But you can't go there. Ever. That's exactly what he wants you to do. You can't keep giving him ammo to use against you."

Tears welled in her eyes, leaking down her cheeks as she made her way to her son, who was knuckles-deep into another ice cream cone.

When they arrived, Atwater let go and stood watch behind her.

"Mom? Are you okay?" Jeffrey asked, his eyebrows pinched and cheeks red.

She wiped the tears from her cheeks and forced them to stop before dropping to one knee. Her swollen face was now level with Jeffrey's. "Yes, Mommy is okay. Just a little sad, but I'm all better now."

"Hi, Mrs. King," Megan said, blinking her almond-shaped eyes at Stephanie. The tiny, dark-skinned girl seemed to be handling the crutches, but the medical brace looked heavy and awkward.

"How's your knee feeling, sweetheart?" Stephanie asked, feeling guilty for not asking earlier. She'd been so wrapped up in her own drama that she'd forgotten to say hi to the child she'd helped rescue from the bus.

"It's really sore, but Doctor Marino said it's just a sprain. I'll be good as new in no time. I just have to use these crutches for a while. It sucks because I can't ride Star for like four weeks."

"I know, baby. Being hurt is no fun, especially for little girls who were really brave on that bus today. But I'm sure your daddy will take really good care of you," she said, cradling Megan's cheeks in her hands.

Stephanie let go after a brief linger, then turned and looked up at Franklin, who was showing a gentle smile. He gave her a simple head nod and touched the soft area near the top of her back. His enormous hand sent a warm, comforting wave of tingles down her spine and into her bones. It felt amazing. Just what she needed.

Right then, Stephanie knew that all men were not like her ex. She had to find a way to let her hatred fade because it was consuming all that she was, turning her into a version of herself that she hated. She needed to focus on surrounding herself with tender, good-hearted men like Franklin.

And maybe even Bunker—a man she barely knew. But clearly a man who was willing to help others at great risk to himself. A man who wasn't consumed with money and power and living life only for himself. A man she might be able to feel safe with. Especially when the penetrating darkness came for her, creeping into her soul during the endless, quiet moments waiting for her in the future.

It wasn't going to be easy, not with her hold on sanity tenuous at best. But she needed to be strong and find a way through this. For herself and for Jeffrey.

After her son finished the last of the cone, she wiped off a splotch of ice cream from his lips, then cleaned up a drip down his chin.

Jeffrey smiled at her.

She wrapped him in her arms and whispered in his ear. "Mommy loves you. I hope you know that."

"I'm sorry I made you sad, Mommy."

"No sweetheart. You didn't make me sad," she said, struggling to keep from blaming the boy's father. She needed to rise above the pettiness and change her outlook, like Franklin wanted her to do.

"Sometimes, Mommy just gets sad and needs a minute to herself. It's never you, honey. You always make Mommy happy. Always. You're my little angel. Never forget that. That's why I love you soooo much."

She let go of Jeffrey and leaned back. Her son nodded, looking adorable. She smiled and brushed a swatch of hair away from his forehead, then stood and turned to Franklin.

Stephanie was about to ask the dark-skinned cowboy for a huge favor, but he beat her to it.

"I think you and Jeffrey should stay with us for a bit. Some time away from this town—and you-know-who—will do you good."

She wrapped her arms around his neck. "Thank you."

CHAPTER 27

Albert wasn't sure how much longer he could take the stale odor of Bill King's breath. Or the man's attitude as the owner of the silver mine continued his tirade.

"I don't care if you went to school with my ex-wife or not, I'd suggest you mind your own business if you know what's good for you," King said.

Albert raised his chin, then sucked in a full breath before tapping his finger on the star hanging from his chest. "Don't forget who you're talking to. I'm not as helpless as your ex-wife."

"Ah, that badge don't mean shit," King said, looking at the other deputy, Dustin Brown. "You got anything to say, slim?"

Dustin shook his head. "Nope. Just what Albert said."

"I figured as much. Just a couple of wannabe rent-a-cops," King snapped before walking away.

Albert flipped him the bird, then looked at Dustin.

"That was intense," Dustin said.

Albert smiled, deciding it was time to push his agenda and start recruiting. "You know, buddy, I think I'm starting to like this gig. Things are finally getting a little . . . interesting."

"That's one word for it," Dustin scoffed, pushing his lips together and to the right. "Any more intense and one of us would be bleeding. Or in the hospital."

"Ah, no worries. I had it covered."

"So, you went to school with his ex-wife?"

"Yeah, she sat in front of me in homeroom. And if I remember right, I'm pretty sure she was in my chemistry class, too. Sat in the back, I think. Though I'm not sure she actually passed the course. At least not with her grades. Rumor had it she was giving out blowjobs for grades." Albert pointed at the back of King, who was now twenty feet away. "That's how the two of them met."

"She gave him a hummer in the back of the class?"

Albert laughed. "No, dude. They met in high school. She was supposedly blowing the chem teacher, Mr. Carson. A real ass-hat of a man."

"Oh yeah. Right. The teacher. Lucky man. Those lips of hers are righteous."

Albert knew he had his hook into Dustin and just needed to set it before reeling him in. "Asshole King over there had a wickedly nice Corvette at the time. And she had the best rack in school. All the guys used to drool over her."

Dustin nodded, licking his lips awkwardly. "I see why. She's fine. We're talking USDA Prime Choice. I could totally tap that."

"Yeah, right. Keep dreaming. She's not interested in guys like us. I doubt she even remembers ninety percent of the guys in school. Her eyes were only on King and his killer ride."

"She remembered you, though. That's gotta count for something."

Albert wished she did for the right reasons. "I doubt she remembers much. Just some fat guy sitting behind her and sweating all over his desk. Until now, I didn't think she even knew I existed."

"Well, she did. Maybe now that she's divorced—"

"Don't kid yourself. That's never gonna happen. She likes the guys with all the toys. You know, endless bling. Something shiny and new to play with and make herself feel important."

"Really? That shallow?"

"Oh yeah. Just like the rest of the *beautiful people*. And then you know what happens? The same chicks sit around and bitch and moan after their looks go and their men get bored with them. And they wonder why they all end up divorced and got nothing."

"I don't think that's what split them up. She's still smoking hot."

"Sure, for now. But it won't last. It never does. Once women hit their late thirties, they dry up like old hags. My guess is that King stuck his wick somewhere he shouldn't have. Not that I blame him. If had his money, I'd never settle for one chick, either," he said, hesitating as a flood of memories filled his thoughts. "But man, even the freshman chicks loved his ride. That black Z06 Corvette was like a two-door magnet, all 700 horses drawing them in. That thing could lay down some serious rubber."

Dustin nodded. "The Vette gets 'em wet."

"Not anymore," Albert said with attitude, letting a smile grow on his lips. He pointed across the square at one of the abandoned cars parked in the street. It was a gray, four-door sedan with its hood sitting open on its hinges. The driver's door was open. "What we have now is a level playing field. And that, my friend, presents us with a unique opportunity."

"With the hot bod?"

"No. I'm talking about business, not snatch. Right now everyone is scrambling around like idiots. A couple of smart men like us should take advantage and get set up now, so we're ready when the shit really hits the fan."

Dustin was looking directly at him, nodding. But his mouth was silent.

Albert continued, thinking of his days in New York and LA. "I've seen it all before. Misery is a great motivator . . . Let me ask you this: how would you like to make some serious fat stacks?"

"Money?"

"Lots of it. More cash than you could ever imagine. Enough money so you can buy ten hot bods and ten Vettes if you want."

Dustin's face lit up, his eyes as big as pears. "What do I need to do?"

"Follow me," Albert said, turning south. "Time to go old school, literally."

CHAPTER 28

Sheriff Apollo turned the knob and opened the door to the Mayor's office. He walked in, ready to answer the summons from his boss like a dutiful servant.

The flickering light from the lamp on the Mayor's desk caught his attention first, reminding him to go check on the town hall's ancient gas-powered generator. Its distinctive engine whine was uneven and slow, dimming the emergency lights with every change in pitch. It was a melodic reminder of how tenuous the situation was for everyone.

Most of the generators in town were newer models with an electric start feature and other integrated electronics, all rendered useless after the event earlier that day. An EMP strike was the official consensus of those in the know, though the group's conclusion was based on circumstantial assumptions and little in the way of hard facts.

Apollo expected to find the Mayor sitting behind his desk, but he wasn't. Buckley was to the left, standing in front of the picture window that overlooked the town square. His back was to Apollo, showing only the rear of his tailored suit. Based on the position of the man's arms and elbows, Apollo assumed the sixty-year-old's hands were tucked inside the front pockets of his dress slacks.

The glistening light from the candles, flashlights, and lanterns outside made the man's silhouette dance across the ceiling in random patterns, occasionally melding together into one extended blob. Apollo felt like he'd walked into a medieval castle, praying for a chance to impress the king before his sentence was delivered.

He cleared his throat. "Excuse me, Mr. Mayor. You sent for me?"

Buckley never turned before answering, still looking away. "Gus, do you think any of them have put the pieces together yet?"

"About the EMPs?"

"Yes, and the possible invasion," he added, his voice deep and grizzly.

"I'm sure some of them have. If not, it won't be long. Not with the handful of civilians in my office earlier when we were decoding the Morse code signal. We both know gossip flies around this town like greased lightning."

"That's what I'm concerned about. In retrospect, we never should've allowed any unauthorized personnel to remain in your office. That mistake is on me. I should have taken charge and cleared the room first."

Apollo didn't want Buckley to assume all the blame. "Well, sir, I was there, too. Trust me, we were all a little caught up in the moment. Neither of us was thinking about a potential information leak."

"That may be true. But it's not how the man in charge should act, regardless of the circumstances. Especially a man who hopes to become Governor of this great state someday. Now there's no way to contain any of this."

"I understand, Mr. Mayor. But it's their town, too. They pay our salaries and all of them have a right to know what's going on."

"Yes, of course. But how are we supposed to protect them if they know the whole truth, and not the version of the truth that will help keep them calm and cooperative when the time comes?"

"I'm afraid I don't understand, sir."

"It's like Bunker said. The masses will panic when tragedy strikes."

"I'm pretty sure he was talking about his hometown. Big cities like LA have millions of desperate, down on their luck people. Nothing like the good folks of Clearwater. I think our neighbors and friends might just surprise you, sir. Even if the worst does happen."

Buckley turned and made eye contact. "I hope you're right, Gus. But from now on, it's best if we hold our meetings in private. We can't let ourselves get caught up in the moment and forget to do our jobs."

Apollo nodded, but didn't answer.

Buckley continued. "It's critical that we control the flow of information in order to protect everyone—from themselves. Too much information is never a good thing, especially when we're talking about everyday people. Even the truth can get twisted around and over-hyped, leading to a situation that neither of us wants. The less specific we are with the facts, the better, I think."

"Sounds prudent, sir. I'd suggest we meet here or in my private office from now on, with only authorized staff and invited guests. It's the only way we can make sure everything is on a strict need-to-know basis. Going forward, that is."

"Exactly what I was thinking, my old friend."

"When Bunker returns, will we be inviting him to our meetings?"

"Yes, for now. He's proven himself capable."

"I tend to agree, but we know so little about him."

"True. But if my gut is right, his military background and tactical skills are something we're gonna need. We should keep him in the loop until he gives us a reason not to. We owe him that, at least."

"I'm sure he'll appreciate that."

"Have you identified any candidates for the reconnaissance teams yet?"

"I'm working on it. However, most of the able-bodied men I've talked to are too busy looking after their own to help. I can probably draft a few volunteers from the new teams we've deputized, but other than that, we'll have to focus our efforts on the younger men. Like your grandson, Rusty. Those without a wife or kids," Apollo said, purposely avoiding the word *expendable*.

The Mayor nodded, but didn't say anything.

Apollo still had his concerns. "However, now that we have our new need-to-know mandate in place, it's going to be difficult to ask for volunteers without telling them some of what's going on. Otherwise, it's going to raise suspicions and that'll just lead to more rumors flying around town."

"I see your point," the Mayor answered, hesitating for a few moments. "I trust you'll use your best judgment."

"I will, sir."

"Let's get those teams out there the minute Daisy and Bunker get back from Tuttle's place. I don't like the idea of being completely shut off and working in the dark. Literally."

Just then, something caught the Mayor's attention outside. He turned and moved to the window, pressing his face to the glass. He looked sharply to the right. "What the hell?"

"What is it, Mayor?"

"There's a group of men walking into town from the north. Very slowly and erratically, like a bunch of mental patients on drugs."

Apollo ran the window, leaning against it with his hands. The Mayor pointed, leading the Sheriff's eyes across the town square and past the ice cream parlor. He counted the new arrivals— six men—walking with an uneven stride, just as Buckley had claimed.

A second later, two of the men on the right passed a group of residents holding candles, showering their faces with light. "That's Rico and Zeke. From my reserve squad!"

"Thank God they're back! What about the others? Are they from your unit as well?"

"Probably, but I can't see them from here," Apollo answered, noticing their clothes were dirty and tattered, like they'd fallen down a mineshaft.

"I wonder what happened to them. They look like the walking dead."

"I gotta get down there," Apollo said, whirling around and tearing across the office floor.

CHAPTER 29

Apollo's feet took him out of the Mayor's office and past the empty receptionist's desk. He flew past the disabled elevator and pushed the exit door open, taking him into the stairwell. After several flights of switchback steps, he reached the ground floor, where he tore through the central foyer of the newly-renovated town hall.

On the left was the closed gift shop, its interior and overhead sign dark. The shelves were stocked with trinkets, periodicals, and souvenirs, all protected by a wall-to-wall security screen.

Circular eating tables stood on the right, covered with plastic chairs sitting upside down. He figured the operator of the stainless steel pastry cart wasn't planning to reopen in the morning, not with the power out. It would be difficult to make coffee and warm up apple fritters without electricity. It also meant Apollo would have to fend for himself when it was time for his morning caffeine and sugar rush.

He took a sharp corner around one of the decorative pillars and cruised between a pair of potted plants standing watch on either side of the twenty-foot-long corridor that led to the main entrance.

Just before he made it to the double exit doors, a platinum blonde appeared in his path. She was stationary, with her hands on the shoulders of a stocky boy with black hair that hung down past his neck.

Apollo recognized the woman with the bandage on her forehead. It was Allison Rainey, the nice-looking waitress he'd planned to ask out. Even in the diminished light, he could see her supple skin, slightly turned-up nose, and perfect cheekbones. Her full lips were in view, too, and beyond them, a perfect set of white teeth.

The blue-eyed goddess was the complete package, leading him to wonder if she'd been a Victoria's Secret model in her younger days. Maybe it was just his aging hormones acting up, but when he was around her, he felt ten years younger, always trying to suck in his gut.

He'd managed to avoid arresting her after the broomstick fight with Grace Charmer in the grocery store, thanks to some quick thinking and a little smooth talking. If he'd been forced to toss her in jail, any hope of a first date would have blinked out the moment he closed the iron cell door behind her.

Apollo's eyes drifted down to the stocky boy standing with Allison. He assumed the kid was her son, but the young man didn't look anything like her. The boy's eyes were dark like his hair, and deep-set in his face, looking European by descent.

He didn't remember seeing this lad when the group of rescued kids walked into town with Bunker and Stephanie. Odd, to say the least, since Allison's mother, Martha, had made such a stink about her grandson being on the overdue bus.

"Sheriff Apollo . . . I was just looking for you," Allison said, holding out a hand to stop his approach.

Gus put the brakes on, skidding his dress shoes across the polished marble surface. He caught his balance only a second before his forward momentum stopped.

Whatever this was, he didn't have time for it. Yet he didn't want to be rude. He needed to act like a dutiful sheriff and greet this woman properly; otherwise, she'd never consider a relationship with him.

Apollo offered up a phony smile. "I've got a bit of an emergency outside, Allison. Can we do this a little later?"

"This won't take long, Sheriff. My son, Victor, has something he wants to say to you. And to the Mayor if he's available," she said, leaning to the left to peer around him, her eyes unsure.

"The Mayor's office is up on three. But you'll have to use the stairs since the elevator isn't working."

She nodded, then gave her son a gentle nudge from behind.

Victor stepped forward, his head hanging low. "I'm sorry, Sheriff."

"For what?" Apollo said, wondering if Allison had just caught him stealing.

"For bailing out like a chicken and leaving the kids in my class behind. I never should've done that, sir."

Apollo took a second to absorb what had just landed on his ears, connecting the facts to something he'd learned earlier about the bus accident. "So you're the one Mr. Bunker told me about?"

"Yeah, that was me. I should've stayed and helped, instead of being selfish and running off like that. I'm sorry."

Apollo looked at Allison. The stunning woman's lower lip was tucked under, her eyes locked on her son.

The Sheriff turned his attention to the boy, leaning down to get a better look at Victor's eyes. "Apology accepted, but I think you really need to say you're sorry to all your friends on the bus. Not me."

"But they aren't my friends. They're assholes," the boy answered in a flippant tone.

Allison slapped him across the back of the head, making the boy's hair flop to one side. "Hey. None of that," she said in a commanding voice.

"Oooow," he said, putting his thick hand on the impact point.

She wagged a finger at her son. "If you think that hurt, young man, just try getting smart again."

Victor answered, just not right away. "Fine. I'll apologize to my friends. Happy?"

Allison looked at Gus and shrugged, looking embarrassed. "Sorry. He never used to be this way. Not until his father passed."

Apollo wanted to know more about the boy's father and how long it had been since he'd died, but now wasn't the time. He kept quiet.

Allison pointed at the far side of the entrance before speaking to Victor. "Go wait over there, while I speak to the Sheriff for a minute."

The kid nodded, then took off in a slow, methodical walk.

Apollo could see the pain in her eyes when she brought them back to him. He wanted to comfort her with some encouragement. "It's good that you're making him take responsibility for his actions. Not a lot of parents are doing that these days."

"Now it's my turn."

"For what?"

"To apologize. What I did in the market was inexcusable. I hope you can forgive me."

Apollo wasn't sure if she was asking forgiveness for the catfight or for allegedly trying to walk out of the store without paying for the Pepsi. "No need to apologize. We're all a little wound up right now. If Grace is cool with the situation, then so am I. As far as I'm concerned, it's all water under the bridge. We can just chalk it up to one hell of a bad day."

She leaned in and hugged him, wrapping her slender arms around his neck. Her touch energized his heart. A moment later, her lips found the side of his neck, planting a soft kiss on his wrinkled skin.

He brought his arms up to give her a reciprocal hug, but stopped when he realized it wouldn't be appropriate. Not while on duty and not with her son watching.

Apollo decided the tingle across his spine would have to be his only reward. Touching her would come later, hopefully. Possibly more.

"Thank you. You're a good man," she said, letting go and walking toward her son. About halfway there, she turned and glanced back, sending Apollo a pleasant smile.

Right then he wanted to ask her out to dinner but couldn't find the strength to free the words from his tongue. His jaw was frozen. So was his courage, leaving him standing there like a slobbering idiot.

In truth, he knew this wasn't the right time or place to begin a new relationship. Not with the town out of power and near panic. The sad thing was, there might never be a good time to pop the question, assuming Bunker and the Mayor were right about a possible invasion. After all, who stops to have a date when the country is under siege by a foreign power?

His heart sank, knowing he'd blown it—again. He'd had countless chances the past couple of weeks but never sealed the deal with her, thanks to his endless foot-dragging and self-doubt. The fear of rejection was a powerful force, turning him into a mumbling pile of Play-Doh whenever she took his order or delivered food at the diner.

All those extra meals at the breakfast bar had accomplished only two things: unwanted weight gain and a perfect view of her shapely figure—both of which would stick with him until the end of time.

Apollo waited until Allison disappeared into the stairwell with her son before bolting outside to check on his late-arriving crew.

CHAPTER 30

Apollo pushed through the crowd around his men, wedging himself between two onlookers at the front. A slew of theories raced through his mind as to what had happened to his reserve unit, none of them good.

When he came face-to-face with Rico Anderson, the brown-skinned deputy he'd known for years, he found him breathing heavily and barefooted.

Apollo grabbed the young leader by the shirt collar, keeping him upright. "You okay, Rico? What the hell happened?"

"Ambush, Sheriff. Out by the landfill on Bluefield Road," the thirty-two-year-old Hispanic said, pushing the answer out with extra air between the words.

"What were you doing out there?" Apollo asked.

"Shortcut to Thompson's place. Zeke wanted to drop him off first. At least that was the plan until his F-150 died—again. You know them Fords."

"Who ambushed you?" Apollo asked, shocked that looting had started already.

Rico touched the back of his head, then rubbed it before licking his lips. He winced. "No clue. They were masked. We were about two miles from Zeke's truck when they came out of nowhere and jumped us. Next thing I know, I'm at the bottom of a wash and my head's killing me."

Apollo looked at Zeke who was standing next to Rico, blinking rapidly. "What about you?"

"Head's still a little foggy, but I'm okay. They must have thrown us down the embankment. I've got bruises everywhere," the twenty-five-year-old man said, his brown hair cropped short and his face covered in a week's growth of beard.

Rico spoke next. "Just wish them assholes had left us some water. They took everything, Sheriff. Even our shoes."

Zeke rubbed his elbow, then squeezed it a few times. "And I was so looking forward to eating that fish, too. My wife is gonna be pissed." A second later, his knees wobbled before he took an awkward side-step to catch his balance.

"At least they didn't kill you," Apollo said, turning to the people behind him. "Someone get these men some water!"

"On it, Sheriff," a woman's voice said from behind. He couldn't see her face before she turned and headed for Charmer's Market, her ankle-length orange dress flopping in the cool night air.

* * *

Stephanie helped her son Jeffrey step across the second cattle guard as they proceeded along the winding mountain road. The path had been smoothly graded and was free of stone and other debris. Someone had taken great care to manicure it, and she figured that person was her friend and proud cowboy, Franklin Atwater. The same man who owned the *Trail Dust Riding Stables,* located a hundred yards ahead, and the same man leading this expedition on foot.

The long-standing equestrian business was the first commercial stop beyond Clearwater's city limits. If she had to guess, most of the locals had been there multiple times, keeping his trail riding and supply store in the black. His prices on hay and other feed were excellent, plus hunters would line up after deer season to snatch up materials and equipment for tanning hides.

Like everything else in the area, the real money was in the tourists. They loved the place, flocking to Atwater's to buy everything from polished saddles and authentic Western clothes to homemade driftwood art and scented candles.

Usually the property was packed in the summer with adventure seekers from all over the West; however, with the recent crisis affecting the electrical grid and transportation, she figured the well-maintained spread would probably be a ghost town.

"Almost there," Franklin said to his daughter, who'd been setting the pace with her crutches. The burly man kept his hands close to Megan in case she started to fall. "If you're getting tired, let me know and I'll carry you the rest of the way."

"No, Daddy. I can do it. I have to. Otherwise, the doctor said I won't get better."

"Kids are way more resilient than we are," Stephanie said, seeing the pride in the man's face. "I would've fallen a bunch of times by now."

"You and me both," he said, giving her a wink.

"Crutches are fun, Mom. I wish I had some," Jeffrey said, catching Stephanie off guard. She didn't want to curb his enthusiasm or take the smile from his face, so she said nothing.

Megan stopped her crutches and pointed straight ahead. "Daddy, look!"

Like Franklin, Stephanie followed the girl's petite finger, seeing the front of supply store. Its door was open.

"What the hell?" Franklin said, steel in his voice.

"I take it the door's not supposed to be open?" Stephanie asked.

"No. I locked up everything before I left. I always do."

"Did someone break in, Daddy?" Megan asked.

"I don't know, but I need you to stay here until I figure out what's going on," the man said, turning to Stephanie. "Can you watch her for me?"

Stephanie nodded, just as three horses galloped across the path ahead from right to left, none with saddles or riders.

"Crap. The horses got loose," Franklin said after spinning his heels in the dirt. A second later, he broke into a full sprint, his enormous boots pounding at the trail.

Stephanie gathered up the kids and bent down to keep them close. Her mind raced with a million thoughts, but one kept bubbling to the surface. What if the burglars were still inside, possibly waiting for Franklin in some kind of ambush?

She wasn't sure if she should take the kids somewhere else. Someplace safer and out of sight. She looked to the left and then the right, seeing only tall pine trees and a smattering of underbrush.

Right then, she missed Bunker more than ever. If only he'd been there instead of on the reconnaissance mission to Tuttle's homestead with Daisy Clark, a woman who always seemed to sabotage anything positive that was happening in Stephanie's life. Whether it was intentional or an accident didn't really matter; she hated that woman.

Before she could consider her next thought, she felt a rush of wind behind her. Someone was there.

"Don't move, bitch," a male voice said, pressing something hard against the back of her head. "Or I blast a hole in your head the size of Texas."

CHAPTER 31

Dustin Brown followed his new friend and fellow deputy Albert Mortenson around the back of the high school. The third building was their destination, the moonlight guiding them through the waiting darkness. "Are you sure you remember where it's at?"

"Yeah, I spent a lot of time in there after school with Mr. Carson. Everyone else hated the man, but for some reason, he and I got along pretty well. Probably because chemistry was easy to me. It's the one thing I'm really good at. Besides Oreo Blizzards."

Dustin spoke in a hushed tone, his voice a purr. "I'm not so sure we should be sneaking around like this."

"Relax, dude. No need to whisper. We're the law now. Besides, who's to say we're not on official business? You know, checking the place to make sure a bunch of lowlifes didn't rob it. That's what cops do—keep an eye on stuff. Nobody should think twice about us being here."

"Oh yeah. I keep forgetting. Like you said, perks."

"Gotta take advantage when the time is right," Albert said, stopping his heft at the third door. "And that time is now. Trust me, nobody is thinking about the high school right now. They're all too busy with their insignificant lives, hoping they have enough supplies to make it through the blackout."

"So what's the plan?" Dustin asked, seeing the stenciled white letters on the window next to the door. They spelled *Chem Lab*.

Albert took a folded black pouch from his pants pocket, opened it, and while covering the palm of his extra-wide hand in leather, fished out a pair of slender pieces of metal. He held them up and let out a thin smile, obviously waiting for a reaction.

"A lock pick set?" Dustin asked, trying to process the revelation.

"It's like they used to say in that old commercial. I never leave home without it," he said, closing the pouch and giving it to Dustin. "Here, hold this a sec."

Dustin watched the overweight man lean forward on his wide hips and insert the twin picks into the door lock, jiggling them a bit. "Just gotta catch it just right, and then . . . bingo." He turned the knob and swung the door open.

"Where'd you learn to do that?"

"Couple of years ago in New York. I had this ex-con working for me who taught me all about second-story stuff."

"Like what?" Dustin asked, wondering what the term *second story* meant.

"Let's just say the man had skills. I learned everything I could before he got jacked by the cops. Word has it, he died in prison a few months ago. Got knifed in the shower, I think. Poor bastard. All his skills were useless inside."

"When you said *worked for you* . . . what did you mean?"

"Don't worry about it. It's not important," Albert said, leading the way inside. He found the light switch and flipped it up. Nothing happened. "Shit. No power. Gonna be hard to break that habit."

Dustin settled in next to Albert, feeling a thunderous heartbeat pounding at his chest. This was the first time he'd ever broken into anything. In fact, it was the first time he'd broken the law—period. Not a single traffic ticket or even an hour of school detention in all his years.

Albert pointed. "It's in the back, on the right. Past the workstations."

"Where? I can't see anything. It's too dark in here."

"Hang on," Albert said, fumbling around in his pocket before pulling out a matchbook. He opened it but didn't strike any of the matches. "See if you can find some paper somewhere. Check the tables."

Dustin moved forward, leaving the comfort of the ambient light inside the entrance. The darkness consumed him as he put his hands out to feel around the smooth surface of the first workstation.

His fingers found the edge of a sink first, then a faucet. He continued to the right, running his hands over a square beaker, two flasks, and then a rattle of test tubes in some kind of rack. He worked around the remainder of the station, but didn't find any paper.

The next worktable was only a few feet farther, taking him deeper into the darkness. Just when he was starting to think this was a fool's errand, he found a loose stack of paper sitting on the second corner he checked.

He whirled around with the paper in his hand and held it up, even though Albert wouldn't be able to see him. "Found some!" he reported before retracing his steps to the door.

"Roll the paper lengthwise, like you're getting ready to blaze one," Albert said.

"Blaze one?"

"Yeah, like a doob."

Dustin froze and didn't respond. He hadn't heard those terms before.

Albert rolled his eyes. "Please tell me you know what a joint is. As in pot? You know, a blunt? Doobie? Spleef?"

"Oh, that," he said, nodding. He twisted the paper lengthwise, winding it tight. "Like this?"

"Close enough," Albert said, striking a match. He held it out. "Hold it still."

The red-hot glow exploded on the paper, tearing at Dustin's vision. Once the paper resembled a torch, Albert took it and began a march through the maze of tables.

The fat man zigzagged a path to the back, where he was greeted by another door. "The supplies we need are in there."

Albert grabbed the knob, but Dustin didn't see it turn. "Locked?"

Albert smirked. "Not surprising. The District makes Mr. Carson keep it locked up. You know, to protect it from assholes like us."

"Yeah, assholes like us," Dustin mumbled, realizing they were about to commit more crimes.

Albert scowled and switched to a more commanding tone. "It's a damn good thing we have these badges on, because it's our duty as duly sworn officers to make sure everything is still here and accounted for. Can't be too careful these days. Damn vandals are everywhere."

Dustin laughed at Albert's twisted sense of humor.

Albert gave the burning wad of paper to Dustin, freeing his hands for the lock pick set again.

As the fire quickly worked its way down the shaft of the giant *doobie*—as Albert had called it—Dustin worried about the flames. The heat was intensifying by the second, bringing his fingers into play. He looked around for a place to toss the paper and found it: the stainless steel wash sink. A Bunsen burner sat next to it, giving him an idea.

He opened the burner's value with a quarter turn, then held the flame over the spout. The gas ignited in a poof, allowing him to dispose of the paper torch in the metal basin.

Dustin cranked the knob on the faucet, but the water pressure failed. Only a momentary trickle leaked out. It landed on the flame with a sharp hiss, sending a puff of smoke rising.

"Good idea with the burner. Gas still works," Albert said, his fingers continuing to work the lock.

"Yep, but not the water. Pumps are out."

"Got it!" Albert announced, straightening his posture. He opened the door, then pointed at the gas burner. "Move that a little to the right and see if you can turn it up a notch. I'm gonna need as much light as I can get."

Dustin slid the burner across the smooth counter, making sure he didn't stretch the rubber gas line too tight. He played with the valve and was able to open it a little farther than before. The flame grew brighter—about twenty percent, he guessed.

"That's about as good as it's gonna get," Dusting said, moving to the supply room's door. He held it open with his backside. The light from the flame penetrated the supply room, thanks to his slender frame.

The storage area was about the size of a racquetball court, with a central walkway down the middle. Both sides of the aisle were framed by a lower cabinet that ran from the front wall to the back. The twin, all-black storage compartments had a series of sliding doors along the front. Metal shelves sat on the countertops, each set back about six inches from the leading edge.

The room was crammed full of supplies, all arranged neatly by item: beakers, test tubes, glass bowls, rubber tubing, spare burners, gas masks, goggles, scales, plastic containers, jars of chemicals, and a host of other paraphernalia he hadn't seen before.

A loose stack of cardboard boxes stood at the far end of the room, each roughly the size of a microwave oven and with their top flaps open.

Dustin guessed the chemistry teacher had recently finished restocking its supplies for the upcoming school year. The empty containers had the same name stenciled along their sides in blue ink: *Blue Husky Supply*. The company's icon showed the head of a furry dog wearing safety goggles.

Albert grabbed a carton from the top of the heap and tucked its flaps inside. He put the box on the leading edge of the counter, using his generous belly to hold the container in place while his sausage fingers worked through the first section of supplies. He must have known exactly what he was looking for, as he worked quickly, with little hesitation between the items he packed. He slid the box over and continued until it was full, then picked it up with a grunt.

Albert brought it over and put it on the floor next to Dustin's feet. "This one's yours." He returned to the cardboard stack, grabbing another carton and prepping its flaps for storage.

He filled the second box with stuff from the other side of the room. About half the items were from the metal shelf sitting on top of the cabinet, but the rest were pulled from inside one of the unit's sliding doors. Dustin found it odd that his new friend never bothered to check the contents of the other doors, sticking only with the one in the middle.

When Albert finished, he carried the box through the door and stood near the burning flame with pinched eyebrows. "You coming, or what?"

Dustin wrapped his hands around the bottom of his box and picked it up, finding it heavier than expected. The abundance of heavy duty glassware clanked together as he moved.

Albert began his walk to the classroom door. Dustin followed, letting the storage room door close on its own behind him. He heard the heavy click of the self-locking mechanism when it engaged.

He was halfway through the classroom when a horizontal light appeared outside. It cut through the moonlit shadows like a knife through butter, its powerful beam dancing around in a familiar up and down pattern. A flashlight—getting closer.

Albert whirled around and whispered sharply, "Get down!"

Dustin followed Albert's lead, dropping to his knees behind the closest lab station. He put the box down and leaned up to take a peek over the counter.

The ceiling lit up as the flashlight went into search mode. Whoever had been outside was now inside and checking out the lab.

Albert turned and spoke in an even softer whisper than before. "We stand up on three. Let me do all the talking. Okay?"

Dustin hesitated, letting the words sink in. They were busted. No doubt about it. He hated the idea of his permanent record being marred with a conviction for breaking and entering. And theft. A stab of pain slammed into his chest when he considered his future—a life behind bars.

Albert tugged on Dustin's arm, snapping him out of his guilt-ridden trance. Dustin locked eyes with his fellow thief, bringing his attention to bear.

"Trust me," Albert whispered. "Just follow my lead. Can you do that? Otherwise, we're both gonna get jacked."

Dustin gulped down a fleshy bulge of mucus, then nodded.

Albert stood up and so did Dustin, though his skinny legs wanted to make a run for it. The door wasn't far away. Albert's abundant size meant Dustin would easily get to the door first—a huge advantage if the flashlight wielder decided to give chase.

Dustin waited for his feet to begin their sprint, but they never moved. A second later, the flashlight beam hit him in the face from somewhere near the entrance door, blinding him.

"Identify yourself!" a male voice called out from behind the light.

"Deputy Sheriff Mortenson," Albert said, his voice terse and to the point. He pointed a finger at Dustin. "And this is Deputy Brown."

"What are you doing in here?"

Albert's voice slowed and turned deeper. "My partner and I were on patrol when we noticed the door to the lab was open. We came inside to investigate."

"Who was in here?" the man asked, his tone gruff. Possibly the night security guard.

"A couple of teenagers. But they took off as soon as we showed up."

"You just let them go?"

"Look at me," Albert said, rubbing his massive belly. He tilted his head as a grin took over. "Do I look like the kind of man who runs?"

"No. I suppose not. What about your partner? He looks capable."

"He's new on the job. I didn't want him chasing the perps down on his own. Besides, they dropped the boxes before they split, so nothing was actually taken. They're right here, behind the tables. I can show you, if you like."

"Okay, but no sudden moves."

Albert picked up his box and put it on the table. "There's another container here, if you'd like to see it."

The man lowered the flashlight, then swung it to Dustin's right, landing it on the active Bunsen burner.

Albert continued the ruse. "We figure the kids lit the gas so they could see what they were doing. Looks like they were here for supplies. My guess is they're planning to cook some drugs."

"Again?" the flashlight man asked.

"This has happened before?"

"Yeah, last summer. Never caught the kids who did it, either."

"Then it must be the same group. With the power out and everyone scrambling, they must've assumed this was the perfect time to come back for more."

"Damn it. I told the Principal we needed to put cameras in the storeroom. But nobody ever listens to me," the man said, moving forward as he brought the light back to Albert. Only this time, the light wasn't aimed at the fat man's face. It was angled to the left and down.

The beam must have been reflecting off something because it was now showering the man's face with light.

He was older, in his fifties or sixties, and Caucasian. Pale white, to be exact. Like he hadn't seen the sun for years. Other than his thin gray hair and handlebar mustache, he looked mostly normal, Dustin decided. No real distinctive traits either, except his albino skin and his gray, weary eyes. They looked pushed too close together, like someone had used a vise on his head.

At least the man wasn't wearing a security guard's uniform. Nor did it appear he was armed. The nametag stenciled on his work shirt said *Wade*.

"I know I'm just the night janitor, but I swear, it's like I'm invisible around here. It gets old. Fast. Just once, I'd like the Principal to listen to me."

"Well, the Sheriff's Department thanks you for your diligence. We can't be everywhere all the time, so it's important for citizens to stay alert and report anything they see. Especially now, when we're in the middle of a crisis. Well done, sir."

Wade smiled, looking relieved. "Thank you. Just trying to make a difference. Though after forty-two years, I still get no respect."

"Forty-two years? On the night shift?" Dustin asked.

"Yeah. I prefer the quiet. Not a big fan of people in general. Or the whiny teenagers and their disrespectful ways. I don't know about you, but I don't think kids should be calling me Dennis. It's Mr. Wade to them."

Dustin had his answer. The pale skin was from decades of working the nightshift.

"Well, Mr. Wade, your dedication to this school is commendable," Albert said, picking up the box from the counter.

"I think that should remain here. That's school property," Wade said. "I don't want to get blamed for it going missing."

"You won't. I'll make sure the Principal knows we have it and how helpful you were tonight. We'll return it as soon as we have the glassware analyzed for fingerprints. These kids might be in the system."

"Oh yeah. Right. Do you guys need any help? With the power out, I'm not going to get my weekly cleaning done tonight."

Albert shook his head. "Nah, we got it. But thanks. If you could light the way, we'll follow you out."

"Don't you fellas have flashlights? They're standard issue, right?"

Albert answered without missing a beat. "You'd think so, but with the budget cuts and all, gear and batteries are kinda scarce. That's why we're usually assigned to the day shift."

"But with the power out—" Wade started to say.

Albert finished his sentence, "—they called everyone in. It's all hands on deck until this crisis is over."

Wade took a few seconds, his eyes darting back and forth. Then he looked up and nodded. "I'll lead you out."

CHAPTER 32

Franklin Atwater ran through the front door of his equestrian store and grabbed a flashlight from inside the solid metal cabinet on the left. He turned the beam on, using it to illuminate the rows between shelving units as he searched for the intruder. He came up empty in all seven aisles, then checked behind the lengthy checkout counter. No sign of anyone.

He didn't understand it. The door was open but nothing had been disturbed. In fact, everything was exactly how he'd left it, both behind the counter and on the shopping floor. All of his inventory was still neatly organized and pulled forward to the front edge of each shelf, making them look full even though they weren't.

It was time to check the office in the back. When he arrived, he found the door open. A knot formed in his gut, thinking about his sales receipts. He'd left them in the safe. A week's worth.

He went inside and was met with a frightening scene. It looked like a tornado had rolled through. Paper was everywhere, covering his desk and the floor in a blanket of indiscriminate white.

Franklin pushed his boots through the layers of agonizing mess, then sat in the roller chair behind his six-foot oak desk. He exhaled, then spun around and removed a strategically placed montage of equestrian photos on the credenza to reveal a hidden wall safe.

The safe's door was still locked, even though the rest of his workspace looked like someone had invited a herd of angry buffalo inside.

He spun the dial to enter the left-right-left combination before turning the handle. The door opened on the first try, revealing stacks of cash inside. Each had been wrapped with a rubber band and a paper receipt showing the bundle amount in his own handwriting. He ran a quick count— seven stacks—all there.

The drawers to his desk weren't closed all the way, and neither were those of the mini-filing cabinet standing nearby. He checked the contents of both—someone had rifled through them, but he didn't think anything was missing. However, he couldn't be sure unless he spent hours putting everything back where it belonged.

Every item in his office had a specific spot assigned to it, something his daughter often complained about after Franklin scolded her about misplacing items. He always felt terrible about the reprimands but couldn't control his unwavering desire for tidiness. It was who and what he was, courtesy of his years spent in the US Army.

If Franklin closed his eyes and slipped into his memories, he could still feel the raw power of his drill instructor's baritone voice vibrating the layers of his skin. The man's daily regimen of preachings had become etched in his soul, none of them more important than *maintain order and discipline at all times.*

Organization was his stress reliever. It wasn't easy keeping a horse business turning a profit, all while raising a young girl as a widower.

When he first purchased the operation from an old-timer who wanted to retire, he had no idea what he'd gotten himself into. At first, the clientele seemed taken aback when an outsider took over. But not just any outsider—a black man from the East Coast with no equestrian experience. It took a solid year of second-guessing and endless mistakes, but eventually he made it work. All was running smoothly. At least until now.

If the intruder was after something specific, he didn't think it was cash or supplies. The safe wasn't touched and the store hadn't been looted. In fact, the inventory on hand appeared to have been completely ignored, indicating the burglar went straight to his office after breaching the entrance.

Since none of the walls were spray-painted and nothing appeared to be maliciously damaged, he was certain this wasn't the work of tweakers looking for something they could pawn. Nor was it bored teenagers, out for a late-night thrill.

Then he remembered it. His vintage 1911. The stunning stainless steel pistol his late wife, Michele, had bought for him as a gift on their tenth wedding anniversary. The same day she told him she was pregnant with their second child.

The .45 caliber firearm was his most prized possession, not only because of its age and model, but because it was the only memento he still had of Michele after their pull-behind trailer caught fire and claimed her life, and the life of their unborn child.

The fast-moving inferno consumed the camper in minutes, destroying everything they owned in the process. Well, almost everything. Everything except the clothes on his back and those Megan was wearing when they went out for a stroll while Michele stayed behind to take an overdue nap. If he hadn't tucked the pistol inside the back of his waistband before their nature walk, it would've been consumed by the blaze as well.

Whenever he thought about his love for her, the unmistakable scent of burnt metal and scorched flesh would invade his senses. The tragedy happened while they were traveling West, shortly after he retired from his stint as a master welder with the Army Corp of Engineers.

Focus, Franklin, focus, he told himself, needing to get a grip on the moment. The painful memory cleared a few moments later, allowing him to focus on the present.

He stood up and pushed the roller chair away. He dropped to his knees, then leaned under the right side of the desk, putting his hand under the oak surface. His fingers went for the Colt, but it wasn't there. The Velcro strap was hanging open. He checked again, feeling around in desperation, but the holster was still empty. His heart sank.

That's what the thief was after—his prized handgun and last memento from the love of his life.

Right then, a new idea came unbidden into his mind. He scrambled to his feet and ran out of his office, then took a sharp right and cruised along the back wall until he made it to the far end of the checkout counter.

He flipped the barrier arm up and made a quick turn before scampering twenty more feet to the cash register. He put his hand under the counter and instantly found what he was looking for—the shotgun nestled in its spot.

Franklin yanked it out, needing to feel the power of the double barrel 28-inch Benelli in his hands. He ran the tips of his fingers over the engraved nickel-plated receiver, its smoothness running from end to end.

He cherished the scatter gun almost as much as his Colt .45, but for a completely different reason. While the Colt was an irreplaceable gift from Michele, the shotgun represented something more recent—the first month his newly-purchased business turned a profit.

Megan helped him pick out the Benelli from the abundant inventory at the High Country Guns store in Denver. She thought it was the prettiest gun on the rack, so he went with her decision. Luckily, he'd brought enough cash along to cover the cost.

He stared at the weapon and couldn't believe it. The thief never bothered to check the most likely place for a shotgun—and a $2,700 customized monster at that.

Its satin walnut stock was still in pristine condition, something a burglar would never pass up. At least not anyone who appreciated the fine craftsmanship that went into a firearm like this.

His mind churned through the facts, leading him to only one conclusion: the bandit was only after his Colt 1911. Nobody left a killing machine like this behind. Nobody. Or the stacks of cash in the safe.

But what about the store's ammunition supply?

Franklin whirled around and took out a key ring from his pocket. He found the one he needed in seconds, using it to unlock the sliding steel door of the specialty made storage cabinet.

When he pulled the heavy-duty compartment open, his eyes found rows of ammo boxes on the shelves, all neatly arranged by caliber, from small to large.

Handgun shells were assigned to the top shelf. Long gun rounds to the middle. Powder and reloading supplies were relegated to the third. Even his generous stockpile of the popular binary explosive, Tannerite, was still where he'd left it, on shelf number four.

He grabbed two boxes of Hornady 12-gauge shells, opened them, and then stuffed the Critical Defense cartridges into his pockets. He knew the shotgun was already loaded with the same ammo, having cleaned and reloaded the beast only a few days before. He finished by taking primer fuse and several sticks of mining explosives, each filled with ammonium nitrate instead of dynamite.

Franklin locked the reinforced cabinet and spun around with the shotgun in his hands. He held it up in front of his chest and readied the weapon, bringing a rush of blood into his system. The Benelli was now primed for action, and so was he, pushing his jaw out with teeth clenched. If the thief was still on his property, he was going to pay for what he'd done. "Nobody steals from me and gets away with it. Nobody."

He snatched the flashlight from the counter and quickly retraced his steps into the retail area, then broke into a sprint as he headed for the front door of the store.

The heartbeat in his chest was at full tilt and so were his feet when they landed on the dirt path outside. He ran to the spot where he'd left Stephanie and the kids, but they weren't there.

"Stephanie?" he yelled, calling out into the lingering darkness. "Jeffrey? Megan? Where are you?"

He waited, but a response never came. He called out again, but like before, heard only silence in reply.

The hairs on the back of his neck began to tingle, tightening the knot in the pit of his stomach. He brought the flashlight down, focusing its beam on the dirt around him.

Franklin took a few seconds to study a concentration of impressions about ten feet ahead. The tracks from his boots were easy to identify due to their size and distinctive shape, and so, too, were the tiny patterns from the kids' sneakers. Stephanie's tracks were thirty percent smaller than his and directly behind the children, just as he expected.

However, there was another set of prints—larger than his, with a heavy tread. The size and shape of the waffle pattern told him who and what had made it—a man and his hunting boots.

Franklin sold a similar boot in his store, though the tread pattern was more in the shape of parallel waves, rather than the intersecting waffle design he was looking at now. But the differing tread didn't change what he knew to be true: someone had come up behind his daughter and friends. And now they were missing.

The knot in his stomach doubled in size as a series of new thoughts boiled in his brain. He didn't want to admit it, but he let someone take them, and it was probably the same person who stole his Colt .45. All of it occurring on his watch.

He looked back at his store, realizing he needed to change his outfit. Something a little stealthier was needed. Something that would give him an advantage.

CHAPTER 33

Jack Bunker followed on his horse as Deputy Clark rode her mount across the wooden slats of the bridge in the burgeoning hours of night. The misty glow of the moon was helping them see—barely—making him glad they'd snatched one of the working flashlights in town before they'd left. He kept the beam trained on Daisy's horse, shining past the animal's legs to light the road ahead.

It wasn't easy to hold a flashlight steady while riding a steed, nor was it easy keeping the cold from creeping into his bones. The sun had long since extinguished its flame for the day, bringing with it a damp chill he knew was only going to get worse.

Despite the patchy darkness, he could see Daisy was an accomplished rider. That much was clear. He watched her work the reins with the grace and control of a well-seasoned orchestra conductor, gliding along in the saddle as if it were a magic carpet in the sky. Her posture was perfect and confident, like she'd been born on a horse.

He, on the other hand, was under siege from the saddle, feeling the polished leather smack into his undercarriage with every step of the great beast. His back was starting to feel it, too, and he found himself wishing he'd never sold his old ride. He needed something he felt comfortable on. Something with far more than one horsepower and something with a reliable, built-in suspension and foot pegs.

If they didn't reach Tuttle's place soon, the pain between his thighs and in his lower spine would continue to rise, threatening his ability to walk right. Or have kids. Even his teeth were starting to hurt, clanking together about every fifth stride.

It had been a tiring day of challenges but thankfully, only one task remained: obtain communications gear from Tuttle, and anything else that could be useful, tactically speaking.

The Sheriff and Mayor were counting on him. So were Daisy, Stephanie, and Jeffrey. Plus all those kids he'd rescued. Oh, and their parents, too. Now that he thought about it, he'd essentially given his word to everyone in town.

Even though he could turn the reins and slip off into the night, he planned to complete the mission. As appealing as a smooth getaway sounded to the old version of him, the new Bunker wouldn't allow it. Not now. Not after the town had claimed him for their own. He was committed. At least for the short term.

More importantly, if an invasion was imminent, where else could he go where there was food, water, shelter, and people who trusted him?

If their theories were correct about the Morse code signal and what was coming across the southern border, going it alone was not the right move. Safety in numbers was the only way to play this, even if the town was filled with a bunch of mostly untrained civilians.

"Tuttle's place is just over there," Daisy said, pointing to the right as they cleared the wooden bridge.

"Good, 'cause my ass is killing me."

She laughed. "On the way back, I'll show you how to sit properly so you can move with the horse and not against him. It's much easier that way."

"I figured there was a trick to this. There has to be. Otherwise, nobody in their right mind would ever take a long ride like this."

"Long ride? This is nothing, Bunker. Some day you'll have to take a trip with me to Thompson Falls. It's about thirty miles from here, across some super tough trail. But it's totally worth it. It's one of the most beautiful places on Earth. When you get there and the trees open up, you'll see this massive waterfall that pours into a crystal-clear lake. All of it surrounded by forest and mountain peaks as far as you can see. I swear to God, you'll think you just found heaven. It literally takes your breath away."

"Yeah, some day," he said, not wanting to be impolite. It sounded amazing, but he doubted he'd ever agree to that level of torture on his backside. Not unless her secret trick for the saddle solved the pain he was in, and did so quickly. Otherwise, he'd never survive the agony of a thirty-mile ride.

She turned, taking her horse down a wide dirt road that faded off into the shadows ahead. The surface was uneven and rocky, with deep ruts from water runoff snaking their way across the road from high to low.

"Down on the right is Rainey's place. I think you may have met her in town. Her grandson was supposedly on the bus. Though now that I think about it, I don't remember seeing him. But I only met him once since her daughter moved to town, so maybe I just missed him in all the commotion," she said, sauntering her horse ahead a few more strides. "North, across the street, is Tuttle's. When we get there, let's get off our horses and stand together. You'll need to stay close and keep the flashlight on both of us so he gets a good look at you. But whatever happens, let me do all the talking. Otherwise, he might just start shooting."

"He's really that twitchy?"

She nodded. "He doesn't like strangers. Well, actually, he doesn't like anyone at all. But I think he has a soft spot for me. At least I hope so."

"Great, just what we needed."

"He's really not that bad. But ever since his wife died of ovarian cancer, he's kinda withdrawn from society. He and Helen were together ever since high school. After all those years, it's gotta leave a big hole that just can't be filled. I can't imagine a love like that."

"Speaking of relationships, is there a Mr. Clark?" Bunker asked her in a smooth, gentle tone, not knowing where the words came from. They just came flying out on their own, making him suck down a quick breath afterward.

She scoffed, sounding amused. "A girl's gotta have a boyfriend for more than a minute if she's ever gonna get married. I'm sure you noticed in town, it ain't exactly full of underwear models. Slim pickin's, if you know what I mean. Most of them missing a few teeth."

Bunker's mind drew him a visual, which he quickly erased. "You ever thought of moving to the big city? Denver isn't that far away. A lot more choices there."

"Nah. I love it here, despite the total lack of men. I figure I'll grow old in Clearwater and then they can bury me next to my dad. He's been gone eight years now."

"And your mom?"

"Eleven years. I miss them both so much. Especially around the holidays. My trailer isn't very big to start with, but when Christmas comes, I feel like I live inside a tuna can. It's just me and my cat, Vonda, who loves—"

"—tuna," he added, interrupting her.

"Exactly. The walls close in like a noose around our necks. Sometimes, I just can't breathe and have to get out of there. You know what I mean?"

"Yeah. I do, as a matter of fact. Sometimes the only thing you can do is say no more and get the hell out of there. Change is good for the soul."

She hesitated for a moment, then swung her head around to make eye contact. "Is there a Mrs. Bunker waiting for you somewhere?" she asked, using the same tone and playfulness in her voice as he did a minute ago.

"Nope," he said, wishing he hadn't opened himself up for investigation by asking her about her love life. Now he was compelled to answer or he'd sound like a complete jerk.

She spoke again, this time sounding more deliberate. "So . . . no one who's waiting for you back in LA? A girlfriend? Friend with benefits? Regular Thursday night stripper?"

He smiled, enjoying her candor. However, he wished it wasn't aimed at him. He needed to end this line of questioning and fast, before he was cornered.

Keep it simple and to the point, he decided. "Nope. Nobody. I don't even have a home back there anymore. I decided it was time for some drastic changes in my life and I left town. That's why

I was on the train when I met Steph and her kid. Just looking to start over. My old life wasn't going the way I planned, so I set out to see where fate would take me."

"And bam, you ended up here. Lucky us."

"Well, I don't know about that."

"Yeah, seriously. Lucky us. Those kids wouldn't be alive if God hadn't brought you here," she said, slowing her horse as a metal gate came into view. "We're here."

CHAPTER 34

Bunker rode his horse next to Daisy, then aimed the flashlight higher, showering the top of Tuttle's gate with light. Beyond the gate were piles of rock and then a tall structure—the barn, he assumed. They were on the left, opposite a singlewide trailer on the right.

The house looked to be sitting on a foundation, but its distinctive shape and style screamed mobile home—a model from the seventies, if he had to guess. The four windows along the front were covered in horizontal blinds, something he figured Tuttle purchased from Home Depot and installed himself, given the rundown look of the place.

In front of the home were three old Ford pickups, sitting bumper to bumper with their driver doors facing the road. Beyond them was a huge stash of gas station and roadway signs. They'd been stacked up vertically, with their faded lettering and logos aimed away from the trailer.

"Tuttle's a serious packrat," he said to Daisy.

"Yeah, no doubt. I'm pretty sure he does it to get under the skin of Mrs. Rainey across the street."

Bunker couldn't hold back a half-smile. "Gotta love neighbors. Doesn't matter where you live, there's always one who pisses you off. Even way out here."

"I think he angled all this junk to shield his place, too. You know, privacy. Rainey is a gawker, supposedly."

"I was wondering why the trucks were parked parallel to the street. A collector would've had the hoods facing the road."

"Yep and those signs are way cheaper than a fence. Plus, I think he gets off knowing she has to stare at them all day."

Tuttle even had a couple of safes lying in the weeds, their reinforced doors hanging open. But there was something else between the house and the trucks—something much smaller and a darker color.

He moved the beam to get a better look. It was a red lawnmower, but it wasn't old and rusted like the rest of the scrap.

Daisy dismounted.

He did the same, taking the reins of her horse so she could focus on Tuttle. Bunker stood to her left, with the flashlight angled up from his waist, showering both of their faces in light.

A single light was burning in the house, near its midpoint. It wasn't flickering or moving, so it wasn't a candle. Nor was it a flashlight or a fireplace. Probably a lamp or some other type of fixed, hard-wired light source. If his assumption was correct, it meant Tuttle had power—backup power—with the grid down.

Daisy took in a deep breath before she spoke in a loud, deliberate tone. "Frank? Are you home? It's me, Deputy Daisy Clark with the Sheriff's Department. From earlier."

They waited for an answer, but none came.

She called out again, this time louder than before. "Frank? We really need to speak to you. This is my friend, Jack Bunker. Sorry to bother you again, but we need to borrow one more thing."

"Rent one more thing," Bunker reminded her quietly. "Not borrow."

"Rent one more thing!" she yelled, correcting herself. "I know it's late, but can you please come out and talk to us? It's super urgent."

Again, there was no answer. She called a third time, pleading with him to show himself. He didn't.

"That's weird. The light's on," she mumbled before turning her eyes to Bunker.

"Probably on battery backup. I don't hear a generator running."

"I don't understand. Why doesn't he answer? He's got to be home. He's always is."

"It's possible he's not inside. Could be out back somewhere. Or he's busy taking a leak."

"Yeah, maybe," she said, laughing. "Probably has his hands full. Sort of." She pointed at the stacks of rocks in the driveway. "Last time, he was hiding in that middle pile. He's got some kind of little hidden bunker thing going on in there."

"A bunker?"

She smiled. "Yeah, *bunker*. Just like your name. Hmmm. How about that? Never dawned on me until just now."

"Is it deep?"

"I don't think so. It's more like a hatch, but I never went inside. Maybe it leads somewhere. Who knows? He did mention something about having more than one stash of supplies. Underground, I think. I just wish I could remember exactly what he said."

Before Bunker could respond, three brilliant flashes caught his attention from inside the house. Two happened quickly, then another one a second later. Each of the flashes was immediately accompanied by a loud bang.

"Get down," Bunker said when he recognized the sound of gunfire. He turned off the flashlight and grabbed Daisy's arm in an instant, pulling her and the horses about twenty feet to the left. He stopped when the bulk of the rock piles were between them and the house.

"Oh my God! Frank?" she said in an emotional voice, pushing large amounts of air out with each word. "We gotta get in there," she added a few moments later, pulling her weapon from its holster. "I think he just shot himself."

Bunker kept his grip on her arm, preventing her from standing. "No. Wait. There were three shots. Not one. When you shoot yourself there's only one. Then it's over."

The fright on her face disappeared and was replaced by concern. "Someone's in there with him?"

Bunker nodded. "That's my guess. Whoever it is probably didn't expect a deputy to show up just now, either. With some other guy."

"Then Frank is d—"

"Probably. Did you notice how the first two shots were close together, then the third?"

She nodded, but didn't say anything.

"When I was in the military, they taught us a technique called *The Mozambique*. It's two to the chest and one to the head. The timing between those gunshots makes me think that's what we just heard."

"Military?"

"Or former military. Then again, could be some lowlife who happens to know what a triple tap is."

"Why would someone do that? Frank's no threat to anyone, except himself."

"Probably robbing the place when we showed up."

Her eyes dropped their focus to the ground, then began to dart from left to right. She stopped and looked up, as though she'd just reached a conclusion. "Then this is all my fault for calling out like that," she said, with her nose pinched and forehead wrinkled. "Damn it. I should've waited and checked everything out first."

"You couldn't have known someone was in there with him."

"I should've followed procedure. He's probably dead because of me."

"Look, we both thought he was out here all alone."

She shook her head, looking determined, eyes wide and face tense. "I gotta do something. I can't let the shooter get away. I have to arrest him."

Daisy tried to stand up again but Bunker wouldn't let her go, noticing she was breathing heavily, with her gun hand shaking. He figured she hadn't been in many situations like this. Not out here in the sticks. Small towns like Clearwater didn't exactly have a lot of shootouts, or murders.

"Daisy, you need to slow down. Think it through," he said, squeezing her arm gently to reinforce his words. "The last thing we need is to make the situation worse. It's just you and me out here and there's no backup. We need to take this step by step and work together."

She nodded, taking a few extra breaths.

He leaned to the right and scanned the area around the house. The light inside was now off, leaving the home shrouded in darkness. He aimed the flashlight at the windows along the front, moving quickly from window to window. Each of the blinds was still closed, but the glass in the far window looked like it had been broken.

Bunker turned the flashlight off and waited for his pupils to adjust. Once they did, he let his gaze run out of focus, switching to peripheral vision.

He'd been taught in the service that peripheral vision works best in near-total darkness. Something about the rods around the retina being more light sensitive than the cones inside the center. He waited for movement, but didn't see anything.

He looked at Daisy. "Is there a back door to the place?"

She pointed at the front of the trailer. "No, just that door in the middle."

"Are you sure?"

"Positive. I used to hang out here all the time with his daughter. It was back in high school, before Misty skipped town with a total jerk from overseas."

"What about windows across the back?"

"Three, I think. But I'm not sure. It's been a while."

He tied the horses to the gate, then checked Tuttle's house again. Still no sign of anyone. "Looks like one of the windows at the far end is broken. You know what that means—"

"—break-in."

"By an amateur."

She nodded. "A pro wouldn't have done that. Too much noise. Probably a meth-head looking for a score. Something they can pawn for some easy cash. Wouldn't be the first time around here. But these types of break-ins don't usually happen while someone is home. And there's normally not a shooting involved."

'Maybe not around here. But where I'm from, they do," he muttered, looking down at Daisy's right hand, staring at the Glock semi-auto. "You wouldn't happen to have a backup I could borrow, would ya?"

She reached down and pulled up her pants leg. "You mean something like this?"

"What's that? A .380?"

She nodded and whispered, "Ruger. LCP. My belly gun." She unwrapped the Velcro strap and pulled it from the ankle holster, then gave it to him.

"Is it chambered?" he asked, ready to rack the slide and inject a round from the magazine.

"Yeah, with Black Talon hollow points."

"That'll work," he said, wishing he had her Glock instead.

The smaller caliber of the LCP meant he'd have to be dead-on accurate and at close range in order to take down the assailant. A .380 round didn't pack a lot of punch, but the Black Talon hollow points would do some serious damage once they were inside the chest cavity and began to sprawl.

That was assuming, of course, the target wasn't wearing body armor. Otherwise, he'd have to go for a headshot. Just under the nose and above the lips was the most lethal shot, severing the spinal cord at the back of the neck in an instant.

"Let's move," she said, moving forward in a crouched position. She climbed through the split-rail gate and scampered to the closest rock pile.

CHAPTER 35

Bunker followed Daisy through the gate. She took a position behind a rock formation on the left. He chose one to the right, peering around the manmade mound while keeping his profile thin.

He looked over at Daisy just as she brought her head around after taking a peek herself. She flashed a hand signal, telling him they were going to move ahead.

Bunker waited until her feet moved, then slid out from behind the cover. He kept low as the two of them worked their way to the pair of rock heaps closest to the barn.

All was quiet, but Bunker knew the gunman was still there, waiting for them with several rounds at the ready. If the perpetrator had military training, they might be advancing into a trap.

He needed to dig deep and remember all the training he received at Camp Pendleton under the dutiful tutelage of the short in stature but lethal Sergeant Haskins.

It was back during the part of his life when he *thought* he knew how the world worked. When it still had honor. Still had meaning. He was straight out of high school at the time, wide-eyed and ready to serve Mother Liberty.

He still remembered how proud he felt when he signed up: his conviction was strong, feeding his desire to walk in the steps of all those brave souls who came before him. His life plan was simple back then—do his part for God and country. Then go to college on Uncle Sam's dime.

Bunker wasn't sure why his mind was thinking about all of this right now, but it was and he couldn't seem to shake it. Before his next breath, a wave of dizziness hit him, making his legs buckle. He landed on his knees and fell forward, ramming his forehead into the rocks stacked up before him.

His breathing ran shallow and his eyes started to ache, forcing him to slam them shut. A series of images tore into his mind, all bloody. Even though they were only momentary glimpses, he knew what they represented—a sequence of events from long ago.

His chest tightened, squeezing his heart just like it had during his final deployment. The crushing pain from years past was now raging in his chest with thunder.

A dozen or so breaths later, the rapid-fire images began to slow before they came to a full stop—much like an old jukebox spinning through a flurry of titles until it found the one it wanted to play.

He'd been through this process before and knew what was about to happen. It was time to relive one of the most painful moments of his life, a moment that changed who he was at the cellular level.

As expected, the vision changed. He was now standing over the bodies of the fallen, the corpses in pieces and stacked up like sandbags in front of a mile-long poppy field, deep inside the Afghan desert. He remembered the scene like it was yesterday. It was the exact moment when he—

"Bunker!" Daisy said in a sharp whisper. "You still with me?"

Bunker snapped out of his flashback. His chest was still on fire and his breathing rapid. Pushing through it wasn't easy, but he managed to regain control just as the last haunting image vanished from memory.

He swallowed hard, then opened his eyes. He looked at Daisy, feeling the drip of sweat on his cheeks. "Yeah, I'm still here."

"Good, 'cause whatever that was—"

"—I know. It hasn't happened for a long time. Not sure why now, but it's over."

"Thank God," she answered, waiting a bit before speaking again. "I need to get in there and arrest the shooter, but I can't do that if you're somewhere else. You gotta keep it together."

She was right. He needed to shake the after-effects and focus on the task at hand. His legs still felt like rubber, but he was confident he could do what needed to be done. "I'm good. Trust me."

She gave him a sidelong glance, looking hesitant.

"I'm good to go," he said with more conviction.

Her uneasiness seemed to fade. "I'm gonna move to the corner of the house first, then to the front door. I need you to cover me and follow me inside. We go on three. Ready?"

He shook his head in disagreement, still feeling a light dizziness swirling inside. "With all due respect, Daisy, going in hot is a mistake. A fatal one at that. It's just the two of us, with only pistols. We don't know where the shooter is and it's pitch black in there. Plus, we don't know the layout."

"Well, first of all, I do know the layout. Inside the door is his living room, which connects to the kitchen and bedrooms. It's probably covered in stacks of old newspapers and ashtrays filled with cigar butts. Second, it may be dark but we do have a flashlight. Third, I can't let this man get away. It's my duty to take him into custody."

"I get all that, but entering a door at night with a flashlight will get us killed. My fire team leader drilled it into us during our tactical training sessions: doorways are the Fatal Funnel—the most dangerous position during an assault. And the flashlight is the last thing we want to use. The shooter will aim for it first. Plus, we don't have any body armor or sufficient manpower to make an effective breach. Now, if we had a complete assault team with night vision goggles, flashbangs, and ARs, we might have a chance. But right now, we're at a complete disadvantage. It would be a suicide mission."

"Okay then, Mr. Military, what do you suggest?"

Bunker took a few seconds to consider the options. They needed to draw the shooter out and control the risk, but the tools and resources at his disposal were limited. Improvisation was needed.

His mind turned to something Daisy had just said about cigar butts and ashtrays. When he looked at all the junk in Tuttle's yard, it gave him an idea. It was a long shot, but worth a try. "I've got an idea. You stay here and cover me."

"What are you gonna do?"

"I don't have time to explain, so just listen." Bunker pointed at the closest window of Tuttle's trailer. "When you see the shooter peek through those blinds, empty the magazine at him. Start high and work your way low. We'll only get one chance at this, so don't miss."

She looked a little confused, but nodded anyway. "I won't. Was second in my class."

He was pleased to hear she was near the top of her class in marksmanship, given he was about to put his ass on the line. Yet he couldn't help driving home one more point to the country cop. "Whatever you do, don't turn that flashlight on. It'll give away your position."

Her eyes were in agreement as she put a soft hand on his shoulder. "Be careful out there."

"I plan to," Bunker said, checking the front of the house again. It looked clear. He took off for the closest Ford truck, angling his path to take him to the driver's door. He opened it and climbed into the driver's seat.

A quick check of the interior didn't turn up much except empty beer cans, a sweat-stained bandana, chewed toothpicks, and some wadded-up aluminum foil lying on the floorboard in front of the passenger seat. There was also a Colorado Rockies baseball cap with a salt lick growing around the brim and pair of work gloves with gaping holes in the palms.

He pulled the ashtray out and found a supply of ashes and two cigar butts sitting in its reservoir. The clues were obvious: Tuttle spent time in this truck, enjoying beer and smoking. Probably after working in the yard, which would explain the gloves, cap, and stained bandana.

Bunker imagined the old man sitting where he was now, laughing at his nosy neighbor across the street, all the while chugging down a few cold ones and belching between smoke rings as he puffed on a cigar. He wasn't sure what the foil wrappers were from—Ding Dongs, maybe?

Bunker leaned over and opened the glove box. Inside he found an old pipe, a zippered pouch of dry tobacco, and a book of matches that said *Billy's Pump and Munch* on the cover. He opened the matches and found four virgin sticks inside. Bingo. Just what he hoped he'd find.

He slid the matchbook into the front pocket of his jeans, then grabbed the bandana and one of the beer cans before slinking his way out of the truck. He'd planned to cut away sections of the seat covering to use as a flammable material, but scoring the old bandana saved him a step.

Once on the ground, he stuffed the do-rag into his back pocket, then took out his knife and used the tip to enlarge the opening on top of the beer can.

So far, so good, he thought. Now he just needed gasoline.

He crawled under the pickup and went in search of the fuel line, starting at the rear of the vehicle. He felt around the tank until his fingers came upon a hose. Bunker followed it down and around to a clamp. A few inches later, he landed on a grommet and clip holding the rubber tube to the frame.

Now that he'd found the low point, he needed to sever the supply. However, his body was directly under the gas line, so he repositioned himself for better access. With the beer can under the hose, he cut the tube in half with his knife, then waited. Nothing came out. *Damn it.* The tank must have been empty.

He sighed, realizing his plan wasn't going to work. Not without a supply of gas. Bunker thought about checking the other trucks for fuel, but they weren't in the proper position for his targeted diversion to succeed. He'd have to transport the gas from one truck to the other, and that was going to take too much time. Plus, he didn't have a hauling container.

Before he could decide what to do, a new thought arrived.

Maybe the tank in the first truck wasn't empty.

Since the vehicle was old and stationary, the gas might've broken down and gummed up the fuel line. He tapped the butt end of his knife on the underside of the tank. The sound was deep and solid, not a hollow ping like he expected. There was fuel. He tapped farther up the side. Same sound. Plenty of gas.

Bunker cut away another section of the fuel line. But again, no fuel ran out. He tried slicing a third section, this time as close to the tank as he could reach, but still nothing. The facts led him to only one conclusion: the blockage was inside the tank.

He opened the pickup's gas cap and leaned in to take a whiff. The odor wasn't what he expected. It smelled sour, like varnish. He was right. The gas had gummed up.

That meant a Molotov cocktail might not work since the fumes inside the tank wouldn't be potent. He figured the gas would still burn, but not without a high-octane ignition source to jump-start the chain reaction needed to cause an explosion.

Just when he thought his diversion plan was doomed, he remembered something from earlier: the red lawnmower. It looked to be a lot newer than the rest of the clutter in the yard. It might have gas in it—fresh gas—a more combustible ignition source.

Unfortunately, the mower was sitting in front of the vehicles and he'd have to expose himself to the shooter at close range. He needed better cover. Or a shield of some kind.

Then it hit him—Tuttle's old signs: they were made of metal.

Bunker put the beer can on the ground and crawled past the second truck. He continued to the back of the third truck, stopping to survey the sign graveyard.

Most of them were too big to carry or were the wrong shape to help him. But there was one he thought he could use—a faded red stop sign, about three feet tall and just as wide. It had two dark spots along the upper left edge. Dirt or rust? He couldn't be sure, not without better light.

Regardless, the idea had potential. Antique roadway signs were made of steel and thicker than the more modern composite aluminum. Better protection. Plus, the stop sign was small enough to maneuver around by hand. He'd have to stay low and keep the shield at a deflecting angle. Of course, if the shooter had armor piercing rounds, the steel wasn't going to provide much protection, even at an angle.

He thought about it for a few seconds. If Daisy was correct and the shooter was a meth-head amateur, then the criminal was probably armed with a 9mm handgun or something similar in caliber.

In that case, the thickness of the sign would protect him, but he'd have to work quickly to avoid successive shots in the same location. They'd cause an ever-deepening dent and eventually penetrate.

Bunker weighed the odds and decided it was worth the gamble. He put his knife into its sheath, crawled over to the stop sign, and grabbed it.

CHAPTER 36

Bunker used the half-inch mounting holes in the center of the sign as a grab point. The tips of his index fingers just fit, allowing him keep the shield in position as he worked his way to the mower in a crouched position.

His fingers were exposed to the shooter; however, he wasn't too concerned. Not if he was facing an amateur like Daisy suspected. The man's hands were probably shaking thanks to the rush of adrenaline pumping inside his arteries. He'd seen it many times before, even in the service. Unexpected duress turns ordinary shooters into cowering sprayers and prayers. Unless the man inside had a precision-guided firearm, like the Tracking Point M1400, accuracy would elude him.

Regardless, Bunker couldn't rely on his assumptions and let his guard down. Not with his life and Daisy's on the line. The sign needed to stay in front of him and angled to help deflect any rounds launched his way.

Daisy was still on the left, positioned behind one of the rock piles in the driveway. Bunker could feel her eyes studying his every move, trying to figure out what he was doing.

He didn't get a chance to lay out the diversion plan before he started on this quest, so she'd have to be patient and figure it out on her own. She was smart and capable. As long as she took the shot when the opportunity presented itself, his plan should work.

After another step, the sign bumped into something firm. He lifted the metal several inches and took a peek underneath. The moonlight was just bright enough to see a pair of black wheels and the mower's cutting deck.

It was time to reverse course and haul the mower where he needed it. He took a deep, invigorating breath and hoisted the sign in one flash of movement, then brought it down on the inside of the handlebar in front of him.

He wrapped his fingers around the mower's grab bar and pulled the machine away from the house, keeping the shield in place. The weeds were thick, slowing the process down, but he was able to drag the cutter behind the trucks where he had better cover. He tossed the sign aside.

Part of him was shocked the shooter hadn't sent a round while he was exposed, but the rest of him was thankful. Bunker couldn't be sure if the intruder was watching him or not, but since Daisy hadn't taken a shot, he assumed no. He figured the target was hunkered down behind a couch, waiting for them to breach.

Bunker found the cap to the mower's tank and twisted it open. He leaned in to smell it. The fumes were potent, making him turn his head away. Fresh gas. Excellent news.

He took the beer can and held it under the machine as he tilted it, allowing the fuel to leak out and run inside the aluminum container. Some of it spilled onto his fingers, but he was able to fill the can halfway. He put the mower back on its wheels, leaving the gas cap off.

Bunker held the can next to the mower and was about to pour it across the ground to make a long fuse, but a new thought stopped him. If he didn't work quickly, the gas would evaporate or soak into the dirt. Either way, it would become inert and not light. But that wasn't the only problem.

The mower's explosion might not set off the old fuel in the truck's tank. For ignition to happen, he needed to bring a high-intensity flame directly inside the tank.

A better solution was needed.

Then he remembered the bandana in his pocket. He pulled the rag out and studied it for a few seconds, letting a new idea form in his brain. He liked it, though everything had to be set up perfectly for it to work.

First, he made sure the truck's gas cap was securely in place. He twisted it tight, locking the varnished fuel inside the enclosed container. Step one complete.

Now he needed to find the weakest point on the truck's tank. He opened the matchbook and struck one of the four remaining matches. It was risky to expose his location for a few seconds, but he didn't have a choice.

When the match head finished its initial flare, he bent down with the steady flame and held it under the truck. He studied the condition of the tank, finding a rusted area about the size of a baseball on its longest side, facing forward. Some of the steel had peeled away, reminding him of petals on a rose, though brown instead of red.

He put the tip of his knife against the tank to mark the location, then blew out the match. He wrapped both hands around the knife's handle and leveraged all his weight to push the blade into the oxidized area.

The tip penetrated slowly at first before the metal gave way, sending the rest of the knife inside with a lurch. The lack of resistance sent his knuckles slamming into the tank, bringing a sharp sting to his hands. He grimaced and withdrew the knife.

The decomposing fuel began to seep out in slow-moving clumps of goo. It reminded him of nearly frozen marmalade jelly, oozing out like sap from a tree.

Now for the bandana. He sliced the smelly do-rag into two dozen strips of cloth, each a half inch in width. Once cut, he twisted them lengthwise between his fingers to form strings, then tied their ends together.

Next up: the beer can and its fuel. He dunked the makeshift fuse into the gas and let the cloth soak for a few seconds. When he took it out, he put one end of the fuse into the mower's tank and draped the rest of it to the ground.

He slid the machine under the truck's gas tank, positioning the mower's cutting deck directly under the fuel icicle that was now halfway to the ground. He spread out the remainder of the fuse on the ground, snaking it around the rear tire and under the tailgate.

It was now or never.

Bunker wiped his hands in the dirt to soak up the petroleum on his fingers, then took the matchbook and folded over one of the remaining matchsticks. He closed the cover and lit the exposed match with a single swipe of his thumb across the contact strip.

Once the flame settled into a steady burn, he angled the rest of the matchbook over the fire, then tossed the burning pack onto the end of the fuse. Bunker crawled feverishly past the other two trucks and positioned himself inside the stack of metal signs.

If he'd set this up correctly, the fuse would burn to the mower's gas tank, setting it ablaze. Once the fire reached a high enough temperature, it should ignite the dripping fuel-cicle and take the flame inside the truck's tank.

He covered his head and waited.

CHAPTER 37

Daisy Clark's focus was pulled to the right when a brilliant flare erupted from underneath the Ford truck closest to her. She knew Bunker was behind the old clunker and working on something big—something he said would bring the shooter to the designated window. The same window where the sights of her Glock were currently aimed.

She thought setting a fire was the extent of Bunker's plan, but then a powerful explosion rocked the property. The truck blew apart along the rear axle and sent the vehicle's rusty bed flipping into the air.

The shockwave hit her first, knocking her to the side and landing on her elbow. The thunderous blast ripped at her eardrums, locking her jaw in an open position as a high-pitched, pinging sound tunneled its way inside. It felt like someone had unleashed a turbocharged dentist's drill against her temple.

She cried out in pain, covering her ears as the back section of the truck flipped through the air, cradled inside a cocoon of flames. Gravity soon took charge and brought it down on top of the second truck, smashing its cab flat.

Daisy shook off the ringing in her ears, then resumed her firing stance behind the rock pile. She brought the handgun back into position and locked its sights on the closest window of Tuttle's home.

A big part of her was worried that Bunker got caught up in the explosion. Even if he was hurt, she couldn't let her attention drift. Her eyes and hands needed to remain where they were, burning a hole in the window's covering.

The beat in her chest was rapid and so, too, was her breathing. If it weren't for the pile of stone acting as a shooting rest, her aim would have been erratic. Impossible to control.

The horizontal blind began to move, pried apart near the midpoint. Daisy took a short breath and let it out before her finger pulled the trigger.

The round left the chamber, tearing a hole in the glass before her finger could squeeze again. The blinds blew apart, sending a spray of red across the window.

She continued firing in rapid succession, smashing more of the glass as she aimed lower with each successive shot. Her wrists absorbed the near-continuous recoil, keeping the sights trained on the destruction path down the wall. When the magazine was empty, the semi-auto's slide locked open.

The blind broke free from its overhead mount and crashed to the floor, almost as if someone had tried to pull themselves up with a yank.

Daisy pushed the release button on the left side of the grip and let the empty magazine fall to the ground. She jammed a new double-stacked magazine into the bottom of the Glock, then racked the slide to fill the chamber with a round.

Bunker appeared in a blur from the right, entering her vision as he worked his way through the weeds in front of Tuttle's place. His backside hit the wall to the right of the door a second later.

Thanks to the light from the truck fire dancing across his body, she could see his Ruger LCP locked in a two-handed grip and held chest high. He waved her to join him, looking unharmed and eager to take down the shooter.

* * *

Bunker waited until Daisy arrived and took position on the opposite side of the entrance. He turned the door handle and pushed it open, keeping his profile thin and out of view.

The blaze behind him was in full burn, creating a concert of shadows to contend with, each dancing in lockstep with the ballet outside. The shadows were a threat, providing dynamic cover for the target.

The shooter was there, somewhere, but not at full strength thanks to at least one bullet wound. Possibly more. Bunker was impressed with Daisy's accuracy, seeing the spray of blood after her first shot.

He remained outside as he worked the doorway by slicing the field of fire into a handful of thin segments, moving both his vision and his aim slowly to the right. It was a tactic called *Slicing the Pie*, a phrase his Fire Team Leader used often.

When he finished his initial visual sweep, he pointed to himself to get Daisy's attention. She nodded. He aimed his finger at the door and swung it to the left, then pointed at her and turned his aim to the right. He ended the covert communiqué by holding up three fingers to indicate a countdown was about to start. She made an okay sign with her fingers.

He started the hand signals in one-second increments, starting with three. At zero, he led the two of them into the home. He went left and she went right, both keeping low with their handguns ready to fire.

The corners were clear of active threats. So were the walls, leaving only two bodies to cover—each motionless and lying in a pool of blood. One was under the window Daisy shot out, and the other was twisted awkwardly on a bearskin rug in the center of the room.

Behind the rug were a tattered sofa, loveseat, and recliner, forming a horseshoe shape around the body. Next to the dark-colored easy chair were four stacks of newspapers, reaching the same height as the chair's stained armrests. Beyond that was the only light in the room—a floor lamp. It was lying on its side with its bulb smashed to pieces.

Daisy was right. The room reeked of smoke and body odor. Years of it—all of it fermenting until it had taken up permanent residence in the paint, the upholstery, and the light-colored linoleum floors. The stench was overpowering and nearly enough to make a billy goat gag.

Bunker pointed at the long gray hair of the body on the rug. Daisy swung her eyes and looked at it. Her look of shock told him the victim was Tuttle.

She lowered her head for a two-count, shook it twice, then brought her focus back to Bunker. The look of alarm was now gone, having been replaced with a fierce, determined stare—almost predator-like.

He knew exactly what she was feeling, having felt it years ago. He remembered the moment well. It was the same day he found himself standing over a heap of body parts, deciding right then to end his deployment in the swirling sands of Afghanistan.

Daisy went to Tuttle's body while Bunker crept forward to the shooter. He kept his trigger finger at the ready, just in case the corpse wasn't a corpse. When he arrived, he found the intruder covered in all-black garb, including a sweatshirt, balaclava, canvas pants, and trail shoes.

Daisy's aim had been spot-on, landing a round in the shooter's left eye. Most of the blood had pooled around his head, forming a near-perfect circle of red.

Bunker pulled the assailant's hood off in a single tug. A large hunk from the back of the skull came off with it, landing on the floor with a thud.

The man was dead all right. No doubt about it. Even a zombie from the *Walking Dead* couldn't function with half his brain missing.

Earlier, when Daisy had suggested the intruder was probably a meth-head looking for an easy score, Bunker thought it was plausible. However, now that he was standing over a body dressed in all black, he wasn't willing to accept that assumption.

He studied the man's face for a moment, then bent down and pried his lips apart. The dead man's teeth were aligned with precision and stark white—both upper and lower. No signs of tooth decay from inhaling endless amounts of methamphetamine.

This was no drug addict or down on his luck outcast. The man's short-cropped hair, all-black clothing, balaclava, trim body, and complete lack of facial hair screamed military. Or former military.

But why break into Tuttle's place like a common thug? He thought about it for a moment and realized something wasn't right. He stood up and looked at Daisy. "You stay here. I'll be right back."

"Is something wrong?" she asked while checking Tuttle's vitals.

"Toss me that flashlight. I need to go check something."

She sent the flashlight flipping end over end. He snagged it out of the air with one hand, then turned it on before starting his trek down the hallway.

He stopped to search the first bedroom. No threats. Only food stores. Dozens and dozens of #10 cans for long-term survival storage. Everything air-tight and sealed. He saw mostly Mountain House labels. However, a few stacks contained inventory from Saratoga Farms. Potatoes and pancakes must have been the man's favorite. Plus beef stroganoff.

Bedroom two had more of the same, except for the pair of backpacks leaning together in the center of the room. Their aluminum frames, adjustable shoulder straps, and padded hip belts were designed for hiking.

Bunker figured they were Tuttle's bug-out bags, both of them camouflage green and stuffed to the seams, with their pouches hanging open.

But why two packs if he lived alone?

When Bunker arrived at the last bedroom, he entered with the Ruger LCP and flashlight leading the way. He scanned for targets. All clear.

Most of the space had been dedicated to the sagging king-size bed. To the left was a single-stack four-drawer oak dresser covered in scratches and dents. A pile of clothes stood next to it—waist-high and soiled. The dingy t-shirt on top looked paper thin with a plethora of holes in it, the white fabric barely holding together.

Poor man's hamper, Bunker mused, figuring it was a couple of weeks' worth of laundry.

Before he could take another step, he remembered a light being on in the house when they'd first arrived on the scene—the floor lamp in the main room, toppled over with bulb smashed.

Tuttle had backup power. Bunker didn't need the flashlight. He found the wall switch and flipped it on, stinging his eyes with overhead light.

The stench of smoke was pervasive and even more pronounced here than in the main room. When he looked at the end of the bookcase-style headboard, he discovered why: a half-length cigar smoldering in a turquoise-colored ashtray.

A black revolver with a wooden grip was huddled next to it. He guessed it was a .357 based on the diameter of the six-inch-long barrel. Just the type of cowboy gun he'd expect an old-timer like Tuttle to own. Plenty of stopping power, too, plus it was quick and reliable. No magazine jams or extractor problems. Just aim and fire, though the trigger guard would sting the hand of anyone not familiar with the powerful recoil.

Tuttle's room wasn't much, but he'd obviously spent a lot of time in it, mainly on the oversized bed. Its white sheets were twisted into a rope-like pattern and pulled to one side, making room for a spread of newspapers. A magnifying glass, yellow marker, 100-pack of push pins, and blue-handled scissors sat nearby.

The scene fit what Bunker saw on the walls—hundreds of newspaper articles, each with yellow highlight streaks and uneven edges from Tuttle's scissors. Push pins held them up in a mosaic pattern, though there were numerous gaps remaining. Some of the cutouts remained a pristine white color, while others hung faded from years of smoke damage.

Bunker took a few seconds to consider the scene. Only one answer came to him: the assailant caught Tuttle in the middle of a cigar while scanning articles in bed.

But how did he get a drop on Tuttle?

Daisy claimed the man lived on the edge and had an itchy trigger finger. If that was true, Tuttle would've been tuned in to any change in his surroundings and grabbed the .357.

Bunker went to the headboard to inspect the firearm, freeing all six rounds from the cylinder. The hollow points were still seated in their brass jackets, none of them fired. He smelled the barrel. No gunpowder odor.

It was clear he was missing something.

Across from the bed were three piles of newspapers nestled against the wall, each about four feet tall with palm-sized rocks sitting on top. He took a paper from the first stack and checked the date. It was from the previous year: May 15. The paper below it was from the week before that. Tuttle was way behind on his reading.

Bunker turned sideways and scooted past the paper stacks to make his way around the bed to the far side. He found three drops of blood on the floor by the window. But that wasn't all. There were also two shards of glass about the size of marbles, though not nearly enough to account for the basketball-sized hole in the window.

After careful consideration, Bunker came up with only one answer: the window was broken from the inside. Possibly during a struggle. A struggle that surprised Tuttle and didn't allow him time to grab his revolver and defend himself.

After a quick retrace of his steps back down the hallway, Bunker closed in on Daisy's position in the main room. He stopped to put the floor lamp on its pedestal base.

He aimed the flashlight down and saw a gash on the middle finger of Tuttle's left hand. His suspicions were correct.

"Something's wrong, isn't it? I can see it on your face," Daisy said in a sharp, concerned tone.

"I think we have this whole situation wrong," Bunker said, pointing at Tuttle. "You see that cut? Tuttle's hand broke the window in his bedroom. Not the shooter. Plus I found a loaded revolver sitting within arm's reach from his bed."

"So what are you saying? This isn't a break-in?"

"Not like we think," he answered, leading her by the arm to the shooter's body. "Look at him. He's no drug addict. He's clean-cut, fit, and I checked his teeth. They're pearly white across the board. Plus his clothes are all wrong. I'm guessing you don't see too many balaclavas in your line of work."

"No, never. Or perps with perfect teeth."

"I figured as much."

"Dentists around here don't see a lot of repeat business, if you know what I mean. Not with everyone struggling to make ends meet."

Bunker nodded. "At this point, it seems clear. This was no simple home invasion. Whatever is going on here is something else entirely."

"Like what?"

"Not sure yet. But there was purpose and intent involved. And skills," he answered, kneeling down next to the body.

CHAPTER 38

Daisy knelt down next to Bunker and joined in the search of the assailant's body. Bunker started with the man's pants, so she decided to explore his sweatshirt and then move to his hoodie.

While her fingers were busy, she couldn't help but stare at the blood trail running down the side of the perpetrator's face. It was all a little too much to take in, especially the gaping hole in his eye.

She'd caused this carnage with the hollow points from her Glock. Now her conscience was stirring inside, slowly taking over. Well, stirring wasn't exactly the right word—*frothing* was a better term—as in foaming with guilt. Like a vat of molten steel, boiling away with ferocious intent.

Daisy sucked in a sudden, deep breath and turned her head, unable to keep a sharp gasp from leaving her lips.

"First kill?" Bunker asked her, turning the man's right front pocket inside out—nothing but lint.

"Yes," she said, taking a few seconds to compose herself. She swallowed hard, then steeled her nerves before looking at the body again. "In the academy, they train us how to handle almost every conceivable situation when we first arrive on a scene. But what they don't teach us—what they can't teach us—is how to handle kneeling over the gruesome body of someone you've just killed."

Bunker stopped his hand search, focusing his attention on her. The tone of his voice changed, now slow and tender. "It's never easy, but you did what you had to do."

She stopped searching as well, feeling the urge to heave. The stomach bile was close to erupting, but she kept it down. "I'm not so sure about that. Maybe if we'd waited until morning, this man might still be alive and I wouldn't feel like puking right now."

"I know you're hurting inside. That's normal. But this was a righteous shoot. This man had already killed one person and did so in cold blood. Plus, it was a friend of yours. Someone you've known a long time. It's going to affect you, like it would anyone."

She agreed, but it didn't ease the guilt raging inside her brain. "I know I had to do it, but it still doesn't change how I feel."

"I've been exactly where you are right now, so I know what you're going through. But we both know he was going to do the same to us, unless we burned him first."

"Yeah, I guess you're right," she said, feeling the knot in her belly tighten even more. "Does it ever get any easier?"

"No. And you never want it to. Taking a life is the last resort. But when it comes down to you or the enemy, you have to take the shot. It's your duty as a deputy, and as a human being, to protect yourself and those around you."

She nodded, feeling a slight decrease in stomach pressure. "I know all that, but this isn't how I thought it would feel."

"It never is. The first is always the toughest."

She appreciated his sympathy, but it really wasn't helping. "I always knew it would affect me, but not like this. I thought I would be stronger."

"Just take a minute. We're in no hurry."

She lowered her head as her breathing became shallow and rapid. A twinge of dizziness found its way into her head, making her blink rapidly to keep her vision clear.

If she'd been at home in her trailer, she would have run to the far end and jumped into bed, snuggling under the covers with a pillow wrapped between her knees until the attack faded. But she couldn't do any of that here. Not while on the job and not with her new friend watching.

Despite how she felt, Bunker was right. She needed to suck it up and be strong. She knew the risks when she applied for this job. Shooting someone was always a possibility, even in a small town like Clearwater.

Her job was to protect and serve and that's what she'd done. End of story. This man chose to enter Tuttle's home and execute him, leaving her no choice but to take him out. This wasn't her doing. It was the shooter's.

Anyone else in my position would have done the same thing, she thought quietly, trying to convince herself she wasn't at fault.

Right then, some of the guilt faded into the shadows of her heart. So did the dizziness.

When she looked at Bunker, a string of words formed on her tongue, then flew out of her mouth before she could stop them. "How many have you . . . uh, well . . . you know?"

"Too many," he said in a downtrodden tone. His eyes moved away and focused into a long stare, not looking at anything in particular. "So many, in fact, it's a miracle I can sleep at night."

Bunker's face turned a few shades whiter than before. Even in the flickering light from the fire outside, it was obvious she'd struck a nerve with him.

Daisy touched his hand, feeling compelled to return the favor of support. "But it was war, right? You did what you had to do."

"At first, yes. That's what I kept telling myself. But somewhere along the way, someone changed the rules of engagement when I wasn't looking. All of a sudden, I found myself in the middle of an unacceptable situation—a situation that I helped create. Like you, I wanted to throw up. There were so many bodies. Bodies of innocents. I hated myself for what I'd helped them do. At that moment, I knew I couldn't continue to lie to myself, so I walked away."

"What the hell happened?"

Bunker hesitated, then brought his eyes back to the corpse before resuming his search again, this time with the shooter's back left pocket. "It's a long story," he said in a breathy voice, sounding like he wanted to talk about something else.

"I'm sorry, I didn't mean to pry. It's really none of my business."

"It's okay. I know you're just trying to make sense of all this. But killing never makes sense. It's just something that happens in the line of duty. And as it turns out, it needed to. You just gotta push it aside and move on. Otherwise, if you dwell on it, the ghosts will never stop haunting you. Trust me, you can never let your guard down. Not for a moment. If that kind of guilt ever gains a foothold inside your soul, it will never leave. It'll change you in ways you never imagined. I'm not sure if that makes any sense—"

"—I think I know what you mean," she said, looking down at the man she'd killed. She let Bunker's words sink in and fester for a bit, until they resonated with her logic. "We all have something inside us that we can't stand. You know, that part of us that makes us sick to our stomach when it comes out. The Sheriff calls it our inner demon."

"Exactly. But that same part—the part we can't stand—also keeps us safe in situations like this. It's who we are as humans, whether we like it or not. We all have a primal beast inside. It's part of our DNA and has been since we first crawled out of the oceans and walked upright. The trick is to not let it take over. It's a tool, nothing more. And every tool has its place. When you're done with it, you put it away so it doesn't—"

"—consume you."

"Yes. That's exactly what happened to me. The guilt took over and turned me into something worse, sending me off the deep end. It almost killed me inside and I wouldn't wish that on anyone. Not even my worst enemy."

She nodded but didn't respond. She couldn't find the words.

Bunker continued, "Nobody should ever have to walk the path of shame like I did. And do it twice. Those who do almost never recover. They spiral completely out of control. In the end, you either eat your own bullet or spend the rest of your days in jail. Somehow, I managed to crawl out of it, but the beast is still there, inside me. Fighting to gain control. I'm gonna have to live with it for the rest of my life, and I'd never want that for you. So please, give yourself time. You'll get through it, but you can't dwell on it. You did the right thing here. This man was going to kill both of us, like he did Tuttle. He had to be stopped."

Before she could respond, Bunker ended his hand search. "What's this?" he said while digging around the inside of the man's waistband. His fingers pulled out a pouch that had been hidden inside the pants.

He opened it and pulled out a thin card. It was the size of a cigarette pack and shaped like a playing card, except its corners were dual tapered, giving it eight sides instead of four. Bunker held the item up. Its purple and yellow cartoon characters were frozen in some kind of action scene.

Daisy recognized it. "A Pokemon card?"

"That's a first," he answered, looking like he was about to start laughing. He turned the card over and examined it closely.

"Why would an assassin have a Pokemon card?" she asked, the tone of her voice a few octaves higher.

"He wouldn't. It has to mean something."

"But what?"

"I don't know, but we'll have to figure it out later," Bunker answered before tucking it into his pocket. His fingers went into the pouch again, this time pulling out a pair of thin metal pins.

"Now that's more like it," she said in a steady tone. "A lock pick set."

"This is how he got the jump on Tuttle. He snuck in through the door and then went down the hall to Tuttle's bedroom. How many meth-heads do you know who walk around with a lock pick set?"

"There's no doubt now," she answered, feeling a tiny lump inside the man's hoodie. "Hey, I think I found something. Hand me your knife."

Bunker gave it to her. It only took a few seconds to insert the tip into the black cotton material and cut around the bulge she'd found.

Her fingers pried the material open and dug out something flat and hard. It was about the size of a flake of instant oatmeal and perfectly square. She held it up for Bunker to see. "What the hell is this?"

Bunker took it from her and studied it. After a short pause, he announced, "I think it's a micro tracker."

"As in GPS?"

He nodded, tucking in his lower lip. "I've never seen one this small before."

"Military issue?"

"Probably. But where's the power source?"

She fished around the shooter's hoodie for another item, but didn't find anything. "Could it be powered by his body somehow?"

"Maybe, but microelectronics is really not my thing. Plus, I've been out of the game for a while now. Who knows what they've developed since then?"

"So it's one of ours?"

"Can't tell for sure, but that would be my guess."

The revelation took her by surprise. She ran it through her mind for a bit, then asked, "Why would our military break into Tuttle's place and execute him?"

"That's the million dollar question. And let's not forget, it happened immediately after an EMP blackout and a plane going down."

"What does it all mean?"

"It means we've stumbled onto something big here."

She agreed. "Something we weren't supposed to see."

"What I really need is a magnifying glass," he said in a matter-of-fact way before standing up.

Daisy did as well, then followed Bunker down the hall to Tuttle's room.

The overhead light was on when Bunker sat on the edge of the bed and reached over for a magnifying glass sitting next to a yellow marker. He snatched it, then held it over the micro tracker lying flat in the palm of his hand.

Daisy sat next to him, waiting for the results of the man's investigation.

Ten seconds later, Bunker finally spoke, his voice energized. "I've seen some impressive tactical gear in my days, but this thing is off the charts. The circuitry is absolutely microscopic and I think it even has an onboard battery unit. Plus, there are two antenna wires on the end."

The words *antenna wires* brought a new idea into her brain. "Bunker? I need to ask you something."

"Yeah, shoot."

"If this man was being tracked, who was doing the tracking?"

Bunker stopped his examination immediately. His eyes shot wide and all the color drained from his face. He grabbed her arm. "We gotta get out of here. Right now!"

The two of them ran out of the bedroom and tore down the hallway. After a quick left and a few more strides, they bolted through the front door of Tuttle's home, with Bunker leading the way.

The instant Daisy's feet landed in the dirt outside, she caught a glimpse of at least a dozen silhouettes standing just beyond the old Ford trucks. Before she could redirect her focus, someone with an automatic rifle opened up on their position from the right, strafing the ground in front of their feet.

BOOM, BOOM, BOOM, BOOM.

Bunker stopped and ducked his head. So did Daisy, just as a bank of vehicle lights snapped on, stinging her vision with beams of powerful energy.

"On your knees with your hands up," a commanding male voice said from the darkness.

CHAPTER 39

Dustin Brown rolled out of bed and planted his feet on the chilly wood floor. It took a second for his vision to clear before he remembered where he was—a spare bedroom in a country home belonging to Albert's mom.

He hadn't planned to spend the night at his new friend's house, but Albert talked him into it after they'd acquired the items from the high school's chemistry lab.

The room was maybe ten feet square and sparsely decorated, with a three-drawer vertical dresser directly in front of him. Its top was smothered with loose stacks of faded baseball hats, plus a glass jar sitting next to the edge, half full of coins.

The single bed under his rear end had a thin white sheet, ergonomic pillow, and pastel-colored comforter that smelled dank and musty. The walls, painted an off-white color, were barren except for a three-foot-wide mirror with a flock of fingerprints dotting the bottom.

The strangest item in the room was the lamp next to the bed. It featured a howling dog's head as the base. Dustin wasn't sure if it was homemade, but the intricacy of the carving was impressive. The lampshade, not so much. It was faded yellow, with a fist-sized hole along the back.

The closet to his right was empty and missing a door. The hinges were there, hanging, but the rest of the frame had been orphaned. He counted eleven hangers dangling from the rod across the middle. The metal kind.

The antique hardware on the bedroom door matched the gaudy crown molding encircling the room. So did the amenities in the hall bathroom he'd used the night before. He couldn't remember the last time he'd seen a seashell-shaped sink, or used a toilet with an overhead tank and pull chain.

Right then, a tickle rose up in his nose. He tried to quell it but couldn't. He sneezed, sending the tiny dust particles on the lampshade spewing into the air. They floated through the air in random patterns, swirling around each other like a swarm of bees.

Everywhere he looked, it was more of the same—dust covered everything. It was clear Albert wasn't much of a housekeeper. But Dustin wasn't surprised. His new pal and fellow deputy didn't take very good care of himself, so why should his deceased mother's home be any different?

Dustin stood up and stretched out his back. It creaked and popped, thanks to the mattress he'd slept on. It was beyond uncomfortable, especially the lumpy middle, leaving his rail-thin physique begging for an eight-hour do-over.

When he went to the bedroom door and pulled it open, a slip of white notepaper smacked him in the face. Albert must have taped it to the door while Dustin was sleeping, and done so precisely at eye level.

Dustin took the note and read it. The handwritten message contained a single sentence scribbled in blue ink: *Meet me in the basement when you get up, Amigo.*

He crumpled the note and tossed it into the corner, adding to a pile of empty plastic bottles and torn candy wrappers. The last person to stay in this room must have had a serious fetish for Ensure protein drinks and Almond Joy bars.

Dustin walked past the kitchen and found the door to the basement. He ducked under an overhead beam just inside the threshold, then started down the stairs.

The instant his foot landed on the fourth step a pungent odor punched him in the nose. It smelled of cleaning chemicals, making his eyes water. He covered his face. "Jesus, what the hell is that?"

Albert turned around and gave him an abrupt hand wave, revealing a dual respirator mask and a lab apron lashed around his generous middle.

Dustin couldn't see much of the man's face, but he thought Albert was smiling. The blue cleaning gloves on his hands were a new addition, but the rest of his ensemble was the same as the night before: jeans and an oversized shirt.

A string of foldout banquet tables stood behind Albert, stretching from one side of the basement to the other. They were sprinkled with lab equipment and supplies, looking as though they'd been meticulously placed and arranged, not like the junk scattered throughout the rest of the home.

Dustin wanted to continue down the stairs, but the fumes convinced him otherwise. He went to turn around, but Albert stopped him by pulling the mask off to speak.

"Grab some gloves. We got a lot of cleaning to do," he said, snatching a second gas mask sitting on the table next to him. He tossed it like a saucer, spinning it into Dustin's hands. "Be sure to tighten the straps on the back. Wouldn't want you passing out before we get the lab up and running."

Dustin put the mask on and secured it, then caught a white apron launched his way. He found the front of it, put it on, and tied the straps around the back of his waist.

The spread of items on the tables was impressive: beakers, flasks, two large glass bowls, three stainless steel containers, measuring scale, tube furnace, some kind of filtering apparatus, and an overhead stainless steel hood, much like those installed over a cooking station in a commercial restaurant.

Wait, why does a basement have an exhaust hood?

Dustin thought about it for a moment before the answer came to him: Albert had been planning this for a while, having gone through the time and expense to have it installed.

"Everything must be spotless before we start our cook," Albert said in a muffled voice, sounding like he was trapped in an underground bunker. "I can't wait to show you my secret voodoo. I'm sure you've heard of Clearwater Red, right?"

"Ah, no. Not exactly."

"Trust me, it's legendary. Every tweaker on both coasts is completely hooked on this blend. With me here, instead of in LA, inventory will be running low soon. We need to get busy and ramp up production. It's time to start raking in some fat-stacks while everyone else is busy trying to deal with the power failure."

"So I take it this is your recipe?"

"Yep. Finally found a way to put my chemistry skills to good use. Couldn't see myself working 9 to 5 for some pharmaceutical company, making them rich off of all my hard work. And genius."

* * *

Sheriff Gus Apollo cut across the street and headed toward the outdoor grill in front of the café. The tantalizing aroma of maple-smoked bacon and sizzling eggs locked on to his nose and pulled him forward.

His stomach had been growling all morning and so had his heart, with thoughts of Allison Rainey. She was the chef slinging food on the wood-fired cooktop roughly thirty feet ahead. Even from a distance, he could see her hands working the spatula with precision, reminiscent of a brain surgeon trying to reconnect nerve endings in a dying patient.

Apollo smiled when Allison turned her head and looked up for a moment, catching his gaze. *Perfect timing*, he thought as she smiled at him.

His day was off to a wonderful start. Next up, an impending surge of high cholesterol and an elevated heart rate, one delivered by the food and the other by the chef who was about to prepare it.

Apollo knew it was a deadly combination on multiple levels, but he didn't care. He needed this moment of bliss before the remainder of the day took over—a day destined to be filled with second-guessed decisions and endless challenges.

When he arrived, he noticed four hands tending the grill, not two. Allison's son, Victor, was helping her.

The tall, lanky kid had his hair tied back into a single ponytail, matching his mom's. It was clear the youngster had slung breakfast before, working in near-perfect concert with his mother. Apollo was impressed. The boy wasn't a complete slacker after all.

"Hey Sheriff," Victor said, only glancing up for the briefest of seconds.

Allison brought her eyes to Apollo again, this time with a look that was all business. "How do you want your eggs, Sheriff?"

He'd hoped for a friendly conversation, but he didn't want to press it. She was busy earning a living and so was her son. "Over easy is fine. Plus some of that bacon, if it's ready. It smells amazing."

"My secret recipe. Hope you like it."

"I didn't know you cooked, too," he said, thinking about all the hours he'd spent sitting at the service counter in the restaurant. She'd only ever waited on him, never venturing into the kitchen during the hours he'd spent on his favorite stool.

"Our regular cook never showed up for his shift. I guess Craig thinks people don't have to eat now that the power is out," she said before grabbing another log from the stack behind her. She put it into the firebox under the cooktop. "Luckily, Billy Jack had this old grill in the basement. Not sure what we'd do without it."

"Sometimes being a packrat has its advantages. I know I've got my share of junk. Haven't been able to pull my truck into the garage for a couple years now."

"It happens to the best of us," she said, handing him a plate with three eggs and four slices of bacon. "Sorry we don't have toast."

"This is more than plenty. Thank you," he said, holding his tongue from releasing the rest of the words in his mind. He wanted to ask her out, but with Victor standing next to her, now wasn't the time.

Hell, it never seemed to be the right time. Something always seemed to rise up and block him. Sure, some of it was because he was a gutless old man. But perhaps it was more. Perhaps the universe was trying to tell him something—or stop him from making a complete ass out of himself.

If she said no, or took offense to his unsolicited advances, then the rest of the town would soon know about it. Small communities are famous for their fast-moving rumor mills, and Clearwater was no exception. As Sheriff, he certainly didn't need to make himself the target of gossip or innuendo. Not with his reputation already paper thin at best. But regardless, his heart wanted what it wanted and he couldn't stop it.

Apollo decided to try another approach. If he chose his words carefully, maybe he could discover a better time to stop by and pop the question. "You working a full shift today?"

"Till ten, when the owner takes over. Unless, of course, Craig decides to show up and do his job."

Apollo smirked, wanting to say something clever. "If he still has one after this."

"Yeah, with my luck, I'll be stuck here all day, every day. At least until hell freezes over."

His heart sank when he heard those words. Crap, she might never be alone. Or have any free time to relax and enjoy a night out. She was clearly stressed out, and Apollo couldn't blame her.

Time to move on, he decided, wondering about payment for the meal. There was no cash drawer nearby. "What do I owe you for this?"

"It's on the house today, Sheriff."

"No, that's really not necessary."

"Yes, it is. I insist. It's the least I can do after what happened in the market yesterday."

"I appreciate that, but department rules explicitly forbid accepting gifts of any kind."

"Even food?"

"Yes. Any gift, including food. Just need to know the total and I'll grab it from my wallet."

She hesitated, beaming her big, beautiful eyes at him. "Fine. A buck, then. That'll cover it."

"Seems a bit low."

She smiled, her face perking up. "For the next minute, we're having a very special law enforcement-only sale. Three eggs and bacon for a dollar. Best deal in town."

He looked around, but didn't see anyone else in the area. At least not anyone in uniform who appeared to be headed his way for breakfast. "One minute, huh?"

She put her hands on her hips and rocked her head from side to side when she spoke. "Fifty seconds, now. Oh, and by the way, we're not accepting tips during this one-minute special, either."

"But Mom, we need the money," Victor said, interrupting the conversation.

Allison shushed him.

Apollo felt a thin smile grow on his lips, appreciating her quick wit and her generosity. "All right, a buck. I'll be right back," he said before walking to the nearest table.

He put the plate down and checked the bills in his wallet: four ones, two fives, a ten, and a twenty. He pulled the twenty and folded it over in his hand, then wrapped it inside a single before returning to her.

Alison put a mason jar on the stainless-steel shelf above the grill and pointed to it. It was at eye level for her.

Apollo tucked the pair of bills inside the glass container and went back to his table. As long as she didn't check the deposit he'd just made, she'd only think there was a buck inside. He needed to eat quickly and leave before she noticed the twenty. Then she couldn't give it back.

He sat down and tore into his food. The eggs were perfectly cooked, with a thin white film over the yolks, and so was the bacon—crisp, lean, and delicious. There was something uplifting about the perfect breakfast. It truly sets the day. Especially when it was prepared by a stunning middle-aged woman who'd captured his heart.

Then again, his stomach *was* on empty and if she'd served an old miner's boot smothered in honey, it would have tasted like heaven. So who was he kidding?

When the last scoop of eggs entered his mouth, a pair of legs came in from the right and parked in front of him. They were covered in blue slacks. Pressed and expensive.

Apollo looked up, choking down the mouthful of food.

"Well, I finally tracked you down," Mayor Seth Buckley said, his face flushed.

"Sorry, needed to eat," Apollo said, wiping his chin with a napkin. His eyes found their way past the Mayor, landing on Allison. He hadn't planned for his focus to wander, but it did. When he brought his attention back to his boss, a sharp comment landed on his ears.

"Something tells me hunger isn't the only reason I found you here. Hunger for food, that is," Buckley said with attitude. "She's beautiful, I'll give you that. But don't you think Allison is a little out of your league?"

"Yeah, probably. But the heart wants what it wants."

"The heart, maybe. But you and I both know that Little Willie is doing all the thinking right now."

The Mayor was spot-on. Apollo couldn't deny it. But his heart was also involved. "True. It *has* been a while."

"For you and me both."

"Are you hungry, Mayor? I'm buying."

"Nah, I'm good."

"Are you sure? A man's got to eat."

"I had a protein bar earlier. Found it in the back of my pantry. It was a little stale, but it'll hold me for a while. Besides, we've got work to do."

"The reconnaissance teams?"

Buckley nodded. "Need to get them in the field ASAP. I need to know what's going on out there. Did Daisy and Bunker acquire the communications gear from Tuttle?"

Apollo shrugged. "Haven't seen them."

"Seriously?"

"Probably still sleeping. I'm guessing it was a long night."

"Then we need to wake them up. Now."

"I'll get right on it, sir. Daisy's trailer isn't far."

"Any idea where Bunker's staying? I want to have a little chat with him. Seems prudent to get to know him a little better. I'm not sure why, but my gut is telling me there's more there than meets the eye. I can't put my finger on it, but something's off."

"You mean like those bandages on his neck?"

"Well, that too."

"He might be staying at Franklin's place."

"Are you sure about that? I thought when he first rolled into town, several parents offered him a place to stay."

"They did."

"Then he could be anywhere at this point."

"True, but I'd still suggest starting at Franklin's. I found a handwritten note in my office this morning from Stephanie King. It was addressed to Bunker and included directions to the horse stables. So I'm betting that's where Bunker is. With Stephanie and her son."

Buckley's eyebrows tightened and so did his chin. "Bill King's not going to like that one bit. Even though they're divorced, we both know he's gonna take exception."

"Not sure I blame him. A stranger in town, and he's hanging around King's only son."

"And his ex-wife, too. You'll need to keep an eye on that situation."

"I will. Anything else, sir?"

"That's it for now. Let's have everyone meet in my office in ninety minutes. We've got a lot of work to do and little time to do it."

CHAPTER 40

Stephanie King stood up in the dark when she heard the distinctive sound of keys jingling beyond the door. Someone was in the hallway and headed her way. She fumbled around like a blind woman and found Jeffrey and Megan on her left. She moved in front of them.

"Are we going home now, Mommy?" Jeffrey asked, his voice trembling.

"Not yet, honey," she answered in a whisper. "But soon. Right now, I need you to be really quiet."

"I miss my Daddy," Megan sobbed in her little girl's voice, tearing a hole in Stephanie's heart.

"I know, sweetheart. I'm sure he misses you, too. I promise, as soon as I can get us out of here, I will. But no matter what happens, I need you to be really brave and not say a word. Can you do that?"

"I think so. But I'm really scared. I don't like the dark."

"Neither do I, baby. Just stay close. I'll protect you," she said, keeping an eye on the thin strip of light leaking in from under the door.

Just then, two sets of shadows appeared from the right, blocking out some of the light creeping in from the hallway. One pair moved slowly. The other jumped around sporadically.

A couple of grunts came next, then the sound of a key sliding into the door lock.

Right on cue, the kids' four tiny arms locked onto the backs of her legs and squeezed tight as the door opened. Stephanie blinked rapidly when the intense light from the hallway overwhelmed her vision.

An imposing shadow appeared in the doorway, almost filling the entrance from floor to ceiling. She'd seen this same silhouette earlier, when they were first tossed into the mysterious room.

The man stood there like a statue. He may have been the same person who kidnapped her in front of Franklin's horse stables. But she couldn't be sure. She never saw his face. He'd snuck up from behind and held her and the kids at gunpoint, then quickly gagged them and put black hoods over their heads.

She knew they were still in Colorado. Somewhere. It only took roughly twenty minutes to get here. Plus, the crunching sound of dirt under the tires never stopped. Neither did the fragrance of the mountain terrain.

The trip included four turns: three rights and a left, plus they'd traveled over a cattle guard somewhere in the middle. She remembered feeling the rumble of the metal grate immediately after she heard the sound of running water on the right. A river, perhaps. However, they never crossed a bridge, so the waterway was alongside the road, not under it.

The kidnapper in the doorway finally moved, putting his left arm out and yanking something into view. It was another person—small in stature, hands tied behind their back. A woman, by the body type, with long hair hanging from the hood covering her face.

The man spun the woman around and used a knife to release her hands, then pulled the hood off. He shoved her into the room. The woman flew forward, tumbling onto her back with her hair covering her face.

Before the guard slammed the door shut, Stephanie caught a glimpse of the new arrival's all-black outfit, but the rest was a blur. Her eyes hadn't fully adjusted to the intense light beaming in through the doorway.

"Are you okay?" Stephanie asked the woman.

A grunt answered, not a voice.

"Did the bad men hurt you?" Jeffrey asked the woman in a trembling tone.

"Shhhh, Jeffrey. Let Mommy handle this."

"Stephanie? Is that you?" the new prisoner asked, her tone weak and slow.

Stephanie recognized the voice, and by extension the all-black outfit. It was a uniform—a deputy sheriff's uniform—a uniform belonging to Daisy Clark. Her nemesis. The woman who'd ruined her marriage.

Stephanie couldn't believe it. How was it possible? She got kidnapped in the middle of nowhere and then ended up in some scary room with the one woman on the planet she hated the most? The situation was already bad enough, and now this?

"I know you're there, Steph. It's me, Daisy."

"Yeah, I know who you are. But just because we're stuck in this hole together doesn't mean I want to talk to you. So just shut up, already."

"Deputy Daisy?" Megan asked. "It's me, Megan."

"Megan? They took you, too?"

"Uh-huh. Is my daddy with you?"

"No, honey. He's not. I haven't seen him since last night. How did you get here?"

Stephanie decided to take over the conversation since Daisy wasn't going to keep quiet like she was told. "The three of us were taken in front of Franklin's place. He was inside the store when someone came up behind us."

"So I take it Franklin's not here with you?"

"No, it's just me, my son, and Megan. Franklin went to check out an apparent break-in."

"I'm sorry you're in the middle of this. All of you."

"What's going on? Who is this man?"

"I don't know. But there's more than one of them. Bunker and I were ambushed at Frank Tuttle's place."

"Bunker? Where is he? Is he okay?"

"I hope so, but I haven't seen him since they took us hostage."

"Let me guess, hoods and handcuffs?"

"Unfortunately, yes. Then they split us up into different vehicles."

Stephanie wanted to ask more questions about Bunker, but couldn't find the words.

"They have vehicles that work?" Jeffrey asked, breaking his mandated silence.

"Apparently. But I'm not sure how," Daisy answered.

"What do they want with us?" Stephanie asked, hoping the slut of a law enforcement officer would know something other than how to sleaze her way into her ex-husband's arms.

"Ransom, I'm guessing. Your husband is rich, right?"

Stephanie couldn't believe the nerve of this woman, bringing up her cheating husband at a time like this. "Well, Daisy, you know he is. So don't play dumb with me. I'm sure that's one of the main reasons you did what you did. Oh, and by the way, it's ex-husband now. So you can have him all to yourself. I'm done with him, forever."

There was a short pause before Daisy responded, "I'm pretty sure I told you before that I ended it right after it started. I'm sorry for what happened, Stephanie. I truly am. I never meant to hurt you."

"Well, you did. And my son, too."

"I know. It was wrong and I feel just awful about it. But I never planned for it to happen. It just did. Can you ever forgive me?"

"No. Not a chance. You need to burn in hell for what you did."

Daisy's voice turned soft. "It was a mistake and I'm sorry. I wish you could forgive me. We used to be such good friends. I just want things to be the way they used to be."

Stephanie snorted an angry huff. "Things will never be the same because of you. Never. You can't go back and undo what's been done."

"I know. It kills me inside. I'm so sorry."

"I'm just glad it's dark in here, so I don't have to look at your face."

CHAPTER 41

A thunderous punch landed on Bunker's gut, making him gasp for air. Then another came, striking his cheek and snapping his head to the right. If his hands weren't bound to the metal frame above his head, he would've returned the beating tenfold.

So far, he'd taken everything the masked men had thrown at him, literally, and hadn't said a word. Only the occasional grunt as their grilling intensified.

He was defiant. Steadfast. Unwilling to crack. All the while, studying the trio between the waves of pain. He couldn't see their faces—only their determined eyes behind the masks.

But that didn't stop him from sensing their frustration or overhearing their comments to each other. Most of them came after they stripped him of his clothes and removed the bandages on his neck. It seemed the blowtorch scars had them more intrigued than the artwork across his body.

Somehow his presence in Clearwater had upset their plans, whatever they might be. And for some reason, they couldn't proceed without discovering his identity first. He knew they were desperate, making him laugh inside.

He hadn't seen Daisy since the two of them were ambushed in front of Tuttle's place, then separated. Probably to keep them from communicating during transport. Perhaps they assumed he and Daisy were a couple, or that Bunker was a law enforcement officer, like her. Her uniform was a dead giveaway and so, too, were the location and timing of where they'd been detained.

He worried Daisy was in another one-window shack and naked like him, being questioned with the same vigor and tenacity. If he was right, then she'd crack soon. She didn't have his years of training—or life experience—leaving her at the mercy of her own pain receptors.

Daisy didn't know much about Bunker's past, and that was a good thing. For him. Not her. Unfortunately, her suffering would continue until one of two things happened: she took her last breath, or they got answers. Satisfactory answers. Answers she didn't know and couldn't give them.

Even though he hated the idea of her being tortured, she knew the risks when she signed up for duty. The same was true for anyone who wore a uniform to work. Whether it be law enforcement or military, they put their lives on the line every day. Still, it didn't make the situation any easier.

So far, these men had kept their interrogation at level one: physical beating. They weren't amateurs by any stretch, picking their impact points with precision to inflict the most agony.

Yet they were running the detainment scenario by the numbers. So far, at least. What they didn't know was that Bunker would never cooperate, no matter what they did to him. He'd been training for this moment all his life, and now it was time for the ultimate test. If it came down to his will against theirs, they were going to lose.

When you don't care what happens to you and you have nothing to live for, it gives you an advantage. An endless advantage. Granted, death would most likely come for him today, but he didn't care. Death was a victory of sorts. His salvation.

Before his next breath, another thump landed on his side, sending a pressure wave through his ribcage to the other side.

When he closed his eyes to suck in the pain, his old man's favorite saying roared in his thoughts: *Born to Fight*. To some, those words might not make sense in a situation like this. But to Bunker, they did, cradling him in reassurance.

Just then, more of his father's incessant preachings came to his thoughts. They played in a rhythmic chant, finding a familiar cadence that cradled his soul.

Pain is your friend.

So is fear.

Both of them keep you alive.

Both of them keep you strong.

A true warrior tests himself.

A true warrior punishes himself.

Because until he knows pain, he doesn't know himself.

Bunker wasn't sure how long he'd been tied to the vertical bedspring attached to the wall of the old miner's shack. More than an hour. Less than a day. Long enough for his captors to do a number on his head and midsection.

Every impact point was sore and bruised, plus the streaks of blood across his body seemed to be growing with each round of strikes. Most of the gashes were on his cheeks, chin, and forehead.

"I can keep this up all day," the man in the middle said in perfect English, readying his cloth-wrapped fist for another round of rights.

The punishers spoke without a hint of an accent, leaving Bunker to guess about who these men were and where they were from. Accents and dialects are important when sizing up an opponent. Accents can reveal an adversary's motivation, or at least their tendencies, since different locales carry their own ideology. Accents give a diligent student an advantage if he's paying attention. And Bunker was, to every word and every movement.

Thus far, the interrogator had kept the one-sided conversation to a minimum, only asking three questions.

"Who are you?"

"What are you doing in Clearwater?"

"Who do you work for?"

The other two men in the room hadn't said much. Must be observers, Bunker figured as another punch found its mark. He steeled the left side of his abdomen, welcoming the pain as it penetrated like a sword.

When the man pulled his hand back in advance of another strike, Bunker locked eyes with him and held his stare. He didn't blink until the blow landed on his cheekbone. The force tore open his skin, sending blood down to his neck.

Bunker wondered if anyone in the room could sense that he was enjoying the hurt. The more they dished it out, the more it bolstered his defiance to tell them nothing.

Little did they know, his extensive military and street training had kicked in shortly after first blood was drawn. He was now deep within his own mind where the pain morphed into something else, something powerful and spiritual—almost transcendent in nature—allowing him to retain control over his fear.

He knew his ability to take the punishment was going to test everyone in the room. Probably more than any prisoner they'd questioned before. Soon, they'd have no choice but to change tactics, once they realized their blows were useless.

The next evolution would no doubt involve the metal framework digging into his back. Ever since they'd removed his clothing, the coiled bed springs had been probing his skin for weakness.

There was only one reason to remove his shoes and socks, then strip him naked: to maximize skin contact before the water buckets were introduced to his feet with the help of high voltage. All of it was designed to enhance the anxiety level—standard procedure during interrogation.

Bunker took a count of the car batteries beyond the buckets: six. Overkill, he figured, but effective.

Two breaths later, the man hitting him said, "Last chance, asshole. You won't like what's coming next."

Bunker gave him a bloody smile, sending a message that he didn't care. If they were going to electrocute him, he welcomed it. It seemed fitting, given his past and all the horrible things he'd done.

"Take a break," the observer on the left said. His volume was low, but not too low, almost as though he wanted Bunker to hear what he was going to say next, accidental like. "Let his pain settle in and do a little convincing for us. When the chief gets here, he's gonna want answers. Especially about all those tattoos. This man better be ready to talk."

"If he's not?"

"Then so be it. We'll get something out of the women. Or the kids."

Bunker's attention locked onto the words he'd just heard.

Women.

Kids.

Plural forms of each term.

He and Daisy weren't the only prisoners.

There were more.

The revelation made his chest tighten, like someone had just parked a school bus on it.

CHAPTER 42

Albert Mortenson gave Dustin Brown the first of three stainless steel trays. The container looked like an oversized baking sheet without the grease. Or the cookies.

"Hold this under the feeder tip and move it around. That way we'll get an even layer across the tray," Albert said, keeping a close eye on the process.

"Like this?" Dustin asked, sliding the tray to the left, then the right, letting the red, gelatinous substance land on the surface and smooth out. It oozed from the tip like a batch of freshly made hot fudge being poured onto a sundae.

"Yeah, that's about right. Just a little slower. Let it collect a little before you move it again. It'll make the next step a lot easier if we end up with a smooth, even layer."

"Reminds me of the taffy my mom used to make. Only this stuff is red instead of purple."

Albert laughed, thinking of a similar time when he and his mom were baking pies in the kitchen upstairs, directly over this spot in the basement. "But this candy is much sweeter, if you know what I mean. And pure. Ninety-seven percent pure, to be exact."

"Both will rot your teeth, too," Dustin added in an upbeat tone, following through with the analogy.

Albert chuckled, feeling their kinship deepen. "But instead of costing you money, this treat will fill your pockets with the kind of cash you've only ever dreamed about. The kind of cash that will buy you anything you could ever want."

"And anyone we could ever want, right?" Dustin asked, continuing to work the tray under the feeder.

"Oh yeah. Even that drop-dead gorgeous deputy you like," Albert said, smiling at his new friend from inside the hood of the hazmat suit.

"Actually, Daisy's your favorite. Not mine."

Albert couldn't deny it. "Ya got me there. I won't lie. I figure a couple grand should do it. Chump change once we start delivery."

"Really? Just throw money at her and she'll drop her panties?"

"Trust me, every chick has her price. Even a deputy. You should've seen the smoking hot little spinner I had in LA. Every inch of her was perfect. And I mean perfect. She was this golden-skinned goddess from Panama and super religious when I first met her. But she caved on all her beliefs once I showed her the cash. Lots of it."

"A spinner, huh?"

"Yep. And let me tell you, Latin chicks are amazing. And fierce."

"I do like them a little smaller."

Albert knew he had Dustin hooked. All he needed to do was continue to tap into the man's primal desire. If he did that, his new pal would follow along like a lost puppy.

"Then that settles it, dog. We'll get you two of 'em with the help of my contacts south of the border. That way you have some variety. But first, we continue production until we have the inventory needed to satisfy my distribution network down in LA."

"How are we going to get it there? It's not like we can just send it UPS. Or drive it there ourselves. Nothing works anymore."

"I got a couple of ideas about that. But let's focus on one thing at a time."

"Wouldn't it be easier if we just sold it locally? We're already here and so is the supply."

"Nah, too risky. We'd have to expose ourselves. And our operation. Never a good idea. Sort of like the old saying, never shit where you eat."

"But I thought the deputy badges were going to help with all that?"

"Not on a street level. First, we have to raise some serious cash, and the best way to do that is out of town, where the network's already set up. Once we have the funds in pocket, we'll import the slingers we need for this neck of the woods."

"Makes sense."

"When you first open a new area, you never recruit locally. Not when you don't know the players. Especially in a small town like Clearwater. One mistake and everyone knows. I've found it's best if the initial pushers are from out of town. That way, the LEOs think the supply is from out of town, too, and they don't start a hard target search. The last thing we want is for the Sheriff's Department or the State Troopers to start sniffing around. Can you imagine what would happen right now if they stopped by unannounced?"

"LEOs?"

"Law enforcement officers."

"Like us."

"Exactly. Only trained and dedicated. Not easy to bribe."

Dustin finished covering the last section of the tray with Clearwater Red. "Okay, that's one. I'm ready for another."

Albert gave him the second tray. "After this, we let it sit. Once the blend is solid, we'll smash the ice into pieces and weigh it. I figure this batch should come in around twenty-five pounds, give or take. Depending on how well we followed my recipe."

* * *

Rusty Buckley parked his racing bike in front of the town hall and lashed it to a lamppost with a self-coiling heavy duty cable chain hanging from the top tube of the frame. He set the tumblers on the lock to a random combination, then took the water bottle from the holder attached to the down tube. It only took a few seconds to swallow a long, refreshing swig, replenishing his fluids.

The past twenty-four hours had been a whirlwind of assignments, keeping him on the padded seat of his lightweight carbon fiber ride. So far, the new Tommaso performance machine had lived up to the hype, giving him confidence he'd made the best choice, given his modest budget.

He wished he could have purchased the top-selling model, but couldn't afford it. The Mayor had offered to help him upgrade, but he turned his grandfather down, wanting to pay his own way. The last thing he needed was rumors flying around that the Mayor stepped in and spoiled him. Never a good idea when you're living in a small town where everyone knows you're the grandson of the most powerful politician.

The intense burn in his thighs tugged at his attention as he walked to the entrance. The muscle strain felt invigorating after the two-mile sprint.

Ever since the blackout, he'd fallen behind on his Olympic training schedule. He decided to make it up by pushing himself whenever he was out on the Sheriff's field assignments. Anytime he approached an uphill grade, he downshifted and began a full-on sprint, much like he'd have to do if he made the U.S. cycling team.

Rusty put two fingers to his neck to check his heart rate, wondering what time it was. His Fitbit Superwatch wasn't working, but he knew he was late for his report. More than a half hour late, he guessed. But it couldn't be helped. Not after what he'd discovered on the latest reconnaissance mission.

His mind churned through the new information, trying to figure out the best way to tell his grandfather what he'd learned. The door to the Mayor's office was only three minutes away, so he needed to hurry. Then again, if he took the stairs one step at a time instead of two, he could delay his arrival time.

When he reached for the handle on the entrance door, a man's voice called out from behind. "Hey Rusty. Great timing!"

He turned, seeing Sheriff Apollo and his familiar smile. Rusty held the door open. "Hey Sheriff."

The chief lawman entered first, turning sideways as he brushed past Rusty's outstretched arm.

"You headed up to see your grandfather?" Apollo asked.

"Yes sir."

"So am I. If you don't mind, we should walk together and catch up a bit."

"Fine by me."

"How's that new bike holding up?"

"Awesome. Worth every penny," Rusty answered, walking next to Apollo as they crossed the foyer.

"I'm sure it is. There's a deep sense of pride when you work hard and save up for something you really want. I'm proud of you, son. We need more young people like you these days. I fear the new generation doesn't appreciate the value of a dollar."

"Yeah, I got a couple of friends like that. It's kinda sad, really. I think it totally affects their motivation. Some of them should be much better racers, but they just don't work hard enough."

"Well, your grandfather and I know how much time and effort you put into your training. Which is why it goes without saying that we appreciate you taking a break from it to assist us. Did you get a chance to talk to your training partners? Are they available to help?"

"So far, they've all blown me off. I tried to convince them it was the right thing to do, but they gave me some lame excuse, like having stuff to do around the house. I think it's really their girlfriends making them stay home with the power out."

"Hey, at least you tried. I know your grandfather is proud of you for stepping up like this."

"Just wish he'd say it once in a while. Sometimes, I feel like I'm invisible when I'm around him."

"Don't sweat it, Rusty. He's a very busy man these days. Trust me, the Mayor talks about you all the time."

"Thanks, Sheriff," Rusty said, following Apollo into the stairwell.

The friendly conversation continued until the two men hit the third floor, where they turned and headed down the hall. The door at the end of the corridor was their destination.

For some reason, the hallway seemed a lot shorter than Rusty remembered. And the Mayor's door looked twice as imposing, like a sentinel for the damned.

When a stab of pain hit Rusty's chest, he realized he'd been too busy chatting with the Sheriff about his Olympic dreams to finish arranging the words in his head for his field report.

Now that the Sheriff was tagging along, it was even more important he didn't sound like a complete idiot and embarrass his grandfather.

CHAPTER 43

Mayor Buckley leaned back in his leather office chair, fighting the urge to swear at Bill King, who was standing across his desk. The wealthy business owner was always a handful, but today's encounter had pushed the aggravation level to an all-time high.

Buckley needed to find his calm and take the high road, not letting the slender man goad him into overreacting. "I get what you're saying, Bill, but you really need to take it up with the Sheriff."

King gasped, shaking his head. His tone turned harsh. "I can't talk to that man. He always seems to go out of his way to blow me off. I think he gets off on it. Why you picked him as the new sheriff is beyond me."

"I thought Apollo assigned a couple of deputies to help you out yesterday. Something about rescuing trapped miners."

King hesitated before he spoke again, his lips thin. "He did."

"Well then, I don't know about you, but that doesn't sound like he's blowing you off to me."

King's eyes rolled, then he shook his head. "That was official business. Lives were at stake, so he *had* to respond. He didn't have a choice."

"Exactly. It was *official* business. Which is why the issues with your wife need to be handled by the courts. Or child services. Not me."

"Ex-wife."

"Yes, ex-wife. My apologies. But I say again, family matters are not in my purview."

"I get that, Mayor. But it still doesn't change the fact that I need to know where she is. She's completely unstable and she has my son."

"Being a father myself, I'm sympathetic to your situation. Now, with that said, you have to realize that the entire town is facing a major crisis, so we've got bigger issues to deal with at the moment."

"What could be more important than the wellbeing of my little boy?"

"That's not what I meant, Bill."

"Okay, then. Explain it to me."

"I meant we've got the wellbeing of the entire town to consider, not just you, and not just your son. With the power still out and equipment down across town, we're sitting on a powder keg that's ready to erupt at any moment. And I can't let that happen."

"But I pay more in taxes than anyone else."

"That may be true, but—"

"No, it is true. Nobody else even comes close. You know as well as I do how many people my family's business employs. If it weren't for the Silver King Mine and all the revenue it generates, this town would have dried up and blown away a long time ago. I don't think it's unreasonable to expect a little extra consideration now and then from the Mayor and his new errand boy. Certainly, you can bend the rules a bit here, Seth, especially since my son's life might be at stake."

Buckley sighed, realizing this conversation was never going to end. King wouldn't back off until he got what he wanted. Buckley needed to defuse the situation.

Before he could blink again, a new idea entered his mind—one he should've thought of when the conversation first started. "Look, it just so happens that I sent someone out to the Trail Dust Riding Stables earlier on another matter. We needed to—"

"What does Atwater's business have to do with this?" King said, interrupting.

"What I was trying to say was that's where I think Stephanie and your son stayed last night."

"At Franklin's place?"

"Yes."

"How do you know that, exactly?"

"Your ex-wife left a note in the Sheriff's office. With directions."

King threw up his hands, looking even more pissed than before. "Damn it. I knew it. The note was for that new guy, Bunker. Am I right?"

"Yes, as a matter of fact. But I'm sure it's not what you think."

"Trust me. It is. You don't know her like I do. The minute I questioned her involvement with that lowlife, it sent her flying into his arms. She'll do anything to aggravate me."

Before the Mayor could respond, a quick knock came at his office door, then it flung open. In walked Sheriff Apollo and Rusty.

A flood of relief washed over the Mayor's bones. Prefect timing. He stood up to greet the new arrivals. "Gentleman, we were just talking about you."

"Did you find my wife and son?" King snapped at Apollo.

The Sheriff stopped walking, looking a little confused. So did Rusty, leading Buckley to hold up his hands at both of them. He needed to keep them quiet until he could subtly read them into the confrontation brewing in his office. He didn't want them exacerbating the situation.

Buckley cleared his throat. "Mr. King and I were just discussing a matter involving his ex-wife and son. I told him we think they might have stayed at Franklin Atwater's place last night."

The Sheriff nodded, his eyes indicating he understood Buckley's delicate lead-in.

His grandson, though, still looked lost so he continued. "Rusty, I'd like you to meet Bill King. Owner of the Silver King Mine."

"Nice to meet you," Rusty said, putting out his hand for a shake.

Bill King didn't respond. Nor did he move.

Buckley kept his eyes on Rusty. "I just told Mr. King that you took a ride out to the stables to check on a few things for me. Isn't that correct?"

"Yes, sir. I did."

"Well? Were they there? My wife and son?" King asked, his tone charged with hostility.

Rusty looked at the Mayor with a blank expression on his face.

"Come on, kid. Spit it out already. We don't have all day," King added.

Buckley sensed Rusty's reluctance and knew the kid was looking for guidance. "Go ahead, Rusty. Tell us what you found out. Just give it to us straight. Don't hold back a single detail."

"Well, sir, when I arrived, I found the store's front door just hanging open. I went inside, but the place was empty. Of people, I mean. I waited around for a bit, but nobody showed. So I checked in the back to see if Mr. Atwater was in his office. You know, working at his desk or something. But he wasn't. It looked—"

"Is that all you have?" King asked, not letting Rusty finish his report.

"Please, Bill. Let him finish," Buckley said.

Rusty cleared his throat, his tone unsure. "It looked like someone had completely trashed his office. Stuff was everywhere. Like they were looking for something. Plus, I saw some of the horses running loose outside."

"Loose?" Apollo asked, finally joining the discussion. "That doesn't sound like Franklin to me. He's a stickler for order and proficiency, ever since his days in the Army."

Rusty nodded. "Something must've happened. Something bad, I think. I even checked the main house, but there was no sign of anyone. It's like everyone just disappeared."

The Sheriff ran his hands across the back of his neck. "I thought for sure that's where everyone was. What the hell is going on?"

Buckley stepped out from behind his desk and put a hand on Apollo's shoulder. "So I take it Daisy wasn't at her trailer?"

"No sir. After my knocks went unanswered, I used her spare key to go inside. I found her bed made, and there were no dishes in the sink. When I checked the coffee maker, it was ice cold and spotless."

"Coffee maker?" Buckley asked, not understanding the relevance.

"Daisy told me she always downs a full pot first thing. It's the only way she can get moving in the morning."

"Maybe she cleaned up; did you ever think of that?" King said, his words frothing with contempt.

"Yes, of course. But that wasn't all I found. There was no coffee filter in the trash and the gas heater's thermostat was turned way down. Plus, her cat Vonda wouldn't stop meowing until I fed her."

"Wait a minute," King snarled. "The power's out. That would've have worked anyway."

"Normally I'd agree but she has an old Onan generator she inherited from her father after he passed. It's from the early 60's and looks like an old tractor, but it still works. No electronics, either. She has a lot of trouble with the grid out there in the winter, so I know she keeps that beast fueled and ready."

"Onan, huh?" King said in a less contentious tone, his eyes tight. "Do you happen to know what model?"

"No, not off the top of my head," Apollo said, pausing before he spoke again. "So, after careful consideration and review of the facts, I came to the only conclusion that made sense. Especially after I found the cat's water bowl empty. Daisy never made it back last night with Bunker."

"Bunker? Seriously?" King asked, resuming his nasty mood.

"Yes," Buckley answered. "We sent the two of them to Tuttle's place last night."

King flailed his arms. "Jesus, Buckley! How much more do you need to hear? We've obviously got a situation here and it is clearly *official business*. Something that both the Sheriff's Department and the Mayor's Office need to address. I'll bet my last dollar Bunker is at the center of all of it."

CHAPTER 44

Bunker snapped awake when someone threw cold water on his face. It took a second to remember where he was. When he did, he realized he must have passed out after the last round of electrocution.

He glanced around the room, but little had changed. He was still naked and bound vertically to the metal bed frame, with his feet soaking in water buckets. The car batteries were two feet away, wired together with electrical cables that ended with a pair of wide-mouth clamps attached to the frame.

There was no way to know how long he'd been out, but the pools of blood on the floor were more distinct than before. The electrical burns across his back and legs were intense, but he fought back the urge to wince or show any sign of discomfort. He didn't want to give these men the satisfaction.

"Status report?" The words came from a short man entering the room through the only door.

"So far, he hasn't said anything. Not a word," answered the man who'd been serving up the torture.

"Sounds like we have ourselves a hero," the new arrival said.

Bunker studied the man who'd just called him a hero. His neatly-trimmed hair was combed from left to right and peppered with even amounts of gray and black along the sides. His wide nose looked pushed in at the top, like a bulldog, and his eyes were set close together, black as coal.

The man's thin lips and narrow shoulders matched the rest of his slender profile, but his most noticeable feature was the pitted scars across his cheeks. They were heavy and deep, much like the collection of wrinkles around his hawk-like eyes.

Bunker could sense the respect the man carried, leading him to believe he was the commander of this group. His black slacks and long-sleeved shirt were pressed and his dress shoes shined, looking as though he'd just come from Casual Friday at some lawyer's office.

"Bring in one of the females. He'll talk," the commander said.

"Which one?" the torturer asked.

"Doesn't matter. Just make it quick."

"Yes, sir," the torturer answered, leaving the room in a hurry.

The commander turned to one of the other men standing nearby, then pointed at Bunker with authority. "Untie him. I want him on his knees for this. Make sure he's secure."

The man farthest to the right stepped forward and began to untie Bunker, while the remaining two guards aimed their rifles at him.

Once Bunker was free, his vision blurred for a moment before his legs gave out. He landed on his kneecaps with a heavy thud. He ignored the discomfort, turning his thoughts to the other hostages—women and children. They needed him, but he decided not to fight back. Not yet. His strength was only just beginning to recover. If he was lucky, he'd get one crack at these men, and this wasn't it.

"Looks like Marco did his job well," the commander said. "Nobody tenderizes meat like he does."

Someone pulled Bunker's hands together behind his back, then secured them with rope around his wrists.

The commander grabbed the back of Bunker's head and yanked, breathing heavy and close. "I can see you take great pride in keeping yourself in shape. And in your artwork. Impressive. But none of that will help you now. I'd strongly suggest you tell me what I want to know before my patience runs out."

Bunker didn't answer, keeping his eyes on the commander's as his chest swelled with adrenaline. Whether the rush was out of anger or pain, he couldn't tell; both were thick inside. Either way, he could feel his strength building with each passing second.

The commander twisted Bunker's hair in his hands, turning Bunker's neck to study the blowtorch scars. When he was done, he yanked on the back of Bunker's hair, nearly ripping the strands out by their roots. "Who are you?"

The pain sent Bunker's breath out of control, making him clench his teeth as air and spittle shot out in rapid bursts. He wanted to kill this man. Yet he said nothing.

"You are one stubborn son of a bitch, I'll give you that. It's obvious you've had extensive training in counter-interrogation, but you'll break. Guys like you always do. Just need to find the proper motivation."

Right then, the door swung open. In came Daisy, still in her uniform and with her hands behind her back. The torturer, Marco, had a grip on her, keeping her under control.

She'd been gagged and blindfolded, her shirt ripped along one of the shoulder seams. Plus, her hair was a confused mess, with clumps hanging about her face and neck, making it appear she'd put up a good fight. Or just gotten out of bed.

"Looks like motivation just arrived," the commander said. He let go of Bunker, shoving his head to the side before turning his wrath to Daisy.

"On your knees," the commander told her.

She didn't move, yelling something into the gag. The words were muffled, but her defiance was clear.

The commander spun to the side with his arm drawn back, then unleashed his fist, landing a sharp blow to her gut.

Daisy gasped, doubling over from the force. She dropped to her knees, her chest heaving to gather oxygen.

Bunker's heart screamed at him to do something, but his logic killed the idea. They'd shoot her if he made his move at the wrong time. Patience was needed.

The commander grabbed Daisy by the hair and snapped her head back to expose her face. "Do not defy me again, woman. Next time, I use my knife."

She didn't respond, still fighting for air in short, choppy bursts.

He let go of Daisy and took the blindfold off.

Her watery eyes found their way to Bunker. When they shot wide, he showed her a raised eyebrow and gave her a slight head shake, hoping she'd know to stay calm.

Daisy's eyes softened and her breathing slowed, even though it was clear she was in considerable pain.

Bunker flashed a stern look at her, then, with only his eyes, directed her attention toward the commander, who was now moving around behind her.

She nodded gently as the man pulled his knife and bent down, putting the blade under her chin.

"Now that we all know each other, it's time to wrap this up," the commander said, tugging down on her hands.

He aimed the tip of his knife at Bunker before he spoke to Daisy again. "Let's hope your boyfriend over there decides to cooperate. Otherwise, I'm afraid your beauty will be a thing of the past."

She said something into the gag, but again the words were garbled.

The commander brought the knife back to her throat, then told Bunker, "Tell me what I want to know, or I start carving."

Daisy struggled against his grip, but the man only smiled, keeping her secure and under his control. "She's a feisty one. Just the way I like them." He moved the tip of the blade from her throat to her right eye, only an inch away. "I think I'll start with her eyes."

Daisy's face went into all-out fright mode, her eyes as big as quarters.

Bunker couldn't hold his silence any longer. "Okay. Okay. I'll tell you what you want to know."

The commander withdrew the dagger and was about to say something when a powerful explosion rocked the building. The blast was close, stinging Bunker's ears and shaking everything around him, including his teeth.

The man in charge flinched, then motioned to his men. "Find out what's going on!" Two of the guards scrambled to the door and disappeared outside, leaving one armed man inside.

Bunker made sure Daisy was looking at him before he yelled, "Now, Daisy!" He sprang to his feet, hoping she'd take action.

Daisy reacted in an instant, snapping her head back to catch the commander in the groin. The man doubled over, groaning, his hands covering his crotch.

Bunker charged the remaining guard with his chest leading the way, ramming him into the wall with a thud. The man fell hard and twisted over to his side.

Daisy swung her feet around and took out the commander's legs, sending him to the floor in a heap. She wrapped her thighs around his neck to pin him in a leg vise.

Bunker kicked the guard lying at his feet, landing a blow to his face. The back of the man's skull smashed into the wall behind. A moment later, the guard's eyes closed and his hands fell to the side, releasing the AR-10 rifle. Bunker kicked it a couple of feet away, in case the man regained consciousness.

Another explosion went off outside, this time farther away. Gunfire erupted next, distant like the blast. It started as controlled bursts of automatic fire, then a pair of powerful single blasts followed. A shotgun, Bunker figured, landing a few more kicks to the guard's face as insurance.

He went to help Daisy, but she appeared to have everything under control. The commander's face was now a deep red color, with the veins along his temples raised and distinct. His tongue was hanging out like a thirsty dog, gurgling sounds emanating from his throat.

She continued applying pressure to his neck with her thighs, while the commander threw wild fists behind his head. She ducked most of the punches, though one did manage to catch the side of her head.

Bunker brought his foot up to kick the man's face, but the commander's entire body went limp before he could unleash his fury.

Daisy kept her leg lock in place for a few more seconds, then let go. She rolled herself next to Bunker, then mumbled a string of frantic words into the gag.

The words were garbled, but he understood what she wanted. He spun around and used his fingers to find the cloth around her mouth. He had to fight through the paracord wrapped around his wrists but he was able to untie her gag and free her voice.

She moved her legs under her before standing up with an awkward step. "They have Stephanie and the kids!"

"Jeffrey?"

"And Megan, too."

"Quick, untie my hands," Bunker said, continuing to hear the distinctive chatter of gunfire outside. The firefight was intense, no longer including shotgun blasts—only intermittent spurts from automatic weapons.

Daisy spun around and tore her fingers into the knot securing his wrists. She worked it loose. "Now it's my turn."

Bunker freed her hands, then grabbed the sidearm from the unconscious guard's holster and gave it to Daisy. She cocked the semi-auto Colt 1911 by racking the slide in earnest.

He snatched the AR-10 from the floor and ejected the magazine to inspect it. It appeared to be full, with twenty rounds of 7.62. His eyes found the chamber next. It was empty. No round present. Odd, given the weapon had been trained on him since he'd been dragged to this location. Had he known the gun wouldn't have fired, he would have made his move sooner.

Bunker rammed the magazine into the lower receiver, pulled the charging handle back and let it snap forward to inject a round into the chamber.

"Which way to Steph and the kids?" he asked, wincing, the sting of the interrogation wreaking havoc on his body.

"I don't know. I was blindfolded," she answered, her tone sarcastic.

Damn it. He should've remembered that fact. It was clear he was out of practice and needed to take a pause to calm himself. Otherwise, his supercharged adrenaline would affect his decision making. Mistakes cost lives.

He drew in three slow breaths, then he was ready. "We sweep and clear. Shoot anything that moves. Don't hesitate, not for a second. We don't stop until we find Steph and the kids."

Daisy nodded, then grabbed his arm to stop him. She pointed at Bunker's privates. "Aren't you forgetting something?"

He looked down. Still naked.

Her eyes were now taking a survey of the artwork across his chest. They stopped moving when they landed on his left pectoral muscle, the location where he had the most damning tattoo on his body. Artwork from his last job—an insignia—one that told the entire world something he wanted to forget.

The emblem featured a white skull with wings, painted red with flames. The words *THE KINDRED* were sprawled above the skull in a curved, downward-facing arc with red block lettering on a dark background. Under the artwork were the words *Brotherhood Forever*, also emblazoned in an arc, only this one faced up.

She took a step back. "The Kindred, huh? I've heard of them. LA biker gang. White supremacists. Shaved heads. Guns. All that."

Shit, his secret was out. "Yes, but that was the man I used to be. A man I hated. I no longer run with them."

Her eyes pinched and so did her nose. "I thought once you're in, you're in for life. Nobody ever quits."

"Well, I did. A few months back, when they decided to start selling meth to kids."

Daisy's inquisitive look was replaced by one of confusion. "So, let me get this straight," she said, her voice now sounding like a suspicious member of law enforcement. "A proud Marine leaves the military and joins a group of white supremacists who ride around on Harleys and break the law. Drugs. Guns. Prostitution. Extortion."

"Yeah, I'm not proud of any of it. That's why I left. Right now, I'm just trying to start over and make up for all the bad decisions I've made."

"So you keep saying."

"Just trying to be honest here."

"What's the story with those scars on your neck?"

"Blowtorch."

She scowled, her eyes tight. "That had to hurt."

"You have no idea. But it was cheaper than a trip to the tattoo removal center."

He expected her to ask another question, but Daisy kept silent, only blinking with her jaw stiff.

"Are we good?" he asked, trying to get a read on her.

She turned and sent a head nod at the guard lying on the floor. "He looks about the right size. You should get dressed." She held out an empty hand, palm up. "It'll be faster if you give me the rifle."

He froze, wondering if her suggestion was simply a ploy to disarm him. After all, she was the deputy and he was the criminal. Or a former criminal. Her viewpoint would depend on if she believed people could change and make amends.

Bunker wasn't sure what to do, but he couldn't stand there much longer. The firefight outside had gone silent. He needed to find Stephanie and the kids and deal with whoever was outside. It was time to take a chance and trust her. He gave her the rifle and waited to see what would happen next.

She tucked the pistol into her waistband and then aimed the rifle at the door. "Come on. Hurry up. We don't have all day."

He began stripping the guard. When he took the man's pants off, he found an extra pouch sewn inside the waistline. It was the same size and shape as the hidden pocket he'd found on the shooter's body when they were inside Tuttle's trailer. Bunker looked at Daisy and pointed.

She nodded, but kept silent.

He opened the fabric compartment and found something familiar. He took it out—another purple and yellow playing card. Eight-sided like before.

"Looks like someone has a serious hard-on for Pokemon," Daisy said in a cynical tone. "Is it the same card?"

"No. The characters are different," Bunker said, studying it for a moment before motioning to the commander's body on the floor. "Check his pants."

While Daisy performed the search on the commander, Bunker tied the unconscious guard's hands behind his back with the same paracord they'd used on him.

He searched the man, finding a heavy duty folding knife in one of his pockets. The stencil on the blade said *Benchmade*.

Someone has good taste, he mused silently as he put the man's pants on. The slacks were a little snug, but he managed to fasten the button at the top. He put the knife in the front pocket with its exterior clip on the outside. He slid the weapon over, positioning it where he could access it easily for a fast draw.

For a moment, he thought about slicing the guard's throat in retaliation for all the man had done. But he chose not to. It would send the wrong message to Daisy. She was already uneasy about his past. A cold-blooded kill would just enflame her doubts.

Bunker put the man's shirt on and buttoned it, then finished with his shoes. They were two sizes too big, but they'd suffice until he could find his own clothes.

Daisy stood up from the commander's body and spun around. "Found them!"

"More than one?"

She fanned them out with her fingers. "Three. All different."

He took the cards and compared them. Daisy was correct. Each card featured a different scene, with various characters and poses. Only the shape of the eight-sided cards and their color scheme were the same.

"What do you think it all means?" she asked.

Bunker took one last look at the cards before sliding them into a pocket. "Beats the hell out of me. But these men are not carrying them around by accident. We'll have to figure it out later. Let's get moving," Bunker said, extending his hand in the direction of the assault rifle she was holding.

She turned to the right, moving the weapon out of reach. "I don't think that's a good idea."

He didn't respond right away, needing a few moments to process her reaction. Deep down, he wasn't surprised. Not when he was standing with a proud deputy who wore her badge with honor.

Her view of him had changed from hero to criminal, all because of some artwork etched into his skin. He couldn't blame her. He hated himself. Why shouldn't she?

Regardless, lives were at stake. She'd need his help to rescue the others and get everyone out of the camp safely. To do that, he'd need a weapon other than the folder knife in his pants pocket.

"Okay, Daisy, I understand your reluctance. But seeing my tattoos doesn't have to change anything if you don't want it to. I'm still the same man who helped save all those kids on the bus—"

"—and helped me take out the shooter at Tuttle's," she said, tentatively, like she was thinking it through.

"Exactly. All that's happened here is that you've learned a little more about my past. A past I left behind. Like I've said before, I'm no longer that guy. I'm trying to start over and make things right."

She didn't answer, her eyes sharp and her posture tense.

"Look, Daisy, we need to work together if we're going to rescue Stephanie and the kids. You can't do this alone. You're gonna need my help and to do that, I need a weapon. Otherwise, there's zero chance we'll get everyone back to Clearwater in one piece. You need to trust me, here. Like you've been doing all along. Nothing's changed."

CHAPTER 45

Bunker led the charge out of the building, his hands wrapped around the assault rifle Daisy had just given him. He'd expected armed resistance from the hostiles once they were outside, but there was none.

He panned the area and waited. No immediate threats were visible. He hoped the men were drawn away by the explosions. However, he wasn't familiar with the layout of the camp, giving him pause, especially since the area contained plenty of hides that could be used against them.

Jets of warm air washed over his neck from behind, pulsating with regularity. They were from Daisy, standing close and breathing hard with her pistol in hand.

She was understandably nervous. Anyone with a pulse would be, and not just because of the predicament they were facing against an armed force.

A minute ago, their budding friendship had suffered a meltdown, then a tentative reboot. And now, here they were, outside and working together for the greater good. Everything going forward would be about reestablishing trust and taking a leap of faith. He'd taken one with her, and she with him. And he wasn't about to let her down.

The sun was almost directly overhead, but not at its midday position. The slight angle indicated the time was around 11 AM or 1 PM. No way to know which of those two it was, not unless he found a patch of trees covered with moss to determine north. Then again, he could drive a long stick into the ground and track its shadow for fifteen minutes.

But there wasn't time for either. Time being the key. Had it been closer to sunrise or sunset, he would have used the low angle of the sun to blind any potential targets, keeping the brightness at his back.

That left him with only his training and experience. Oh, and of course, Daisy. Odds were, none of it was going to be enough. Not in hostile territory against an unknown enemy. Weaponry and ammo were limited and they were without body armor, tactical gear, explosives, and air support.

"Which way?" she asked.

"Let's work left to right. I'll take point. You cover me," he answered, eyes scanning the sprawling camp that covered a full acre.

Three wooden shacks stood to the right, opposite from the two on the left. Each looked like the wooden hovel they'd just escaped from: decaying walls and rundown roofs with steps leading up to the front door. The vertical slats filling in the walls were a dull gray instead of a vibrant brown, showing signs of extreme weathering.

Everywhere he looked, Bunker saw piles of junk dotting the landscape. Most of it was old mining equipment, rusting after years of neglect. However, there were also strands of broken fences, several toppled water barrels, and at least five stacks of rotting lumber.

Beyond the last pile of wood sat an old-fashioned windmill with two of its four blades missing. Its dilapidated base had it leaning to one side, preparing it for certain death after the next windstorm.

Wild grass and waist-high weeds had taken over most of the clearing, covering the dirt between the buildings like an invasion of green carpet. He could see several trampled paths cutting through the foliage, connecting the buildings to each other. The fresh condition of the paths meant the enemy had only been in camp a few days. Otherwise the crushed stalks would have died and blown away, exposing the dirt to the sun.

Bunker was thankful the wind wasn't an issue at the moment, the air crisp and still. Had the flora been swaying in a breeze, spotting movement would have been much more difficult. A calm landscape allowed him to use his peripheral vision, watching for discrepancies as he began to move forward.

Ten steps later, something caught his eye—an out-of-place shadow in the weeds ahead. Just then, it changed on its own, shifting positions and getting smaller.

He stopped and dropped to one knee, holding up a closed fist to Daisy to tell her to freeze. He put out an arm and lowered it with his palm facing down, instructing her to get low. He turned to check on her. She'd followed his commands. He pointed his index finger at the terrain ahead.

"What's wrong?" she asked in a whisper, crouching low.

"Movement ahead," he answered quietly, wishing she'd stick to hand signals to avoid unnecessary conversation.

"Where?"

"In the grass. Ten o'clock. Just this side of the windmill."

"I don't see anything."

"Someone's there, trust me. The shadows aren't right."

"Okay then, why aren't they shooting?"

"Good question. They've had plenty of opportunity."

"What if it's the kids? Or Stephanie?"

"Doubtful."

She hesitated for a few moments before speaking again. "Yeah, you're right. They'd be calling out to us by now."

"Yes, they would, assuming they could somehow manage to escape on their own. Not likely," Bunker said, pointing at the small building to the left. It was about fifty feet away. "I'm gonna make my way over there and see if I can get a better angle on the target."

Daisy pointed to the right with the pistol, at a pile of decaying lumber. "I'm gonna set up there. Better sightlines. They could come at us from anywhere."

Bunker agreed. "Aim small, shoot small," he told her, hoping to instill caution since she only had a handgun with limited range and ammo. She'd have to make every shot count.

Daisy nodded with confidence before moving in a crouched stance to the stack of 2x8s with weeds surrounding it on all sides.

Bunker brought the rifle into firing position, nestling the butt of the stock into the soft flesh of his shoulder. He kept both eyes open as he looked through the red dot optics mounted on the top rail of the weapon. He advanced, using a low profile tactical stance with knees bent. His trigger finger was straight and positioned above the trigger guard, waiting for a target to present itself.

Along the way, he came across a wooden platform, about four feet square. Someone had cleared the weeds in the immediate area, then placed four equally sized rocks as posts for the corners of the half-sheet of plywood. The wood had seen its better days, rotting from years of exposure to rain and sun, but it looked relatively level. There was a black letter painted across the center—a large X, with a two-foot diameter circle drawn around it in black. It wasn't faded or distressed, so it was new.

He wasn't sure what to make of it. It looked like a shooting target, but there weren't any bullet holes in the plywood. Plus, someone had built a rock base for the platform, indicating it was meant to be horizontal. Then again, perhaps they just wanted to keep the wood out of the mud when it rained.

Bunker continued, making it to the corner of the building without issue. He pressed his back against the wall to register a zero signature, giving his adversary nothing to shoot at. He peered around the corner to see if he could spot the target from the new location. The shadow was still there, hiding in the weeds. Whoever it was hadn't moved.

The tightness in his chest had him on full alert. He knew advancing from here would take him directly into the line of fire. A trap could be waiting, possibly a triangulation of fire if the person wasn't alone.

Bunker brought his eyes around and checked on Daisy. She was still behind the lumber, peeking over the top layer of boards with her pistol at the ready.

Before he could get her attention, she swung her head and looked behind her, then checked the forest to each side.

He waited until her eyes were forward again, then flashed a series of hand signals to inform her he was going to advance on the enemy's position.

Daisy nodded, then repositioned herself a few feet to her left, near the end of the lumber stack.

Bunker dropped to the ground and began a commando crawl into the grass. Once inside, he broke off a handful of weeds and stuffed them into the collar of his shirt as camouflage. He did the same with his hair, weaving stalks at angles to hide his head and neck. He finished with the sleeves of the clothing he'd stolen, stuffing them as well.

Once the makeover was complete, he took a moment to reflect on the changes to his outfit. The improvised camo wasn't perfect, but it was better than nothing. Oh, what he wouldn't give for a forest green Ghillie suit right about now. Or a few grenades—smoke or flashbang, either would work. Hell, if he had a 50cal or a .338, he'd lay down a spray and cover the target in lead.

Next, he took the knife he'd recovered from the guard and dug it deep into the soil. He cut around in a circle to loosen the soil and tear a clump of grass free. He shook the dirt loose, then draped the clump over the end of his rifle before knotting the longer roots to secure it around the barrel.

When his eyes spotted a dozen or so pebbles in the vicinity, he decided to pick them up and stuff them into his pocket. They might come in handy.

If it had rained recently, he would've finished by smearing wet dirt across his face. A little battle paint would've bolstered his chances, helping his white skin blend into the surroundings.

All that was missing was the wind. If he had the religious conviction of Stephanie King, he'd ask God to kick up a swirl to help to cover his approach. Without it, the target might notice a change in the landscape when Bunker closed the thirty yards of distance.

Even with his stealth crawl, there were no guarantees. All it would take was the snap of a twig to give away his position. The success or failure of this operation was going to come down to one thing: who spotted the other first.

He sucked in a deep breath and held it, focusing all his thoughts. His warrior self was hiding inside—somewhere—buried deep under a glacier of guilt. He hadn't felt the beast since the moment he was discharged from active duty, even during his days riding with the Kindred.

It took a few seconds, but he managed to summon the demon. Its raw strength poured into his body, supercharging his heart with energy. He wasn't sure how long it would remain, but he planned to unleash hell while he had it under control.

Someone was dying in the next few minutes, and it wasn't going to be him. Or Daisy. Or any of his other friends.

CHAPTER 46

Bunker continued his slither through the underbrush, figuring he was about fifteen yards from the last known position of the shadow. A shadow that didn't belong. A shadow with death on its agenda—his and Daisy's.

He brought another knee forward, then his opposite elbow. So far he'd been ultra quiet during his approach, feeling confident the target wasn't aware of his position.

Bunker stopped moving when more of the dark figure came into view. The weeds and grass didn't allow him to see every detail of his opponent, but someone was there all right, allowing Bunker to begin a tactical assessment.

The person's legs were to the left, but their shoes were pointing up, not down or to the side as expected. The shoes were heavy soled and a black color, just like the rest of the tango's clothing.

Bunker leaned to the left, changing his angle to peer through the stalks. He could only see the middle portion of a face. The broad, distinct nose and the size of the feet told him it was a man, his eyes facing the sky. He didn't appear to be moving, either. Time to find out why.

Bunker took three of the pebbles from his pocket and lobbed them into the sky at his target. They sailed past the man as intended, thanks to the force behind his throw. He heard them land, snapping a twig and crunching some grass.

The target should have reacted to the sounds, but he didn't.

Was he dead?

Unconscious?

Or just playing possum?

There was no way to be sure. Not from this distance and not with the thicket of weeds in the way. Regardless, if Bunker took the shot now, he could end the threat.

He brought the cold steel of the AR-10 into position, resting the barrel on a thick mound of grass. It only took a second to bring the sights to bear.

Normally, he'd aim for the most lethal area on the human body—the gap between the nose and mouth, where a bullet could penetrate quickly and sever the spinal cord. But that location wasn't an option. A temple shot was his only choice, though the limited sightlines would make a precision shot difficult.

His plan was to engage after an exhale, once everything with his body was calm. To do that, he focused his breathing, pacing each breath until his hands steadied.

When he was ready, he brought the tip of his finger down and lightly put it on the trigger. The brush of metal against his skin felt amazing.

Just then, a haunting phrase from his drill sergeant echoed in his brain. *Bullets are forever. Verify your target.*

The nostalgic words connected with his logic, making him move his trigger finger back to the safe position. He brought his head up and looked over the weapon's optics to take one last look at the man in the grass.

The target began to stir a moment later, sitting up in a hunch, torso leaning over its legs.

Bunker reacted, snapping twigs as his eyes and hands worked together to bring the red dot back to its target. The instant the sights were lined up, his brain sent the command to fire to his finger. The instant he felt the resistance of the sear engage, the man turned his head and looked at Bunker.

Shit! It's Franklin Atwater! Megan's dad!

Bunker jerked the rifle as the hammer sent the round down the barrel. The recoil rammed the folding stock into his shoulder, thanks to the awkward, unsteady rifle position. When the shot was over, Bunker turned the muzzle toward the sky and held a quick breath, waiting to see if his friend had been hit.

Franklin never moved. Not a flinch. Not a duck for cover. Instead, he just sat there, blinking, his eyes glazed over and locked into position, staring at Bunker.

Bunker exhaled, letting a wave of relief enter his body. The round must have missed; otherwise, it would have sent Franklin twisting to his right side when the sudden impact of a 7.62 round tore into him.

Bunker crawled forward, crossing the distance between them with vigor. It would've been faster to stand up and run, but without knowing who else might be stalking the camp, he needed to stay low.

"You okay, Franklin?" he asked in a whisper upon arrival, checking the man's condition. There was blood on his right shoulder, just above the top of the bicep.

"Took one earlier," Franklin answered in a low, thready voice, his hand moving to the wound.

Since it was on the opposite side of where Bunker was aiming, it couldn't have been from his shot. "I damn near killed you."

"I know. I swear I felt it whiz by. Good thing your aim sucks."

Bunker smirked, not because it was funny. It was more about relief. Relief that he'd pulled the rifle away in time, making him a bad shot by design. "You're the last person I expected to see out here."

"I could say the same thing. You alone?"

"No. Daisy's here, too."

"I'm guessing you're here for the same reason I am. To get our people back."

Bunker nodded, but decided not to waste time mentioning their capture. Or escape.

Franklin continued. "Been tracking these assholes ever since they took my little girl."

"Do you have a count?"

"Eight down. Three remaining," he said, looking at the blood oozing from his shoulder.

"Well, you can scratch two more off the list, thanks to Daisy and her killer thighs."

"I'm sorry, what?"

"Never mind. Long story, but they're no longer a threat," Bunker told him, running the facts through his brain. "So I take it that was you on the shotgun earlier."

"Yeah," he said with a grimace, the pain in his shoulder obvious. "Used explosives to draw them out, then took down the first two with my street howitzer."

Bunker saw an assault rifle lying nearby, not a scattergun. It looked identical to the AR-10 he was holding. He figured Franklin picked it up from one of the kills and used it from there. "Where's the last one?"

Franklin pointed. "Lost him over there by that shack. Tried to follow, but my legs gave out. I'm pretty sure I winged him. Just need to follow the blood."

Bunker wrapped his hands around Franklin's shoulder, applying pressure with his grip. "Speaking of blood, we need to get this stopped."

Franklin tore Bunker's hands away, then spoke in a deep, controlled voice. "Look, this isn't the first time I've found myself on the X. I know what to do. You need to go. Now. Save Megan and the others. They're here, somewhere. I can feel 'em. If that guy gets to them first—"

Bunker understood. "Roger that. Will do."

The large black man gave the spare rifle to Bunker. "Here. Take it. There are a few rounds left in the mag."

* * *

Daisy waited, her eyes searching the area near the base of the old windmill.

What the hell is going on out there?

First there was a single gunshot, then the sway of brush from left to right. Since then, nothing.

Was Bunker down?

Or the enemy?

She wanted to charge forward, but her training kept her feet still. More information was needed; otherwise, she might walk straight into an ambush. All she could do was watch and listen for a sign.

Another handful of seconds went by, then the crown of a head appeared, just above the tops of the weeds, peering in her direction. A hand came up next, waving. A person rose up, showing more of their chest and arms. It was Bunker, signaling for her to join him.

She checked the area behind her and to the sides. All clear. Time to move. After a short trot through the grass with knees bent and head low, she was at his position.

Daisy knelt down next to the former biker, expecting to see a lifeless body at his feet. However, that wasn't the case. The target was still alive and looking at her, smiling. Though it looked like a painful smile.

"Franklin?" she asked, her mind not believing what her eyes were reporting.

"Hey Daisy."

"What the hell?"

"This is what happens to old men who forget to duck," Franklin Atwater said, holding his left hand on his right shoulder.

Daisy looked at Bunker, who now had two rifles instead of one. "You shot him?"

"Wasn't me," he said, pointing at a building nearby. "There's one left. Apparently wounded. You ready to finish this?"

"Ah . . . sure," she said with a stammer, her mind still processing the facts.

Franklin pointed at her pistol. "So it was these guys?"

"What do you mean?" she asked.

"They stole that 1911 from my office. My wife gave it to me."

She held the gun out. "It's all yours."

He took it from her. "Thanks, now go find my daughter and finish the job."

CHAPTER 47

Daisy stood to the left of the door leading into one of the mining cabins. Bunker was on the right, reminding her of their breach into Tuttle's place. Granted, this was a different day and a different location, but they'd both taken the same positions on either side of the entrance. This time, however, they were armed with assault rifles and the target was contained within a much smaller space. Better odds, to be sure.

They'd followed the blood trail to this location, just as Franklin had suggested. A single threat remained inside—an injured man, wounded at the hands of the burly, bleeding cowboy who was hunkered down in the weeds, waiting for his daughter, Megan, to be rescued—again.

First the bus accident. And now this. The poor little girl was going to need counseling after everything that had happened to her the past couple of days.

All Daisy's thoughts were on the wellbeing of the two kids. Well, them and Stephanie. A woman who hated her guts.

However, before they could perform a rescue, the lone remaining gunman needed to be neutralized. And to do that, she would team up with Bunker as they entered the shack with clear intention to engage.

Bunker held up three fingers and mouthed a silent countdown. When he reached zero, he spun out and brought his leg up, then kicked open the door in one massive strike.

Daisy moved into position, entering the building with the rifle leading the way. She was ready to fire, but held the trigger when she saw a thick, bearded man with a shaved head holding a blindfolded girl at gunpoint. It was Megan, sobbing quietly.

The stocky white man wasn't dressed like the others in camp, nor was he as trim. His black muscle shirt showed off his endless hours in the weight room pumping iron. He looked to be covered in tattoos, like Bunker, investing thousands.

The Neanderthal was on the floor with his back against the far wall, his wounded leg outstretched and bleeding. Megan was on his lap, crying into the enormous hand covering her mouth.

Stephanie and Jeffrey were also there, huddled on the floor to the left. Both of them were bound and gagged. Daisy couldn't see their eyes, not with the blindfolds in place.

"That's far enough!" the man yelled, the handgun pointing at Megan's right temple.

Daisy froze, unsure what to do.

Bunker slid into the room behind her, then took position on her right with a rifle held tight against his shoulder.

"Bulldog?" the hostage taker asked in a surprised tone, his eyes locked onto Bunker.

"Grinder?" Bunker answered, looking confused. He lowered his gun a few inches. "What the hell?"

"I could say the same thing, pal."

"I can't believe you're still alive."

"Yeah, me either. It was touch and go for a while, but the prison doc managed to put me back together. I've got enough metal in me now to make The Terminator jealous."

"You know this man?" she asked Bunker, keeping her sights trained on the perpetrator.

"Yeah. We used to ride together."

Daisy scanned Grinder's tattoos again, specifically, his upper left chest area. There was a small portion of a winged tattoo sticking out from the under the edges of his tank top. She missed it before, but now that she knew more about this man, it was easy to complete the rest of the emblem in her mind. It was a Kindred tattoo, like Bunker's.

Grinder moved the gun a few inches away from the little girl's head, though it was still aimed at her. He spoke to Bunker, using Megan as a shield. "That we did. A long time ago. Imagine my surprise when I got released and found out you'd disappeared. Not cool, brother. Watts is pissed."

"I figured as much," Bunker said, his face relaxing a bit. "What are you doing here in Colorado? This isn't Kindred territory."

"Watts sent me here to strike a deal. Just arrived when this shit-storm happened. Next thing I know, lead's flying and someone puts a hole in my leg. I'm pretty sure I dropped the shooter. He's out there in the grass somewhere. You need to finish him off."

"I'm afraid I can't do that."

"Why not, brother?"

"That person is a friend of mine."

"You're part of this?" the hulking man snapped.

Bunker nodded. "Your pals should've never taken these hostages."

Grinder's face pinched together. "Hey, I wasn't involved in any of that."

"Except now you are," Daisy said. "That girl in your lap is the daughter of the man you shot outside. And they're friends of ours. We're here to take them back."

"Look, I had no idea."

"Well, now you do. Time to do the right thing, Grinder," Bunker said, taking the rifle from his shoulder and aiming it at the floor. He took one hand off the weapon and held it out, in a peaceful, non-threatening manner. "Come on, Grinder. Let the girl go. There's no need for any of this."

"Sorry, Bulldog. No can do," he answered, nodding in the direction of Daisy. "Not until your hot little friend there drops her piece."

"Not a chance," Daisy said, adjusting her feet and keeping her trigger finger ready. All she needed was for Megan to move to the left and she'd have a clear shot at his head.

Bunker shot Daisy a look, one that said not to add any more tension to the situation. He returned his eyes to Grinder. "Let the girl go, Grinder. There's no reason this has to escalate."

The man didn't answer.

"You can trust me, old friend. Put the gun down."

"Trust you? After you just up and disappeared? And then you show up with some cop? You got some big set of balls, Bulldog. I'll give you that. At least that hasn't changed."

"Yes, I'm still the same man. The same man who put in a lot of miles with you over the years. I've always had your back, and you of all people know I'm a man of my word."

Grinder's face softened a bit, but he didn't answer.

Bunker continued. "Look, you're injured and at a severe disadvantage right now. There's no need for any of us to die today. You and I have been riding together way too long for something like this to come between us. So please, put the gun down and let these people go. We can all walk out of here together," he said, taking a step closer to Grinder.

Grinder's eyes dropped, looking as though he was deep in thought.

Bunker took another step, this time with the rifle hanging limp along his right side. He held out his free hand. "Come on, buddy. It's time to end this. Just give me the gun."

Grinder paused for what seemed like thirty seconds. Then the tension in his face disappeared, just before he let go of the girl and gave the pistol to Bunker.

"You made the right decision," Bunker said, tucking the pistol inside the back of his pants. He motioned for Megan to come to him.

Megan stood up and hopped to Bunker on her good leg, wrapping her arms around his legs.

Bunker leaned the rifle against the wall to the right. "Are you okay, sweetheart?"

Megan nodded, tears visible on her cheeks.

Bunker pried her loose. "Your daddy's outside. Deputy Daisy will take you to him."

A sudden chill washed over Daisy when she heard Bunker's words. She wasn't about to leave. Not with two bikers and more hostages in the room. "I'm staying here," she told him, keeping a close eye on the position of everyone.

"Daisy, I've got this," Bunker said, motioning for her to leave the shack with Megan.

"Megan, sweetheart, wait for me outside," she told the young girl.

"What's wrong?" Megan asked in a scared, curious tone.

"Everything's going to be okay. Just go outside and help your dad. Right now. Like I said."

Megan didn't hesitate, hopping past her and out the door. "Now the others," she told Bunker, motioning with the rifle in her hands.

Bunker hesitated for a second, like he was sizing her up for something. Then he walked to Stephanie and Jeffrey, freeing them as well.

Daisy expected Stephanie to say something when she stood up, but the woman kept quiet. So did Jeffrey, possibly stunned and traumatized.

Bunker took a step back. "Franklin's going to need your help, Steph. He's by the base of the windmill. Go. Now."

Stephanie nodded, then corralled Jeffrey with her arms and escorted her son toward the door. She didn't make eye contact with Daisy as they cruised by and went out the door.

The instant the hostages were safely outside, Daisy moved forward and put the barrel of the assault rifle against Bunker's forehead.

"Whoa, wait," he said, raising his hands.

"Give me the pistol, and no sudden moves."

CHAPTER 48

Daisy took a step to the right, allowing her to keep an eye on both Grinder and Bunker. She wasn't sure where Bunker's loyalties stood, not with a longtime friend and fellow Kindred gang member in the same room.

"Bulldog, huh?" she asked, buying herself more time to formulate a plan.

"Nothing's changed here, Daisy."

"See, I told ya. You can never trust a cop," Grinder said with pain in his words, his bullet wound bleeding on the floor. Just then, he lunged for the rifle leaning against the wall and grabbed it.

Daisy spun to shoot him, but Bunker grabbed the end of her rifle and snatched it from her hands before she could fire.

"Now that's the Bulldog I remember!" Grinder said with a full smile on his lips. He aimed the rifle at Daisy and pulled the trigger.

She flinched, expecting to be torn apart by a high velocity round, but the weapon never fired.

Bunker pulled the pistol from his pants and fired a single round at Grinder, nailing him in the forehead.

The goliath's head snapped back, spraying brain matter and blood on the wall behind him. He slumped over with his head hanging limp and to the side, exposing a swastika tattoo on his neck. Daisy wondered if that was what Bunker burnt off his neck—Nazi signs.

"I told you I had it covered," Bunker said in a calm, controlled voice, his pistol hand still aimed at Grinder.

It took Daisy a few moments to catch up to the facts, not believing the speed with which Bunker reacted. First, he grabbed her rifle before she could blink. Then he pulled his pistol and shot Grinder like it was nothing. Right then, the answer came to her. "You planned this, didn't you?"

"Of course. I had to test him and see if he'd go for the rifle the second my back was turned. I just didn't want you involved if he did. Not after what happened in Tuttle's place. It's hard enough to free yourself of the guilt from one shooting. But two, that's an entirely different story. I was trying to spare you."

"But you let him grab the rifle and fire?"

"Yes, but I'd put the weapon on safe before I leaned it against the wall. That's why I waited until after he gave me the pistol and released Megan. To control the situation."

She wasn't sure what to say, so she kept silent.

Bunker continued, his tone turning soft. "His name was Grinder for a reason. He preferred things up close and personal. Fists usually, or knives. Guns were not his thing, and certainly not assault rifles. I knew he'd forget to take it off safe."

She felt like an idiot. "You wanted him to make the first move."

"To see if I could trust him. Obviously, I couldn't."

"There's a shock," she said, still processing the events. "But I guess in the end, the shoot was justified."

"Exactly, but you were supposed to be outside. I didn't want you to be a part of it."

"I was afraid you were going to let him go. You know, brothers and all that."

"In truth, I was thinking about it. But I needed to be sure."

"I get that."

"Looks like my suspicions were correct. The first thing he would've done was let the brotherhood know where I am. You heard him. They're pissed and looking for me. They would've come to town and painted the sidewalks red. Trust me, it had to end like this. There was no other choice."

"I'm sorry. I didn't know. I thought I needed to do something. You might've turned on us."

Bunker's face flushed red, then his shoulders sagged. "I'm not sure what else I can do to prove myself. I'm not that man anymore."

Daisy now understood why he chose to inflict such pain on his neck with the blowtorch. Everyone judges by what they see, not what they know. Or don't know in this case. She felt embarrassed and small-minded. "Like I said, I'm sorry."

He exhaled, his jaw stiff. "People can change, Daisy. You really need to think about trusting me."

Daisy nodded. "I will. I promise."

"Fair enough. Let's get everyone back to town."

CHAPTER 49

Jack Bunker held up a closed fist to stop his two-person search team, but not because of a possible threat ahead. Rather, he needed to give his ribs a rest and catch his breath. The aftereffects of the brutal interrogation were spreading across his body like a determined pathogen after the containment seal was broken.

The adrenaline high had kept the pain at bay and his mind focused. But now that he'd escaped and neutralized the enemy, only the reality of torture remained. Reality that came with wave after wave of stout reinforcements: bruises, scrapes, and electrical burns.

"You okay?" Deputy Daisy Clark asked, grabbing his elbow.

"Yeah, just need a second," Bunker answered, taking in another gulp of air. He held it, letting the cool mountain freshness settle in before the next exhale. He adjusted his grip on the assault rifle, feeling as though the killing machine's weight had just doubled. It was clear fatigue had settled in, taking residence next to the pain. He needed food, water, and sleep—none of which were available at the moment. They needed to find the insurgents' vehicles and return to the others.

She let go of his arm. "Need to get you to medical as soon as we get back to town."

"I'll be okay. It's Franklin you should be worried about. Even though it was a through and through, that shoulder isn't going to heal itself."

"Thank God it wasn't a few inches lower; otherwise, we'd be consoling his daughter right now. And I think we both agree, Megan's been through enough the last couple days."

"Roger that. Just need to find their rides. Got to be around here somewhere."

"Otherwise, we'll have another situation with too many riders and not enough horses."

"Like they say, history repeats itself," he added, remembering the long walk to Clearwater with the herd of kids.

"You got that right. It's too bad Franklin didn't think to bring more than one."

"I'm sure once they grabbed his daughter, he was totally focused on search and recover. I know I'd be. Probably didn't think it all through."

"If it comes down to it, Megan will be the one to ride. The rest of us can walk. We can't have her trying to hop all the way back to town in that leg brace."

"I might be able to make some crutches. Just need some lashing material and a couple of tree branches. If not, I'll carry her back to town, like before."

"Yeah, like that's gonna happen. You can barely keep yourself upright. They really did a number on ya."

"Trust me, this ain't nothing. The Kindred's Circle of Doom makes today feel like a Thai Massage. The kind with a happy ending."

She laughed before her face turned serious. "Circle of Doom, huh? What's that, some kind of initiation?"

"I guess you could call it that. It's more about proving your toughness against an overwhelming enemy."

"Yeah, how does that work exactly?"

"The entire brotherhood stands in a circle and takes shots at you. And not just one at a time. It's a free-for-all. Talk about a beating, with chanting and laughing the entire time. All you can do is stand there and take it as a blur of pain comes at you from every direction. Fists. Feet. Elbows. Head butts. Nothing is off limits. I think there was a lead pipe involved, too. Everyone comes out with at least a concussion. Usually worse."

"So that's what happened to your nose," she quipped in a sarcastic tone.

"Among other things."

She shook her head, looking shocked.

Bunker continued. "One guy ended up with serious brain damage. Poor bastard. Our leader, Watts, just dumped the asshole in the alley behind the bar we were drinking in, then just left him there when we took off for the next town. That guy obviously never rode with us again."

"Why would anyone ever want to do any of that? And for what?"

He shook his head. "Not my finest hour. But I was so lost at the time. In fact, I wanted the beating. I figured I deserved it for what happened during my last tour. After that, it was all about being part of a brotherhood. A place to call home. A place where I felt I belonged, for better or worse."

"With a bunch of thugs?"

"Yeah, I wasn't in my right mind at the time."

"Probably from the Circle of Doom."

"Sure. That was part of it. But in truth, there was more. A lot more. A person's past can change them at the cellular level, pushing them places they never thought they'd go. Even to the dark side, like me. I know it's all a poor excuse for the shit I've done, but what I went through actually happened. And it was real. I can't tell you the hurt that was boiling inside me at the time. Clear down to my soul. It was like some creature had taken control of my insides, eating away at my guts. And my heart. I was so angry at the world. And myself."

"I can't imagine."

"But I finally managed to crawl out of that hole. It wasn't easy, but here I am. Broken and bruised. Just trying to put the pieces back together. All I can do now is move forward and try to find the man I used to be. The kind of man my father would be proud of. I hope you understand."

A minute of silence filled the air before Daisy spoke again. "Maybe we should split up to cover more ground?"

Bunker was happy she'd changed the subject. "I thought about that, but I don't think it's a good idea for you to be out here alone. Not until we know the area is secure."

"You heard Franklin; he said we got them all."

"Maybe, but he *was* down for a while after taking a bullet. There could be more of them out here."

Her head snapped back, as she shot him a fierce look. "Hey, I can take care of myself. It's you who shouldn't be out here. Not in your condition. I've seen drunks on a three-day bender who can move faster than you."

He laughed, harder than he wanted, waking up a string of pain across his midsection. He grimaced. "Don't make me laugh."

"Sorry, can't help it. Watching you right now is like a comedy act. Seriously, maybe you should head back to camp and send Stephanie to help."

He hated that idea. "Not a chance. The last thing I need is for the two of you to be out here alone. And armed. It's pretty obvious that Steph wants to kill you right now."

Daisy paused before she answered. "I know, and I feel terrible about it. But I'm not sure what else I can do. I've apologized like a million times."

"You gotta give it some time. Sleeping with her old man wasn't cool. I'd be pissed, too," he said, resuming his trek through the forest. "No, I'm afraid it's just you and me. Steph needs to stay back and keep an eye on the kids. And Franklin."

Daisy checked the AR-10, inspecting the magazine after ejecting it. "Well, at least we've got thirty little friends who can help. Armor piercing friends, at that."

He wanted to laugh again, but held it back to protect his ribs, offering up a smirk instead. "Let's hope we don't have to use 'em."

Bunker turned and resumed his march through the uneven terrain of central Colorado. Daisy followed three steps behind, with her rifle in a firing position.

Before he could take another step, Bunker heard a twig snap, then the heavy tread of something moving in the forest. He swung his focus to the right, seeing the backside of a naked man running at an angle away from him. The back of the man's head was bloody; so was his neck.

Bunker knew who it was—the guard he'd overpowered in the torture shack, his hands still bound behind his back. "Shit, I forgot about that guy!"

"I got him," Daisy said, taking off after him.

Bunker followed, though his pace was slower than hers. Every stride tore at his wounds, sending the pain into overdrive.

Daisy raised the rifle and took a shot, never stopping her uneven jog. The blast echoed across the landscape, bouncing off the tall, majestic trees and embedded rock formations.

The man's speed didn't change, his bare feet tiptoeing through the countryside with a hurried step. He looked like a streaking Olympic hurdler, racing cross-country over broken glass.

When the trim guard's path took him up a gentle slope, more of his nakedness came into view.

Daisy took another shot.

This time the escapee went down, twisting forward with his right shoulder leading the way, his legs the last to disappear from sight.

"He's down!" she said, picking up her pace.

"Hold on—don't approach without me."

She did as he asked, coming to a halt next to a wide tree stump, eight feet high. Check that—it was a mound of termites, building an impressive fortress amongst the greenery. They'd been at it for a while, the colony's exterior walls bustling with trails of activity. From a distance, it resembled a miniature rock formation—something you'd see in Monument Valley, though this shrine had a collective mind of its own.

He memorized its location out of habit, just in case the group needed an impromptu source of protein. The kids would probably gag if he stuck his hand inside one of the towering walls and pulled out a wad of eusocial insects.

So would Stephanie, but he figured the capable deputy would be a willing participant. Eventually, the entire group would partake in the live feast. Hunger would transform everyone's mindset, especially when faced with no alternatives.

"Where is he?" Bunker asked when he arrived at Daisy's position.

She pointed with the end of the rifle. "Two o'clock. Fifteen yards out. By the base of that willow with the wishbone branch in the middle."

"On me," he said in his most authoritative voice, dragging his sore legs forward. They weighed a hundred pounds each, feeling like they'd been stolen from someone else's body, filled with cement, and sewn onto his.

Bunker crept through the underbrush with the barrel of the gun aimed in the same direction as his eyes, waiting for the man's bare skin to arrive in the sights.

Even though Daisy landed a round on the target, it didn't mean the man wasn't a threat. Caution was needed. He could reappear at any time and from any direction, breaking through the cover provided by the natural landscape.

The deadfall ran thick in spots, requiring careful placement of each step. The foliage scratched at him, reminding him it was searching for unprotected skin. Skin it could tear open and penetrate.

His days in wilderness survival training had taught him a great many things, none more important than Mother Nature is always in control. Whether you were prepared or not, she was gunning for you.

Her mercy kind, but her vengeance wicked, his team leader would say.

Bunker couldn't believe how the day had kept evolving, starting with a beating and ending with one of his captors on the run. It all felt a little too surreal, as if his destiny was unfolding on the pages of some twisted Hollywood screenplay.

He knew nothing would ever seem normal from here on out. Not after the Area 51 plane crash and corresponding EMP attack.

* * *

Daisy stopped her march and stood alongside Bunker after he'd taken position near the base of the willow tree.

The man she'd shot was lying on his stomach with a gaping bullet hole in his right shoulder. Even though she wasn't trying to wing the target, she was glad she did. A fortunate result of her second shot, taken on the run, over uneven terrain.

Yet the shoulder wound wasn't the man's only injury. A piece of skull had been cracked open across the back, courtesy of Bunker and his relentless kicking in the torture shack. It was a miracle the guard could even walk, let alone make a break for it in the woods.

Bunker pressed the barrel of his rifle into the man's back, but the body didn't move. Bunker tried again, this time with more force. No response. He tucked the rifle down to his side, then bent over and used a free hand to roll the man onto his back.

When the victim's face came into view, Daisy turned her head away in disgust. There was a hunk of wood sticking out of his right eye—thick, sharp, and bloody. His fall must have taken him face first onto an exposed branch, perhaps a root, impaling his eye.

"Oh man, that had to hurt," Bunker said, using a buoyant tone. "Nice shot, Daisy. Nailed him twice."

"Not what I had in mind," she answered, wishing she'd never seen the results. "I take it he's dead?"

Bunker checked the man's vitals. "Yep, and then some." He moved a step to the left and pointed at a fallen sapling. Its trunk had been snapped in half, exposing a jagged base. "Poor bastard. Must have landed there. Talk about bad luck."

Daisy expected guilt to rage inside her like before, yet all felt calm inside. Well, calm mixed with queasiness. She wondered if they were going to keep searching for the trucks, or drag the corpse back to camp. "What about the body?"

Bunker didn't hesitate, answering a millisecond later as if he was already thinking about it. "Let the animals take care of it. I give it a week, then there will be nothing left."

"And the others?"

"Toss them out here, too. It'll be a forest buffet for the critters. Going to be some fat coyotes running around."

She didn't like the answers, but she was too tired to argue. Rules and procedure had been tossed aside a while ago, leaving her at the mercy of Bunker's decisions. Decisions being made by a former Marine turned white supremacist biker.

CHAPTER 50

Franklin Atwater sat with his arms wrapped around his daughter, his shoulder pulsating with the thump of his heart. The bleeding had stopped, but not the constant sting, reminding him of how much damage had been done by the shooter's bullet. A shooter named Grinder, according to Daisy after she and Bunker had emerged from the miner's shack.

One question kept nagging at him. How did Bunker know the man's name was Grinder? Who offered up their name when they were holding a gun on a little girl? His little girl.

"I hope they're back soon," Megan said in her sweet little voice, nestling her head against the uninjured side of his chest. "I wanna go home, Daddy."

"I know, me too, sweetheart. But we need to wait just a little bit longer. They'll be here soon. I promise."

The temper in his chest boiled as he visualized the scene with his daughter. Megan must have been scared senseless, wishing her daddy would come inside to rescue her from the clutches of a bad guy. A bad guy she'd most certainly never forget. A bad guy whose face would haunt her dreams for years to come.

Had Franklin been in Bunker's shoes, shooting the man would not have been his first choice. No, a more personal form of justice was warranted. One involving as many blows as his fists could dish out.

Primal instinct is a powerful weapon, especially when it's delivered with ruthless efficiency—efficiency infused with extreme prejudice.

He imagined the beating in his mind, landing punch after punch, not stopping until one of two things happened: he broke every bone in his hands, or the man's face caved in like a rotting cantaloupe.

Sure, to some, his vengeful daydream might seem harsh, disproportionate, or even unwarranted. But deep down, he knew he was right. Every parent knows that no punishment is too great for those who would hurt innocent children. Retribution was the only answer.

Every cell in his body was tuned into his rage, but he kept all signs of it hidden from his fragile little girl. Megan was the only thing in his life that mattered and he would never do anything to compromise her future or her happiness.

And yet, he'd come within a trigger pull of losing her. Likewise, she almost lost him. Different bullet, but same shooter.

The rest of what he had in his life was just a pile of useless possessions. Meaningless spoils of years of hard work. All of it could be replaced. All of it except the Colt 1911, the gun his wife had given him right before she died in a tragic fire. If he'd only been there when the pull-behind trailer ignited, she'd still be alive.

If he closed his eyes and focused, he could remember every agonizing night since then. The long, sleepless hours ticking by like frozen molasses. But not just for him, for Megan, too. His memories were filled with endless hours of his little girl crying herself to sleep in the bedroom next door, her face buried in the pillow, trying to muffle the sound of her misery.

The pain in his heart was real. There was no denying it. So was his guilt. All of it stemming from one mistake. His mistake—one that had turned into a flaming dagger, anchoring itself to his soul for all of eternity.

If only he'd been diligent and stayed on top of his game. Then Megan would still have her mom. And he, his wife. The only woman he'd ever loved.

His situational awareness skills had become rusty. Not just once, but twice. First with his wife and the trailer fire, and now with his daughter's kidnapping. These failures couldn't continue. Not with the Universe apparently on a rampage against him.

If it weren't for Bunker, a man who just showed up and took residence in their lives, Franklin would have nothing. It was almost as if God himself had handpicked a savior, sending him to Clearwater just when the town needed him most.

Before the next thought arrived, Franklin heard a sound. It was off in the distance. Mechanical. Closing.

Megan sat up in his lap. "Daddy? Do you hear that?"

"Engines," Stephanie King said, whipping her head to the side to investigate. "Working engines. Sounds like more than one."

"Mr. Bunker must have found them," Jeffrey added, the freckles on his cheeks dancing with each syllable.

"Well, let's hope it's Bunker," Stephanie said, pulling her son closer.

"It is. Gotta think positive," Franklin said. "That man knows what he's doing. So does Daisy."

"I know, but what about those gunshots earlier?" Stephanie asked.

Franklin could see the worry smothering her face. "I'm sure they're okay. Probably did a little hunting while they were out there. Deer, I would guess."

Steph's eyes tightened before a short pause. "Good, 'cause I'm starving. We all are," the woman said, wiping a clump of hair away from her son's face. "This day just needs to end."

Thirty seconds later, a pair of identical trucks broke through the trees across the clearing, their engines growling in low gear. They plowed across the rolling terrain, crushing stalks of starter growth with the roll of their tires.

Franklin recognized them, having owned one in his younger days—1965 Land Rovers. The 109 Series, if he wasn't mistaken. Each a four-door Sedan model, complete with a winch affixed to the front bumper and a white roof rack.

The paint was a beautiful Grasmere green color, though the wide splash of mud along the side covered up most of it—so much so, it was difficult to see where one door ended and the other began.

Franklin stood up. So did Megan, Stephanie, and Jeffrey.

The trucks pulled to a stop fifteen feet away, giving Franklin a priority view of the oversized, heavy-tread tires. They looked new, including the spare attached to the hood.

The driver's window rolled down in successive, uneven bursts before Bunker stuck his head out, wearing a smile. "Someone call a cab?"

"A cab?" Stephanie asked in a sarcastic tone. "Who calls cabs these days? Uber would be more like it."

"Okay then, Uber."

"You're late," Stephanie added, letting out a thin smile. "Don't expect a tip."

"Traffic was a bitch," Bunker said, playing along.

"I was getting a little worried there for a moment," Franklin said.

"We heard gunshots," Megan said.

"Everything okay?" Franklin asked Bunker.

"Had to take care of some unfinished business," Bunker said, stepping out of the vehicle.

"So . . . you weren't hunting after all," Stephanie said.

"Well, sort of. Just not for something we can eat," Daisy added, exiting her truck and joining Bunker.

Stephanie put up her hands. "Someone please tell that woman that I'm not talking to her right now. Or ever."

Bunker shook his head, looking at Franklin.

Franklin shrugged. "Let's get everyone loaded up and back to town. It's a long drive south."

"Daddy, what about Tango?" Megan asked. "We can't leave him out there all alone."

"I'll come back for him later, sweetheart."

"But your shoulder?"

"I'll ride him to town for you," Bunker said, taking a step forward.

"Seriously?" Daisy snapped, giving him an exaggerated smirk, then pointing at his backside. "Haven't you had enough punishment for one day?"

Bunker rubbed his butt, twisting his mouth before he spoke. "I'll be okay."

"Are you sure? I doubt you can take another argument with a saddle."

Bunker laughed. "Right now, my rear end hurts the least of everything. Another ride will just even out the pain. Besides, someone has to do it. We can't leave a valuable horse out here."

"Thanks, Bunker. We appreciate it," Franklin said, pointing to the right. "He's tied to a tree just beyond a stream. Look for a huge oak tree lying on the ground. Can't miss it. It's massive. Tango's right behind the stand of blueberry bushes."

"Got it."

"Tango loves blueberries," Megan said, looking at her father.

"That's why I left him there, darling. So he could eat. There's a stream, too, for water."

"Don't you think we should stay together?" Stephanie asked, her tone tense. She cleared her throat, shooting a sharp glance at Bunker. "So none of us *accidentally* wanders off on their own."

Bunker shook his head, ignoring her obvious reference to him. "You guys go ahead. I'll catch up. I need to finish a few things around here before I head out."

"For the buffet," Daisy said, nodding in a matter-of-fact way.

"Exactly."

"What buffet?" Stephanie asked.

"I'll explain later," Bunker said. "Just not in front of the kids."

"Oh, right," she said, nodding tentatively, though her tone suggested she wasn't sure what he meant.

CHAPTER 51

Mayor Buckley waited in front of *Bubba's Repair and Restoration*, his feet just outside the entrance to the first garage bay. He kept his head turned away to avoid a dangerous case of welder's flash, waiting for the gas-infused hiss of the crackling torch to run quiet. A few seconds later it did, filling the garage with an echo of silence.

"I'm a little busy here, Mayor," a male's voice said, his tone terse and to the point.

Buckley brought his eyes around until he found the owner of the auto repair shop, Burt Lowenstein. He was down on one knee with his welding mask tipped up, his face unevenly tanned and soiled.

Burt wasn't wearing a shirt, only a pair of shop coveralls with the straps wrapped around his wide shoulders. There must have been two dozen burn scars across his arms, round belly, and powerful biceps, making Buckley wonder why Burt chose to weld steel without a shirt for protection.

The bruise around Burt's left eye was colorful and notably swollen, courtesy of the Sheriff's nightstick from a few days prior. Yet the injury didn't diminish the intensity of Burt's penetrating stare. Nor did it lessen his body odor or gruff demeanor.

The Mayor wasn't looking forward to this conversation, but it needed to take place. "Sorry to interrupt, Burt, but I need to speak to you about something."

"It's gonna have to wait, Buckley. Got a schedule to keep," the mechanic said with sharp words. The man brought his eyes down to the triangle-shaped project in front of him that featured two mountain bike wheels on the end of an axle. His hand came up to the open mask along the side, his fingers wrapping around the edge.

Buckley assumed he was about to flip the mask down and resume his work. The Mayor needed to stop him and continue the conversation.

However, before the Mayor could utter his next word, Sheriff Apollo arrived and joined him at his side, his voice charged with volume. "It can wait, Burt. The Mayor can't. I'm afraid this is official business. So I'm gonna have to ask you to put down the torch and have a little chat with us."

Burt never looked up at Apollo, keeping his head low and shaking it slowly. It was clear the man wasn't happy about the interruption. After a three-count, the grease monkey stood up, tearing the mask from his head and tossing it onto the workbench behind him.

Burt huffed, then ran his hands through his unruly hair before making eye contact. "Okay, but make it quick. You're costing me money here."

"We can appreciate that, but this won't take long," the Mayor said in an authoritative voice, stepping inside the open garage bay. Apollo followed him as they walked to Burt's location.

Burt grabbed a red shop towel from a rolling work cart next to him and wiped the sweat from his brow, then turned the cloth loose on his filthy hands and fingers.

Buckley decided to forgo the customary handshake, not wanting a messy transfer of grease to take place. He knew Burt wasn't a fan of meet-and-greets anyway, so he figured the man wouldn't take offense.

Burt was a carbon copy of his dad, Bartholomew Lowenstein, the entrepreneur who started the repair shop some twenty years prior. At first blush, one might think the senior member of their family would have been tagged with the nickname Bart, but that wasn't the case. Everyone called him Bubba. Buckley wasn't sure why.

The Mayor remembered the old man's funeral like it was yesterday. A brawl broke out in the church pews halfway into the service. The melee started as an argument over the previous presidential election. Something about gun control, if Buckley remembered right.

As usual, Burt was at the center of the fisticuffs, taking on his toothless cousin Dave. It took an act of God to pry the burly combatants apart, etching the day into Buckley's memory until the end of time.

"Is this about what happened with Albert?" Burt asked, his eyes focused on the Sheriff's duty belt.

Buckley figured the sweaty professional wrench was looking for Apollo's nightstick, worried that another beat-down was forthcoming. "No, this is about another matter."

"How's the eye?" Apollo asked, sounding genuinely concerned.

Burt tightened his chin, and his eyes. "Hurts like a motherfucker. How do you think it feels?"

"I wish it hadn't been necessary, but you can't assault a deputy like that," Apollo said.

"Deputy? Albert's not a real deputy. Who are you trying to fool? He's a lazy dumbass. Everyone knows that. And you just gave him a badge? Seriously?"

"Yes, I did and it was the right thing to do. We've got a serious situation in town, in case you hadn't noticed. And I have a town to protect."

"With Albert and that other spaz?"

Apollo hesitated, looking like he was fighting back his temper. "You know, Burt, you should be grateful that I didn't toss your ass in jail and file charges. There was certainly probable cause to do so."

Buckley needed the tension to disappear. "Gentlemen, what happened at the gas station is ancient history now. We need to move on."

Burt pointed at his face. "Yeah, well, tell that to my eye. I've been seeing double ever since. Gotta close it when I'm using my torch."

"Yes, that's unfortunate. But we can't dwell on the past. There are more important things to discuss."

"Then let's get on with it, Mayor. I don't have all day," Burt said with more air in his words than before. He tossed the wipe away, depositing it on a loose pile of soiled towels sitting a few feet away.

"First of all, thank you for repairing the town hall's generator. It's working much better now," Buckley said, giving Burt a pair of hundred dollar bills from his pocket.

The man snatched the money. "The invoice was for three hundred, Mayor. Where's the rest?"

"I'll have it for you tomorrow. We're a little low on petty cash at the moment."

"That's not what we agreed on," Burt snarled. "I thought you were a man of your word."

"I am. You just need to be patient until I can send my assistant to the bank to restock the cash box. Should be tomorrow afternoon, at the latest."

"Fine. Is that it?" Burt asked.

"No, there's another matter we need to discuss," Apollo said, pointing at the two-wheeled frame on the floor. "You're building a rickshaw, am I right?"

Burt shrugged, looking smug. "Yeah, so? No law against that."

"Actually, there is," Apollo answered in a sharp tone.

The Mayor decided to explain in more detail, just in case Burt hadn't been informed of the new conservation policy. "Since we don't know when the next tanker truck will arrive, if ever, I've designated the town's fuel supply off limits to everyone. Except, of course, in case of emergency."

Burt rolled his eyes. "Yeah, good luck with that. People are gonna need fuel."

"I've already instituted a rationing system, based on need. Everyone seems to be adjusting."

"Well, good for you. What's that got to do with me?"

Apollo spoke next. "We know about the 1932 Indian Chief motorcycle you just bought from Stan Fielding."

"That's what this is about? And old ride I bought from a buddy who wanted to sell it? He needed the cash and I needed the bike."

"We know you're going to use it to pull the rickshaw," Apollo said.

Burt stood there for a moment, blinking. Then he answered. "Hey, people still have to get around, so I thought I'd lend a hand. You know, fill a need."

"For money."

Burt nodded. "It's called free enterprise, Sheriff. Even you can't stop a man from earning a living."

"That motorcycle will take fuel. Fuel we can't afford to spare," Buckley said.

"Wow. You guys are really looking to bust my balls. Over nothing."

"Wasting fuel is more than nothing," Apollo said.

"Look, I figured there's some easy money to be made offering rides around town. So I'm showing a little initiative. What's wrong with that?"

"We'd prefer that you didn't. Others might follow your lead," Buckley said. "And that will cause a run on the town's fuel supply. So I'm afraid we can't allow you to do this."

"Look, I'm not planning on using any of your precious fuel. So get over yourselves."

"Okay, how's that exactly?" Buckley asked, wondering if the man was going to build a wood gasifier for the motorcycle, or possibly some other form of alternative fuel system.

"Got my own supply out back. Topped off the thousand-gallon tank last week, long before any of this craziness started."

Buckley wasn't aware of Burt's fuel storage but still needed to stop the man, for his own good, if nothing else. "Don't you think you should conserve the fuel you have and not waste it on a fleeting endeavor?"

Burt's face flushed red as fire erupted in his eyes. "Fleeting endeavor? Are you serious? I'll tell you what's a fleeting endeavor . . . being an auto mechanic in a small town where all the vehicle electronics have been fried. And I mean totally fried. I can't fix any of it, even if I had the parts, which I don't and probably never will. Even my tow truck is useless. So no, I can't just stand by and do nothing. Only an idiot would do that. Unless I come up with something quick to replace the income, I'll be hanging a Going Out of Business sign on the front of my old man's building. Even you can't possibly think I'm gonna let that happen."

Buckley looked at Apollo for guidance. The Sheriff didn't offer any.

Burt continued. "So the way I see it, you've got no legal standing here. I'm using *my* fuel for *my* motorcycle that I purchased legally to pull *my* cart that I made with *my* own two hands. As long as I'm not breaking any traffic laws and the bike is licensed, which it is, I don't see how you can stop me from using my setup any way I please. In fact, if this idea takes off, and I think it will, I'll build a fleet of these rigs."

"Well, we could always close down the streets," Apollo said, looking at Buckley. "Make them pedestrian-only zones."

Burt laughed, shaking his head. "Sure, that'll go over well. You'll end up with a bunch of pissed-off citizens on your hands. I'm sure you realize there are a lot of old people in this town who can't get around without assistance. They're gonna need my new taxi service. Maybe I'm wrong here, but it seems to me that closing down the streets just to stop my ride sharing business is the last thing you wanna do, especially with the Mayor's reelection coming up next year."

Buckley didn't have an answer.

Apollo was silent, too.

Burt tilted his head and shot Buckley a look of superiority. "Okay then, if there's nothing else, I need to get back to work."

Before Buckley could respond, a gentle female voice spoke up from behind the group. "Excuse me, gentlemen. Are we interrupting something?"

Buckley whirled around. It was Allison Rainey. She was with her mother Martha and her son Victor.

The woman looked at Apollo. "Looks like we meet again, Sheriff."

"Allison? What are you doing here?" Apollo said, stammering over his words.

"I heard Mr. Lowenstein is giving rides to people who need them."

Burt stepped forward, looking damn proud of himself. "Looks like my first customer has arrived. What can I help you with, folks?"

"We need a ride out to my mother's place on Old Mill Road. She needs to feed her animals and get her meds."

"Are all three of you going?" Burt asked. "Round trip?"

"Yes, if you wouldn't mind. How much would it cost?"

"Let's see . . . Three people . . . Old Mill Road . . . Round trip . . . we're looking at fifty bucks."

"Fifty?" she repeated.

"Whoa, that's too much," Buckley snapped.

"Yes, it is," Apollo added.

Burt ignored Buckley and the Sheriff, keeping his eyes on Allison. "It's a long way out there lady, plus I have to wait around for you to finish your business and bring you back. My time ain't cheap. So it's gonna cost fifty. Take it or leave it."

Allison dug around in her purse. "I've only got thirty. Been a little slow at the diner."

"Well then, looks like it's gonna be a one-way trip."

Allison hesitated, looking at her mother and her son. They both nodded. "Then I guess that'll have to do."

"Wait a minute," Apollo said, pulling out his wallet. "I've got a twenty you can have."

Allison shook her head with vigor. "I can't let you do that, Sheriff. Especially after that huge tip at breakfast. That was too much earlier. I can't let you do that again."

Apollo held the bill out in his hand, shaking it. "I insist."

"No Sheriff, we can't take your money."

"So what's it gonna be?" Burt asked her.

Allison's face softened a bit. "Can you come back to my mother's house in a couple of days? I'll need a ride back into town for my next shift at the diner."

"Sure, I can do that. Probably offer you a discount, too, assuming this is gonna be a regular thing."

"Thanks, I appreciate it."

"I'll need a little bit more time here," Burt said before pointing at his project. "I've got some more work to do, then it'll be ready. Why don't you have a seat in my office and let me finish?"

"Thank you," Allison said, shooting the Sheriff a friendly look before leading her family toward the office access door.

Burt turned to Buckley, letting a thin smile grow on his lips. "Like I said, filling a need."

"No, that's not filling a need. What you're doing is highway robbery."

"Supply and demand, Mayor. What choice do they have? Other than walking all the way out there."

"Still doesn't make it right."

"You guys know your way out, right?" Burt asked, angling his head at the open bay door.

CHAPTER 52

Bunker lowered the last of the bodies from the mostly chestnut-colored horse using a rope assembly he'd fashioned from the leftover paracord in camp. The makeshift pulley system was a godsend, giving his back and shoulders a reprieve from the pain. The corpse landed on the others, flopping to its side in an awkward position.

He was impressed with the power and willingness of Franklin's steed—an American Paint Horse, according to its owner. Tango was more than capable and not nearly as skittish as he expected when Bunker first approached him in the forest. He was able to walk right up to the white-legged animal and mount the saddle, without the slightest hesitation.

Good thing, too, otherwise hauling the dead bodies by hand to this well-used game trail would've been a time-consuming chore, not to mention exhausting—the path was nestled at the bottom of a steep ravine.

The horse seemed to instinctively know what Bunker wanted him to do, working with speed and precision, no doubt because of Franklin's training.

Bunker didn't know Franklin all that well, but the towering cowboy's attention to detail was obvious. Not just in his appearance but in the way he carried himself. His daughter Megan was as sweet as they came—another testament to the man's steadfast nature.

"It's all about dedication and effort," Bunker's old man used to say, preaching something along those lines on a daily basis. "They're the keys to success. Got to test yourself, Jack, then see it through."

Franklin must have believed in those virtues as well. Let's face it, being a black man in a small town in Colorado was a test in and of itself. But running a horse stable and supply business in redneck country—that took guts. And balls.

Bunker wondered what his old man would say now if he were still alive. Bunker's past had certainly taken a few wrong turns. No denying that, but here he was, working with a bunch of near strangers in the forest of Colorado. Funny how life takes you down paths you'd never imagine.

Bunker was happy to be back wearing his own clothes, having found them during a search of the camp. It was the first thing he did after the others headed back to Clearwater in the pair of ancient Land Rovers. Thankfully, both women knew how to drive a stick, keeping Franklin from having to drive with a wounded shoulder.

Thus far, the cleanup was going according to plan. He'd found more of the Pokémon cards hidden inside pouches on all but one of the men. Only Grinder's body didn't have a card, but that wasn't a shock since his old riding partner had apparently just showed up at camp before Bunker was forced to burn him with a single round to the forehead.

From what Grinder had said, his old gang leader, Watts, sent him to make some kind of a business deal with the unidentified insurgents. Bunker figured that meant The Kindred were expanding their territory again, obviously not expecting the sweeping EMP attack to hit the countryside.

Just then, before Bunker could take another step, the saddled beast backed up in a lurch, snorting and bucking his head. Bunker stumbled sideways from the sudden weight shift, yanking on the reins to catch his balance.

"Easy there, Tango," he said, running his hand along the animal's neck. He looked around but didn't see anything that could've spooked Tango, other than the lifeless meat sacks lying nearby.

Bunker pampered the animal with long, even strokes of his fingers. He continued talking to the animal using slow, tempered phrases, timing the movement of his hand to match the melodic delivery of his reassurances.

Tango looked him in the eyes, almost as if he were judging Bunker's sincerity. The magnificent creature was an imposing combination of muscle and force, able to trample him at a moment's notice. However, Franklin's ride gave off a different aura. It was one of tranquility, as if Tango was content with just being alive and available to help.

"We'll head out soon, boy. Just need to spread these bodies out, so your friends can have a go at them. Everyone needs to eat."

He admired the symmetry of the rounded spots of white, offsetting the chestnut base with balanced perfection. It was almost as if Picasso himself had painted this stunning portrait, and done so for the sole purpose of Bunker's admiration. He'd never noticed such beauty and elegance in a horse before. Then again, he'd never really been this close to one, either.

It was possible his newfound connection with Tango was simply the product of his exhaustion and raging soreness. He couldn't be sure. Not that it really mattered. He liked how it felt, his emotions guiding him down a new, undiscovered path. A path where four-legged creatures suddenly took on a profound magnificence in the world around him.

Bunker took a moment to soak it all in. Then a new idea stormed into his thoughts.

Maybe it was okay to rely on someone else for a change.

Even if that someone was a non-stop fly-swatting machine, its tail flapping at every insect in the area.

After Bunker swiped his hand through Tango's thick, luxurious mane a few more times, the quadruped let out a blow, nodding like he understood all that Bunker was thinking and feeling at the moment. It was a strange sensation, washing over Bunker like a fresh ocean breeze, caressing his skin with contentment.

Bunker shook off the moment of unexpected tranquility, then tied Tango to the closest branch. It was time to turn his attention to the pile of bodies. He had work to do.

The dead were lying at odd angles in a tangle of arms and legs, reminding him of a loose pile of deli meat, fresh from the butcher's slicer.

The instant Bunker's mind focused on the word *butcher*, a wicked spin of dizziness took over.

The forest around him blurred into a swirling green haze, sending him to the ground on his knees. A razor-sharp headache exploded between his eyes, then shot to the back of his skull. When it traveled down his spine, Bunker slammed his eyes shut and wrapped his arms around his head, trying to stop what was about to happen.

But it came at him regardless.

Images.

Hundreds of them.

Snapshots.

Memories.

Played in rapid succession.

Amplified in color and brightness.

He knew what it was, having endured it all before. It was a vivid replay from Afghanistan—the night before he was due to rotate out. The horrific scene continued to flood his thoughts, stampeding his already exhausted synapses.

One after another, the images flashed. Severed arms. Mangled legs. Headless torsos. Stacked up like sand bags. All of it bloody. All of it his fault.

Bunker fell into the grass with his jaw clenched, writhing in silence. The visual onslaught went on for what seemed like minutes, never taking a moment off.

Then, just as quickly as it had started, the playback stopped. A few heartbeats came and went, then the headache dulled to a speck of numbness. So did the dizziness.

He sat up, his chest heaving and hands shaking.

Tango snorted, then neighed twice, acting like he was concerned.

For some reason, Bunker felt compelled to console his new friend. "I'll be okay, buddy. Just some human bullshit to deal with."

Bunker kept his eyes closed as he took in a long draw of air. He held it for a three-count before letting it out slowly. He ran the sequence again and again, needing to collect himself.

A wet nose pushed at the back of Bunker's head, softly at first, then harder. Bunker pried his eyes open and found Tango standing next to him. A broken branch hung from his bridle, tangled in a knot of leather.

"Clever boy," Bunker said, realizing he'd underestimated his mount.

The stallion pushed at him again and again, this time snorting with attitude.

Bunker freed the broken limb from the reins and tossed it aside before wrapping his hands around Tango's prominent nose. He gave his new friend a tender rub with his thumbs, traversing the streak of white on his snout. "I'm working on it, boy. Just need a minute."

Bunker waited for the energy to return, then stood with knees wobbling. The ache along the back of his neck was at level seven, almost matching the sting in his ribs.

Yet, none of the discomfort surprised him. He'd been through this type of episode before, knowing the weakness would pass. So would the aches and pains, but this time he couldn't wait until they did.

He walked to the bodies and began spreading them out in even rows with space between. Better access was needed for the moment when the game trail came alive with activity.

The feeding frenzy would begin once the sun gave way to the moon. The nighttime air would settle in like a blanket of thick mosquitoes, hovering with a chill over those creatures who called the darkness home.

Nature's garbage disposal, he thought. Fast, efficient, and indiscriminant. Human or not, meat was meat. All of it fair game for those with a thirst for blood and tissue.

The last body he arranged was that of Grinder. The wound in the bald man's forehead was no longer bleeding, but the gaping entry wound was still there, staring at Bunker like a judgmental third eye.

Bunker had known the tattooed brute for four years at last count, sharing hookers and whiskey bottles at various roadside establishments across southern California, some gloomy, others seedy, but each of them welcoming riders who wore their colors.

If someone had asked him a few months ago if he ever could've imagined a moment like this, he would have responded with an emphatic *HELL NO!*

So much had changed over such a short time. One minute he was riding his Harley through the car-clogged streets of LA, and now this.

He shook his head, letting the insanity of the situation soak in. The more he thought about it, the more the long string of unbelievable events came together in his mind, forming a logical roadmap. A roadmap drawn just for him.

Somehow the craziness made sense, almost as if destiny had reached out and touched him. Yet, despite the epiphany, it was time to press on. The past was history and so was his former life as Bulldog, fifth in command of the infamous Kindred biker gang.

He gave Tango a pat on the side of the neck. "Ready to go, stud?"

The horse lifted its nose, sending a huff into the air.

Bunker smiled. "Just try to take it easy on me. I'm not the rider Franklin is. Or Megan, I'm guessing."

Bunker stood frozen for a moment, contemplating his next move.

Suddenly, he wasn't convinced heading back to Clearwater was the best course of action. He'd done his part and saved his new friends, then disposed of the bodies. Surely, they could venture on without him at his point. They were capable and they all had each other. Small towns were like that, pulling together in times of crisis so no one was alone.

Bunker figured Jeffrey would get over it. So would Stephanie, once she stopped dwelling on it. They'd all understand if he decided to quietly slip away and resume his walkabout, a term Jeffrey had used.

Perhaps the biggest reason for leaving Clearwater was Daisy—a unique bundle of grace and power. A bundle with a badge who knew his secret.

It was obvious she no longer trusted him, and he couldn't blame her. He didn't always trust himself. Why should she be any different?

Bunker figured it wouldn't be long before the Sheriff and Mayor were read into the facts she'd uncovered. Eventually, she'd have no choice. The facts would find their way to the surface. So would the truth—it always did, no matter what bullshit was tossed on top of it.

Bunker might be able to keep Daisy at bay for a while, but not all three of them. They'd gang up against him—eventually. No matter how many people he saved.

Sure, his Code of Honor was nagging at him to head back to town like he promised, but his heart wasn't into it. Neither was his logic. He didn't have the energy or time to overcome their doubts, needing to head somewhere quiet. Somewhere he could enjoy some serious shuteye and recover from the beatings.

And maybe grab a steak, too.

And a beer.

There had to be a friendly rancher around here somewhere, someone with a few chores needing to be done. He figured a trade was in order—a little manual labor in exchange for a bed and breakfast. He liked the idea.

"What do you think, boy? Will Franklin mind if I borrow you for a little while? Maybe head to Denver or Kansas City. See what's what. I'm sure we can find a nice stable for you. Someplace with a hot little filly for you. You'd probably like that, wouldn't ya?"

The horse didn't seem to care, only blinking its eyes and flapping its tail at another round of bothersome flies.

"Or we go back to town," Bunker said, wondering if the horse could sense his dilemma.

He stood there another ten seconds, pondering what to do. Once he'd reached a decision, he folded the reins in his palm before addressing the mount with a firm grip on the saddle horn and a foot in the stirrup. He yanked, hoisting himself up with his right leg over first.

The molded leather of the seat settled in under his backside, reminding him he still had plenty of healing to do across his undercarriage. And elsewhere. He still didn't feel confident in the saddle, but was starting to get the hang of it. Of course, it helped getting to know Franklin's horse a bit.

Bunker was about to nudge Tango in the sides with his heels, but stopped when he heard the grind of an engine. But not just any engine—a high compression diesel engine, chattering and knocking as it processed the heavy fuel within its bowels.

Tango's feet became restless and his ears twitched, turning from side to side like a pair of radar dishes in search of an unidentified object.

Bunker leaned forward and rubbed the equine's neck, wanting to keep the twelve-hundred-pound locomotive quiet. And still. The attention worked, allowing Bunker to study the sonic waves vibrating through the humid atmosphere of the forest.

The engine noise was a constant rattling chug, traveling somewhere beyond his field of vision. Even though the pitch wasn't changing, the angle was, indicating the vehicle was headed north. North meant the traveler may have been on an intercept course with the miner's camp—a locale choking in blood and guts.

He ran through it in his mind, crunching the possibilities. It couldn't be Stephanie. She never would've returned to the camp, not with the children and Franklin in tow. The huge cowboy needed medical attention and the kids sanctuary.

It probably wasn't Daisy, either. The Land Rovers were gasoline engines, not diesels. Unless, of course, she changed her ride before doubling back.

But how? Theoretically nothing else was working. They were fortunate to find two working trucks as it was, so that likelihood seemed remote at best.

No, the vehicle cruising nearby belonged to someone else. Someone with an EMP-proof machine. It was also possible the vehicle wasn't within the blast area when the electromagnetic pulse hit. Possibly stored underground or in a metal barn that doubled as a faraday cage. He figured it was one of the anonymous men in black. Men who had a hard-on for Pokémon, as Daisy had quipped. Men who were prepared for this EMP event.

When the engine whine faded, it gave way to the harmonic timbre of the Rocky Mountains. Birds chirped, whistled, and sang, sending invitations of courtship to each other, their ballads interrupting the near-constant backdrop of the breeze pushing its way through the dense thicket of leaves.

Bunker tugged the reins to one side, swinging Tango around to investigate the new arrival. Two taps of his heels sent the animal forward. Two more sent him into a fast trot.

CHAPTER 53

"I wish I could disagree," Buckley told Apollo as they walked into the Sheriff's Office together. "But you're right. Burt isn't going to stop taking advantage of people. Not if there's money to be made."

Apollo nodded, not looking happy about it. "There's not much we can do about it if the citizens are desperate enough to hire him." The portly uniformed man sat in his chair behind the desk, letting his backside land on the cushion with more force than was necessary. He spun around to face the window that peered into the town square with his hand on his chin.

Buckley took a seat on the end of the desk, his knees facing the same window. "Who I worry most about are the older folks. Most of them are on fixed incomes."

"Aren't we all," Apollo smirked, his eyebrows pinched and nose wrinkled.

Buckley cleared his throat, hoping to avoid a conversation about salary. "On a different matter, Gus, I don't think we can wait any longer for Daisy and Bunker to return on their own."

Apollo didn't hesitate. "Agreed. Time to send out search teams."

"Who are you thinking?"

"Me, for one. And I'd like to commandeer your grandson, if that's all right with you. Rusty's already been to Atwater's ranch and I figure I can use his eyes and ears. Plus I'll need to know if anything has changed since he's been out there. He's our only real witness."

"I know he'll want to help."

"Do you know if he can ride a horse?"

Buckley didn't know the answer for sure and didn't want to mislead his second in command. He decided to answer with more than a simple yes or no. "Probably, but I'm betting he'll want to make the trip on his racing bike."

Apollo sucked in his lower lip before he answered, nodding slowly. "I'm sure we can make that work. Though I'm still taking a horse, because pedaling up and down these hills isn't gonna cut it for this old dog."

Buckley laughed, the smile growing by the second. "Yeah, you and me both. Like Mother Nature, Father Time does not negotiate."

"Nor does he take prisoners. This getting older thing sucks," Apollo added, his tone friendly. "Had I known what this would be like when I was younger—"

"No need to go there, Gus. I'm already way ahead of you."

"Good to know we're on the same page. About a lot of things."

"You know what they say, great minds and all that."

"Definitely," Apollo said, sitting forward in his chair with his eyes locked on the bustle of activity outside. "I'll go round up a couple of my deputy teams and get them moving as well. We've got a lot of forest to cover."

"New or old teams?"

"New, I'm afraid. Doc Marino wants the reserve unit to rest. They'll need several days to recover from their hike back to town. Dehydration is some seriously nasty business."

"Sounds prudent. Though I'm not so sure about those two, Albert and Dustin. They're not exactly what I would call physical specimens, plus they're a little green around the edges."

"Yes, they are. But I'll get them up to speed, eventually. Assuming I can ever find the time to do a little training. So far, this train wreck of a situation hasn't stopped for a moment."

Buckley couldn't hold back a nod. "I'm sure Bunker would agree. Train wreck and all."

Apollo stood up and faced the Mayor. "Rusty and I will investigate Tuttle's place first. Then we'll head over to Atwater's stables. I wanna get a look at everything first hand."

"Tuttle's place, huh? Isn't that across the street from Martha Rainey's place?"

"Yes, as a matter of fact."

"You're obviously worried about her fine-looking daughter, Allison," Buckley said, refraining from ribbing Apollo about his obvious infatuation with the new waitress in town.

"Her and everyone else. Wish I could've stopped her from heading out there until we knew more about what's going on, but that's where her mother lives. People are gonna do what they do. There's only so much I can stop legally."

"Roger that," Buckley said, taking a few seconds to run a few more thoughts through his mind. There was one more scenario they needed to cover. "What if Daisy and Bunker happen to stroll into town while you're gone?"

"If that happens, then great. But make sure they stay put. I'm gonna want a full report when I get back."

Buckley paused, his eyes drifting into a long, unfocused stare. He suddenly felt a thousand years old, his energy levels draining the needle toward empty.

"Is there something else, Mayor?" Apollo asked, his tone genuine and concerned.

Buckley exhaled a slow breath, letting the words line up on his tongue. "I don't know, Gus . . . right now, it feels like we're swimming in quicksand."

"What do you mean?"

"Every time we try to take a step forward, it seems like we're dragged three steps back."

"I know how you feel, Mayor. It's exhausting."

"The word exhausting doesn't begin to cover it. Just look at all we're facing. We've got important people missing, no communication equipment, a fuel supply under threat, citizens doing their own thing, no power, no electronics, no real transportation, limited manpower, limited food and medical supplies, and our plan to send out recon teams in all directions has gone nowhere. Oh, and let's not forget, a possible invasion," he said, feeling his blood pressure spike. "Even I'm starting to wonder if we're the right men for the job."

"We are, sir. I'm sure of it," Apollo answered, his tone confident. "We're just a little shorthanded, that's all. Eventually something will break our way. Until then, I think it's important that you and I stick together and stay the course."

"No, you're right, Gus. A united front is the key."

"Absolutely. As long as we make sound, rational decisions, I'm confident everything will work out. You know what they say—two heads are better than one."

Buckley nodded, feeling better than he did a few seconds ago. "Because if we don't take the lead, who will?"

"Exactly, sir. The good citizens of Clearwater are counting on us, whether they realize it or not."

CHAPTER 54

Albert Mortenson put his hand on the lift handle of the garage door, twisting it ninety degrees before yanking it up. The four-panel steel door slid open, allowing the sun to flood the space. The rays of light instantly highlighted the dust in the air, showing a medley of swirls and streaks dancing in the turbulence.

He stood on his toes to push the door into its overhead locking position. It would've been much easier if his dad had installed backup power on the property when he was alive. A generator. Solar. Something. Anything to avoid the constant manual work to open and close this heavy door.

At least the door was insulated. So were the walls, keeping the temperature inside the garage from getting out of control. Drafts of air still found their way into the car shelter, but it was better than it would have been without the extra attention to detail.

Fellow deputy and legendary string bean Dustin Brown walked in first, heading for the lengthy, tarp-covered vehicle parked inside. "How long has this thing been in here?"

"Since before I was born. Dad would only take it out on Sundays," Albert said, following his new friend and rookie meth cook. "Dad bought it brand new from a Plymouth dealer in Denver when he and Mom first got married. I swear he loved this car more than her. Definitely more than me."

Albert rubbed a layer of dust away, then grabbed the strap on the front of the cover. He pulled it back, revealing his father's most prized possession, a 1957 Plymouth Sport Suburban four-door station wagon.

The tarp caught air as he tugged on it, floating atop the vehicle's massive hood. He continued to remove the wrap, giving Dustin a prime view of the abundant glass surrounding the seating area and the acres of nearly-flat steel making up the cab.

"Holy shit, that's big," Dustin said, running his hand across the red paint. He traced his finger along the flaking white of the vehicle's pinstripe, tracing the contour of metal from the front fender well to the set of rear vertical fins. "Even has a luggage rack. Cool."

"Not that we ever took a trip in it."

"I wish I could've seen this thing back when it was new. It must have been beautiful. Look at all that chrome."

"Yeah, Dad was really proud of it. I'm pretty sure it was his first and only new car."

"Can't be many of these on the road anymore. In fact, I don't think I've even seen one before."

"Most people haven't. At least not our generation."

"With all that steel, I'll bet it feels like a tank when you drive it."

"I wouldn't know. Dad never let anyone but him take the wheel."

"How many miles on it?"

Albert tossed him the keys. "I don't know. Why don't you get in and find out?"

"Really?" Dustin asked as the keys hit him in the chest. He made a wild two-handed stab for them but missed, sending them to the concrete floor in a jangle. He picked them up and unlocked the door. When he opened it, the hinges creaked and groaned like an old man trying to get up from an afternoon nap in an easy chair.

Dustin sat inside, gripping his fingers on the vintage steering wheel. His eyes looked down at the dash. "Wow, only 21,066 miles."

"Like I said, only on Sundays. When he was alive, at least."

Dustin hesitated for a moment before he spoke again, his fingers playing with the knobs on the dash. "When did he pass?"

"A little over a year ago," Albert responded, wondering if he should share the cause of death. If he did, it might add to the bond they were forming. "Dropped dead during a church volleyball game, if you can believe that shit."

"Your parents were religious?"

"Not exactly. Dad was there to weather-strip their doors when one of the nuns talked him into playing in a charity match. I guess someone didn't show up and they needed one more guy."

"Jesus, that must have been a shock."

"Yeah, it was. Mom went six months later and ta-da—I inherit everything. Well, after the state did its thing during probate. Took forever, but it's all mine now. Including this old clunker."

"I'm sorry about your parents."

"Don't be. I really wasn't that close to them. All we did was argue whenever I was around. Usually about my weight. Or my choices. Especially my dad. He never really approved of anything I did."

"Most fathers don't."

Time to change the subject, Albert decided. "I have to say, you look damn good behind the wheel. Why don't you go ahead and start it?"

Dustin smiled, then inserted the keys into the ignition. His eyes flared as he turned it. Nothing happened. Not a sound. "Hmmm, battery must be dead."

"Actually, I'm sure the whole engine is dead. This thing hasn't been started in a long time. Cars are machines and you have to use them or they seize up."

"So . . . how exactly is this station wagon going to help us with our transportation problem? I mean, I get that's it's big and all, with tons of room for our first batch of Clearwater Red. But it seems kinda useless if it doesn't run."

"Remember the guy who tried to break my thumb at the gas station?"

"You mean Burt?"

"Yep. He's the best mechanic around."

"You think he can fix it?"

"No doubt."

"But how? He hates your ass."

Albert reached into his pocket and pulled out a Ziploc bag filled with brilliant red crystals. "A trade."

"He's into meth?"

"Wouldn't put it past him. He's obviously a weak-minded man with self-confidence issues. The perfect customer."

"What if he isn't?"

"Then I'll convince him to sell it and make some serious cash. Either way, I'm sure he'll get this sled running for us."

CHAPTER 55

Bunker slowed Tango to a trot as they grew closer to the deteriorating miner's camp. He continued the slower pace for another hundred yards or so before he decided to pull back hard on the reins. Tango responded, allowing him to dismount in one smooth motion. He secured the horse to a stout branch of a seasoned cottonwood tree, its broad canopy providing a welcome respite from the sun's fiery glow.

He decided to use a Clove Hitch, something he learned to tie during his extensive underwater training sessions. It was the preferred knot when attaching detonation cord to an obstacle and he figured it was strong enough to hold Tango. As was the branch he'd chosen, unlike the overgrown twig he'd used before.

His traveling companion was a clever escape artist, but Bunker couldn't afford to let Tango work himself free again. Not until he figured out what was going on with the new arrivals.

Bunker grabbed his rifle and headed up a long, steep incline, pushing his burning thigh muscles to their breaking point. The steep ridge ahead overlooked the camp, a fact he learned while Daisy and he were searching for the insurgents' vehicles.

When he neared the apex, he put the AR-10 in his left hand, then dropped into a low-angle crawl, slithering the remaining twenty feet on his belly.

A stand of underbrush was his target—scrub oak, packed together like a skirmish line on the edge of the ledge ahead. Their orange leaves were interspersed with patches of brown and red, giving them a festive aura. The flora's rainbow of colors would help conceal him, he figured, as he neared the steep drop-off. His arms trampled a handful of discarded acorns. They were yellowish-brown with shallow, warty cups, flattening against the hardpan soil as he moved.

Once in position, he allowed himself a few seconds to take in the view. The scene was almost beyond words. Majestic peaks rose like imposing sentinels in every direction, proudly reaching to the heavens. Trees of every shape, size and color lined the undulating tapestry, huddled together like willing soldiers on a march.

The blue sky held wisps of cirrus clouds, each with curling streaks of moisture leading the way. They looked like massive sprays of paint, floating free in the jet stream as they worked their way toward oblivion.

Birds with mighty wingspans were soaring—four sets of them—spread out across the blue in pairs. Their all-black wings banked hard around a different surface point, waiting for their respective prey to draw its last breath before they swooped in for an easy meal.

The pair of airborne carnivores circling above him might have been eying him, thinking his health was failing. He was moving slow like a dying animal, drawing them ever closer.

Bunker brought his eyes down to the clearing before him. The miner's camp had visitors. Men, by their size and stature. However, they weren't dressed in all-black civilian garb like the last group who'd taken residence here. These were troops, fully armed and covered with tactical gear. Head-to-toe forest green camo was their outfit of choice. A few carried assault rifles with grenade launchers attached, other's without.

Yet seeing troops in camp wasn't the only surprise. They'd arrived in three GAZ Tigr all-terrain infantry mobility vehicles plus a heavier armored personnel carrier. It was a fifteen-ton BTR-80. Russian made. Amphibious. Formidable.

Its high-angle turret, twin deployment doors, 7.62 coaxial machine gun, and 30mm cannon were easily recognizable. So was its welded steel hull and eight-wheel design, something he hadn't seen since his stint in Afghanistan.

"Looks like we were right," he mumbled, wondering how many more Russians were in the area. If this wasn't a lone patrol, then the enemy might already be in country en masse.

He imagined whole armored divisions clogging the interstates, driving up from Mexico with scores of infantry and command personnel, tanks, APCs, mobile missile systems and artillery. He figured they'd brought along plenty of supply trucks, too, and let's not forget radar and air defense batteries. All of it would be needed, and more, especially for an assault on a land mass the size of the USA.

If he was right, then the apparent Russian-coordinated computer hacks and EMP assault had left the US military and its civilians without communications and basically defenseless, except for small arms and munitions, a smattering of EMP-proof vehicles and other limited tech and, of course, explosives. None of which would matter in the end, against an overwhelmingly superior force. Anyone who resisted would be mowed down like animals.

Bunker prayed that Daisy and the others hadn't run into any of these squads. Otherwise, he'd have yet another rescue mission to plan. Or more dead bodies to handle.

His heart wanted to let the emotions in, but his brain fought them back. Now wasn't the time for concern. He needed to think positive, keeping his head clear and mind sharp. Plenty of time had passed since his friends departed. Chances were, if they'd kept driving and never stopped, they made it back to Clearwater before the Russians arrived in this area, he convinced himself.

Normally advance units didn't travel solo, meaning this Russian unit was off on its own, possibly sent here to rendezvous with the men in black. Yet the team he'd killed spoke perfect English—not a hint of Russian—so he wasn't sure if this Russian team would consider the Pokémon Squad friend or foe.

Could be either, he decided, wishing he'd gotten into position sooner. If he'd been able to observe how they first rolled up into the camp, he'd know the answer based on their approach tactics.

The buzz of activity below was furious, with three-man squads scrambling to the various cabins with their long guns held high and tight. Each team took position around the entrance to a different building, moving methodically and with purpose.

Their entry protocols were the same each time: one soldier would approach the doorway, spin around backwards, and kick the door open before stepping aside. The other two operators would immediately scramble inside from flanking positions and sweep left and right to clear.

A lone soldier stood in front of the vehicles, barking orders with his arms folded and legs still. His booming voice was confident and deep, echoing a hail of Slavic syllables across the clearing. Bunker didn't speak Russian, so the words were nothing more than gibberish when they landed on his ears.

Ramblings of a commander, he decided, keeping his eyes locked onto the scene below.

A troop flew out of a shack on the right, carrying something other than an AK-47, the preferred weapon of communists. It was about the size of a small toaster, though flatter and a white color.

Bunker was too far away for an accurate assessment. He didn't have a pair of binoculars or a scope on his rifle—only the non-magnified Leupold DeltaPoint Pro sight, designed for close quarter battles. Compact, durable, and rugged. Not ideal for long range targets or surveillance.

He thought about working his way closer, but his options were limited. The ridge in front of him dropped off sharply and he didn't have climbing gear. So that idea was out.

The only other path he could see was to his right. It led down to the clearing, but the forty-foot-wide rocky trail was devoid of cover. They'd see him coming and unload a barrage of hurt. He was no match for the armament they carried, or the manpower. They'd overrun his position in minutes.

If he had a Barrett .338 Lapua Magnum with a full tactical setup and a spotter, he would have been tempted to take a sniper shot aimed at the commander. But his rifle's range was limited, and so was his marksmanship, leaving him only to observe.

The commander took the device from the soldier and walked a number of paces away from the front of the BTR-80. He stopped next to the wooden platform Bunker had discovered earlier that day.

Bunker could see it clearly from his elevated position—a raised plywood structure with the letter 'X' painted across the middle.

The commander began to fiddle with the device in his hands as more of his men gathered around, forming a semi-circle behind him. A full minute ticked by before any of them moved again. This time, they all craned their necks, including the commander, focusing on something in the sky.

Bunker looked up to see a black speck high above. It wasn't one of the predatory birds he'd seen before. This was something else. Something hovering. Something that wasn't riding the air currents in a hawk-like fashion.

Its altitude began to drop, heading down with focused speed and direction. When it reached the height of the surrounding trees, it gave off a constant whirling hum.

"A drone," Bunker muttered, realizing the commander was holding the remote-control device. The drone and its controller must have been more hardened pieces of equipment, capable of withstanding an EMP event. On the other hand, they might have been stored in a protected area, then launched after the pulse hit the area.

The man's body language gave Bunker the sense that the Russians came here specifically for the drone, as if it belonged to them. If his revelation was correct, then the Pokémon men were part of this incursion and not adversaries. The ramifications were huge—Americans colluding with a foreign military. Americans who knew the cyber-attack and subsequent EMP was scheduled to take down society.

He'd heard about the Deep State within our own government but never thought they'd act against innocent civilians. Someone planned this—traitors. Men and women planning against America with subterfuge on their minds, simply to further their own agenda of control at all costs.

The descent of the four-prop mini-craft was balanced and precise, and it landed on the platform's 'X' with a gentle touch. The drone's footprint covered the entire half-sheet of plywood, telling Bunker it was four feet in width.

The commander waved his hand at the soldier who'd brought him the control unit. The man promptly went to the drone and picked it up. He turned the quad-copter sideways, then retrieved something from its underbelly and gave it to his boss.

A storm of ideas roared in Bunker's mind, none of them good. Either the aerial unit was hovering in standby mode when Bunker and his team took out the men in camp, or it was on a long-range mission and had just been called home by the commander.

If he remembered correctly, civilian models required an operator at all times. Plus, they were limited in range, speed, and battery time.

However, military versions could remain airborne much longer and be preprogrammed with specific mission specs. Many of them carried night vision cameras, while others could be outfitted with an array of lethal weaponry.

If the micro-copter was hovering in standby mode and included a high-resolution camera, then the soldier had just retrieved the video card. If that was true, then everything he, Daisy, and Franklin had done must have been recorded.

Bunker gulped, realizing he'd made a grave mistake.

CHAPTER 56

Deputy Daisy Clark put her foot on the brake pedal of the Land Rover, then depressed the clutch to allow the antique vehicle to coast into a slow, rolling stop. She moved the shifter knob to the center position, testing for resistance to make sure it was in neutral.

Stephanie King was in charge of the Land Rover parked in front of her, having pulled over to the side of the road only seconds before. Jeffrey and Megan were with her, their heads barely visible above the top of the back seat.

"Why are we stopping?" Franklin Atwater said from the seat in the back, his tone weak.

"Not sure," Daisy answered, engaging the parking brake while keeping her eyes locked on the Land Rover in front.

Stephanie opened the driver's door and hopped out, then sprinted across the two-lane road to a stand of bushes. The woman disappeared inside, her hands tearing at the top button on her jeans.

"Looks like another pee break," Daisy announced to the black man lounging in pain behind her.

"That's what? Number three?" his voice cracked.

"Yep. Small bladders. Maybe we shouldn't have spent all the extra time hydrating before we left. Paying the price now."

"It sure would be nice if she could coordinate the stops with the kids."

"A group pee? Yeah, good luck with that."

"It *is* possible, even with kids."

"As a father, you have to know that's never gonna happen, right? Not in a tense situation like this. Even I've been holding it back."

Franklin hesitated before he spoke again, sounding defeated. "Yeah, you're right. Just wishful thinking."

Pop! Pop! Pop! Pop!

"What the hell was that?" Daisy snapped, whipping her head around to the right. Her eyes went in search mode, looking past the steel guardrail protecting the vehicles from the steep cliff just beyond.

"Sounds like gunfire!" Franklin said, groaning. "Quick, help me out of the truck."

Stephanie stumbled out of the bushes with her hands pulling at her pants, trying to hoist them up from her thighs. She headed for the open door to her Land Rover, her stride uneven and awkward, no doubt due to the friction from her skinny jeans.

When Daisy got out of the truck, more gunfire rang out, sounding like a string of firecrackers going off.

She ducked out of instinct, then yanked the passenger door open and helped Franklin out. The man's knees wobbled, but he was able to stand, his left hand pressing on the wrap around his opposite shoulder. The cloth was a deep shade of glistening red, indicating the wound had started bleeding again, probably from his sudden movement.

"You don't look so good," Daisy said, keeping her arm wrapped around the towering man's waist.

"I'm okay. Just a little lightheaded. Get me over there. I need to see what's going on."

When they reached the steel barrier, the sound of gunfire changed in pitch from distant pops to powerful bangs, echoing across the landscape below. Her eyes followed the roadway as it snaked its way lower, navigating the contours of the mountain range.

Franklin must have done the same thing, pointing at an angle across her body. "There, three o'clock."

Daisy followed his finger and found the cause of the ruckus, about two thousand feet below their position. There were four military-style vehicles parked side by side, their camouflaged hoods aimed at the forest nearby.

"What the hell is going on?" she asked, seeing a series of flashes from both sides of the battle.

"Some kind of standoff."

"Is it the Russians?"

"Could be. Or it's just some kind of roadblock. Possibly the National Guard. Can't tell from here."

"Why would civilians be firing on the National Guard? They're the good guys."

"Good point. They wouldn't. Not unless there's a serious threat."

"Then it must be the Russians."

"What's going on?" Stephanie King asked from the left, just as the gunfire stopped.

Daisy swung her eyes, finding Stephanie's. The woman stood near the back of her truck, leaning against the rear quarter panel with her hands latched onto the sides of the metal.

Daisy looked, but didn't see the two kids with her. A good thing, she decided, figuring Stephanie told them to stay inside and keep low. She flashed a quick hand signal, directing

Stephanie to the guard rail. "Looks like there's a standoff between the military and civilians. About a mile below us on the road."

"What did you mean a second ago when you asked Franklin about the Russians?"

"Didn't Bunker explain it to you?"

"Explain what?"

"The possible invasion."

"Invasion? Are you serious?" Stephanie asked, ducking her head lower as she stepped closer. Three more gunshots rang out, this time sporadic and spaced apart.

"Yes. Now stay back. Let us handle this."

"How? How can you handle it? Franklin's barely able to walk. Even if he could, we can't fight the Russians. We need to get the hell out of here. Right now!"

"And go where?"

"Anywhere but here! We've got kids to protect."

"She's right," Franklin said, wincing in pain. "We need to get moving."

"What about Jack?" a boy's voice asked. It was Jeffrey, standing behind his mom with eyes wide.

Stephanie whirled around in a flash. "Jeffrey, I told you it wasn't safe out here."

"But we have to warn him, Mom. He's all by himself."

Stephanie grabbed her son by the shoulders, turned him around, and nudged him back to the Land Rover. "Go back inside right now like I said. I need you to help keep Megan safe."

"Boy's got a point," Daisy said to Franklin, hoping for some advice.

"Bunker can look out for himself. We need to get Steph and the kids out of harm's way. That's our number one priority right now."

Daisy felt a sudden increase of weight on her shoulder. Franklin was getting weaker and leaning on her. She turned him around and led him back to the truck. "Where do you suggest?"

Stephanie was now standing with Daisy, pointing at the firefight below. "Well, I can tell you one thing, we obviously can't continue back to town. Not with all those men down there."

"My place," Franklin said in a matter-of-fact tone. "I've got food stores and a decent first aid kit. We're gonna need both."

Stephanie shook her head, looking defiant. "I don't think so. The last time we were at the stables, my son and I were kidnapped. So was your daughter. And you both know how that turned out. No, you need to pick a better place; otherwise, we're not going."

"Wait, I have an idea," Daisy said. "One that's closer. On Old Mill Road."

"Tuttle's place?" Franklin asked.

Daisy nodded as the video player in the back of her mind played an image of Tuttle's corpse lying on the floor in a pool of his own blood. She and Bunker had killed the men involved with that home invasion, so it might be a safe place to hold up for a while. "That man has been prepping all his life for a moment like this. He's got a massive stockpile of just about everything, including guns and ammo. My gut is telling me we're gonna need it."

"Can't argue with you there," Franklin said.

"Yes, I like that idea, too," Stephanie added.

Franklin continued. "But we should stick to the back roads. Wouldn't want to run into another armed convoy. If there is one, you can bet—"

"There's more," Daisy said, finishing his sentence. "Good thing these trucks have four-wheel drive."

"And plenty of gas. Let's go," Stephanie quipped, turning and walking toward the Land Rover parked in front.

Daisy made a mental note to drive ahead of the others as they got close, planning to run inside and hide the bodies. That was assuming, of course, they were still there. The men in black could've moved them after they took her and Bunker hostage for interrogation. Daisy wasn't sure what she was going to do about all the blood on the floor.

CHAPTER 57

Ten minutes earlier . . .

Misty Tuttle turned her head and locked eyes with her fiancé, Angus Cowie, as the two of them hugged the leaf-covered ground with their chests, her hand squeezing his.

She was thankful for a great many things in her life, but nothing more so than the massive oak tree they were hiding behind at the moment. It was one of the biggest trees she'd ever seen in Clearwater County. Had they'd taken a different evasive route, they never would have found it before the hunt patrol stopped to take position on the two-lane highway. Sometimes you make your own luck and other times, luck finds you. This was the latter.

Her logic screamed at her to get up and run, but her heart kept her body frozen in the spongy bed of oak leaves, nestled cheek to cheek with the love of her life. She worried that the troops gunning for them could hear her heartbeat thumping away in her chest, nearly breaking free from its cage.

Misty knew this might be their last moment together, so she gave Angus a slow, tender kiss. She wanted to remember how magical his lips felt for all of eternity.

His touch was heaven, filling her heart with levels of bliss she never thought possible. Every time he was near, her body electrified, igniting something deep inside that she never knew was there.

The feeling was beyond spiritual, something that words could never explain. Even after their years together, her love for him had never waned. Not for a second, completing all she was as a woman and as a human being.

She pulled away from the kiss and ran the tip of her finger across his slightly upturned mouth. Every inch of him was beautiful, even the smallest of details. She looked into his soulful eyes, her voice now a whisper. "I love you, sweetheart. I have since the moment we met on the side of the road that day."

"I'm sorry I got you into this mess," he answered in his distinct Australian accent, his volume low and purposeful. "I should've known this would happen. Only an idiot would think they'd stopped looking for me, even back here in the States. Everyone in the trades knows the rules—no one steals from Mother Russia and gets away with it."

"I know baby, but you did it for the right reasons. That's all that counts. I'm so proud of you."

Her mind suddenly went into flashback mode, remembering the day they first met. It was shortly after high school, back when her life was out of control and without meaning. Beer bongs and casual sex had filled her weekends up to that point, leaving her yearning for something more out of life. That's when he came along and gave her existence meaning. She couldn't help herself, latching onto the most amazing man she'd ever met.

Misty originally thought Angus hailed from Great Britain, his sexy accent stealing her heart with the very first syllable. Of course, she soon learned she was wrong. The dark-haired, physically fit man was from a small town in Australia, someplace far removed from Europe or anything London related.

The lure of Angus was more than just the way he talked, his voice reaching inside her soul. Even though she'd characterize his appearance as rugged and imperfect, he was a beautiful man, both inside and out, connecting with her on a deep, emotional level.

Angus was unlike anyone she'd ever met before or since. His drive to succeed was only outdone by his intense ability to focus on a task and see it through. But that wasn't all. It was almost like he could read her mind and knew exactly what she wanted at all times, both in the bedroom and out.

She'd never traveled anywhere beyond the borders of Colorado before he came storming into her life, literally, one rainy afternoon in July. If it weren't for the mudslide that had stranded his vehicle, she never would have stopped to help the stranger in need.

Fate had stepped in that day, much like today, when the two of them smuggled themselves back into the USA by hiding in the bowels of a Swedish cargo ship. Their plan was working perfectly, until they ran into a roving patrol of Russians on the hunt for him.

She wasn't sure how they knew Angus had returned, but they did, somehow zeroing in on his location before the two of them could make it to her hometown.

"The EMP should have been the first clue they were already here," he said in a whisper. "I'm sorry, honey bear. This is all my fault. I was fooling myself, thinking they weren't going to want retribution. We never should've returned."

"We had to. For everyone's sake," she said, letting go of his hand. She was the one who'd convinced him to return, wanting to expose the Russian plans among other things. Angus wasn't at fault; she was, secretly needing to see her father while they were here.

"Maybe so, but I should have made this trip alone. I never should've put you at risk like this."

"But I had to come. You don't know my contact in NORAD. He'll only meet with me, nobody else," she said, thankful Angus never asked about why the covert meeting was to take place in Clearwater.

"But what if he doesn't listen?"

"He will. He trusts me. Ever since high school. I took the blame for our senior prank so he wouldn't lose his West Point scholarship."

"Still, I've acted irresponsibly, breaking every rule of my training."

"None of that matters anymore, my love. Trust me, I knew the risks and so did you, but I'm exactly where I want to be and I wouldn't trade a second of it. Even if right now is our last minute on Earth, I'm content to spend it with you."

He grabbed her hand and cupped her palm around his cheek. A moment later, a hailstorm of bullets ripped up the landscape around them. Splinters of wood filled the air from the nearby trees as the two lovebirds buried their heads together in a tangle of arms. Leaves exploded to the right, then to the left, sending dirt onto their backs in clumps.

He whispered into her ear while the thundering gunshots continued in rapid bursts, "I'm going to give myself up so you can get away. They only want me."

Misty shook her head, latching onto his arm. "No, they'll kill you."

"I have to, babe. It's the only option. I'm not letting you die today. When I surrender, you need to run as fast as you can. Don't look back."

"No, I'm not leaving you." Misty looked beyond her feet, scanning the tapestry behind them. There was a narrow path about twenty yards away and it led to a stand of greenery near a gathering of mature birch trees. She knew it was a long shot, but she'd rather die trying to escape than let him be murdered or captured, only to rot in some foreign jail cell. "If we keep low, I think we can make it to those trees. Looks like it goes downhill from there."

Angus shook his head, his eyes tense. "We'll never make it. They'll shred us to pieces."

"I don't care. I'm not letting you go. No matter what," she said, grabbing his hand with all her strength. "But I really think this big oak tree will protect us. Maybe long enough to make it to the bushes. We have to try, honey. We have to. We can't give up. Too many lives depend on it."

He shook his head with a steadfast look on his face.

Misty knew what that meant—he'd made up his mind and there was no way to change it. His determination was set, but she had to try again, even if it meant telling him something she'd been saving for the right moment. Granted, this wasn't that moment, but she couldn't wait.

"You have to go. There's no choice now," she said, hoping to penetrate the fortress he'd built around his decision to lay down his life for hers.

He flared a concerned look at her. "Why? What are you saying?"

"I'm pregnant," she confessed, waiting to see his reaction.

He froze, bullets ripping up the landscape around him. Then a smile grew on his lips.

She kissed him on the cheek. "That's why I arranged the meet in Clearwater, so I could tell my dad at the same time. I wanted both of the men in my life to hear the wonderful news at the same time."

He nodded, his face turning soft. Tears welled in his eyes.

Right then, she knew she'd cracked his defense armor and touched his heart. She continued, this time with more urgency in her voice. "That's why we have to escape together. Right now. Our child can't grow up without a father."

When the shooting stopped for a few seconds, she took action, crawling away from the oak tree with Angus in tow. Her free hand, lead elbow, hips, and both knees pushed through the leaves, leaving only half of her body exposed above the surface.

One of the attackers yelled something in Russian, then the shooting started again, bombarding her eardrums with random bangs and pops.

A few rounds whizzed past her head, one finding its way through a patch of her shoulder-length hair, dangling to the side. The round's inertia tugged at her scalp, making her duck.

Misty continued the desperate crawl to safety, working her body even faster as the firestorm intensified. Somehow, she and Angus were still alive, even though an endless stream of lead was tearing up everything around them.

More Russian voices rang out from the road behind them, their words reaching her ears between the machine gun bursts. Even though she didn't understand Russian, their tone and inflection told her they were desperate and pissed, frothing at the chance to take down the man who'd stolen their top-secret information.

"Keep moving," Angus said, "They'll try to flank us."

She made it to the bushes, then let go of Angus' hand and dug her way through the branches. Her fiancé was right on her heels, taking the same path she was making with her hands.

"Faster, don't stop," he whispered, his tone desperate.

When her feet made it through the foliage, she discovered she'd been correct about the downhill grade. Unfortunately, it was a steep drop-off, taking the ground away in an instant.

She fell feet first, sliding down the embankment on her backside with only the force of gravity in control. The path was Teflon slick, thanks to a bevy of compacted pine needles and oak leaves covering its surface.

Misty brought her arms up to block a gauntlet of branches from whacking her in the face. Tree after tree flew past, some on the right and others to the left. The slide path banked sharply around a stand of boulders, taking her with it like an engineered bobsled course.

She took a peek behind her to check on Angus. He was still with her, though he was sliding headfirst, his groans intensifying with each passing second. At least the sound of gunfire was fading, the mountainside taking them away from harm.

Misty wasn't sure how long they'd been falling when she finally spotted the end of the ride coming at her. She lifted her legs and landed butt first in a low spot, only a short distance from the edge of a river.

The leaves were thick when she hit, cradling her in a blanket of softness up to her neck. She thought she might sink deeper into the compost, but her shoes found the hardpan below.

Angus arrived next, his right shoulder catching hers as he zipped past. He tumbled out of control and disappeared into the leaves.

She waited for him to make an appearance. But he didn't, sending her into a panic. Her hands dug into the leaves as she searched from left to right. She hoped to find skin or clothing, but only discovered a cold dampness between the leaves.

"Angus!" she cried out, continuing her hunt with a step ahead. She fished around the leaves, tossing them into the air as she dug. He had to be here, somewhere.

Another minute went by before something inside her made her crane her neck to look up. Her eyes scanned the ridge above. All clear. No Russians. Not yet, anyway, but she knew they'd appear soon.

She moved a foot to her left to tunnel into another area. Right on cue, her fingers made contact with something round and hard. Wait, check that. It was soft with hair—his head. She moved her hands lower and found his shoulders, digging her reach under his armpits. It took all her strength, but she managed to pull him to the surface.

When his eyes finally came into view, she gasped. They were closed. He must have been knocked out cold, probably due to the four-inch gash on his head, the skin hanging open and bleeding in spurts.

Just then, a thought came unbidden into her mind. He could have been dead. She couldn't tell. Her heart beat at an even faster pace. Regardless, there wasn't time to find out, not with the Russians hunting from above. She moved her hands into a rescue hold, much like a lifeguard would use to save a drowning victim. She tugged at his frame, dragging him free from the mound of leaves and onto the sand that bordered the river.

Misty put his limp body down and checked the ridge again for activity. Still no sign of Russians. She needed to get Angus out of here while there was still time, but she didn't know how. Carrying him wasn't an option. He was too big and she wasn't strong enough.

That only left the river. The current was swift with whitecaps popping across the raging water. Maybe they could float downstream a few miles, far enough to escape the reach of the Russians. She'd have to keep his head above water and avoid any rocks. A risky option to be sure, but the only one. So far, luck had been on their side. Maybe it would continue.

Misty bent over, latching onto his torso from behind. She yanked with all her strength to begin the haul to the river. The water would be cold, so she steeled herself for the shock that would come next.

CHAPTER 58

Mayor Buckley opened the front door to Charmer's Market and walked inside. He counted five customers milling about, each with a portable food basket draped over their arm.

Some of the store shelves were noticeably empty, but that didn't seem to dissuade the shoppers, whose eyes were locked like heat-seeking missiles, scanning the aisles for targets.

One of the customers was William King, the curly-haired owner of the Silver King Mine. The candy aisle had the lanky man's undivided interest, his back turned at an angle to Buckley.

Grace Charmer waved at Buckley from the cash register that was located just inside the front door. Her thin smile and welcoming eyes indicated she was in good spirits, probably because the stampede of food sales had finally slowed down.

The gray-haired widow wasn't getting any younger, and after the broomstick fight with Allison Rainey, she certainly needed a vacation. If nothing else, some sedatives and a good night's rest. Or two.

Buckley gave her a friendly nod, then cruised past the register on his way to King's position. When he arrived, he cleared his throat and waited for the blond man to finish dumping two candy bars into his basket.

When King turned around, Buckley said, "I've been looking all over town for you, Bill."

"Well, what do you know? I was just about to head over to see you, Mayor."

"Then I guess this is good timing,"

"Do you have some news?"

"Well, that's what I wanted to talk to you about. Unfortunately, we haven't been able to locate your ex-wife or your son."

The man's face turned a deep shade of red. "Shit, I knew it. That bitch skipped town for good. I should've had her arrested when I had the chance."

"Easy now, Bill. We really don't know if she left town or not. All we know for sure is that they are still unaccounted for."

"Well, she did it once, so it's not a stretch to assume she did it again," King snorted, his eyes darting back and forth. "It's that damn Bunker guy. He's the reason for all of this. I know it."

Before Buckley could respond, Grace yelled from the cash register, "Hey, look!"

Buckley turned to see her pointing at the front window just as a full-sized semi-truck rolled past the front of the store. The white tractor-trailer had a series of four blue letters stenciled on it, which were highlighted by a blue stripe running diagonally from low to high.

"Are you kidding me?" King asked. "FEMA?"

"Damn, that was fast," Buckley muttered, letting the revelation sink into his brain. With communications down, the town had no way to call for help, yet the Federal Emergency Management Agency was here with vehicles that worked after the EMP took down everything. He was impressed with their disaster planning and reaction time, both right on the mark, bringing them here when the citizens needed them most.

Two more massive vehicles drifted by on the pavement outside, the rumble of their weight sending a slight shimmy into his feet. The second truck was another lengthy tractor-trailer with the same four letters and blue accents as the first.

However, the next one was about half as long, with the words EMERGENCY OPERATIONS stenciled on its side in bold red letters. The radar dish mounted just behind the cab was facing the rear of the vehicle, drawing Buckley's eyes to the access ladder attached to the back.

"This has to be some kind of all-time record," King said in a sarcastic tone, standing next to Buckley. The shopping basket was still in his hand. "It took FEMA, what, like a week to show up after Katrina hit?"

"Yeah, something like that," Buckley answered, never taking his eyes from the window as the parade of trucks continued, one after another.

"Jesus, it looks like they sent the whole fleet," King said, his eyes pinched. "A fleet that still runs after the EMP. Someone was prepared."

The hairs on the back of Buckley's neck started to tingle, tickling the skin around them. The feds must have prioritized Clearwater's situation somehow. Even though he was thankful for their quick response, he wasn't sure if their sudden appearance was a good thing or not. He needed to find out. "I should probably get out there."

"I'll come with you," King said, putting his basket down on the checkout counter as they walked past the register.

"Hey, you need to pay for this," Grace said, holding up the basket.

"Later," King told her, pushing through the door first. Buckley followed.

King came to an abrupt stop on the sidewalk, grabbing at the sleeve of the Mayor's suit coat. The mine owner pointed to the right, down the street. "Check it out. That's not going to make old Doc Marino happy."

Buckley spun on his heels to see yet another style of truck approaching. This one was just as long as a traditional semi, except its trailer wasn't a perfect rectangle. It had two areas along the sides that stuck out, like a retracted sleeper extension on a RV.

The words MOBILE MEDICAL UNIT were written in red on the side, just under the blue FEMA name and logo. Buckley tried to peek inside its windows as it drove past, but they were tinted black—so much so, he couldn't see inside, even through the windshield. He figured the blackout tint was done as a security measure.

Just then, his mind went into imaginary mode, visualizing the convoy rolling into a federal disaster area, where a horde of desperate citizens suddenly comes out of nowhere to swarm their vehicles. Tactically speaking, the tinting now made sense to him.

"I wonder if they think there's some kind of radiation leak," King said. "You know, after the EMP took everything down. Don't forget, Fort St. Vrain is just north of Denver."

Buckley needed to reign in King's wild theories before someone else caught wind of them. "It is, but that nuclear plant was shut down in 1989."

"I know, but they still store tons of nuclear waste stored there, deep underground. Don't you remember the protests? The news couldn't get enough of it."

"You're reaching, Bill."

"Then there's the uranium mining. Let's not forget what that material is used for."

"I thought those mines were shut down in Colorado?"

"Not all. There's at least one that's still operational. And it's a lot closer than you think."

Buckley wondered if King was hinting at something. Something to do with the Silver King mine. If he was, then King must have gotten caught up in the moment, sharing information he probably shouldn't have. "I guess we'll know more shortly."

The Mayor checked the rest of the seemingly endless convoy for the stenciled letters of *CDC* on the sides. He didn't see any. FEMA was clearly running the show.

Buckley watched the vehicles complete their slow lap around the town square and park single file. The doors to each vehicle flew open and two men wearing dark sunglasses got out of each cab. He didn't see any women and everyone appeared to be dressed the same—plain black pants and shirts—long-sleeved. "I think we have our answer."

"Yeah, no Hazmat suits. Must be something else."

"Like I figured. This isn't about radiation." There was more he could say to take a few shots at King and his crazy theories, but Buckley held his tongue.

The swarm of newcomers quickly spread out and tended to their duties, each moving quietly and without hesitation. Buckley got the feeling this rollout had been rehearsed—a welcome change from what he'd read about after the failed deployment in New Orleans when Katrina hit in August 2005.

Some of the men put orange safety cones around their vehicles, while others carried clipboards as they walked to the rear of their trailers. One by one, the cargo doors were opened, releasing even more men wearing the same casual uniform.

Next came ramps from two of the trucks, pulled out by hand and lowered at an angle to the asphalt. The men stood aside as several all-terrain vehicles drove out of the trailers and down the ramp. Each four-seater featured bright yellow paint and a heavy roll bar design.

"Looks like FEMA did a little Christmas shopping," King said. "Those are just like the two I own, right down to the paint job and 28-inch tires. We're talking top of the line equipment."

"What are they?" Buckley asked.

"Maverick Max Xs. Each one of those bad boys carries 131 horses of turbo-charged kick-ass. Only theirs are still working."

Buckley shook his head as his inner politician took control of his thoughts. "Leave it to the government to spend as much as they can on every piece of equipment. No wonder we owe over twenty trillion in debt."

"Yeah, those rides are about twenty-seven grand a pop, depending on add-ons. Maybe more." King hesitated before he spoke again. "I wonder if those trucks are shielded in some way. It would explain why their Mavericks are still running."

Three more trailer doors opened, only this time off-road vehicles didn't roll out. Bodies did—live bodies—men dressed in all-white lab coats and black shoes.

"Medical is here," King quipped.

"Must have been one hell of a ride in the back of those trucks."

"Probably short on transportation, so they had to make do. We should feel lucky they sent anything at all."

Buckley agreed. "Exactly what I was thinking. Clearwater can't possibly be a priority for the government."

King shrugged, looking amused. "Well, today, we apparently are. That's the first piece of good news I've heard since this whole thing started."

Buckley wanted to rejoice, but something inside was holding him back. "Let's hope it's good news."

"What do you mean, Mayor?"

"Not sure. This just seems a bit off to me."

"Ah, you're just being paranoid. Which, by the way, is usually my job. Funny how quickly things switch."

"Can't argue with you there," Buckley said, holding back what he really wanted to say. When you're the Mayor, you must choose your words—and your battles—carefully, not letting your true feelings and true self bleed through when unexpected situations arise. That's how elections are lost. He put a friendly hand on King's back. "Let's go see what's going on."

CHAPTER 59

Sheriff Apollo stood at the river's edge and waited for his horse to finish a long drink. If Apollo inched his toes forward, they'd be underwater and touching his aging, portly reflection staring back at him.

He locked eyes with his mirror image, his mind wandering to memories of the stunning Allison Rainey. His heart wanted to take over the moment, but he quickly quashed the idea. And the vision. There wasn't time for daydreaming. He needed to stay sharp.

Rusty Buckley was to his left, sitting on a protruding rock with his mountain bike parked a few paces behind. The kid scooped up another handful of water and draped it across the nasty case of road rash on his knee.

The boy's kneecap looked swollen and must have been painful as his fingers pulled out a collection of pebbles from the bloody recesses.

Apollo didn't want to say anything, but the Sheriff's badge on his chest was screaming at him to make a safety point. "Next time, let me take the lead downhill. Your grandfather will have my badge if you don't come back in one piece."

"Yeah, had no idea that rock would be there. Just came out of nowhere, like it was trying to send me flying."

"Slow and steady wins the race, my young friend."

"Not in the Olympics," Rusty shot back a split second later, his face looking as though he regretted answering so quickly.

"True. But out here, we take our time and make the trip safely. Understood?"

"Yeah, sure. I get it. I'll take it slow. I promise. Just anxious to get there, that's all."

"I know, son. But we have a job to do and we can't do it if we're dead. Or seriously injured."

"I'll be okay. I've jacked myself worse than this lots of times. Usually though, it's from catching the tire of a racer in front of me, not some stupid rock in the dirt."

"Still, no more craziness or next time, you're on a horse like me. And I'm sure neither of us wants that. But from here on out, safety must be job number one."

Rusty nodded, his youthful eyes turning to the massive figure standing behind Apollo.

Apollo followed Rusty's gaze up to Dick Dickens, the third member of their team. The temporary deputy's shadow seemed to stretch across as much of the shoreline as the horse he was sitting on.

The faithful steed's pant was heavy and Apollo wasn't surprised. The animal had been working double-time thanks to the nearly three hundred pounds of chiseled muscle on its back.

Apollo had known Dickens for as long as he could remember. Over the years, he'd grown accustomed to his imposing stature. However, to the uninitiated, namely Rusty, the prominent veins in his biceps were like a magnet for the eyes, twisting and contorting like cords of rope every time he moved.

Apollo decided to address Dickens by his nickname, wanting to keep the conversation light. "You're up, Dicky. Might not be another chance for water until we get to Tuttle's place. Make sure your horse gets a good drink."

"You got it, chief," Dicky said, his tone sharp and to the point.

The thirty-year-old behemoth never said much and Apollo was okay with it. Rusty talked enough for all three of them. If Dicky suddenly became a chatterbox, Apollo's patience would evaporate.

It's one thing to coddle a youngster's natural inquisitiveness, but having to deal with a grown man's diarrhea of the mouth, well, that's a different animal all together—a dangerous animal wearing a deputy badge.

If provoked, Dicky could probably break him in half with one punch. But as town sheriff—hopefully, a smart one—he knew better than to test his staff like that. Certainly not the team members who carried an impressive girth across their frame.

Lead by example and never piss off the giant was the new motto he just decided to adopt. He liked it. Plus, it was even more applicable when the bodyguard was a semi-famous offensive lineman.

To a stranger, Dicky may have appeared to be as gentle as a sack of flour. But Apollo knew better, especially when someone got under his skin. Or in his face. Apollo remembered several defensive linemen who'd made that mistake over the years, their season ending after a series of forearm-led concussions.

Apollo liked to call that side of humanity *The Demon Self*—that thing inside that all of us have, but none of us ever wants to set free. Not until the shit hits the fan.

Before the Sheriff could utter the next phrase forming on his lips, echoes of gunfire erupted. They were off in the distance, but distinct. It was a heavy barrage that was originating from upstream, somewhere beyond the trees.

The echo of the rapid-fire pops told him they were from a machine gun. Possibly more than one. The pops were not close by, but not far either, factoring in the uneven terrain of the mountain range and the bend in the waterway.

"What was that?" Rusty said, standing up on the same rock he'd been using as a triage chair.

Dicky hopped down from his mount and moved in close to the kid.

"Automatic weapons," Apollo said, pulling his horse from the water.

"What should we do?" Rusty asked in a hurried voice, his eyes pleading for an answer.

Apollo gave the reins of his horse to Dicky, then pulled the gun from the holster on his hip. "You two stay here. I'm gonna go have a look."

"By yourself?" Rusty asked. "On foot?"

Apollo didn't want to elaborate, deciding to keep the answer short on words and detail. "I'm sure it's nothing. Probably just some yahoos out here testing their new machine gun. I'll be back in a few minutes."

"What do you want me to do?" Dicky asked, his square jaw stiff and ready for a fight.

"Keep an eye on our young friend here. Make sure he doesn't wander off. If I'm not back in twenty minutes, then use my horse to get him back to town on the double. Don't wait for me. Understood?"

Dicky nodded, grabbing Rusty with his oversized hand. The kid didn't struggle, following the man's lead.

A moment later, a woman screamed, "Help us! Please! Help us!"

Apollo tried to locate the female's position, but his eyes came up empty.

She called out again for help, this time sounding even more frantic.

Dicky pointed upstream about fifty yards. "There. In the water. Two of them. Just passing the rapids near the shore."

Apollo spotted them, their heads bobbing together on the surface. The woman waved one of her arms, while the other was wrapped around the neck of the second person.

"Quick, outta my way," Apollo ordered, planning to run into the river for a rescue.

Dicky held out an arm bar, not allowing the Sheriff to pass. "I got this, sir," he said, giving one set of reins to Apollo.

Dicky hopped on the other horse and jammed his heels into the side of the animal. The beast shot into the water, taking a stance perpendicular to the flow. Dicky leaned down, hanging his arm low with a hand just above the waterline.

Apollo liked the deputy's idea, but worried the man might miss. "Don't move," he told Rusty as he climbed into the saddle. He took his horse into the river, positioning himself about ten yards downstream from Dicky's position.

It took several tries, but Apollo was able to convince his oversized gut to give way to his intentions, allowing him to bend down with a hand extended like Dicky had done.

"Grab my hand!" Dicky yelled to the pair in the water.

"Save my fiancé," the woman yelled, holding up the other person's hand. "He's hurt."

Dicky grabbed the man's hand, sending the pair of refugees into an uncontrolled spin between the horse's legs. The animal got restless, moving forward a step and braying. "Easy boy," Dicky said in a stressed voice.

One of the woman's arms was now free, flapping in the strong current as she tried to correct her balance. She screamed, her other hand holding onto to her fiancé's shirt.

"Just let go," Apollo said, waving a hand at her. "I've got you."

She didn't answer, her eyes wide and showing excesses of white.

Apollo could see Dicky struggling to hang onto both of them, despite his incredible strength. "My deputy can't lift you both up. Not with the river pulling on you. You need to let go and aim for my hand."

The woman shook her head, but didn't respond.

"Trust me. I've got you."

"No! No! No!" she screamed, her face full of panic.

"Please. You have to trust me. Just let go. I'm not going to miss."

She hesitated for a two-count, then nodded and let go. The current brought her quickly toward the Sheriff with her hands held high, then spun her around without warning. She screamed again as the position of her hands was now off course, making Apollo have to lunge at her before she raced past him.

His palm landed on hers, their fingers searching for an interlock. A millisecond later, their hands came together in a tight squeeze. Her grip was strong, no doubt supercharged by the adrenaline pumping in her veins.

The water took her past the belly of the horse, flipping her body around feet first. When their arms straightened from the downstream force, the mass of her body tripled. The sudden weight shift startled his horse, its feet moving back a short, corrective step.

Apollo grunted, sending all his strength to his right hand to keep the river from sweeping her away.

"Don't let go!" she screamed, her face buried in a tangled mess of wet hair.

Apollo wanted to reassure her verbally, but all his focus was on their hand hold. He tried to pull her up, but the river's tug was too strong.

Right then an idea came to him as his grip began to loosen. The horse's corrective step a moment ago. It was the solution.

He tugged back on the reins with his free hand, hoping his mount would know what he wanted. The beast did, backing up one half step at a time until the woman was safely out of the raging water and lying on shore.

Apollo let go of her and sat upright, his lungs burning after the ordeal. Apparently he'd forgotten to breathe during the struggle to hang on to her. Or maybe it was his belly, compressing his diaphragm and keeping the air from his lungs.

A few seconds later, Dicky arrived on land with the woman's fiancé draped across the front of the saddle.

"Rusty, help him," Apollo said in a breathy voice, slowly dismounting with his chest heaving. He dropped to his knees to help the woman crawl free from under the horse. He put his hand out.

She wiped the hair from her face, tucking the wet clumps behind her ears to reveal her eyes. There was a hint of familiarity in her face, but he couldn't quite place her.

Her eyes lit up when they met his. "Gus? When did you become Sheriff?"

The voice registered in Apollo's brain, igniting a flood of memories. "Misty? What the hell?"

"Is my fiancé okay?" she asked, leaning to her right to look past Apollo.

Apollo turned to his deputy, who was now off the horse and kneeling beside the unconscious man. "How is he, Dicky?"

"Not sure, Sheriff. He's breathing, but not very well. It's kind of all over the place."

Apollo pointed at the gash on the man's head. "Get some pressure on that wound. We gotta stop the bleeding."

Dicky leaned forward on his knees and put his enormous hand on the victim's forehead.

Misty crawled through the sand and latched onto her man. "Angus, sweetheart, please wake up. Come on, I need you to talk to me. Right now. Right this very minute."

Angus never moved.

She hugged him, rocking him slowly in her arms as tears rolled down her cheeks.

"What happened?" Apollo asked.

It took a second for her trembling lips to respond. "The Russians."

Apollo didn't believe what his ears just reported. He must have misheard what she'd said. "I'm sorry, what did you say?"

"We were on our way to Clearwater when they found us and started shooting. We tried to get away but—" she said, stopping her response in mid-sentence when Angus opened his eyes.

"The formula? Safe?" Angus asked, his words weak and disjointed. His eyes were glazed and not looking at anything in particular, almost like he was in some kind of waking dream state.

"Don't worry about that now, baby. Just rest until we can get you some help."

"My head," Angus said, closing his eyes a moment later, his head tilting to the left, limp. His chest was still moving, the breaths short and choppy.

Rusty stood up, looking confused. "Russians? They're here? In Colorado?"

Apollo shook his head. "Easy now, everyone. Let's not get ahead of ourselves."

Misty brought her watery eyes up for a moment, aiming them at the Sheriff with purpose behind them. Her voice turned sharp. "They're the ones who set off the EMP."

"Why? Why would they do that?" Rusty asked, his face locked in denial.

She looked at Rusty and hesitated for a beat, her voice sounding apologetic now. "We stole their formula."

"What formula?" Apollo asked her in a cynical tone, worried she was delusional from all the trauma. Sure, Bunker had theorized about a Russian invasion, but he couldn't believe they would start World War III over a stolen formula, assuming any of this was true.

"It's called Metallic Hydrogen. Angus stole it from one of their secret labs."

"Why would he do that?" Apollo asked, his eyes burning a hole in the unconscious man's face.

"And then bring it here?" Dicky added.

"We were trying to get it to my friend who works for the Pentagon. That's why they're trying to kill us. They're going to use it. That's why we came back. To stop them," she said, shooting the words out in spurts. She let Angus slip out of her arms, carefully putting him on the ground. She crawled to her feet, then looked at Dicky. "Can you help me get him on the horse? We need to go. They'll be coming for us."

"Doc Marino?" Rusty asked Apollo, sounding like he was seeking approval.

Apollo nodded, his mind working in slow motion, still chewing on the facts. "If we head toward the lake, it'll take us straight to route six."

"No!" Misty snapped. "We can't. They're setting up roadblocks everywhere. We'll never make it to town."

"Roadblocks? Seriously?" Rusty asked, shooting Apollo a look of panic.

She pointed. "We should go to my father's place. He has plenty of medical supplies."

"As a matter of fact, we were just on our way there," Apollo said without much thought. His attention was elsewhere, still processing the landslide of revelations.

Misty continued, her eyes sharper than before. "If Martha is home, she can help, too. She's a former nurse. Used to patch me up all the time when I was little."

Apollo nodded, though he still needed a few moments to think this through carefully. Their lives were in his hands and he couldn't make any mistakes. Not with access to town being blocked and armed insurgents taking control.

Of course, all of this was assuming he actually believed Misty and her formula excuse. She seemed genuine and he'd known her a long time. She wasn't one to exaggerate, at least not when her father wasn't around.

The scope and implications of what she just revealed were beyond anything he could have imagined. It all seemed preposterous, almost beyond belief.

There had to be more to the story.

CHAPTER 60

One of the vultures that had been circling overhead landed on a tree branch, thirty feet above Bunker's position. The bird must have thought it was safe to approach its intended meal, since Bunker hadn't moved in a while.

He ignored the scavenger, knowing the meat eater couldn't get to him, not with the scrub oak surrounding his head, neck and body. He was nestled in and protected, from the bird and hopefully from the men in the miner's camp below.

Bunker kept his attention on the Russians, who now were standing around a computer that a soldier had retrieved from one of the trucks a few minutes earlier. It sat on the same lumber stack that Daisy had taken position behind when they first escaped from the Pokémon men.

The commander stood in front of the console, watching something on the screen. Bunker assumed it was the high-definition video from the drone, but from this distance it was simply a guess.

Bunker could also see something in the man's hand, next to his ear. Probably a field radio. If so, it seemed likely that he was calling in the details from the flash memory card.

Was it a video of Bunker and Daisy's killing spree?

Or something else?

Before Bunker could decide what to do next, a loud series of sounds erupted behind him. It was Tango, neighing and nickering in a panic.

Bunker turned his head out of instinct, snapping a branch in the process.

The vulture above him screeched, then took off from its perch, flapping its mighty wings with a swooshing sound.

The Russian commander yelled something from the clearing. Bunker brought his eyes around and peered down to see a squad of rifle barrels pointing up at the ridge. Two soldiers brought binoculars up and pressed them against their eyes, scouring the hillside for threats.

Three men ran to one of the trucks and retrieved a new piece of equipment with a tripod configuration at its base. It was an infantry mortar. The turret of the APC's 30mm cannon was moving his way, too.

Bunker froze, figuring the scrub oak's color array would keep his exact location a secret. He waited, hoping the Russians would decide he wasn't worth the hassle. Or the expense.

Ten seconds ticked by.

Nothing happened.

Thirty seconds.

Again nothing.

Maybe he was in the clear?

Just then, one of the binocular-wearing men pointed at the ridge and said something in Russian.

The commander didn't hesitate, pointing at the ridge and yelling commands. The troops fired their AK-47s in earnest, unleashing a world of hurt at the ridge.

Bunker ducked, burying his head in his hands.

The chatter of automatic fire tore at the countryside, lighting up everything in sight. Rocks split apart, bark exploded, and tree limbs shattered as the barrage intensified all around him. Some rounds hit close, others not. He knew the Russians were spraying and praying, hoping to land a lucky shot from afar.

When the men fired their grenade launchers, mounts of dirt started to fly apart. He decided it was time to bug out. He slithered away from the ridge, keeping his face buried in the surface clutter as bullets whizzed past his head. It wouldn't be long before the mortars were brought into the fray.

He hadn't planned an emergency egress like he should have, failing rule number four of SERE training. SERE stood for *Survival. Evasion. Resistance. Escape,* the latter of which, escape, was taking up the most space in his mind at the moment.

The only choice was to make a run for it, then hop on Tango and gallop away through the dense forest. It would take the Russians some time to work their way up to the ridge, so it might give him a decent head start.

Bunker stood in a crouched position to run, but as expected, a salvo from the mortar launcher delivered its first shell. A tree exploded to Bunker's left, its wide base disintegrating in a cloud of dirt and smoke.

The shockwave smashed into Bunker, sending him flying, tumbling through the brush like a football squib kick. He flipped, spun, and skidded, somehow missing a tree stump and a pile of rocks that would have brought a swift and painful halt to his momentum.

Once he came to a stop, Bunker rolled over to his knees, planning to get to his feet, but the high-pitched squeal in his ears kept his balance from returning.

His body wasn't responding to commands from his brain, either, no doubt overloaded by the compression wave and the disorientation flooding his senses.

Two more rounds from the grenade launchers hit the forest. They weren't close, but the damage was visible.

A second later, another mortar shell landed on the ridge, this time to the right, far enough away that Bunker wasn't caught up in the destruction zone.

More guesswork by the Russians, giving him a glimmer of hope that he might make it off the ridge without having his body ripped apart like string cheese.

The sound of the explosions tearing apart the forest, however, still nipped at his eardrums. He covered his ears with his hands, sucking in a half-dozen breaths in an attempt to quell the pain. It seemed to work, his legs finally listening to commands from his brain. He got to his feet and staggered forward.

It would only be seconds before the troops in the clearing readied another mortar with his name on it.

He ran in an unplanned zigzag pattern, his balance erratic, stumbling with irregular foot plants. A straight line would have been preferable, but he'd take it. Distance was good, any type of distance, and in any direction that led away from the clearing. The range of the weaponry wasn't endless, but he still had a long way to go to escape the field of fire.

Another round hit, this time dead ahead, slamming into the side of a small rise in terrain just beyond a pile of boulders. The earth flew apart, sending rock, grass, and other debris in every direction.

The blast knocked him back, twisting and flipping in the air. He felt his legs rotate once around before they found the ground again, landing sideways on his knees. Bits of rock slammed into his left shoulder, feeling like someone was peppering him with golf balls.

Each impact stung, but he shook it off and got to his feet again, deciding to take a different route than before. He ran parallel to the ridge, figuring the Russians were assuming he was retreating in a straight line away from the ridge and adjusting their trajectory accordingly.

Bunker's new flanking route would take him to the far left, then he'd turn right to head away from the ridge. Eventually, he'd turn right again, zeroing in on Tango's location. That was assuming the horse was still where he'd left him.

The animal must have been frightened to death, each explosion causing an even greater state of alarm. Bunker imagined Tango rearing up on his hind legs, flailing his front legs and kicking to free the reins.

The Clove Hitch was strong. So was the branch, but when twelve-hundred pounds of pure muscle got angry, there was no telling how much damage could be done.

Another shell went off—farther away from his position, just as Bunker expected. He could see the impact point, shattering a mighty oak in half in a cloud of smoke and dust. He dove behind a pile of deadfall to avoid the concussion wave and any possible shrapnel hurled his way. So far he'd been lucky, but he knew it was only a matter of time before something took him down.

The automatic weapons fire finally stopped, leaving the detonation sound of the latest mortar shell echoing across the mountaintop. Bunker listened for Tango but didn't hear him. He wasn't sure if that was a good thing or not, but he'd know soon enough.

He resumed his dash through the forest, running another hundred yards or so to the left. Another shell landed in the distance, proving his theory to run an evasive flanking route was the right choice. He kept his pace, turning right while tracking the number of seconds between bombardments.

The timing seemed consistent, providing him with a sense for when the next detonation would arrive, which was now. He dropped down behind a pair of large rocks with moss growing on one side, steeling his mind and his body in preparation for the next round of incoming.

The blast arrived on schedule, blowing apart another area on the ridge. He wasn't sure where this one hit since he was behind cover, but it wasn't close. The sound was much less intense than the last, indicating the enemy was working a different area of the ridge.

He got up and took off, making good time down a natural game trail, its brush trampled and dirt exposed. His energy level was holding, no doubt due to his fight or flight response taking over.

The adrenaline pumping in his arteries felt invigorating, giving him more speed and determination as his body pain faded and his muscles came alive.

Just then, he heard the sound of water on his left. A stream, he figured. Wait, check that, more like a river. Something with rapids or possibly a waterfall. He changed course, planning to take cover and then grab a drink after the next shell landed.

Bunker stepped around a smattering of birch trees, then stumbled through twenty feet of thick brush, using his arms as pry bars and as shields to keep the branches from cutting into his face.

He expected the water source to appear next and it did, in a deep ravine ahead, down a nearly vertical embankment that led to a stand of bushes with red berries on them.

Bunker wasn't sure if he should classify the water source as a river, but it was certainly a heavy stream. He couldn't judge its depth, but it was somewhere close to thirty yards in width. Not that it mattered. The current was heavy, with several rocks protruding up from the water, each reaching at least fifteen feet above the surface.

Their stoutness impeded the flow's swiftness, creating trails of bubbling whitecaps to the left, their color and length reminding him of fading contrails in the sky.

His eyes locked onto one of the bigger rocks across the waterway, near the far bank. It was shaped like a giant finger pointing at the sky. It even had a pair of wide knuckles jutting out along its midsection.

Everywhere he looked he saw collections of dead trees, branches, and garbage on the upstream side of the rocks, huddled together and pinned against the stone by the force of the water.

Before he could take another step, a blast landed to his right. The explosion was uphill from his position, digging a massive crater into the hillside.

Dirt, rocks, and plant life were sent airborne. So was he, twisting backward and to the left like someone had tied a bungee cord to his pants and yanked it with the force of a semi-truck.

His solo flight seemed to go on forever, with time ticking in slow motion. Then a shredding pain tore into his left forearm just as a cool splash of water flooded his legs.

Bunker's backwards momentum stopped an instant later, snapping his head back against something hard.

He closed his eyes to contain the pain from the whiplash and the impact, then everything went black.

CHAPTER 61

Mayor Buckley ignored the growing crowd of townspeople behind him as he waited for the oldest of the FEMA representatives to finish his conversation with three other men.

Buckley couldn't help but stare at the circular bandage along the left side of the man's neck. It was tan-colored and about the size of a nickel, positioned just under the earlobe.

When the pale fellow with thick, gray hair locked eyes with him, Buckley stepped forward to engage. "I take it you're the man in charge?"

"Yes sir. John Howard. Field Commander," the man answered, his words thick with an English accent. His slightly down-turned eyes and broad, wrinkled forehead gave him a distinctive, intelligent look. Almost professorial. "And you are?"

The Mayor put his hand out for a shake, holding it strong to send a message. "Mayor Seth Buckley."

Howard grabbed it, giving it a firm shake.

Buckley took his hand back. "What's going on here, gentlemen?"

"No reason to be alarmed," Howard said, his eyes sharp and focused. "This is just a precautionary deployment."

"For what?"

"Is there somewhere we can chat in private?"

Buckley hesitated for a moment, his mind churning through the request. A private chat? There was only one reason for a FEMA Field Commander to say those words. Something was seriously wrong. Howard didn't want others to hear their conversation. Buckley's heartbeat skyrocketed as he pointed to a building across the square. "How about my office?"

"That'll be fine. Lead the way, Mr. Mayor."

Buckley wanted a second pair of ears in the meeting with the FEMA commander, so he motioned to the tall blond civilian standing next to him. "This is Bill King, one of our most prominent business leaders. I'd like him to join us."

"That's fine, Mayor. It's your call," Howard said and redirected his hand to King, shaking it as well. "Pleasure."

King shook it twice, but said nothing. Buckley figured King had become concerned about the private meeting as well, keeping his lips silent.

Buckley turned and began the trek to his office with King and Howard following behind. He ran a quick visual check of the other FEMA men nearby. Each of them had the same circular bandage attached to their necks as Howard, and they were in the same location. He wasn't sure what it meant, but he planned to find out as soon as they were behind closed doors.

All three men were silent until they stepped inside Buckley's office on the third floor of the Town Hall.

King spoke up first, his tone light and probing. "Sounds like you're from across the pond. I'm guessing London."

"Australia, actually. From a small coastal town called Wollongong."

"Never heard of it," King responded in a gruff tone.

"You're a long way from home," Buckley said without hesitation, wanting to defuse any potential offense from King's demeanor. He had a million questions to ask Howard, but one found its way to his tongue first.

"How did you end up working for FEMA?" he asked, realizing the question was probably the least important one he could ask at the moment. He wasn't sure why his lips uttered that query before any of the others. Maybe his heart had decided to trump his logic in some kind of stall maneuver, not wanting to have this conversation.

"Actually, my team and I are on temporary assignment. We were in country training when the EMP swarm hit. I'm sure you can imagine that US Emergency Services are spread rather thin at the moment. They needed volunteers, so here we are."

Buckley didn't like the sound of the word *volunteers*. "Well, we appreciate the help and the quick response, though I have to admit, I'm a little more than astonished that you're actually here, in Clearwater. Certainly there are more prominent communities needing help. Like Denver. Or am I missing something?"

Howard paused before he spoke, looking as though he was searching for the right answer. "I'm not sure how they do things here in America, but where we're from, we go where they tell us. We don't ask questions."

"I understand, but why exactly are you here?" Buckley asked, avoiding a different question burning a hole in his mind. The word *volunteer* was the cornerstone of what he really wanted to ask about, but he needed to tread lightly until he knew more about these men and their mission.

"We've been tasked with containment."

"Containment of what?"

"There's been an incident in Denver."

"Incident?" King asked in a sharp tone, flashing an intense look at Buckley.

"When the EMP swarm hit, it created a minor breech in a CDC bio-containment facility."

"I'm sorry, what did you say?" Buckley asked, not believing what he'd just heard. The word *swarm* was out of place and brought an even higher state of alarm to his chest, especially when it was followed by the word *breech*.

"One of their storage units failed. We've been sent here as a precaution to inoculate the residents of Clearwater in case the hazard cloud makes it way here."

"Jesus Christ!" King snapped. "Hazard cloud? Are you frickin' kidding me? We've got families living here. Women. Children."

"Like I said, we're here on a precautionary basis. Nothing to be alarmed about. The CDC has protocols in place for such an event as this. So does FEMA. My men are setting up the medical unit right now."

Buckley pointed at the man's bandage. "I see you guys already got your injection."

"Yes, it's standard procedure for all first responders to be treated before they head into the field."

"What exactly is involved in this treatment?"

"A simple injection every day for the next thirty days. We have plenty of supply."

"Thirty days?" King snapped again, his face looking even more agitated than before. Buckley figured the high-strung man was about to blow. Not that he could blame him.

Howard tightened his eyes, checking his watch with a flash of attention. "The lengthy protocol protects against any possible contagion."

There was an extended pause in the room.

"Are we talking anthrax, or what?" King asked with fire in his eyes.

"No sir. Nothing like that. However, I can't elaborate since the compound being stored is of a classified nature."

"Do you hear what they're saying, Mayor?" King said, throwing his hands out to the side.

One of Howard's men came through the office door and handed him a clipboard. The commander flipped up the top page and studied the page below it for a few moments, then gave it back to his underling. "Let's move the timeline up. Make sure everything is ready. We begin in five minutes."

The FEMA assistant nodded, never uttering a word. The young, dark-haired man turned crisply and walked away, heading for the door.

Howard looked at Buckley. "We'll need to start with the children and the elderly, then move on to the more able-bodied residents."

"So tell me this," King said, folding his arms over his chest. "What happens if we refuse these inoculations?"

"Then you'll suffer the effects when the contamination makes its way here. Trust me, you don't want to be in that situation."

"When it makes its way here? I thought you said this was precautionary?"

"It was. However, my second-in-command just informed me that the winds have shifted. We no longer have the luxury of time."

"Are we talking fatal?"

Howard nodded, his face devoid of emotion. "Unfortunately, yes. Everyone will need treatment. No exceptions. I have my orders."

"What about livestock and pets?" Buckley asked, trying to gauge the nature of the threat.

"They won't be affected."

King grabbed Buckley by the arm and led him to the far corner of the office. His voice went into a whisper. "Do you buy any of this?"

Buckley's gut wasn't sure, but his logic was. "FEMA and the CDC obviously sent these men and their equipment here for a reason. We need to listen to them."

"But they're a bunch of volunteers who aren't even from the US."

King was right. Buckley didn't like what he was hearing, either. But as Mayor, he couldn't let his suspicions take over without more concrete facts. He had a job to do and that meant he needed to show strength, even though his emotions were boiling over just like King's. "I understand what you're saying, but I don't think we can gamble with the lives of everyone in town. There's obviously a threat. A serious one. Why else would the feds send in all these resources? I think we should be thankful they're here so quickly."

"I see your point," King said after a short pause, his words less uptight.

"Then it's settled?" Buckley asked, not wanting to pull rank and overrule the man's apprehension. The day would go much smoother if King was onboard.

"What about the people out of town, like my son? If we do this, FEMA can't just focus on whoever happens to be in town at the moment."

"Of course not. My grandson, Rusty, is out there, too. So are the Sheriff and a number of other people."

"I think you need to demand that they take those four-wheelers out with the vaccine right away. If a hazard cloud is on its way here, then the out-of-town people are at the greatest risk."

King was right, again. "Let me see what I can do." Buckley walked back to the FEMA commander. "Mr. Howard," he said, taking a moment to formulate the words he wanted to bring to bear. "Are you aware that we have residents who are outside of town right now?"

"Yes, Mr. Mayor. I am. We have a list. Nobody will be skipped, trust me. My orders are clear."

"What about those four-wheelers?" King asked, not waiting for Buckley to address them. "Why don't you send them out first?"

"We plan to do just that. In fact, we're gearing up now."

Buckley nodded, feeling a sense of calm wash over him. His logic was correct. These men had it handled.

King held quiet, though he still didn't look convinced.

"Is there anything else, gentleman?" Howard asked in his thick Australian accent. "I need to get back to the staging area."

Buckley looked at King, waiting for an answer.

King shrugged, then nodded.

"I guess that about covers it," Buckley said. "But if we have more questions—"

"Just find me and I'll answer them. We're here to help," Howard said, not waiting for Buckley to finish his sentence before he headed for the office door.

CHAPTER 62

Burt Lowenstein stood on the paved forest road, staring at his recently purchased 1932 Indian motorcycle with his hands on his hips. He was fresh out of ideas after spending the last twenty minutes tinkering with the engine after it quit.

Luckily the motor failure happened after he dropped off his first paying customers—the Raineys—at their remote homestead on Old Mill Road. Otherwise, word would have flown around town that his new rig was unreliable.

There were piles of money to be made with his new taxi service, but breakdowns weren't an option. Not when ferrying around the elderly and the lazy.

He figured he was at least ten miles from town, but couldn't be sure. The bike's odometer was useless since he didn't get a chance to hook up the speedometer before the first fare. Allison Rainey was in a hurry and so was he, needing to jump on the cash flow immediately.

Even if he had a working odometer, he wasn't paying attention to the time or distance traveled during the trip back to town. His mind had been focused elsewhere, mainly on the power and speed of the antique machine purring between his legs.

There was something exhilarating about a maiden ride through the mountains of Colorado, the lush peaks and their magnificent scenery zipping past in random flashes of sunlight, offering glimpses of nature's splendor in his peripheral vision.

He could still feel the adrenaline pumping in his chest after navigating the seemingly endless series of blind turns, each one challenging his willingness to push the throttle even farther with a rickshaw in tow.

Stan Fielding sold him the old bike at a rock bottom price and now Burt knew why. Somewhere inside this aging beast was a flaw. One serious enough to stop the engine cold, but small enough that he'd missed it during his initial assessment.

Burt conceded that he'd been blinded by greed, thinking he'd hit the mother lode with a functioning motorcycle—one of only a few in the entire area, he figured, after the EMP had fried everything else in sight.

Burt was confident he could fix the problem, but he'd need his shop tools and the time to diagnose. He prayed it wasn't anything involving new parts. They'd be scarce for an antique like this. Plus, with communications down and transportation choices limited, he couldn't order them. At least not anytime soon. Fabrication would be the only answer. Or cannibalization. To accomplish the latter, he'd need a second bike that matched the first.

Regardless of the cause of malfunction, an adjustment was needed to the deal with Stan. Burt needed to decide on which type of adjustment he'd deliver to his old high school pal.

"Head or gut" was usually the question when one of them had a grievance to settle—a question Stan would most certainly understand.

Burt's old pal had softened a bit after the birth of his twin girls, but that wasn't going to change anything. Not from Burt's perspective. Rules were rules and Stan had to know an adjustment was coming.

Some might think a sharp jab to the seller's face might be overreacting, especially since Burt hadn't taken the time to inspect the bike thoroughly with a vigorous ride at high speed. But he wasn't overreacting, nor was it too harsh, not when someone gave you their word and then shook on it.

Small towns run on deals made man-to-man, and they only hold water if you enforce the trust aspect of the agreement. Friend or not, Burt needed some payback. Payback in the form of a little chin music.

It was time to get the motorcycle to the shop, but that meant pushing the two-wheeled tank up and down hills—a grueling trip to be sure.

Normally, he'd just leave the bike on the side of the road and come back for it with his tow truck, but the flatbed wasn't an option after the EMP had turned it into a 9500-pound boat anchor.

Burt unhooked the homemade trailer from the custom hitch he'd welded onto the rear of the bike's frame, pushing the rickshaw off the road and onto the soft shoulder.

He figured it would be safe until he returned. He hadn't seen anyone on the road since he'd left town with old hag Rainey and her pushy daughter. The kid wasn't much better, but at least they paid in cash.

Burt took a few seconds to visualize what it was going to take to get the bike back to town. He sighed, then shook his head.

The next part was gonna suck, no two ways about it. He walked to the handlebars and latched on with a firm grip before releasing the kickstand he'd customized with a flip of his foot. "Come on, Burt. Suck it up and quit complaining like a little bitch. Just get it done already."

A mile or so later, he stopped to catch his breath. The last uphill grade had kicked his ass, reminding him how out of shape he'd become since high school. Burritos and beer were a mean combination, even though he spent a few sessions a week pumping the dumbbells in the shop's office. Curls were his favorite, with tricep extensions coming in second.

Just then a male's voice came at him from the trees on the right. "Well, look who broke down. The mighty purveyor of all things grease and steel."

Burt snapped his head around to see who it was, following the near continuous sound of pine needles crunching underfoot. It was Albert Mortenson, the grossly overweight rent-a-cop, and his pencil-thin friend.

"Are you shitting me?" Burt said quietly, his tone sarcastic. He sucked in his lower lip, fighting back the urge to utter an angry comeback. Every fiber in his being wanted him to lash out—it was who and what he was, never taking grief from anyone. Even in jest.

Yet he needed to keep his cool now that help had arrived. Three men pushing the machine back to town would make the trek a lot easier, and faster, even if two of the group weren't exactly prime physical specimens.

"Did you remember to put gas in it?" Albert asked with barbed words, laughing at the end of his question. "It's that cap thing on top of the tank."

"Of course I did," Burt answered, visualizing what he could do to this smartass. But he had to let the anger go and focus, at least until they delivered the bike back to his shop. "Just died. Not sure why."

"That thing looks ancient," the skinny deputy said, the straps of a backpack clinging tightly to his nonexistent chest. A deputy's badge hung loosely from his shirt, almost like the tin star was embarrassed to be associated with the guy, trying to get as far away as possible.

"Yeah, but it still ran after the EMP hit," Burt answered, wanting them to know he understood the situation and was smart enough to take advantage of it. "People are going to need to get around and I intend to provide a solution. For a steep fee, of course. A man's gotta earn."

"So you agree? An EMP?" Albert asked.

"Me and everyone else in town. That seems to be what everyone thinks. Why don't you guys help me get this bike back to Clearwater? It'll be a cinch with three of us pushing."

"I've got a better idea," Albert said as his hand went into his pocket. He pulled out a clear plastic baggie with red crystals in it.

"Is that what I think it is?" Burt asked, not believing what he was seeing—or hearing, wondering what Albert meant by *a better idea*. Was he talking business or pleasure?

"Yep. Clearwater Red. A full pound."

"Wasn't sure there was any of that left in town. The supply dried up a while ago."

"That it did, and for good reason."

"I'm guessing it's back and you just used that new badge of yours to steal it from some junkie in the area."

"Not exactly, but that's what I wanted to talk to you about. We were coming to see you."

"Oh really," he said, putting the bike's kickstand down to free his hands from the handlebars.

A sudden thought came storming into his brain—this might be some kind of trap. Albert hated his ass and he needed to be ready to take these chumps down. "What does Clearwater Red have to do with me? You know I never touch that stuff."

"Yeah, right. Come on, Burt. Everyone knows you partake in a little ice now and then," Albert said, holding the baggie up and shaking it.

Burt couldn't seem to stop staring at the crystals. Their glistening red color was almost hypnotic. "Ah, you got no evidence of that. Look, you two need to turn around and go try to fool someone else. I'm not gonna fall for it."

Albert scoffed. "This isn't a sting operation, Burt."

Burt took his eyes from the bag and scanned the tree line, looking for shadows that didn't belong. He pointed, moving his finger from left to right. "So I'm guessing the Sheriff is hiding out there in the woods somewhere. Probably the Mayor, too."

"Why would you think that?"

"Because you and Slim over there would never be stupid enough to try to arrest me way out here, by yourselves."

Albert shook his head, sending his long, curly hair into a wiggle. "I already told you, we're not here in an official capacity. We're here with a business opportunity. Nothing more."

"That's a little hard to believe, especially with those badges on your chests."

"I'm telling you the truth. Dustin and I are here with only your best interests at heart."

Burt rejected the obvious lie, turning his head to the right. He sucked in a full breath to charge his vocal cords, then cupped his hands around his mouth. He knew the Mayor and Sheriff would do anything to stop his new rickshaw service and it was time to force their hand. "Come out now, Sheriff! I know you're there. This ain't gonna work, so you might as well show yourself. I'm not falling for any of this."

Albert's eyes tightened and his voice grew more to the point, emphasizing each word with more volume than before. "You said you needed to earn. That's what I'm proposing here—a chance for you to earn. Especially since the EMP fried your main source of income."

Burt thought about it for a moment, his defense systems still on high alert. He didn't trust this guy and neither did his gut, nagging at him that something wasn't right.

Despite all of that, Albert was correct about one thing—he did need to make some cash, and quick. His repair shop had become a ghost town after everyone realized what took out the vehicles and electronics in town.

Burt took a long second to think about it, then made a decision to listen to Albert's pitch. He didn't think it would hurt to hear the man out. "Okay, I'm all ears, but this doesn't mean I'm admitting to anything."

"I understand completely. But trust me, you won't be sorry. I know we've had our differences in the past, but there's no reason for any of that to get in the way of generating some seriously fat stacks of cash. Lots of it. And we think you're exactly the kind of man we need."

"Come on, dude. Out with it. You don't have to lube me up so hard. What the hell do you want?"

"Two things. First, you're going to need a new front operation. Something that will help you hide all the money we're gonna make for you. You know, to keep the eyes of the law off you."

"You mean like you guys?"

"If you want to label people, then sure, guys like us. However, I'm talking about others in town who are not going to be involved with the second part of our little venture."

Burt nodded, feeling his interest pique. "The Sheriff and the rest of his staff."

"Exactly."

"I knew you two were never legit."

"Yeah, like they say, looks can be deceiving. And as it turns out, that's a perfect analogy. These badges help us hide in plain sight."

Maybe Albert wasn't a complete waste of skin after all. "What's the second part?"

"I have a connection to get as much Clearwater Red as we can move. But we're gonna need a distributor with the muscle and the motivation to get this done. That's where you come in."

Burt stood a little more erect than before, tugging on the end of his shirt sleeve with pride. Finally, a little respect coming his way. "Okay, I get that. You guys obviously recognize the skills."

"But you'll need to forget the motorcycle. We have something better. Something that will not only allow you to give more comfortable rides to more people, but also serve as a transport for the second part of the business."

"What kind of transport?"

"It's a 1957 Plymouth Sport Suburban four-door station wagon. I'm sure you know what I'm talking about and why."

"No electronics," Burt said, sifting through his memories. "Seems to me, I remember working on a classic like that for your old man."

"Yep. It's sitting in my mom's barn, just waiting to be brought back to life. If you can get it running, we'll have the perfect vehicle not only for your new taxi service, but also to move the ice where we need it."

"And do so in broad daylight," Dustin added.

Burt understood where these two clowns were going with their proposition. "You want me to create hidden storage areas inside your old man's wagon, then use the taxi service as a cover while we're moving the drugs."

"You catch on fast, my friend."

"Well, I wouldn't go that far."

"About what?"

"The friend thing. We might end up being in business together, but we'll never be friends."

"Sure, if that's what it takes, I can live with it," Albert said, swinging his eyes to the man standing with him. "What about you, Dustin?"

"I'm good. All that matters is that we build a network we can trust. Something safe and reliable. There's plenty of money to spread around."

Burt was starting to like this idea, but he wasn't done putting restrictions on the deal. "Then we might just be able to work something out. But I'll need my tools and it's a long way back to town. You guys up for it? I'll need help getting everything I'm gonna need to your father's place. My tow truck is useless."

"That won't be a problem. We gotta do whatever it takes to get set up. Anything else?"

"Yeah, there's one more thing. If you guys try to screw me, I'll dig a hole in the forest and bury you in it. We do this 50/50, and none of that bullshit you pulled in high school when you had me expelled."

Albert put his hand out for a shake. "Then we're in agreement."

Burt took Albert's hand and squeezed it with a firm grip. He shook it three times, then said, "I'm deadly serious, Albert. I'll kill you where you stand if this is anything other than what it appears to be."

"Won't be a problem. Just do your part and we'll all make tons of money."

Burt let go of Jumbo's hand and pointed at the motorcycle. "Okay, then let's go. I'll grab the handlebars and you guys push."

"I thought we were leaving the old clunker behind," Albert said.

"Not a chance. I won't use it in the new business, but I'm not leaving it out here for some asshole to come along and steal it. This belongs to me. I paid good money for it. Do you have a problem with that?"

"No, it's cool."

CHAPTER 63

Daisy turned the wheel of the Land Rover to the right, cruising by the same wooden sign she'd ridden past on the mountain bike. This time, though, pebbles weren't landing on her back like before and she was grateful. So were her thighs, not having to pedal like a madwoman with people hanging on.

Old Mill Road wasn't exactly a smooth ride, but the suspension on the ancient vehicle was doing its job. Stephanie was in the truck behind her, piloting the second vehicle, her beautiful but perpetually angry face centered perfectly in Daisy's rear view mirror.

Somehow Daisy could sense Stephanie's thoughts. They were focused on her and what she'd done, bringing a sharp pain to her chest. Daisy wasn't sure how many more times she'd have to apologize for her embarrassing interlude with Steph's ex-husband, but she planned to keep soliciting forgiveness until it found its way to her.

There wasn't much else she could do other than keep trying to fix things between them. She knew it might never happen, but it was the right thing to do, regardless of the odds. There was no way around it—she'd done wrong and hurt one of her oldest friends.

Daisy swallowed hard, wishing she could unwind the hands of time and eliminate that one mistake. A huge mistake. One that had smothered her soul in a shroud of darkness, erasing all the good she'd done in her life.

Bill King wasn't the most handsome man she'd ever met, but he could be unbelievably charming when he wanted to—usually when a pair of legs and other assets were in his crosshairs.

How could she have been so stupid?

She knew his reputation.

And yet, she let herself fall victim to his unsolicited advances, smearing her reputation in the process. She'd only let her fence down for a moment, giving him the small opportunity he needed to climb past it and establish a toehold in her life.

Daisy flushed the pity party from her thoughts, then pressed the brake pedal and slowed the lead vehicle before pulling in parallel to Tuttle's gate.

"We're here," she announced to Franklin Atwater, the hulking black man who was stretched out horizontally on the seat behind her. "I'm gonna go have a quick chat with Steph."

"About what?" the injured cowboy asked, his concern obvious.

"There's something I need to go take care of before she brings the kids inside. Will you be okay for a minute?"

"Yeah," he grunted in response, his hand pressing on the bullet wound in his shoulder. "I think I have the bleeding stopped. For now, anyway. Go do what you need to do. I'll be okay." He worked himself into a sitting position, the grimace on his face intense.

"I'll be right back," Daisy said, hopping out of the truck and heading to the second vehicle with a fast stride, arriving in seconds.

She rapped on the glass of the driver's window, expecting a response.

Stephanie never moved, her eyes fixed on the road ahead.

Daisy knocked again, this time with a set of more determined knuckles. "Come on, Steph. We need to talk. It's important."

"I've got nothing to say to you," Stephanie said, her lips pressed together into a pucker. She pointed at the car parked in front, whipping her finger in an arc from back to front. "So I'd suggest you just turn that big butt of yours around and go take care of Franklin. The kids and I will follow you inside."

"That's what I wanted to talk to you about. I need you to keep the kids out here for a bit, while I go clean up inside. There are some things they shouldn't see."

Stephanie still didn't bring her eyes around to look at Daisy. If the woman could breathe fire, Daisy figured the hood of the Land Rover would be engulfed in flames by now.

Daisy wasn't about to give up, despite the woman's justified anger and resentment. "Look, you don't have to talk to me, but we have others to think about here. So we have to find a way to work together."

Stephanie remained perfectly still, not moving or blinking.

Daisy's chest grew heavy, making every breath harder than the last. "Come on, Steph. I've said I'm sorry like a million times already. We have to get past this, for everyone's sake. Even if it's only for a few minutes. You can hate me again tomorrow. But right now, we have to do what's right. For the kids and for Franklin."

Stephanie turned her head, landing her piercing eyes on Daisy. They flared a bit as she tilted her head with attitude. "I'm listening."

"Can you watch Franklin while I go do what I gotta do? He looks stable for the moment, but I'd feel better if he weren't alone."

"Alone? Like you left me? And my son?" Stephanie snapped in a quick, terse tone, her head bobbing left and right as she spoke.

Daisy sighed, her shoulders slumping. This was going nowhere. "I said I'm sorry. I don't know what else I can do."

Stephanie didn't answer.

Daisy looked at the kids in the back seat. The alarm in their eyes was all-consuming. Sparring with Stephanie wasn't going to help the situation.

It was time to give up on the apology route. She'd done all she could, but this approach clearly wasn't working. No matter what she said or did from this point forward, she would always be the slutty mistress of Clearwater and would always be the one to blame for breaking up the Kings' marriage. What had happened couldn't be undone, no matter how hard she tried. Stephanie was never going to let this go.

Guilty or not, Daisy decided it was time to take charge like a Deputy Sheriff should do and protect the citizenry. Franklin needed medical attention and she needed to go inside and clear out the bodies and wipe up the blood.

Her voice energized with strength and the pain in her chest evaporated in an instant. "Enough already, Steph. I screwed up and I apologized. But this is where it ends. As a duly sworn officer of the law, I need you to watch Franklin and make sure the bleeding doesn't start again. That's an order."

"What's going on?" a new female's voice said from behind.

Daisy whipped her head around, seeing Allison Rainey standing two feet away. Allison's aging mother and long-haired son were also there, posing as curious bookends on either side of her. Daisy figured the nosy neighbors must have seen the trucks pull up and walked across the street to investigate.

Daisy needed to explain, but not within earshot of the kids, so she pulled Allison aside and stood close to her. She pointed at the lead Land Rover, then changed the tone of her voice to a whisper. "Franklin Atwater is hurt pretty bad."

"What happened?" Allison asked in a hush, her words nearly silent.

"Took a bullet in the shoulder."

"Someone shot him?" Allison asked, her eyes wide.

"Yeah, a little while ago."

"Who?"

Daisy didn't want to go into the details about the Pokémon men and their kidnapping exploits, so she redirected the focus to something more urgent. Something she hoped Allison would latch onto and help with. "We got the bleeding stopped, but we really need to get him inside before it starts up again. We're hoping Tuttle has a medical kit somewhere. But first, I need to go clean up some blood and bodies. Don't want the kids to see them."

"Blood and bodies? Cool," Victor said after stepping forward and joining the conversation, his youthful eyes full of excitement.

"Bodies?" Allison asked, looking stunned.

Daisy nodded, realizing she was relaying too much information. "From an earlier incident."

"Who's doing this? Are we in danger?"

Before Daisy could answer, Martha Rainey joined them, angling her shoulders to squeeze her way into the whisper group. "I can help."

Daisy wasn't sure how, remaining silent as she took a few moments to decide on a proper response. She wished Allison's son wasn't part of this conversation but wasn't certain if she should ask him to leave.

Martha didn't wait. "I used to be a trauma nurse."

Daisy welcomed the news, not only because of the professional medical assistance, but because the old woman had just changed the subject, keeping her from having to answer Allison or scold the boy for butting in. "Oh. Okay, cool. We can use the help. Do you have a med kit at your place?"

Martha shook her head. "Unfortunately, no. Just a basic first aid kit."

"Why didn't you take Franklin back to town?" Allison asked, her tone skeptical. "Why bring him here?"

Daisy knew the truth about the insurgents wouldn't serve any useful purpose, so she decided to soften her answer and spin. A gentle lie was needed to keep everyone calm and cooperating. For Franklin's sake, and the kids'. "This was closer. We had to act fast."

Allison grabbed at Daisy, latching her thin fingers around Daisy's wrist. "What if someone followed you here?"

"They didn't. Trust me, nobody knows we're here."

Martha unhooked Allison's hand from Daisy, then looked at her daughter. "We've got work to do, sweetheart. People need help. The deputy knows what she's doing. We need to listen to her and do exactly what she says."

Allison nodded and exhaled, her eyes turning soft. Her mother was obviously in charge and carried a lot of persuasion. It was too bad that level of control didn't extend to Martha's grandson, listening to every word being said.

Allison looked at Daisy, her eyes focused and brows pinched. "What do you need me to do?"

CHAPTER 64

Bunker stirred awake with his eyes shut and head spinning. He tried to lock onto his thoughts, but they were popping in and out of focus as a swirling fog filled his mind. The pounding thump across the back of his skull wasn't helping either, keeping his face scrunched and eyes tight.

A minute or so later, his thoughts gained a foothold, triggering the rest of his senses to come alive. Sensory information came at him all at once, feeding his mind a stream of data: birds tweeting, water trickling, crickets chirping, and bees buzzing. Plus there was the scent of pine trees, wild jasmine and musky decay, lingering humidity, smoke, and the distinct stench of feces. He was obviously still in the forest—somewhere.

Gravity told him he was vertical, not horizontal. Yet he wasn't standing. It was more like he was cradled in something. Or tangled, if he factored in the pressure across his back and the tightness encircling his legs.

Two heartbeats later, a new flash of pain registered. This time it was from his left forearm, originating from a single spot near the midpoint. There was also pressure associated with the ache, feeling as though it was expanding outward.

A tightness rose up from his stomach, but it wasn't from pain or stress. It was a different kind of discomfort—hunger. Level ten and climbing. The kind of hunger that makes you think about eating a pile of bear scat, if given the chance.

Bunker tried to open his eyes, but they wouldn't budge. They were stuck together, like glue, taking all the control away from him. But that wasn't all; his eyelids felt heavy and dry, like something was covering them.

A sudden rustle of leaves came at him from the left. He sucked in a breath and turned his head, listening for clues. Just when fear was about to make an appearance, he felt a gentle brush of air tickle the skin on his cheek. It flowed over his nose, building in force as it ran from one side to the other.

He relaxed, letting the oxygen run free from his lungs. It was just the wind, not a Slavic fire team on the hunt. Or a bear needing to fill its hunger for meat. Otherwise, he'd hear the directional sounds of twigs snapping and foot plants, not just the gentle pulse of air moving through the trees.

He tried to bring his hands up to clean off his eyes, but only his right arm moved. His left was not responding, defying him like a petulant child. He tried to move the arm again, but it sent back a howling sting instead, making him grimace.

Bunker used the fingers on his free hand to wipe his eyelids clean of a dry, crusty substance. It felt like mud, caked on like pancake batter.

Sunlight poured in after he pried his lids apart, storming his vision in a flood of white. He turned his head and blinked, waiting for the parade of spots and blobs to fade. Eventually they did. So did the tears, though not as quickly.

He looked to see what was wrong with his left arm. It was ramrod straight and out to his side, rising up at a forty-five degree angle. A moment later, he saw it—a bloody stick protruding through the skin in the middle of his forearm.

The branch was about a half-inch in diameter, wide enough to take out the center of his Harley-Davidson tattoo. The capital letters Y and D had been obliterated, almost as if the branch had been aiming for them. He could still move his fingers and didn't see any bone exposed, so he figured it wasn't broken.

He looked down to take a visual survey of the rest of his condition. His body was stuck in a thicket of driftwood, his legs tangled in a nest of branches. Thankfully, his feet were holding up his weight; otherwise, he would've felt like a side of beef hanging from a meat packer's hook.

The water was a handful of inches beyond his feet, but it wasn't flowing like he expected. It was calm and shallow, with a layer of gravel and sand below its glimmering surface.

Several tiny fish swam about, cruising in and out of the shadows as they scoured the pool for food. A few yards away was a grassy bank, angling down from the nearby tree line.

Bunker thought about it for a few moments, trying to remember what had happened before he woke up. When the answers came to him, they streamed up from his memories in a series of brilliant flashes.

The Russian mortar landing close.

The hillside blowing apart.

Flying backwards through the air.

Searing pain in his forearm.

Wetness on his legs.

His head hitting something hard.

The data points lined up in his brain, telling him the explosion must have jettisoned him into the river, where he landed on one of the collections of branches that had been trapped in front of a boulder. That's how he ended up impaled.

He figured the momentum of his impact must have broken the wood pile free from the rock. That's when it drifted downstream, taking him with it until they both ran aground on a sandbar.

The facts seemed to fit the scenario he was in, but they didn't explain how mud got caked on his eyes. The only answer he could come up with was that the branches had been tossed around by the current, rolling and tumbling like a beach ball.

At one point, he must have been upside down with his head in shallow water. He ran his fingers through his hair to confirm. Yes, mud was present. Caked on and dry. His forehead was full of silt, too. But not his cheeks, nose, or chin.

The facts were obvious. He'd been underwater, just deep enough to cover his eyes and hair in mud, but not deep enough to drown him.

Damn lucky.

Almost as lucky as what happened when he was on the ridge. The Russians sent their arsenal his way but somehow, not a speck of shrapnel hit his body.

He'd heard of that happening before on the battlefield, but he always thought it was a complete fabrication, somebody's inaccurate version of the truth. Possibly a sick joke invented to keep the new recruits calm and compliant while advancing on their target with less fear in their bones. Let's face it, hope is a powerful tool. It can trump fear, even a mountain of it, but only if a foundation is set first—a foundation formed in lunacy.

There was a reason they were called FNGs, or Fucking New Guys, because cannon fodder was too harsh a term, regardless of its accuracy. He'd seen his share of FNGs come and go, usually on a stretcher or in a body bag.

For all that shrapnel to miss him like that on the ridge, he must have gotten more than lucky. Almost as if God himself had stepped in and erected an impenetrable force field, deflecting the metal away. He didn't understand any of it, but yet, here he was. Alive and in one piece—well, sort of.

The odd thing was, he was completely dry. Not a hint of moisture on his clothes. He distinctly remembered his legs being wet before he passed out.

Plus, if the cocoon of branches surrounding him had been floating, bobbing, and rolling, more of his clothes must have gotten wet. Lack of moisture meant time had passed, long enough for the sun to dry his clothes.

But how much time? Hours? Days? He couldn't be sure, not after blacking out from a head injury. Regardless, it was time to get moving.

First up on his to-do list was to liberate himself from the wilderness spear in his arm. He brought his free hand over and cupped the underside of his forearm with his palm, his fingers spread out evenly around the entry point.

Bunker took a deep breath and yanked with every ounce of energy he could rally. The pain exploded when his arm slid up about an inch and then stopped. He groaned with his jaw clenched, keeping a four-alarm scream from leaving his lips.

Three rapid breaths later, he closed his eyes and let his head sink. The blowtorch incident was the worst pain he'd ever felt, but this was a close second. Anytime your body is punctured by an object of significant size, it'll convince you to reevaluate all your decisions. And do so based on expected pain levels.

"There has to be a better way," he mumbled between breaths, visualizing the dynamics inside the wound. Several inches of the stick remained above his arm, its coarse bark ready to tear apart the sensitive tissue inside. At this rate, he'd need another handful of tugs before he was clear, each one sending his agony into orbit.

He sighed, realizing his luck had become a fickle mistress.

Right then, a new idea entered his mind, flashing an image of his knife. He might be able to use it to cut the branch off just below his arm. Once free, he could bring his arm in front and pull the stick out with one thrust. It would hurt either way, but he'd have better leverage to remove it quickly, minimizing the duration of the torture.

He dug his hand into his front pocket, expecting the knife to be nestled inside. It wasn't.

Shit. Must have fallen out.

Only two choices remained: continue the excruciating process of jerking his arm up until it worked itself free, or snap the branch in half somehow. He didn't like either choice, but he had to do something.

After careful consideration, he decided to try breaking the branch. But he'd need to do it in one quick motion, like ripping off a Band-Aid. Otherwise, he might change his mind in mid-stream once the pain overwhelmed his resolve.

Bunker made a fist with his free hand and drew it back. He ran a silent countdown from three, summoning more and more of his strength as the numbers dwindled.

When zero arrived, he unleashed a swift punch, while simultaneously pulling his injured arm forward to create a pressure point. His knuckles slammed into the branch just below his arm, splintering the wood with a loud crack.

He held his wounded arm in the air until the pain bled off, then brought it down and positioned it in front of his abdomen.

His knuckles were still throbbing in anger, but he didn't want to wait. He grabbed the stick and pulled it straight up. The wood ripped through his arm, sending blood and tissue into the air behind it. He tossed the branch away, puffing air from his lungs to disperse the pain.

Now it was time to free his legs. He bent down and began to untangle the knot of roots around his shins. Some of them were loose and easy to remove, but others were tight—boa constrictor tight—taking extra time to unravel with only a single arm available.

Once liberated, he crawled off the driftwood pile and stepped into the shallow water. The cold flooded his feet, rising up to the middle of his calves where tender flesh met the hardness of muscle. The Arctic blast felt invigorating, keeping his feet moving as he made his way to shore.

Ten feet away was a flat rock about two feet square. It was next to a half-dead spruce tree with rotting bark and mostly barren limbs. He walked to it, spun around, and took a seat facing the sun so he could examine the wound in his arm.

The puncture hole was impressive in a sick, twisted sort of way. The gaping tunnel went all the way through, though some of the damage path had been fettered by loose clumps of tissue inside. He figured he could stick his finger all the way through if he chose to, though it wouldn't be very sanitary.

Speaking of sanitary, he needed to clean and disinfect the wound from one side to the other. He had no way to know how long he'd been a human shish kabob, but it had been long enough for extreme hunger to settle in, taking over many of his thoughts.

Great hunger meant significant time had passed, certainly long enough for whatever bacteria and microbial life were on the branch to make a home in the damage path. Sepsis would come for him soon, so he needed to turn to bush alternatives for a first aid kit.

There was plenty of running water around, so that wasn't an issue as long as he boiled it first. However, since he didn't have any medical swabs for a manual cleanout, he would need to irrigate the wound in some fashion.

The final step in the process would involve a natural poultice—something to protect his injury from the elements and also draw out any infection that might be forming.

When he first woke up, he remembered a number of distinct odors, one of which was smoke. It was faint. Possibly a campfire nearby. Upwind, most likely. Plus, he heard the sound of bees buzzing. Those memories gave him an idea.

CHAPTER 65

Bunker bent down on one knee, scooping up water in his right hand to feed his mouth. He felt like a hound dog lapping up water from its owner's hand. The thirst inside was almost as intense as the hunger, but he knew a fill of water would help stem the craving for food.

The water was cool to the touch and tasted fresh, but it wasn't clear by any stretch. Specks of dirt, leaves, and other particulates landed on his tongue, making him wonder if it was clean enough to drink, even a sip.

The current had a decent flow to it, plus he hadn't seen any sign of beaver around, so he wasn't too worried about Giardiasis. But there were countless other waterborne pathogens that might be lurking. He decided to stop his consumption, despite the water's apparent freshness.

He stood and headed upwind, keeping his nose tuned to every scent around him. Most of the odor was that of his own body, or from the surrounding fauna. Yet the aroma of charcoal was noticeable, too, and it was growing with each step. He didn't see any smoke rising in the trees, at least not yet, but he had a strong sense that a campfire was nearby, possibly around the next bend in the river.

He continued upriver, wading through shallow pools of water along the bank. The slippery stones below the surface were a challenge, having been worn flat by the nonstop erosion and covered with a Teflon-like film of algae.

But the slippery walking surface wasn't the worst obstacle in his path. It was the trees lining the bank—specifically, their army of branches, searching out his skin. Blocking them with only one good arm was laborious and time consuming, but he forged ahead, trying to keep his thoughts on the mission.

Staying focused wasn't easy, though, not with the pangs of hunger eating away at his insides. It felt like a school of piranhas had spawned inside and were swimming around in the small amount of water he'd just ingested. His intestines were on fire, feeling as though the underwater carnivores were well into their feeding frenzy.

After he climbed over a fallen log, something shiny caught his attention. It was dead ahead, about thirty feet away, the sun reflecting off its surface.

It sat between two oversized rocks, just to the right of another tangle of driftwood. He wondered if it was his knife, having fallen from his pocket sometime after the Russian mortar shell sent him flying. His paced quickened, as he kept his eyes locked on the location of the glint.

When Bunker arrived, he scoffed, unable to hold back a roll of his eyes. It wasn't his knife. In fact, it wasn't any kind of metal. It was plastic—a water bottle. Simple human garbage tossed away by some jerk who thought the forest was his personal dumping ground.

He bent down and picked it up. Its cap was still attached but the container was empty. The label said *Fiji, Natural Artesian Water.*

"Privileged asshole," he mumbled, shaking his head. Despite his hatred for anyone who littered, the plastic bottle was a godsend. His mind filled with a list of potential survival uses as he untwisted the cap and put it into the river. The water seeped in, slipping past the air escaping in plops. Once it was full, he put the cap on and continued his trek.

The scent of smoke was stronger now, telling him he was getting close to the source. He continued until a thin dirt path appeared on the right, heading up a steep incline that disappeared into a heavy stand of oak at the top of the hill.

Another game trail, he first thought, until he saw footprints in the soil. They were human tracks, not animal. Sneakers, if he had to guess. Someone with feet smaller than his.

He bent down and inspected the ridges of the tread pattern, using the tip of his finger to test their crispness. They flaked apart easily, with little indication of moisture.

This meant the tracks weren't recent; otherwise, they'd show more resistance to the touch. He decided to follow the prints up the trail, figuring they'd lead him to the source of the charcoal smell.

When he made it to the top of the hill, the mighty oaks gave way to a small, flat clearing that featured two patches of grass some fifteen feet apart. A tree lay in the dirt to the right, the center portion of its four-foot diameter trunk rotting and falling apart. In front of it was a circle of rocks with mounds of gray ash and extinguished coals inside.

A campsite, all right, with footprints everywhere. Garbage, too—stacked neatly to one side and left to rot with a couple of rocks sitting on top of the pile.

The shoe patterns were all the same and seemed to travel in a thin, repetitive course around the campfire stones. Someone had been here solo, probably dancing around the flames like some kind of Pagan fool, hoping to ward off evil spirits. Had Bunker gotten here earlier and under better circumstances, he would've shown the littering idiot the meaning of an evil spirit.

He found more of the empty water bottles in the pile of garbage, so the camper wasn't using the river for drinking. Must have hiked down to the water to clean dishes, he figured. Or take a leak—in the same water source from which Bunker had just taken a drink. Right then, a rancid flavor rose up out of nowhere and landed on his tongue.

Bunker reacted in an instant, curling a wad of saliva and sending it flying from his lips. He knew the acrid taste was psychosomatic, but he didn't care, completing a second round of saliva ejection for good measure.

Bunker used a stick to dig around and check the rest of the trash. He found a few items he recognized—mostly food wrappers from energy bars, plus a clear plastic wrap from some kind of creamy Danish that had a price sticker on it that said *Billy's Pump and Munch*. But that wasn't all. There were aluminum wrappers from gum. Lots of them, like the person had a serious addiction. He grabbed a handful, then spotted a few crumpled twists of Kleenex.

The tissue had snarls of yellow and brown in it—some loose but all of it dry. However, there was one red splotch, spread out across the cotton fibers. It too was dry. The Pagan freak must have had a serious sinus infection, expelling gobs of putrid discharge that would keep even the hungriest of vultures away.

There was also an empty Red Bull can and a single sandwich bag that contained bread crumbs and specks of what smelled like turkey inside. He dumped the remnants from the baggie and tucked it inside his pocket. He also kept the can and a few gum wrappers, figuring he might need them as well.

After a little more rubbish flipping with the stick, he spotted something plastic and pink with an assembly of metal on one end. It caught his eye like a beacon of opportunity.

The object's spark wheel, guard, and hood were unmistakable—a Bic lighter. Yet it was neon pink. Odd. He'd spent countless hours around strippers, hookers, and more than his share of gotta-have-it biker babes, but never once did he remember any of those chain-smoking strumpets having a pink Bic lighter.

Bunker ran a quick visual check of the area but didn't see any cigarette butts around. No cigar butts either. The camper wasn't a smoker. If he was right, then the pocket torch was used to start the campfire. He picked it up and shook it.

Its weight was next to nothing—fuel reservoir empty, just tossed away by its owner after its usefulness ran out. He put his thumb to the spark wheel and pressed down on it. As expected, a spark flashed, but a flame didn't catch.

Bunker tried to light it two more times. Again, no success. He wasn't surprised, nor was he going to throw the lighter away. It still had survival uses. He stuffed it into his pocket until later.

Next to the lighter was a condom. Unfortunately, it wasn't wrapped. Nor was it devoid of fluid, its dried white contents visible in the sunlight.

It took Bunker a second to wrap his head around the soiled contraceptive. He knew the camper had been out here alone, so why the condom? Only one answer came to him. The man must have self-gratified until he shot his seed into the latex. Then he left it for the animals to enjoy.

Granted, it was revolting and perverted, but not the strangest wilderness story he'd ever heard. Grinder and some of their other pals in the Kindred had done far worse, usually in the mountains with others around.

He remembered the stories like they were yesterday—a handful of brothers sitting around the clubhouse bar, bragging about their most disgusting exploits after a few rounds of tequila had set in, each man wanting to top the other's debauchery. He flushed the memories from his mind and returned to the task before him.

Condoms had a long list of survival uses, but he wasn't going to touch this one. The lighter, Red Bull can, baggie, gum wrappers, and water bottle would suffice. He'd also need some of the used Kleenex—the cleaner part, that was—which he promptly tore off and stuffed in his pocket.

Bunker reversed his path and headed downstream to find the source of the buzzing he'd heard earlier when he'd first woken up. He needed to be extra careful, not wanting to anger a hive of bees, assuming that was the source of the sound.

Their most precious asset—the honey—was his target.

CHAPTER 66

Daisy Clark finished mopping up the last of the bloody scene in the center of Tuttle's main room, planning to take the mop out back and dispose of it next to Tuttle's body.

The old man didn't weigh much, allowing her and Martha Rainey to haul the carcass outside a few minutes ago without too much trouble. Martha took the feet and she took the arms, dragging the lifeless hunk of wrinkled meat through the kitchen that was filled with dirty dishes. They couldn't take the body out the front door, not with the kids waiting outside, so stuffing it through one of the back windows was the only option.

The biggest problem thus far hadn't been where to dump the body. It was the stench. His body in the midst of decay, filling the room with a smell unlike any other she'd witnessed. But the stink didn't end there. There was his ripe body odor, too, mixed with layers of stale cigar smoke.

She wasn't sure how long it would take to rid the old trailer of the disgusting aroma, but she assumed it was going to take a few gallons of Febreze, at least. Or some other kind of industrial de-stink-a-fier. It was all she could do not to turn her head and throw up. At least she was almost done, thank God.

Next up, bury her friend.

The pastures behind the home were lush, meaning the ground should be soft enough to dig a quick grave site, assuming she could find a shovel. There had to be one around the homestead somewhere. Probably in the man's massive barn that was stocked full of every supply known to humanity. Well, maybe not that much, but close enough.

Her previous glimpse of the inventory was still fresh in her mind—stacks and stacks of supplies from floor to ceiling. A ceiling that was four stories high.

"What do you think happened to the other body?" Martha Rainey asked from her knees, her glove-covered hands wringing out a bloody sponge. The red, viscous liquid dripped into the mop bucket with a string of clumpy tissue leading the way.

"I figure his accomplices hauled it away," Daisy answered. "Probably to cover their tracks." She hadn't told Martha that she was responsible for taking out Tuttle's killer. Nor had she mentioned the Pokémon cards or the fact that she and Bunker had been taken hostage by the same men.

"Makes sense," Martha said, taking the mop handle from Daisy. "I'll dump this out. You go get everyone."

"Shouldn't we bury the body first?"

"Don't worry about it. I got it covered."

"Really?" Daisy said, not sure if the woman understood her words. Or her official standing as deputy.

Martha flashed a look with her eyes, squeezing them like she was starting to get upset. "Yes, I'm not some helpless old woman. I can dig a hole with the best of them."

"No, of course not. Not what I meant. I just thought it would go faster if we both took turns digging."

"You're the deputy, Daisy, and you need to focus on the safety of everyone. That's your job," Martha said, pointing at the door. "And your job is out there, right now, waiting for you. I can handle the burial."

"That's true, but I think it would be best if you used your nursing skills to help Franklin. I can't do that. Only you can. You should go get everyone and I'll get rid of the body."

Martha shook her head, her tone turning sarcastic. "We need a medical kit first. Do you see one around here?"

"Oh yeah, right," Daisy answered, hoping there was one in the supply barn.

Martha grabbed the handle of the mop bucket as she stood up. "You go find the med kit and I'll dispose of Tuttle. It's the best use of our time."

Daisy didn't respond, wanting a moment to think.

"Go on now," Martha said in a hurried tone, waving her hands to shoo Daisy out the door. "You know I'm right."

Daisy turned and headed for the front door, wondering if she should've protested more. Martha's logic made sense, but it still seemed like she was caving too much. Not just to Martha, but to Stephanie and everyone else she knew.

A deputy has to make decisions—for everyone—and then stand behind them, no matter what comes her way. That's how you protect and serve. And lead. Nobody respects a person who can't make a decision. Or who always cowers to the will of others.

Daisy stopped her march and whirled around, her spine full of confidence. She held up a finger and said, "On second thought . . ."

Martha was no longer in the room.

Hmmm. Already taking care of business, Daisy thought. *Made a decision and then stuck with it. Like I need to do.*

Daisy let out a grin, feeling a tingle of warmth wash over her. The manner in which Martha carried herself was impressive. And encouraging. Plus, the gruesomeness of the scene didn't seem to faze the former nurse. Almost like it never happened.

Daisy figured it was due to Martha's years of trauma conditioning in the ER. Conditioning Daisy would never acquire. No wonder she almost threw up when she walked back in Tuttle's home.

Wait a minute, she thought. *That can't be right.*

Maybe it wasn't simply the woman's former job. It had to be more. It had to be. Otherwise, there was no hope that Daisy would ever become the kind of deputy she wanted.

Just then, her logic chimed in, adding to her thought process. It was probably age and wisdom. Plus some serious life experience. All of that was something Daisy would acquire, eventually.

It was just like Bunker had said after she'd killed the assailant with her perfect shot through the blinds, his baritone voice still echoing in her memory. "Just give it time, Daisy. Don't dwell on it."

Time and experience—that's the key.

That's how you solidify your resolve in the face of tragedy. Or loss.

Nobody is born with this skill.

You learn it, acquiring it over time, assuming the savagery that tragedy brings with it doesn't consume you first.

CHAPTER 67

Mayor Buckley took a step back with an arm outstretched, waiting for the next family in line to move forward and enter the FEMA medical station.

Most of the residents hadn't wanted his help, but a few had taken it, the last of which was an elderly couple who found the metal steps a challenge. They'd been fetched from their home and delivered to the staging area by one of FEMA's four-wheeled ATVs, apparently complaining the entire way.

Other than assisting the old, Buckley felt useless, much like an old-time usher at the movies—a man who took up space near the entrance but offered little in terms of real value to the procession.

The line had been over a block long ever since the inoculations began, but FEMA's medical staff was working with precision and speed to handle the demand. He was impressed with their assembly line organization, using a three-member squad to process each patient.

The first medic would start by marking off the resident's name on a digital list being displayed on a computer tablet, then rubbing a cotton swab containing some form of sterilizing agent with numbing properties across the side of the person's neck.

The patient would then be passed to the second station, where medicine was injected with a needleless gun. Each time the high-tech unit fired, it emitted a momentary swooshing sound that was followed by a hollow click.

Buckley knew air was being used to deliver the drug, but the hollow click was odd. Perhaps the injector had to lock itself back into position for the next round of treatment, causing the metallic sound of metal on metal.

The process finished with the third guy applying a peel-and-stick circular bandage over the entry point, then checking the resident's name off a secondary list.

The procedure was slick and rehearsed, always ending with the third man uttering the same seven words: "Leave the bandage on for 24 hours." The tech's words carried an Australian accent, matching that of the FEMA commander.

A few residents had asked the bandage man a follow-up question, but he'd only respond with the same seven words in response, then direct them with an outstretched finger to the exit door on his right.

Buckley understood the medic was ultra-focused on keeping pace, but the guy didn't have to act so detached and uninterested, ignoring the worry in the patients' voices. Sure, FEMA had a job to do and unnecessary questions would just slow the process down, but the man's bedside manner needed work.

Regardless, Buckley chose not to say anything. It really wasn't his place. Everyone had a role to play, including him, and there wasn't a moment to waste. The hazard cloud was still rolling this way and they had plenty of residents to inoculate.

Stan Fielding stepped forward with his twin daughters, Beth and Barb, his eyes locked onto Buckley's. His mouth was slightly agape, as if he were debating whether or not to speak.

Buckley decided to take the lead. "Do you have a question?"

The man stopped his feet. "As a matter of fact, I do. Lots of them."

Buckley waved his hand from right to left, motioning Stan and his kids toward the steps leading into the medical unit. "I'll answer what I can, but we need to keep the line moving forward."

Stan and his twins resumed their pace, matching the people in front of them. "Is this medicine safe for my girls?"

Buckley nodded, walking along with them. "Yes, perfectly. Nothing to worry about."

"What is it, exactly? Some kind of penicillin?"

"It's called MH2. It's an anti-contamination protocol, whatever that means. I wish I understood more about the treatment, but we're really pressed for time here, Stan. With the hazard cloud on its way, we need to process everyone quickly. Trust me, these men know what they're doing."

The look of concern faded from Stan's face as he nodded in response. Yet he still chose to pull his daughters in close to his legs.

Buckley was aware of everyone's trepidation and he didn't blame them. It wasn't every day that FEMA showed up with a fleet of trucks and then unveiled equipment to treat everyone you knew against a lethal contaminant.

One of the twins, with tears in her eyes, said, "I'm scared it's gonna hurt, Daddy. I don't want to do this."

"It'll be okay, honey," her father told her in a gentle voice, pointing at the people coming out of the trailer. "Look, they're not in any pain, sweetheart. These doctors know what they are doing. I promise. We all need this medicine to keep us safe."

"He's right, young lady," the Mayor added, wanting to support the single father. He turned his head and pointed to the bandage on the side of his neck. "See? I got mine and I promise you, it didn't hurt at all. All it feels like is a puff of air on your neck."

The girl didn't answer as the trio went up the steps, her face frozen in fear.

Buckley didn't enter with them. Instead, he ambled to the left and traveled around the outside of the trailer. He waited at the bottom of the exit stairs, praying the girls wouldn't come out too upset, especially since they'd need to go through this same process every day for the next thirty days.

He wasn't sure if the FEMA timeframe was etched in stone or not; the commander never confirmed after he'd asked a few minutes ago. Maybe they'd adjust it once they had a chance to collect more data about the threat. Or the winds might shift, taking the cloud in a different direction. One could only hope.

When Stan Fielding and his girls came out, the tears were gone and circular bandages were present. Buckley bent down to address the twin redheads, not able to tell them apart. He wasn't sure which one of them had been crying before, so he addressed them both with solid eye contact. "How did it go? Did you feel anything?"

The girl on the right answered. "No. It was okay, but I was still really scared. Do we really need to do this every day?"

"Yes, you do. It's how we are going to keep you and your sister safe. We're all proud of you for being so brave."

"And keep my daddy safe, too," the other girl said, wrapping her tiny fingers around her father's hand.

Buckley felt a warm sensation fill his chest when the girl said those words, pushing a full smile to his lips. "Yes, and your dad. We all have to stay safe and this medicine will do just that."

Stan seemed pleased, or perhaps it was relief. "Thanks for the assist, Mayor. I can't thank you enough. Sometimes they need to hear it from someone other than me."

Buckley gave him a quick nod before changing the subject. "Hey, there's one more thing we need to discuss, if you have a minute."

"Yeah, shoot. Got nowhere to be at the moment."

"That motorcycle you sold recently," Buckley said in his most serious tone.

"The 1932 Indian?"

"The very same."

Stan's eyes lit up. "I've got two more if you'd like to buy them. They're up for sale. My girls and I could really use the money."

Buckley didn't need to hear the man's words of financial desperation, or see it in the eyes of his little ones. It wasn't going to make the next part of the conversation any easier, but it needed to be addressed, regardless. "No, that's not what I wanted to talk to you about."

"I guess I don't understand then."

"The town would appreciate it if you didn't sell any more of them to Burt. I know he's your buddy and all, but we need to slow down his plans for a taxi service."

"Why? Is there a law against what he wants to do? He needs to earn a living, too. And like I said, we need the money."

"We have no problem with you selling them to raise cash. Just not to Burt."

"With all due respect, Mayor, I don't think that's something you can really control. It's a free country and I can sell them to anyone I please."

"Yes, you can. But his new service is going to use a lot of fuel. And right now, everyone needs to conserve, including Burt. It's for the good of everyone in town."

Stan didn't respond, but he no longer looked upset.

"Can I count on you to help us out, Stan?"

The man hesitated before he spoke again. "I'll see what I can do."

"Thanks. The residents of Clearwater thank you."

CHAPTER 68

"Guys, I need a break," Albert said, letting go of the back of the motorcycle seat. He bent over with his hands on his knees, gasping for breath. The burn in his lungs was strong, and so was the strain in his oversized thighs as he watched the bike roll up the steep grade. Burt was pushing on the left and Dustin on the right, pressing on without him.

"Come on, Jumbo. Suck it up," Burt shot back in his usual condescending tone, his head never turning to look at Albert.

Albert wished he had a semi-automatic in his hand, feeling the need to shoot the man in the back. Pulling the trigger would feel amazing right about now, as his body reeled from the lack of oxygen.

A handful of breaths later, Albert was able to speak, albeit barely. "Would it . . . be too much to ask . . . that you stop calling me that? It's not helping . . . the situation. After all, we're in business together now . . . So how about a little civility?"

"Wow, a little touchy, aren't we? I thought you were a tough guy now?"

Albert ran a few more breaths through his lungs before responding. "That has nothing to do with it . . . The slurs . . . they just get a little old after a while. Yeah, I'm fat . . . So what?"

Dustin let go of the bike and stopped walking, folding his rail-thin arms over his chest, looking defiant.

"What's your problem, Slim?" Burt said to Dustin, stopping his feet. He put the kickstand down and let go of the handlebars before turning to face him. "Come on, out with it."

Dustin finally spoke up, though the tone of his voice sounded like he was unsure whether to speak or not. "Albert and I have had enough of your constant insults and put-downs."

Burt turned his attention to Albert. "So what is this? A mutiny?"

"If you want to call it that, then sure. A mutiny," Albert said, sucking in more air. "You need to start treating us with respect; otherwise I'll be forced to rescind our agreement."

"Yeah, right," Burt said, rolling his eyes. "You guys need me a lot more than I need you."

"I seriously doubt that," Dustin added.

"Look, we all need each other," Albert said, not wanting to admit the brute was right. They needed Burt. More than he would ever confess.

Yet Albert also knew that in order to deal from a position of strength, he could never show a glimmer of weakness. He needed to use his opponent's greatest desire as a weapon to suffocate the man's mounting arrogance and need for control.

"Look Burt, the situation is pretty clear. Money doesn't flow into your pockets unless we work together. You know that. It's business 101."

Albert was finally able to stand up straight, his lungs back to normal. "We all want the same thing—to make money. And I'm talking about more money than you could ever make on your own. Like a thousand times more. And none of that happens unless we proceed ahead like adults. So no more of your third-grade bullshit. We're tired of it."

"Wow, there's a shock. I'm working with a bunch of wimps," Burt snapped, shaking his head. He craned his neck, looking up at the sky. "I swear to God, the universe must hate me."

"So, what's it gonna be?" Dustin asked the mechanic, slipping out of his backpack and putting it on the ground. "Because me and Albert can just walk away right now and you can go fuck yourself."

Albert couldn't believe what Dustin just said. The dude actually found some backbone and did so in the middle of nowhere, with little in the way of backup. Not the best timing, but impressive nonetheless.

Albert decided to reinforce their stand against the slimy dictator with one last comment. He pointed at Dustin, while looking at Burt. "Like he said, show us respect or we walk."

"Respect is earned, not demanded," Burt quipped.

"Yeah, you should talk," Dustin said, his chin stiff.

"So, what's it gonna be?" Albert added, not letting a second of dead air linger after Dustin's last comment. "Last chance to man up and do the right thing. Money and success, or slams and poverty. Your choice. We're not kidding around here."

Burt looked at the steep hill ahead, then down at the Indian motorcycle. His head dropped to his chest and his shoulders slumped for a bit, as he mumbled something to himself. When he brought his eyes back, he answered, "Fine. No more jabs. Let's just get this done already."

"There, that wasn't so hard, now was it?" Albert said, walking to the rear of the bike, his eyes locked onto Dustin's backpack. He couldn't help but lick his lips in anticipation.

Dustin must have noticed Albert's gawk, opening the pack and giving Albert one of the water bottles inside.

Albert twisted the cap off and took three full swigs. The water was heaven, exactly what his body needed. He took one last drink, then put the cap on and gave it to Dustin, who quickly stowed it in the pack.

"You should drink, too," Albert told his assistant.

Dustin shook his head forcefully. "Nah, I'm good. Don't want to use it all up at once. We've got a long way to go."

Burt put out his hand. "I'll take some. My mouth is so dry, I can barely talk."

If only, Albert thought to himself.

Dustin flashed a look to Albert, obviously waiting for a response. Or approval.

Albert nodded. "We're gonna need to share if we have any hope of getting all of us back to town."

Before the next heartbeat, a rumble cut through the mountains, vibrating the road beneath Albert's feet. He put out his hands as if his balance was about to vanish. "You guys feel that?"

"Hell, yeah," Burt answered with eyes wide. "We've got company." He turned on his heels and tore up the asphalt grade, heading in the direction of the sound.

Dustin did the same, leaving Albert to hold up the rear as all three went to higher ground.

When Albert made it to the top, Burt grabbed him by the shirt collar and yanked him down to his knees. "Get down," Burt said in a sharp whisper, tugging at Dustin as well.

"What's wrong?" Albert snapped, prying Burt's fingers loose from his shirt.

Burt pointed. "Check it out."

"Jesus, look at all of them," Dustin said, his eyes watching the procession of military-green trucks coming their way.

"Yeah, but those are not ours," Burt said, his voice full of anxiety.

About a half-mile ahead, Albert could see a long line of vehicles, including tanks, with soldiers marching alongside.

"How do you know they're not ours?" Dustin asked, his voice as low as a purr.

"The tanks—those are definitely not ours. I was always building models when I was kid and I can guarantee you those are not US tanks. The size and shape is all wrong."

"Maybe they're something new. Let's face it: it's been a while since any of us were kids."

"Bullshit," Burt said, his tone low and words fierce. "I doubt we would ever roll tanks and troops through the streets like that. Not here. Not in the middle of nowhere. Not unless we were at war."

Albert searched for the end of the procession but couldn't spot it with the road winding itself around and out of sight. There was a two-lane bridge between their position and the convoy ahead, making him wonder if the structure could support all the weight once it arrived.

The sheer number of troops and equipment brought a new idea into Albert's mind, one he thought Burt might want to consider "What about martial law? It's possible after the EMP attack."

"Out here? In the mountains? You can't be serious. What would be the point?"

"Just tossing out ideas."

"Not a very good one," Burt said, never taking his eyes from the danger marching their way. "Just look at those transports. We don't have anything like that. I'm pretty damn sure we use Humvees for personnel, not those eight-wheelers."

"Who do you think it is?" Dustin asked.

"China? Russians, maybe? I don't know."

Dustin pinched his pointed nose and furrowed his brow. "So this is some kind of invasion?"

"This far inside our borders?" Albert asked in a sarcastic tone.

"Obviously, yes. They're right there. Plain as day," Burt answered, looking at Albert.

"The Russians? Invading Colorado?"

"Or China," Dustin added, obviously on board with Burt's theory.

"Do you know how nuts this all sounds?" Albert asked, his mind not able to process what Burt was suggesting.

"Yep. But the facts are the facts."

Albert didn't buy it. "I'm not sure I'd call any of this fact. Somebody has to know these guys are here. They just can't march around like they own the place. I think you're reading too much into the situation."

"We should get a better look to know exactly what we're dealing with here," Burt said, ignoring Albert's redirect.

"We?" Dustin asked.

"Yeah, but not from here," Burt said, pushing back ten feet before getting up and running downhill to the motorcycle. Albert and Dustin followed.

The three of them pushed the bike off the road, using a natural opening that led into the forest. They hid the machine behind a tall stand of bushes, making sure it couldn't be seen from the road.

"What now?" Dustin asked.

Burt pointed. "See those boulders?"

"Yeah."

"We should be able to hide there and watch them pass by. Then we'll know more. Let's go." Burt didn't hesitate, starting a hike toward the turquoise-colored rock formation.

Burt took center position behind the smallest of the four boulders, with Dustin on his right. Albert decided to crawl to the other side of Dustin, keeping Burt as far away as possible.

The man's stink was stifling, almost to the point of making him want to gag. He knew he had to suck it up as Burt had suggested, but it wasn't going to be easy. The space was limited, but at least they had cover.

If Burt was correct about the military presence heading their way, keeping out of sight was job number one. He just hoped Burt wasn't going to do something stupid and get them all killed.

The man's arrogance was only outdone by his willingness to go out of his way for a fight, as if he was in constant need of a physical altercation, like it was some kind of affirmation of his manhood.

Somewhere deep inside Burt was a root cause, Albert figured, buried under a mountain of anger and pain.

The guy was in serious need of a hug, but Albert wasn't going to be the one to give it to him. A knife to the gut would be more along the lines of what Albert was thinking at the moment.

He took a second to imagine himself sticking the blade in deep, pressing harder and harder until the soft flesh gave way to hard bone. Then he'd twist it slowly in a circle, watching the life run out of Burt's eyes with every degree of hurt delivered.

It was a glorious vision, but one Albert knew would never happen. He wasn't a killer, no matter how badly he wanted it.

Even though he was sure everyone in town would agree that Burt was a first-class asshole and probably deserved it for all the pain he'd caused to everyone over the years, Albert wasn't going to take on the role of the Reaper. That wasn't who he was. He was more into the cerebral side of altercations, using wit and cleverness as a defense. And a disguise.

Killing would have to be someone else's job, like the new guy in town that he'd heard about, Jack Bunker. Albert hadn't met the drifter yet, but everyone was abuzz about the brute's military background and his bravery.

Albert imagined a towering hulk of a Marine with a chiseled chin, hawk-like eyes, and shoulders that could carry an endless amount of weight. Someone who could bring hell down on anyone who got in his way. Sure, it was a second-hand guess at the man's size and stature, but from what he'd heard, it fit.

The road below them was about fifty yards away and at a slight decline, giving Albert a straight-line view of the blacktop through the trees. He figured as long as they stayed out of sight and quiet, the military convoy should pass them by without incident.

Albert kept his head low as the three of them waited for the fleet to arrive. Dustin didn't seem too willing to poke his head out, either, but Burt did, unable to keep his eager eyes from peering over the top of the boulder. Albert couldn't decide if he should say something or not, his mind visualizing the enemy's first round finding its way into Burt's forehead.

His vision was both wonderful and horrifying, giving him pause. Tissue and blood would spray everywhere, etching the ghastly memory into Albert's synapses for all eternity—a gruesome thought to be sure.

Yet he wasn't entirely sure if a decapitated Burt was a bad thing or not. It would all depend on which side of his conscience was in charge at the time of the decision.

Albert reached past Dustin and tapped Burt on the shoulder. "You need to get down. You're gonna give away our position."

"Relax, Jumb—" Burt said, stopping his words in mid-sentence. "—I mean, Albert. Unless they're looking right at us, they'll never see us up here."

"You can't possibly know that," Albert snarled, trying to burrow his way through the man's wall of pride. "These men are trained killers. This is what they do, look for assholes like us."

"I need to find out who they are and that can't happen unless I keep an eye on them."

"He's right," Dustin said, swinging his eyes around to Albert. "Sorry, dude, but we have to know who we're dealing with."

"You're taking his side in this?"

Dustin shrugged.

Albert wanted to say more but realized it was useless. He was running with a pair of clueless bastards and one of them had just thrown him under the bus. "I'm outta here," he said, backing away on his stomach, his legs and hands moving in concert.

"Where you going?" Dustin asked.

"Anywhere but here. You guys are nuts." Albert got to his feet and headed for higher ground. He decided to angle to the left, choosing an area where he wouldn't end up directly behind the line of fire when the barrage was unleashed.

He prayed he was wrong about the troops spotting his team behind the rocks, but his gut knew better. In fact, it was screaming at him to climb faster and higher, so he did, pushing his thighs through the pain.

The combination of altitude, weight, and terrain took the air from his lungs quickly, but he couldn't stop, sounding like a racehorse, wheezy and puffing its way down the home stretch of a high-stakes race.

Twigs snapped and needles crunched as he pressed on, finally reaching the summit of the climb. He took position behind a fallen tree, lying on his back to allow his mouth to have priority access to all the air it could take in.

He'd never been so tired in all his life, feeling a squeeze in the center of his chest as a river of sweat emptied from the pores of his skin. Three breaths later, dizziness found him, and so did an ocean of stars in his vision.

Albert closed his eyes and fought the raging nausea building in his stomach, but then the blackness came and he passed out.

CHAPTER 69

Deputy Daisy squeezed her thin frame past the next stack of heavy, reinforced pallets in Tuttle's barn, wondering how many more she'd have to check before finding items that could be deemed tactically useful. Specifically, she was searching for communications gear—something she'd been tasked to find on an earlier visit with Bunker.

If it weren't for the Pokémon men and their assault rifles, this electronics hunt would have been completed a while ago. So would a lot of other things, she figured, knowing that critical town plans had gotten interrupted when everything went sideways at the miner's camp.

"Better late than never," she mumbled, thinking of the near-lethal interrogation they'd escaped from in those old shacks. The term *never* was the word tearing at her heartstrings, knowing they could've all been killed, children included.

Thank God for Bunker and his quick reaction skills. Otherwise, there would be several funerals on the docket. Hers included.

Her thoughts turned to the lonely man from Los Angeles and his wicked set of tattoos—the colorful Kindred emblem front and center in her mind. She hadn't seen or heard from the troubled soul since they'd split up after Grinder's death.

She didn't know if Bunker was hurt, lost, wandering around, back in town, or captured again. No way to know, so she'd just have to stay positive and wait for him to make an appearance.

Hopefully, he hadn't skipped town. If he did, she wouldn't blame the guy. She'd pulled a gun and was ready to shoot him, her apprehension about his past taking over in a moment of weakness.

She hoped they had put the unexpected confrontation behind them, but the former biker might have decided to take off. In that case, it would be her fault and she'd have to live with it. She'd overreacted and wasn't proud of it, but sometimes a woman needs to take a step back and take a moment to be sure. Especially when it has to do with someone brand new in your life—a man whose past wasn't what she expected, and neither was his gallantry for that matter.

Tuttle seemed to have a little bit of everything stored in his pole barn, but so far, she hadn't found a single electronic device. Not a one. The first three columns of inventory had proven fruitless, leading her to stack number four.

Her eyes scanned the contents of each plastic-wrapped bundle, stacked neatly from the floor to the ceiling. Nothing of interest caught her eye, though she couldn't see much detail on the pallet near the top.

"I'm getting tired," Jeffrey said from Daisy's left. "I don't want to look anymore. Can I go back to my mom?"

"Not yet, sweetheart. Not until we find what we need," Daisy said, wanting to keep the kids occupied while Martha, her daughter Allison, and Stephanie King tended to Franklin Atwater's injuries.

"But we already found the bandages and stuff. Why can't we go back?"

"Because your mom and the Raineys are busy helping Mr. Atwater. We need to let them do their work so he gets better. It won't take long, I promise. Just keep looking."

Daisy returned to the front of the stacks to check on Megan. The young girl hadn't said much since they began this forage, obviously worried about her dad.

Her tiny backside sat centered on top of a small crate near the barn door, her crutches lying at her feet. She wasn't crying but the traumatized look on her face told Daisy all she needed to know.

"It'll be okay, Megan. Mrs. Rainey is a really good nurse and she's going to help your dad. He'll be good as new in no time."

"I know," Megan said. "I just wish we were at home, where it's safe. I don't like it here."

Daisy wasn't sure what to say, so she said nothing. Sometimes trying to comfort someone else's child backfires when you meddle without the proper experience or frame of reference. Right now, the smart move was to keep quiet. Otherwise, she might say the wrong thing and upset the girl.

In truth, the safest place for everyone right now was here, at Tuttle's place, but she didn't want to argue the point. Megan was calm and waiting patiently, exactly what everyone needed.

"I really miss my horse. I hope Star is okay," the dark-skinned girl said, her tone depressed. "He was probably really scared when someone let him loose. I'm afraid he ran far away."

"I'm sure he'll find his way back home," Daisy said. "Horses are really smart. He knows that you love him. He'll come back."

"Yeah, but unless I'm there, I think he might try to find me or something. It's really scary out in the woods when you're all by yourself."

Daisy was at a loss for words again. The girl was pushing the conversation down a path she wasn't sure how to handle.

"What's he gonna do, Daisy? He's got nobody to feed him. Or give him water."

"He'll find a stream to drink in, sweetheart, and there's plenty of grass around. Horses know instinctively what to do. They used to run wild before we corralled them and put saddles on their backs."

Megan nodded, her lips turning silent as she fiddled with the heavy leg brace. Her tiny fingers tugged at the metal, straightening the alignment around her sore knee.

Maybe Daisy had finally found the proper words to bring comfort to Megan's broken heart. Daisy's heart was feeling it, too. So much happening and so little of it good. Everyone was reeling but they all seemed to be holding it together.

Strength in numbers was the phrase that seemed the most appropriate at the moment, though *misery loves company* would also work. Let's face it, sometimes too much drama all at once drowns a person, suffocating their ability to think or even act. But her friends were pushing through it.

The girl's comments about food and water reminded her that they needed to tend to Tuttle's chickens and pigeons out back. It would also give the kids something to do while everyone waited for Franklin's recovery.

Before Daisy could blink again, she heard the unmistakable sound of hollow tin, banging away. It was coming from the left, yet it was distant, somewhere near the back of the barn if she had to guess. Jeffrey must have been rapping on something made of metal.

At that moment, her memories fired, reminding her of something she'd seen the first time she'd walked through the barn with Frank Tuttle as her guide. The sealed storage cabinets near the hatch to the man's underground bunker. Each cabinet featured twin doors whose seams had been covered with metal-reinforced tape.

Her memory changed again, flashing the letters *TEOTWAWKI*. It was the term she'd seen written across the doors—an acronym that meant *THE END OF THE WORLD AS WE KNOW IT*.

The banging continued, louder this time.

"Hang on, Jeffrey, I'm coming to you," she said, breaking into a full sprint to the ten-year-old's location.

When Daisy arrived, she found the boy hitting one of the cabinets with a three-foot-long piece of 2x4. Black magic marker ink had been scrawled across its knotty surface, spelling the phrase *Master Story Stick*. Under that phrase was another pair of words, *CC Legs*. She wasn't sure what the chicken scratching was for, but Tuttle's handwriting was a mess. Almost like he was in a hurry. Or drunk.

"It's locked," Jeffrey said, taking another whack at the cabinet. His aim caught the center of the left door, creating a more pronounced dent than before.

She held out her hand. "Here, let me try."

The boy gave her the lumber, taking a step back after he did.

Daisy wrapped both hands around the end of the wood and brought it back past her shoulder like a baseball bat. Her target was the pair of handles in the middle where the doors met, specifically, the one on the right. It featured a key slot.

After a full swing and a loud clang, a tremor-like reverberation shot through her arms. It made her elbows hurt and her hands release, sending the 2x4 to the ground with a hollow thud.

She brought her eyes to bear and looked at her target. The locking handle had been bent slightly to one side, but it appeared to be holding firm against her attack.

Daisy bent down and picked up the makeshift hammer to swing again. This time she let out a powerful grunt as she unleashed her malice with more force.

The lever sheared off in pieces, pinging a death song across the cement floor when it landed. Their collective journey came to an abrupt halt when the pieces slid into a stack of thirty-pound bags on the floor—mostly white and evenly placed in a crisscrossing pattern.

The blue stenciling on the bags told her the weight and the name of the business that Tuttle had purchased them from—some place called Dewey Farms in Arizona. Under the brand name was the word *FERTILIZER* with chemical formula *$NH4NO3$* with *34% N* printed after it.

"Nice shot!" Jeffrey said.

"All those summers of girls' softball really paid off," she quipped, reliving a painful moment of glory from her youth. It was back when she ran headfirst into a heavy girl at home plate. Bethany was her name, if she remembered right. Actually, it was Big Bethany, the official nickname of the opposing team's immovable catcher.

Daisy's team lost that game in the city finals when she was thirteen. That was the last time she ever picked up a glove or bat. The collision was the main reason, though her focus would soon switch from sports to boys.

That legendary impact had changed her life, but she wasn't sure if it had been for the better. Her luck with the opposite sex hadn't exactly been good; she always seemed to choose the wrong guy. Maybe she only attracted assholes, reeling them in like an expert fisherman with all the right bait.

Daisy used the sharp corner of the 2x4 to cut through the tape along the middle seam. Once she had a loose piece to work with, she was able to pull the remaining tape away from the cabinet, working it free from the center out.

The instant the restraints were removed, the doors, no longer held in place, plopped open an inch. Daisy finished the reveal, swinging the doors open until the hinges stopped the movement. Inside were five shelves, spaced evenly apart from top to bottom.

"Now that's more like it," she said, seeing an array of electronic equipment on each level. She figured Tuttle stored them inside the steel structure and used metal-infused tape to complete what she assumed was another one of his homemade Faraday cages.

"Hey, what's this?" Jeffrey asked, pointing at a bulging orange manila folder hanging on the inside of the door. A strip of two-inch clear tape was holding it in place along the top, but the folder was loose otherwise. The boy yanked at it, freeing the paper from the grip of the sticky packing tape.

Daisy took it from him and put her hand inside, sliding past the open flap on one end. Her fingers found a wad of papers partway down. But not just one batch. There were two, folded in half separately. She yanked one of them out.

"What is it?" Jeffrey asked, his curious eyes round with excitement. "Let me see."

Daisy bent her knees and brought herself down to Jeffrey's level, letting the helpful boy get a good look at his discovery.

He smiled at her.

She unfolded the fold of papers. There were eleven pages, all handwritten on white letter-sized notepaper. The cursive writing was precise, curly, and easy to read.

Daisy figured it was a woman's handwriting—Helen's—knowing from the 2x4 that Tuttle's penmanship was a disaster. Like most men's.

Must be part of their DNA, she decided—bad penmanship and horrible relationship skills. Oh, and let's not forget embarrassing table manners, and last but not least, disgusting bathroom etiquette. The term *spraying and praying* entered her mind, carrying a cruel dual meaning.

Daisy scoffed silently, realizing that God had a wicked sense of humor, pairing women and men together with an invisible, yet unbreakable attraction for each other. It was a bond that had been forged by the Almighty in heaven, then laced with passionate heat and unending turmoil.

How any of that worked was beyond explanation, with both sides polar opposites in every respect. It was a wonder anyone on Earth got along for more than a minute without shooting each other. Especially couples.

Jeffrey pointed his stubby finger at the first line on the page, aiming its tip at the first two words, both of which were underlined in black ink. He read the phrase aloud, sounding out the words using medium speed. "Inventory List."

Daisy hesitated for a moment, the kid's reading catching her off guard. "You can read longhand? I didn't think they taught that in school anymore?"

"They don't. But my mom teaches me at home. Well, actually, my tutor did before Mom kicked Dad out of the house. Now she does it."

"Well, good for her," Daisy said, finding a new appreciation for her former best friend.

Stephanie King may have been royally pissed off at Daisy, and the rest of the world for that matter, but her motherly skills and devotion to her son were clear and evident. Even the most unstable person has something in their life that they excel at, even if it's only one thing.

Jeffrey was a pleasant, happy boy, his manners honed and politeness always on display. Easily a win on any mother's résumé.

Even though Daisy didn't have any children, she knew that pride in one's offspring was hard-earned, just like respect, requiring time, dedication, and patience.

Kudos, Stephanie, she thought, her heart skipping a beat.

Daisy figured she'd never get a chance to be a mother since her taste in men was a bigger disaster than the federal deficit. However, if she was ever lucky enough to find someone worthy, she hoped she could be half the mother Stephanie was—without the hysterics thrown in, of course.

Before her next breath, a loud, forceful voice came tearing at Daisy's ears from the right. "Jeffrey Thomas King! You get over here right now!"

Jeffrey looked up in a flash of panic, the color in his cute, freckled face drying up in an instant.

"I'm not going to say it again," Stephanie King demanded, her lips pinched and her hands on her hips.

Jeffrey took off running to his mother's position. When he arrived, his quick feet stopped with simultaneous plops, his head hanging low. "I'm sorry, Mom."

"It's okay. He was being good," Daisy said in a matter-of-fact way, wondering why Steph was so upset—over nothing. After all, Stephanie had sent the kids in here to get them out of the way while Allison, Martha, and she tended to Franklin's injuries. Daisy didn't understand the problem.

Stephanie put her hands on her son's shoulders. "I need you to take Megan inside. Mr. Atwater is awake now and wants to see her."

"But Mom, we just found—"

"Right now, young man. Megan needs your help. Go, do what I said. Mommy needs to have a little talk with the deputy."

"Okay," Jeffrey answered, walking to Megan. He picked up her crutches and gave them to her. The two of them left a short minute later.

Daisy felt the heat in Stephanie's eyes when the curvy pile of fury turned her way.

CHAPTER 70

When Bunker found the location where he'd woken up, he put the materials he'd scavenged in a pile along the bank, then followed the incredibly loud buzzing sound. It led him west, into the forest, where he found the hive a few yards beyond the first stand of trees.

It was huge, at least ten feet long, dangling its succulent nectar under a low-hanging willow branch that ran left to right. It was shaped like a pregnant panda bear, holding on for dear life against the pull of gravity.

The white area near the middle was the only section not covered with worker bees. That would be his entry point. However, he'd need a few things first.

First up, a makeshift knife—something he could use to gently slice into the honey reserve and harvest its sweetness without pissing off the residents. If he wasn't careful, he'd jostle their home and ignite their pheromones, sending them into an all-out attack.

There had to be at least a hundred thousand bees, possibly a lot more, each one carrying a painful stinger with his name on it. His mind flashed a vision of him running blind through the forest with a black cloud of tiny drones swarming around his head.

He returned to the creek and walked along the shoreline until he found a bed of exposed rock with hundreds of stones scattered about. The search took a few minutes, but he located a flat stone made of what he assumed was shale. The dark gray rock was about the size of his palm and had a polished, smooth surface. Its oblong shape was perfect, giving him two opposing ends to work with.

Two feet away was a semi-flat stone about the size of a dinner plate, though it wasn't round. It was shaped more like a kidney, with a noticeable divot in the middle. It would serve as the anvil base for the bipolar percussion process.

All he needed to complete his knife-making kit was a heavy striker rock, one about the size of his hand and made of a denser material than the shale. It took a bit of foraging, but he found a potential hammer stone.

He tested its hardness on another piece of shale, striking it multiple times until it broke in half. The force needed was more than he expected, but he knew it would do the job.

Now it was time to make the knife. He took the target stone and adjusted its oblong shape between his fingers. Its two opposing ends were now standing vertical, with the lower point sitting in the divot of the anvil stone.

He moved his hand out of harm's way with a loose two-finger grip before grabbing the cantaloupe-sized striker rock. The stone filled his grip as he hit the top of the shale rock repetitively, using more force with each strike.

The pressure waves eventually worked their magic, shearing off a piece that jettisoned to the right. He picked up the shale offspring and examined it. Its fine edge was razor sharp to the touch, traversing one side of it from end to end. Its size was roughly fifty percent of the original rock—almost a perfect slice, its shape just like the parent, only thinner.

Bunker had planned to fashion a handle for it out of a piece of driftwood, but the size of the cutting stone looked to be large enough to hold on to as he cut into the honeycomb. Skipping the handle would save time and energy, so that was what he decided to do. However, before the beehive could be penetrated, he needed to make sure the bees would remain docile and unthreatened by his activity.

Since there wasn't a beekeeper's suit handy, he'd need an alternative. Smoke was the only answer and would keep the insects oblivious and calm, letting him cut into their hive and extract what he needed.

He went back into the forest and gathered up a generous bundle of dry sticks for kindling. He snatched some brown grass, too, before returning to the flat spot by the creek where he'd left the Red Bull can and the other objects. He cleared off an area of river rock to expose the dirt underneath, making a four-foot-wide circle.

Bunker took the Kleenex out of his pocket and put it in the center of the campfire ring. Next, he stacked the dry grass over the tissue, fluffing the stalks to create air gaps. He finished by building a pyramid of sticks around the pile, leaving one side open for direct access to the Kleenex.

Now he needed an ignition source.

Bunker had several choices, one of which could have been the condom in the camper's trash pile. Had it not been soiled, he would've turned the latex into a water balloon, then used it to focus the sunlight into a single point, acting like a magnifying glass. It would've taken a bit of finagling, trying different angles and finger pressures, but it would've worked on a sunny day like today. He could have done the same with the bottle of water, but it too would have taken trial and error.

The Bic lighter was a faster, better choice.

He took it out of his pocket and held up it up for close examination. It had been a while since he'd done what came next, but he still remembered the basic process.

Even though the camper had thrown the lighter away when it ran out of gas, Bunker knew there was at least one more flame hiding inside.

First, he'd have to use the lighter's fork assembly to open the jet port all the way. That would allow the last bit of gas to find its way to the striker. The fork was positioned just under the spark wheel and was flat by design to fit a person's thumb. However, it was protected by the hood guard, which he pried off with his fingernail.

Once the fork assembly was exposed, he loosened it with his thumb, popping it free from its seated position. He moved it to the side, allowing the jet port to be pushed up a notch by its spring, then he brought the fork back to its starting position. He repeated the same process one more time, exposing more of the jet port to maximize the potential gas flow.

He held the lighter close to the Kleenex and engaged the spark wheel, spinning it against the flint. A brilliant, two-inch flame shot out from the end of the lighter and lit the Kleenex on fire, spreading quickly to the mound of grass.

Bunker watched the fire work its way up to the kindling he'd arranged. Once the sticks were fully engulfed, he carefully stacked more wood on top until he had a roaring fire. Now he just had to locate the remaining items needed to make a torch.

He found a stand of pine trees about fifty yards east of the beehive. The second tree on the right had what he needed—tree resin—gobs of it, smothering an area along its bark approximately six inches in diameter.

The resin was part of the tree's natural defense system to protect it against invading insects, acting as an impenetrable bandage after one of its lower arms had been sheared off. Probably from high winds, Bunker decided, stepping over a fallen branch whose thickest end appeared to match the damaged area on the tree.

So far, so good, he told himself, knowing the resin was only part of the equation. He needed a pinecone and a live branch, too, both of which he could salvage from this location.

He chose one of the smaller branches on the tree, just to the right of the resin glob, breaking it at the spot where it attached to the trunk. The limb was about an inch in diameter and still alive, just as Bunker needed. It took effort to bend it back and forth, but he was able to work it free, ending with a twist.

He took the sharp stone he'd made earlier and sawed a split into one end of the live branch, stopping after cutting down about five inches. He tested his progress, prying the split end apart and stuffing the pinecone inside. "Perfect," he said, storing the cutting rock inside his pocket.

He put the branch aside, then leaned his chest against the base of the tree. He had to stand on his tiptoes in order to reach the resin, but his fingers were able to tear off a hunk about the size of a baseball. It felt sticky, smearing across his fingers like an invading swarm of Gorilla Glue.

The campfire was still roaring when he returned with the items he'd found. As planned, the unmodified end of the torch slipped into the pour spout of the aluminum can, making it simple to pry its wide-mouth lid open. He worked the stick around until he had clear access to the bottom of the aluminum container.

Bunker put the resin inside, then placed it near the campfire, leaving an air gap so the resin would melt slowly and not catch fire. He stirred the contents with the handle of the torch until it had a runny consistency that resembled sticky paste.

Bunker freed the pinecone from the end of the torch he'd made, then dipped it into the resin and swirled it around inside the can. The substance transferred as expected, coating the pinecone.

"Time for a little honey," he mumbled, jamming the resin-covered pinecone back into the end of the torch. He put it aside and went to the creek, where he dipped his fingers into the cool water and rubbed them together until the tackiness went away.

Bunker dried his fingers on his pants, then returned to the fire. He held the torch over the flame until the resin smothering the pinecone caught fire. Smoke billowed from the improvised torch, filling the air above him in puffs of white. He figured he'd have about ten minutes of burn time. Maybe fifteen.

"Drum roll, please," he announced to the forest, taking in a long breath and letting it out. He spun on the balls of his feet before heading uphill.

His destination—the beehive. His goal—the honey.

CHAPTER 71

"Rusty, get the gate," Sheriff Apollo said, waving a hurried hand signal at the Mayor's grandson when they approached Tuttle's homestead. The kid hopped off his mountain bike, right on cue.

Apollo wondered if the angry relic who owned the place was watching with his shotgun at the ready. The man's reputation as an eccentric recluse was legendary and well-earned. Even though it was imperative to get everyone off the road in case they were followed, Apollo needed to take it slow.

So far, he hadn't seen any sign of the owner and that, by itself, was a good thing. His badge and gun were probably a good deterrent, he figured, despite what Daisy had told him about Tuttle's propensity to shoot first and ask questions later.

Tuttle may have been living on edge and fighting reality on a daily basis, but the old codger wasn't crazy enough to shoot at the Sheriff and a bunch of innocent people from town. Was he?

Not likely, Apollo decided. *Act like nothing is wrong and Tuttle will behave himself.*

Rusty worked the latch free on the gate and pushed the barrier open. Apollo stood guard as each member of the group made their way inside, passing next to him.

First, newly appointed Deputy Dick Dickens went through, the former football star who took point on his own. Then Misty and Cowie entered on their horse, the man's head hanging low and bobbing from left to right, matching the stride of the great steed.

Rusty went in last, pushing his bike along with caution, keeping a three-foot distance from the hind legs of the mammal in front of him.

The look on everyone's faces told Apollo the same thing—they were exhausted from the trip. He couldn't blame them. They'd covered a lot of distance on foot, plus he was sure everyone was worried about Angus Cowie, the Australian man who never regained consciousness before they'd arrived on Old Mill Road.

The trip had been stressful ever since the foreigner's rescue from the river. They stopped occasionally to let Misty Tuttle's arms rest and for Apollo to check for pursuers, the upstream gunshots fresh in his thoughts.

Misty had been holding the wounded man upright in the saddle ever since she'd climbed onboard and took position behind her fiancé. Her selfless dedication to her man's every need was impressive, her attention and hands never wavering. Not for an instant.

There's love there, Apollo decided, his soul absorbing the words as he thought them. Their love was the kind of love he wished he'd find for his sorry old ass.

Apollo's eyes drifted across the dirt road on their own, lingering for a few seconds as a daydream about Allison Rainey began playing on the video screen in the back of his mind.

Right now, across the street was the one woman in the world who might fill what he was missing in his life—someone to love and care for, and maybe provide the same in return.

He couldn't stop thinking about the middle-aged goddess—the waitress with the heart of gold, her face dominating his every thought. She was a mere two-hundred yards away and off duty for a change.

He sighed, letting the torment of the moment sink in. Asking her out sounded easy in theory, but he knew better. Every time he tried, his backbone would crumble, leaving his desires orphaned and alone, rendering him some kind of dumb mute. But not just any mute. An overweight, balding mute with little in the bank to show for his life's work.

It had been the same excuse over and over—wait for a better opportunity—wait for the perfect opening. That's what he needed. The perfect opening. Then he'd surely get her to notice him on a more meaningful level. God knows he needed it, because their current waitress / patron basis wasn't cutting it. Not by a long shot. He needed more.

If he could somehow pull it off, then he'd have a chance at a full, meaningful existence on this rock. It wasn't like being town sheriff didn't have its rewards, but in the end, they meant nothing. Not compared to the rewards of having somebody to share your triumphs with, or someone soft and warm to lean on when your mistakes reared up and took a painful chunk out of your sagging backside.

The barbed thoughts swirling in his head were basically a rerun of his entire life, cutting and burrowing their way from his brain down to his heart.

Enough already, Apollo scolded himself quietly, deciding it was time to stop the adolescent fantasy. Your life is what you make it, and so far, he'd taken the easy way out. Nobody to blame but himself. It only took a second to wipe the romantic scene from his mind and turn his focus back to his sheriff duties.

Cowie's bleeding was slow but relentless, releasing his life-force one droplet at time. The horse he and his girl were riding didn't seem to mind the blood, its redness painting a random montage of gravity-fed stripes down the beast's side.

Franklin Atwater had trained the powerful horse well. Its calm temperament was on full display, despite the strangers on its back and the tension in the air.

Apollo wasn't an expert when it came to training equines, but he was almost certain this animal was a cut above the rest, something that only a proud, steadfast man like Franklin could achieve.

Once they were all inside the gate, Rusty shut it behind the group. Apollo led the way around the first two stacks of rocks in the old man's driveway, but stopped when he noticed something to his right. Something out of place—a black circle in the weeds. Flat. Charred. Distinct.

But that wasn't all.

Just beyond the scorch mark was the twisted hull of an old Ford truck. Its grille resembled the two Ford pickups that were parked nearby, facing him.

Rusty caught up a few seconds later with the handlebars of the off-road bike in his grip. He tapped Apollo on the elbow and pointed at the same pile of steel. "Is that a truck?"

"What's left of it."

"What happened?"

"Looks like Mr. Tuttle had himself a little bonfire recently, and it must've gotten out of control. I'm guessing that old truck was sitting where the charred area is, and then boom. The tank exploded."

"Should have used some rocks around it."

Apollo nodded, never taking his eyes from the burn mark. "A little attention to safety would've helped contain the fire."

"I just hope the old dude is okay. If he was standing close to it—"

"Then he was seriously injured."

"Or worse."

"That's what I'm afraid of," Apollo answered, wondering if Tuttle had set the fire on purpose. A man of Tuttle's temperament and years might have been distraught after losing his wife. It wasn't a stretch to think Tuttle might have hurt himself.

"We should go inside and find out," Dick Dickens said, joining Rusty and the Sheriff in the gawk fest.

Apollo stopped his deputy from advancing with an outstretched hand. "Wait a second, Dicky," he said after spotting the bumpers of two vehicles tucked behind the corner of the barn. The paint across the rear of the vehicles looked new, both a greenish color.

He pointed, leading Dicky's eyes to the cars. "I don't think those are Tuttle's. They are too new and he'd never spend money on two of them, not after Helen died."

"That doesn't look right either," Dicky said, aiming his enormous index finger at the window closest to their position. The glass was missing and so was its blind, the window next to it still intact and covered.

"The explosion?" Rusty asked in a leading manner.

"I'm not so sure," Apollo said, pulling his weapon from its holster before addressing Dicky. "I need you to get everyone behind the rocks while I go check it out. I need you to keep an eye on the road, too. I'm pretty sure nobody followed us, but we better not take any chances."

Apollo had planned to head to the front door of the home, but changed his mind when he heard a loud crash coming from Tuttle's massive barn. The noise sounded like wood breaking.

When he heard a smattering of grunts, whacks, and a woman screech, he took off running for the double doors along the front of the barn. His mind ran through a dozen scenarios in search of an explanation for the scene they'd stumbled on, but nothing seemed to fit.

When he arrived at the structure, the noises inside were louder and more intense than before. He heard a few more crashes, then more grunts and a loud thud. A second later, he heard a painful scream.

Just then, the slats of the wall broke loose in front of him, showering him in a spray of splinters and planks. A body came flying out at the same time, tumbling backwards and rolling into a heap at his feet.

It was the body of a woman—a voluptuous woman whose hair was twisted around and hanging in clumps, covering her face from his vantage point. Her curves were prominent, drawing his eyes in an instant.

Apollo tore his gaze from her cleavage and aimed his sidearm at the hole in the building. He wondered if Tuttle had hurled this woman through the wall. Possibly for trespassing, the same thing he and his group were doing.

He was about to yell a series of commands at Tuttle, instructing him to come out slowly with his hands up, but the woman at his feet grabbed his ankle. Her moans were soft but her grip hard, her face still obstructed from view.

Apollo kept the gun trained on the hole in the barn as he knelt down and brushed the hair away from the woman's face. When her eyes came into view, he recognized her. "Stephanie?"

"Hey Sheriff. Long time no see," she quipped back, sounding as if her situation was normal and expected. Her upper lip was bleeding from a half-inch scrape along the side, and so too, were the middle knuckles on her right hand.

"What the hell is going on? Did Tuttle do this?"

"No, it wasn't Tuttle," another female's voice said from in front of him, the tone and pattern familiar. "It was me."

When Apollo looked up, he saw a bloody face staring back at him, peering out of the barn through the ragged hole. It was his number two in charge, Daisy Clark, the cut on her chin dripping blood in sets of two.

She smiled, showing her pearly whites, a stark contrast to her left eye, which was noticeably swollen. One of her teeth had a smear of red on it. It was faded and almost pink in color.

Stephanie King let go of Apollo's ankle and crawled to her feet in an awkward stumble, nearly toppling over after her arms swung to one side.

Apollo put his gun away in a flash, then latched onto the shoulders of the unstable woman, using his brawn to keep her upright. "You okay?"

"I am now," she said, laughing after she spun her head and spat out some blood in a pucker. She worked herself free from Apollo, then moved forward with deliberate feet and put her hand into the opening in the wall, thumb facing up. She held it still, only inches from Daisy's position.

Daisy grabbed Stephanie's palm, pulling herself through the gaping exit hole in the barn.

"That was some kick," Stephanie told Daisy in a friendly tone after the two of them came together outside.

Daisy rubbed her chin, her fingers just missing the blood on one side. "Nice punch. I didn't think you had it in you."

Stephanie smiled and spoke again, her tone amplified. "Try living with the asshole I was married to and you'd understand why."

"I hear you, Steph. Again, I'm sorry for everything that happened."

"No, I'm sorry. Taking this all out on you was wrong. I know you just got caught off guard. You're not the one I need to be mad at."

Daisy didn't respond, her face unsure.

Stephanie continued, "The way I see it, you did me a favor. A huge favor."

"Then we're good?"

"Yeah. We're good," Stephanie said, putting her arms around Daisy and pulling her in for an extended hug. "I've missed you."

Daisy brought her hands up as well, finishing their embrace in a tangle of blood, hair, and arms. "I missed you, too. It was killing me inside."

Apollo wasn't sure what to say, so he kept his mouth shut, content to let this play out on its own.

Rusty slid in next to him, with Dicky on the far side. Both of them looked as dumbfounded as Apollo felt at the moment. These two women just beat the hell out of each other and now they were acting like nothing had happened.

Stephanie put an arm around Daisy's shoulders as the two of them walked away, making a beeline for the front door of the house. Daisy's arm was around Stephanie's waist, the two of them laughing and chatting like schoolgirls.

"What was that?" Dicky asked, throwing his hands up in confusion.

Apollo shrugged. "Beats the hell out of me."

"Women," Rusty said in a sarcastic tone.

"You got that right, son. Obviously, there's some history between them. Let's just hope whatever that was is over," Apollo answered, figuring Bill King was at the center of it. The man usually was, and the cryptic exchange between the women appeared to confirm that assumption.

Regardless of what had started it, Apollo was thankful he didn't have to break up yet another fight between two women he knew.

He snickered after shaking his head.

One catfight per week was his new over/under limit, as he decided he needed to set quotas for all things unexpected and sheriff related.

Apollo waved a signal at Misty to bring the horse forward, then turned and locked eyes with his stout deputy. "Dicky, you and Rusty help her get Cowie inside. Find a couch or bed. Somewhere with decent light. Keep his head elevated."

"You got it, chief."

The Sheriff closed his eyes and let out a soft exhale, taking a few moments to let his mind catch up to the facts pouring in. A million questions formed instantly, coming at him all at once.

He wasn't sure where to start. So much to cover. However, since Daisy was here at Tuttle's, then maybe Bunker was as well.

"Yes, Bunker," he mumbled, realizing he needed an impartial observer. Someone who wasn't part of the town. Someone with the skills and experience to explain all the craziness, both with the people and with the events of the day.

CHAPTER 72

Bunker slowed his pace as he neared the low-hanging, horizontal branch of the willow tree. So far, the bees hadn't noticed him, allowing him to continue his advance unscathed. He wondered if their incredibly loud buzzing had kept the noise of his approach a secret. If the pitch was a little higher, he figured it would have sounded like a gas-powered weed whacker in action, mowing down the forest one clump of grass at a time.

He brought the torch up, moving it slowly from side to side to spread out the smoke, not knowing how much was needed to keep the bees calm. But regardless, he couldn't dillydally.

There was a finite amount of burn remaining in the torch; plus, he still needed to be able to see what he was doing. Too much smoke would exceed both of those limits, so he decided to just go for it and hope he was close to deploying the proper amount.

After four more steps and a full waist bend, he put the torch underneath the swarming hive, leaning it against the base of the trunk. He waited as the smoke floated up to the target, gently surrounding the hive in a cloud of white.

He'd expected the smoke to slow the hive's activity down, but that was not what happened. The instant it hit a tangle of bees, they took off in unison, zipping away with a much higher pitch to their wings than before.

Everywhere the smoke went, the bees abandoned their posts, retreating in formation for safer air. They must have thought a forest fire was headed their way.

He hunched and waited for them to attack, ready to run for cover. The bees were zipping about but apparently too busy avoiding the smoke to care about him.

Bunker let out the breath he was holding, then took out the cutting stone. He held it in his hand with the sharp edge leading the way, while a squadron of bees circled around the far side of the smoke cloud and doubled back.

They buzzed his head, neck, and shoulders in a swirling pattern, sending his blood pressure a level higher. He froze for a few moments, waiting to see if one of them would bring a stinger his way. Their flight paths were chaotic and near, but none of them seemed interested in testing the resistance of his skin.

It was hard to concentrate with non-stop fly-bys obstructing his vision, but he continued to the middle of the hive wall facing him. He gently pushed the cutting stone into the surface.

A runny yellow substance leaked out and landed on his hand, then oozed a trail to his wrist before sliding down his arm. He ignored the leakage, slicing deeper into the substrate until he found a firmer area inside.

Before his next blink, a bee swooped in and landed on the bridge of his nose.

Bunker drew in a short breath, seeing only a dark smear an inch or so from his eyes. He could the feel the drone's tiny feet on his skin, moving down his nostrils before taking a sharp left and crawling onto his cheek.

He thought about shaking his head to send the bee into flight, but decided against it. Right now, the insect appeared to be calm, almost like it was curious, casually checking things out. If the drone changed its mind and stung him, the others would detect the release of threat pheromones and swarm.

The bee took off a moment later and joined the others, flying in random patterns to avoid the smoke cloud. He let go of the breath in his lungs and continued slicing until a one-foot-long chunk fell to the ground. He cut a second piece off as well, then picked up both pieces and made a hasty retreat.

After a quick jog back to the campfire, Bunker put his take on the ground, then checked his hair, shirt collar, and the rest of his clothing for unwanted guests.

All clear.

He'd done it.

No stings.

A smile erupted, his body energized with the thrill of victory. It took a minute for his heart rate to calm, then he sat down next to the fire to admire his score.

The first batch of honeycomb had a waxy covering. Beeswax, he figured, to seal in the honey. He wasn't sure if that was the right term, but it didn't matter.

Bunker scraped off a small amount of the wax with the cutting stone, giving him access to the golden nectar. He dipped his finger inside for a sample and tasted it.

"Wow, that's frickin' good," he mumbled, savoring the sweetness on his tongue.

He couldn't remember from his survival training if he could eat the honeycombs, too, but the hunger in his belly convinced him it was worth the risk.

Bunker scraped off more of the wax, then took a bite. His teeth worked through the fibrous texture, releasing a supernova of flavor that exploded on his tongue. It was fabulous, better than any store-bought honey he'd ever tasted.

He continued eating like a madman, until every ounce of the first cutoff was in his stomach. Damn, he was in heaven and wanted more, but he knew he had to stop. The rest of what he'd stolen was destined for the wound in his arm—a wound he needed to treat before it became infected.

Punctures are notoriously difficult to keep clean, especially in a woodsy, humid setting like this. Yet keeping his injury clean was the last step in the treatment process, one that could only start after he dealt with the bacteria lurking inside the damage path.

He removed the cap from the water bottle and stood the container a few inches away from the campfire by leaning it against one of the larger rocks.

It would take a few minutes to bring the water to a boil, so he used the time to clean off the wax on one side of the remaining honeycomb.

Once the water came to a boil, he used one of his socks as a glove to move the bottle away from the fire. He waited until the boiling stopped, then picked up the container again with the sock on his hand.

Bunker took a series of deep breaths to summon all his strength, then brought the underside of his forearm over the bottle's opening. He made sure to align the plastic opening precisely with the wound.

The plan was to fold his wounded arm up with his hand next to his ear, then instantly shoot the water through his arm with the upside-down bottle. Pressurized hot water was the key to flushing out his injury. But it would come at a cost—pain. Level ten and excruciating, but it was necessary to rid the wound of bacteria.

It was now or never.

Bunker sucked in a deep breath and then, all in one motion, folded his arm up and squeezed the water bottle in one firm crush of his hand. A water jet shot into the hole in his forearm and out the other side.

"Yeeeeeeooooooowww," he cried through clenched teeth, muffling the cry to keep the decibel level down.

He squeezed the bottle again, sending another flush of water through. The pain was just as intense the second time, but he was able to remain quiet, even though he was seeing a burst of stars in his vision.

After the two power flushes, the container had about fifteen percent of the water remaining. Probably enough for another go, he figured.

He thought about it for a second, but decided he'd had enough of the crush and flush, bringing his arm down and removing the plastic from his skin.

Bunker looked to his left to check the results of his work. The water had been forced through his arm as planned and landed on the neighboring rock, but it was no longer a clear liquid. It was more of a washed-out red color, with hunks of tissue mixed in.

"Looks like it worked," he said, feeling relieved the process was over, despite the throb in his arm. Pain he could deal with, but microscopic bacteria and unrelenting sepsis was another matter. What he'd just put himself through was worth it, assuming it was enough.

Once the water cooled, he brought the opening of the bottle to his lips and chugged down what remained inside. The liquid quenched his thirst—a thirst that had been building ever since he'd woken up.

He got up and went to the creek to fill the container again, then returned to the fire, where he put it next to the same rock for another boil. His hydration levels were low, and he figured it was going to take several more rounds to properly replenish his fluids.

While he waited for the water to heat up again, Bunker decided to prep his wound for travel. He broke off a hunk of the second honeycomb loaf, then angled it to allow the honey to leak out and land on his arm. He used the honeycomb as a swab, pushing more and more of the anti-bacterial remedy inside the damage path.

Once he'd packed it tight, he flipped his arm up next to his ear and did the same to the other side. The process was a sticky mess, but the bush remedy was necessary.

He finished by slicing a strip of cloth from his shirt and tying it around his arm as a bandage.

"That should do it." He turned his eyes to the leftover honeycomb, licking his lips before tearing into the treat.

Ten minutes later, the sugar rush kicked in like a pressure wave. The newfound energy felt amazing, giving him a much-needed mental boost. He downed the last of the boiled water, then stood up, ready to head out.

From what Franklin Atwater had told him earlier, it was a long walk south to Clearwater. Bunker knew he could make the grueling trek, but after the last twenty-four hours of beatings, electrocutions, mortars, bullets, and impalement, he figured a shortcut was in order. A shortcut by the name of Tango.

Unfortunately, hitching a ride on the horse meant another fight with the saddle. He wasn't looking forward to it, but it was better than trying to hump his weary ass back to town on foot. Just the act of breathing would become more difficult after his adrenaline waned, leaving him to argue with a snarl of injuries.

Guilt sprang up inside when he remembered the Russians unloading on the ridge. Bunker prayed the horse got away, sprinting into a full gallop when the firepower was unleashed. If Tango wasn't able to pull himself free from the branch, then he was probably down. Possibly dead.

The thought of Tango lying on his side with his guts exposed tore at Bunker's heart. He closed his eyes and shook his head, taking in a series of deep, slow breaths, trying to free his mind of the imagery. And the remorse.

The Clove Hitch he'd chosen was a sturdy knot, almost impossible to defeat. But maybe the clever steed managed to pull himself free, or chew through the reins.

He figured the Russians were long gone from the miner's camp, but he still needed to take it slow in case his assumptions were wrong. They most certainly sent out search teams after he was blown off the cliff, scouring the ridge for clues after their barrage ended.

If they followed his tracks through the forest, they would have ended up where he'd taken his last step. Bunker hoped they decided to give up their pursuit, thinking he'd floated away with the current, while surrounded by a bloody run of body parts.

There was no way to know how far he'd drifted downstream, so he'd have to make an educated guess as to where he first landed. He remembered seeing bushes with red berries lining the shoreline closest to him, and a huge boulder sticking up like a finger on the other. It even had knuckles, though they were fat and uneven.

Granted, everything would look different from ground level, but he should be able to spot those two elements. Especially together. After all, how many giant finger rocks with twin knuckles exist in nature? Not many, he decided, starting his hike upstream.

He planned to stay on the same side of the waterway as the berries. That way, they'd be the easiest to spot. A prudent plan, he decided, since the finger rock might not look the same from a downriver position.

CHAPTER 73

Albert felt a gentle weight on his shoulder, then a light jostle, rocking his extra-large frame with each round of pressure. A voice followed a second later—a male's voice, tone soft and inflection concerned.

When his hearing connected with his memories, a name attached itself to the words he was taking in. Albert opened his eyes to confirm the answer, seeing Dustin Brown kneeling over him.

The skin on his friend's face was a deep red color and his eyes were energized with worry.

"You okay?" Dustin asked in a whisper, his words charged with air.

"Yeah, sort of. What happened?" Albert groaned, his body reacting to commands in slow motion.

"I don't know exactly. When I came up here, you were out cold. At first, I thought you were dead."

"What about the troops?"

"Never came. Burt went to find out why."

Albert rolled to his side, needing a moment to let his body catch up to his intentions before he stood. "We gotta get moving. They're gonna spot Burt and he'll just lead them back to us."

Dustin put both hands on Albert, applying light downward pressure. "You need to stay here and rest. Burt said he'd be right back."

Albert swatted the man's hands away. "That's what I'm afraid of. That cement head is gonna get us all killed."

"I really think you need to give him a chance."

Albert couldn't believe what he just heard. His new friend had already turned on him, joining the team of assholes led by Burt. It was hard to accept, but Albert wasn't going to wait around and worry about it. If that's what Dustin wanted, then fine. "Well, you can, but I'm getting the hell out of here."

"What about our new business? We're going to need him."

Dustin's choice of words stoked a glimmer of hope inside Albert. Maybe their friendship wasn't over quite yet. He decided to give it one more chance, not willing to let all the work he'd put into Dustin go to waste.

"Not if we're dead, Dustin. Let's go. We'll figure out the rest later," Albert said, getting to his feet in a stumble. He waited a few seconds to see if Dustin would seize the opportunity to salvage their relationship, but he said nothing. Nor did he move.

I guess that's it, Albert thought, putting his hand into his pocket, confirming the baggie filled with ice was still there. He wondered if Clearwater Red would still be a viable product now that an apparent invasion was underway.

Probably not, he decided. Everyone would be too busy defending themselves to buy his special blend of meth. If he was right, then Burt was two-hundred pounds of baggage he no longer needed. So was Dustin.

Before Albert could take a step, a crunching sound came from the bushes on the left. Both men spun to see Burt, huffing his way up the last ten yards of the hill.

"Miss me?" Burt asked in a breathy voice, looking proud of himself.

"That didn't take long," Dustin said, his voice cracking in the middle of the sentence.

"Like I said, I just needed to take a peek. I told you it was nothing to worry about. You guys need to chill. I got this."

Albert flashed a penetrating stare at Dustin, realizing his fellow deputy had raised the very same concerns to Burt about getting too close to the military convoy. "Give him a chance, huh?"

Dustin didn't answer, his eyes confirming what Albert assumed had happened.

Albert turned to Burt, wondering what revelations he'd uncovered, if any. "What did you find out?"

Burt continued his approach, stepping over a foot-tall sapling in his way, then pushing his feet through a stand of grass. "It's the Russians. No doubt about it. They're setting up a roadblock on the other side of Mason Bridge. But that's not all. They're forming a massive perimeter as far as I could see from my position. Tanks, troops, missile launchers—you name it. They brought a little bit of everything."

Albert wasn't ready to accept Burt's report or his assumptions. The burly man could easily be wrong, though the term missile launchers did take Albert's concern to an entirely new level. "Little bit of everything, huh? What for?"

Burt stood with hands on his hips, his chest working overtime to restock the air in his lungs. "To keep everyone out, obviously. It's called a roadblock for a reason, or didn't they teach you English in that chemistry class of yours?"

Albert let out a short chuckle. The man's stupidity was even worse than he thought, demanding a quick retort.

"Keep everyone out of Clearwater?" Dustin asked before Albert could say anything.

Burt sucked in more air, nodding slowly. "Yep. I can't imagine what's going on in town right now, but I'm glad we're here."

"Why on Earth would the Russians care about a shit-stain of a town like Clearwater? It doesn't make any sense, Burt. Denver or Colorado Springs would be better targets, especially NORAD."

"The Silver King mine would be my guess. It's the only thing of value in our neck of the woods."

"So let me get this straight," Albert said in a terse tone, glancing at Dustin for a moment, then turning his eyes back to Burt. "You think the Russians came all this way to invade our country and risk World War III, just to get their hands on the silver in our mine? Even a high school dropout like you has to realize they could get silver in a million other places, and do so without risking a war."

"He's right," Dustin said, moving his eyes from Albert to Burt.

Burt shrugged, looking smug. "Maybe they're after something else in those mineshafts. A by-product or something. I don't know. But it's the only thing we got worth something around here. So it *has* to be the reason."

"Unless they're after the people," Dustin added. "For slaves. Or food, like in that old movie *Soylent Green*."

"That's even a dumber idea. You guys are totally reaching here," Albert said, stunned by the absurdity forming on the ridge. There was more he could say, but he held it back, figuring the dust-filled brainpans standing with him wouldn't understand the logic.

Burt continued, "Maybe so, but the Russians are here for a reason and they brought along a shit pile of firepower to make it happen. Whatever is going on took a lot of planning and a lot of guts to pull off. They have to be after something important."

"And they needed to set off the EMP first," Dustin added, nodding his head in earnest.

"Yep, to get *this* done, whatever *this* is," Burt said.

"What do we do now? We can't go to town with the road blocked," Dustin asked the mechanic.

"We work our way around and take a closer look at what's happening in town. We need more information, then we can form some tactics we can use."

"Tactics? Really?" Albert snarled, pointing at the road below. He wanted to leave these two behind, but for some reason, he felt compelled to stay and argue. "While you stand around and talk about tactics, those professional soldiers down there practice logistics all day, every day, just waiting to unleash holy hell on anyone dumb enough to get in their way. You ever heard of the term *Force Multiplier?*"

Burt seemed unfazed by Albert's perfectly worded rebuttal. The man motioned to the mountain behind them. "That climb looks do-able. We should head up there. I figure we can make town by nightfall, if we hurry."

"Then what?" Albert asked, wondering what it was going to take to get through to the brute. Dustin was obviously enamored with the man, leaving Albert to fly solo on the island of opposition.

Burt sounded sure of himself when he spoke again. "We take action, depending on what we learn. Simple enough."

"The three of us? Take action? Are you insane? You can't possibly think taking them on is a good idea."

"We gotta do something. We can't stay here."

Albert huffed, holding back his anger. He needed to get through to Dustin; otherwise, his friend would end up dead if he followed Burt. "The smart move would be to head back to my mother's place and stay out of sight. But we need to avoid the roads because you can bet your last dollar there are more Russians around. If they *are* forming a perimeter around Clearwater like Burt said, then Mason Bridge won't be the only roadblock. They probably have heavily-armed roving patrols, too, so we need to be careful. Don't want to find ourselves as human targets."

"So you're coming with us?" Dustin asked.

"Only if the plan makes sense. And right now, what Burt is suggesting is totally nuts."

"Hey, we're all on the same team here," Burt said.

Yeah, the team of nut jobs, Albert thought.

"What about food, water, and supplies?" Burt asked. "I'm guessing your mom's place isn't exactly a prepper compound, now is it? Heading back there is a huge mistake, Jumbo. Support hose and a dresser full of fake wigs ain't exactly gonna cut it."

Albert didn't respond to the obvious insults about his dead mother—the greasy jerk wasn't worth the effort or the time. He needed to get moving and fast, with or without Dustin.

Burt continued, his words keeping Albert's feet anchored in the soil. "We gotta be smart here and think this through. We're gonna need guns and ammo, too."

Dustin cleared his throat, his gaze now aimed at Albert. "You know, when we were in town before, I overheard the Sheriff talking to the Mayor about Frank Tuttle's place. Supposedly he has a stockpile of just about everything. Maybe we should go there?"

"That's not a bad idea. It's about the same distance, just in a different direction," Burt said without hesitation, looking at Albert.

Albert took a minute to run it through his mind. Dustin's plan made sense, even though Albert didn't want it to. And since it wasn't Burt's idea, he decided to consider it. "Going to Tuttle's place has some merit, but it would be one hell of a climb to get there."

"Yeah, we just take our time. No big deal," Burt said without an ounce of concern in his voice. "Look, at this point, it doesn't matter where we go. I just know we can't stay here."

"That much we agree on."

"Plus, nobody should be out here alone. We have to stick together," Dustin said.

"Then we go? Tuttle's place?" Burt asked, his tone genuine.

Burt's tone and his willingness to take a vote surprised Albert. Maybe there was hope after all.

Then Burt spoke again, ruining the moment. "Is everyone in agreement, or do I need to start knocking some heads together to get you guys to see the light?"

"Hey, no reason to make threats," Dustin said.

Burt huffed, tossing his arms out to his sides. "Come on, get over yourselves. We need to make a decision already. So what's it gonna be?"

Albert hated the idea of keeping Burt around, but Dustin was right. Going it alone was a mistake. He needed to make sure everyone was onboard and fully aware of what was needed to make this new plan work, despite his loathing of Burt. "We need to stay as far away from the Russian perimeter as we can, so we can't take any shortcuts. That means taking the long way around."

"What about water?" Dustin said, taking his backpack off and putting in on the ground. "We don't exactly have a lot of it."

Albert was in full agreement. "If we run out, we're screwed. Maybe we need to rethink this idea. I'm not sure if you guys know, but wilderness survival comes down to the rules of three. Three minutes without air, three days without water, and three weeks without food."

Burt shook his head. "Look, I've hunted in these mountains all my life, so I know them like the back of my hand. There are a couple of natural springs between here and Tuttle's place, so we can refill our water bottles along the way. And trust me, it's not going to take three days to get there. I know a few old logging roads we can use to shorten the time. Shouldn't be a problem."

Dustin locked eyes with Albert again. "Well? What do you think?"

Albert was out of objections. The idea might work as long as Burt could deliver on his promises. "Old man Tuttle's not gonna like us showing up uninvited. I hear he shoots first and asks questions later."

"Trust me, I can handle one crazy old man. Besides, I've fixed his tractor a bunch of times—usually at a discount—so I figure he owes me. Big time."

"All right, let's do it," Albert said after a three-count. Even if their plan wasn't complete or even sound, it was better than staying where they were, just waiting for the Russians to find them.

A smile appeared on Burt's lips. "Excellent. Then it's settled. We arm ourselves and fill our bellies at Tuttle's, then sneak back to town to see what's what."

"Lead the way," Albert said, deciding not to debate the mechanic's last statement. There was no chance he'd agree to head back to Clearwater from Tuttle's place, but Burt didn't need to know that fact. The first order of business was to get everyone out of here safely and to a secure location with food, water, and shelter.

If that meant letting Burt erroneously think they were going to town after that, it was Burt's problem. Albert couldn't care less.

CHAPTER 74

Mayor Buckley stood in the shadow of the towering statue of Cyrus Clearwater with his right elbow resting on the top of the blue mailbox. The first of four ATVs tore past him, each vehicle loaded with FEMA techs and a stash of MH2 inoculation equipment and supplies.

He was still having trouble reconciling the speed and efficiency of the emergency response crew. Their collective efforts were impressive to say the least, hardly speaking to each other in their Australian accents as they worked to complete each task.

"A well-oiled machine," Buckley mumbled, thinking of his own failure to run the small town he'd grown up in. Especially during this latest emergency.

He and Sheriff Apollo had done their best thus far, but the results were less than acceptable. So many failures and the list was growing. The only reason the situation was under control was because of FEMA. Not him.

His thoughts turned to his faithful grandson, Rusty. He wondered how the kid was doing in the wilderness. Thank God Apollo and Dicky were with him, otherwise the greenhorn would've surely struggled with the new reality facing them all. No power, no electronics, and no transportation. Buckley just hoped FEMA would find his missing family and friends before the toxic threat reached the surrounding area.

His mind tried to turn to visions of Rusty dying a horrible, painful death if the contamination cloud found him unprotected, but Buckley quickly flushed the idea.

A layer of guilt tried to take its place, but again, he wouldn't let it settle in and begin to fester. Mayors don't have the time or the luxury to second-guess themselves. Or grieve, if their decisions turn out to be dead wrong after an emergency strikes.

If his current stint at the helm of Clearwater, Colorado was a prelude to an even higher office at the state level, then he needed to continue bringing his leadership skills to bear and stay sharp. Hundreds of lives were counting on it, many of whom were family and long-time friends.

He sucked in a deep breath and held it, wanting the suffocating pressure of the moment to sink in and fortify his determination. A second later, he let the air escape before turning and heading to the FEMA Mobile Medical Unit.

The last of the in-town citizens had worked their way through the injection station ten minutes earlier, leaving the line in front of the trailer empty. But not just empty of people—empty of worry and terrified faces. Mostly little ones.

"Day one complete," he said, projecting out the mountain of work ahead for everyone involved, needing to finish the remaining twenty-nine days of treatment protocol. So many injections to administer. So many lives to save. All because of an EMP that took down a CDC containment facility in Denver.

For the briefest of moments, he thought about blaming the federal government for the mess they were in. But he couldn't. Not when the same government had quickly responded and taken care of everyone in town. A town he doubted that few in the state government even knew existed. Certainly not the federal government or their respective agencies. Except FEMA. His mind still couldn't wrap itself around that fact, not after a lifetime of assuming that every federal agency was corrupt and inept, just like he'd read about in countless newspaper articles.

If it weren't for the Silver King Mine and annual rush of tourists seeking refuge from the blazing heat down south, Clearwater would have dried up and blown away long ago—and taken his political career with it.

He owed everything he was to this quaint little town where "nothing ever happens." Except it did happen this week, when the residents found themselves at the mercy of some kind of coordinated attack, if he chose to support Bunker's compelling theories.

The bustle of activity inside Charmer's Market and Feed Store had been slow but steady, though the shelves were emptying quickly. Grace Charmer was going to need a restock soon; otherwise, the elderly widow would be hanging an Out of Business sign in the window.

Despite the desperate need for inventory, it clearly wasn't happening anytime soon, not without communications and transportation. Clearwater needed help.

Buckley went inside the medical truck to address that very need, climbing the metal steps with purpose and determination. He needed to find FEMA's Field Commander, John Howard.

The three medics who'd manned the injection station had their backs turned to the entrance door. Their hands were busy putting items away, stuffing them into locking compartments along the sides of the truck.

A biohazard container the size of a 30-gallon trashcan sat nearby. Buckley knew from watching the men work that it contained hundreds of cotton swabs and other medical waste from the day's activity.

Buckley cleared his throat. "Excuse me, gentlemen."

One of the techs turned his head and looked at Buckley. The others seemed to be ignoring him, almost as if they were in a hurry to get home and nothing else mattered.

"I'm looking for your boss. Have you seen Commander Howard?"

The tech pointed to the left, then spoke in a crisp tone, his Australian accent rushed. "He's in communications. Two trucks down."

"Thanks, I appreciate it. And thanks for all the hard work today. You guys did a bang-up job, especially with the kids. I know some of them were terrified. You guys obviously know what you're doing."

The tech nodded, but didn't respond, his eyes looking content and proud. Buckley understood the lack of response, the man wanting to remain professional and detached.

Buckley took the steps down to street level, then turned and traced a straight line to the second truck, just as the medical tech had instructed.

The communications dish mounted on the back of the trailer was moving when he arrived, turning south a few degrees in measured increments. Someone was inside, that much was clear. But who?

The side access door to the truck was closed.

Buckley knocked. "This is Mayor Buckley. I'm looking for Commander Howard. If he's in there, I need to speak with him. It's urgent."

The door opened a few seconds later. Commander Howard's eyes met Buckley's. "Can you wait a bit, mate? I'm just finishing up my communiqué. I'll be with ya in a flash."

"Sure," Buckley said, getting his response out only a split second before the door slammed shut in his face. The rush of wind smacked him in the face. So did the rudeness.

Buckley blinked, taking a moment to calm his temper. Sure, he didn't have an appointment, but the man had told him earlier to ask for help anytime he needed it. It was back in his office, when they were meeting privately with Bill King in attendance. The same resident who was now headed his way.

King looked calm, but something inside Buckley told him that was about to change. After all, this was Bill King. Nothing about the man was ever easy. Why should this moment be any different?

"There you are, Mayor," King said after he stepped close.

"Yes, here I am. Like I've been ever since FEMA arrived."

"That's what I wanted to talk to you about. FEMA."

"I figured as much. It's all anyone wants to talk about. Not that I blame them."

King pointed at the techs across the square—three of them on the left. Then he aimed his finger at nine on the right. "Notice anything?"

"Yeah, they're busy. Like everyone else."

"Look again," King said, hesitating before he spoke again. "Putting stuff away."

"Yeah, the day's injection work is finished. Seems reasonable to expect a cleanup."

"But why? They're supposed to be here for the next twenty-nine days. Why not leave everything set up? It's not like someone around here is going to steal anything."

Buckley nodded, thinking it through. The man was right. He didn't want to admit it, but the FEMA crews did appear to be closing up shop. And now that he thought about it, so were the three med techs in the injection station, their hands working quickly to stow items away. "Okay, I see your point. What do you want me to do about it?"

"Find out why."

"As a matter of fact, I was just waiting for Commander Howard," Buckley said, sending a quick head nod in the direction of the communications truck. "He's inside making a call. Just waiting for him to finish."

"I don't think we should wait. If these men leave, we all die."

"I see your point."

King pounded an angry fist on the door of the truck. He waited for a two-count, then pounded again with heavy thuds. "Open up. We need Commander Howard out here on the double."

Howard finally opened the door and stepped out, closing the door behind him. His face was usually the bastion of calm, but right now he looked pissed. King's pounding on the door was surely the cause of the sudden change in mood.

"I said I would be out when I was finished," Howard said, sliding past King and taking position a foot in front of the Mayor. He pointed at King, his eyebrows pinched. "Why is he here?"

"He has a question to ask you. And frankly, so do I. We need some answers."

"Fine, make it quick."

"See, that's just it," King snapped, moving around and taking a position next to Buckley. "We're wondering why it appears that you guys are leaving. And in a hurry."

"Our work is done."

"For the day, or forever?" Buckley asked, needing clarification before he took the conversation to the next level.

"I thought I explained it all before. In your office. This is a thirty-day process. Was I not clear?"

"Yeah, you were. But why pack up now?"

"Look, Clearwater isn't the only town in danger."

King shook his head. "Nice try, Howard. But you've still got those turbo-charged Mavericks out in the field. There's no chance you're leaving those expensive toys behind."

"We're not. They will be joining us at our next stop. Everyone has their orders, including me."

"Will you be back tomorrow?" Buckley asked. "Same bat time. Same bat channel."

"I'm sorry, what?" Howard asked with a look of confusion.

Before Buckley could explain his superhero reference, a rumble hit town. It was coming from behind him, somewhere down the street near the entrance to the town square.

The Mayor spun his head.

So did King. "What the fuck?"

"Wal-Mart?" Buckley quipped, counting five semi-trucks rolling into view. Each one had the mega store's logo stenciled on the side in trademark blue.

"I'm guessing one of the items you wished to speak to me about was a resupply of the local supermarket. Charmers, I think you call it. Well, gentlemen, may I present to you the mother of all resupply convoys—Wal-Mart."

"Here? In Clearwater? Just like that?" King asked, shaking his head the entire time.

"Wow," Buckley said, his tongue unable to find any other words to say. Once again, FEMA had surprised him, calling in supply trucks right on cue.

King didn't look as impressed. "So let me get this straight. Not only do you guys show up within hours of a disaster to save all of our lives, now you just happen to have more big rigs around that work after the EMP? And they belong to Wal-Mart? Filled with stuff we need? Seriously?"

"Gentlemen, it's been a pleasure today. Please see to it that these supplies get where they need to be," Howard said, turning for the open communications door. One of the techs inside was standing in the doorway. "Let's roll out," Howard told him. "Stage two is a go."

Buckley watched the FEMA drivers start their engines and pull away. The Wal-Mart trucks waited until the FEMA trucks left the town square before pulling into position around the grassy area.

King put a hand on Buckley's shoulder. "Normally, I hate all things Wal-Mart related. All they do is run the little guy out of business. But today—"

"I know, Bill. You don't have to say it. Lifesavers come in many forms. Ours just happens to be FEMA and Wal-Mart. I'm sure Grace Charmer is dancing a jig right about now. All that free inventory headed her way."

King didn't appear to be listening. "I wonder which town FEMA is going to next?"

Buckley didn't really care. "More importantly, I think we should be asking ourselves will FEMA be coming back?"

"You know, now that I think about it, Howard never did answer that question, did he?"

"Nope. It was almost like he was stalling until Wal-Mart showed up. I wonder if that's who he was talking to inside the communications truck."

"Probably. None of this is happening by accident," King said, shaking his head slowly.

"I'm starting to get the sense that we are all pawns in some master plan, whether intended or not."

"Yeah, I hear ya. It's like we're on a roller coaster, heading toward the end of the ride with zero control over anything."

"I hate roller coasters," Buckley said, tugging on the cuffs of his suit coat before adjusting his tie.

King nodded. "Me too. They always make me puke. Sort of like Wal-Mart."

"Except not today," Buckley added. "Let's go help these drivers get where they need to be."

CHAPTER 75

Bunker climbed over a dead, mangled tree lying on its side, then dragged his weary feet between two moss-covered rocks along the bank of the river. He'd been hiking for what seemed like hours, but the sun's position hadn't traveled far enough in the cloudless sky to support that assessment.

Either way, he figured he had to be getting close to the original spot where he'd been knocked off the cliff. He had to be; otherwise, he was just wasting time, looking for a horse that was probably long gone.

He took another step, then spotted a thicket of waist-high bushes along the shoreline ahead. Green bushes with red berries—lots of them, glistening in the sun for all to see.

Was this the location?

He craned his neck to look up, checking the ridgeline above. It was certainly high enough, but the mountains were full of scenes like this. No way to be sure. Not from here.

Bunker picked up the pace, taking longer strides through the uneven terrain. A glint of sunshine slammed into his eyes from something shiny. It was nestled in a twist of deadfall ahead. Deadfall that had collected in a heap along the shore, acting as some sort of marker leading to the next bend in the river.

He changed course, heading for the object while keeping the reflection locked in his vision. Last time he'd seen something like this, it was only a plastic water bottle—refuse discarded by some punk who only drank the premium stuff.

The bundle of branches stopped him cold when he arrived, its tangle of thorns heavy and imposing. The reflecting object was deep inside but visible, the sunlight bouncing off its flat surface. It was made of metal all right, and lying sideways, but he could only see about an inch of its length peeking out from beneath the collection of wood and leaves scattered on top of it.

Bunker slid his hand inside, figuring he'd need to bury his arm up to the bicep in order to reach it. The thorns tore at him, ripping the top layers of his skin as he penetrated deeper and deeper into their lair.

The farther he went, the more they attacked, sending stabs of pain racing up his forearm and into his shoulder. Despite the backlash, he wasn't about to stop, not until he recovered the object.

When the tips of his fingers made contact with the steel, a cold dampness came with it. He brushed away the leaves and other decaying matter, exposing the compact shape facing him. It looked half-buried but intact, the clip visible on top. He moved his hand a few inches over, digging his fingernails under one end.

Right then, his mind turned to thoughts of his trusted k-bar knife, its handle inscribed with the letters J and T. Those were initials from his former life. His life before the fabricated legend of Jack Bunker came into existence. J. T. stood for Jack Terrier. His birth name. AKA Bulldog if you happened to wear the colors of The Kindred and ride a Harley.

"Bingo," he said, grabbing hold of the Benchmade folder knife and pulling it free, focusing less on the safety of his arm and more on the value of the edged weapon.

Blood dripped from his arm as he released the blade with a satin finish. He opened it and tested the Reverse Tanto style edge with his fingernail. It was still razor sharp and ready to go to work.

He closed the knife and tucked it into his pocket, feeling as though his life was starting to merge itself back together with some sort of equilibrium. Eventually, the universe rights all the wrongs, he figured. The question was, which side of that correction would he end up on?

Time to get moving, he decided. This was the spot where he'd landed after the mortar shell nearly tore him apart. The towering boulders he could see across the river loosely resembled fingers sticking up, but from this low angle they looked different than they would from high up.

Regardless, the hill before him wasn't going to bend over and give him a lift up. He needed to climb. It wouldn't be easy, not with sore arms and an exhausted body.

It took twenty minutes or so to traverse the ridge, dragging his legs over the top edge and onto the semi-flat plateau of rock and dirt. He stood up and admired the view, seeing the familiar rock formations standing proudly in the water below.

This was definitely what he remembered—fingers pointing at the sky, aiming their intent at the Almighty. This was the exact spot where he'd been launched into a new possible future, courtesy of the Russians.

He spun his head to the right and let his eyes find the crater from the last impact. Dead ahead and up a noticeable incline was the detonation point. Trees were missing and several tons of dirt had been relocated as well. He still couldn't believe it—no shrapnel from the near-miss explosion.

"Sometimes you get lucky," he mumbled, thinking about how close he came to being torn apart. But of course, luck was a matter of perspective. It all depended on your expectations out of life and what you figured was due to come your way.

If someone had asked him a week ago, he would've said he welcomed a brutal, painful death, figuring he deserved it for all the hurt he'd caused. That's what he had coming. No doubt about it, hitting a new low point in his life.

He remembered the moment well, the despair so profound that he figured he'd never feel normal again.

But of course, normalcy was an illusion. It was something only happy people felt. For all others, misery dragged them along, leading them to make one bad decision after another even though they were fully aware of the dark, unforgivable path before them.

A guilty conscience was a powerful thing, secretly driving people to destroy themselves. He wasn't sure if that propensity toward self-destruction was simply human nature, or something specific to him. Regardless, that was the old Jack Bunker.

The new version had found a renewed purpose in life and he wanted to hang on to it. Clearwater may have just been a sleepy mountain community that few on the planet knew existed, a town barely on the map and filled with regular people who had no idea who he was or what he'd done.

But to him, Clearwater was more than that. It was a salvation of sorts. His salvation. At least, that's what it felt like inside. He didn't have the words to accurately describe it, but it was there and it was real, something he'd never experienced before.

He took a few seconds to search his memories, but couldn't pinpoint when the change took place. But it had.

Maybe it was when the kids on the bus wrapped their arms around his legs to thank him.

Maybe it was Stephanie and her judgmental ways getting under his skin.

Maybe it was Jeffrey and his bright blues. And his endless questions.

Daisy was part of the equation, too, covering his six during battle, then pulling a gun on him in a moment of weakness.

The Mayor and Sheriff had earned some credit as well, always trying to do right by the people they served.

Then there was Tango—a powerful, graceful force with a simple goal in life—just live another day. Maybe that's when it started? A gentle rub of his hand while looking into the serenity that filled Tango's eyes.

Then again, maybe all it took was the simple act of setting foot inside the town limits of Clearwater. At the time, Bunker was more than desperate to find a new place to call home. Someplace where he could start over and find meaning to his life.

Guilt used to be the driving force in his life, speeding him toward annihilation. But now it was Clearwater pulling him toward something else. It felt like a powerful magnet, latching onto his hardened soul and drawing him in.

One word kept popping up in his thoughts—survival. That was his motive now. Not penitence or retribution. Maybe it was time to stop hating himself.

Before he could turn around, he heard the ratcheting sound of a rifle bolt being pulled back and rammed forward to close the chamber. Then the snap of twigs. Someone was armed and standing behind him.

"Hold it right there, mister!" an agitated male voice said. The high tone and pubescent inflection of the words indicated a young person, teenager maybe. "Put your hands up where I can see them."

Bunker froze for a moment, needing to formulate a plan.

"I said, hands up," the voice said again, this time with more urgency in the words.

Bunker did as he was told, raising his arms slowly.

"Now turn around, but no sudden moves. I'll shoot if I have to."

Bunker spun slowly, bringing the gunman's face into view. It was a young male, as he suspected. But this boy couldn't have been more than thirteen, his round, puffy cheeks peppered with acne. His eyes were wild with fright and his finger was resting on the trigger of a hunting rifle. The bore of the barrel suggested a 30-06 or something close in caliber. Enough to kill just about anything in the area. Including him.

"Easy there now, son. Let's not get trigger happy," Bunker said, keeping his tone soft and even.

"I'm not your son, old man," the kid said with a snarl, raising the rifle higher against his shoulder before sliding his eye behind the rear of the scope. The weight of the rifle was giving the kid fits, his arms straining to keep it locked into position.

"Look, I'm sorry. I meant no disrespect. Just take it easy. Please."

"Who are you?"

"My name is Jack Bunker."

"What are you doing here?"

Jack figured this kid's family owned the land beneath his feet. He needed to make sure the boy knew his trespassing was a mistake and part of a rescue mission. "I'm looking for my friend's horse. His name is Tango. Have you seen him?"

"No. I haven't. So are you with them?"

"Who?"

"The Russians."

"No. I'm American, like you."

"I don't believe you."

"Listen to my voice. Do I sound Russian?"

"No, but that doesn't matter. My dad told me they have camps set up where everybody learns English until they speak it perfectly."

"I don't know what to tell you, but I'm American, one hundred percent, through and through. Go ahead and ask me anything. About sports or whatever. Let me prove it to you."

"Okay, so tell me this . . . where's your friend? How did he lose his horse?"

Not the question Bunker expected, but it gave him an opportunity to prove he wasn't with the Russians. "Well, he didn't. I did, actually. It was after the Russians tried to kill me a little while ago on this ridge. I barely escaped when they bombed the hillside."

"So you're the one?"

"One what?"

"The one they were looking for."

"Shit," Bunker said, realizing this ordeal with the insurgents was far from over.

The kid nodded, his eyes filled with dismay. "Yeah, shit. Because of you."

"I'm sorry, I don't understand."

"They came to our farm house a little ways downriver. I was in the barn when they showed up and started shooting. They killed my dad and took my sisters and my mom when they left. I wanted to help, but I didn't know how so I just stayed in the barn and watched. They kept asking about who was on the ridge. When my mom couldn't answer, they started hitting and kicking her."

Bunker's heart skipped a few beats knowing that he'd brought more pain and suffering to people he didn't know. Fallout from his continued presence in Colorado was spreading.

The young man continued, reaffirming what Bunker already suspected. "They thought my family was hiding you on our property somewhere. When they started searching, I hid in the secret underground armory my dad built. I was so scared I couldn't move."

"I take it they didn't find you."

"No. I got out when I heard their engines leave, but there was smoke everywhere from our house being on fire. So I grabbed my dad's hunting rifle and I ran."

"I'm so sorry," Bunker said, realizing that every decision he had made or would make was critical, even when he chose to do nothing. Act or react, it didn't seem to matter. The universe was gunning for him and leaving a wake of collateral damage in its path.

"You're the reason my family is gone," the red-faced youngster snapped with his jaw clenched, his finger moving in and out of the trigger guard. It was clear the boy was considering whether or not to pull the trigger, trapped somewhere between fear and anger.

Bunker needed to diffuse the situation, if he had the time. And the words. "I'm sorry about your family, I truly am. But you have to believe me. The Russians were trying to kill me first. I did nothing to them other than watch what they were doing."

"Then why'd they come to our house? Why did they kill my dad?" When the tears came, the boy's hands began to shake and so did his knees. Slowly at first, but the intensity ramped up quickly.

Bunker let out a long exhale. He couldn't deny it any longer. The kid deserved the truth. "You're right. This is all my fault for getting spotted up on that ridge. I had no idea the Russians would do what they did. If I could, I'd go back in time and stop all of this from happening by giving myself up. But I can't and for that, I'm truly sorry. All I can do now is help you get your family back, if you'll let me. But first you need to put down the gun. Nobody has to get hurt here today. We are on the same side," Bunker said, sharpening his words and his stare. He needed to reach this kid before the adolescent's raw emotions turned this standoff into a killing. "The Russians are the enemy. Not me."

Bunker waited a few seconds before he continued, waiting for a sign that the kid's paranoia had softened. "I have friends out here, too. Probably captured, like your sisters and mom. If we work together, I think we can get everyone back. But that can't happen unless you put the gun down and trust me."

The kid hesitated, the tears worse than before. "You can get my sisters back? And my mom?"

"Yes, I think so."

"How?"

"I used to be in the military and I know a few tricks. The government spent a ton of money training men like me so we could stand up against enemies like this and protect the innocent. Innocent people like your mom and sisters. There are tactics that can be used against a hostile enemy. It won't be easy, but I give you my word that I won't stop until I do. What happened to your family was an accident, but it was my fault, so let me make it right. Please," Bunker said, pausing to let the words sink in. He needed to personalize the situation and cut through all the turmoil boiling in the kid's heart. "What's your name?"

"Dallas."

"Okay, Dallas. Like I mentioned before, my name is Jack. We are on the same side. I can help you, but I can't do that if you shoot me. If you want to get your family back, then you have exactly one chance here. Put the gun down and let's work together. We can do this, son, but only if we work as a team."

"I said I wasn't your son. Quit calling me that!" the kid snapped, the fury returning to his face.

Before Bunker could respond, a rustle of noise came storming in from the left, blurring a path to Dallas' position. It was Tango at full speed, snorting and bucking his head with each stride.

"Tango! No!" Bunker shouted, just as Dallas dove sideways and landed on his stomach. Four angry hooves landed in the dirt next to Dallas' head and neck, barely missing him as the horse galloped past in trample mode.

When Tango's feet slowed and turned sharply to the left, Bunker realized he was circling around for another attack.

Bunker ran to Dallas and grabbed the rifle from his hands, then tossed it several yards away. He stepped in front of Tango, holding up his hands and standing firm.

Tango's feet came to a full stop, knocking a spray of dirt loose in the process. The horse reared up on his hind legs, then flailed his hooves with wild swings and kicks, occasionally ramming them together in a powerful clack.

"Easy now, boy. Easy," Bunker said between the horse's blustering neighs and nickers. The kicks continued for another twenty seconds before Bunker's soothing phrases started to calm the mighty protector.

When Tango finally stopped his tirade, he stood motionless, with his tail flapping from one side to the other. Bunker moved forward, taking slow, even steps with eyes transfixed and hands steady.

Tango held his temper long enough for Bunker to make contact, then rub his hand across Tango's neck from high to low. "Easy does it, buddy. Everything is okay."

Tango nodded once, then snorted a quick huff, as if Bunker's words and his touch were exactly what he needed.

"Good boy," Bunker said, continuing his rub of Tango's chest and sides—not a mark on him from the Russian mortar attack. He could feel the heat in the animal's fur, his heart thumping away. The horse rolled his head into Bunker, nudging gently. "Everything is okay, Tango. You did good, but now it's time to rest. We're all friends here."

Bunker swung his head around to check on Dallas. The kid was still on the ground, only now he was tucked in a ball, covering his head with his hands.

"It's okay, Dallas. You can get up now. Tango won't hurt you."

Dallas uncurled from the fetal position and brought his terrified eyes to bear.

Bunker could sense what the teenager was thinking and feeling, knowing the look of pure panic all too well. "It's over now. You're safe. My friend's horse was just defending me. That's all. Like I said, we're all on the same team here. You. Me. Tango."

Dallas stood up in measured increments, moving slowly and never taking his eyes from Tango. He wiped the tears from his cheeks, then stood motionless, looking as though he was trying to decide whether to stay or take off running.

Bunker waved at him with one hand, patting Tango's neck with the other. "If you rub his neck, he'll know you're a friend. Tango's not dangerous unless you're trying to hurt someone he cares about. Since we're all friends now, he's not going to hurt you."

Dallas shook his head in silence, taking a step back.

"Trust me. Tango won't hurt you, but you need to come show him that you're a friend. Just rub his neck a few times and he'll understand."

Dallas took two steps forward, then stopped.

Tango never flinched.

Dallas continued forward until he was able to put his hand out and make contact with Tango. Bunker grabbed the kid's hand and helped him get started with the petting process.

Tango responded, letting out a slow, non-threatening breath, his eyes blinking and tail swatting a few determined flies.

The tense look on Dallas' face vanished in an instant, his hand working the rub even faster now.

Bunker waited a bit before he turned the conversation to a more pressing topic. "As much as I'd like to hang out here and just chill, I need to know more about what happened when your family was attacked. Did you see which way they went?"

"Yeah. They took the service road that eventually leads back to town."

"Clearwater?"

Dallas nodded as a few tears returned. "Dad has an office there. He builds underground shelters, or at least he used to."

Bunker put a hand on the brave young man's shoulder. "I know it hurts, but you need to stay strong. For your mom and for your sisters. Do you think you can show me exactly which way they went? I want to follow their trail and see if I can't find a way to rescue your family."

"You're really going to do that?"

"Yes, of course. I gave you my word."

"I thought you were just saying that because I had a gun."

"If a man is any kind of man at all, his word is his bond. That's what my dad taught me. I'll bet your father taught you the same thing."

"Well, sort of. He was more about making sure you show up on time and get the job done. Otherwise, you don't get paid."

A bit shallow and greedy, Bunker thought, but close enough. "That's really the same thing, Dallas. It's a promise that you keep to someone who's depending on you."

Dallas nodded, the tears consuming his face.

Bunker stepped aside. "I think you should ride first. I'll walk. Tango needs to get used to you."

"We can't."

Bunker tilted his head, trying to find meaning in the cryptic phrase. "Can't what?"

"Follow them."

"I thought you said you knew which way they went."

"I do. But I had to stop. They are setting up roadblocks everywhere."

"Like a perimeter. Around town?"

"Uh huh, every bridge into town that I tried was blocked."

"How many men did you see?"

"Uh . . . all of them, I think. They're everywhere. Tanks and missiles, too."

Bunker paused, needing a moment to think it all through. The EMP. The plane crash. The grid failure. Technology useless. Grinder in the miner's camp with the English-speaking Pokémon men, most of them dressed in tactical black. The BTR-80 and support vehicles arriving later, the Russian mortars across the hillside, and the drone being recalled from its overhead position.

And now to top it all off, a perimeter was being constructed around a small mountain community that was little in the way of a threat to anyone, except themselves.

It didn't make sense, especially the targeted execution of Tuttle at his trailer. The tightness in Bunker's gut was screaming at him that something was missing. Something critical. A second later, the answer came to him: the US military and the National Guard.

Even with a coordinated computer attack and EMP strike, some of the US armed force's equipment and vehicles should have survived. He knew for a fact that certain transports, communications gear, and mobile weapon arrays had been designed to be EMP-proof. They had to be, given the always-present nuclear threat.

Plus, somewhere along the way, someone had to notice a Russian battalion marching across the border. Unless, of course, they were already in country and just waiting to deploy.

Before his next breath, a flashback to an old news report he'd seen roared in his mind: *Jade Helm 15*. The largest military training exercise ever conducted on US soil.

At the time, he remembered endless conspiracy theories erupting across the Internet, everyone focused on the reason for the volume of troops and equipment being deployed across seven Southern states. Martial law was the favorite answer offered up by the bloggers and loonies, but what if it was something else entirely?

If Bunker was right, it meant the central question about Jade Helm 15 had just changed from *why* to *who*. As in whose assets were being moved? The US' or someone else's?

Regardless of the answer, someone must have put up some form of resistance by now, but it didn't appear to be so. Not from what he'd learned thus far.

He didn't understand any of it. It was almost as if the insurgents were given a free pass to take over.

Bunker looked at Dallas, waiting for the kid to bring his eyes around before he spoke again. "You mentioned something about your dad building an underground armory. I'm assuming he stocked it with guns and ammo."

"Yep. Lots."

"Did it survive the fire?" Bunker asked, figuring they needed to bury the kid's old man while they were there. Then he planned to grab some gear before stashing the young boy somewhere safe.

"I think so. But I didn't stick around very long."

"Can you take me to it?"

"Okay," Dallas said in a tentative voice, looking like he was dreading it. Bunker couldn't blame him; his emotional wounds were fresh and gaping.

He felt sorry for the kid. And responsible. In truth, Bunker caused this to happen when he decided to take position on that ridge and spy on the miner's camp filled with Russians. This young person's life was now in his hands.

A smarter man would have known this result was coming since every decision has a consequence, some known and others not. This was both, wrapped up into a single teenager's life. A life without his father and quite possibly without his sisters and mother.

Bunker's first instinct was to protect Dallas from what would come next. But deep down, he knew that was the wrong move. Especially in a society without power and an apparent invasion in progress. More death was headed their way. Endless amounts of it.

If he could help Dallas learn to face the finality and suddenness of death, Dallas would be stronger for it. It was what Bunker's father would have done.

"Death comes in waves," his father used to preach before each of his wilderness exercises. "Both physically and emotionally. Nobody is immune."

Those words were never truer than this exact moment in time, as he looked at Dallas' shock-covered face. Bunker hated to put the kid through it, but it had to be done.

At least Dallas wouldn't be alone. Even the shoulder of a complete stranger to lean on was better than none at all.

CHAPTER 76

"Where do you want this?" Mayor Buckley asked Grace Charmer, resting the shipping carton of powdered milk on his hip. This was the heaviest load thus far of the eleven he'd made since the Wal-Mart trucks arrived.

She pointed at the floor next to an empty stand that used to contain a display of green apples. "Just put it there. I want to rearrange some things before I stack it up."

"You got it," Buckley said, depositing the box precisely where the store owner had indicated. He wiped the sweat from his brow and stood more erect, his back howling after the latest haul across the town square.

If he had a handful of ibuprofen, he'd slam them down in a heartbeat, not stopping to count them first. Not that he should be surprised—middle age is a culmination of all the decisions we make, physical ones, too.

As we get older, we are the sum of all our parts, even those that are less than functional after decades of pushing a pencil behind a desk. Too many bagels with cream cheese and not enough exercise—a receipt for health problems, none more common than near-constant back pain, flaring to level seven anytime he engaged in something physical.

The day was far from over, but he needed to finish what he'd started. Someone had to help Grace out and so far, only two had. The last pair of Wal-Mart trucks were emptying fast and would pull away soon, so he needed to pick up his pace, despite the lower back twinges.

"I can't thank you and Rico enough," Grace said to Buckley. "I could never do this by myself."

"Least we can do, Grace. We all have to pitch in when we can, including me. We're all going to need each other before this is over."

"I just wish I knew who stole the hand trucks, but I'm afraid I was distracted when the Wal-Mart trucks showed up," she said in an apologetic tone.

"Me too. I should've been paying more attention. I still can't believe how low some people will sink when trouble hits."

"Yes, it breaks my heart but we really shouldn't blame anyone. They're just fending for themselves. We all know the blackout isn't going to end anytime soon. People gotta eat."

"That much is true," Buckley said, watching the buzz of activity outside. It looked like a swarm of ants emptying the remaining Wal-Mart trucks. "But it still doesn't make any of this right. People need to step up and help their neighbors in a time of crisis. All this selfishness makes my skin crawl. I'm sorry, Grace. I expected more from this town."

She smiled, though it looked forced. The widow was obviously tired and frustrated, her gray hair tattered and hanging in disarray. "I put your suit coat in the back on the coat rack my late husband used every morning when he came in to work. It seemed like the right place for such a nice garment. I hope you don't mind."

"Not a problem at all. Thanks for looking out for it," Buckley told her, watching her sagging, thin arms work nonstop. The woman was relentless, working day and night to keep her dead husband's store alive after her staff quit when the original inventory ran out.

Sheriff Apollo's reserve team leader, Rico Anderson, brought in another box from the truck, struggling to carry its weight. The stenciling on the side of the container said it was bar soap. The anti-bacterial kind. "Where should I put this, Mayor?"

"Grace?" Buckley asked, not wanting to assume he knew the answer.

"By the boxes of deodorant. I'm going to start a new row in a minute."

Buckley looked at Rico. "You heard her. By the pit spray. If nothing else, everyone in town will smell good, even though their actions stink."

Rico laughed through the pain, his recovery still ongoing from bruised ribs and a head injury.

Buckley had tried to talk him out of this transport duty, but the man refused to stay in bed. Old Doc Marino's post-concussion orders were clear, but Rico chose to ignore them. He volunteered without hesitation. "It's not too late to go out there and stop them. I'll do it, Mayor. Just give me the word."

"I appreciate that, Rico. But the food belongs to everyone. I don't have the legal standing to stop them. Nor do I want to. They have a right to feed their families, no matter how much it disgusts me to watch. Just wish a few of them had stepped up to help us."

"I get that, sir. But when it all runs out—"

"Then it runs out. They'll have nobody to blame but themselves."

Rico paused for a moment, his nose pinched and eyes tight.

Buckley knew what the loyal thirty-two-year old was thinking. "I know, it sounds cold. But that's the reality of the moment. Unless more trucks arrive, I'm afraid this is just a temporary reprieve from what's headed our way."

"Yeah, no doubt. Things are going to get dicey."

Buckley nodded, the skin across his chest tightening as he brought more words to his lips. "Count on it. People I've known for most of my life will most certainly turn on each other when the food runs out. I guess I shouldn't be surprised. It's human nature to look out for yourself and your own. To hell with everyone else."

"Maybe we need to consider the cattle ranch as a solution. Plenty of meat out there."

Buckley pointed outside, his tone turning even more cynical. "It's a wonder none of them have latched onto that idea. If they had, we've have dead cows everywhere. Can you imagine the carnage?"

"Hey guys, look," Grace said, snapping to attention in an instant. She pointed at more trucks rolling into town. "Looks like our prayers have just been answered."

Buckley watched the new procession arrive. Like before, these were full sized tractor-trailers, at least ten of them, only this time the Wal-Mart stenciling was missing. The trailers were all-white and pristine, like someone had just painted them.

"I wonder what goodies they're bringing us this time?" Rico asked, stepping in close to Buckley.

"I suppose it's too much to ask for some quality booze. A little Jack and water right now might be just what the doctored ordered, if you know what I mean."

"I do, Mayor. Been a long couple of days."

"You got that right. Just hope your boss makes it back to town soon with my grandson."

Before another word was said, the convoy came to an abrupt stop, one of the trucks positioned directly in front of Charmer's Market.

Rico shook his head. "That's strange. Why not park in the same location as the others? There's plenty of room after the empties left."

"Good question," Buckley said, moving to the window to get a better view of the activity. Rico joined him. So did Grace.

A second later, the doors on the back of each trailer opened. Out flew dozens of armed soldiers dressed in full military garb, tactical vests and all. They began yelling orders to each other, but the words weren't in English.

They were in Russian.

CHAPTER 77

Sheriff Apollo pulled Daisy aside, leading her out of the kitchen at Tuttle's place and through the front room where the window blind had been destroyed. He opened the front door and the two of them stepped outside.

"What's up, boss?" she asked, her feet coming to a stop in the weeds.

He looked around to make sure they were alone before he spoke. "I need you to fill me in on some things."

"Sure, anything."

He pointed at the scorch marks in the front yard. "Let's start with those. What the hell happened here? Where's Tuttle?"

"He's dead, sir. When Bunker and I arrived to get the communications gear, someone had executed him."

"Who?"

"We don't know exactly. I killed the man who did, but he didn't have any ID when we searched him."

"And the burn marks?"

"Bunker blew up one of Tuttle's old trucks as a diversion. It drew the assassin to the window so I was able to get a good shot at him. Worked like a charm."

"Clever. Where's the body? I should probably take a look."

"See, that's the thing. When Stephanie and I pulled up with the kids and Franklin, the man's body was gone. I figure the rest of the intruder's team hauled it away."

"There was more than one? Here? At Tuttle's?" Apollo asked, wondering if these men were the same group who attacked Rico and Zeke and stole their shoes while they were on their way back to town from their annual fishing trip.

"Yep. They took me and Bunker hostage, then started interrogating us at some remote camp they'd taken over. We eventually got loose. That's when Bunker and I took out whoever was left after Franklin got the party started."

"Seriously? Franklin? He was there, too?"

"Ten-four. That's how he got shot. Apparently, these same men took Steph and the kids from his property, so Franklin went after them. He took out most of the men before he took a bullet.

That's when Bunker finished off the rest of them. Though I did have to kill one trying to make a run for it at the end."

"Where's Bunker now?"

"He stayed behind to dispose of the bodies and then go find Franklin's horse. We needed to get Franklin back to town before he bled to death. That's when we ran into trouble and decided to head here instead. It was the only place I could think of where the kids might be safe. They needed food, water, and a place to sleep."

"Good choice, as long as you weren't followed."

"We weren't. Since we'd eliminated everyone involved in what happened here and at the camp, I figured it was safe to return. I had to clean up the blood and get Tuttle buried before the kids could come inside, but I think it worked out okay. Martha Rainey has been a huge help. So has Allison."

"So I'm guessing Bunker doesn't know you're here."

"No sir, he doesn't. He thinks we went back to town. That was the plan, anyway. I just hope he didn't run into any more trouble."

"If he did, I'm sure he can handle himself."

"Yeah, he can. Though, on second thought, he might have decided to just take off while he had the chance. You know, resume his life. As much as we need him around here, he's probably done more than enough for our little town."

Apollo agreed, but wanted to change the subject to something else. Bunker was the least of his worries. "What about those trucks parked out back?"

"We stole them from the miner's camp. That's how I got everyone here so quickly."

"Good thinking."

She shrugged. "I mean, it's not like those men were going to be using them anymore, right? I figured we could use some working vehicles after the EMP strike."

"What about that little skirmish with Stephanie?"

"Yeah, that never should've happened. I thought she just wanted to talk, but then she attacked me, so I had to defend myself."

"Do you want to press charges?"

Daisy shook her head without hesitation. "That won't be necessary."

"Are you sure? Assaulting a peace officer is a serious felony."

"Well, I really wasn't a deputy at that point. I was just me. I figure I had it coming, anyway, after what I did with her ex. Can't blame her. I would've done the same thing."

"Okay then, if you want to give her a pass, then that's what we'll do."

"I appreciate it, boss."

"Truth is, I'm shocked it took this long to come to a head."

"You knew about the affair?" Daisy asked with eyes wide.

"Of course. Everyone knew. It's a small town. Can't expect any secret to remain that way for long."

"No, I suppose not. It's so embarrassing."

"I'm sure it is. Those types of slip-ups get around town quickly. You know how rumors are. They take on a life of their own. Especially in Clearwater."

Daisy's eyes turned soft, tears welling inside. "I never meant to hurt her. But I did. God, how could I have been so stupid?"

Apollo wasn't sure if she was fishing for sympathy or not, so he kept his mouth shut.

"I swear, I only let my guard down for a second and next thing I know, I'm in bed with her husband."

"But that's all in the past now, right?"

"Yes sir. All in the past. I can't even stand to look at his face."

"That's good to hear. For everyone's sake," Apollo said. "What about the fight?"

"I think Stephanie and I just needed to let it all out. A once and for all type thing. In a strange way, I think it helped. Like we both needed it or something. It's hard to explain."

"No explanation needed. I'm just glad it happened inside the barn so the kids didn't have to see it."

"Speaking of the barn, there's some stuff I need to show you. I found a few things you should see."

"Lead the way," Apollo said, holding out an extended arm. He followed her around the corner of the house and over to the massive barn Tuttle had built.

"Damn, this thing is huge," Apollo said as they angled a path to the front. Tuttle's reputation as a cheapskate was well-earned, but he'd spent some serious money on this structure.

"Wait till you see what's inside. It's mind-blowing."

The double doors along the front were already partially open, allowing Daisy to turn her frame sideways and easily step through. The lights were off, but Daisy had already told him about Tuttle's backup power. He figured her first task would be to find a light switch, hopefully by the time he wedged his wide hips past the entrance.

Daisy turned to the right and disappeared into the blackness as expected. He continued behind her and entered the building. When the lights snapped on as expected, he heard a shotgun being pumped behind him, then felt something hard press against the back of his head.

"Hold it right dere, Sheriff," a man's firm voice said, the words laced with twangs and broken syllables.

Apollo raised his hands and turned his head to the right, seeing another man with a rifle to Daisy's head. In total, there were three intruders, all wearing black masks and country attire: flannel shirts, jeans, leather work gloves, and weathered boots.

Only one of them had a pistol; the others held long guns. Apollo guessed the all-black six-shooter was a forty-five caliber based on its massive barrel.

"Looks like you was right, cousin," the man with the pistol said.

Shotgun man tapped the muzzle against Apollo's skull, like he was trying to loosen a bolt inside. "I told ya. Dey be coming in here next. Dey always do. Gotta take what don't belong to dem."

"Don't forget. I want dey shoes. Need 'em for my collection. Specially da Sheriff's. I like them shiny ones."

"I won't forget. Let's get dem out front and round up da others. Now dat we have da law under control, da rest is easy."

The comment about taking shoes rang true in Apollo's mind, connecting with something that Rico and Zeke had told him when they stumbled into town. The men who had attacked them stole their valuables, including their shoes. These must be the same men who ambushed Rico's group, then tossed them down the bank of a gully.

"Let's go. Outside. Both of ya," shotgun man said, shoving Apollo forward. The man holding Daisy hostage did the same thing.

Apollo kept his hands up, moving slowly while he ran it through his head. If these were the same men who attacked his reserve unit, then they were just here to steal, not to kill or anything else. They'd let Rico and Zeke live, so Apollo decided to play along and make sure this ended peacefully.

Word was obviously spreading across Clearwater County about the treasures at Tuttle's homestead, meaning he'd need to fortify a perimeter before the place was overrun with scavengers and thieves. But first things first. He needed to keep his cool and play along to diffuse the situation.

Shotgun man gave Apollo another shove. "Come on. Keep movin'."

Pistol man spoke next. "We should take da women with us dis time. Dey worth a fortune at the Outpost. Their paying good money for da young ones."

Their comments about kidnapping the women burrowed a hole into his heart. Apollo was obviously wrong about their intentions. This wasn't going to end peacefully. At least not for the women. And probably for the kids, either. He needed to act before the rest of his group was dragged into the middle of this.

He whirled around and tried to knock the shotgun out of the hands of its wielder, then pull his sidearm and shoot, but a powerful jab smacked him in the face in an instant. The force of the punch sent him to the dirt in a heap. He landed on his left side, then rolled before a fleet of stars swarmed his vision.

When he looked up to get his bearings, he saw the bottom of a foot coming at his face. The man's boot heel smacked him in the forehead, turning everything black.

CHAPTER 78

When Sheriff Apollo woke up after getting kicked in the face, he found himself on his knees with his hands secured behind his back. His feet had been laced together as well, plus someone had a firm grip on his shirt collar, keeping him upright.

The raging headache pounding at his skull made it difficult to focus his eyes and his thoughts. He blinked rapidly, trying to clear the blobs and specks, but it wasn't helping. Neither was the intense pressure across his forehead. He could only assume his face was swelling from the impact, making him look like an aging boxer who just got pummeled in the ring.

Then again, a more accurate description might have been that he resembled a modern version of a Neanderthal, complete with heavy brow ridges and minimal intelligence. He was hearing echoes in his mind, his brain processing everything in slow motion.

He tried blinking again to clear the spots, this time keeping his eyes closed for a few seconds. It helped, his vision returning to almost normal. Only a single fizzy spot remained in his right eye.

He turned his head to peer to his left. Dicky was next to him, only inches away. The giant was also on his knees with his hands behind his back. Apollo couldn't see Dicky's feet, but he assumed they were secured as well.

At least Dicky was awake, his eyes staring straight ahead and blinking. However, there was a deep gash across his cheek. He must have put up a fight, possibly taking the butt end of a rifle to his face.

Rusty was on the far side of Dicky. The kid was also on his kneecaps and most likely tied up since Apollo couldn't see his hands. His face didn't appear to be injured, but when the kid leaned forward and looked at Apollo, his eyes went round and showed an unusual amount of white.

Everyone else was huddled about ten yards in front of him, sitting on the ground in a loose circle with their hands behind their backs. Daisy, Stephanie, Allison, Misty, and Megan were to the left, while Jeffrey, Victor, and Martha were separate and to the right. Misty's face was full of tears and so was tiny Megan's.

"What do you guys want?" Apollo asked the shotgun man, who was standing a few yards away with his back turned.

The man spun around and looked at Apollo, his eyes black as coal. The rest of his features were hidden by the dark-colored ski mask covering his head, but that didn't stop Apollo from trying to memorize as many details as he could. The man appeared to be about six feet tall and stocky, his chest and shoulders broad. His hands were white, though they were weathered like an old pair of leather work gloves.

"Let's finish dis," the pistol man said, walking out from behind Apollo and entering his field of vision. The man took position about three feet away with his .45 aimed at Apollo's forehead.

The third man stood in front of Dicky with his bolt-action rifle in a firing position. He was shoulder to shoulder with pistol man, lining up for what Apollo assumed was an execution. Shotgun man arrived last, aiming his pump-action scatter gun at Rusty's face.

"Wait! We can work this out," Apollo snapped. "You don't have to do this."

"Ready," shotgun man said, straightening his posture a bit. "On three."

"Please don't shoot!" Rusty cried out. "I don't want to die."

Dicky was dead silent, apparently ready for the firing squad to begin their evil deed.

The women were crying with their heads down, while Jeffrey had his head buried in Martha's shoulder.

"Please! Stop! We'll give you whatever you want!" Apollo said, hoping to reach one of the men before the countdown started.

"We already have what we want," shotgun man answered.

Apollo closed his eyes when he heard the countdown starting, his lungs pumping out of control. He wanted to say more, but he couldn't find the words, not with his headache escalating right along with his blood pressure.

"3 . . . 2 . . ."

Just before shotgun man's voice reached the count of one, Apollo heard a momentary whizzing sound, then the echo of a gunshot coming from the left. He felt a wetness land on his cheeks and chin, then heard three different thumps hit the ground in succession.

When he opened his eyes, he couldn't believe what he was seeing. All three attackers were lying on the ground with huge chunks of their necks missing. Blood and tissue seemed to be everywhere, hanging in clumps along the sides like red cheese.

"We're still alive?" Rusty asked, his voice unsteady and full of anxiety. "How?"

Apollo looked at Dicky, then at Rusty. Neither appeared to be injured. However, blood splatter had found its way to them as well.

"I don't know exactly," Apollo said, turning his eyes to the women and children. They all looked stunned but unharmed, their tears flowing.

"Someone took a shot," Dicky said, turning his head hard to the left.

"Yeah, an amazing shot. Killed all three," Rusty added. "How is that even possible?"

"That's got to be what, a thousand yards?" Dicky asked, never taking his eyes from the tree line in the distance.

Rusty turned his head to peer at the trees as well.

Apollo did the same, keeping watch for whatever happened next.

Just then a spotted horse appeared in the distance, sliding out from the backdrop of green. There were two riders, one large and one small. The larger person appeared to have a rifle in his hand. Apollo couldn't make out much detail otherwise, not from this distance, his old eyes watering from the strain.

The horse began a full gallop a moment later, heading straight for them. Apollo wanted to stand up and greet the visitors, but his feet were still tied.

When the shooter closed about half the distance, Daisy spoke up with excitement in her voice. "Hey, is that who I think it is?"

"Bunker!" Stephanie said an instant later. "That's gotta be him."

Apollo waited another twenty seconds to be sure, but Stephanie was right. Bunker was atop the horse with the reins in one hand and a rifle in the other. There appeared to be a young boy sitting behind him, hanging on with his arms wrapped around Bunker's waist.

When Bunker arrived, he circled around the back side of the women before coming to a complete stop in front of Apollo. "Everyone okay?"

"Yeah," Daisy said. "Barely."

"Where the hell have you been?" Stephanie asked, her voice full of attitude.

"On my way here with a new friend."

"You took the shot?" Rusty asked.

Bunker nodded, then helped the boy off the horse with his free hand. "Take your knife and cut my friends free. Start with the girls."

"Okay," the kid said, his feet moving quickly.

Bunker looked at Apollo, his face stiff and devoid of emotion. "All I can say is it's a good thing I happened to spot those men in time. If I hadn't realized what they were about to do—"

"You don't need to remind us," Apollo said, his heart still pounding in his chest.

"Nothing like waiting until the last second," Stephanie said, looking pissed.

"Had to get into position. Figured I'd only get one shot. Luckily, they lined themselves up perfectly so I could burn them with one round. Not sure what would have happened if I'd had to reload."

"Or missed," Dicky added.

Apollo couldn't seem to pull his eyes away from the bolt-action rifle Bunker was holding. The tan-colored death machine had grabbed hold of his eyes and wouldn't let go, even with the headache pounding at his skull.

The rifle's collapsible stock, sleek lines, and long barrel were stunning. The scope sitting on top was beyond high-tech, unlike anything he'd ever seen before. "What kind of rifle is that?"

Bunker held it up in front of his chest, looking like a proud papa. "It's a TrackingPoint M1400. Been a while since I had a chance to shoot a .338 Lapua Magnum."

"I've never seen anything like it."

"It's a precision-guided sniper rifle that basically aims itself. Just follow the optics inside the scope and it's dead on. Even a grunt like me can make a shot like that. Every time. Without fail."

"Yeah, no doubt," Rusty said, his eyes locked onto the dead bodies.

"Can even take down moving targets," Bunker said, getting off the horse. He let go of the reins and used his knife to free Rusty's hands and feet with a few swipes of the blade.

Bunker gave the rifle to the Mayor's grandson after the youngster got to his feet. "Here. Hold this for me, but be careful. That's over twenty grand of firepower you're holding in your hands."

Rusty smiled, leaning to support the weight of the weapon.

Bunker freed Dicky next, then Apollo.

"Where the hell did you get it?" Apollo asked, his brain still not functioning at full speed. There were better questions to ask, but that was the first one to land on his tongue.

Bunker pointed at the new boy, who was busy freeing the women. Only Misty and Martha remained. And, of course, Jeffrey and Victor. "From my new friend over there, Dallas. It was his father's. The man had quite a collection, God rest his soul."

"I take it something happened?"

"Yeah, the Russians happened. They're here already."

"We know," Apollo said matter-of-factly.

"They took the kid's mom and sisters. Because of me."

"How's that exactly?"

"They were searching for my sorry butt when they came across his parents' place."

"Why would they care about you?"

"When I was policing the bodies from the miner's camp, they showed up in force. I took cover on the ridge above, but they spotted me and unleashed a firestorm. For whatever reason, they didn't want a witness getting away."

"What did you see?" Dicky asked, breaking his silence.

Bunker shrugged. "Not much. They searched the camp, then recovered a drone that was in flight. That's about the time when they noticed me."

Apollo pointed at the makeshift bandage around Bunker's forearm. "Is that when this happened?"

"Roger that. A shell sent me flying into the river. Got impaled when I hit bottom. Took a while to find my way back after floating downstream, and that's when I ran into Dallas. Couldn't just leave him there all alone."

"I understand. He's your responsibility now."

Bunker nodded, taking a full second before he spoke again. "At least until we can get his mom and sisters back. I hope you don't mind."

"Not a problem. Just add it to the to-do list."

"How did you know we were here?" Daisy asked.

"I didn't. I was bringing Dallas here for safety."

"Yeah, but why here?" Rusty asked.

"This is one of the few places I know in the area. I had to take him somewhere safe and this seemed like the best choice after the Russians burnt the kid's place to the ground," Bunker said, turning his focus to the Sheriff. "I know why I'm here, Sheriff, but what about everyone else?"

"That's a good question."

"We're all here for different reasons," Stephanie said, stepping forward with Jeffrey in tow. She let go of her son's hand and wrapped her arms around Bunker's neck. "But at least we're all together. Well, sort of."

"Hey Steph," Bunker said, bringing his arms up to hug her. Her grip was tight, so he returned the favor.

Jeffrey joined the hug-fest, his tiny arms trying to reach around his mom's legs and Bunker's.

When Stephanie spoke again, her voice was muffled due to her face plant into his neck. "I thought we were never going to see you again. But as usual, you show up just in the nick of time."

"Hey, I try."

"You know, people are gonna start to expect this now and that can't happen unless you're here. Like permanently."

"Well then, I guess I'd better stick around for a while. I'd hate to disappoint everyone."

When those words landed on Apollo's ears, his heart warmed and his headache eased; he was unable to hold back a grin. He let out a long exhale before turning his attention to Daisy, who was still with the other women.

The deputy's eyes were sharp and focused, but not on the people standing with her. They were locked on Bunker and his long embrace with Stephanie. Daisy looked lost. Or maybe she felt forgotten, her eyes telling an emotional story.

Apollo wondered if Daisy was purposely staying away from Bunker, letting Stephanie have a tender moment with him first. Given their history of violent love triangles, it was certainly a possibility.

If he was right, then things were going to get complicated—again.

CHAPTER 79

The heat from Stephanie King's beating chest soaked into Jack Bunker's skin as the reunion hug continued in front of Tuttle's place. He was happy to see her, too, and the rest of the gang who hailed from Clearwater, Colorado. Her son's ten-year-old arms couldn't reach all the way around Stephanie's legs, let alone Bunker's, but it didn't stop Jeffrey from trying.

Everyone else had tears in their eyes, including the Sheriff and his deputy, Daisy—the same woman who'd pulled a gun on Bunker after learning his darkest secret at the miner's camp.

Bunker thought they'd patched things up after the incident, but was still worried she might turn on him now that she knew he used to ride with the infamous Kindred biker gang.

Or at the least, share his background with the town's chief law enforcement officer, Gus Apollo. Keeping one law enforcement officer on your side is hard enough. Trying to manipulate two would be impossible. Something would go wrong. It always does when you're lying about your past.

Until a second ago, Bunker thought the emotions pouring out of those in attendance were a result of the near-fatal execution he'd just stopped with his long-range sniper shot. It was a work of perfection. Part shooter, part weapon, especially when that weapon was a TrackingPoint Precision Guided Rifle.

When you take down three masked men with a single long-range shot, a sense of relief should have been permeating the atmosphere. Yet it wasn't. The air felt stale and heavy. Almost putrid.

Stephanie pulled back from the tender embrace, her eyes filled with tears. Her tone turned somber when she spoke. "We needed you here ten minutes ago."

"Why? What happened?" he asked, his gut tightening after hearing the words.

Stephanie didn't answer. She turned her gaze to the women in attendance. Daisy and a gray-haired woman he'd seen in town were on their knees, consoling Megan and a mysterious brunette he didn't know.

Sheriff Apollo aimed a firm eye at Stephanie, lifting an eyebrow. "Where are Franklin and Cowie? Are they okay?"

Stephanie shook her head. Her eyes indicated she wanted to speak, but something was holding her back. Something painful.

Bunker pushed past Stephanie with his focus on the tiny black girl, Megan, and her innocent face.

Stephanie let go of his hand as Bunker continued, moving closer to the precious soul he'd saved from certain death on the bus. He stood motionless behind the old woman hugging Megan.

Every tear that rolled down Megan's cheek impaled his heart with the savagery of a red-hot dagger. Normally the ten-year-old was a beacon of joy, filling the air with her exuberance. But that wasn't the case at the moment.

Megan was absent, both mentally and spiritually, her eyes locked in an empty stare, focused on something over the shoulder of the woman cradling her in her arms. It was clear the entirety of Megan's being was under siege, suffocating the poor girl.

Apollo asked again, "Where's Franklin? Cowie?"

More seconds ticked by without a response from Stephanie. Everyone else seemed to be avoiding the question, too, not wanting to speak or make eye contact with Apollo.

Bunker knew the situation meant only one thing—bad news. Terribly so. The kind of bad news that squeezes your chest a few seconds before you hear the actual words.

He knew from his days in the military that the all-consuming feeling of dread had a habit of transcending time and space, breaking the laws of physics to arrive early. The earlier it arrived, the worse the news, giving everyone in attendance a sensation of impending doom.

Someone must have died.

It was the only conclusion that made sense. Otherwise, there would've been a response to Apollo's question by now. From someone: the kids, the women, the men.

A group of this size would never remain silent, not after what had just happened with the bloody, last-second deaths of the attackers.

"They're inside," a long-haired boy said in a slow and deliberate tone, breaking the quiet. A tall blonde woman stood behind him, her hands resting on the tops of his shoulders, squeezing at random.

Bunker recognized the young lad from the bus crash. He was the kid who tossed his backpack out of the broken window and took off in a flash, before Bunker could stop him.

The boy pointed at the old woman consoling Megan. "My grandma was there when it happened. Franklin is d—"

"That's enough, Victor. You don't need explain," the woman standing with the boy said. "He knows what happened."

"Both of them?" Apollo asked Dicky, the large man standing next to him. Apollo's expression indicated he wanted to ask a different question, but settled on this one.

Bunker figured the Sheriff had tailored his words to protect the children from having to endure any more drama than was necessary. Especially with all that had happened recently. These kids always seemed to be in the center of everything, taking the brunt of death head-on.

Dicky's head slumped before he finally spoke to Apollo. "Sorry boss. They came out of nowhere."

Bunker knelt next to the old woman and Megan, avoiding the girl's injured leg and its heavy knee brace. His mind searched for the proper words, but all that came back was a cloud of dust.

His tongue was empty, but not his heart, feeling compelled to comfort the child in some way. Yet he wasn't sure how. Former hardcore, white-supremacist bikers with no kids and a bloody stain on their military record usually don't have a deep connection with children they just met. Or adults, for that matter. But Megan Atwater was different, and it wasn't solely due to her rescue from the bus.

The old bag let go of Megan and stood up, as if she did so specifically to give Bunker access. He raised his hands a few inches, then pulled them back, not sure if the emotional girl wanted a hug from him.

Stephanie and her motherly instincts would know exactly what to do for a child in need, but he had no clue. Before he could make a decision, Deputy Daisy appeared next to him, throwing her arms around the other woman sitting next to Megan. A brunette. Distraught. About thirty. Someone he didn't know.

"I'm so sorry, Misty," Daisy said, the two of them starting a symbiotic cry inside an arm-filled hug. She pulled away for a second, then shot Bunker a nod before she spoke again. "Bunker and I tried to save your father, but we got here a second too late."

The woman's familiar name and Daisy's words came together in Bunker's mind. He knew who the girl was: Misty Tuttle. Frank Tuttle's daughter. The woman who threw away her lifelong friendship with Daisy when she ran off with a foreigner shortly after high school.

"Was it these same men?" Misty asked the deputy, pushing the words through her trembling lips.

"No, it was someone else. Earlier."

Misty turned her eyes to the old woman who'd been comforting Megan. "Angus *and* my dad? Both of them?"

The lady shook her head, the skin on her cheeks sagging.

"Please Martha, tell me it's not true. Please."

Martha's face flushed a deep red color. "I can't. I'm so sorry."

Misty's cries shot up a level, her hands shaking against Daisy's shoulder blades. "Oh God! No! Please no!"

"It'll be okay," Daisy said, her voice cracking through her tears. "I'm right here. Just let it out."

"This is all my fault. We never should've come back."

"It's not your fault, Misty. It was these men," Apollo said, standing with Dicky, Dallas, and the Mayor's grandson Rusty, who Bunker had met a few days earlier in town. "They did this and now they got what was coming to them."

"But I never got a chance to tell my dad . . ."

"I'm sure he knows how much you loved him," Daisy said, her tone confident.

"It's just not fair."

"No, it's not. But you'll get through this. I promise. Look around. You have a lot of friends who will be here for you, every step of the way."

Misty cried for another minute before she spoke again. "But you don't understand. We just got engaged. That's part of why we came back. I wanted Dad to know. From me. About the engagement and everything else."

Stephanie broke her silence, her tone soft yet to the point as she addressed the long-haired kid from the bus. "Victor, maybe you and your mom should take Megan to your grandmother's house. Where it's quiet. She needs to lie down and rest for a bit. She's been through a lot today."

"I'm sure we can make room for both of them," Martha said, looking at Daisy, then motioning to Misty. "Everyone should eat something, too."

Daisy nodded.

"Can I help, Mommy?" Jeffrey asked, his nose sniffing as he wrapped his hand around his mother's.

Even though Stephanie's son had just been through yet another traumatic, death-defying incident, the boy didn't seem scared or withdrawn. Bunker wasn't sure if Jeffrey had become immune to the nonstop evil or not, but the boy was showing incredible strength. Far more than he was at the moment.

Kids are much stronger than adults think, he decided. Most adults, that is. Bunker's dad never cut him any slack, about anything. Everyone else in the neighborhood back then seemed to shield their kids from the harder aspects of life. And death. In the long run, he didn't think that approach prepared young people for the harshness of humanity. A harshness that would continue to escalate after the apparent cyber-attack and EMP that had taken down society.

Before Stephanie could answer Jeffrey's lingering question, Megan brought her pear-shaped eyes to Bunker with a crane of her neck. A second later, the girl's emotions came to a boil and let go all at once.

Megan's mouth shot open in a silent, sick-like grimace as her eyes ran thin. Then the waterworks exploded, sending streams of tears down her cheeks, more than double the amount before.

She leaned forward and wrapped her rail-thin arms around Bunker's neck, then bawled into the soft of his shoulder, the volume intensifying by the second.

Bunker held her tight, her chest heaving in concert with the uncontrollable waves of misery flooding out. His chest, arms, and hands could feel the pain escaping from every pore in her body. Her emotions bled into him, racing past his defenses and taking residence deep inside his heart.

When the tears came to Bunker's eyes, he knew he wasn't going to be able to hold them back. Her pain was now his pain, even though he hadn't known her long. All he could do was hold this child and wait for the turmoil to pass. It might take minutes or hours, but he wasn't going to let go of this precious girl.

Sure, if he had a choice, he wished he was somewhere else, but Megan needed him. So did the others, their lives inexplicably commingled with his, well past the point of no return.

CHAPTER 80

Megan slowed her crying and leaned back from the hug she was in. She looked at the towering white man who'd saved her from the bus, Jack Bunker. He was almost as tall as her father, but his muscles were bigger.

Despite his scary tattoos, she could tell he was a nice man, not a mean one like the others who had hurt her and her dad.

When Jack was around, she felt safe. Not just because he'd saved her and her friends more than once. It was more than that.

She wasn't sure what it was called, but when she was in his arms, it felt like home. A home that was now missing her mom and her dad. She couldn't believe it. Both of them were dead. Even her favorite horse, Star, was missing. All she had left was Jack and her dad's favorite horse, Tango.

Megan wanted to go inside Tuttle's trailer to see her father, but she was scared to look at his body. Or his face. The bad men had shot him. There'd be blood everywhere and a big hole from the bullet. It would be too gross. She didn't think she could do it. She wanted to, but she didn't know how.

"Jack?" she asked in a weak voice, her lips shaking.

His tone was gentle and fatherly. "Do you need something, sweetheart?"

The tightness in her chest wouldn't stop growing, making it hard to breathe. It hurt. A lot. Her lips were trembling even more now as the words arrived, air shooting in and out of her mouth in bursts. "I, uh, think I want to go see my papa. But I'm not sure I can do it. Will you come with me? I don't want to go alone."

"Sure, Megan. Anything you need. I'm not going anywhere."

"Ah, no. That's not a good idea," Stephanie King told Jack in a firm voice, her hand still latched onto Jeffrey's. "Little girls shouldn't see those kinds of things."

"No offense, Steph, but I think you might be overreacting a bit," Jack said.

"How do you figure that?"

"Kids are stronger than you think."

"Really, now. And I guess that observation is based on all your years of experience? Being a parent, I mean."

Jack shrugged, his eyes drifting into a long stare. "It's what my father would have done. He believed in facing everything head-on. Especially tragedy. Regardless of age. You can't outrun death."

"Well, then. That explains it," she said with attitude.

"Explains what?"

Stephanie opened her mouth to say something, then closed it as if she'd just had a change of heart. After a couple more seconds went by, she shook her head and said, "Never mind. It's not important."

Jack looked confused, his eyes squinting. "Not important, huh?"

"No, it's not. Let's move on. Okay?"

"Look, my old man might have been more than a little tough on me, but facing things is what makes you stronger. Sure, most people didn't understand him and more than a few hated his guts, but he was always fair. No matter what the situation."

"Sure, whatever," Stephanie said after a long exhale, rolling her eyes. "They're both in the master. Down the hall on the right."

Jack nodded, flaring his eyebrows before he spoke again. "Megan, sweetheart, are you positive you want to go inside? It might be pretty hard to see."

She wanted to be strong for herself, but more so for Jack. He was brave and she wanted to be like him. "Yeah, I think so. As long as you come with me."

"Well, you need to be sure because I don't want you to be scared. We don't know what the bad men did, exactly. Maybe I should go inside first and check it out?"

When Jack let go of her and tried to stand up, Megan grabbed his hand and wouldn't let him leave. He just couldn't leave. *Bad things always happen when Jack leaves*, she thought. *He's got to stay.*

"Please, don't go, Jack. Don't leave me here. Take me with you."

"It'll be hard, darling."

"I know, but papa needs a goodnight kiss, like we did every night before I went to sleep. Otherwise, he'll have bad dreams. Forever."

Jack sucked in a sudden breath, then turned to Stephanie, his voice different than before. He sounded sad, like she'd hurt his feelings. "Sorry, Steph, but I'm doing this. I'm taking her inside."

"That's a mistake."

"Maybe, but she needs to say goodbye to Franklin. You heard her. He needs a goodbye kiss. We can't deny her this one chance, no matter how hard it is."

"I don't think you're hearing me. She'll be traumatized."

"I hear you, trust me. I just went through this with Dallas after what happened to his father. But in the end, we all have to face this—eventually. Even little girls. More so now than ever before with everything that's happening out there. We can't shield them forever."

Stephanie dropped her head and shook it. When she brought her eyes back up, she looked tired and maybe a little upset. "Don't say I didn't warn you."

Jack bent down and slid his arms under Megan before picking her up. Her bad knee was sore, but he was being gentle.

Megan wrapped her arms around his neck, avoiding the scars on each side. They looked like they still hurt, the skin rough and ugly. She wanted to ask about them, but didn't want him to get mad or be embarrassed.

Like her papa always told her, it wasn't really any of her business. "Some people are just different, that's all," he'd say. "Don't stare. It's impolite."

Sheriff Apollo came forward and stepped in front of Jack, his hands adjusting the waistband of his pants. "Do you need some help?"

"Nah, I got this, Sheriff."

"Are you sure?"

"Yeah. A little privacy is probably a good thing."

Sheriff Apollo nodded, his eyes looking away as if he was thinking about something else. "You're probably right."

"Though you might want to get some ice on your forehead. Looking pretty swollen, Sheriff."

Apollo rubbed his hand across the raised area above his eye. "Yeah, they got me good, that's for sure."

"Let me take a look at it," Martha Rainey said without hesitation.

Jack flashed a strange look at Apollo. Megan thought he looked confused. Probably wondering why the old woman would get involved like that.

"She's a trauma nurse," Apollo said, sounding like he was proud of her.

Martha put her hand on the side of the Sheriff's face, not letting him move. "Former trauma nurse, though nowadays they'd call what we did back then a Physician's Assistant, just without all the extra pay. I was born a generation too early, I'm afraid."

Apollo pulled away from her as if her hand was bothering him. "I appreciate the help, but the gash on Dicky's cheek takes priority. Gonna need a lot of stitches."

Martha swung her head and glanced at Dicky, craning her neck in the process. She was going to need a stepladder to reach the big man's face, his head way above everyone else, including Jack's.

Megan's mind filled with a flash of memories, each one showing Martha stopping by the supply store on her father's ranch for a can of saddle soap. The last time she came by, her grandson Victor was with her, but he didn't look happy about it.

Megan didn't think the Raineys had horses, so they wouldn't have saddles, but every month the old lady would buy some, regardless. Always on a Wednesday for some reason. And always the same brand: Kiwi. Martha would step up to the counter with her purchase, while whistling a pretty, soft tune. She'd stop the melody long enough to smile before taking out a bag of homemade taffy and offering a piece to Megan. It was sticky and gooey, but yummy.

Jack tapped the Sheriff on the shoulder. "You guys might also want to think about setting up a perimeter. We need to start focusing on a defensible position with access to town cut off. This is about the only choice to make camp."

"Or make a stand," Apollo agreed with sharpness to his words.

"Exactly. We both know this is going to get a lot worse before it gets better, so it's up to us to provide a safe place for these kids."

"I agree. Tuttle was well prepared," the Sheriff said, stepping aside. "Let us know if you need anything."

"Will do."

"Jack?" Megan asked, after the Sheriff disappeared.

"What's up?" he answered on the way to the front door of Tuttle's house.

Megan wasn't sure if she should ask, but decided to anyway. It was important. "What about Misty? She lost somebody, too. Doesn't she need to come inside with us? You know, to say goodbye."

"I don't think she wants to, honey."

"But she needs to, like you said. We all have to be strong and face stuff like this."

"Deep down she probably does want to say goodbye, but sometimes people just can't bring themselves to do it. That's her choice, Megan, and we have to respect it. Everyone's different when it comes to bad things that happen. Some people are extra brave like you and want to go inside, while others need to stay outside. Not everyone is the same and we have to let her deal with this in her own way. Does that make sense?"

"Yeah, well, sort of. I just hope she's okay. It's not good to be alone when you're sad."

"She's not. Daisy is with her. They're BFFs from a long time ago."

"I wish I had a best friend, but there aren't many kids out where we live."

He grinned. It was a little smile, but she liked it. She thought he should do it more often so he wouldn't look so scary to people who just met him.

Jack's smile grew bigger when he said, "Isn't your horse your best friend? What's his name again?"

"Star. Yes, he is. I just hope he's okay."

"Maybe when this is over, you and I can take Tango for a ride and go find Star. Would you like that?"

She couldn't hold back a grin, though her heart was still hurting. "You'd do that for me?"

"Of course I would. We just have to make sure it's safe first."

"You promise?"

"Yes, I promise."

She hugged him as they continued through the front door and went inside.

The house had a strange smell to it. It was gross, but she'd smelled worse. Usually in the stables when she was cleaning out the stalls.

She figured most people didn't know that horses are super messy and they poop a lot. Tons of it and it really stinks. There was so much when she did her chores that it would fill the wheelbarrow all the way to the top. It was really heavy, but she was able to take it out back and dump it all by herself.

It was hard work, but her father said she had to do it. Even when she was tired. He wanted her to grow up big and strong and be able to handle stuff on her own. Sort of like now. She didn't want to go inside, but she needed to. It's what big girls do.

At least Jack was here, so she didn't have to go alone. He was strong and would protect her, like her papa would have done.

CHAPTER 81

Bunker turned his body at an angle to make room for the cargo he was carrying down the hallway of Tuttle's place. The girl in his arms was dead quiet, lying on her back with her head to the right, keeping an eye on where they were going.

For some reason, his heartbeat was out of control, thumping as if he'd just run a thousand-meter dash. But not just any dash. A dash through the hostile streets of Afghanistan with a loaded rucksack on his back.

Normally he was in control of both his pulse and his breathing, but right now, right here, he was struggling, even though he'd been in far more precarious situations than this.

Before his next breath, a scene from his past rose up and landed in his thoughts. When his eyes blinked, the entire incident played out in an instant, filling his mind's eye with a rush of vivid imagery.

White trails of smoke following a fresh salvo of RPGs.

Explosive impacts shaking the air as the rocket-propelled grenades destroyed the foundation of a building not far from his squad.

The bitter smell of propulsion that followed, hanging above the combat zone like some kind of pestilence.

The horrendous claps of .50 caliber machine guns sending round after round downrange, each bullet creating pressure waves that traveled faster than sound.

Headset squawking in his ears.

Commands arriving across the airwaves and men responding.

The clatter of equipment and boots scrambling for cover.

Flashbangs going off in the distance as another entrenched terrorist got what was coming to him.

The rattle of M16s.

Pops of pistol fire.

The stench of burning tires and rotting garbage in the street. Strong enough to make a billy goat gag.

Bloodcurdling screams coming at him from every direction. Some in English. Others not. All of it intense.

For some men, the sensory overload during combat was more than they could bear. A few froze in the heat of a battle. Others would break down. Some got tunnel vision, focusing only on their primary target and forgetting to listen to commands or pay attention to changes in their surroundings.

Falling victim to any one of those symptoms meant you were probably going home in a body bag, or hauled to medical on a stretcher covered in blood.

If someone asked, Bunker would tell them he didn't believe in *Fog of War*, as most would call it. To him and his fire team, it was more along the lines of *Mutually Assured Chaos*. Or Big MAC Attack for short. Sure, it was a private term his team tossed around, but it fit.

Despite the intensity, Bunker never had an issue staying focused and advancing to do what was needed, regardless of the indescribable bedlam surrounding him.

He assumed his battle hardness was due to his father's relentless preaching, training, and of course, pop inspections. He'd come to learn over the years that everything his father had put him through was done for a reason—to prepare him for what would come next, in all walks of life.

Bunker was born to fight.

He knew it.

His old man knew it.

Yet here he was, in a singlewide trailer with a fragile girl in his arms, carrying her to a rendezvous with the body of her dead father. A man Bunker knew and respected. A man who'd just been executed without a second thought by a band of thugs in the mountains of Colorado.

Bunker had seen his share of corpses, most riddled with holes and body parts askew. But this face-off with death was different. Something inside him had set his adrenaline on fire. He wasn't sure he could keep it under control.

When he looked down at the injured girl, his eyes met hers. He wondered if she was staring back at him in order to draw strength in some fashion, like some kind of emotional conduit.

"You okay?" he asked her, faking a steady voice. Her tears were gone, but the wetness down her cheeks remained.

She nodded with her upper lip tucked under, but said nothing. He understood what she was feeling. She didn't have to say it.

"It'll be okay. I promise," Bunker told her as they arrived at the open door to Tuttle's master bedroom. He didn't enter. Not yet. He wanted to take a quick survey while she couldn't see inside.

Like Megan, this room had seen its share of turmoil in the past few days, first with Tuttle's ambush by the man in black, and now Franklin Atwater's murder. So much blood and violence in close proximity to kids. Innocent kids who were forced to grow up all at once with an invasion looming and countless other threats waiting in the shadows beyond Tuttle's property.

Sure, there were other actionable items and several friends needing his attention, but none of them were more critical than this mission.

It's the little things that count, he told himself quietly. Important things. Things that keep your sanity in check, and your humanity. Not just Megan's, but his. The others would have to wait a few minutes, especially the adults.

Two bodies lay lifelessly in the bed. The closest was Franklin. He was in the prone position and shirtless, with his muscular shoulder covered in a wide bandage.

The wrap was bloody, but not nearly as red as the discards stuffed in a wastebasket sitting a foot from the bed. The wire-mesh receptacle was half-full of red and white cloths. Martha must have been busy trying to stop the bleeding before the hillbillies showed up, tossing the old rags away like unwanted bills.

He smirked. Some good it did for the proud Army vet lying dead in the room occupied by a former recluse—a country hermit who was obsessed with all things conspiracy related. If the swatch of newspapers on the walls could talk, they'd tell a tale few would believe.

The other body was on the far side of the bed, twisted over in an awkward position with its right side facing up. Bunker had never met the man known as Angus Cowie, but given what he'd learned, the corpse belonged to Misty Tuttle's boyfriend from overseas.

The blood splatter on the wall behind Cowie indicated he'd been shot sitting up. It meant the man must have regained consciousness and probably saw the gunman coming for him. The hole in his right palm supported that theory, most likely caught in the bullet's damage path while trying to protect his face.

It was a gruesome scene to be sure, but what he worried most about was the gaping hole in Franklin's head. It was visible from the doorway. So was the blood on the cowboy's face, his head propped up by a pillow. His eyes were still open, but looking in two different directions after his ocular control had let go upon his death.

Stephanie was right. The girl shouldn't see this.

"Megan, I don't know about this. It's pretty awful, honey. I think we should go back outside."

"No, Jack. I need to do this. Take me in, please. I have to say goodbye."

Bunker held back a response. He didn't have the words, her voice cutting through his armor and squeezing his vocal cords.

"Please, Jack. Please," she said, tears taking over her eyes once again. She continued her appeals, her voice like acid, eating away at the petals of his heart.

He wanted to deny her request, but couldn't find the strength, his insides a swampy mush. "Okay. But if we do this, I need you to close your eyes for a minute. There are a couple of things I need to do before you open them. Can you do that for me?"

"Uh-huh," she said, her eyelids slamming shut.

"All right, keep them closed until I tell you to open them."

"I will. I promise."

He walked through the door and put her on the floor at the foot of the bed. Her eyes were still closed, so Bunker went to Franklin's body as planned.

First up, he needed to cover the hole in the man's forehead. After a quick scan of the room, he realized the items he could use were limited.

Martha had left a pair of scissors on the headboard and some used bandages in the waste bin, but little else. He had hoped to find medical tape—the preferred item—but he didn't see any rolls.

A pile of pushpins, a magnifying glass, and a yellow marker were in the room, sitting on a stack of unread newspapers by the broken window on the far wall. They'd been moved since his initial visit with Daisy. However, unless he was going to complete Tuttle's article review, they weren't going to be of much help.

The blood around the entry wound was still fresh and glistening, giving him an idea. He tore off a six-inch strip of newspaper from one of the nearby articles on the wall and folded it over several times, until it was slightly larger than the wound.

He tucked the edges under so they locked together in a fold, then put the wad of paper on the wound. The blood worked like glue, adhering the makeshift bandage to the man's skin.

Not bad, he decided. It reminded him of the mornings when he decided to shave. Inevitably, he'd have to use tissue to cover the cuts from the perpetually dull razor. Otherwise, the bleeding would run down his chin.

Unfortunately, the cover-up wasn't perfect, blood seeping into the newsprint along the edges. Yet it was better than letting Megan catch a visual of the gunshot hole in her old man's face.

A traumatic image like that would stick with her until the end of time. This was going to be hard enough as it was. Bunker didn't want the memories of her father jaded any more than they had to be. Not if he could lessen her pain in some way.

He ran his finger over Franklin's eyes to close the lids, then grabbed a handful of used bandages from the trashcan. He lifted Franklin's head and wiped up most of the blood and tissue, then tossed the rags back where he'd found them. He turned the pillow over to the cleaner side, then repositioned the dead man's head so it looked natural.

Bunker had done all he could for his Army pal. Now it was time to fix the deadly scene on the other side of the mattress. He walked past Megan and headed to the far side of the bed.

"Can I open my eyes now?" Megan asked.

Bunker figured the sound of his footsteps and the rush of air past her cued her question. "Not yet. Hang on. Almost done."

"What's taking so long?"

"Just another minute or so, sweetheart. Don't open your eyes yet." Bunker rolled Angus onto his back, then positioned the man's hands across his chest, like a mortician would do. Then, as he did for Franklin, Bunker covered the forehead wound with folded newspaper.

Next up, he needed to devise a quick solution for the blood splatter on the wall. Some of it had landed on the nearby paper, but the rest had stuck to the naked drywall.

He tore down the newsprint that had red on it, then turned his attention to the area of drywall covered in blood and tissue. The gruesome mess covered about six square feet and had spread out in all directions.

If he had a sponge and a mop bucket, this would have been an easy fix. Cleaning supplies were probably stored in the mobile home somewhere, but Bunker didn't think he had the time, nor did he want to leave Megan in here alone. She was already running out of patience. If he left the room now, she'd almost certainly open her eyes too soon.

He had a better idea. One involving the eleven pushpins remaining in the clear plastic tray that sat on top of the stack of papers behind him.

Bunker grabbed eight of the pins, along with three full-sized sheets of newspaper, then put them on the wall to cover the splatter in large, overlapping squares. The sheets were from a section of the paper that featured dark-colored ads, obscuring the red splotches behind them. The pins slipped into the drywall without much pressure, making quick work of the evidence.

After a final survey of the room, he believed he'd done all he could in the time allotted. He returned to Megan's side of the bed and took a knee next to her, his heart still running in overdrive. "Okay, I'm finished. You ready?"

Her eyes remained closed when she said, "Uh-huh."

When Megan's hands came up for him, he obliged, slipping his arms under hers to pick her up.

Bunker wondered if she was actually going to see this through. It wasn't going to be easy, but not just for her. In truth, a big part of him hoped she'd ask him to turn around and haul her outside before she opened her eyes. "Last chance to change your mind."

"I'm okay," she answered in a timid voice.

He exhaled, letting the anxiety ease a bit before he stood her next to the bed, just beyond Franklin's right side. "Open your eyes when you're ready. But remember, we can leave anytime. Just let me know. I'm right here."

Her weight leaned into his as Megan took control of her balance. When her eyes opened, Bunker expected her to break down instantly, but she didn't. Instead, the ebony skin across her cheeks held its solemn look as the tears came.

Megan reached out for her father's hand, her fingers shaking with tremors of grief. Unlike Cowie, Franklin's arms were down along his sides, lying in wait next to his hips.

Her grip looked soft when she made contact, almost as if she was afraid she might hurt Franklin in some way.

"Papa? It's me, Megan. I'm here now so you're not alone anymore." After a two-count, she twisted forward and took a seat on the edge of the bed, her injured leg angled away from the mattress.

Bunker took a step back to avoid her knee brace and give the girl some privacy. It felt wrong to stand there and watch her torment, but he wasn't sure what else to do. He hoped she'd give him a sign if she needed him.

When she spoke again, the words were chaotic and uneven, gasps of air breaking up the delivery. "I'm sorry it took me so long to come in and say goodbye, Papa," she said in a trembling voice, sniffing twice before she continued. "But I was really scared at first."

Megan picked up his hand and held the back of it to her cheek. "I know I'm supposed to be brave, but it's so hard. I don't know what I'm supposed to say."

Bunker sucked in a breath and held it, his gut twisting into a knot. He wanted to speak up and guide her along, but the words failed him. Nothing sounded right in his head.

Her tears intensified, streaming down her cheeks and landing on Franklin's hand. "I'm sorry I made you mad before we went to church last Sunday. I was gonna pick up my room, but I forgot. I didn't do it on purpose, Papa, so please don't be mad at me. I'll do better. I promise."

Bunker turned his head away for a moment, hoping some newfound strength would find him. Megan's words were killing him, even after surviving the bloody sands of Afghanistan and years of knock-down, drag-you-away-on-a-stretcher street brawls with The Kindred.

He couldn't believe it. This was who he had become—a giant, tattooed marshmallow, eaten alive by the words of a tiny young girl saying goodbye to her father.

When he brought his eyes forward again, he saw her kiss the back of Franklin's hand gently, holding her lips against his dark skin. A few seconds went by before she adjusted her grip, opening his fingers and putting his palm against the curve of her cheek.

Her voice trembled, matching the shake in her hands. "It's time to sleep now, Papa. Don't be afraid. The angels are coming for you."

Bunker fought back the tears welling in his eyes, using a quick wipe of his fingers to usher them away. He was thankful nobody else was in the room.

"When you see Mommy in heaven, tell her I miss her every day. I'm gonna miss you, too, Papa. You've been the best daddy in the whole world."

Just when Bunker thought Megan was going to get through this goodbye without a breakdown, it came. Not all at once, but in waves. Her stomach started to convulse and so did her sobs, the tears gushing out from somewhere profound.

She looked up at Bunker, her face twisted in a full-on grimace. Her cries were silent at first, waiting for air from her lungs as her chest began to heave. When the sound arrived, it came with the volume of a wolf howl, her cries uncontrolled.

When she reached out for him, Bunker flew to her side in a flash. He wrapped her in a hug and held her tight. "It'll be okay, sweetheart."

"I'm sorry. I tried to be strong, Jack, but I can't."

"No, honey, you're being super brave. Just let it out until there are no more tears left. We have all the time in the world."

CHAPTER 82

"That poor girl," Stephanie said after hearing the wail from inside Tuttle's place. Megan's cries were not only deafening but heartbreaking, consuming every molecule of air in front of the trailer. "I tried to warn him."

"Bunker was just doing what he thought was right," Sheriff Apollo said. "It's all any of us can do at the moment."

"Maybe one of us should go in there?" Rusty asked.

"I'll go," Dicky said, taking a step forward with his back straight and chin stiff.

"Not until I'm done," Martha said, straining to draw another suture through his check as he moved.

"I'm sure that's good enough," Dicky answered, his hand stopping hers.

"You need a couple more stitches."

"Nah, just cover it and I'll be good."

"That'll leave a nasty scar."

He lifted up his shirt, giving everyone in the yard a prime view of his six-pack abdomen and impressive chest. He pointed at a ten-inch scar along his torso, running vertically across his slender ribcage. "You mean like this?"

"Yeah, like that. What happened?" Martha asked, her wrinkled hands cutting the suture with a pair of scissors.

"ATV accident. It's what happens when you're not paying attention to the sand dune in front of you."

"What did we miss?" a new voice said from behind the group, its tone loud and laced with sarcasm.

When Stephanie whirled around, she saw Albert Mortenson, the heavyset deputy she knew from high school. He was puffing noticeably. "Albert? What are you doing here?"

"Trying to stay alive," he said, pointing at the burly man walking next to him. "Not an easy feat when you're walking with a guy whose sole purpose in life is to piss off the Russians."

Stephanie recognized the stocky man. It was Burt Lowenstein, the town mechanic.

The third member of the new arrivals was the skinny deputy she'd met earlier when Albert and he broke up the argument with her ex in front of Doc Marino's clinic. She thought his name was Dustin, but wasn't sure. His hands were fiddling with a knapsack strapped to his back.

"I take it you ran into them," Apollo said.

"Yeah, you could say that," Burt answered, his grin looking forced.

"Anyone hurt?"

"Just their pride after we gave them the slip."

"Are they close?" Rusty asked, his eyes pinched and head turned slightly.

"Doubt it. We took the long way around. Made sure they weren't following us. I know a few shortcuts."

Albert rolled his eyes. "Well, I don't know about that. They're not shortcuts if we took the long way around."

"They got you here in one piece, didn't they?" Burt snapped.

"Barely," Albert said, his lungs still working to catch up. He pointed at the skinny deputy. "Am I right, Dustin?"

Stick boy didn't answer.

Before another word was uttered, Misty stood up in a flash of movement and pushed away from Daisy's embrace. Daisy got to her feet as well, then the two of them took off in a rush, entering the front door to Tuttle's place.

"Was it something I said?" Albert said in a smartass tone, throwing up his hands.

"I'm afraid a lot has happened," Apollo said, his tone firm.

"Obviously. Was it the Russians?"

"No. Somebody else. We got ambushed by some lowlifes," Victor added with a flip of his hair, his mom shooting him a piercing look after he spoke.

"Misty's boyfriend was the first to be shot," Stephanie said.

"Misty? As in Misty Tuttle?" Albert asked. "That was her?"

"Yep. Back from her trip overseas apparently," Stephanie said. "I feel for her. First her father and now her fiancée."

"Frank's dead, too?" Burt asked, his face twisted.

Stephanie nodded. "I'm afraid so. But he's not the only one."

"Who else?" Dustin asked, his voice as thin as his shirt.

"Franklin Atwater," Apollo answered. "Bunker's in there with Megan right now."

"Poor bastard," Burt said.

"The guy with all the horses, right?" Dustin asked Albert.

Albert sent him a nod, then turned his focus to Apollo. "So, Bunker's here? Cool. I've been wondering when I might meet the man with all the tattoos. And a big pair of balls, apparently."

Apollo didn't react to Albert's attempt at humor. "Well then, I guess today is your lucky day. But I'd suggest checking the attitude a bit. He's been through hell, too."

Stephanie walked to Martha and Allison Rainey. "What about that food you mentioned earlier? We should all eat something, and I'm sure these kids need to rest. I'd suggest your place. You know, until we get things arranged over here."

"You mean more digging," Martha said in a matter-of-fact way.

Stephanie nodded. "Something tells me we're going to be doing a lot of that around here."

Martha put a hand on her daughter's arm, just below the elbow. "Allison, why don't you bring Megan over when she's done inside?"

"Okay," Allison said before turning her head and looking at her son.

"I'll watch Victor," Martha said. "You go. Take care of the girl. I'm sure Bunker could use a break."

Allison turned her shoes and headed for the entrance to the trailer.

"Jeffrey, come here," Stephanie said, waving her hand three times until he responded.

"You too, Victor," Martha said.

The other kid, Dallas, stood with feet frozen, looking as if he was waiting for his name to be called.

Stephanie made eye contract with the quiet boy, then asked, "Are you hungry?"

"Yeah. Starving."

"Then why don't all you kids head over to Mrs. Rainey's place? She'll fix you something to eat."

Apollo pointed at Dicky. "You go with them and keep an eye on things."

"You got it, chief."

"If anyone approaches, notify me immediately."

Stephanie held Jeffrey's hand as Martha led the group to her place across the road. Victor and the new kid, Dallas, were right behind Martha, chatting about something like old friends. Their voices were low so she couldn't make out the words, but they were definitely excited.

Dicky followed beside her, his hands holding a rifle flat against his bulging chest. He kept watch on the area ahead, scanning to the left first, then the right. He repeated the same process a few more times before she decided it was time to say something.

Stephanie looked up at her escort, marveling at his sheer size. She knew Dicky from town, but had never been this close to him. Nor had she relied on him for anything before. Certainly not her life and that of her son.

The threat of death changes a person's perspective. And their awareness of anything new, she decided, noticing her view was about a foot shorter than his. Bunker's stature was intimidating, but nothing like this guy.

She motioned at the rifle in his hands. "Tell me you know how to use that thing?"

"Yeah. Been hunting all my life. Shouldn't be a problem."

She wasn't as confident, but didn't want to upset the man by questioning his skills. A different approach was needed to drive home her point.

"I hope you're right, because these particular animals can shoot back."

CHAPTER 83

Mayor Buckley stood in the trampled grass of the town square, wondering how much worse this day would become. Bill King was on his left and Doc Marino on his right, both having a hard time standing still, as were the rest of the residents of Clearwater.

Everyone was packed in tight, including Stan Fielding and his twin girls, who were huddled only a few inches in front of the Mayor.

"Seriously?" Buckley mumbled, as another set of unmarked trucks pulled up, this time arriving from a side street that dumped into the center of town, directly adjacent to the Catholic Church and its soaring bell tower.

Now that the Russians had taken over, he wondered if Pastor Green would ring the bronze-colored bell before service this coming Sunday. Then again, maybe Sunday Mass would be suspended altogether. He wasn't sure. The Pastor might cancel.

As expected, a flood of Russian troops scampered out of the arriving trucks, adding to the imposing force already occupying town. The additional military presence made the side of his neck itch, the sensation centered on the same spot where FEMA had injected him with their MH2 treatment. He scratched with vigor, digging his fingernails into the skin around the bandage, but not enough to draw blood.

When Buckley turned his head to Doc Marino, he found the physician's dark, inset eyes trained on him. It felt as though the healer was monitoring his actions for signs of derangement.

Or maybe Marino was gathering vitals with his eyes. Hard to tell when you're standing next to an ancient doctor who was content with small town medicine, despite his Harvard education. The man was an enigma and always on duty, even while stuffing his face at the annual Forth of July picnic.

"It's not your fault," Doc said in a whisper, his Italian accent evident. Even after all his years as a naturalized citizen, he still sounded like a foreigner—an overly slender, mild-mannered Italian who stood only 5' 5" tall. His one vice: homemade brew—the kind with double the alcohol content and a sugar level sure to give steady drinkers chronic liver disease.

"Yes. It *is* his fault," Bill King added, looking at Doc. "Buckley screwed the pooch, big time."

"You don't have to remind me, Bill. Nobody feels worse about this than me. Though I do remember you being there with me. I know you won't admit it, but it wasn't just me who got fooled by the FEMA rollout."

"Hey, I raised concerns—a couple of times. Especially after the Wal-Mart trucks showed up. But no . . . as usual, nobody listens to me."

"At this point, it doesn't matter, gentlemen," Doc said, the words heavy in his accent. "We need to stay focused and work together. All these people will need leadership."

"Let's just hope this doesn't get any worse," Buckley said.

"Any worse? How is that even possible?"

"That's how," Doc Marino said, pointing to an eight-wheeled transport pulling up, its diesel engine grinding to a stop in front of the crowd. The camo-green vehicle featured a massive gun with a cannon that seemed to stick out a mile. A squad of men shot out of the transport and scampered to the raised platform that had been erected at the head of the square.

Most of the new arrivals were outfitted like the others already in town, heavily armed and wearing tactical gear. All except one. The lone exception carried only a sidearm and was smoking a cigar with vigor. He had the forearms of a bodybuilder, though the rest of him looked slender.

"Must be their leader," King said after a twitch of his eyes. "Looks like a real asshole."

Another soldier moved across the stage and gave the Commander a megaphone, his steps measured. The cigar man turned the unit on and held it up to his mouth, while a brigade of Russian flags doubled as a backdrop behind him.

After a momentary squeal from the speaker, the man's voice rang out in English, though the words carried a heavy Russian accent that obscured the crispness of the syllables.

"Citizens, my name General Yuri Zhukov. This town under Russian control. Follow orders and you not be harmed. Food, water, supplies are here. More coming. You are safe, but must follow orders."

Buckley's shoulders relaxed a bit. "Okay, at least they're not here to harm anyone."

King shook his head before he spoke in a whisper. "Yeah, until we hear his demands. You heard him. We have to follow orders. God knows what those are going to be."

"Quiet!" Doc said in a sharp whisper.

Zhukov continued, the device amplifying his voice louder than before. "I repeat. This is Russian territory. Disobey and we shoot you."

The crowd buzzed after the last statement, mumbles and whispers erupting in every direction. The tension in the square rose, everyone moving closer to each other, as if huddling provided some form of sanctuary against the great red menace.

Buckley's mind turned to a conversation he'd had earlier with Bunker about the coordinated, high-tech attack. Bunker used his theory to explain why US troops hadn't made an appearance, or the National Guard, and now it appeared he was right.

Under other circumstances, Buckley would have expected the military to be involved by now. Somewhere along the way, someone would have noticed the Russians rolling across the countryside. Hell, even the State Troopers would have intervened.

He didn't want to believe it, but Bunker's theory seemed to fit—a cyber-attack was unleashed before the EMP to take down the eyes and ears of everyone who could pose a threat to the invasion force.

Then again, there was a chance the US Army had engaged the invasion force somewhere along the way, possibly even local law enforcement, but lost badly.

Sure, he conceded that his idea might be nothing more than wishful thinking, but the hypothesis wasn't a total stretch. Not if he factored in the size of the incursion needed to pull off something like this—assuming of course, this rollout was happening across the country.

The obvious problem in defending the continental USA stems from the fact that American forces are spread out across the states, usually involved in some kind of on-base training exercise. It wouldn't take much for domestic forces to become complacent, not expecting a localized attack. All eyes would be on the borders and in the sky, not focused on the streets beyond the security fence.

With a good portion of our active forces deployed overseas, and busy hunting the latest terrorist to take up residence on the high priority target list, domestic security might have suffered. If so, it would be easy to be compromised by an enemy with the will, the might, and the balls to green-light their plan.

Zhukov stood silent for a minute as another soldier wheeled a two-shelf cart across the stage. It was about ten feet long, with a set of batteries occupying the lower shelf. The second shelf contained a bank of electronic gear, though its power must have been off since none of its lights were illuminated.

The General ambled to the cart and flipped a switch, bringing a bank of lights to life across the front of the equipment. He turned to the crowd and spoke through the loudspeaker once again, skipping certain connector words in his version of broken English.

"Compliance agent injected," he said, pointing to the left side of his neck. "We track you. You leave without permission, explosive detonates. Try to disable, also detonates."

Buckley stopped scratching his neck when he heard those words, yanking his hand away.

"So much for those thirty days of injections. I guess that was all bullshit," King said. "I knew something wasn't right with that whole thing."

Stan Fielding turned around and stared with intense eyes, his face flushing red. He pointed at the circular bandages on his girls' necks. "You let them do this. How could you, Mayor?"

Buckley didn't have an answer for the single father. The man was right. He'd let this happen. Just another failure on his already full resume.

At this point, his seat in the Governor's office was nothing more than a pipedream. Not that his future political aspirations mattered in the grand scheme of things. Lives were at stake. So was everyone's freedom. The Russians were here for a reason and *this* was just getting started. Whatever *this* was.

There was one consolation, though. At least now he knew why he'd heard a metal click when the FEMA injections were administered. They were implanting the tracker and explosive.

"Remember when FEMA mentioned they had a list?" King asked, his question coming out of nowhere.

Buckley took a few seconds to locate the memory. "Yeah. It was after we asked about treating the residents out of town."

"How could they have that information?"

"Not sure. But this was obviously well planned."

"No shit, Sherlock. But not only that, they must've had help from someone. You know, on the inside. Otherwise, how could they get their hands on a detailed list like that? I'm pretty sure our government doesn't track that type of stuff. Not real-time info about who's in or out of town. So the Russians couldn't have stolen it from some computer hack."

"Or maybe they do track us," Doc said without hesitation. "The skies are covered with satellites. Who knows what they are really watching? They've admitted to spying on everyone. Nothing is sacred. Every phone call. Every Internet post. Every email."

"Or they could've had spies in town. For a while now, setting this up," King said.

Buckley agreed with King, but he wasn't about to cave to the man's pressure. "Okay, I see your point, but what do you expect me to do about it?"

"I don't know, show a little concern maybe?"

"Trust me, every cell in my body is concerned right now. For everyone. Including you."

"I'll bet the new guy, Bunker, is part of all this. I mean, come on. He just shows up out of the blue and bingo, we're invaded. Sounds a little suspicious to me. Plus, now we have this General trying to bribe everyone with truckloads of free food and supplies like he's our best buddy. Then he tells us we'll explode if we don't follow along like sheep. Seems damn clear to me. None of this is by accident. They've been planning this for a while and must have had inside help to pull it off."

"Trust me, Bunker is not part of this," Buckley said.

"Yeah, you say that now, but how do you really know? This was all orchestrated with precision. They could've easily placed sleeper agents in town just waiting for the go-ahead to take action."

King had a point. Buckley shrugged.

"What if our government is in on it somehow?" Stan Fielding asked, his tone serious.

Fielding's theory had merit. "It would explain a few things," Buckley answered.

Stan nodded. "And you have to ask yourself, why send a General? This town can't be that important."

"Unless it is," King added.

Zhukov aimed the megaphone to the side, pointing it at another truck pulling up. This vehicle was a long flatbed, loaded with a stack of poles that stretched from one end of the rig to the other.

Buckley figured they were at least fifty feet long since they hung over the rear of the trailer by a couple of feet. They could have been made of steel or plastic; he couldn't be sure.

Behind the flatbed was a ten-wheeled mobile crane, its hook swaying in front of the windshield as it crawled along under its own power. The lowercase letters "anipsotiki" were stenciled on both the front of the cab and the side of the crane's main boom.

Following the crane was yet another flatbed, this one transporting two rectangular pieces of cargo that filled the trailer from front to back. Each section was wrapped with a red tarp and strapped down in multiple directions.

Buckley watched a team of men remove the straps, then pull the tarps away with a theatrical flair.

King didn't hesitate. "Generators. Big suckers."

"At least we'll have power again," Fielding said.

"Looks like they're gonna be here a while," Buckley said, thinking of the residents who were out of town. The Russians had sent out patrols in their ATVs looking for them. He hoped that God had stepped up to keep them safe. Or Bunker had, assuming the man was still alive and in the area. Nobody had seen him since the Sheriff sent him with Daisy to Tuttle's place.

King lowered his eyes and stared at the ground for a few seconds. Then he shook his head before aiming his focus at Buckley. "Jesus Christ. We are so fucked. So is my son, wherever he is. We're gonna have to do something, and fast."

CHAPTER 84

Daisy Clark found the light switch at the bottom of the ladder and turned it on when her feet found the loose dirt at the bottom of Tuttle's hidden bunker in the barn.

Everywhere she looked, the room was brimming with treasure—not just any treasure; this was the type of stash that could inflict endless amounts of damage and death.

"Jackpot!" she announced, hoping Sheriff Apollo could hear her from his position above the trap door in the barn.

"What did you find?"

"Everything! You need to get down here."

"On my way," he said, his feet appearing on the top rung of the ladder a few seconds later.

Daisy waited for his arrival, then held out her hand to lead his eyes to the inventory. "Look at all this."

Apollo didn't answer right away, his mouth agape. He walked to the wooden rack of weapons installed on the wall, then ran his fingers over two of the rifles stored vertically on the left, their barrels pointing up. They were both pump action shotguns, their distinctive slide-action fore-end evident.

The next three guns were assault rifles, 5.56 caliber, if Daisy had to guess, bringing Apollo's hands to them quickly. She estimated their barrels were only sixteen inches long, perfect for gunfights in tight spaces.

"M4 Carbines," he said, snatching one in his hands. "Colts." He played with the folding stock, then held it up to his shoulder. His eye went behind the sights as he pretended to search for targets in the room.

He brought the weapon down, with his attention lingering on the twelve-inch secondary attachment hanging under the front of the barrel. It had its own trigger and the word "Havoc" stenciled on the side.

"A flare launcher, sir," Daisy said in case her newly-appointed boss had questions.

Apollo nodded, then studied the hundred-round drum installed in front of the trigger guard. He ejected the firepower upgrade and inspected its contents for a three-count. After a flash of his eyebrows, he mounted the magazine back to the weapon with a firm hand. "He spent a bundle on this stuff."

"Must have thought World War III was coming," she quipped, pointing to the pile of the banana-shaped magazines sitting on the shelf below the rack. They looked to be of the thirty-round capacity, but there were at least five more hundred-round drums as well.

"Bunker's gonna love this," Apollo said, putting the rifle back in the rack. "And the communications gear we found upstairs."

Daisy agreed, thinking about the radio sets and the working batteries they'd discovered. She nodded slowly. "Thank God Tuttle was a paranoid nut. Those homemade Faraday cages really did the trick. I didn't know you could turn a storage cabinet into one of those."

"Then again, was Tuttle really so paranoid? After all, what he feared would happen, did."

"True. It's like they say, it's not paranoia if you are actually being followed. He looks like a genius now."

"I don't know if I'd go that far. There's a fine line between insanity and genius," the Sheriff said, walking to the far end of the rack, bypassing at least a dozen rifles.

The longest of the barrels belonged to hunting rifles, Daisy decided as she followed her boss. Each had a high-powered scope and a sling for carrying.

The second cabinet was smaller than the first and built differently. It was more of a display case and angled for presentation, featuring a line of semi-auto handguns. Glocks mostly, though there were a few Rugers and Colts mixed in.

There weren't any revolvers and that surprised her. Tuttle obviously liked them, having a cowboy gun at his bedside before he died—a .357 magnum revolver, maximum firepower for a man of his size. Perhaps Tuttle only kept the semi-autos down in this bunker. His revolver stash may have been somewhere else.

On the floor beyond the weapons cache were at least fifty cardboard boxes of ammo, still sealed in their bulk shipping cartons. Some were critical defense loads with hollow point rounds to inflict maximum damage once they entered the body cavity. Others were standard-tipped. All of them were lethal if the shooter's aim was accurate.

Apollo knelt down and inspected the first column of containers, his eyes taking in the black lettering that indicated the manufacturer, caliber, grain, and quantity of rounds. He seemed most interested in the .223 caliber ammo, his fingers ripping open the top seal on the 1000-round container. His hand went in and pulled out one of the rifle rounds. He held it up in front of his eyes. "Full metal jacket. Green tip. That'll do some damage."

Daisy wasn't shocked by the amount of ammo on hand. Nor was she surprised by the illogical order of the stockpile, the boxes mixed and stacked haphazardly. She would've arranged them by caliber to allow for quicker restock.

At least the waist-high collection of green-colored ammo cans was organized, their grab handles facing up. She snatched the top one. It was heavy. She opened it. Inside were 30-06 rounds. Mostly for hunting. Another ammo can held .223 rounds. The third one she checked had the larger .308 rounds, yet she didn't remember seeing a rifle chambered for that ammo.

Must be around here somewhere, she thought to herself as she continued walking behind her boss. She figured all the ammo cans were full and ready to go, which would explain why the 1000-round boxes of bullets hadn't been opened yet. They were being held in reserve, for when Tuttle's version of World War III started.

A clothing rack with four caster wheels stood in the adjacent corner, its line of garments hanging from the central aluminum bar. However, this wasn't your typical lineup of clothing. It was tactical apparel, at least two dozen forest-green camo shirts of various sizes to the left, with just as many pairs of pants to the right.

An unmarked container the size of a dishwasher sat just beyond the end of the rack. Its top lid was open, giving Daisy an angled view of the tactical vests sitting loosely on the box.

Tuttle must have inspected the delivery, but never bothered to stuff the items back inside. Again, not surprising given the disheveled state of the man's home.

Apollo picked up the first vest and inspected it, testing the Velcro seals on the magazine pouches. He then turned his attention to the cross-draw holster along the front.

"Are any bulletproof?" she asked, wondering if Tuttle had finished his purchase with some body armor. Since the Russians had cut off access to town with roadblocks, they wouldn't be able to get to their gear room inside the Sheriff's office.

Apollo dug through the rest of the box of vests, then reported, "Not that I can see."

Gas masks, hiking boots, gloves, safety glasses, and scores of earplugs rounded out the garb, all of it sitting in clumps nearby. The man even had a few thousand feet of paracord bundled and ready to go. It was sitting on a thick, folded stack of cargo netting—camo-colored, of course.

Apollo went to the backpacks leaning against the third wall and picked up one of the six. The pull of gravity on the straps told Daisy they were full, much like the two hiking packs in Tuttle's middle bedroom. However, these were camo-colored and about half the size.

The Sheriff opened the top zipper to inspect its contents. "The man has been busy. I'll give him that," he said, angling the open pouch toward Daisy.

Her eyes ran a quick check as Apollo pulled items out one at a time, her mind making a detailed list of the inventory.

Magnesium fire starter kit.
Quart-sized plastic drinking bottle.

Smaller metal water bottle with a strap and twist cap.

Mobile water filtration system and pump.

Three feet of rubber tubing.

Three green bandanas.

Pack of water purification tablets.

Container of waterproof matches.

Chainsaw in a can.

Mini-fishing kit.

Three military ready to eat meals.

Two energy bars.

Three granola bars.

Handful of beef jerky.

Advil to go pack.

Metal cup.

Small cooking pot.

Magnifying glass.

Folding knife with a belt clip.

Heavy-mil garbage bag.

Blue 10x10 tarp.

Two pairs of wool socks and gloves.

Orange beanie.

Pack of steel wool.

Mobile first aid kit.

Reflective survival blanket.

Dog tag reflector with a compass.

Spool of twine.

Fixed blade survival knife and sheath.

Head lamp and strap.

Extra batteries.

Glow sticks.

Pouch with twenty $5 bills.

Folded area map.

Notepad and pencil.

Can of bear spray.

Small measuring tape.

Can opener.

Toothpaste and brush.

And finally, a bar of soap.

"That's one hell of a bugout bag," Apollo said, standing with his hands on his hips, admiring the inventory.

"Yeah, good luck getting all of that back inside," she said with a smile, her boss rolling his eyes.

"He obviously spent a lot of time putting this together. I'm guessing the other packs have the same items."

The last of the unexplored walls grabbed Apollo's eyes next, specifically the six-foot banquet table. Its foldout legs appeared weak and its wood veneer top had several deep scratches. On it were a stack of bundled white paper, each three feet long and rolled lengthwise, with a rubber band around their middle.

The Sheriff took one of the rolls and slid off the binder. The paper unspooled as he pushed the other rolls to the side, then laid the paper out on the table.

Daisy stood next to him, her eyes drawn to the same discovery. It was an area map of Clearwater County showing the rivers, lakes, mountains, forest, roads, bridges, and the mines in the area. But someone had drawn on it in red ink, creating a loose collection of shapes resembling circles and ovals. Eleven of them, to be exact.

Apollo pointed to the farthest one on the right. "Silver King Mine."

Daisy nodded, then pointed to the ink in the middle. "Mason's Bridge. Where Stan's wife died."

The Sheriff continued with the next one, moving left. "Patterson's Meadow."

"As in Jim Patterson?"

"Yep. The one and only," he answered.

"Isn't he dead?"

Apollo nodded. "Eight years ago, if I remember right."

She tapped her finger on the meadow. "Why do you think he circled it so many times?"

"Not sure."

"I guess it would make a nice spot for a hunting cabin. The mountains around it would protect it from the winds," she said, checking the other circles. All but one of them was indicating another bridge in the area. The last circle was for the abandoned Haskins Mine, an old phosphate pit that had long been extinct. "What does all this mean?"

"Not sure," he said, unspooling another map. It also showed Clearwater County, only it was a topographical map, defining the contours of the terrain, including elevation.

The third map contained climate information for the entire state. Apollo tossed it away, moving on to the fourth, which was a detailed road map. It showed the roads, highways, and railways in the area, each in a different color.

There was more ink on this map, too, only Tuttle hadn't drawn circles. Instead, he drew long, squiggly red lines that seemed to run from point to point, many of them connecting at common locations.

Daisy pointed at one of them. "What do you think these are?"

"My guess . . . Frank was marking the old logging roads."

"Why?"

Apollo shrugged. "The only reason I can think of is to move his supplies without anyone noticing."

"Or as escape routes," she added.

* * *

Victor Rainey waved at his new friend Dallas to keep up as he turned a corner around another stack of pallets in the rear half of Tuttle's barn. He could hardly contain himself. "The best stuff is back here."

"How do you know all this?" Dallas asked, his legs working double-time to catch up.

"When Tuttle was done working outside, he'd sit in his old truck and drink a bunch of beer. I could see him from my grandmother's porch with a pair of binoculars. All I had to do was wait until he went inside to tap a nap, then I'd sneak in here. Tuttle would be out for hours."

"Old people tap a lot of naps."

"Yeah, my grandma, too," Victor said, nodding. "If my mom was in town working, I usually had plenty of time to explore before she got home."

"Didn't the old guy keep the doors locked?"

"Yep, but picking a lock is easy. My dad showed me how before he died. Tuttle was so clueless, it wasn't funny. As long as I put everything back the way he had it, he never noticed."

"Can you show me how?"

"It takes a lot of practice."

"I don't mind. I wanna learn."

"Maybe later. There's something really cool I want to show you by the workbench."

They ran by a dozen more pallets of shrink-wrapped boxes, taking two more turns on their way to the workshop. The last set of items they passed was a wall of stackable water containers. Victor didn't know if the five-gallon jugs were full or not, but there were a lot of them. Enough that he couldn't see over the top.

Tuttle had built his workbench out of 2x4 lumber, with a vise on each end. The workspace stretched from one end of the wall to the other and had to be thirty feet long. All kinds of stuff cluttered the top, thrown into piles on the surface.

Tuttle had a ton of hand tools, plus heavy spools of electrical wire and several rolls of electrical tape. A box of screwdrivers sat by the rolls of duct tape, and next to them, three hammers, a mound of wrenches, and at least twenty boxes of nails and screws.

To the right was a hacksaw, pair of vise grips, a box full of measuring tapes, six box cutters, a pack of magic markers, red shop towels, three cans of motor oil, and a bunch of other crap.

The Husqvarna chainsaws at the far end must have been in for repair, one of the three missing the chain. Victor had seen them elsewhere in the barn before today, but never back here. At the time, he thought about starting one of the heavy, tree-eating machines, but never did. The noise would have woken Tuttle up from his afternoon nap.

A coffee maker and pot sat on a rolling cart in front of the bench, complete with two cans of coffee and a stack of filters on the shelf below. The coffee in the pot looked like it had dried onto the glass.

Above the bench were open storage cabinets crammed full of junk. Everything was a mess. The man must have been collecting for years, especially the batteries, steel wool, and axle grease. He had gobs of it, just thrown in the cabinets like a madman.

"Is this what you wanted to show me?" Dallas said, standing in front of the workbench. He looked confused, his eyebrows pinched as he stared at the endless clutter.

"No, it's over here," Victor said, turning left and walking to a bunch of items covered up with faded yellow sheets. He pulled the cover off the first to reveal a four-foot-long piece of equipment. It looked like an ancient sewing machine with a few parts missing along the top.

It was made of cast iron and sat on its own integrated pedestal, with a pair of foot pedals installed below and a metal seat out front. Victor had played with its various handles and wheels before, so he knew they worked and hadn't rusted shut.

"What is that?" Dallas asked.

"A foot-powered lathe."

"For what?"

"Turning metal and wood. They make bowls and junk with it."

"Really?"

Victor nodded. "Saw it on YouTube before the Internet went down. I think this one can make stuff out of metal, too."

"Looks old."

"Yeah, I'm thinking from the 1800s, just like old man Tuttle himself."

Dallas laughed. "No doubt."

"Tuttle was just like my grandma. Old people never throw anything away and need projects to keep themselves busy. Otherwise, they fall sleep in front of the TV. Grandma's into jigsaw puzzles."

"I hate those. They're so boring."

"No lie. I like to take one of the pieces when she's not looking, just to mess with her. That way, when she's almost done, I get to finish it with the missing piece."

Victor worked his way around to the far side of the lathe. "Help me push," he told Dallas, peering down at the caster wheels mounted to a sheet of plywood holding the lathe.

The two of them moved the machine about fifteen feet, leaving it a foot away from the welding equipment on the other side of the shop. Tuttle had several torches of different sizes. Some had tanks, while others had a long electrical cord. He wasn't sure why the man needed so many.

Victor returned to the next covered item. He knew it to be a ten-inch wood joiner made of cast iron steel. It was old, like the lathe, but it was electric and not foot-powered. He pulled its protective sheet. "Tuttle has them all on wheels so he can move them. Let's get this one out of the way, too."

It took some effort, but the boys got the heavy joiner rolling. They wheeled it across the workshop and parked it next to the lathe. Had they chosen a spot farther to the left, they would have run into the man's blacksmithing equipment. Tuttle's anvil was pitted and a little rusty. So was the pounding hammer. Like the other equipment in the room, the forge was also on wheels and looked ancient.

Victor pointed at the base cabinet exposed after the equipment move. It featured two plywood doors with a latching mechanism made out of a bent nails and hooks. "Check out what's in the bottom."

Dallas went to the door on the right and opened it.

"What do you think?" Victor asked.

"What is that?" Dallas asked, his tone energized.

"Samurai sword."

Dallas put his hand in and pulled at the weapon, but it was stuck. He angled his arm sideways to work the item through the door of the cabinet. He spun around and held it up, still in its protective sheath.

Victor smiled. "Go ahead. Pull it out."

Dallas didn't hesitate, sliding the blade free. He put the sheath down on the workbench and wrapped both hands around the grip.

Victor remembered the first time he held the sword. "Pretty, cool, huh?"

"For sure," Dallas answered, slashing the blade back and forth before pretending to stab someone with it. "I'll bet this thing is worth a fortune."

"That's what I was thinking. Now that Tuttle's dead, someone needs to take good care of it. I was thinking maybe you should."

"Really? Me?"

"Yep."

"Awesome," Dallas said, putting the blade back into its protective carrier. The kid brought his eyes to Victor. "I'll bet Tuttle has a lot of other cool stuff. Maybe even some guns."

"So far, I've only found the sword. But I do know where there are lots of guns and ammo. Explosives, too."

"Where?"

"At Franklin Atwater's store."

"The horse stables?"

Victor nodded. "My grandma took me there a bunch of times."

"You still think it's all there? You know, after what happened to him."

"It was a few days ago when I was there. I found a pistol hidden under his desk."

"Can I see it?"

"I wish. It fell out of my pants when a bunch of men in black showed up and started chasing me."

"We should go look for it. Must be around there somewhere."

"If those men didn't take it."

CHAPTER 85

"We're gonna need more men if they're serious about staying here," Albert said to Dustin as the two of them leaned against the front of the fertilizer stacks, watching the activity in Tuttle's barn.

"Yeah, seems like a long shot. I know this Bunker guy is one serious badass, but how in the world are we going to stop a convoy like the one we saw back on the road?"

"We won't. They're nuts."

"As nuts as Burt wanting to head back to town?"

"So you finally agree with me?" Albert asked.

"Of course I do. We're partners."

"That's not how it came across before."

"I know, but that was different."

"How's that?"

"We're not stuck in the woods."

"Oh, I see. Your loyalty shifts depending on which way the wind is blowing. That's pretty weak."

"Dude, you really need to chill. I'm on your side."

"Only until something else pops up. Then you'll bail again," Albert said, unable to stop his disdain from fueling the words.

Dustin didn't say anything, his lips running quiet as his eyes dropped to the ground. After a long pause, he looked up and pointed at the mammoth of a man, Dicky, who was busy directing a forklift out of the barn. "Maybe we should think about lending a hand. You know, do something constructive."

"Nah, looks like they got it handled."

The new guy, Bunker, was behind the wheel of the machine, its engine churning under the strain of a massive spool of barbed wire hanging from the forks. It was clear Bunker was running the show with his endless barking of orders.

Albert motioned at Bunker, waiting for Dustin to catch up with his eyes. "I don't like that guy."

"Who? Bunker?"

"Yeah. Something seems off to me. I get that everyone is in love with the guy, but he rubs me the wrong way. I mean, who is he really, other than some overgrown testosterone sack?"

"He seems okay to me."

"Of course you'd say that. The wind just shifted."

"Maybe if you got to know him better, you'd feel the same way."

"I doubt it. He just runs around giving orders and telling everyone what to do. Like he owns the place. It's really starting to piss me off."

"I don't know; he looks like the kind of guy you wanna have on your side, not the other way around."

"Why? Because he's tall and slicks his hair back?"

"Well that, and he's pretty big. Those tattoos are kinda intimidating, too."

"Dude, just because you look tough does not mean you are tough. Trust me. Some of the guys I used to work with were half his size and they were some of most feared badasses in Southern California. I know. My crew used to have to deal with them all the time. Like I've said before, looks can be deceiving."

"Yeah, maybe you're right."

"Of course I'm right. You just need to listen to me once in a while."

Dustin shrugged, his tone changing to one of guilt. "I still feel like we should be doing something."

"Don't worry about it. They'll ask if they need something, especially the new guy, Mr. All Bark and No Bite," Albert said in a flippant tone, his eyes locked on the tattooed man with scars on his neck. He watched Bunker work the controls of the forklift with precision. Right then, an intense sense of déjà vu washed over him. "Damn, he looks familiar."

"Bunker?"

"Yeah, can't seem to place him though." Albert wasn't sure if he'd seen the black-haired man in one of the many warehouses or back alleys he'd been in during an exchange, or in some other capacity. But the man was familiar in some way. No doubt about it.

"Hey Sheriff, check it out," Daisy shouted from somewhere in the barn behind Albert. Apollo and the hot deputy had had been in the back for the last half hour, searching for something.

"Good work," Apollo told her, his voice wandering through the stacks of pallets. "Looks like the inventory map was out of date."

"Probably hasn't been updated since Helen died," she answered.

"Then we need to keep looking. No telling what else is in here. See if you can find some rechargeables."

Albert pulled his feet in as the Mayor's grandson Rusty walked past with a red, heavy-duty toolbox in his right hand, grunting and leaning hard to the left with every step he took. The kid had tree trunks for legs, but they weren't helping with the weight of the metal box. Rusty followed the forklift, heading for the entrance to the barn.

"That kid's gonna wreck his back walking like that," Dustin said.

"If someone asked me, I'd have Dicky carry it. That brute wouldn't break a sweat," Albert said, turning his eyes to Dustin. "Now, let me tell you, that guy is *tough*."

"How do you know?"

"Used to watch him mow down opposing teams back in high school. He has this switch inside of him, that once it goes off, watch out. He sent more than one defensive lineman to the hospital back in those days."

"You went to the football games?"

"Sure. Wasn't much else to do on Friday nights. Though I usually had to sit by myself. But of course, that shouldn't surprise you, right?"

"Nope. Had the same problem, which is why I skipped the ten-year reunion. Figured what was the point? I couldn't stand most of those assholes anyway."

"What high school again?" Albert asked, realizing he didn't know where Dustin was from. He knew the stickman had moved to Clearwater recently, but that was the extent of the guy's background.

"Arcadia High School. Phoenix."

"Hot down there."

"You got that right. You never stop sweating from March to November. But everyone has a pool, so that doesn't suck."

"Really? A pool, huh? I can't picture you lounging by a pool."

"That's because I never did. Not a big fan of the whole swim trunk thing."

"Yeah, me either," Albert said as Bunker parked the forklift just beyond the door.

The man jumped off the vehicle, laughed, and then slapped Rusty on the back after the kid delivered the toolbox with a grunt.

"That'll put some hair on your chest," Bunker joked.

"What's in this thing?" Rusty asked.

"Hopefully not rocks," Bunker said, taking a knee. He opened the box and dug around inside, pulling out a pair of hand tools and giving them to Dicky. He stood up. "Why don't you get started? I've got a couple of things to take care of inside. I'll be right back."

Bunker walked through the door and made his way toward the fertilizer stacks. Along the way, he snatched two shovels that were leaning against a crate of bleach, ammonia, Tide detergent, and other cleaning supplies wrapped in clear plastic.

Dustin stopped slouching against the fertilizer bags and stood upright when Bunker arrived.

Albert remained in a causal slump.

"Looks like you two need something to do," Bunker said, his tone deep. He forced a shovel into Dustin's hands and tried to do the same with Albert.

Albert pushed the handle away. "Sorry, dude. Diggin' ain't my thing."

The shovel came at him again. "Well, today it is. Everyone has to chip in if we're gonna get this place ready."

Albert refused to grab it, even though Bunker was pushing it with force against his chest. "You do know that this is all just a humungous waste of time, right? Only a complete moron would think any of this will accomplish a damn thing. Especially with what's out there right now. Ever heard of the term *Force Multiplier*?"

Bunker's chin tightened as he spoke through clenched teeth. "Yes. As a matter of fact, I've lived it. On both sides, my friend."

"Well, first of all, I'm not your friend. And second, if you lived it, it means you served, so you know I'm right. We don't stand a chance against the Russians and all their firepower. It doesn't matter what we do, we'll be slaughtered like mindless sheep."

"Look, I don't have time to explain it all. But trust me, I've got it covered. Right now, we have a few dead to bury and you two just volunteered. I need five graves out back. On the double."

Albert couldn't believe the audacity of this man. He tapped the tip of his index finger against the star on his chest, then pointed at Dustin's badge as well. "In case you haven't noticed, we're both Deputy Sheriffs. So tell me again, who put you in charge?"

"It just so happens, your boss did."

Albert smirked, unable to hold back his attitude. "In charge of what? Landscaping?"

"Of all things tactical and practical. So I'd suggest you two get digging."

"Graves are not tactical," Albert answered, swinging his eyes to Dustin for a few seconds. "Can you believe this guy? Talk about dense."

Bunker's eyes twitched, reminiscent of a cowboy preparing to draw down in a Wild West gunfight. "They are, if the right bodies are being dumped into them. As it stands now, we only need five, but I could easily make it seven."

Dustin's voice cracked when he spoke. "Albert, maybe we should do what the man says."

Albert held up a hand to shut Dustin up, never taking his eyes from Bunker. "Why don't you get Dicky and that Buckley kid to do it? They look like a couple of eager beavers. Dustin and I are taking a break. Been a long day, if you know what I mean."

Bunker looked at Dustin, then back at Albert. "Now, I've asked you nicely. More than once."

Albert wasn't worried. "Like I care. You really need to get over yourself, dude."

"Albert? Come on. Let's just do this," Dustin said.

Albert grinned, feeling emboldened. He wasn't sure why, but something inside was driving him to confront this man. It felt primal, almost as if he was being compelled to expose the man's temper.

"At this point, Bunker, it's all about mind over matter. Right now, I don't mind and you don't matter. So run along now and go impose your will on someone else. Dustin and I are busy."

Bunker flew forward, grabbing Albert by the shirt collar. His powerful arms swung Albert around and pushed him back a good ten feet, until something hard smacked into his back.

Albert put his hands up. "So now what? You gonna hit me?"

"Thinking about it."

"Well then, take your best shot. But I should warn you, you might just regret it."

Dustin voice was more agitated now. "Albert, please. Let's just go outside. It's not a big deal, really."

Bunker shook his head in disgust, his deadpan eyes burning a hole into Albert's face. "You know what, Albert? I've decided that I don't like you. Or your attitude."

"The feeling's mutual, bub. Now let go of me and back the fuck up."

Burt walked into the barn with a partially eaten apple in his hand, his teeth in chew mode. "Well, well. What do we have here?"

Dustin ran to Burt. "You gotta do something. Bunker's gonna kill him."

Burt chuckled. "Let me guess, jumbo opened his big mouth again."

"You could say that," Bunker answered, his eyes still locked on Albert. His grip tightened, lifting Albert to his toes.

Burt stopped his approach, then leaned against a crate with his elbow on top. He crossed his feet, his teeth tearing into the fruit for another crisp bite. "Go on boys, don't let me interrupt," he said with his mouth full.

"So what's it gonna be?" Bunker said, his words warming Albert's cheeks.

Dustin ran back to Bunker. "I'll dig the graves," he said, his tone frantic. "Just let Albert go. We're all friends here."

Albert took a deep breath, keeping his fear in check. Something in Bunker's eyes wasn't legit. He could sense it. The man wasn't going to turn physical. "See there, now we have a real solution. One that didn't involve me bowing to your one-sided demands."

Bunker paused for a few moments, then let go of Albert's shirt. He backed away a second before Rusty and Dicky came into the barn.

"Seriously? That's it? Well, that wasn't worth the price of admission," Burt said, turning and walking toward the exit.

Sheriff Apollo appeared at the door, meeting Burt just beyond the doorway. "What's going on?"

"Nothing, unfortunately," Burt said, stopping for a moment to relay the answer as the Sheriff cruised past him.

Albert waited for the Sheriff to arrive, then motioned at Bunker. "Your guard dog here just physically assaulted me."

"Why?"

Albert huffed, making sure his tone drove the point home. "Because I told him no and he didn't like it."

"Maybe you should do what Jack says. I did put him charge for a reason."

Albert turned to Apollo, eyes squinting. "So you're going to go with him over your own deputy?"

"Thanks for reminding me," Apollo said, his hand snatching the star from Albert's chest. He did the same with Dustin's badge. "Been meaning to repo these for a while now."

"So that's it? We're fired?" Albert snapped.

"I warned you up front. This duty was only temporary."

"See, I told you this would happen, Albert," Dustin said after the Sheriff walked away.

"Yeah, it sucks. So what?" Albert said, flipping his head to the side when he spoke.

An instant later, Bunker took a step forward. He leaned in close, his heated breath filling Albert's nostrils. "Like I said before, we all need to pull together. No exceptions. So I'd suggest that both of you *embrace the suck* and get those graves done before you and I have another problem. Am I clear?"

"Crystal," Dustin said, tugging at Albert's arm. "We'll get it done."

Albert didn't respond. Nor did he move, tearing Dustin's fingers from his arm.

Bunker turned and followed the Sheriff's path out of the barn. Rusty and Dicky followed him.

Bunker's odd choice of words about *embracing the suck* echoed in Albert's mind. He was certain he'd heard that phrase before. Even the tone of the man's voice rang true, anger and all.

It took a few more seconds before a visual appeared in his mind, linking Bunker's face to a name from his past. "That's it! That's where I know him from!"

Dustin's eyes lit up. "Where?"

"From LA. The Kindred biker gang. Bunch of skin heads."

"The Kindred, huh? I'm pretty sure I've heard of those guys."

"The entire West Coast has, unless you're living under a rock," Albert said, letting the memory play out in his mind. "I told you I recognized him. Though I never knew the man had hair."

"I can't imagine him bald."

"Oh, he was. Completely. Like the others. I know it was their trademark, but still. It completely changes his look."

"Those nasty scars on his neck are pretty noticeable. I'm surprised it took you so long to place him."

"He didn't have them the last time I saw him."

"Must be burn scars. I wonder what happened?"

"He didn't like the ink, that's what happened. Swastikas don't exactly get you the red-carpet treatment. Not unless you're running in the proper circles. And I'm not talking about with Wall Street types, either."

"He must have really wanted them off to put himself through that."

"Or someone did it to him."

"You mean, like against his will?"

"Yep."

"I can't even imagine what that felt like."

"Oh, and by the way, his name wasn't Bunker back then either. It was Bulldog."

"Was he a slinger?"

"Nah. Just muscle. Damn good at it from what I heard. The man had a seriously nice hog and one of the hottest girlfriends on the planet. Can't remember her name though, but she could stop traffic. We're talking USDA Prime Choice. Fake tits and all."

"Figures."

"If I remember right, he used to ride with a mouth-breather named Grinder. If those two apes showed up for a collection, someone was going down. Big time."

"What the hell is he doing here?"

"The only thing I can think of is he went rogue. Otherwise, I can't see him running without his colors, or his bike."

"Or the girl."

"Her, too. Must have had to change his name and appearance when he left."

"I'm sure he had to."

Albert nodded. "Because once you're in the brotherhood, it's damn near impossible to get out. They'll bury you first."

"You think he recognizes you?"

Albert shrugged, pondering the ramifications if Bunker had. "I never spent a lot of time with him one on one. He might remember my street name as Tin Man, but not my face."

"Tin Man?"

"Yeah, the legendary meth cook without a heart."

"That fits, I guess."

"He was always busy providing perimeter security when my crew met with his boss, Connor Watts. Now *that* guy had a seriously bad temper. It seemed like every time we had an encounter with Watts, it almost ended in a shootout. Talk about stressful."

"Now I see why you want Burt involved."

Albert patted Dustin on the back. "I'm glad you agree, because you can never be too paranoid in this business. When you step balls-deep into that world, muscle and guns are the only things that keep guys like us safe."

"It's too bad you just pissed him off. Otherwise, he might have wanted to join our little business. If I had to choose, I'd take Bunker over Burt."

Dustin was right on both counts, but Albert wasn't going to admit it. There wasn't any point. "Nah, I doubt it. He's obviously not the same man. Something's changed."

As it stood now, their future business prospects looked bleak with the Russians moving in. Access to the demand in town had been cut off, and transportation of the drugs to other cities and states would be difficult with checkpoints and roving patrols everywhere.

However, there was one alternative. If he could figure out a way to sell the crystals to the occupying force, then he could trade one set of addicts for another. It would also make him useful in the eyes of the Russians. And necessary. Both would keep him alive.

Albert had read somewhere that young, inexperienced troops are beyond anxious when in-country and living under the ever-present threat of snipers, IEDs, ambushes, and uprisings.

The unending pressure of being one of the hated occupiers takes its toll, resulting in drugs, alcohol, and women being a constant problem for their commanders. Especially since some of those same troublemakers were down on their luck outcasts, signing up to escape their past.

Our lives on this rock are a collective sum of our decisions over time, some good, others not. Those with weak moral fiber are doomed to repeat themselves, their relentless black cloud following them into service.

Let's face it, everyone needs a diversion from their own flawed existence now and then, usually when the pressure gets to be too much. That's how Albert made his living, tapping into that primal need to escape.

Sure, the article he'd read was focused on US troops overseas, but there was a chance it applied to the mighty Russian Army as well.

It's just human nature, he thought to himself.

Maybe his plans for Clearwater Red weren't dead after all.

CHAPTER 86

Several hours later . . .

Allison Rainey put a fresh towel on the floor in front of the fridge in her mother's kitchen. The defrost cycle had begun in earnest shortly after the customized backup generator Tuttle had sold her mom ran out of fuel.

Allison was certain the crotchety old fart had jacked up the price when Martha bought it from him the year prior, but the machine survived the EMP just like Tuttle claimed it would.

Yet the generator couldn't overcome the lack of fuel, despite its enhanced capabilities. That may have been the reason why Tuttle decided to sell his only generator—a move some might find strange. Then again, Tuttle was the pinnacle of strange.

At least the drip had slowed considerably since it first started, though the leak was still active, mocking her as if to say it was never going to stop. Only two dry rags remained in the laundry cabinet. Hopefully they'd be enough.

She turned her focus to the remaining dishes in the sink, resuming her casual hum to cover up what she was feeling inside. The impromptu funeral for Cowie and Franklin Atwater was finally over, and nobody was more relieved than she was.

Allison didn't know either of them well, but most of those in attendance did. Mainly Megan and Misty, their grief on full display, filling Allison's eyes with tears.

You don't have to be close with the deceased to be affected by their loved ones' anguish. It's natural to be sucked into the torment of a loss like that—unless of course, you had a heart of stone.

The new guy, Bunker, seemed to have that trait, his jaw stiff and shoulders broad. The man was a rock during the service, never leaving Megan's side the entire time.

Megan had held up fairly well during the emotional burial, but Misty was another story. The woman was a total wreck, kneeling before the grave of her dead fiancé, bawling her eyes out for what seemed like an hour. It was a tough scene to witness. For everyone.

Often times watching someone else's pain is worse than dealing with your own. Even the strongest person can break down when they see misery consuming someone they know, especially in the eyes of little ones.

The compassionate Sheriff eventually had no choice but to carry Misty across the road from Tuttle's, then haul her upstairs to Martha's bedroom. Misty fell asleep quickly, thank God, buried under a mound of covers and Kleenex.

The dishwater in the sink was no longer clean but the soap bubbles stood strong, caressing Allison's hands. The scrub rag in her hand was as dirty as the water, both symbolic of the world around them. The coldness of death had soiled a once-beautiful countryside, its relentless hunt for prey ongoing. The citizens of Clearwater were the primary targets, some more than others.

Everything was normal a few days ago, and now this—chaos and death swirling outside. However, just like her need for more water from the riser spigot outside, more funerals would be needed to cleanse the heartbreak she feared was headed to the town of Clearwater. In droves.

Megan appeared stable on the outside, but Allison could sense the child's pain. It was obvious: the girl's lingering stares at nothing. But that wasn't the only indicator. Megan's delay when answering questions was another clue. So were her occasional, random sniffs.

Megan was trying to show strength, but Allison knew it was only a matter of time before the child broke down, again.

Whenever it arrived, she prayed someone was there for her. Bunker or otherwise, it didn't matter. Megan would need a shoulder to cry on from one of the adults.

Allison might need a good cry herself, assuming the men failed in their duties to secure the area, or failed to run power from Tuttle's solar array to her mother's house, as they promised. Otherwise, the well pump would forever be useless, leaving her to fetch water the old-fashioned way.

When you've been spoiled by indoor plumbing all your life, it's difficult to go without. The same could be said for overhead lights and hot water. Oh, and a working fridge. All of it essential to feeling human.

She shook her head while her humming continued. What she wouldn't give for a hot soak in the tub right about now. Maybe a few scented candles, too, plus some classical music and a tall glass of Cabernet Sauvignon.

"Heaven in a ten-by-ten room," she mumbled.

"Thanks for the P, B and J, Mrs. Rainey," Megan said after Allison put another dish in the plastic tray on the counter. "It was good."

"Did you get enough, sweetheart?" she asked, wondering how long the ebony darling would hold it together.

"Yeah. But I'm not sure your son liked it very much. Or the new boy, Dallas."

Allison knew it couldn't have been easy for Megan when Dicky and Burt lowered the body of her father into the shallow grave behind Tuttle's barn. That type of finality really hit home, reminding Allison of her own father's funeral.

It was a little over six years ago—the entire congregation standing as one outside of the church. Once the coffin was in the hearse and it pulled away, a collective cry erupted. Watching the vehicle slowly make its way around the parking lot to the street was one of the hardest moments in her life. It was the end of her father, his remains heading down the street for cremation.

Allison broke out of her daydream and whirled around, realizing she hadn't heard the boys in the last few minutes. The two hellions were no longer in the kitchen, their chairs empty and pushed back at an angle from the table.

Their porcelain plates held partially eaten sandwiches, the peanut butter leaking out and mixing with the grape jelly in long smears. They must have snuck out while she was humming. She never heard a sound.

"Where'd they go?" she asked Megan, the girl's knee brace holding her leg straight along the side of the chair.

"I think they went to help Jeffrey get some eggs."

Allison smirked. "Oh, really now."

Her son Victor was many things, but he wasn't anything close to being helpful. Not unless he was getting paid to do so, like the last time he donned an apron and slung hash browns with her on the wood-fired grill in front of Billy Jack's Café.

It was the very same morning when Apollo snuck a twenty-dollar bill into her tip jar after the power went out. She had planned to return the money to the kindly Sheriff, but it was her only tip of the day. Everyone else seemed content to skip that part of the process, leaving her short on cash to pay for the ride home by the smelly mechanic, Burt.

Deputy Daisy walked into the kitchen with Allison's mother, Martha. Neither of them appeared gloomy or depressed, acting as if the dual funeral hadn't just happened—or a last-second shot by Bunker hadn't killed three masked men.

Allison figured the women were putting on a strong front for Megan. That, too, was human nature after a funeral, everyone preferring to move on and not dwell on the pain. No matter how traumatic the deaths, friends and family always rally around those suffering the most.

"What's wrong, Ally?" Mom asked, obviously sensing her frustration.

Allison didn't want Martha to sense her grief, so she wiped the concern from her face in an instant. She pointed at the table to change their focus. "The boys."

"I wondered how long they'd actually sit still. Looks like they hardly touched their food."

"Why am I not surprised?"

"Boys will be boys."

Daisy stood next to Allison in front of the wet dishes. "Can I help?"

Allison gave her a dishtowel to start drying. "Those two better not have gone far, or I'll have their heads."

"I'm sure they haven't," Daisy said, her tone confident and to the point. "Probably out helping Bunker and my boss."

"You know, just once it would be nice if a member of the male species did what they were supposed to do. That's all I ask. Just once. Is that so hard?"

Daisy finished another wipe down before stacking the dish on the counter. "You wouldn't think so, but we all know that's impossible when men have the attention span of a flea."

Allison laughed, bringing a twinge of peace to her heart. There's nothing quite like a fellow sister telling it like it is.

Martha took a seat at the table with Megan, choosing the chair formerly inhabited by her grandson, Victor. "You two need to relax. There are good men around; you just have to look a little harder. Sometimes it's difficult to spot the gems, with all the jerks in the way."

Allison rolled her eyes. "That's easy for you to say, Mom. You only had Dad to deal with the past forty-five years. Trying being a single mother in the world these days."

"I know, sweetheart. It's hard. But trust me, being married to your father wasn't always easy. I learned to say 'yes dear' even when I didn't want to. Remember that, girls. Once in a while, you just gotta let things go. Especially the little things."

"Different generation, Mom. Things are not the same anymore. There are no *little* things."

"You're right, the world is not the same, but people are. Sometimes, the best men are standing right there in front of you, only you're not paying attention."

"Right there in front of me? I think that's a little bit of an oversimplification. Don't you?"

"Not really. It doesn't take much to blind yourself to the answer, especially when you're focused on the wrong question."

Allison pouted, "I don't even know what that means, Mom."

There was a long pause in the room until Daisy cleared her throat. "Allison, can I ask you something?"

"Sure."

"I know you're not fond of men at the moment, but have you ever thought about getting something going with the Sheriff?"

"What do you mean? Like a date?"

"He's super sweet on you, in case you didn't know."

"Really? Gus?"

Daisy nodded, then smiled. "Why do you think he stops in every night after work to have dessert?"

"He's kinda cute and all, but I thought he just had a sweet tooth."

"Well, he doesn't. In fact, until you arrived in town, he'd been planning to get into shape and drop a few pounds."

"I had no idea," Allison said, seeing a vision of his beaming smile in her mind. He was a gentle soul, to be sure, but she'd never given him much thought. Until now. "He hardly ever says anything."

"That's because he's shy."

"The Sheriff? Shy? But he deals with people all day long."

"Yeah, he does. But don't let the badge and gun fool you. He's a big softy inside. Like a squishy teddy bear."

Allison didn't know what to say, so she said nothing.

Daisy continued. "In fact, he's one of the nicest guys you'll ever meet. Hell, if he was a little younger, I'd take a run at him myself."

"What does age have to do with anything?" Martha said from her seat.

Daisy paused before she spoke again. "It doesn't, really. But I know for a fact he only has eyes for Allison. Plus, there's the whole *no fraternization with a co-worker* regulation."

"Excuse me for saying this, Daisy," Martha said, her tone motherly, "but from what I hear, you don't exactly play by the rules when it comes to men."

"Mother!" Allison snapped.

Daisy latched onto Allison's forearm, squeezing gently. "It's okay, Allison. Everyone knows."

"I'm sorry, but sometimes my mom doesn't have a filter."

Daisy turned to face Martha, her hands working the dishtowel across a plate. "You mean Bill King?"

Stephanie walked through the back door only moments after the words flew from Daisy's lips. The conversation dried up an instant later, an eerie hush hanging in the air.

Stephanie stopped and put her hands on her hips. "You ladies were just talking about my ex, weren't you?"

Daisy nodded.

"It never ceases to amaze me how that jerk finds his way into almost every conversation. Even way out here."

"I'm sorry to bring him up, Steph. I know we had a deal."

"No, I get it. People need to gossip."

"It wasn't gossip, exactly," Allison said. "My mother was just being—"

Daisy didn't let her finish. "Actually, we were talking about the Sheriff and his crush on Allison."

"The Sheriff? Really?"

"Yep. Really."

"And Bill's name came up?" Stephanie asked, looking mystified.

"What did Mr. King do?" Megan asked, her sweet voice hanging in the air. "Was he bad?"

"Never you mind, little one," Martha said, snatching the boys' half-empty plates from the table. She grabbed Megan's, too, then carried the stack to the sink and dumped them into the brown water.

"Maybe we should talk about something else?" Daisy said to Stephanie, putting a handful of clean dishes into the cabinet.

"As long as it's not about my ex, then I'm good with it."

"I second that," Martha added.

"Then the ayes have it. Motion carried," Allison said without hesitation, beaming an ear-to-ear smile. "See now, ladies. That's how the newly formed Clearwater Women's Group handles its decisions. Collectively and without a second thought to anyone who relies on testosterone to get up in the morning, if you know what I mean."

Stephanie laughed.

So did Daisy.

Martha turned a deep shade of red before walking to the cabinet next to the leaky fridge. "Speaking of which," she said, opening the door and pulling out a box of Band-Aids. She turned to Daisy. "I think you should take these and go keep an eye on the men. Someone is bound to need one."

Daisy laughed, then took the bandages.

"At least we don't hear any power tools outside," Allison said in a sarcastic tone.

"Good heavens, can you imagine?" Martha quipped, her grin in full bloom.

"Do you remember what Dad used to say? *If I'm not bleeding, I'm not trying.*"

Martha laughed. "Yes, every time he went outside, I swear."

Allison agreed. "When I cleaned out the garage after he died, I must have found a dozen extension cords that had been cut in half by the hedge trimmer."

"It's a wonder he still had all ten fingers when we buried him."

"We cremated him, Mother."

"I know. It was just an expression."

"Sort of like my testosterone joke a minute ago."

"Yes. Exactly."

Daisy motioned with the box of bandages. "I guess I'd better get out there before someone loses a limb."

"And if they do, pick it up and smack them over the head with it," Martha said, laughing after the last word left her lips.

CHAPTER 87

Bunker waited for Rusty to step out of the way before he finished the metal tie on the barbed wire. It completed another barricade at the end of Old Mill Road. "One more set after this and we're done prepping this side of the bridge. We'll need to keep them out of the way until we're ready for final positioning."

Apollo brought another 4x4 post into position, holding it at a forty-five degree angle. Rusty bolted it to a matching piece of lumber running the opposite direction. The two posts formed the letter 'X' lying on its side. Once a pair of ends was made, they'd string wire between them to complete the barrier.

"When we're done here, I should probably get back to Clearwater," Apollo said, his voice barely above a whisper.

Bunker needed him to stick around. "You really think that's a good idea, Sheriff?"

"No. But my duty is with the town. It's my job and I should be there. With everyone else."

"It's not going to be easy to avoid the checkpoints. Probably have a number of patrols out, too. If their orders are to shoot on sight—"

"I can get him there," Burt said before Bunker could finish his sentence. "Like I said before, I know a few shortcuts. Logging roads, mostly."

Apollo seemed to like that idea. His eyes locked onto Burt's. "Tuttle has some area maps we can use to plot a course around the roadblocks we know about. Going to need everyone's input."

Bunker wasn't sure how to respond. He didn't want either of the men to take off, but knew it wasn't his place to stop them. Despite the fact that the women and children needed maximum protection.

He decided to take a neutral, noncommittal approach, giving him time to come up with a plan to change their minds. "We'll figure something out once we get the perimeter secure."

Dicky lowered his rifle slightly and glanced back over his shoulder, his eyes meeting Bunker's. The huge man sent a head nod, bringing a welcome confirmation Bunker's way.

The TrackingPoint rifle looked good in the goliath's hands, his powerful grip keeping it secure and ready to fire. Bunker didn't know the man very well, but thus far Dicky had been easy to work with. He wasn't afraid to jump in and help with any project. Or take guard duty—Dicky volunteered before Bunker had to ask.

"Is this how you made them in the Army?" Rusty asked Bunker.

"I was in the Marine Corps, not the Army. That was Megan's dad. He was a master welder, if I remember right."

"Marines, sorry."

"It's okay, kid. I knew what you meant."

"So, did you?"

"Yeah, sure. Made my share of just about everything once or twice. It comes with the job. They teach us how to defend against all kinds of threats, and not just with a rifle. My favorite part was when we needed to improvise in the field. It never ceased to amaze me what your mind can accomplish when you're desperate."

"Or hungry, I'll bet," Apollo added.

"That, or trying to avoid hypothermia. The high-altitude wilderness training was the worst. Nearly froze the boys off that first night."

"Did you ever have to shoot anybody?" Rusty asked, catching the attention of Dallas and Victor as well. They stopped their work, turning their heads to listen.

"Yes, but it's not something I like to talk about."

"That had to be pretty intense. I'm not sure I could do it."

"My guess is that you could, if you had the right training."

"Maybe. But still, pulling the trigger has to be hard."

"For some it is, but they usually get over it if they want to stay alive. We had this saying, *The more you train in peace, the less you bleed in war.*"

"Makes sense."

"And trust me, we were always training. Sometimes, that's all we did for weeks on end."

"Sounds a little boring," Dallas said.

"At times, it was. But that is what's needed to protect this country. Our government spent piles of money making sure our minds and bodies were prepared for what we had to do. In the end, you have to act without hesitation, otherwise you have little chance to survive combat. There's no time to think. It has to be second nature."

Rusty nodded, but didn't ask another question.

Bunker continued, feeling the urge to share information about his father. He wasn't sure if the compulsion stemmed from the fact that none of these boys had a father around or not. But it seemed like the thing to do. "Then there are the truly great Marines. Those with the mindset to never give up, no matter what they face. Like my father. Before he became a firefighter, he was a member of SEAL Team Two. Men like him have this switch inside that kicks in when the shit hits the fan, always driving them forward regardless of the odds. But not everyone is born to fight," Bunker said, looking down at the letters tattooed on his knuckles: B-T-F. "Only a few have what it takes."

"How do you know if you're one of them?" Rusty asked.

"That's a good question. It starts deep within, somewhere inside your core. I'm not sure how to explain it exactly, but my father knew I had it. He was on me every day, always testing me to see what I was made of."

"Sounds harsh."

"Yeah, once in a while. But a man can accomplish anything if he is willing to push himself beyond his limits. I think that type of person makes the best warrior."

"It's sort of like my racing. I have a couple of friends who take way too many days off from training. I'm always out there riding, but it seems like I'm the only one. It's almost impossible to get them out of bed and away from their girlfriends."

"Exactly. Whether it's sports or combat, those who excel are dedicated to accomplishing the mission. And to do that, you must never stop pushing the envelope."

"To find your limits."

"Yes, because you don't know your limits until you fail, and that takes blood, sweat, and tears. That's what my old man taught me."

"You were lucky to have a dad like that."

"Though I did get tired of the constant preaching and pop inspections," he said, rolling his eyes. "Especially the dreaded almond duty."

"Almond duty? What's that?"

Bunker laughed after an intense memory flashed in his mind. "Every night when my father came home after his shift at the fire station, he'd inspect the ground around the almond trees. If a single nut was on the ground, there'd be hell to pay. The type of hell would vary, but when a former SEAL is dishing it out, you can bet your ass it would be tough."

"Every almond?"

"Shell or nut, it didn't matter. The ground had to be spotless. Those trees are the reason why I hate almonds to this day. I can't even stand to look at them, let alone put one in my mouth. I swear, I had nightmares about giant almonds crushing me for years, all because of those damn trees."

"I can see why."

"As I got older, the almond inspections didn't happen as often, but the punishment for failure went up. It forced me to overcome the anxiety that came with those random inspections, devising new and better ways to keep the birds out of the trees and the nuts off the ground, even in the wind."

"Were you a SEAL, like your father?"

"I planned to be at first, but then a different specialty found me. Something with a unique challenge attached to it. I decided to become a *sapper*."

"What's that?"

"Basically, it's a combat engineer. My job was to clear the way into battle for the infantry to follow. Most of the time that meant engineering a way into the combat zone using explosives and other techniques. To get past the enemy's defenses."

"Was your dad disappointed you didn't become a SEAL?"

"If he was, he never said anything. He knew I liked to be first into the fight. So becoming a sapper seemed like the logical choice. It's an important job. One that requires you to use your brains and your balls to clear a path for those behind you. Most of the time, we'd end up fighting alongside the grunts afterward, but there's something honorable about being first man in. Plus, we got to blow shit up."

"I can see why you liked it," Victor said.

"We also spent time fortifying our base defenses, plus looking for IEDs and other booby-traps. You'd be surprised how clever those booger-eaters can be over there. Almost anything can be turned into a bomb: bicycles, sidewalks, electrical transformers—you name it. For some reason, learning all that stuff really appealed to me. I'm not sure how to explain it exactly. It just fit."

Burt Lowenstein brought another stack of 4x4 posts from the barn, each cut off at the four-foot mark. The man had some serious pipes, his biceps bulging with every movement of his arms. His sagging gut was another matter; he obviously skipped the cardio portion of his workouts.

"That should be enough, Burt," Bunker said, pointing at the spot where he wanted them.

"You know, Bunker, I was doing some thinking about those Land Rovers behind the barn. Tuttle has a seriously nice torch I could use to make some adjustments. A little fortification, if you know what I mean. There's a shitload of steel plates out back."

"Good idea, but first we need to use the Rovers to push Tuttle's old trucks into position."

"I can do that. Where do you want 'em?"

Bunker pointed to the far end of the wooden bridge. "One on each side, funneling traffic to the middle. Once the Fords are into position, disable their tires and drive trains. If you can weld some of those plates onto the door panels, it'll be extra protection in case we get in a firefight."

"Tuttle's also got an old Massey Ferguson Combine out back, if you think it'll help. That harvester is from the '60s and built like a tank, but it should still run. At least it used to the last time I worked on it for the old man."

"What about the EMP?" Victor asked.

Burt shook his head. "Should be fine. No electronics in that beast."

Bunker agreed. "Just make sure you leave a path wide enough for a horse to get through. But not too wide. I don't want any vehicles making their way across the bridge."

"Why funnel them down the middle?" Victor asked.

"For easier kill shots. We need to concentrate our firepower in one spot, if they decide to come across," Bunker said. He pointed, aiming his finger at a mighty oak tree to the right, its branches thick with leaves. "If we build a hide up there, a sniper can cover that position with the TrackingPoint rifle. However, once the enemy zeroes in, he'll need an escape route. A fast rope down the back ought to do it. That wide trunk will provide excellent cover."

"I could reinforce it with some steel for protection," Burt said. "Then our sniper might be able to take out a few more of them fuckers."

Bunker liked that idea, except for one problem. "Might be tough hauling up all that weight."

Burt didn't hesitate. "We can use Tuttle's chain hoists in the barn. Just need someone to shimmy up there with the rigging to get us started."

"I can do it," Dallas said, raising his hand to volunteer. "I climb trees all the time."

"Then we should make two," Bunker said, pointing at another oak tree.

"For crossfire," Burt added.

Bunker nodded, wishing they had two of the M1400 TrackingPoints. "Redundancy is important."

Deputy Daisy showed up with a box of bandages in her hand. She held the delivery out.

Bunker locked eyes with the capable brunette. "Are those for me?" he joked.

Daisy gave the Band-Aids to Sheriff Apollo. "Actually, they're for all of you. Compliments of Mrs. Rainey."

"Martha obviously has the utmost confidence in us," Apollo said with a slight grin, taking the gift.

"We all do. Well, sort of," Daisy said with a smile. "How's everything going out here? Need any help?"

Bunker knew her last question was coming. Daisy wasn't shy about getting her hands dirty. Or bloody, for that matter. "Sure, we can always use another pair of hands. Just working through some logistics on how best to secure the area."

"What about explosives for the bridge?" she asked. "In case our defenses don't hold."

"I was *just* going to say that," Victor said, shooting a look at Dallas.

"That's a good idea," Sheriff Apollo said. "We might get ourselves into a position where we need to blow it."

Bunker didn't agree with Daisy's idea entirely. But it had some merit. "It would have to be as a last resort. Because once we cut ourselves off from the rest of the planet, we'll have no way across the river. Like with the sniper hides, it's important that we maintain at least one escape route."

Albert and Dustin arrived with bottles of water. The first one went to Bunker, the second to Daisy. She twisted off the cap and took a swig while the fat man's attention lingered on her figure.

Bunker waited for Albert to bring his eyes to him, but he never did. Bunker got the sense that it wasn't an accident. Maybe their altercation in the barn earlier had calmed the fire inside of Albert. Bunker hoped it did. For everyone's sake.

Burt spoke next. "If we rig up some ropes, we might be able to Tarzan our way across the river. If it came down to that."

"That's a terrible idea," Albert snarled, his tone sharp.

"You don't even know what we're talking about," Burt snapped. "Why don't you go hang out with the women, where you belong?"

"Guys. Let's keep it civil, please," Apollo said.

"We'd have to hide the rope in the trees," Dicky said, breaking his silence.

"And have some way to get to them," Rusty added.

Bunker shook his head. "In theory, that might work if the enemy doesn't spot them first. Otherwise, we're defending two entry points instead of one. Either way, I'm not sure it helps the women and kids. They'll struggle to make it across."

"So will I," Albert said.

"Me too," Dustin said. "It'll take too much upper body strength."

"Well, at least some of us could get the hell out of here if the bridge is taken out. It's better than nothing," Burt said.

"How much rope do you have?" Albert asked Burt, his flabby cheeks wiggling with each syllable.

Burt shrugged, his eyebrows pinched. "I don't know exactly. It's coiled up."

"Take a guess. Are we talking a hundred feet, or what?"

"More like a thousand. Tuttle has a bunch."

"What are you thinking?" Bunker asked Albert, trying to forget the heavy man's insults from the barn earlier. It wasn't easy to let those feelings go, but he needed to take the high road.

"A suspension walkway and a catapult. But we'd need explosives and a delivery system. Something we can use to launch the ropes over the river."

Burt scoffed. "Okay, genius, how do you anchor it on the other side? It's gotta hold weight."

"They're called grappling hooks, dumbass. You *do* know how to weld, right?"

"Of course I do."

"Good. Then all we have to do is shoot a couple of ropes across with hooks to catch on the trees. Then a couple of guys crawl across with lead ropes so they can secure everything. Then we pull the rest of the walkway across. Some wood planks and a little bush engineering should do the trick. Even the women and kids could use it."

"And your fat ass," Burt said.

"Yeah. Even me. I don't think it'll be that hard, as long as we use the proper amount of explosives. Hell, I could even mix some up, if I had the proper chemicals."

"He's a chemistry genius," Dustin added, his eyes searching for someone who was listening. "Tin Man is the bomb."

CHAPTER 88

When the nickname *Tin Man* landed on Bunker's ears, a memory stirred in his mind. It was a vision from his days in The Kindred biker gang, back when he provided security for his boss, Connor Watts, whenever Watts attended a business meeting.

The drugs-for-money exchanges always took place on the south side of LA in the abandoned warehouse district. Plus, they usually involved the crew of the infamous meth cook who went by the name *Tin Man*, a legend who pioneered the formula behind the purest form of ice ever to hit the streets, Clearwater Red. Occasionally Tin Man would attend the meetings himself, passing Bunker at the checkpoint he'd set up.

Bunker studied Albert and let his eyes take in every contour of the guy's round face. He'd only seen Tin Man a couple of times, but this unimpressive deputy could be the same guy.

Bunker also needed to consider the name of the drug, Clearwater Red, and the name of the town he'd stumbled into after the train incident. Was it purely coincidence that they matched, or was it another clue?

If Albert was Tin Man, he wasn't showing any indication that he recognized Bunker, or knew his secret past. Otherwise, Albert never would've gotten in his face in the barn over grave digging duty. Only an idiot would antagonize the head of security for The Kindred biker gang and expect to live through it.

Then again, there was a rumor floating around that Tin Man was a Tae Kwon Do expert. If that was true, Albert couldn't be the legendary meth cook. A man of his size would never be nimble enough to carry out the moves required.

No, it was more likely Albert knew of Tin Man's reputation and decided to impersonate him. To what end, Bunker couldn't be sure.

It would be easy enough to test Albert's chemistry skills by having him mix some of the improvised chemicals Bunker was thinking about deploying in their fight against the Russians. Assuming it came down to that.

Of course, that test would only happen if Tuttle had the necessary materials on hand, and Bunker could find a suitable ambush point. There was a lot to figure out before he brought his ideas to the rest of the group, but at least a plan was starting to form.

"We'll need Burt to fabricate some launch tubes," Apollo said, snapping Bunker back to reality.

"Not a problem," Burt answered. "Saw some steel pipe in Tuttle's bone yard."

"There's a huge stack of old pallets we could use for the boards," Dallas said. "They're in the back, just past the pile of fifty-gallon drums and some wooden spools."

"Spools?" Burt asked.

"Yeah, the kind the cable company uses on the back of their trucks for their wire. My dad made a backyard table out of one of them. Tuttle must have been collecting all that junk for a while."

"We'll need to find a place down river a bit," Bunker said. "If we need to egress quickly, we'll want a head start and effective cover."

"Guys . . . that's all well and good, but we still need explosives," Albert added, his eyes holding onto Bunker's.

Bunker nodded, noticing the odd look from Albert. He turned his attention to Apollo. "Did you notice any when you and Daisy were taking inventory?"

"No. But it wouldn't surprise me if Tuttle has them around here—somewhere. He seems to have everything else."

"Probably hidden," Daisy added. "When I was here the first time, he hinted at a secondary bunker. Not just the one in the barn."

"I know where we can get some," Victor said.

Apollo whirled his head around to peer at the longhaired boy. "Where?"

"At the stables. I know for a fact that Atwater has a cabinet full of stuff in his store. Plus, a ton of ammo. Even some guns. Nice ones."

"How exactly do you know all that?" Apollo asked, his tone reminiscent of a detective grilling a suspect.

"Ah, well, uh," the kid stammered, fumbling the words. "I think I heard Megan talking about it on the bus. You know, before it crashed."

"So, let me get this straight . . . a little girl, who you probably don't know very well, just so happens to mention explosives, guns and ammo on the bus? Out of the blue?"

"Yeah, Sheriff. But it wasn't to me. It was to one of her friends, I think. I don't know exactly. I wasn't super close when she said it."

Apollo raised an eyebrow and then shot a troubled look a Bunker.

Daisy cleared her throat. "Excuse me, gentlemen, but I think you're overthinking the problem. There's an easier solution for an escape route."

"Oh, yeah? What's that?" Burt asked, his delivery gruff and condescending.

"Since we're in the Rocky Mountains, I'm guessing there are some trees near the ledge. I heard they grow in these parts."

"Yeah, no shit," Burt quipped.

Daisy didn't seem to care about his attitude. "Couldn't we just cut a few of them down to use as the foundation for a bridge? I'm guessing one of you knows how to chop down a tree?"

Apollo pointed at one of his newly appointed deputies. "Seems to me Dicky worked at a logging camp a few years ago. I'm sure he can handle it."

"Yes sir, I did. In Alaska. Spent three summers running chainsaws."

The expression on Daisy's face indicated she'd expected that answer. "Just make sure they land where you need them. If they're tall enough, they'll span the gap, right?"

Daisy's idea about dropping trees gave Bunker an idea. Not for their escape route, but for setting up a Russian ambush. He filed the idea away, saving it until later.

"Absolutely, they'll be tall enough," Dicky answered. "We can pre-cut most of the branches, too. Just need to make a climbing harness so I can get up there."

Burt threw out his hands. "But we still have to get across. We can't just tightrope our way over a drop like that."

Daisy's piercing eyes scanned Burt from head to toe, pausing for a moment on his well-worn shoes. "No, of course not. But if you had sections of the walkway already built, then we could just slide them into position and nail them in place as we go."

Burt didn't respond.

Daisy finished her explanation. "I'd suggest making them a bit wider than we think we'll need so they'll cover the width of the tree spacing if Dicky's aim is off a smidge. Seems easy enough, assuming there's a chainsaw around here that still works."

"Dallas and I saw a few of them in the barn on a workbench," Victor said.

Bunker looked at Burt, needing to deliver a directive while he was thinking about it. "When you're finished with the Land Rovers, we'll need to park them on the other side of the river as part of our x-fill."

"After I fortify them, I'm assuming."

"Roger that."

"Should probably hide the keys somewhere close, too."

"Actually, no. I need you to rewire them with a quick start mechanism."

"A push button type thing?"

Bunker nodded, thinking of the Humvees in Afghanistan. "We won't have time to deal with keys."

"Wouldn't that make it easy for someone to steal them?" Victor asked.

Burt motioned with two fingers. "I could design it so a pair of buttons on the radio have to be pressed while you start it."

"That's a cool idea," Rusty said. "I didn't know you could do that."

"Sure. People do that all the time. Usually when they're tired of their cars getting jacked. I'll have to run all new electrical, though. But it shouldn't be a problem."

"Tuttle has a bunch of electrical wire in his workshop," Dallas said. "Big spools of it."

A new idea flashed in Bunker's thoughts after he heard the words *big spools of wire*. "Guys, I have a slightly different idea. It's based on all of your suggestions, which were excellent by the way. Instead of dropping those trees with a chainsaw, how about we use the Massey Harvester like a winch and lower a premade walkway into position."

"Like a drawbridge," Daisy added.

"Exactly."

Burt nodded, his upper lip tucked under. "I see where you're going with this. The harvester's weight should anchor everything in place, then we use its engine and the gears on the header out front to let ropes drop the bridge into place. It'll take a lot of welding to build the framework we'll need."

"Can you do it?"

"As long as I can find the parts in the boneyard, I don't see why not. Though I'm going to need some help if I'm gonna get the sniper hides built, the Rovers fortified, and the other stuff done any time soon."

"Rusty? Victor? Dallas?" Bunker asked, flashing a look at all three kids.

"Sure, happy to," Rusty answered. The other two nodded in earnest.

"But before I do, Bunker. Can I talk to you in private?"

Bunker nodded, then the two of them stepped away. "What's up?"

Burt's eyes tightened as he spoke. "I don't mind helping out, but I don't work for free."

"I can't pay you, if that's what you're asking."

"No, not exactly. I was thinking more about a trade."

"Okay, we might be able to arrange something."

"I want the TrackingPoint rifle when this is over."

Bunker didn't like the idea, but he didn't have much of a choice. Without Burt's skills, there was little chance any of them would survive an encounter with hostiles. He held out a hand for a shake.

When Burt grabbed it, Bunker said, "Agreed."

Burt let go of his hand, but didn't return to the group. "Oh, and there's one more thing."

"What?"

"I want to be the one in the first sniper hide. If I'm building it, then I get to take out the first Russian."

"Have you taken a shot like that before? At a human target?"

"No, but I've been hunting all my life. And just so you know, I rarely miss."

"Shooting a man is not the same as taking down a deer, Burt."

"Ah, bullshit. You aim. You fire. How hard is that? Especially when it's them or us. Trust me, it won't be a problem."

Bunker disagreed, but needed to soften his objection. "I've seen stronger men than you freeze in the heat of battle. It's not as easy as you think."

"Then they were a bunch of fucking pussies."

Bunker didn't respond.

"Look, it's simple. If you want all this welding work done, then that's the deal. It's non-negotiable."

Bunker paused, needing to consider all the angles. Burt seemed sure of himself, but trusting an untrained civilian with the security of the group was not the right move.

Yet, on the other hand, the TrackingPoint rifle would greatly increase the odds of success. "Okay, you have a deal. But I'll need to bring you up to speed on that rifle. Apollo, too. It's not like anything you guys have shot before."

"Why Apollo? I thought we just agreed on me?"

"As backup. Cross-training is important."

"Fair enough," Burt said after a pause. "As long as you don't try to fuck me out of this deal."

"My word is my bond," Bunker said, following Burt back to the group. However, before he could issue the next directive, Jeffrey arrived with a basket full of eggs. "What's going on?"

"They're talking about building a drawbridge," Dallas told him.

"Cool," Jeffrey said. "I wanna watch."

Apollo shook his head. "I don't think that's such a good idea, Jeffrey. Your mother's waiting for those eggs."

"But I wanna see."

"You need to run along now, son. Let the grownups handle this."

"But Victor and Dallas aren't grownups," Jeffrey whined.

Apollo hesitated for a moment before he spoke. "No, they're not, but they're helping Mr. Bunker and me, just like you need to go help your mom. We've all got our jobs to do. And yours is to help your mother."

Jeffrey dropped his head and turned away.

Bunker noticed a brown stain on the kid's hands, and across his clothes. "Hang on, Jeffrey. What's that on your shirt?"

Jeffrey stopped his departure. "Rust."

"From what?"

"This handle thing I found in the chicken coop. I tripped over it at first."

"What kind of handle?"

"It was round and sitting on a bunch of boards."

"Stacked up boards, or were they flat?"

"Flat. Like a door. I tried to pull it up, but it was too heavy."

Bunker flashed a look at Daisy. "Secondary bunker?"

CHAPTER 89

The armed escort tugged at Seth Buckley's arm as the Mayor was led down the corridor on the third floor of the Town Hall.

General Yuri Zhukov had summoned Buckley for an unscheduled meet-and-greet. They were headed to the largest office in the building—the one at end of the hall—Buckley's former office.

The guard grabbed Buckley by the back of the shirt collar and stopped him just short of the door. An empty nameplate holder stared back at Buckley.

A crisp Russian command found its way through the door from the inside. The door flung open and the guard forced him inside with a firm jab to the back of his neck.

Buckley took an off-balance step forward, landing in the grasp of yet another guard. The trim man with a huge, mangled nose led him to the front of the desk—an expensive desk that belonged to Buckley.

A high-ranking Russian officer with thick forearms and a square jaw sat behind the work surface. His rear end was nestled in the high-back executive chair, its leather plush and inviting.

General Zhukov's head was down, buried in a stack of paperwork. His right hand was busy scribbling across the paper with a pen, while his left worked a grip training device, squeezing the spring-loaded handles in rapid-fire succession.

Despite the squeaks of metal, the time between compressions held steady at about one every half second. Zhukov's short-cropped hair may have been laced with peppered gray, but he was obviously in terrific shape—at least his hands and forearms.

Buckley wasn't sure if he should speak, so he kept quiet and took the opportunity to look around his former office. All of his belongings were missing, including plaques, awards, certificates, artwork, knickknacks, and family pictures.

The bookshelves were empty, with only a smattering of dust remaining. The credenza was now to the right and turned around against the adjacent wall, its sliding doors facing the drywall.

Both visitor chairs were gone, probably to intimidate anyone who entered, forcing them to stand with nervous legs like Buckley. Nothing looked the same except for the placement of the desk and the brand-new chair he'd ordered from Amazon two weeks prior.

Two armed soldiers stood behind Zhukov, their eyes facing the picture window. The rumble and hum of activity outside told Buckley another convoy of supply trucks had rolled into town. He figured the two soldiers were keeping an eye on the truck deployment below.

Two equipment towers rose up into view beyond the glass, each recently erected by the occupying force.

Razor sharp concertina wire and other barricades were now encircling the town, with armed checkpoints established at every entry point. Sandbags, heavy trucks, machine guns, scanning equipment, spotters, snipers, and a slew of support troops kept watch on everything. Nobody was getting in or out, not without the Russians knowing about it.

Tri-color flags hung on buildings all over town, one dangling from the arms of the mammoth bronze statue commemorating Cyrus Clearwater, the town founder.

The flag's equal-sized horizontal white, blue, and red stripes may have looked plain and non-threatening, but that was not how they felt. Sure, the former Soviet Union's golden hammer and sickle was gone. So was the red star on top, but this version of Russia's flag still carried fear for anyone unfortunate enough to be trapped under its rule.

To the left of Zhukov was another man in a drab-green military uniform, only he wasn't carrying an assault rifle like the others. His lone weapon was on his hip: a black pistol in a holster. Some kind of satchel hung across his chest, its leather strap running from upper left to lower right.

Buckley could feel the weight of the man's eyes wash over him. He checked for a nametag on the observer's shirt. However, as expected, it wasn't there. None of the Russians he'd come across had displayed any form of ID, stenciled or otherwise.

He found that odd, given the number of troops in town. They couldn't have all known each other by face, could they? He didn't think that was possible and certainly not while in full tactical gear, including helmets and sunglasses. If he was right, then they had another method of identification. Something less obvious, but reliable.

The Mayor's desk contained at least a dozen stacks of folders and three rolls of white paper—each about three feet long. Buckley assumed they were maps, with Russian lettering on the outside. He could also see a bleed-through of various colors. Some were irregularly shaped, while others were blocky. Typical of a topographical map.

Zhukov looked up, his face stiff and focused as he continued the grip training. He motioned to the man on the left to move forward, which he did, snapping to attention once he arrived.

The General gave him a command in Russian, the syllables quick and to the point. The guard gave a single head nod in response before leaving the room with a hurried step.

There was no doubt who was in charge of this occupation. Likewise, there was no doubt about the precision and planning that went into this event. Nothing seemed to be happenstance or an afterthought.

Zhukov moved the hand squeezer to his other palm, never taking a second off. He sifted through one of the stacks before pulling out several files, each one with a streak of red ink running across the tab. Other folders carried different colors: yellow, green, and blue.

Zhukov opened the first of the red-labeled folders and spun it around to face the Mayor. He cranked out a dozen more grip compressions, before he pointed and said, "Missing."

The left flap contained a photo of Daisy Clark, its edges held in place by a series of staples. She was in uniform and talking with a pair of elderly women on the street, both of whom carried shopping bags. Charmer's Market and Feed Store was the backdrop in the photo.

The right side of the folder held a light stack of papers. They'd been attached with twin hole-punches at the top and a metal fastener. If Buckley had to guess, he'd say there were about ten sheets of paper in total.

On top of the stack was a pre-printed form that featured various black-lined boxes of differing size and placement across the white. The words inside the rectangles were Russian, the strange symbols evident. So were the interspersed occurrences of the letter R, written in reverse.

Even though he couldn't read the foreign text, it was obvious the paperwork was some kind of dossier on the Sheriff's deputy. The snapshot was an action photo taken at a distance, not a still portrait as expected. Someone had been taking undercover shots.

Zhukov put the second folder next to the first and opened it, once again saying the word "missing." Like the first file, it was red-inked with a photo to the left and a writeup to the right.

Buckley recognized the full-color portrait of Gus Apollo. It was the same image of the Sheriff from the town's website. The Russians must have been trolling the Internet for information, where they grabbed the photo online.

The General continued, laying out folder after folder. Each was related to citizens he recognized: Dick Dickens, Stephanie King, Jeffrey King, Martha Rainey, Burt Lowenstein, Franklin Atwater, Megan, and the Mayor's grandson, Rusty.

Most of the images were action photos, again taken covertly at a distance. Dicky's and Burt's folders were redlined in ink, as were Daisy's and Apollo's, but the rest were color-coded in green. Buckley assumed the colors represented each person's threat level, with red being the highest.

Zhukov presented another series of files featuring residents who lived beyond the city limits, most in the surrounding forest. One was a redlined file, but the remainder were marked in green or yellow.

Another row of paperwork was put before the Mayor, this time with faces he didn't recognize. He assumed these were some of the remote families living off the grid, their photos taken in the forest.

After Zhukov stopped his presentation, he put the hand grip device down and leaned back in the office chair and said, "Need location."

Buckley hesitated. He needed to think this through. Every word he said from here on out might put people at risk.

He shrugged. "I don't know. Some of them are probably on vacation. People come and go all the time around here. It's not like we have checkpoints to log people in and out. This is the United States of America, or at least it used to be."

Zhukov brought his elbows up and put them on the armrests. He sat up with his back straight, then put his hands together and cracked his knuckles, his stare even more intimidating than before. "Location, Mayor. Now."

Buckley took a moment to study the open files once again. He noticed a few people were missing: Allison Rainey and her son Victor, plus the odd pair of temporary deputies, Albert and Dustin. They were not accounted for in the open files, either. Neither was Jack Bunker, but that wasn't a surprise since he'd just arrived after the EMP.

The incomplete set of files meant the Russian intel wasn't up to date or accurate, especially since they didn't have a folder dedicated to longtime resident and legendary fruitcake, Frank Tuttle.

Buckley wasn't sure if the Russian information gaps were a good thing or not, but it meant there was hope. They still needed him. Perhaps he could leverage their deficiencies to his advantage. To do that, he needed to play it cool and not show fear.

Zhukov snapped his finger in the air with a quick flip of his wrist.

An instant later, Buckley felt something hard press against the back of his head. He assumed the guard behind him was holding his rifle in a firing position, its sights trained on the back of his skull.

Buckley gulped, then took in a full draw of air. "As I said before, I don't know where these people are. Hell, I don't even know half of them."

Zhukov nodded at his guard, who promptly pressed the barrel of the rifle harder against Buckley's scalp.

Buckley knew that the longer he stood there in silence, the harder it was going to be to keep his panic in check. His lungs wanted to pump out oxygen at full tilt, but he managed to regain control of his breathing. "Look, General, if you shoot me, then I can't help you. And trust me, from the looks of it, you're gonna need my help."

Buckley pointed at the files on the desk to reinforce his words. "Not only with finding the missing people, but with maintaining order. People around here don't like being told what to do or where they can go. They *will* resist and I'm sure neither of us wants that. So let me help you, General. Give me some time to check around. Maybe someone knows where these people are."

Zhukov didn't answer but kept his eyes on Buckley, his face locked in a scowl. He picked up the grip trainer and went to work again with his fingers.

Buckley got the sense that these soldiers practiced their facial expressions for hours on end, all in an attempt to maximize their intimidation level without ever having to say a word. It was working, the tingle across Buckley's spine intense and growing. So was the tremble in his hands.

He brought his fingers together and began a rub—hand over hand—pretending to lather up with soap. He had no idea if Zhukov could sense his anxiety, but Buckley decided to continue his ruse.

Zhukov twitched his eyes, then sent his free hand into another stack of folders, this time pulling out a file with a streak of black ink along the tab. He stood up, his height rising several inches above Buckley's.

The General opened the file and put it on the front of the desk. The folder held two photographs, one attached to the left and one to the right. Buckley didn't see any paperwork associated with either image—just the snapshots.

Zhukov jammed his index finger into the photo on the left. As usual, the general kept his words to a minimum. "Identify."

Buckley studied the image. It was an overhead shot of some kind of forest camp. He counted six small buildings spread out across the landscape. Shacks possibly, he couldn't be sure.

He also thought a broken-down windmill was present, not far from two people near the entrance to one of the structures. The pair were standing apart, on either side of what he assumed was the door. Both of them had dark hair and clothing, and looked to be carrying rifles in their hands.

Buckley moved his eyes to the photo on the right. It was a snapshot of the same scene, only this time the camera's focal point was much tighter and held in a zoom, yielding a grainy portrayal of the two unidentified individuals. Their faces were blurry from the resulting pixilation, but the shadows told him one of them was shorter than the other.

A man and woman, he surmised, noticing the longer hair on the smaller figure. The man had dark splotches on his forearms. He thought the duo might be Bunker and Daisy.

Behind them was another figure several yards away, only this person wasn't standing. Buckley could see an outline of legs and arms surrounded by a brown and green fuzz. Someone must have been lying in the grass.

Buckley flipped the image up to see if another photo might be stacked underneath. There was. Again, it showed the same camp from altitude, only this time there were five people in front of the shack. One of them might have been a kid based on the much shorter length of the shadow. Wait, check that, two of them were children.

The person lying in the grass hadn't moved despite all the activity. Must have been a corpse. Or a very patient sniper.

Buckley brought his eyes to the Russian commander. "What am I looking at here? Where is this?"

"Camp. Identify," Zhukov said, sounding impatient.

Buckley shrugged. "Can't see their faces. Could be anyone."

Zhukov grunted, but didn't respond.

Buckley decided to continue, wanting to show confidence and strength. "You're going to need better satellite photos than this, General. Otherwise, I can't help you." He wanted to take a shot at the Russians for their inferior technology, but decided against it.

He knew US satellites could zoom in on a squirrel's penis from a hundred miles up, a fact he assumed the General knew all too well. Rubbing it in would accomplish nothing, other than getting him shot.

"From drone. Not satellite," Zhukov said, tossing the grip tensioner onto the desk again.

"Still, I can't see anything."

After a two-count, the General looked at his guard and motioned to the right with his head. The metal against Buckley's head pulled away, but the guard didn't, his boots still visible behind Buckley's polished dress shoes.

The door to the office swung open and in walked the observer from before. He wasn't alone. A female soldier was following close behind—a slender blonde with soft eyes and a petite, sculpted nose.

She was devastatingly pretty, despite the lack of makeup. Her cheekbones were her most noticeable feature, defined and alluring. So were her shapely lips and bronze skin. If he didn't know she was Russian, he would have taken her to be a Brazilian goddess. Someone you'd see dancing half-naked on a street during Carnival.

The blonde came forward with a field radio in her hand and put it on Zhukov's desk. The General had a short conversation with her in Russian, after which she turned to face Buckley. "General Zhukov would like me to translate for him. He finds English to be torture for his tongue." Her words were crisp and easy to understand.

Zhukov immediately snapped at her, his eyes fierce.

Her face tensed as she stammered to get the words out. "I misspoke, Mayor. The General finds English distasteful and inefficient."

"Okay, sure. I get it. Whatever the General needs," Buckley answered. "I have to say, your English is excellent."

"I studied English for three years at the university in Kiev."

"They taught you well."

"Thank you. The General arranged it for me. I owe him my career."

"I'm Mayor Seth Buckley. Pleased to meet you," he said in a friendly tone. Despite his trepidation, he thought it best to stay cordial and establish a possible friendship. Yet it didn't seem appropriate to offer his hand for a shake, so he kept it at his side.

She gave him a single head nod and a slight smile. "Valentina Zakharova, Communications Officer."

Zhukov interrupted the pleasantries with a two-minute diatribe filled with hand gestures, obviously frustrated about something. His eyes dropped to her small but shapely chest, lingering for a full second before they focused on something else.

Valentina nodded at her boss before speaking to Buckley. "General Zhukov has sent out patrols to locate the missing residents. It would be helpful if you could assist in the search by providing coordinates of each person's current location. Your assistance would help keep the situation calm."

Buckley shook his head. "Good thing you're here to translate because the General must not have understood me earlier when I said I don't know where they are. People come and go all the time around here. This is Colorado, not Russia. We don't keep tabs on everyone."

Zhukov responded in Russian.

Valentina translated. "The General says he understood you perfectly. However, he doesn't believe you. You are the Mayor and in command of this town."

Buckley couldn't hold back an involuntary snort. "In command? Me? Hell, half the people didn't even vote for me. If it weren't for a few extra votes in the runoff election three years ago, Billy Jack would have been elected Mayor, not me. So no. I'm not in command. Not like the General thinks. I wish I could help, but I can't."

"I understand. I will relay to the General that you refuse to cooperate."

His chest tightened before he threw up his hands. "Wait! Wait! That's not what I said. I'd like to cooperate, I just don't have the information he's looking for."

She paused, blinking her pleasant eyes as she stared with intensity at something over his left shoulder.

Right then, the hairs on the back of Buckley's neck sent a shiver down his shine when he realized she was looking at the guard behind him.

He sucked in a short gulp of air and held it as he followed her gaze to check the location and status of the guard behind him.

The slender man hadn't moved, still holding the same position as before. Buckley wasn't sure why she was looking at the guard in that manner. Must be her concentration look, he figured, letting out the breath from his lungs.

The observer in the corner walked to Valentina. He leaned forward to whisper something into her ear in Russian. She nodded a few seconds later, then spoke to Zhukov, though the length of her communication seemed to be twice as long as what Buckley had just told her about his desire to cooperate.

Perhaps she was adlibbing. Hopefully for the better, trying to get his point across to the short-tempered General. Then again, the observer had just intervened with the murmur in her ear. Who knew what he told her?

When she finished relaying her message, Zhukov scoffed before he shot out from behind the desk. He began to pace the room, his hands locked together behind his back. At the end of each run, he'd look at Valentina and hold her eyes, like a father deciding on a punishment.

Buckley kept an eye on the deliberate steps of the commander, waiting for the man to say something. Buckley thought he'd been believable and had laid out a good case for his continued involvement. However, with legendary Russian arrogance filling the room, there was no way to know how the General might react.

It was also possible that Zhukov knew more than he was letting on. If that were true, then this was probably some kind of test. A test Buckley might have just failed by holding back key information.

Those drone photos could have been part of Zhukov's fishing expedition, only showing Buckley the long distance, grainy shots to sample his willingness to help. The test theory would explain why the Russian tech seemed inferior, when in fact it wasn't.

Then again, maybe the shots weren't taken from a Reaper-type, high altitude attack drone. It could have been one of the smaller, portable copter-types. If so, then maybe it was hovering at high altitude and those images were the best it could generate. That alternative explanation made sense as well.

Regardless, Buckley could have made an educated guess as to the whereabouts of the residents in the photos. Even though he didn't know the exact location of the missing persons, he could have sent the Russian patrols in the right direction. Or offered up Daisy and Bunker as the armed persons in the camp photos.

He weighed the odds of each of his theories as the General made his fourth pass. His gut was telling him that the Russians were actually in need of help. Otherwise, he'd be dead by now. A Russian commander doesn't have one of his guards hold a gun to a prisoner's head and then not pull the trigger when the answer isn't what he was expecting.

No, they needed him alive. He was almost sure of it. Someone had to fill the obvious gaps in their intel, and he was the best candidate. That's why they brought in the Mayor of Clearwater. The commander of the town in their eyes.

If Buckley could prove his value, the occupiers might bring him into their inner circle. He knew they'd never trust him, but maybe he could pick up some cross talk or hints about their plans. Then he'd need to figure out a way to get a message to the Sheriff, Daisy, or Bunker. Assuming any of them were still alive.

Part of him hoped his friends had decided to head away from Clearwater. Somewhere safe and not within the reach of the Russians. However, his gut knew better. Those three would never abandon the town. Or their friends. Even Bunker—the man he knew the least about.

Zhukov stopped his pacing and returned to the desk. He sat down in the swivel chair and spoke to the observer at length. The observer nodded mostly, but he did get in a few words before he turned and headed for the office door. A few seconds later, the man was gone from sight, the sound of his boots making quick work of the hallway outside.

The General brought his focus to Valentina. She stepped forward, her posture snapping to attention. Zhukov relayed his orders; her eyes locked and focused.

When the General finished speaking, he waved a quick hand at her before turning his attention to the paperwork on the desk. The man's eyes never came Buckley's way, almost as if Buckley wasn't standing in the room.

Valentina spoke to the guard, again in Russian, then turned her stunning face to Buckley, pausing before she spoke. "The guard will escort you out of the building."

The guard latched onto Buckley's arm.

Buckley tried to pull away, but couldn't. "So that's it? We're done here?"

She gave him a single head nod. "The General is a busy man. You are dismissed."

The guard spun Buckley around and hauled him toward the office door.

Buckley glanced back at Valentina, hoping to glean some information from her before he left his former office.

Valentina's beauty was on full display, filling the room with splendor, but that's where the information ended. Her eyes were devoid of emotion, not giving up a single detail or any impression he could use.

He should have expected as much. These Russians were cold, calculating, and well-trained.

The guard brought him through the door and into the all-white hallway he knew all too well. He'd traveled this same corridor a thousand times before, only this trip was different. He'd just failed biblically. Sure, he'd taken this walk after a failure many times, but never after a fiasco that might affect the lives of everyone in town—and a few who weren't.

He thought he'd kept his cool and played the situation correctly. The Russians' failure was a clear opportunity to work himself inside, but apparently his tactics were wrong. He must have missed something. A hint. A phrase. A look. Otherwise, the guard wouldn't be pulling him along like a prisoner heading for the gallows.

Just then, Bill King appeared at the far end of the corridor. A guard was escorting him as well, but they were heading the opposite way.

The facts lined up in an instant. General Zhukov must have summoned the Silver King Mine owner to his office. A man who would do anything to save his own ass. Or the ass of someone he cared about. Like his son Jeffrey.

A twinge hit Buckley's chest after he realized what he'd missed. The Russians didn't need to rely on him after all. There was another person in town with the stature, the brains, and the balls to work out a deal, and probably sell out everyone else in the process.

The adrenaline soared in Buckley's veins, giving him the strength to pull free from the guard. He flew at King and pushed the slender blond man against the wall with the force of a linebacker taking down a quarterback.

King's back smacked into the wall with a thud.

Buckley's chest was pumping with fire when he looked up and let the words fly from his lips. "Don't you dare, Bill!"

King grunted, then brought his hands up in an attempt to free himself from Buckley's grip, but his effort failed.

Buckley felt a strength he'd never felt before, wanting to pull back a fist and land a punch in the center of this man's face. He wasn't sure where this anger was coming from, but it was long overdue. "You can't do this, Bill! Those are our friends out there! People you've known a long time!"

"Yeah, and one of them is my son."

The guards pulled them apart, tossing Buckley to the floor in a heap. His shoulder slammed into the base of the wall, sending a sting of pain into his body.

King adjusted his shirt collar, while shooting a look of superiority down at Buckley. The man turned and continued his trek to the General's office with determination in his step.

Valentina was in the hallway, just outside the office door. She must have seen everything, yet her face looked numb. Almost like she'd expected the altercation to happen.

CHAPTER 90

Bunker waited for Sheriff Apollo to pull open the wire mesh door of the metal fencing that surrounded the chicken coop in Tuttle's back yard. Once the hole was large enough, Bunker slipped inside the structure Tuttle had built as a Faraday cage.

Daisy was right behind him, the two of them heading for the secondary door that led to the actual chicken coop.

The birds went wild as two sets of legs invaded their space, clucking and running in random directions. Bunker couldn't believe the raw pandemonium, wings flapping and feathers flying.

"Can you imagine doing this every day?" he asked after his mind flashed a scene of old man Tuttle hobbling his weary bones through the two sets of doors.

Chickens are a high maintenance food source that require regular attention. Building a secondary cage around the coop made little sense, not when you must feed, water, and fetch eggs daily. That's what a normal person would think. Of course, not everyone in Clearwater saw Tuttle as normal. He was anything but.

However, the farther Bunker dug into Tuttle's life, the more he believed Tuttle wasn't simply a crazy old man like everyone thought. A *mad genius* might be a better term, even if Tuttle had a tendency to go overboard.

The working theory was that Tuttle had built this wire structure to appear crazy, when in reality he was hiding something. Something important enough to bury under a mound of chicken shit. On face value, the idea seemed absurd, but after Jeffrey showed up with rust on his hands, they decided to investigate.

Bunker figured Apollo was thankful for his wide hips and extra girth, relegating him to doorman duty since he'd never fit. Yet, given the look on Apollo's face, Bunker was sure the Sheriff wished his nose wasn't downwind. The stench of feces was strong, permeating the yard.

Daisy tapped Bunker on the arm and pointed to the left. "Jeffrey said it was over there, near the watering station."

When a rooster came at Bunker with its beak in attack mode, he swatted at it with a backhand. The bird dodged the swipe, but didn't back down. It came at him repeatedly, each time landing a blow near the bandage wrapped around Bunker's forearm. "Damn, El Chappo is pissed."

Apollo laughed.

"Maybe I can herd him into a corner. Hang on," Daisy said, moving her feet quickly with hands outstretched. The bird changed direction and ran the other way.

"See if you can keep him there," Bunker said, sending his hand into the straw. He fished in the sticky mess until he found a ring of metal, then reported, "Got it!"

A second later Bunker had the door open, its hinges complaining in a squeal of metal on metal. The straw and other clutter clung to its surface, no doubt held in place by the abundance of excrement.

Even if the man in black hadn't gunned down Tuttle, Bunker didn't think the chicken coop would've been kept any cleaner. There had to be a month's worth of crap on the floor, literally. Given the mess inside the home, Tuttle obviously didn't prioritize neatness. It was going to take a firehose and a scrub brush to clean off his shoes.

"What's down there?" Apollo asked.

"Not sure. Can't see the bottom. The hatch is angled."

Daisy joined Bunker, her eyes focused on the opening below with her hands on her hips. "Huh, not what I expected. I figured there'd be a regular ladder like what we found with the weapons cache. Not those metal rungs."

"It reminds me of a submarine hatch I once climbed into, though this one doesn't smell like the ocean."

She laughed. "Yeah, I'm guessing there weren't too many chickens onboard a sub."

He smiled, feeling the need for a little humor. "Well, not the kind that still have their heads."

"Do you think he stocked this one with guns and ammo, too?"

"Probably. You never want to keep them all in one place." Bunker bent down and knocked on one of the all-white walls. A deep-toned hollow sound answered back, his knuckle test vibrating across the steel. "Just what I thought."

Daisy knelt down and ran her fingers across the metal. "Nice powder coat."

He nodded. "Some serious cash went into this."

"Prefabricated?"

"That would be my guess. Rust-proof and air-tight."

"What else do you think is down there?"

"Only one way to find out," he said, holding out his hand. "Ladies first."

She shook her head. "Not today, Bunker. Age before beauty."

"Well then, I guess we have more chickens running around here than I thought."

She smacked his arm with a light swat. "Hey watch it, buddy. El Chappo's not the only one who bites."

Bunker couldn't hold back a grin. "Promises. Promises."

Daisy didn't answer.

Bunker let go of his smile, then turned his attention to the trap door when something new caught his eye—something he hadn't noticed before—a steel plate underneath, glued to the boards instead of screwed.

He wasn't sure why Tuttle decided to give the illusion the door was made of wood, but he was happy to see a trio of hydraulic-assisted hinges connecting the thick plate to the walls. Otherwise, the door would have been much harder to open and more dangerous when someone climbed down—like him.

"Watch the door for me," he told Daisy, swinging around to put a foot on the top rung of the down ladder.

She held the door as he descended using the thirty all-white metal rungs, each welded to the walls and spaced about a foot apart.

If he had to guess, he'd estimate the walls to be running at a thirty-degree angle. The design made the climb safer but seemed to be a waste of engineering. A vertical shaft would have been much more efficient and easier to build, especially for something buried thirty feet deep.

The instant his foot landed at the bottom, a series of lights snapped on behind him. He found himself standing on a wood plank in an eight-foot tall tunnel made of corrugated steel. It looked like a giant culvert—the kind of pipe you'd find buried under a roadway to carry runoff water from one side to the other.

He was at the far end of the tunnel, where a bright yellow sign had been hung on the wall next to the ladder. It was about a foot wide and had a set of black, upside-down triangles and the words FALLOUT SHELTER stenciled on it.

A hand-carved wooden plaque hung to the right of the warning sticker. It said *MUD ROOM*.

Directly behind him was a single showerhead hanging from the ceiling. It was centered over a drain in the floor. The words "Decontamination Station" flashed in his mind.

To the right was a stainless steel, thirty-gallon garbage can with a lid on it, plus a whiskbroom and dust pan. Beyond the dust pan was a two-foot piece of plywood with a dense patch of nails sticking up in the center, their tips covered in dried clumps of mud.

"Wait, that can't be right," he muttered. There was no mud above the hatch—only chicken crap, so mud couldn't have been on the nails. That meant it was dried shit, scraped off by Tuttle after running his shoes over the sharp points.

Bunker took advantage of the bed of nails to rid his shoes of a sticky layer of feces, then washed them off with a blast of water from the showerhead. He used the broom and dustpan to quickly sweep up the mess he'd made, then walked across the wooden plank posing as a floor. His destination—the other end of the tunnel.

The corrugated steel corridor came to a stop at a two-way junction. His choices were to turn left or right, then take another corridor like the one he was in.

The two connecting tunnels had overhead lights, each appearing to be about twenty yards in length. He figured they took another sharp turn at the far end, but he couldn't see it from his position.

Bunker returned to the down ladder and craned his neck up. "You gotta get down here and see this."

Daisy climbed down in seconds, her face smothered with anticipation when she arrived. "What is this place?"

"Some kind of underground bunker. I'm not sure if Tuttle built this himself or not, but it looks to be huge."

She held out a hand. "Lead the way."

He pointed to the nails and then the showerhead. "You might want to clean off your shoes first. Close quarters and all."

Daisy did as he suggested before they ambled to the two-way junction, with Bunker leading the charge. He went left and walked to the far end of the connecting tunnel, where it took a ninety-degree turn to the right as expected.

When Bunker found the end of the next tunnel, he came upon a closed door. But not just any door. This was a sealed hatch, much like what you'd find between compartments on a nuclear submarine.

He grabbed the handle in the middle and spun it until the door released. He pushed it open and went inside, stepping over the lower edge of the bulkhead.

The next section wasn't round like the tunnels. It was rectangular and spacious, with heavy beams supporting the steel walls and ceiling in two-foot increments—no doubt engineered to support the weight of the dirt outside.

"Holy crap!" Daisy said after she stepped through the hatch and found her way next to Bunker.

"That's an understatement," Bunker said, taking in the scene before him. The walls and ceiling might have given off an ugly industrial look, but the rest of the space was better appointed and modern. Well, Frank Tuttle's version of modern.

Plush, tan-colored carpet covered the floor from wall to wall. In the middle of the room were a pair of leather couches and a love seat. Three La-Z-Boy chairs completed the seating area, along with two floor lamps and a central coffee table, complete with a glass top. The eight-foot-long dining table in the far corner was a nice touch. So was its overhead chandelier and stable of high-back chairs. A stereo system and flat panel TV hugged the wall in front of the couch, providing a prime viewing angle.

There was even a fancy, curved bar in the corner. The mirrored wall behind it held a shelf full of booze. Bunker counted at least twenty bottles, mostly whiskey based on their familiar labels.

Rows of glasses hung upside down from a wooden rack, directly above a handful of knickknacks sitting on the bar's surface. One of them was a miniature statue of a fat man wearing a white apron. Below the figurine was a placard that said, "Frank's Bar and Grill."

"Now this is what I call a man cave," Bunker said, his tone energized. "Cave being the operative word."

The black and white artwork on the walls failed to match the expensive carpet and modern furnishings. They were military photographs from the 1940s, if Bunker had to guess, each protected in a simple wooden frame.

The action scenes were all different but portrayed the same theme—a beach landing, with troops and equipment storming the sand.

The massive room reminded Bunker of Senator Gray's game room in Laguna Beach, California. He'd only been to the career politician's house on Rivera Drive once with his boss, Connor Watts, but it was a memorable visit. If Bunker remembered correctly, the Senator purchased the mansion for sixty million and wasn't shy about sharing that fact with just about everyone he met.

Bunker spent most of that night standing watch outside of the home, while Watts and Gray drank copious amounts of alcohol and smoked Cuban cigars in celebration of their newfound alliance. When the two-man party was over, Bunker hauled his boss back to their clubhouse to sleep off a wicked hangover.

Tuttle's country version of the Senator's room was almost as nice, if Bunker chose to ignore the bland steel construction. Oh, and the black and white artwork. Senator Gray preferred Picassos.

Bunker and Daisy continued forward, passing the seating area before opening the hatch on the opposing wall. They went through another tunnel that took them to the sleeping quarters.

This section was round and made of corrugated steel like the connecting tunnels, only triple the diameter. Its layout was much more efficient than the living room, with three sets of bunk beds lining the walls on both sides.

Daisy hesitated for a second, pointing at each bunk bed in rapid succession. "This sleeps, what? Eighteen?"

"Tuttle must have been expecting company."

She fiddled with the mattress on the upper bunk closest to her. "The kids are gonna love this."

Just past the third set of beds was a shower, tub, and dual toilets. None of them had privacy walls or curtains.

Bunker pointed at the first toilet. "Yeah, but I'm not so sure about this. I don't know about you, but certain things need to be done in private."

"I won't argue with you there."

The next compartment was the kitchen. It wasn't nearly as spacious as the main room, but featured top-of-the-line Viking appliances and a matching full-sized, built-in double-door fridge—all of them Cobalt Blue.

"I don't know who designed this place," Daisy said, "but I would've added in more counter space and storage. Feeding eighteen people won't be easy."

Bunker pointed at the intersecting point of two of the floorboards. "Looks like storage is underneath."

Daisy bent down and put the tip of her finger inside a plastic recess taking the place of one of the corners. She pried the floorboard up, revealing a two-foot-wide storage space underneath.

Inside were at least two dozen #10 long-term food cans lying on their side with labels facing up. Mostly pasta and potatoes, though there were a number of veggies, too.

Bunker turned the knob on the faucet in the sink and ran his hand under the stream. "Instant hot water. Nice touch."

"I got first dibs on the tub," Daisy quipped. "Heaven knows I need a bath."

Bunker laughed. "You mean the tub without a curtain?"

"Yeah, we'll have to solve that little problem first."

"If not, we can find a volunteer who'll gladly stand guard for ya. I'm pretty sure Albert's been checking you out."

Her face went tense as she wagged her index finger at him. "Oh, don't even go there, Bunker. Not unless you wanna see me pull my gun again."

Bunker smiled, then opened the door to the fridge. He scanned its interior. The shelves were stocked, but not with food. Bottled water and cans of beer were the only two items. The contents of each shelf alternated from one type of beverage to the other, filling every square inch with inventory.

"The man obviously loved his beer," Daisy said in a jovial tone.

"Don't we all."

"At least it's not that crappy light beer. Might as well drink water at that point."

Bunker appreciated her taste for what he considered God's beverage. Though he did enjoy his share of whiskey, too. "Nothing quite like a cold one. Especially on a hot summer day."

She put her hand inside and snatched a can, then held it in his direction. "My treat."

His mouth watered when he thought about popping the lid and downing it quickly. The cool mountain freshness of this particular brand would have been heaven. "Nah, I'll pass. We got too much work to do. Need to stay sharp. Maybe when this is all over, we can indulge in some serious brain cell killing. But for now, we need to keep moving."

Daisy put the can back on the shelf and grabbed two bottles of water. She gave one of them to Bunker. "I figured as much. But I needed to be sure."

"So, what? That was a test?"

"Yeah, but not just for you," she answered, removing the cap and taking a few swigs of water.

"I see. You wanted to slam one, too."

"Was thinking about it."

Bunker took a drink, swallowing hard in preparation for another round. "Like I said, later."

She paused, tilting her head a bit. Her eyes ran soft before her lips grew into a smile. "It's a date, then."

"Copy that," he said, holding back the rest of what he wanted to say. He took a step toward the next compartment, but stopped his feet when he noticed the puzzled look on Daisy's face. "Something wrong?"

Her eyes darted around the kitchen. "Can I ask you something?"

He worried it was going to be a personal question after her comment about a date. "Yeah, shoot."

"How exactly did Tuttle get all this stuff down here? It's not like the fridge or stove could fit through that hatch."

"Good question. Must be another entry point somewhere."

"Yeah, maybe," she said, pausing. "But he still couldn't have hauled them down the narrow tunnels. Or pushed them through those bulkheads. They're too small."

She was right, leaving only one answer. "Must have been pre-installed before they lowered this section and buried it."

Daisy nodded. "Makes sense."

"I'm sure that's why he spent the money on these high-end appliances."

"Because replacing them would be next to impossible."

Bunker agreed. "He needed stuff that would last."

They continued their exploration of the subterranean base, working their way out of the food prep area through another airtight blast door.

Tuttle had planned this horseshoe-shaped complex well, every section spaced out and protected from the previous. It was almost as if he was expecting some kind of catastrophic event to take place underground.

Whether that be a fire, a virus, invasion, or something else, Bunker wasn't sure. The fire extinguishers hanging on the walls before and after each blast door had him leaning toward fire. Regardless, he was impressed with Tuttle's madness. A madness masquerading as genius, if Bunker chose to look hard enough.

After a ninety-degree right turn, they traveled into another rectangular section containing a generous supply of equipment and hardware—both large and small—everything from nuts and bolts on up to refrigerators. A workbench sat to the right, with a sheet of pegboard hanging behind it on the wall. Hand tools, saws, and tape were the most prevalent items, each hanging from a hook.

"Looks like you were right," Daisy said, moving her feet toward the stack of Cobalt Blue appliances in the corner. Tuttle had two of everything. "These are the same models we saw in the kitchen." She looked at the blast door again, her hands up and spaced apart. "Still won't fit."

"He's using them for parts."

She nodded after a short pause, then her voice dropped in pitch and developed an accent, as if she were trying to imitate a country man. "A man's got to have backups, Daisy."

He laughed, appreciating her theatrics. "Tuttle?"

"Yeah. Something he said to me a few days ago."

"Well, he's right. Redundancy is important."

"He obviously believed it."

"I can't imagine how long he's been at this."

"Or how much he spent."

"I guess when you live alone and never leave your homestead, you can get a lot of work done."

"If the walls don't start talking to you first," she said, laughing.

Electrical panels covered the wall opposite the bench, with a handful of conduit piping linking them together. The three Tesla Powerwall v2.0 battery units installed down the center caught his attention. "I was wondering when we'd run into his battery array. Looks like he went all out."

Daisy didn't respond, her head down and feet moving for the exit door of the section. He wasn't sure if something was pulling her forward, or she simply wasn't interested in Tuttle's tech. Either way, he decided to follow her lead.

The next corridor had a blast door at the far end as expected. However, this tunnel had a feature not found in the others—a junction at its midpoint. It branched off to the left, which was odd since every turn they'd taken since the first intersection was a ninety-degree right. Bunker assumed the series of right turns would complete a closed horseshoe shape that would take them back where they started.

"Hmmm. I wonder what's down there?" Daisy asked, standing shoulder to shoulder with Bunker.

"If I had to guess, another way out. The main hatch can't be the only access point. Not if Tuttle planned this as well as I think he did."

"Which way should we go?"

"Straight ahead. Let's see what's in the next compartment. If my bearings are correct, it's the last section before we head back to where we started."

She marched ahead without hesitation, her hands making quick work of the spin wheel in the center of the door. She opened it.

Bunker waited for her to step inside, but her feet didn't move. He put a hand on her shoulder, letting her know he was in position and ready to proceed. She still didn't advance. "Something wrong?"

She nodded with her knees locked, her eyes never wandering from the view into the next room. "Uh . . . we might want to take a minute and think about this."

Bunker pushed in next to Daisy, leaning past her arm. He peered inside, his vision filling with stacks of wooden crates and barrels—dozens them—each with black lettering stenciled on their sides.

It took a few seconds for his brain to catch up to what his eyes were reporting: TNT, gunpowder, charcoal, and Tannerite.

When his mouth finally joined the party, he said, "Now that's a stockpile."

Bunker stepped over the bulkhead and took position to the right. He wanted to swing his head around to check on Daisy, but couldn't pry his eyes from the four containers labeled IMX-101.

It wasn't long before he heard footsteps coming his way, then a rustle of air wandering in from the left.

"What's IMX?" she asked.

"If I'm not mistaken, it's a new high-grade explosive I've read about. Something new since I served."

She took a step toward the door. "Sounds dangerous."

"Actually, just the opposite. It stands for Insensitive Munitions Explosive. The Army wanted something much more stable in their arsenal. But I didn't know it was already in the field."

She bent down and picked up a series of clear plastic bags, each filled with powder inside. "What's all this for?"

Bunker could see their labels as she picked them up in pairs: Red Iron Oxide Fe2O3, Barium Nitrate BaNo3/2, Sulfur, Potassium Nitrate KNO3, and Aluminum Power, 30 Micron. "Base chemicals to mix, in case he ran out of the final product."

"You can buy all this stuff?"

"Everything but the IMX. It's military-issue only."

"How did Tuttle get his hands on it?"

"He couldn't. Not unless he had a source inside the Army."

"Or former Army. Like Franklin," Daisy said.

"I suppose, but that would mean they were involved in some kind of black market sales of munitions. Does that sound like them?"

She paused for a moment, then shook her head with vigor. "Tuttle was a little unhinged, but he wasn't a criminal. Neither was Franklin."

"Are you sure?"

Her eyes lit up. "Positive. There's no way either of them was an arms dealer."

Bunker couldn't stop the next set of words from leaving his lips. He felt compelled to take a shot at his own past. "Sometimes, people aren't what they appear to be. Even close friends."

"Yeah, I know. Tell me about it," she said in a steady tone, raising one eyebrow in the process. "But not Tuttle and Franklin."

"Then this must be something else."

"It has to be," she added.

"At least now we know why he designed this place with the blast doors," Bunker said, taking an unplanned step toward the first container of IMX. He didn't know why, but he suddenly felt the need to check its contents.

Daisy grabbed his arm, stopping his advance with a firm squeeze. Her tone turned deliberate, matching the intensity in her eyes. "Maybe it's time we head out, Jack? This stuff could be unstable."

Bunker let her words soak in and resonate, his mind still churning through the potential uses of the IMX. Her concern was understandable, not having his experience around explosives.

The desire to inspect the stash vanished from his chest. "You're right. This can wait."

She nodded, her eyes turning soft. "We need to check that connecting tunnel, then get back to the Sheriff. I'm sure he's starting to wonder what's going on down here."

Bunker agreed, reversing course. He led the way out of the chamber, taking a quick right at the midpoint of the previous tunnel.

A chemical odor hit his senses about halfway to the next blast door. He stopped and held up a closed fist out of habit. "Do you smell that?"

"Yeah, chlorine," Daisy said after a hand came up to her nose. "But why would Tuttle have chlorine? It's not like he has a pool."

"To decontaminate water, among other things."

"He must have a lot of it," she said, blinking a few times before she spoke again. "Maybe we should turn around?"

He thought about it for a moment, but his curiosity overruled his logic. "You wait here. I'll check it out."

She didn't argue. "Be careful."

The chlorine scent continued to grow, but it wasn't enough to stop his advance. In fact, the increase was only a slight amount, making him wonder if the odor had drifted into the hallway from its source.

However, that theory didn't make sense, not with a closed door in front of him. The seals should have kept the smell from seeping into the tunnel, assuming it was an airtight door.

If he was correct, then only one explanation remained—someone must have moved through here recently, bringing along the chlorine cloud. Probably from the supply room he figured was on the other side.

He opened the door and stepped inside to find another mud room, about half the size of the first one they'd encountered beneath the chicken coop. As expected, a series of metal rungs led up to the surface at a thirty-degree angle. This room also had a decontamination shower, but the shoe-scraping board with nails was missing.

"A second entrance," he mumbled before calling out to Daisy. She came to his position in seconds.

He pointed at the ladder. "The chlorine is up there."

"Wait a minute," she said, taking a step back. "If these doors are sealed—"

"My thoughts, exactly," he said, stopping her in midsentence.

"Then someone else was just down here."

"One of the boys, I'm guessing. You know how they like to explore."

Bunker climbed the ladder and opened the hatch at the top. The chemical smell tripled as soon as the air from above landed on his nostrils. He minimized his breathing while climbing out. Daisy was right behind him, her shirt collar pulled over her nose.

A small wooden shed about eight feet across and just as wide surrounded them. Sunlight poured in through a series of cracks in the boards along two of the walls, showering the room with streaks of light.

Bunker took a visual inventory, counting seventeen buckets of chlorine tablets, twenty-two gallons of liquid chlorine, and sixty bottles of pure ammonia. All of them pushed up against one of walls.

Daisy pointed at the exit door, her eyes watering. She coughed. "Let's get out of here."

Bunker agreed and followed her through the door where a grassy pasture met his feet.

The back of Tuttle's trailer was a least a hundred yards away, with the pole barn standing proudly to the right. The chicken coop was on the left as expected, confirming Bunker's suspicions about the horseshoe shape of the underground complex.

The Sheriff and several others were huddled around the chicken coop, their backs to him. Two of the gawkers were Victor and Dallas. He figured one or both of them had just been in the escape hatch.

"That was intense," she said, coughing three more times. "I can see why he stored all those chemicals way out here. If the wind shifted, the smell would completely overtake his house."

"I don't think that's why he did it."

"What do you mean?"

"He wanted to keep trespassers away."

She turned and looked at the small shed, then at the chicken coop. After another round of coughing, she said, "To conceal the escape hatch."

"Smart, if you think about it."

"Just like hiding the entrance under the chickens."

"Roger that. None of this is by accident."

"Obviously. But I never expected ammonia," Daisy said. "Pure ammonia at that."

"Seems to me, if you dilute ammonia in water, it can be used as fertilizer."

"That would mean he's stocking it as backup to the ammonium nitrate in the barn."

Bunker smiled, his tone turning light as he delivered his best rendition of Daisy imitating Tuttle. "A man's gotta have backups, Daisy."

CHAPTER 91

Mayor Buckley stood with sore knees in front of the window in the back of the Sheriff's Office, his lungs struggling to process the ever-thinning air of the building.

Three Russian checkpoints were visible inside the city limits, carving up the streets into designated control sectors, each with razor wire and barricades. Troops with assault weapons stood at the ready, their eyes watching everything around them. Most of the soldiers were older, with grizzled faces from years of service. The younger men looked unsure, their heads twisting at the slightest noise.

The pain in his heart doubled as he watched a three-man team in tactical gear escort a man, his wife, and two children from one point to another—all four civilians under the threat of a bullet. Other citizens roamed free, though everyone knew their activity was under watch by the eye in the sky.

Construction of the video monitoring system began once the signal towers were in place to track the transponders injected into everyone's neck. General Zuhkov's men quickly deployed a centralized, tethered hot-air balloon with a remote-controlled gyroscopic camera attached. The technology wasn't daunting to say the least, but it was efficient to deploy and covered a wide area. Too much high-tech would be complicated to mobilize and maintain, which is why Buckley figured they'd chosen the simpler balloon route.

The Russian tech meant a central monitoring station was operational in town. Buckley hadn't seen it yet, but it didn't mean it wasn't there. He thought it would be within cabling distance from the mobile generators, their diesel engines purring in the background.

The latest trucks to arrive were a pair of flatbed tractor-trailer rigs. Their cargo—a skid-mounted water treatment plant made by a company called Evoqua. Buckley presumed the equipment was a combination of filtration and reverse osmosis, designed to keep the Russian troops safe from contaminated water.

The need for a purified water source made sense, given their unwelcome presence. It wouldn't take much for a lone saboteur to poison an unprotected water supply, taking out a large group of soldiers without firing a shot.

Water and food are just as important as guns and ammo when you're the invading force. He thought about the logistics of their arrival and realized water would have been too heavy to transport. Plus it would have run out quickly, leaving the invaders at the mercy of the town's water supply. That left only one choice—mobile equipment for onsite filter and decontamination before the water touched the lips of their men.

The buzz of activity continued outside, with scores of citizens and troops doing what they needed to do to survive one more day. So far, no shots had been fired—on either side—but he worried the situation might soon change.

Clearwater may have been a peaceful town that rolled up its sidewalks at night—a town where life eased forward at its own leisurely pace. Even so, these were Americans under duress. Proud. Resilient. Free. It wouldn't take much to spark an altercation, which is why he figured the inoculations had been launched first.

FEMA's contagion alarm was a masterful stroke of genius, designed to add a layer of control to what would surely be an angry population. At the time, everyone in town was thankful for FEMA's help, lining up willingly for what they thought was a life-saving inoculation.

Of course, that perception changed once the residents realized it was only step one of the Russians' occupation plan. As it stood now, anyone considering resistance would think twice with lethal explosives and tracking devices buried in their necks.

He wondered if the FEMA plot would have been successful if Bunker and Apollo had still been in town. Buckley obviously wasn't prepared for the misdirection, nor was he paying close enough attention when it unfolded right in front of him. Bunker and Apollo might have made a difference, noticing that something was off with the FEMA rollout.

All Buckley could do now was stand back and let the Russians expand their grip of terror. He was outgunned, outmanned, and outsmarted by a band of arrogant Slavs who'd arrived from a land far away.

He used to be the man in charge of all things Clearwater-related. A man people respected and looked up to on a daily basis. But that status evaporated the instant the Russians snuck into town.

Their show of force had everyone cowering to their demands, including him. There was one exception though—Bill King, the Silver King Mine owner. The same man who had his own private audience with the General.

There was no way to know what transpired in that meeting, but his gut told him that King wouldn't hesitate to sell out everyone in order to save his life and that of his missing son. He might have managed to turn a profit in the process, too.

Buckley leaned his butt against the edge of Apollo's desk, giving his back and his legs a rest. Thus far, the Sheriff's Office hadn't been commandeered by the invaders like the Mayor's Office had been. However, that didn't mean General Zhukov had forgotten about this space.

His men had already searched the office, removing the pistols, rifles, ammo, tear gas, gas masks, batons, Tasers, Kevlar vests, riot gear, and other equipment. Basically, anything that could be used against their forces, including the letter opener in Daisy's top drawer.

The Sheriff's Office was now a useless relic, with only historic significance behind its name. Much like he felt at the moment. Obsolete. Moth-balled. Forgotten.

A triple knock came at the door behind him. "Mr. Mayor. We need to speak with you," a man's voice said in perfect English. His tone was deep and gravelly, indicating someone of advanced age.

Mayor Buckley chose to ignore the visitors since the hail was devoid of a Russian accent. He needed whomever it was to go away and leave him be.

The knock rang out again, this time turning into heavy bangs on the door. "Mr. Mayor. We know you're in there. We need to speak to you."

Buckley exhaled, letting his shoulders slump as a dull headache began to establish a foothold in his brain. The pounds hit the door again and again. Finally, Buckley decided to speak. "Go away. I'm busy."

The man's voice changed its pitch and its cadence. Someone else was speaking now, the tone softer and younger. "Seth, it's me, Stan Fielding. I've got my two girls with me and we really need to speak to you. It's urgent."

Buckley didn't respond as more fist pounds hit the office door, then all went quiet. The Mayor relaxed, thinking Stan and the other man had given up.

Thirty seconds of silence ticked by, then the pounding and verbal demands started up again. It was clear Stan and company weren't going away.

Buckley needed to take action; otherwise, the incessant noise would soon send his headache into orbit. "Enough already, Stan. Come in. The door is unlocked."

The hinges creaked before footsteps entered the workspace. Buckley turned to make eye contact with Stan, but his focus found the innocent faces of the man's twin redheads, Barb and Beth. Their freckled, pre-teen faces were round and puffy, as if they'd been crying only moments before.

Four other people had followed in behind Stan and his girls—two older and two younger, all men. Their expressions were identical—they wanted answers.

Stan held up a white sheet of paper, waving it as if it were a priority communique from the President of the United States. The other visitors did the same, their hands clutching single sheets of paper.

"Have you seen this?" Stan asked.

Buckley suddenly found the energy to reengage his former life as Mayor. He walked out from behind the desk and met Stan halfway. "What is it?"

"Work assignments," Stan said, giving the paper to Buckley. "For everyone on my street."

Stan turned sideways and held out a hand toward the pair of men on his right. "These are my neighbors, Jack Koehn and his eldest son Don." He moved his arm again. "This is Phil Wright and his son Bret."

"Pleased to meet you," Buckley said in his mayoral voice. He held out a hand for a shake, but there were no takers.

Stan continued, "The Russians are going door-to-door with dogs to confiscate our weapons and ammo. Then they're handing out these notices before they move on to the next house. Everyone is scared, Mayor. You need to do something."

Buckley wasn't surprised by the confiscation of weapons, not after they'd done the same thing to the Sheriff's Office. He was more concerned about the piece of paper Stan had just given him.

His eyes scanned the words on the page. Unlike the dossiers he'd seen on Zhukov's desk, everything was in English, with the name of Stan's street printed in bold letters at the top. Below it were four columns of names—resident names—grouped together and listed by surname, with a number immediately after it.

Stan's last name was near the bottom of the first column: *FIELDING: 3*. Two other families were listed ahead of his, bringing the count of persons in their group to ten. Above their names was the heading: *Ore Transport. Sector 4. Shift 2.*

"What am I looking at here?" Buckley asked in an effort to stall, even though he knew what this paperwork represented.

"We're all supposed to work the mine, starting Monday. Even my girls."

"Why would they need to assign workers? Bill King has plenty of men for that already."

"This isn't for the Silver King Mine."

"Why would you say that?"

"One of my neighbors speaks a little Russian and overhead some of the soldiers talking. They plan to bus us daily to the abandoned Haskins Mine."

"The old phosphate pit?"

"My girls can't be working in a mine, Mayor. It's too dangerous. You have to stop this."

Buckley's mind took a minute to process the information, not wanting to believe what he was hearing. "Your neighbor must have misunderstood what they were saying." He held up the paper and pointed at the task assignment printed above Stan's group. "Why would the Russians need workers for *Ore Transport Duty* at a phosphate mine? There's no ore. It doesn't make sense."

Stan looked at the other men standing with him, then brought his eyes back to Buckley. "We think there's something else in that hole. Something important enough to risk invading the United States."

Buckley gulped after remembering something Bill King had said earlier, when the business owner let it slip that at least one uranium mine was still operating in Colorado, and it was a lot closer than anyone realized.

Anyone except the Russians, apparently.

CHAPTER 92

"Do you think Sheriff Apollo will let me have a gun?" Victor Rainey asked the big man, Dicky, whose powerful hands were holding the precision-guided TrackingPoint rifle in a firing position. The tree line beyond the Old Henley Bridge was the target of the rifle's scope.

Dicky brought the high-tech weapon down from his shoulder, then took a swig from one of the three water bottles sitting behind the barbed wire barricade. "You'll have to ask him. I'm not sure what he'll want to do."

Victor flipped his head to the right, sending the longest part of his hair to the side. "Don't you have some pull with him? I mean, you're a deputy. Doesn't he listen to suggestions?"

"Actually, kid, I'm only a temporary deputy. So no, I don't have any influence with the Sheriff. Like I said, you need to ask. Not me. I just do as I'm told. Something I'm guessing you need to learn to do as well."

A high-pitched squeal of hinges rang out from behind Victor's position, then the hollow ping of steel hitting steel. He turned his head in a flash. As did Dicky, both searching for the source of the noise.

The Sheriff was on his way from Tuttle's front gate with a pair of rolled-up papers in his hands. The Mayor's grandson, Rusty, was walking with him, the handlebars of his high-end mountain bike in his grip.

"Looks like you'll gonna get your chance," Dicky said, his tone terse and to the point.

Victor swallowed hard, forcing down a knot of saliva. "Not exactly what I was hoping for."

"I know, but if you want to get somewhere in this world, you need to take ownership of your actions. That means manning up when the situation calls for it. Like now. What's the worst that can happen?"

"He says no."

"Then he says no. At least he'll know you want to help. It's a start."

Victor nodded as he waited for the Sheriff to arrive. Dicky was correct. Nobody was going to give him any respect unless he did something to earn it. He wasn't sure if asking for a gun was all it would take, but he planned to ask.

"Any activity?" the Sheriff asked Dicky when he arrived.

"No sir. All quiet."

"I figured as much. No news is good news," the Sheriff said, tapping Victor on the back with one of the papers. "Right, sport?"

"Yeah, no news is good news."

Apollo pointed at the bicycle. "I thought having Rusty's bike down here was a good idea to speed up the notification process."

"Yes sir," Dicky said, sounding more like a soldier than a deputy. "Much faster than running. Every second counts."

"What do you think, Victor?"

"Sure. I guess. If that's what you need. But seems to me that using the walkie-talkies you found would be better."

"Bunker and I discussed that, but we decided to save the batteries."

"They're rechargeables, aren't they?"

"Yes, they are. But charging them takes time and power away from other things—more important things. We also don't know if the frequencies are being monitored. If they are, it wouldn't take long to get a fix on our position, and we can't afford that. So we decided to keep them off, for now."

The Sheriff motioned to Rusty.

Rusty gave the bike to Victor. "Just don't wreck it."

Victor took the bike by the handgrips, his foot fumbling for the kickstand.

"You do know how to ride a bike, don't you?" Rusty asked, his brow furrowed.

"Yeah. No problem. Everyone knows how to ride a bike."

"But this isn't just any bike."

"I know. I'm not stupid."

"Good then," Apollo said before Rusty could respond. "If anything pops up, let me know immediately." He held up the rolled paper. "We're heading inside to go over these maps with Bunker. There's something interesting I need to show him."

"Good luck, sir," Dicky said, nudging Victor on the shoulder.

The Sheriff brought his eyes down to Victor. "Is there something else?"

Victor's lips started to answer before he was ready. "Ah, yeah, well, uh . . . I was wondering if I could maybe get a gun? You know, to help protect the bridge and all that. Like Dicky."

The Sheriff shot a glance at the towering guard before returning his focus to Victor. "Do you think you're ready for a gun, young man? It's a lot of responsibility."

Victor felt emboldened by the man's question. He decided to deliver his words like Dicky would have done. "Yes sir, I am. A hundred percent."

"I appreciate your gumption, son, but the answer is no. I don't feel comfortable with a weapon in your hands. I'm sure your mother would agree with me. And so would your grandmother."

"But you don't understand. Grandma showed me how to shoot last summer with her .22. It's not hard. I hit every can at least once. Ask her."

"I'm sure you did. But chances are, you need a lot more practice. Shooting cans is a lot different than being an armed guard."

"What, you don't trust me?"

"It's not that, Victor. There are procedures in place to make sure someone's ready to carry a gun. Especially someone your age. But even more importantly, I'd need to run it by your mother first, and I think we both know what she's gonna say."

"Yeah, you're just like everybody else. You don't trust me."

Apollo didn't respond.

"Look, I apologized, but I guess that doesn't count for anything."

Apollo took a second before he spoke. "You mean for what you did at the bus accident."

"I said I was sorry. If I had known what Bunker was going to do, I would've stuck around. But I didn't. He was just some guy who showed up out of the blue. How did I know he wasn't going to push the bus over the cliff?"

Apollo gave the maps to Rusty, then cradled Victor with an arm around the shoulder. He pointed at a flowering bush ten yards away. "Let's have a little chat, shall we?"

The two of them moved away from the group, then Apollo spoke again, this time with a much softer voice. "I know you don't think anyone trusts you, and maybe they don't, but that's because of what you did."

Victor shrugged. "I said I was sorry."

"And we all appreciate that. But it takes more than just words to earn trust."

Victor wasn't sure if he should say anything, so he didn't.

"Trust is about honesty and how you conduct yourself when it really matters. You have to show responsibility and quit taking the easy way out. That means no more lying and no more stealing. I know your mother is at the end of her rope with you."

"I didn't steal anything."

"Yes, you did. Be honest."

Victor held his tongue.

"We all know you broke into Franklin's store and stole his gun."

"That wasn't me. That was someone else."

Apollo dropped his head and shook it before he made eye contact again. "You see, this is exactly what I'm talking about. When you lie, people don't trust you. No matter how many times you apologize afterward. Do you hear what I'm saying?"

Victor nodded.

Apollo continued, his tone more serious than before. "It's time to grow up and be accountable for what you did. So right now, I need you to be honest and answer me. That was you in Franklin's store, wasn't it?"

Victor considered his options, pausing before he answered. "Yeah, Sheriff. It was me. I broke in, but I needed a gun so I could protect my mom after what happened. Wouldn't you have done the same thing if you were me? It's not like my dad is around anymore to protect us. So I had to."

"Okay, some of that is justifiable, but why did you destroy the office?"

"What? I didn't destroy anything."

"Rusty told me about what you did. He was there. The place was a complete mess."

"All I did was take the gun under the desk. I didn't touch anything else. I swear. Took me like ten seconds, then I was outta there. I knew right where it was from what Megan was saying on the bus."

Apollo didn't answer.

Victor continued, "It must have been the men in black. They showed up right after I got there. That's how I lost the gun, when I started running."

"They chased you?"

"Well, sort of. I'm not sure. I didn't stick around to find out."

"I see," Apollo said, his eyes indicating he was deep in thought. A handful of seconds drifted by before the man spoke again, this time tugging Victor by the arm. "All right, come with me."

Apollo directed the next question to Rusty. "When you first arrived at the horse stables, was the front door open to the store?"

"Yes sir."

"Did it look like force was used, or did someone use a key?"

Victor knew what the Sheriff was suggesting and decided to tell his side of the story first. "I crawled in through a window in Franklin's office. He always leaves it open."

Rusty looked at him. "That was you?"

"Yeah, but I never trashed the office. That part is a lie, Sheriff."

"There were papers everywhere. I saw it," Rusty said, his tone elevated.

Apollo held up his hands. "Easy boys. Nobody is accusing anyone of anything. I'm just trying to understand what happened."

Victor could sense the Sheriff's distrust. "I already told you, Sheriff. I went in through the window and took the Colt that was under the desk. When the men in black came into the store, I went back out the window, but lost the gun in the bushes or something."

"Maybe someone needs to head back there, Sheriff, and take another look? I'll go if you need me to," Dicky said.

Apollo didn't hesitate, shaking his head. "I don't want anyone leaving without an escort. But since we only have one horse, our choices are limited."

"What about the Land Rovers?" Rusty asked, giving the maps back to Apollo.

"We'll only use them if our camp is overrun. Otherwise, they sit right where they are."

Dicky nodded. "Too much noise."

"Exactly. We can't risk using them unless we know precisely where the Russians are. No, I'm afraid horseback is the only choice. For now."

"It's too bad we only have one," Dicky said.

Apollo shot a nod at Rusty. "Let's go have a chat with Bunker." He looked at Dicky and Victor before he departed. "Stay sharp, men. Everyone is counting on you."

"You got it, sir," Dicky answered.

Victor waited until Rusty and the Sheriff were out of sight. He looked up at the giant. "You believe me, right?"

"I'd like to. But at this point, the jury is still out."

Victor dropped his head. He knew most of this was his fault, but some of what happened wasn't. "It seems like no matter what I do, I get in trouble. Even before we moved here, it was the same thing. Everyone judging me all the time. Even when I didn't do shit. It was always my fault. But not this time. All I was doing was trying to protect my mom. That's all. It's just not fair."

A heavy silence hung in the air for what seemed like a minute.

"Hey, I'll tell you what," Dicky said, holding out the rifle. "You hold this and stand guard while I go take a major leak. All that water is running right through me. My back teeth are floating."

Victor took the gun and smiled. "Really?

"Yes. But don't let me down."

"I won't. Thanks for trusting me."

Dicky pointed to the rifle. "That's the safety. It won't fire as long as it's engaged."

"Okay, got it."

"But let me be perfectly clear," Dicky said, pointing at the stand of trees on the other side of the bridge. "The safety stays on unless you see the entire frickin' Russian Army coming through those trees. Not some rabbit, or a bird. Am I making myself clear?"

"Crystal. Safety stays on."

"You'd better have both feet intact when I get back. Hands, too," Dicky said, turning to head toward the tallest oak tree in the area—the same tree Bunker had selected for the first sniper hide.

Victor leaned his weight under the heavy rifle and held it up to his shoulder. The scope was a million times bigger than the one mounted on his grandma's .22. He looked through it. The image was clear and bright, allowing him to see every detail across the bridge.

Right then, something Dicky said tore into his mind. It was his earlier statement to the Sheriff about the need for more horses.

Victor's thoughts filled with an idea. One that would surely earn him the respect of everyone in camp. Even the Sheriff.

He brought his eyes around to check on Dicky's position. The man was almost to the base of the oak tree, his hands working the front of his pants. A few seconds later, Dicky was behind its wide trunk and out of sight.

Victor leaned the rifle against the wooden posts of the barricade, being careful to brace it so it wouldn't fall over. He grabbed one of the water bottles and twisted off the cap. After a quick swig, he used the remaining liquid to fill the orange water container hanging on the downtube of Rusty's bike.

He gripped the handlebars and flipped the kickstand up with his toe. A few seconds later, his butt was on the seat and his right foot on the pedal, ready to take off for the far end of the bridge, and beyond.

If he hurried, he figured he would be back before dark. However, he needed to buy himself some time so Dicky wouldn't miss him and send out search parties.

Victor turned his head in the direction of the tree masquerading as an outdoor toilet. "Hey Dicky! I gotta pee, too, and check on my mom. I'm gonna ride back to house. The rifle's right here for ya."

"Okay. Grab some more water while you're there."

"Will do."

CHAPTER 93

Sheriff Apollo unrolled one of the maps he'd brought to Martha Rainey's house from the hidden bunker beneath Tuttle's barn. He held it down with a spread of his hands, its footprint spanning almost the entire length of the dining room table.

The second map was still rolled and standing in the corner of the room, its center bound by a rubber band. He was saving it for later, once he had a chance to test a theory he was working on regarding Tuttle's maps.

Bunker stood across the middle of the table from Apollo, sandwiched between Stephanie and Daisy, both of them leaning forward, eyes glued to the map.

Apollo made a mental note to pull Bunker aside later and have a discussion about the new information he'd uncovered about the theft of Franklin's Colt 1911 and the subsequent appearance of the men in black at the store.

He also needed to verify Victor's testimony with Megan—the part about the girl giving up the secret location of the gun. Something was nagging at him about the words Victor had used. Most notably, his statement about the office window *always being open.*

Victor couldn't have known that fact unless Megan told him on the bus, or he'd been using that entry point to break in on a regular basis. Either way, Megan needed to confirm.

Albert was next to Daisy, looking nervous, with his skinny friend Dustin on the other side of him. Both men stood erect, with their arms folded across their chests.

Martha Rainey took position at the head of the table, just as the matriarch should do, with her daughter Allison manning the opposite end of the six-foot-long mahogany surface.

The Mayor's grandson Rusty hovered only inches beyond the reach of Apollo's right elbow, with Dallas and Jeffrey pushed in close on his left, their hands pressing down on the map.

Megan Atwater and her knee brace sat in the dining chair in front of Stephanie King, her eyes wide from the mounting excitement. Megan glanced up and sent Bunker a smile over her shoulder. He reciprocated with a grin of his own, then put a soft hand on the top of her back.

Misty Tuttle remained upstairs after her breakdown during the burial of her fiancé. Apollo could still feel the run of tears on his arms, having carried the distraught woman up those same steps earlier.

"This is what I was telling you about," Apollo told Bunker, shooting a long, extended look at the map on the table.

Martha put a candleholder on the end of the map in front of her, while Allison used a thick photo album to secure the other.

Apollo pulled his hands away and gave Bunker a black magic marker from his pocket. He'd found it in Martha's kitchen drawer.

Bunker removed its protective cap, then flashed a look at Burt and Albert. "Where did you see the convoy?"

Burt pointed at a road cutting through the mountain range on the left, just above a bridge symbol printed in black. "It was about here."

"Actually, it was here," Albert said, aiming his finger an inch lower. "We hadn't quite made it to the bridge."

Bunker looked at Burt with one eyebrow raised, obviously waiting for confirmation.

The mechanic's eyes tightened for a few seconds before he answered, moving his finger on the map to match Albert's correction. "I hate to admit it, but Albert's right. They set up the roadblock here, just past the bridge. We were coming up a rise on this side when he spotted them."

Bunker drew the letter 'X' where Burt had indicated, smothering Mason's Bridge in ink.

Dustin smiled. "Yep. That's where we were." He pointed about a quarter inch to the right. "The boulders we hid behind were over here. I'll never forget that moment for as long as I live. Talk about intense. Especially the tanks."

"How many tanks?" Bunker asked.

"Three, I think."

Bunker nodded. "Sounds about right. What did the chassis and turret look like?"

Dustin shrugged. "Not sure. They looked kind of old, but we weren't exactly close."

"Does it matter?" Apollo asked.

"Yeah, it does. If it's a classic T-72, it might not have reactive armor. If it's newer, then all bets are off."

"With our luck, it'll be the newer model," the Sheriff said.

"I wouldn't say that. The T-72 may be old, but it's still their most popular main battle tank. There are literally thousands of them still around, so I wouldn't rule it out. Those things are damn reliable," Bunker said, looking at Dustin again. "Did you see rectangular, raised objects covering the hull? They'd look like pillows, or wedge-shaped packs around the turret."

"I don't remember any of that," Dustin answered. "But Burt got a better look at them."

Burt nodded. "Flat hulls, for sure. Plus they had steel drums attached to the back. Two of them."

"For extra fuel," Bunker said before looking at Apollo. He nodded. "I'm betting T-72."

"That's good, right?"

"Possibly."

Stephanie King spoke up next, her finger aimed at a spot not far from the first roadblock. The map legend in the corner indicated its distance was only a handful of miles away. "I think this is where we stopped for a potty break. Right, Daisy?"

Daisy took Stephanie's hand and moved her finger an inch closer to the first roadblock. She brought her eyes up to Bunker. "Do you think it was the same convoy?"

Burt spoke before Bunker could respond. "Did you see any tanks?"

Daisy shook her head. "No, just a few trucks. But they could have been there, and we just didn't see them."

"Tanks are kinda hard to miss," Burt replied, his tone sharp and to the point. "Unless you're asleep."

"Burt's right," Bunker said, tracing his finger along the roadway. When he came upon another bridge named Royal Palace Bridge, he stopped.

Dallas joined the conversation, tapping his finger next to Bunker's. "That's the first roadblock I saw." The kid moved his finger down another inch on the map. His voice cracked when he said, "My parents' house is here. At least it used to be."

Bunker drew a second X on the map to cover the Royal Palace Bridge, then put a hand on the kid's shoulder. "We'll find them, I promise. Just need to be patient."

Dallas nodded, sniffing. His hand went back to the map, touching two different points. "The other roadblocks I ran into were here and here." Both of his touches landed on landmarks, the first being Kay's Crossing Bridge and the other Union Towers Bridge.

Bunker drew two more X's, each over the designated bridge. He looked up at Apollo. "Where did you find Misty and her boyfriend?"

Apollo took a second to find his bearings on the map, looking for a waterway that followed the river flow he remembered. When he found a match, he put his finger on it. "Dicky, Rusty, and I were here."

Bunker's eyes followed the river upstream several miles, then his finger landed on the paper next to another landmark. "I wonder if they were headed to Rickman's Bridge before they spotted Misty and Cowie," he said, circling the bridge and drawing a question mark inside the ring.

"No, they weren't," a new female's voice rang out from behind Apollo.

Apollo turned his head.

It was Misty Tuttle, her feet landing at the base of the stairs. The bedsheet wrinkles on her right cheek were distinct, no doubt due to some serious sack time. Her eyes were puffy and her hair was a tangled mess, sticking up at odd angles.

Misty ambled across the floor and squeezed in next to Allison. "The Russians weren't headed to some bridge. They were hunting for us. They wanted us dead."

"Why?" Bunker asked, sounding skeptical.

Apollo didn't wait for Misty to answer. "Because allegedly, they'd stolen a formula from the Russians."

"We did steal it. Well, actually, Angus stole it, but I convinced him we needed to get it here, to NORAD. I have an old friend who works there," she said with conviction. Her hand traced a path from Colorado Springs to Clearwater. "I wanted to see my dad while we were in the area, but they found us first. Almost like they knew we were coming."

"What kind of formula?" Albert asked.

"It's probably a new kind of bomb," Burt added. "The news likes to say the arms race is over, but they're full of shit."

Misty shook her head, looking frustrated. "No, it's not for a bomb. Why do men always assume it's a bomb? That's exactly what my friend in NORAD asked me when I first texted him about it."

"Well, it is the Russians after all," Albert said, shrugging. "That's what they do. Develop new and better ways to kill the planet. Just like we do."

Misty seemed to ignore Albert's statements. "It's for something called Metallic Hydrogen."

Albert sucked in a breath, his eyes flying wide. "What did you say?"

"Metallic Hydrogen. They've figured out a way to make it."

"That's not possible," Albert snapped. "The pressures required are enormous. Plus, you'd need to keep it super-cooled."

"What's Metallic Hydrogen?" Dustin asked Albert.

"A theoretical phase of hydrogen," Albert answered, his eyes never leaving Misty's face.

"I hate chemistry," Burt mumbled, though Apollo heard it clearly.

Albert continued. "Basically, it would be a new kind of liquid metal, made entirely of hydrogen. A Quantum Fluid with nearly unlimited superconductivity. At least, that's what the theoretical physicists said in the article I read."

"Sounds like a bunch of gobbledygook to me," Burt said.

"We're talking cutting-edge stuff. One of the scientists went on to say that if we could solve the manufacturing process, we might be able to use it to create a quantum bridge that could tap directly into zero-point energy. Of course, the man was just speculating, because nobody has a clue how to actually make Metallic Hydrogen. We just don't have the technology."

"Well, they do now," Misty said. "They're making it in Russia as we speak. And from what Angus told me, they've figured out a way to avoid supercooling it. It has something to do with a rare Earth element found in only certain parts of the world."

"Are you talking about some kind of subatomic stabilizer?" Albert asked.

She shrugged, the corners of her mouth turning south. "I don't know. Angus mentioned a new kind of nano-particle, but it was all over my head. I wish I could remember more."

Albert looked at Apollo, his voice charged with intensity. "If she's right, do you know what this means?"

Apollo shook his head.

"It means the Russians would have access to almost unlimited amounts of free energy. Something they could sell to the rest of the world at a fraction of the cost of oil."

"Holy shit! They'd put the Middle East out of business," Dustin said.

"And the United States," Bunker added. "We have more oil reserves than anyone."

Burt smirked. "I'm not sure putting all the oil companies out of business is such a bad thing."

"Except for all the jobs we'd lose. And tax dollars," Bunker said.

"I'm betting it would crash the stock market, too," Albert added.

Dustin laughed. "Rich people always hate it when someone tries to turn them into poor people."

"Once the oil companies are out of the way, Russia could raise the price to anything they wanted," Martha said.

"And control the world," Albert said.

"So this is all about money?" Allison asked.

"It usually is," Bunker answered. "Money and power, though most of the time they are the same thing."

"He who controls the energy has the power," Albert said, his tone deliberate. "In more ways than one."

Misty continued, "Angus stumbled across a classified file while he was working as a contractor in one of their joint research labs in Australia. When he told me about it, we decided to get this information to my friend in NORAD. Someone needed to know about it."

"Why NORAD, if it's not a bomb?" Burt asked.

Misty rolled her eyes. "Weren't you listening? I had to tell someone in the government, and he's the only one I knew. Plus it was close to my dad's house. That way I could kill two birds with one stone."

Kill being the operative word, Apollo thought. Franklin and Cowie—two unintended victims of the techno-invasion. "That explains why they were hunting for you, but it doesn't explain why the Russians decided to invade the US." He looked at Bunker, hoping for insight.

Bunker nodded, slowly. "Unless the two are related somehow."

Daisy spoke next. "Maybe that's what the Morse Code signal was for."

Apollo nodded, though he was still having a hard time processing the meaning of the new information. "If those coordinates were to deposits of the rare elements—"

Bunker finished his sentence. "—it would be worth the risk of invasion."

"I need to get a look at that formula," Albert asked Misty. "It might not be what you think it is."

Dustin patted his friend on the back. "Tin Man will figure it out. He always does."

"Tin Man?" Allison asked.

"Just a nickname from high school," Albert said in a downtrodden voice, shooting a look at Bunker. "Something I'd like to forget, but some people won't let it go." He moved his eyes back to Misty. "That formula? Can I see it?"

Misty shook her head. "I don't have it. Angus kept it hidden. He said it was safer if I never laid eyes on it."

"So let me get this straight. You never actually saw it, yet you came all this way and almost got yourself killed in the process, for something that might not even exist," Albert said in a patronizing tone, shooting a look of doubt at Apollo.

Misty's voice shot up a level. "Angus wouldn't lie about something like this."

Albert huffed. "Well, he *was* a spy working for the Russians. Not exactly a ringing endorsement for the truth."

Burt nodded. "Albert's right. Spies are experts at lying. That's what they do. All day, every day, to everyone. Even you."

"Like I told you guys, he was a contractor. Not a spy."

"Same thing," Albert quipped. "He obviously was part of all this, somehow. Nobody is that innocent. Especially if they're working in some secret advanced research lab with the Russians."

"How many times do I have to say it? He wasn't a spy!"

Burt laughed. "You do realize that if he was a spy, he'd never tell you. So you really don't know for sure."

"Neither do any of you!" Misty shot back. "But I know my Angus. He was a good man who just wanted to do the right thing."

"We should search his clothes," Apollo said.

"They're upstairs. In the hamper," Martha said, "waiting to be washed."

"Seriously, who washes the clothes of a dead man?" Burt asked.

"Habit, I guess," Martha answered.

"I'll get 'em," Rusty said, leaving the table an instant later.

Daisy tapped Bunker on the shoulder. "Maybe you should show everyone what we found in those pouches."

Bunker paused for a few moments, then reached into his pocket and pulled out several brightly colored items. They looked like playing cards, except for the extra angles cut into each of the four corners. He tossed them onto the map, sending them into a spray of color.

"Pokémon cards?" Dustin asked in a stunned voice.

"Dude, you can't be serious," Albert said to Bunker.

"I know. It seems ridiculous, which is why I hadn't brought it up before now. But the men in the miner's camp had these sewn inside their pants. Someone put them there for a reason."

"Yeah, some nut job," Martha Rainey said. "Sounds like something Tuttle would do."

"Mother!" Allison said before looking at Misty. "I'm sorry. She didn't mean it, Misty. Sometimes my mom just says things without thinking."

"It's okay. I know my dad can be a little eccentric," Misty said, her eyes tearing up. "I mean, could be."

Bunker continued. "Bottom line, these cards are no accident. Neither was the observation drone in the miner's camp. Someone planned this."

"And sent an assassin to Tuttle's place," Daisy said.

Bunker looked at Daisy, then at Apollo. "This is all connected somehow."

Daisy turned her eyes to Misty. "Do you think the men in black went to your dad's place looking for Angus?"

Misty choked back the answer, only nodding in response.

"God damned KGB," Burt snapped.

"Actually, it's the FSB," Albert said. "They took over for the KGB."

"Sorry guys, but you're both wrong," Bunker said. "The FSB is for internal security. The SVR handles foreign security. Then again, if this was under the control of their military, the GRU is responsible."

Apollo didn't want to mention the obvious, so he kept his mouth shut. In the end, Misty got her dad killed, regardless of which Russian intelligence service was involved. An assassin was in his home, torturing him for information he didn't possess.

An extended silence sucked the oxygen out of the room until Jeffrey grabbed one of the cards and held it up to the light of the chandelier. "Cool. There's a—"

Stephanie snatched it from his hands and put it back on the table. "What did I tell you about asking first?"

"Sorry, Mom."

Bunker gave two of the cards to Jeffrey. "Knock yourself out, kid."

Dallas took one of the cards from Jeffrey, then reached into his pocket and pulled out a device that looked like a small gun. He pressed the lever on the handgrip, sending out a brilliant blue and yellow flame from the opposite end. He aimed it at the lower corner of the card. "Ever see what happens when you burn one of these?"

Apollo grabbed the pocket torch from Dallas before the card caught fire. "Where did you get this?"

"Found it in Tuttle's kitchen."

"No more fire. You hear me?"

"Yes sir. Sorry."

"And no more snooping." Apollo gave the mini-torch to Bunker, then walked to the corner and grabbed the remaining map. He brought it to the table and held the roll up to grab the group's attention.

Apollo let his eyes wander around the table, making eye contact with everyone. "There's something else I want to show you all, but I've been saving it until after we had our discussion. I didn't want what's on this map to influence anyone's input."

"Come on, Apollo. Let's see it already," Burt snapped, making a stab for the roll.

Apollo pulled the map back, keeping it out of Burt's reach. "Before I show you what's on this map, everyone needs to prepare themselves."

Burt rolled his eyes, his waist bent forward with both hands on the table. "Jesus Christ, Apollo. What's with all the drama?"

Apollo slid the binder from the middle of the roll and uncoiled the map, spreading it over the one already on the table. He kept his hands on the corners so it wouldn't spool up on itself. He peered down at the lines and ovals written on the map by Tuttle. "Anything look familiar?"

Bunker grabbed a corner of the new map and pried it up. He scanned the map underneath, then brought the corner down to look at the top map once again. He repeated the process three more times, then said, "The marks I made are almost identical to the ones on top."

"What does this mean?" Stephanie asked Apollo.

"It means Tuttle knew this invasion was coming. Or at least, he was trying to figure out how it might be done. That's why he marked up the top map. This is no coincidence."

"Are you serious?" Martha asked.

"Now we know why he had all the supplies in the barn," Daisy said.

"And the weapons in the two underground bunkers," Apollo added.

"Let's not forget the Faraday cages, too," Bunker added. "He knew something was coming."

"For a while now," Albert added.

Misty looked at Martha, flaring her eyebrows as she spoke. "Still think my dad was a nut job?"

Martha's face turned soft, her head lowering a bit. "I'm sorry. I never should have said anything. Sometimes my mouth gets the better of me."

"You know Martha, living across the street from you was never easy for my dad. I didn't get many letters from him while I gone, but when I did, your name always came up. So it wasn't just your mouth. He knew you were watching everything he did. Nobody likes to be spied upon. Especially by some old witch who lives across the street."

"Hey, you can't talk to my mom that way!" Allison said, walking toward Misty.

Apollo grabbed her, keeping the women apart. "Easy now ladies, let's not do something we'll all regret."

"This doesn't concern you Sheriff," Misty said, her tone sharp.

"I said I was sorry. I hope you can forgive me," Martha said, pulling her daughter back from the Sheriff's grip. "I couldn't help it. It's not easy living out here all alone."

"Found 'em!" Rusty yelled as he made his way down the stairs with a wad of clothes in his hands. He plopped them onto the table, breaking the tension in the air.

Allison backed off. So did Misty, almost like the heated exchange never happened.

Bunker, Apollo, and Daisy began a hand search of Angus' shirt, pants, and shoes, turning pockets inside out, checking seams, and yanking out soles.

A few minutes went by before the trio came to a collective conclusion, one that Apollo announced to everyone else in the dining room. "Nothing here, folks."

"I told you this was a wild goose chase," Burt said.

"It must still be on him," Albert said, locking eyes with Apollo. He tilted his head, sending a signal that resembled a question.

Bunker nodded. "He's right."

"No. No. No," Misty said, holding up her hands and taking a step back from the table. "You're not digging him up."

"We have to, Misty," Apollo said.

Misty shook her head, looking like she could breathe fire. "No, I won't let you. It's sacrilegious."

Apollo looked at Daisy and Stephanie, then shot a nod at the staircase. "Ladies? A little help, please."

The women didn't hesitate, moving to Misty and grabbing her arms. Misty fought against their control, twisting her body in defiance.

"I'm sorry, Misty, but there's no choice," Daisy said as she and Stephanie led the emotional woman up the stairs and out of sight.

"That was intense," Dustin said to Burt.

"Too bad the Sheriff didn't let them throw down," Burt answered. "My money was on Allison."

"Like in the market, with Grace. You should have seen it. That was a pretty good cat fight," Dustin said, turning to Albert. "Right?"

Albert ignored the comment, focusing on Bunker instead. "It's your turn with the shovel, dude. Dustin and I dug the last round of holes."

"Follow me," Bunker said, leading the group out of Martha Rainey's house and across the street to Tuttle's.

The shovels were still leaning against the back wall of Tuttle's house when they arrived, only a few feet from the fresh graves they'd dug next to Tuttle's. He scanned all six gravesites with his eyes. "Anyone remember which one it is?"

Martha pointed at the first grave. "That's where I buried Tuttle."

Dustin aimed a hand at the second. "That's the black cowboy's."

Rusty walked from Martha's position to the far end of the graves. "These last three are the guys Bunker shot."

Bunker nodded, then stood over the lone unidentified grave. It was the third one from Martha's position. "Then this is where we start." He lifted the shovel above his head and brought it down with force, penetrating the darker colored dirt at its midpoint.

His eyes came up to Burt. "Grab the other shovel. We've got work to do."

CHAPTER 94

Apollo slid the top half of the body onto the ground, while Burt took care of the legs, both men sidestepping the gravesite just uncovered. Albert and Dustin took a step back to make room next to the hole.

The clean bed sheet they'd used to wrap the deceased was now a brownish color, with moisture splotches and other defects marring the all-white tapestry of the cloth.

Bunker began to unwrap Cowie, starting with the end of the sheet nearest to the head, then unwinding the material in a diagonal pattern.

Dallas and Rusty took positions next to Bunker. The boys' willingness to help suggested they weren't fazed by the exhumation process. Not in the least.

Apollo couldn't say the same for himself, wishing they didn't need to dig up the corpse. His apprehension wasn't because of some religious belief. It was more about respect for the dead.

Once a body was in the ground, he believed that's where it should remain. After all, that's why they call them "the remains." However, countless lives were at stake and the only clues to the madness behind the Russian invasion might lie with this cadaver.

Burt held the lower half of the body off the ground, while Bunker's hands completed the sheet removal process. Once the man's naked body was exposed to the air, Bunker gave the soiled bed sheet to Apollo.

Apollo coiled the material into a loose ball, then put it over the man's privates. Sure, a dead man can't feel embarrassment or become chilled from a draft, but it still was the right thing to do.

"What are we looking for?" Burt asked Bunker. "He's obviously not carrying anything."

"My guess is the formula is hidden on him."

Burt threw out his hands and shrugged in an exaggerated motion. "Okay, but where?"

"Check the bottom of his feet and between his toes. If the formula is still with him, it's not going to be obvious. Could be very small, too."

"We have to think like a spy," Albert said. "Check inside his lips and eyelids."

Dallas whispered something into Rusty's ear. The two boys laughed.

"What's so funny?" Burt asked, his hands prying apart each set of toes on the right foot.

Rusty shook his head, his lips not willing to answer. Dallas was still laughing, though it was more of giggle.

"Come on, out with it. What's so funny?" Burt asked, his tone serious.

Dallas pointed at the bundle of cloth covering Angus' midsection. "Check his butthole."

Burt shook his head, then looked at Bunker. "Everyone's a comedian around here."

"Actually, Dallas might be on to something," Dustin said. "Seems like the perfect place to me. Nobody would ever want to check there."

"Why am I not surprised?" Albert asked in a cynical tone.

Bunker shook his head at Dallas. "Maybe I shouldn't have taken you back to your father's house. I'm starting to think too much desensitization is not a good thing."

"He's right, boys. This is no time to be joking around," Apollo said.

Dallas dropped his head, his tone somber. "Sorry."

Apollo knew the boys were just being boys, using humor to cover up their anxiety. "Let's stay focused, shall we."

"But I wasn't exactly joking. It's possible, right?"

Bunker sounded frustrated when he said, "Sure, just not likely. If he has it on him, it would be someplace a little more accessible."

"At least they're getting along okay, which is pretty amazing under the circumstances," Martha said to Apollo, nodding at Rusty and Dallas. "More than I can say for Rusty and Victor."

"Among others," Bunker interjected, his focus landing on Albert.

The big man locked eyes with Bunker, but didn't respond. Nor did his facial expression change, obviously not wanting to address the comment sent his way.

It was clear something was going on with Albert and Bunker. Apollo wasn't sure what was fueling the tension, other than their near fisticuffs in the barn earlier. He thought their heated exchange was a thing of the past, but their odd looks, head turns, and cryptic comments seemed to indicate their distaste for each other hadn't eased.

"Dallas, why don't you and Rusty go check Tuttle's bathroom," Bunker said.

"For what?"

"See if you can find some shaving cream and a razor. We've got some hair to remove. I'll need scissors, too."

Dallas laughed again. So did Rusty.

"It's not for that," Bunker said, looking less than amused. "We need to check his scalp."

"Good idea," Albert said in a deliberate tone, his eyes never leaving Bunker. "I'm sure there are plenty of guys who've hidden stuff under their hair. Stuff like scars. Birthmarks. Lumps. Hell, I'll bet even a few tattoos. Nobody would ever suspect it, either."

Bunker hesitated for a good three seconds, his eyes lingering on Albert. Then he motioned at the boys with a quick wave of his hand. "Go on. Get the stuff we need."

Dallas and Rusty took off a moment later, taking a path between the end of the trailer and the barn.

* * *

"Wait! You don't have to do this," Mayor Buckley screamed, his feet churning at top speed across the grassy square. Deputy Rico was only a few feet behind him, both men trying to stop what was about to take place in front of a growing crowd of Clearwater residents.

"Ready . . . aim . . ." a Russian soldier yelled in broken English. A three-man squad stood before him, their rifles aimed at an equal number of prisoners, each on their knees with hands tied behind their backs. The commander's accent was thick; so were the blindfolds covering each of the captives' faces.

Buckley called out again, his lungs gasping for air. "Don't do this! Please!"

A second later, the order to fire was given. Gunshots rang out and brain matter exploded when the invaders' bullets let loose with their rage.

The crowd turned away, gasping in unison, the unarmed prisoners toppling over in death.

The energy in Buckley's legs vanished in an instant, stopping his gallop with a slam of the ground into his knees. A stabbing pain filled his heart, his mind unable to comprehend what he had just witnessed.

"No! No! No!" he screamed in a fading voice, his lungs starving for oxygen.

Rico plopped down next to him, the expression on his face mirroring how Buckley felt. Rico covered his eyes with his hands and began to sob. Slowly at first, then more tears came to him as the seconds ticked.

Buckley wanted to console Rico, but the rage in his chest convinced him to get up and keep moving. Answers were needed and he couldn't get them from his current position.

He resumed his trek with weak, unbalanced strides, his eyes unable to look away from the blood-covered corpses. When he arrived, two guards turned their rifles on him. The third grabbed Buckley by the suitcoat and stopped his advance with a straight arm.

"What did you just do?" Buckley asked, his voice charged with grief.

Valentina came into his vision from the right, seemingly out of nowhere. "These men were charged with sedition and sentenced accordingly."

"Sedition? What are you talking about?"

"They refused to report for work duty, then resisted arrest when the General's security team took them into custody. One had a concealed knife. A forbidden weapon."

"So you just shot them? In cold blood?"

"All resistance will be met with swift justice."

"On whose authority?"

"General Zhukov's."

"Take me to him! I demand to speak with him this very instant!"

* * *

Bunker drew the razor across the crown of Cowie's head, his hand holding the razor at a consistent angle. The shaving cream gave way under the even pressure, the edge removing the hair in one pass.

He wouldn't quite classify the remaining hair as stubble, but it was close after the scissors had done their job to give him better access. He figured another swipe or two and the man's head would be completely bald.

The process reminded Bunker of his days riding with The Kindred. Every morning he'd stand in front of the dingy mirror and drag a razor across his lumpy head. The sound and vibration of stubble ripping across his scalp was a unique sensation, one still fresh in his memory.

Martha Rainey came around the corner of the trailer. "That didn't take long. Find anything?"

"Nothing yet," Bunker said. He brought the razor up and positioned it for another draw. About halfway through the next pass, something appeared beneath the shaving cream. It was an all-black tattoo, but not one he'd seen before. This one was perfectly square and filled with patterns of dots and squares.

"A QR code?" Rusty asked, his voice an octave higher than usual.

Dustin looked just as surprised. "What the hell?"

Albert folded his arms across his oversized gut before raising an eyebrow. "There's a first time for everything."

"Wow, I didn't expect that," Apollo added.

"None of us did," Bunker said, his eyes drawn to the detail of the artwork.

"What's a QR code?" Martha said, her question defining her age.

"It stands for Quick Response code," Albert answered.

Dallas added, "Normally you use a smart phone to scan it, then it takes you to a website on the Internet."

"Didn't Japan's auto industry invent it?" Dustin asked.

Albert shook his head. "I don't think they invented it, but they were the first to use it widespread. At least before the Internet crashed their party."

"Well, that's pretty frickin' useless," Burt said. "No Internet. No website."

"Angus obviously didn't expect the EMP," Bunker said, running through the logistics in his mind. The man must have created a special webpage somewhere on the Internet that contained the Russian formula, then had a tattoo artist draw the code on his head. "It's damn fine artistry."

"Time to fill the hole back up. Then I need some food," Burt said, looking at Martha.

"Look, just because I'm a woman doesn't mean I'm stuck with all the cooking duties."

Burt laughed. "Your daughter then. She's had plenty of experience at Billy Jack's."

Martha stopped her approach next to Bunker, then answered Burt. "You'll need to take that up with Allison. But I'm pretty sure she'll tell you the same thing."

"To go fuck myself," Burt said in the middle of a chuckle.

"You said it, not me," the old woman answered, leaning in close to the tattoo. She held her eyes on the matrix of squares for a few beats. "Are these supposed to be all black?"

"Yep, just like any other barcode," Albert answered.

Martha stood upright and said, "Well gentleman, I hate to tell you, but that's not a QR code."

"How the hell would you know?" Burt snapped. "A minute ago, you didn't even know what it was."

Martha pointed at the upper left corner of the tattoo, drawing Bunker's focus. "You see here, the center of that larger square is not black like everything else."

Bunker studied the dot before he spoke again. "Looks black to me."

She scoffed. "No. It has a tinge of burgundy to it."

Bunker shook his head. "I don't know. Black is black."

Albert laughed hard.

"What's so funny, dude?" Dustin asked.

"Most people don't know this, but women can see shades of color that men can't. More so in the red spectrum. It's all about them rods and cones."

"Okay, if it has some red to it, what does it mean?"

Bunker answered Dustin, "It means I need a magnifying glass."

"What are you thinking?" Apollo asked.

"A microdot."

"Something a spy would use."

"You'll need more than a magnifying glass," Albert said with confidence.

"A microscope?" Dustin asked.

Albert nodded. "Got one back at my place."

Bunker agreed with their line of thinking. "Just need transportation."

Apollo spun to face the fenced-off area of Tuttle's back yard where Tango stood with his snout buried in the short grass. "I'm guessing four-legged transportation. Not four-wheeled."

Bunker laughed. "We'll need to map out a route. Figure I'll do some scouting while I'm out there."

"I can help with that," Burt said.

"Actually, you need to get back to work on the projects. There's a lot more welding to do."

"Hey, wait a minute."

"A deal is a deal, Burt. That TrackingPoint rifle isn't free."

"If we follow the routes Tuttle put on the map, I'm hoping we can get you where you need to go," Apollo said.

"Time to gear up," Bunker said, getting to his feet.

"All the gear is in the bunker below the barn," Apollo said.

"I'm glad you've decided to stay," Bunker said to the Sheriff. "Someone needs to keep an eye on things till I get back."

"It's not that, exactly. I still need to head back to town, but since we only have one horse, I'll wait for now. Besides, I don't think Tango wants my fat ass on his back, too."

Bunker smiled. "Or mine, either."

"Yeah, as if."

"What about my mom and sisters?" Dallas asked. "You promised."

"Don't worry, I'll look for them. They're probably in town, if my hunch is correct."

The kid nodded, but didn't respond.

Bunker held out his hand. "I'll need that photo you found."

Dallas took it from his pocket and unfolded it. The scorch marks on three of the corners obscured some of the scene, but the rest of the image was useable. Well, mostly useable, if you discounted the heavy crease down the middle. The kid had obviously opened and closed the photograph a number of times, cherishing the lone surviving memento from the house fire.

Dallas gave it to Bunker with a trembling hand. "Mom's hair is black now."

Apollo cleared his throat. "You might want to talk to Daisy before you go. I'm guessing she needs someone to swing by her trailer and feed her cat, Vonda. I left food and water out when I was there before, but I'm sure it's running low by now."

"I'll take care of it."

Burt huffed. "You guys are worried about some cat?"

Apollo ignored Burt's jab, still speaking with Bunker. "I'm sure she'll appreciate it."

"I'll make the rounds with everyone before I head out. Make sure they're all on the same page."

"Well, that and say a few goodbyes. Just in case. God forbid."

"Copy that."

Martha pointed at Cowie's bald, naked body. "I think you're forgetting something, Bunker."

"Oh yeah. Right." Bunker moved to Cowie's feet, then motioned to Burt. "Grab the other end. Let's get him inside."

CHAPTER 95

"Where are we going?" Mayor Buckley asked Rico Anderson after they entered the main entrance to Charmer's Market and Feed Store.

Rico didn't respond.

Buckley hadn't planned to visit this establishment today, not with a pending meeting with the Russian General on the horizon. But Rico convinced him to follow along, claiming it was Priority One.

The mercantile owner, Grace Charmer, waved a quick hello as Rico led the Mayor past the front registers in silence.

Buckley nodded back at her.

The nervous, red-faced look on Grace's face sent a chill down his spine, almost as if the old woman had just been sentenced to life in prison for mass murder. It was the strangest feeling. One that Buckley couldn't shake.

"Hopefully everyone is here," Rico whispered, his feet marching down the center aisle. The man's step was deliberate. So were his words.

"For what?" Buckley asked, his gut telling him the stockroom door was their destination. It stood between the grain bags and the animal feed piled along the rear wall. He remembered those stacks well, he and Rico carrying the inventory through the store when the Wal-Mart supply trucks arrived in town.

Rico stopped, then glanced around with hunched shoulders and determined eyes, obvious paranoia fueling his movements. "Not here, Mayor," he said, his voice barely a purr. "Wait for thirty seconds, then follow me in through the back door."

"Why?"

"Could be sympathizers around. Can't be too careful."

Buckley nodded, even though he had a long list of questions boiling in his brain. Especially about the word *sympathizers*.

He looked around to see what had Rico spooked. Three customers occupied the same aisle as he did, two of whom held baskets in their hands. The other was behind a full-sized cart, all of them seemingly busy with their shopping duties.

Unlike the chill he'd received from Grace's body language, everyone else in the store appeared engrossed in their own worlds. Nothing out of the ordinary.

Buckley stood firm as Rico turned and walked away, continuing his original path down the center aisle. At the end, he took a ninety-degree right.

Buckley could see the top of the Hispanic's jet-black hair moving above the racks as Rico made two lefts, then a right. A handful of seconds later, the door to the back room opened and Rico's head disappeared from sight.

"Afternoon, Mayor," one of the residents said as she slipped past the Mayor with her shopping cart leading the way. One of the front wheels fluttered in epileptic mode, shuddering side to side in a lightning quick wobble.

Buckley recognized the overweight eighty-year-old woman. She was Jane Flacco, a round-faced senior who always kept her gray hair short—short enough to resemble a recruit fresh out of Basic Training. No makeup either—a scary thought to say the least.

"Afternoon, Jane. How's George doing these days?"

She tucked in her upper lip before she spoke again. "Meaner than a God damn snake. That's how he's doing."

Buckley expected a negative response since this woman never seemed content about anything, except when she took down the prize at Bingo and ran with gusto to the front of the hall to collect. The sight of all of her extra weight flopping and wiggling was a sight he could never un-see. "I take it his gout is acting up again?"

"Yeah, that and the fact that he's a total pain in my ass. I've had hemorrhoids I liked better."

Buckley held back a laugh, remembering the celebration party involving the Flaccos from the year prior. "Didn't you two have an anniversary recently?"

She nodded. "Sixty-one, if you can believe that."

"That's quite an accomplishment, Jane. Congratulations."

She shook her head. "Just between you, me and the lamppost, I'm pretty sure that ass-hat of a man won't make it to sixty-two. But you didn't hear it from me."

Buckley smiled out of courtesy, having heard her same rhetoric a number of times over the years. Yet the Flaccos were still alive and still married, despite their loathing for each other.

He figured the very nature of their tumultuous relationship was the one thing keeping them both alive. That communal hatred gave them something to look forward to when each new day arrived.

Buckley had learned over the years that most people only need a single reason to crawl out of bed and keep plowing forward, even if it's one filled with nausea for another.

Mrs. Flacco snatched two items from the shelf in front of her and put them into her half-full shopping cart as Buckley started a silent count to thirty.

One of her items was a shovel and the other was a length of braided rope. The rope landed on top of a bear trap. The shovel nestled in next to a king-sized container of lighter fluid, its metal moving the plastic bottle over an inch.

The rest of her cart was full of items that Buckley could classify as weapons, if he didn't know the woman: framing hammer, black-handled axe, crowbar, and a blue nail puller. Not a single morsel of food.

She pointed at the front windows of the store. "You gonna do something about all those cock-sucking Russians? Those assholes are really starting to piss me off."

Her heavy tone didn't catch him off guard, but her extra foul language did, sending his tongue into a stammer. "Uh, well, yeah . . . I'm working on it."

"Well then, work faster. Some of us don't have all day."

"I'm doing my best, ma'am."

When Buckley's count hit thirty, he found his way to the back room where Rico was waiting inside with two additional members of the Sheriff's full-time deputy team: Zeke Dawson and Russell Thompson.

"Good to see you guys up and about," Buckley told them, their eyes glassy and movements slow. The roadway bandits did a number on them, but at least they'd found some shoes to wear. "I didn't expect Doc Marino to release you so soon."

"He didn't," Zeke said. "But we couldn't wait any longer."

"What's going on?" Buckley asked, his eyes landing on each man in succession, hoping for some insight into this clandestine meeting.

Rico waved his hand. "Follow me, Mayor."

Buckley did as he was told, following Rico through the mess of empty boxes covering the storeroom floor, then into the small break room along the back. Rico stopped in front of the door-sized refrigerator on the left.

The stainless-steel model had been built into the wall and featured a pair of magnetic Green Bay Packer stickers along its front. Below them was a series of football schedules from the previous three years.

Buckley expected Rico to reach for the handle on the door, but that was not what happened. The man's brown-skinned hand went under the cabinet on the right, where his fingers yanked on something. Buckley heard a dull noise that sounded like a latch giving way.

Zeke grabbed the back edge of the fridge and pulled with an outstretched arm. The entire unit swung open, frame and drywall included.

The depth of the steel fridge reminded Buckley of a bank vault door opening. Behind it was a short passageway that led to another door.

"Seriously?" Buckley muttered.

"Leads to a panic room, sir," Rico said, stepping inside the chamber first. "Grace's husband had it built when they remodeled this store."

"Grace said he barely got it finished right before he died," Zeke added. "Poor bastard."

"After you, Mr. Mayor," Russell said, extending a hand toward the opening.

"I take it Grace knows about all this?"

Rico didn't hesitate with the answer, his face looking even sterner than before. "Absolutely. She's the one who offered the space, so all of us could meet in private."

Buckley went inside. "All of us?"

Zeke and Russell followed, closing the secret door behind them.

Rico opened the next door, then stood aside as if he expected the Mayor to react. Three men were huddled inside, standing around something about four feet high and covered in a padded moving blanket.

Two of the men had their backs to the door, so Buckley couldn't see their faces. One had extra-long gray hair pulled back into a single ponytail that hung down to the middle of his back. The other was a tall, shorthaired blond with a thick waist and broad shoulders.

The third man was facing Buckley. It was Bill King, the Silver King Mine owner.

Before Buckley could blink, his feet took off in a sprint, bringing him to King's position in a flash. Buckley hands came up on their own, planning to wrap the traitor's throat in a stranglehold. However, before his fingers made contact, the stout man with short blond hair spun on his heels and jumped in front of Buckley.

When Buckley's eyes took in the man's face, his heart skipped a beat. It was Bill King's convict of a brother, Kenny.

The man's powerful hands latched onto Buckley's chest, stopping his approach. "Easy there, Mayor."

"Kenny?"

"Hey Seth. Miss me?"

"When did you get out? I thought your parole hearing wasn't for another month, at least."

"Got released early," he said, his tone grizzled and deep. A grin crept up on his lips. It was slight and maniacal, but a smile nonetheless. "On account of bad behavior."

"Actually, he escaped," Rico said, without a hint of concern. "After the EMP hit, the Department of Corrections lost containment of the facility. He just made it here this morning."

"Sneaking past the Russian checkpoints wasn't easy, but here I am," Kenny said. "It pays to know every nook and cranny of this town. Russians missed a few."

Buckley took a step back when a series of flashbacks from Kenny's drug trafficking trial flooded his memories. The Mayor had taken the stand as one of the federal prosecutor's character witnesses, feeling obligated at the time. He looked at Rico, then Zeke. "Why isn't this man in handcuffs?"

Kenny stepped forward, holding his wrists together. "If you're man enough, Seth, go for it. Nobody here will stop you . . . except possibly me."

Rico stepped between the two men. "I think you need to hear him out, Mayor."

The longhaired man on the left finally turned around to reveal his identity.

Buckley recognized the leather-skinned entrepreneur with several teeth missing from his crooked mouth. "Billy Jack? You're involved in this?"

His country twang filled the room when he spoke. "Like Rico said, you need to take a minute here, Mayor. We got a lot to discuss."

Buckley turned for the door behind him, but Zeke intercepted his departure. "Please, Mr. Mayor. This is important."

Buckley froze, needing a moment to think about the dynamics at play. Blood adversaries were working together, including members of the Sheriff's Office, and nobody seemed concerned. Kenny King was not a man to be taken lightly. By anyone.

Zeke motioned for Buckley to turn around.

Buckley spun, just as Kenny put his hand on the crown of the blanket covering the item next to him. He removed it with a yank to reveal an unconscious woman strapped to a chair with her head hanging limp.

The petite blonde had blood dripping from cuts on her cheeks and above her badly swollen eye. The large slit across the front of her military uniform revealed her porcelain skin, almost to the point of exposing her breasts.

It was the General's interpreter, Valentina—beaten and unconscious.

"What the hell is going on here?" Buckley asked.

"Getting some answers," Kenny said. "The old-fashioned way."

"By torturing a woman?"

Kenny's eyes turned fierce. "No, Mayor. We're extracting information from the enemy. In case you haven't noticed, the town is crawling with them."

Buckley shook his head, his mind running through a number of retaliatory scenarios the General would unleash because of their actions. "You guys can't do this!"

"The hell we can't. This is war, Mayor," Bill King said, breaking his silence. He pointed at the exit door. "Right now, outside this store, people are dying in the streets. You were there, Mayor. They just gunned down some of our friends. People who voted for you."

"Still, this isn't right," Buckley said, pulling the hanging piece of Valentina's shirt up. "She's just the interpreter. This woman didn't pull the trigger."

"No, she didn't, but she's still guilty as hell," Kenny said, taking a step closer to Buckley. "Trust me, I know guilty, Seth. I was surrounded by it for years after you and Fielding testified against me."

"Look, I was just doing my job. You left us no choice. We had to protect this town from the evil you were selling."

"And now, I'm doing my job," Kenny said. "Like you, I'm just protecting this town from the evil the Russians are selling. After you let them stroll right in and take over, I might add. What kind of man just stands by and let's that happen?"

"A coward. That's who," Bill King snapped.

Buckley looked at Bill first, then at Kenny. "I'm sure you don't know this, but your brother had a private meeting with General Zhukov. He sold us all out, like a traitor."

"Nice try, Buckley. But you don't know what you're talking about," Bill said.

Buckley pointed at Bill, his eyes still locked on Kenny. "I was there. I saw him. He's working with the Russians. You can't trust him for a second."

Bill shook his head, his voice calm and cool. "All you saw was me in the hallway, but you have no idea what was said in that meeting, if anything. You're reaching, Buckley. It's pathetic and weak."

"I'm pretty sure I know what was said. It's what men like you do to save your own ass. You'd give up everyone you know without a second thought. Even your brother."

Bill pointed at the door. "Are you forgetting I have a son out there somewhere?"

"That's exactly my point. To save him, I'd bet my last dollar that you gave up Bunker and Daisy when the General showed you the photographs. Even your own brother, if it came down to him or you."

"What photographs?"

"From the drone."

"That's enough," Kenny said to Buckley. "You're wasting your breath, Mayor."

"What I'm telling you is the truth," Buckley said. "You guys are being misled. You can't trust anything that man has told you."

"Even if he did try to save Jeffrey, none of that matters now," Kenny said, his eyes turning to the bleeding Valentina.

"Wait—" Buckley said, trying to get through to Kenny and stop this madness. "I don't think you realize who she is."

"I know exactly who she is," Kenny said without missing a beat.

"You don't understand. She's not just some Russian you've grabbed. She's part of the General's personal staff and I get the strong impression she's important to him. More than just professional, if you catch my drift. If you do this, he'll take it out on the town. Tenfold."

Kenny spun to grab Buckley by the neck with force. "I said that's enough! We're doing this. End of discussion. Am I making myself clear?"

Buckley couldn't breathe with the man's powerful grip squeezing his windpipe.

"You're either with us or against us, Mayor. You need to decide before I lose my patience. And trust me, that's the last thing you want to happen right now."

Buckley nodded in a panic.

Kenny let go after a three-count, his chin locked in a forward position with clenched teeth.

Buckley gasped a sudden, deep breath, then bent over and coughed before his lungs recovered.

"Now, where was I?" Kenny said to the group, his eyes turning to the captive in the chair.

Rico grabbed the Mayor by the bicep and spun him around. The Deputy shook his head and sent a silent message with a flare of his eyes not to push the situation.

Buckley wasn't about to give up. Not yet. There had to be a way to stop this, but he needed to try a different tactic.

Bill King was a liar and a cheat. There had to be a secret to expose. Something that might allow him to get through to Kenny and the others, but he needed to dig to find it. Dig like a Special Federal Prosecutor, combing through political files in search of a crime. One had to exist somewhere, if he probed hard enough. If nothing else, if he kept the attention on himself, maybe they'd stop their assault on Valentina before they killed her.

Right then, his mind replayed the steps Rico had taken when they'd first entered the market. They were careful and guarded. Plus, the deputy had used the term *sympathizers*, which brought a new question to Buckley's mind. One he sent Kenny's way. "How did you get Valentina in here without anyone noticing?"

Bill King tilted his head, then raised an eyebrow at his brother.

Kenny nodded in response, as if to give his approval to answer the question.

"The Russian bitch wandered into the store on her own. Grace took her down in the back when nobody was looking. Then she came to me for help."

"Grace?"

"She's a true American Patriot. Unlike others I know," Bill said, aiming his barbs at Buckley. "Kenny was cleaning up after his long walk home when Grace showed up. She filled us in on what happened, then we came here to get answers."

Right then, another flashback rose up from Buckley's memory. The vision showed Grace standing by the register with that strange look on her face. A guilty, downtrodden look. "I still can't believe Grace started this."

Bill laughed. "Didn't think the old bag had it in her. Obviously, I was wrong."

Buckley took a moment to run it through his mind. Granted, Grace was a little high-strung and had attacked Allison with the broomstick shortly after the EMP took down the grid, but a disagreement over stolen Pepsi was lightyears away from attacking a Russian officer.

Grace's look of guilt could have been the result of any number of things. Probably from letting these miscreants use the back of her store for torture. "I've known Grace for years. She'd never do this." He shook his head with force, letting his words hang in the air for a beat. "No. I don't believe a word you're saying. Not for a second."

"It really doesn't matter what you believe, Seth. What's done is done," Kenny said.

Buckley looked at Zeke and Russell, then turned his eyes to Rico. "You guys okay with this?"

Rico's eyes tightened. "It's them or us, Mayor. We've got to make a stand before it's too late."

"I get that, but this isn't the way. We can't start torturing people. It'll only make things worse. There has to be another way."

Kenny shoved at Buckley's chest. "I suppose you just wanna stand around and talk the Russians to death."

"Yeah, as a matter of fact, I was waiting to have a chat with General Zhukov. To lodge a complaint about the executions. I'm sure I can reason with him. We have to try."

"I thought as much. That's all you politicians ever want to do is talk, talk, talk," Kenny said, rolling his eyes. "The minute they pulled the trigger and shot our people in cold blood, they declared war. The gloves are off, Mayor. It's time to take back our town."

"I get that you want revenge. We all do. But do you really think you have a chance against the Russian Army?"

"Fuck the Russians. Americans don't back down from anyone."

"You need to stop and think here," Buckley said, throwing up his hands. "What are you gonna fight with? They've confiscated all the weapons."

Bill King shook his head, laughing. "If you really think they found all the weapons, you're dumber than you look, Mayor."

Buckley paused, unsure how to respond.

"And don't forget, our family owns a mine. Weapons aren't the only thing we have," Kenny said.

"Explosives?" Buckley asked.

"More than you know."

Buckley felt a glimmer of hope spring up inside. "But that still doesn't change the situation. How many lives will be lost trying to kill them all? Ten? Twenty? A hundred?"

"I doubt we'll have to kill them all," Zeke said. "We just have to make them miserable enough that they'll want to leave. It's about destroying their morale, Mayor."

"Hit and run," Kenny said. "We know where they are, but they don't know where we are. Or who we are, either."

"Home field advantage," Bill King said.

Kenny slapped his brother on the back. "We hit them hard and fast before we disappear into the woodwork. Then repeat."

Russell Thompson added, "It's what happened in Afghanistan. The Russians eventually withdrew after a bunch of sheepherders broke their will."

"It's still a huge gamble. You're putting everyone in danger."

"They obviously need us for slave labor, so the last thing they'll want to do is kill off their workers," Kenny said. "We can take advantage of that."

"They'll hunt you down."

"But they'll never find us. They don't know this town like we do."

Buckley pointed to the side of his neck. "I don't think you realize that we, unlike you, have trackers in our necks. And explosives."

Kenny scoffed. "Damn it, Seth. You'll believe anything, won't you?"

"I'm not following."

Kenny pointed at his brother's neck. "Show him, Bill."

Bill turned his head, exposing the left side of his neck.

Buckley counted six stitches. "You removed it?"

"Didn't have to."

"Because there's nothing there," Kenny said. "They went through all that injection bullshit to convince everyone not to resist. You really didn't think any of that was real, did you?"

Buckley didn't answer right away, shrugging. "Seemed legit to me."

"That kind of technology only exists in a James Bond movie, Mayor. None of it was real."

"I'm pretty sure it does exist. We just don't know about it yet. It's not that far-fetched, with how fast technology is advancing these days."

"Even if it did exist, it would cost a fortune to use it on a mass scale like this."

Kenny had a point, but Buckley still didn't believe the man would risk his brother's life like that. "So let me get this straight. You just took a knife and started digging around your brother's neck, hoping the implant was fake?"

"No, dumbass. Your girlfriend Valentina told us," Kenny said, pointing at the small dinette table in the corner. The First Aid kit was sitting on its surface and had its lid open. A bloody knife sat next to it, with some gauze covered in blood. They'd obviously used it to patch Bill up after cutting into him.

Bill King pointed at his neck. "Doc Marino's handiwork."

"He's in on this, too?"

"Oh yeah, he knows what's at stake."

"Anyone else I should know about?"

"No, that about covers it."

Kenny took a step forward. "I want to keep this small and efficient. Otherwise, the Russians will find out that we know about their fake injections."

Buckley wanted to respond, but couldn't after his mind filled with a scene of a bloody massacre in the town square. Bullets flying everywhere. Bodies ripping apart. Children screaming.

In his vision, he found himself walking through the grass in horror, the eyes of the dead looking up at him. "Aren't you forgetting the balloon outside? They're watching everything we do. They'll know she came in here and never left."

"No, they won't," Rico said without hesitation. "It's centered over the square and their cameras can't look directly down."

"We're in a blind spot," Kenny added.

"You can't know that for sure."

Kenny pointed at the unconscious Valentina. "That's why you extract information from those who do know."

Rico nodded. "She said they're using it mostly for intimidation."

"And to watch the perimeter of town," Zeke added.

"A sniper can take it out easily," Russell said.

"It's time someone stands up to them," Bill King said, now shoulder to shoulder with his brother. "And you, you God damn son-of-a-bitch—we're tired of your leadership. So consider this your recall election."

"I thought we had an understanding, Bill."

"What, like we're friends or something?"

"More like a coalition for the good of the town."

Bill huffed an angry breath. "Not after you testified against my brother in open court."

"Look, I wasn't the one accusing your brother of anything. That was Stan. I was only providing background information."

"More like character assassination."

Kenny grabbed Buckley by the shirt collar, pulling him forward until the two of them were nose to nose. "Don't think for a second that I've forgotten a single word of what you and Stan said on that stand, Mayor. I've had years to plan my revenge."

Buckley gulped as the shirt around his chest tightened under the man's grip.

Rico put his hand on Kenny's wrist. "We're going to need everyone, Kenny. We have to pull together, despite our differences."

Kenny hesitated for a few seconds, breathing heavily. He let go of the material with a shove. "Trust me, there will come a time when I take my revenge against all those who stood up against me."

"Welcome to the Resistance, Mayor," Zeke said, moving in front of Kenny.

Rico and Russell joined him in a show of solidarity.

CHAPTER 96

Bunker filled the remaining pouches on one of Tuttle's tactical vests with ammo magazines, then packed his rucksack with a slew of supplies for his reconnaissance mission. He wasn't sure what he'd face once he left the compound, but he needed to be prepared.

Tuttle had stocked the bunker with just about everything a warrior could need, though most of the weapons and gear were civilian models, not the same high-end military-grade equipment he'd trained with. But it would do. At least the Steiner 8x30 binoculars were first-rate, their built in rangefinder and compact size a welcome addition to his load-out.

He planned to travel weapons-light for speed and agility, needing only a reliable semi-auto handgun and a tactical rifle. He figured a Glock .40 and a 7.62 should be sufficient, mainly because if he found himself in a situation where he needed more firepower, then he'd probably be surrounded and outgunned by a Russian strike team.

Tuttle had mounted a red-dot Vortex scope on the AR10. He took a moment to consider upgrading to a high-powered model, but decided to keep the optics as-is. Long-range marksmanship wasn't his specialty, so the CQB setup was preferred.

Where he was going, a Close Quarters Battle was the most likely scenario he'd face. Hopefully, it wouldn't come to that, but he took along extra batteries for the scope and magazines just in case.

Daisy arrived in the supply bunker, her hands buried in her pockets. "Looks like you're just about ready."

"Just need to pack a few more items. I'll head out at dusk."

"Under the cover of darkness. Smart." She snatched a head-mounted device from the stack next to her and tossed it at him. "Don't forget this."

He caught the night vision goggles in his left hand. "Thanks." He put the Gen2 device into his pack, along with a change of civilian clothes and a Colorado Rockies ball cap.

"Think you'll need those?" she asked.

"I might have to blend in as a civilian and I can't do that wearing this," he said, glancing down at his forest-green camo and rattling gear.

She hesitated before she spoke again, her eyes watching every movement of his hands. "The Sheriff and Burt have mapped out a plan for you. They're waiting in Martha's dining room."

"Tell them I'll be there in a flash."

Daisy moved closer and wrapped her arms around his neck, then kissed him on cheek. It was only momentary peck of her lips, but there was feeling behind it.

"What was that for?" he asked in a whisper.

Her hug grew tighter. "Just wanted you to know how much I appreciate you stopping by my place and checking on my cat."

Not the answer he expected, but it made sense. At least the situation didn't spin sideways and get emotional. "No problem. I'm headed that way."

She let go of the embrace, her eyes focused on the floor around his feet.

Bunker wondered if his lack of reciprocal hug offended her. "Is there anything else you need me to do, while I'm there?"

Her eyes came up and met his. "Just make sure the gas is off."

"Consider it done."

"There are bowls in the cupboard by the sink. Vonda won't overeat, so go ahead and leave extra food and water for her. That should hold her for a while."

"I can bring her back if you'd like."

"No. She'll just slow you down."

"Are you sure?"

Daisy shook her head, though the shrug that followed looked tentative. "She's only a cat, Bunker. It's not worth the risk. We've got way more important things to deal with right now."

Her callous answer was unexpected. The woman had a big heart, that much was clear, but he figured she'd react like most pet owners—overly attached and willing to risk life and limb to save the animal.

"Will do," he said, letting the question go so he could shift focus back to his packing.

"Stephanie and Megan are getting Tango ready."

"Excellent. One less thing I have to worry about."

"Speaking of worry . . . I don't think either of them wants you to leave. Things could get a little weird before you head out."

Bunker didn't respond, needing a moment to think.

"At least that's the impression I got when I stopped by to check on their progress."

"Did they say something?"

"No. Just a feeling."

"Okay. I'll deal with it. Thanks for the heads-up."

A suffocating silence hovered in the room as Bunker stared at Daisy and she at him. There was another topic he needed to cover with her, but he wasn't sure if this was the right time.

Daisy spoke before he could decide. "All right, then. I guess my job here is done." She turned and walking away.

"Hey Daisy?" he asked in a delicate tone.

She stopped and turned in an instant, her eyes filled with anticipation.

"There's one more thing I need to say."

"Okay, shoot."

He cleared his throat, waiting for the words to line up on his tongue. "Thanks for believing in me. I know we've had our moments, but your trust in me means more than you'll ever know. I won't let you down."

She smiled, her tone turning confident as her face flushed red. "I know you won't. Otherwise, I'd have to hunt you until the end of time, *Bulldog*."

He sent back a smile, appreciating her not making this goodbye any more difficult than it already was. They both knew the mission was dangerous and some words were best left unsaid.

* * *

"Where's Victor?" Sheriff Apollo asked Dicky when he arrived at the guard station at the end of Old Mill Road.

Dicky pointed in the direction of Martha Rainey's house. "He went inside a while ago. Should be back anytime. Hopefully, he'll remember the water."

"Ah, no. He's not inside."

"What do you mean?"

"His mother sent me here to check on him."

"Shit," Dicky said, looking down at the empty spot of dirt formerly occupied by Rusty's bike.

Apollo shook his head, not wanting to ask the next question. "Tell me he didn't take off?"

Dicky shrugged, then pointed at the oak tree designated for the sniper hide. "I was over there taking a whiz when the kid told me he was heading back inside to check on his mom. I thought that's where he went."

"Jesus, Dicky. How could you let this happen? I assigned him to this spot so you could keep an eye on him."

Dicky dropped his head. "Sorry, Sheriff. I fucked up."

Apollo thought about continuing the reprimand, but chose not to because it wouldn't change anything. Besides, this failure was his for trusting Victor and leaving the flight-risk kid with a volunteer deputy. "Do you have any idea where he went?"

"No sir. Just what he told me. I thought he rode the bike back to the house to check on his mom."

Apollo paused, putting on his detective hat. A set of tire tracks angled around the barricade and led to the bridge. "What were you two talking about right before he took off?"

"Nothing really. He was feeling down after you refused to give him a gun. I know he thinks that nobody trusts him, so I put him in charge of this station when I went to take a leak. I thought it might cheer him up."

"Anything else?"

"That's about it."

"When was this exactly?"

"Right after you left earlier."

Apollo ran through the conversation with the kid, replaying the words exchanged. "I laid into him pretty good, didn't I?"

"He needed to hear it, boss. Otherwise, he'll never grow up."

"Yeah, maybe so. But I didn't need to be so harsh."

"At least he admitted to the break-in. That's a start."

"I suppose it is. But if he thinks none of us trusts him, then there's no telling why he took off."

"I'm sure he's just trying to find a way to prove himself. I was like that back in the day, always trying to figure out where I belonged."

Apollo agreed. "It's not easy at that age, especially when you don't have a father figure around."

"Down deep, I think he's a good kid."

Apollo felt a knot form in his stomach as he peered over his shoulder, his eyes landing on the Rainey homestead. If Victor took off because of what Apollo had said, then whatever happened to the boy was his fault.

He let out a slow breath, his mind a whirl. "I better go have a chat with Allison."

"I can go explain it to her, Sheriff. You shouldn't have to. This was my bad."

"No, this one's on me."

"Are you sure? Because I don't mind taking the heat. I was in charge and he skipped out on my watch."

"I appreciate the offer, Dicky, but I got this. It's my job as Sheriff," Apollo said, the pain in his abdomen intensifying. "Stand watch until I send Daisy here to relieve you. Won't be long. She's helping Bunker get geared up."

"You got it, boss. Again, I'm sorry."

CHAPTER 97

Apollo took Allison Rainey by the crux of the arm and led her away from the other members of the compound who were standing around the dining room table in Martha Rainey's house. The area maps were spread out across the surface and ready for Bunker, but he hadn't arrived yet from Tuttle's place.

"Where's my son?" Allison asked, her tone tense and suspicious. The depth of concern in her eyes was obvious, almost painful.

Apollo needed to soften the news and find a way to explain his complete and total failure. The last thing he wanted was to inflict undue emotional trauma on the woman he'd been planning to ask out on a date ever since she landed in town. He swallowed hard, then licked his lips in a stall maneuver until he found the proper words. "That's what I wanted to talk to you about…"

"Is he hurt?"

"No, no, no," he stammered. "That's not it."

The volume in her voice shot up a level. "Then what is it, Sheriff? Is he dead? Oh my God, he's dead, isn't he?"

Martha Rainey joined the conversation an instant later, touching her daughter's forearm with a soft hand. "What's wrong? Is it Victor?"

Allison nodded, looking at her mother with fright in her eyes. "Yeah, something's terribly wrong. I can sense it. But I can't get the Sheriff to tell me anything." Her eyes swung to Apollo. "Why won't you tell me?"

Apollo opened his mouth to answer, but Martha beat him to it, not letting a millisecond of silence drift by. "You need to tell us, Gus. Right now. This very instant!"

"I'm trying to—" Apollo said, wishing they'd let him respond before their mounting hysteria ran them over. "Victor took—"

"Damn it, he stole something again!" Allison snapped, throwing up her hands. She shook her head at her mother. "I told you he'd do it again. I told you. It just never stops with that boy."

Martha's eyes softened, compressing some of the wrinkles along her temples. "It'll be okay, honey. It's not your fault. You're a good mother."

Allison stuck out her chin and pinched her lips before she answered, her breathing more exaggerated. "If I'm such a good mother, why does he keep doing this?" She paced a bit, her feet moving in a circle, tears beginning to show on her cheeks. "I thought we were making progress. He promised me."

Apollo brought his arms up to stop the woman's trek, but Martha got in the way when she wrapped her arms around Allison's neck and spoke into her ear. "Trust me, Allison. You've done everything you can. None of this is your fault."

Allison's arms were hanging limp, not returning the embrace. "Yes, it is my fault. I'm his mother and I'm responsible for everything he does. I just wish I could get through to him, Mom, but he's just like his father—stubborn, and he doesn't listen to anyone. I don't know what I'm going to do with him."

The hug ended before Allison shifted her focus to Apollo. "He's going to jail, isn't he?"

"Hang on a minute. I never said that," Apollo answered, trying to break through the madness running amok.

"But he stole something, didn't he?"

"Yes, as a matter of fact," Apollo said, taking a step closer to Allison. He needed to penetrate the panic surrounding her and explain, "but you need to listen to me—"

Martha put out an arm, pressing her palm on Apollo's chest before he could finish his sentence. "We appreciate your concern, Sheriff, but this is a family matter now—a *private* family matter. You need to step back and let me deal with this."

Apollo pushed her hand away. "All right, just stop. Both of you! You're getting way ahead of yourselves here."

Martha's lips ran quiet and her eyes shot wide.

Apollo continued while there was a moment of silence in the room. "Both of you need to shut the hell up and let me talk."

Allison looked stunned.

Martha folded her arms across her chest and stood more erect than before. "I suppose that's an order?"

"If it has to be an order to get the two of you to listen, then it's an order. But for heaven's sake, let me talk for a minute."

Apollo peered at the others by the table. Each of them was staring at him, their faces covered with shock. "Everything is okay, folks. No need to be concerned. Just a little situation, but we've got it under control."

He took a moment to make sure Allison and Martha were listening before he continued. "What I was trying to tell you is that Victor borrowed Rusty's bike and went for a ride."

"A ride?" Martha asked before pointing toward the front of her home. "Now? With everything that's going on out there?"

"Yes, he took off and we're not sure why. But there's no reason to start a panic, ladies."

"When did he leave?" Martha asked.

"A while ago."

"And you're just telling us now?"

"I would have told you earlier, but I just found out myself."

"You need to go look for him, Sheriff," Allison said, grabbing him by the hands with a tender wrap. Her fingers squeezed his, grabbing his attention. "He shouldn't be out there all alone. It's too dangerous."

Her skin was smooth and supple, just like he'd imagined. Her touch was a distraction to be sure, but he managed to push through it and regain his focus. "I plan to. But first, I wanted to let you know that he's missing. But we'll find him, you have my word."

* * *

Bunker opened the front door to Martha's house and waited for Daisy to enter first. When he stepped inside, he found Apollo standing to the left with Martha and Allison. The Sheriff's hands were holding onto Allison's, all three of their faces flushed red.

Jeffrey, Stephanie, Rusty, Burt, Albert, and Dustin stood to the right, holding position near the dining room table. Their faces looked numb. So did Megan's, her butt planted in the same dining room chair as before.

Bunker looked at Apollo, the tension in the room thick and palpable. "What did we miss?"

"I need to go take care of something, then I'll get right on it," Apollo told Allison, ignoring Bunker's query.

She nodded, then let go of his hands.

Martha wrapped an arm around Allison and pulled her close.

When Apollo arrived at Bunker's position, he said, "There's been a development."

"The Russians?" Daisy asked.

"No, it's Allison's son," Apollo said, the volume in his voice less than before.

"Did he get hurt?" Bunker asked, lowering his voice to match the Sheriff's.

"No. He took off with Rusty's bike while Dicky's back was turned. I had them both on guard duty."

Daisy took a step closer, leaning in close to Apollo. "Did he run away?"

"Not sure. But we're going to need to send out a search party."

"How long ago was this?" she asked.

"Too long, unfortunately. I just found out when I went out there to check on things."

"Why didn't Dicky say something?"

"He didn't know, apparently. Victor waited until he was behind a tree doing his business, then pretended he was taking the bike back to the house to check on his mom. That's when he took off. Tracks head across the bridge."

"Why would he do that?"

Apollo took in a slow breath, then let it out. "I think it has something to do with a little chat he and I had with about him stepping up and taking responsibility."

"Franklin's 1911?" Bunker asked.

"That, and other things. I might have been a bit too rough on the kid."

"So the boy got pissed and just took off?" Daisy asked.

"I'm afraid so."

"It's possible he might come back on his own, Sheriff," Bunker said. "I'm not sure sending out a search party is the right move. Not with me leaving."

"He might, but I promised his mother we'd look for him. We got a kid out there who needs our help."

Bunker nodded. "Then we'd better hurry before it gets dark."

"Dicky and I will handle it, Bunker. You need to get moving as planned."

"What about me?" Daisy asked.

"I need you to relieve Dicky."

"10-4."

Apollo looked at Bunker. "Burt and I have outlined some waypoints for you. The map's on the table."

"Okay, show me what you got."

CHAPTER 98

"Excuse me, General," Colonel Sergei Orlov said in Russian after knocking, waiting for clearance to enter the newly acquired office of his commanding officer.

General Yuri Zhukov was not a patient man by any stretch, but Orlov hoped today might be the exception. Then again, maybe the General would deny this unscheduled meeting, one Sergei preferred not to have with the ruthless leader.

Usually Sergei stood in the corner of the General's office in silence, waiting for orders. It happened recently when the guards dragged the Mayor in for a light interrogation. Then again when the Silver King Mine owner tried to negotiate his way out of the occupation.

It was degrading for an officer who had achieved the rank of Colonel to stand at attention for hours on end, but it was an honor to serve Mother Russia in whatever capacity she needed. And right now, she needed him to suck it up and support the narcissistic, overconfident General during *Operation Gospodstvo.*

It was the single most important mission in Russian history, one that drew his full attention the instant he learned it involved taming the American beast on American soil.

What kept him moving forward in this demeaning role was the knowledge that once their battalion had acquired what it needed, they'd return home with the spoils of a victorious mission. His name, and the names of his junior officers, would live on in the history books for all those who came after.

Sergei tried hailing his commander again, this time raising his voice and knocking four times instead of three. "General Zhukov. I have important information."

"Enter," Zhukov said in Russian, his voice thready. His words sounded painful.

Sergei adjusted his uniform, making sure every crease was perfect before he stepped through. When his feet landed inside the threshold, his eyes found a naked man lying face-down on a massage table. A white terrycloth towel covered the man's midsection, leaving his upper back and sandy-white calves exposed to the Colorado air.

A rail-thin American woman in an all-white outfit chopped at the man's back with the downward edge of her hands. The reddish glow in the blonde's cheeks intensified as she worked the area just above the towel in a rapid-fire motion, pounding the stress away.

Sergei wasn't sure how the narrow-hipped resident could work her hands with such speed and precision, but the woman was obviously a professional.

Typical, Sergei thought to himself, having witnessed the General's taste for blonde women and massages before. Russian Foreign Intelligence had developed detailed files on every Clearwater resident and he was certain the General used the SVR-gathered information to select this woman as his personal masseuse.

Sergei had his share of body hair, but nothing close to that of the General's. It looked like the masseuse was pounding at a Persian rug instead of someone's spine.

He cleared his throat, keeping the conversation in Russian, not only due to its classified nature, but because the General despised English. He couldn't blame his boss. He wasn't fond of it either, but like he preached to his men, it was part of their duty.

Technically, learning to speak English was an order that came from the highest levels of the Kremlin—one every officer in this command had accepted without question. It wasn't easy preparing for this most prestigious mission, not when a year of endless language sessions was involved. "General, sir. Sorry to interrupt."

The masseuse stopped her hands when the General raised his head and brought his eyes to Sergei.

Sergei felt the eyes of the woman on him. He turned to confirm, seeing her tuck two unruly strands of hair behind her ears, exposing more of her face.

She was attractive, but much too thin for his taste. He preferred women with wide hips and a little meat on their bones. Yet he knew she was just the type of woman the General preferred, having witnessed the man's selection process before. The man loved to sample the local cuisine. Both with his lips and other body parts.

"Can't you see I'm busy?" the General snarled.

"Sorry, sir. But this can't wait."

"Make it quick, Colonel."

"Sir, the information I carry is classified." Sergei could have provided more information to his commander, but decided against it. Their pre-mission briefing had been explicit and clear—a small percentage of Americans speak Russian. He wasn't to assume his conversation was secure when speaking his native language.

Zhukov waved at the masseuse to leave the room. The woman didn't hesitate, backing away and taking one of the hand towels from a stack next to her. She folded the towel in half, then used it to dab the beads of sweat on her brow as she walked to the office door and disappeared outside.

The General rolled to his side and sat up. The towel fell from his lap when he stood up and strolled behind his desk, never bothering to cover up.

The leather chair squeaked when Zhukov's naked backside slid across the upholstery. He flashed a scowl. "I don't have all day, Orlov."

"Sorry, sir," he said, handing the General a single sheet of paper containing eleven items on the Daily Action Report. "An incident has been reported that warrants your immediate attention."

He watched the General's eyes, waiting for them to land on the last item. The other notices were fairly routine, given the nature and location of their mission. He'd seen it all before when in-country. So had the General.

Flare-ups with residents and troop misconduct were predictable when dealing with command and control of foreign civilians. The newest recruits were usually the problem. It developed like clockwork, usually within days, leading him to classify the troops in one of two groups: those who were overly committed to their first assignment, or those struggling with their own inner demons.

Not every Russian who puts on the uniform can handle the relentless pressure of being in-country, especially when you're looking into the eyes of innocent women and children.

However, when an officer goes missing—a female officer—everyone takes notice, even the new recruits. Patriotism trumps morality every time. Especially when it's the General's interpreter. He'd hoped to have a resolution before stepping into this meeting, but his pair of investigators came up empty.

"When was this reported?" Zhukov asked.

"Forty-five minutes ago. Officer Zakharova failed to appear for a scheduled duty assignment. Our initial search came up empty."

Zhukov slammed the paper down on the desk. "That's unacceptable, Orlov! Find her! Tear apart this town if you have to. Task whatever resources you need, but I want her found. Now!"

"Yes, sir."

* * *

Burt Lowenstein stood next to Bunker and across the table from Apollo and Dicky as he put his scarred finger on the map. Mechanic work ages a man's hands quickly, leaving them broken, bruised, and beyond salvation. Constant grease and soap were only part of the problem. Wrench slippage near an engine block caused far more damage, tearing skin from bone upon impact.

Burt traced a path along a series of black lines he'd drawn on the map earlier, purposely avoiding the red circles Tuttle had added when the old coot was still alive.

"This is the way I'd go, Bunker. It's the safest route back to town."

Bunker nodded slowly, then pointed at a clearing bordered by mountains on all sides. "What can you tell me about this?"

"That's Patterson's Meadow. But you'll want to avoid it, too." Burt drew a line from north to south, taking Bunker's eyes through a narrow gap in the topography. "It's a death trap, with only one way in or out. A guy could get himself killed in there."

The answer didn't appear to faze Bunker, almost as if that was the answer he was expecting.

"What's with all the circles around the meadow?" Stephanie asked, putting a hand on Bunker's back as she leaned in next to him.

Burt saw her smile at Bunker, then rub her hand across his back. The man didn't seem to notice. Or else he chose not to react to her friendliness.

"Daisy thought he might be planning to build a cabin on it," Apollo said from across the table. "But we really don't know for sure."

"Okay, I get that," Stephanie said. "But why highlight all the bridges and the other stuff?"

"It's important to know the area, especially the egress points," Bunker said, his tone slow and even, sounding as if he was running it through in his head.

Apollo nodded. "If a forest fire hit, his options would be limited."

Bunker walked to the other side of Burt, leaving Stephanie's hand dangling. "I'm going to need to take a closer look at it."

Burt wasn't sure why. The meadow was much too close to town to be used as any type of base camp, if that's what Bunker was thinking.

Stephanie put her finger on the lines representing the highway near it. "At least it's close to some pavement. I don't know about you guys, but driving these dirt roads would get old after a while."

Burt disagreed with the buxom beauty. The clearing was much too close to the paved highway—would be easy pickings for the Russians. He'd choose something more remote.

Bunker put the tip of his finger on Burt's original path, then drew an imaginary line from it to the mouth of Patterson's Meadow. "Is there anything to worry about in here?"

"Not really. Just avoid the highway." He took the protective cap from the black marker and added another line to the map. "This logging road is one of the nicer ones in the area. The Forest Service maintains it regularly."

"How wide is it?"

"It's pretty wide. At least forty feet. Maybe more. The ATV riders fly up and down it all the time. At least they used to whenever I was out there hunting. Those assholes always scared off the game in the area."

"Wide enough," Bunker mumbled, his eyes locked onto the map.

"Wide enough for what?" Burt asked.

"It's not important," Bunker said, straightening his posture. He rolled up the map. "How are the projects coming along?"

"I'm getting there, but it's a ton of work," Burt said. "All I can say is that you better come through with that rifle. Otherwise, you and I are gonna go a few rounds."

Apollo answered instead of Bunker. "No reason to go there, Burt. A deal is a deal. It's yours when this is over."

Bunker's eyes darted around the room. "Has anyone seen Albert? I need to have a chat with him."

"He's down the road, hanging out with Daisy," Dicky said.

Apollo rolled his eyes. "Why am I not surprised?"

"I don't know how she puts up with it," Burt said. "Even I don't drool that bad."

Apollo looked at Bunker. "While you're doing that, I'm gonna check on Allison and her mother before Dicky and I head out to look for Victor."

"I'm sure they'll appreciate that. Just don't overcommit on the search. Can't risk everyone's security for the sake of one troubled boy."

Apollo's eyes signaled he agreed with the assessment. "There's a fine line. But we gotta try."

"Good luck," Bunker said, holding out his hand for a shake.

"Keep your head down out there," Apollo said, grabbing his hand and shaking it twice. Dicky did the same. The two men left the room in a rush.

Bunker looked at Stephanie. "You wouldn't happen to know if Martha has a pen and some paper around here, would you? I've got a laundry list to write."

She pointed at a curved entry table hugging the wall by the front door. "Try the drawer. That's where I'd keep them."

CHAPTER 99

Fifteen minutes later . . .

Bunker grabbed the assault rifle leaning against the wall by the front door of Martha Rainey's place and loaded a magazine from his vest with a firm shove of his hand. He headed outside with the map lashed to his rucksack using the Velcro straps along the side.

Shortly after his feet hit the pavers outside, a tug landed on his right arm. The force was enough to turn him sideways.

"You got a minute?" Stephanie King asked, her son fiddling with the Pokémon cards a few yards away. Dallas was huddled with Jeffrey, shining a flashlight at the underside of one of the cards.

"Sure, but I need to get moving. The sun is almost down." Bunker didn't see Megan, but he knew she was around somewhere. He planned to say goodbye to the ebony child who had captured his heart.

"So . . . you're really going to do this?" Stephanie asked in a defiant tone.

"I'm coming back, Steph. Don't worry."

"You say that, but you really don't know for sure. It's dangerous out there."

Bunker held up his rifle. "That's why I have this."

She hugged him without warning, her ample chest pressing hard into his tactical vest.

He brought his arms up and wrapped his forearms around her back. He put his free hand on her back and rubbed, making sure she knew he appreciated her concern. "I know you're worried, but this is what I'm trained to do."

"But it's the Russians."

"Trust me, they have no idea who they're dealing with."

"Please be careful. We need you to come back in one piece."

"I will," he said, as the hug continued.

"Jeffrey would be heartbroken if you got yourself killed."

"Yeah, I'm pretty fond of that boy, too," he said, debating whether to say the next three words lining up on his tongue. He decided to set them free. "What about you?"

She leaned back from the embrace but didn't answer, her face only inches from his. Her watery eyes never moved. He stopped his breath as her stare lingered for what seemed like a minute, their lower bodies pressing together.

"You two gonna kiss, or what?" Dallas asked.

The words broke through the awkwardness to end the stare-down. Bunker pulled his arms away and stepped back.

Stephanie did the same, looking like she had an hour's worth of words she was holding back.

Bunker exhaled, letting the breath he'd been holding escape.

Someone tugged at Bunker's pant leg.

He looked down.

It was Jeffrey, hovering only a foot away, with Dallas next to him. The freckled boy brought his hand up with the deck of Pokémon cards in his clutch. "These are yours, Jack."

"No Jeffrey, you hang on to them until I get back. Someone needs to keep them safe."

The boy nodded, then spread the cards out in his hand. He took one from the stack and held it up. "I want you to have this one."

"For good luck," Stephanie said a millisecond later, her tone pushy and to the point as usual. She snatched the card and gave it to Bunker.

Bunker knew he couldn't refuse. He took it and studied the colorful scene. The cartoon character portrayed a demon-looking squirrel creature with a fiery tail. "Which one of them is this?"

Jeffrey's face lit up with excitement. "That's Charmeleon, my all-time favorite."

"He looks fierce."

"He is. But there are a bunch of other characters I like, too. My second favorite is Metapod. But Parasect is cool, too. Oh, and Arcanine. He's really fast."

Bunker never paid much attention to the Pokémon craze. Why should he? He didn't have any kids and Pokémon wasn't a high priority for the members of the brotherhood. The Kindred had other hobbies, so to speak, usually with names like Candi or Jasmine. "How many are there?"

"Over eight hundred."

"Wow, that's a lot more than I thought," Bunker said, figuring this kid was a collector. He seemed to know a lot about the Pokémon phenomenon. "How many do you have?"

Jeffrey held up the cards Bunker had given him. "Just these. Mom won't let me collect them."

Bunker smiled at the boy, then slid the Charmeleon card into one of his pockets. "Thank you, sport. I'll be sure to keep this one safe for you."

"Don't forget my mom and sisters," Dallas said.

"I won't," Bunker answered, figuring he'd run across them along the way. Most likely in town, with the other residents. When you're the occupying force, a centralized detention zone is the most efficient strategy to maintain order.

Stephanie leaned forward and whispered in Bunker's ear. "I'm sure Jeffrey would like a hug."

Bunker nodded. He bent down on one knee and waited with arms outstretched. Jeffrey knew instantly what to do, flying into Bunker's embrace.

After their hug ended, Stephanie said, "Megan wants to say goodbye, too. She's waiting for you by the corral."

Bunker stood. "She's not by herself, is she?"

"No, Rusty's keeping an eye on her."

"I'll head there shortly." Bunker turned his feet toward the end of Old Mill Road. "Wish me luck, everyone."

Stephanie didn't answer as Bunker walked away.

Neither did Jeffrey or Dallas.

CHAPTER 100

Bunker waved a quick hello at Daisy when he arrived at the guard station by the Old Henley Bridge, but didn't send any words her way. He aimed his focus at Albert instead. "Can we talk a minute?"

The fat man paused before he nodded, then walked with Bunker using his trademark waddle.

When Dustin started to follow, Bunker held up a hand. "Why don't you hang back a minute, Dustin?"

"Oh, okay. Will do."

After twenty yards or so, Bunker stopped and turned, keeping Albert in a direct line between him and Daisy.

"I sense a question coming my way," Albert said, his tone confident.

"You could say that."

"I'm all ears."

"I think it's time for the two of us to clear the air."

"About what?"

"About something you and I have been dancing around for a while now."

Albert blinked, but didn't respond.

Bunker ran through a half-dozen variations in his mind about the question he wanted to ask, before deciding to keep it simple and direct. "Are you really Tin Man?"

Albert's breathing stopped as he angled his head to the side, staring at the ground in silence.

"It's not that hard a question," Bunker said, recognizing the stall maneuver. "It's either yes or no."

Albert brought his eyes to bear, letting out the inhale he'd taken in. "Are you really Bulldog, enforcer for The Kindred?"

Bunker couldn't hold back a short chuckle. "I think you already know the answer to that question."

"As do you, to mine."

Bunker should have expected the non-committal rhetoric Albert was slinging. If he was Tin Man, then he'd probably spent his share of time in front of curious law enforcement—as had

Bunker. That type of intense scrutiny hardens your resolve, teaching you to remain calm and choose your words carefully, if you decide to speak at all.

Detective teams are masters at spins, lies, and deceit, able to say almost anything to entrap their suspect. Self-incrimination is one of their most powerful tools.

Only those suspects who keep their wits about them while being grilled in the hot seat will survive the hours, sometimes days, it takes until the public defender makes an appearance. For those who rode with The Kindred, a hired barrister would arrive within an hour to end the questioning and ensure the gang's secrets remained a secret.

A smirk landed on Bunker's face.

The corners of Albert's mouth turned up. Yet it wasn't a grin. It was more of an *I'm smarter than you* look.

Bunker decided to change tactics, choosing a flanking maneuver instead of an all-out frontal assault. "Look, you and I both know you're not Tin Man."

"Then why are you asking?"

"Because we're a long way from the streets of LA and these people deserve better, one way or the other."

"I'm sure that's true. But since I don't have a map in front of me, I'll defer to your expertise on the matter."

Bunker shook his head. "So the dance continues."

"Are we done?" Albert asked, looking bored.

Bunker wondered if there was another way to confirm Albert's identify. The heavy man wasn't going to give a direct answer.

Right then, his mind connected with a memory from the past. Rumor had it the legendary meth cook possessed certain physical skills that would be easy to confirm without wasting time on any more words.

Bunker made a closed fist and threw a punch at Albert's head.

Albert responded in a flash, bringing his hands up in a lightning-quick defensive maneuver, deflecting the punch with a hook block. The big man countered by closing the gap between them, moving into Bunker's center position with a twist of his body.

An instant later, Albert locked Bunker's outstretched arm in a wedge position, then leveraged his considerable weight to drive Bunker to the ground on his back.

Albert brought a knee down on Bunker's chest, while simultaneously unleashing a swift right jab that stopped less than an inch from Bunker's nose.

"Satisfied?" Albert said a moment later, his eyes focused and fierce.

Daisy ran to their position. "What the hell is going on?"

"Just testing a theory," Bunker said from the prone position, the rucksack pressing into his spine.

Albert withdrew his fist, then stood up before extending an open palm.

Bunker grabbed it, letting Albert pull him to his feet.

Daisy moved between the two combatants with her arms outstretched and hands pressing on each of their chests.

Dustin joined the circus, his eyes wide in disbelief. "Jesus Christ! Where did that come from, Albert?"

"Are you okay?" Daisy asked Bunker, her hands grabbing at his vest and backpack.

"I'm good."

She turned to Albert. "And you. Explain yourself."

Albert flared an eyebrow, his face looking smug. "Just answering a question."

"What question?"

Albert ignored Daisy, keeping his eyes on Bunker. "Are we good?"

Bunker sent a nod of respect to Albert.

"So that's it?" she asked, her gaze alternating between Bunker and Albert.

"That's it," Bunker said in his most solemn tone. "Time for me to get moving."

She held for a moment, then huffed before stomping her way to the guard station.

Albert slid around Bunker to change places, now facing the end of Old Mill Road, his eyes peering at Daisy's position behind Bunker.

He put a hand into his pocket and pulled out a plastic bag filled with red crystals, dangling it from his fingertips. "I'm thinking you might need this."

Bunker recognized the infamous red crystals—Clearwater Red, the purest form of meth ever to have hit the streets. "For what?"

Albert lowered his voice. "To bribe your way past a checkpoint. It's my finest blend, but I'm sure you already know that."

Bunker took the gift and tested its weight with a bounce of his hand. It was roughly a pound, he figured, having held the same quantity on a number of occasions when he rode with The Kindred.

"Trust me," Albert said in a confident tone. "That will get you wherever you need to go."

Bunker knew Albert was right, but didn't want to openly admit it, even though the history books were filled with countless examples of military drug use. Most of it heavy. All of it dangerous. Especially during wartime or occupation. He'd seen it firsthand during his tour of duty, despite the public zero-tolerance policy of the Pentagon.

Drugs put a warrior's life in danger from either fatigue, over-stimulation, or euphoria. But it didn't end there. A grunt's comrades were also affected, relying on the addict to cover their six.

At this point, there was no reason to think the Russian troops would be immune to the epidemic of drugs. They were human, like everyone else, regardless of their reputation as ruthless, unfeeling, and ready to kill.

It would come down to pride and honor versus fear and anxiety, both sets of terms representing the primal instincts of a warrior and the root emotions of an addict. A fine line, indeed.

Some of the troops would need an escape from the stressors of constant threat. Others would be looking for temporary relief from the hours of endless boredom between duty shifts. Either way, these crystals would come in handy, if Bunker chose to use them.

Despite the clear advantage of supplying the insurgents with a powerful mind-altering substance, he knew the results would be difficult to control. More than that, it would be dangerous to seek out those troops in need. If he made contact with the wrong soldier first, it would not end well. He'd need to choose his initial target well.

Even if he could manage the outcome, fostering the use of Clearwater Red was something he preferred to avoid. Not because of potential law enforcement issues. But rather, because it would be a constant reminder of why he left The Kindred—drugs and children. Two things that should never mix.

Anytime drugs are accessible, even by accident, the potential for underage abuse is a clear and present danger. A danger he would be responsible for if he kept this gift from Tin Man.

After careful consideration, Bunker decided to hang onto the drugs. Leaving them in Albert's hands would be a mistake. Bunker needed to get the meth out of camp before one of the kids got their hands on it.

If, later on, the crystals just so happened to come in handy with the Russians, then so be it. A bonus, he decided. But his first objective must be securing the drugs, then stowing them somewhere safe.

Bunker slid his pack off and stuffed the baggie inside the upper pouch, keeping his body between the pack and Daisy. She'd only just started to trust him again after learning his secrets. If she caught a glimpse of the drug exchange, it would tear down the foundation he'd rebuilt.

"Is there more?" Bunker asked Albert in a whisper.

"No. That's it. But I can cook up another batch if we need it."

"That won't be necessary."

"I wouldn't be so sure. Once those soldiers get a taste, they're gonna want more. Just need someone to escort me back to my lab."

"Like I said, we're good."

"Suit yourself," Albert said, pausing. He glanced at Daisy, then back at Bunker. "Does the smoking-hot deputy know?"

"About what?"

"Your past."

Bunker nodded, holding back his distaste for Albert's sexual description of Daisy. "Most of it. But she's the only one."

Albert's mouth flopped open. "You told her?"

"Didn't have a choice after we ran into one of my old friends, Grinder."

"No, I guess not," Albert answered, his eyes indicating he was deep in thought. "Then I trust she doesn't know of mine?"

"Not that I'm aware."

"Good, then I hope we can keep it that way."

"I'm sure that can be arranged. But I'm going to need something in return."

"Name it," Dustin said, breaking his silence.

Bunker gave three sheets of folded paper to Albert. He'd found the paper in the drawer of the entrance table by Martha Rainey's front door. On the parchment, he'd written a long list of items and detailed instructions. "If you're as good as you say you are, then I'll need you use those chemistry skills to mix up some special ingredients that Tuttle has on hand. Something exotic, if you know what I mean."

"And deliberate, I'm guessing. Russian deliberate," Albert said after a head nod, his eyes tracking down the list. "Toads, really?"

"Can you handle it or not?"

"Sure. For Bulldog, anything." Albert folded the documents until they were the size of a smart phone, then stuffed them into his pocket. "Anything else?"

"That's it for now. Just have it ready when I get back. Ask Daisy if you need help. She knows where a lot of that stuff is."

"I'm sure I can handle it."

Bunker glanced at Daisy, then brought his attention back to Dustin and Albert. "I need to go have a chat with her. She looks a little stressed."

"Good luck with that," Albert said. "She's a unique bundle."

"That's an understatement," Bunker answered after a roll of his eyes.

He turned and headed to Daisy, needing to smooth things over before he went on his recon mission. If she had any questions, he needed to answer them to eliminate any fear or suspicion that might be building. If he didn't calm her down, she might turn to someone else—someone like the Sheriff—and fill him in on a number of things Bunker wanted to keep secret.

* * *

Dustin turned to Albert after Bunker was halfway to Daisy's position. He lowered his voice. "I can't believe you gave our entire supply to Bunker."

"Wasn't doing us any good, now was it?"

"What about our deal with Burt?"

"That's over with. Even he knows it. That's why we haven't spoken about it since we got here. He's moved on to something bigger and better. I can sense it in his eyes. Just watch him when he thinks nobody is looking. It's pretty obvious."

"The welding projects? I thought that was only for the rifle."

"And why do you think he wants it?"

"Not sure."

"To make a name for himself. Slinging ice for us is the last thing on his mind. I'll bet my last dollar he thinks that kind of firepower will allow him to rule Clearwater County, or some crazy shit like that. But first, he'll need to take out anyone who stands in his way."

"Like the Russians," Dustin answered in a likeminded tone.

"And anyone else who might be in a position to stop his plans."

"You're talking about the Sheriff, aren't you?"

"He's one."

"Daisy, too?"

"That would be my guess."

"What about Bunker?"

"Yep. And the Mayor."

"Seriously? How do you know all this?"

"It's simple. You just have to think like a narcissistic sociopath who is never satisfied with anything. There's no such thing as enough."

Dustin took a second to consider what Albert was saying. "You're right. He doesn't need us anymore."

"Exactly, which is why we step out of the way and stay off that hit list," Albert said, his eyes still on Bunker. "No, I'm afraid the Burt experiment has come to a close. Permanently."

"Still doesn't explain why you gave the batch to Bunker."

"He's the new Burt, whether he knows it or not."

Dustin didn't understand the connection. "I'm sorry, what?"

"He'll do what Burt could never do—get those crystals into the proper hands. Then we'll have some major demand."

"The Russians?"

Albert nodded.

"That's why you told him to use the drugs to get past the checkpoint."

A sly grin grew on Albert's lips. "Imagine the power we'll have if the entire Russian Army gets addicted to our blend! And I'm not just talking about here, in Clearwater County."

"You think it'll spread to other camps?"

"Count on it," Albert said. "We'll be able to name our price. And not just in terms of money, either."

Visions of women, cars, food, and guns raged in Dustin's mind. The scene changed a moment later, showing him sitting on a throne, receiving his weekly homage from the thankful peasants. "I see your point."

"Bunker is perfect for this. He's tougher and smarter than Burt. Plus, he's gonna do all the work."

"And take the heat."

Albert laughed. "Without a cut, no less. All we have to do is prime the pump, then stand back and let it happen."

"It *is* perfect," Dustin said, appreciating the guile of his partner. "No cut means a hundred percent profit."

"You catch on quick, my friend."

Dustin flashed a smile, but it quickly faded when a new idea filled his brain. "But what if he decides to get rid of the meth and not distribute it?"

"Then we're right back where we started. No harm. No foul. Plus, we look like the good guys since we tried to help."

"So basically, there's no downside."

"Bingo. Zero risk and potentially endless profits. All for letting a former biker take a bag of Clearwater Red with him."

* * *

"You okay?" Bunker asked Daisy when he arrived at her location.

She pointed at Albert. "What the hell was that?"

"A little history that needed to be sorted out."

"New history or old?"

"A little of both."

"Does he know about your past?"

"Yes, but only part of it."

"How?"

"That's not important."

She flared her eyes. "Everything is important, Jack. We're all depending on each other."

"I get that, but—"

"Look, I don't like working in the dark with all these secrets floating around."

"No, that's understandable. I don't like it either."

"I think you know by now that honesty is important to me. I don't think that's unreasonable to expect from you. Not after all we've been through."

Bunker paused, running it through his mind. She had a right to know, but he didn't want to lose Tin Man's help by betraying his confidence. Bunker needed to find middle ground to keep everyone happy. "All I can tell you for now is that Albert has certain skills we're going to need, if we have any hope of keeping everyone safe."

"What does that mean, exactly?"

"It means . . . I need you to trust me on this. I have a couple of things to verify on my way to town, then I'll fill you in on my plan when I get back."

"And the Sheriff?"

"Him, too. But first I need to be absolutely sure of something. And to do that, I need you to be patient and let me do what I need to do."

She didn't answer.

"Please. Everyone's life is at stake and this is the way it has to be . . . for now anyway."

Daisy put her rifle down on the butt of its stock, leaning the barrel against the edge of the wooden barricade.

She took his free hand in hers, rubbing his fingers gently. "I hope you know I do trust you. More than you know. But you can't keep putting me in these difficult positions. It's making me question everything I am as a law enforcement officer, and as a woman. Sometimes I just want to throw up."

"You're right. This is not how it should be."

"No, it's not. I'm your friend and I believe in you. But I'm also a deputy sheriff. That means I'm going to need a certain amount of confidence that I'm doing the right thing, Jack. For everyone. It can't just be about you and me."

"I completely understand. But I do have a plan."

Silence filled the air for the better part of a minute, her eyes fixed on his. He could feel her soul reaching out to his, trying to find some level of comfort. Faith is never easy, especially when you're staring down the promise of death.

Daisy squeezed his hand before she spoke again. "Okay. I'll go along for now, but when you get back, everyone comes clean. No more secrets. It's the way it's gotta be."

Bunker wasn't sure Albert would agree, but he decided to accept to her deal. Otherwise, she'd turn against him and that was something he couldn't let happen. Not with the lives of children at risk.

In the end, he saw it as a binary choice. Either his plan was sound and they would defeat the threat, or everyone died. At that point, regardless of the outcome, nobody would care about his checkered past. Or Albert's. More so if his plan failed, because the dead never complain.

He shook her hand loose, then pulled his pack around and set it on the ground. It took a minute of digging to find the set of long-range handheld radios he'd stuffed inside. He gave one to her.

"What's this for?" she asked, inspecting both sides of the device with her eyes.

"To get hold of me while I'm in the field."

"I thought we were keeping these for emergency use only."

"We were, but I think it's wise for the two of us to stay in touch. You know, just in case."

"Okay. If that's what you want. But shouldn't the Sheriff have this?"

"That was my original plan, but he'll have his hands full now that Victor went missing. Your name is next on the list."

She nodded. "What about the batteries?"

"They're fully charged."

"Not what I meant."

"Oh, you mean how long?"

"Yeah, like in hours or days."

"Ten hours at least, depending on talk time," Bunker answered, thinking about how well Tuttle had been prepared. The man even had a spare charger in the metal file cabinet where these radios were stored.

"What if you're gone longer than that?"

"That's why we're only going to turn them on for five minutes at the top of every hour. If you need me, that's when I'll be listening."

"All right, but what if you need me?"

"Same thing. Turn the unit on at the top of the hour and wait. If I need you, you'll know. Don't call out to me. The Russians will most likely be monitoring signals. If we're too active, they'll get a lock on us."

"Aren't these encrypted?"

"Our voices, yes. But not the signal. They can still triangulate if we broadcast too long. That's why we keep communications short, if at all."

She nodded.

"Ideally, if would be better if these civilian models had frequency hopping built in. But since they don't, we'll need to use them even more sparingly."

"Okay."

"I've already set the frequency and keyed in the encryption sequence."

"Cool. What is it?"

"314159265358979."

She laughed. "You don't really expect me to remember that, do you?"

"It's the first fifteen digits of pi."

She tilted her head, sending him a smirk.

He thought it was simple enough, but understood her doubt. "It's stored in the flash memory so you shouldn't need to remember it."

"But what if I do?"

Bunker thought about it, then the answer came to him. "Albert can help you out. I'm sure he knows it."

"Or I could write it down."

"Fine, just don't keep it on you."

"Is this how you did it in the field?"

He shook his head. "Not exactly. Our tech was far superior, plus we changed the code daily."

"That must have been a huge hassle."

"Not really. It was all done by computer so there were no codes to input. A central laptop would dump the new daily encryption keys to a small block device, then we'd plug the block into each radio and update the day's code. It was pretty slick, as long as everyone remembered to have their radio updated each morning."

She tapped an index finger on her naked wrist. "Aren't we missing something?"

"Oh shit. Almost forgot," he said. His hand went back into the pack and pulled out a pair of Luminox Colormark watches. He put one on his wrist and she did the same. "I've already synchronized the time."

She winked. "Good, then I'll know if you're late."

CHAPTER 101

Bunker ignored the reins in Rusty's hands as he walked past Tango inside the corral behind Tuttle's place. He took a seat next to Megan on the end of the feeder station. The homemade box felt solid under his backside even though the set of 6x6 posts framing the wooden platform looked weathered. At least the galvanized timber spikes holding them together didn't show any sign of wear.

The front side of the box spilled into an open trough filled with oats. Wait, check that, half-filled, now that Tango had enjoyed his late afternoon dinner, no doubt with Megan overseeing the feeding process. Next to the box was a tub of water. It, too, was less than full.

"Are you okay?" Bunker asked the ebony child, who was adjusting her knee brace. He knew she was in both emotional and physical pain, but he still had to ask.

The girl pulled her hands from the brace, then looked at Bunker with those innocent, almond-shaped eyes of hers, tears welling inside. "I miss my papa."

Megan's confession wasn't a surprise, not with the layers of anguish he knew were smothering her heart. "We all do, sweetheart. He was a really good friend to all of us."

She dropped her head and sniffed a few times, her tiny hands fiddling with each other. Her fingers looked lost, like her, unsure of what to do.

Bunker wrapped an arm around Megan, then took a finger and put it under her chin. He applied a light upward pressure, bringing her eyes up to his. "Your father was a very special man who loved his little girl very much. I hope you know that, right?"

She nodded, then sucked in a short breath and sniffed again, never taking her gaze from his. "Uh-huh. But I'm still scared."

"I know you are, but there's no reason to be scared. You have a lot of people around here who care about you. Like Rusty and the Sheriff. They won't let anything happen. I promise."

"What about you?"

"Me too. And Daisy."

"But I don't want *you* to leave, Jack. Bad things happen when you leave."

The pressure around his heart intensified, her words cutting into him. "I have to go, Megan."

"But why?"

"To find Star, for one. Plus, I need to check on Daisy's cat and see if I can find Dallas' mom and sisters. They're all missing and scared, Megan. Don't you want me to help find them? Bring them home?"

"I do, but the bad men are out there."

She was correct, but he didn't want to reinforce her fears with acknowledgment of the danger. "I'll be careful. Nothing's gonna happen to me."

"Promise?"

Bunker nodded, never taking his eyes from her. "Promise. But I need you to be strong and take care of yourself until I get back. Can you do that for me?"

She nodded.

Bunker pulled his arm away from the mini-hug, then took out a chocolate-covered energy bar from one of the pockets on his vest. "I brought you a present."

A beaming smile took over her face, her misty eyes locking onto the treat like a heat-seeking missile.

Bunker shook the bar like a finger wave.

She snatched it in a second.

"You need to eat more, to keep your strength up. Otherwise, your leg won't get better."

"I will. I promise," she said, tugging at the wrapper. It wouldn't open. She tried again, this time clenching her teeth as she struggled. Still no luck.

Bunker took the bar and ripped an edge free, pulling the paper down along one side. He gave it to her, feeling like a father tending to a helpless child. Sure, this wasn't his kid and the girl was far from helpless, but that didn't change the fact that she was in need.

Megan took a bite and began to chew, looking as though he'd taken away some of her pain, if only for a few seconds.

Somewhere along the way, they'd formed a connection that had grown by the hour. He knew he could never fill the role of Franklin, but taking care of her still felt like the right thing to do. Someone had to take the lead and his heart was telling him that it was his job to do so. One he planned to undertake after this crisis was over. For now, everyone had to chip in and keep her safe.

Bunker waited until she finished enjoying the treat before he spoke again. "It's getting dark, Megan. You need to get inside where it's safe."

"Are you leaving now?"

He gulped and nodded, not wanting to answer.

She spun and wrapped her arms around his neck, squeezing hard enough to choke off some of his air.

The instant Megan let go, she got to her feet and hobbled on her crutches to Tango. She gave the horse a goodbye hug across his snout, then continued on, never looking back.

* * *

Stan Fielding flinched, dropping the fork in his hand when a loud thud rang out near his home. It took a second to realize where the noise had come from—the front door of his modest three-bedroom home on Lake View Drive.

He flew out of the kitchen chair and grabbed his twin girls when a second thump slammed into his house. He corralled Beth and Barb into the corner beyond the dinette table and spun around with his hands behind his legs to keep the girls in one spot.

A third, more powerful bang hit the door. This time it was followed by a powerful crack, then the sound of wood splintering.

Footsteps grew in intensity as they pounded across the tile floor of his living room, carrying with them the clatter of metal. Glass broke and voices were heard—Russian voices.

Barb screamed as four men scrambled into the kitchen. They quickly fanned out side by side, with their rifles aimed at Stan's face. Three of the men were several inches taller than Stan, including the one with a red goatee.

Stan put his hands in front of his chest. "Please! Don't shoot! Please!"

The shortest of the four approached in silence, his calloused, clean-shaven face buried behind the mini-scope on his rifle.

"What do you want?" Stan asked him, his eyes focused on the man's trigger finger.

The other three circled around in a flanking maneuver. The man with red goatee spun to open the pantry room door, his rifle in a shooting position.

"*Vse chisto*," the solider said in a commanding voice, closing the door behind him.

A spread of hollow thuds raced across the floorboards above. Stan couldn't be sure, but it sounded like three men were searching the second floor and possibly the tiny attic space on the third floor. Doors squeaked open and then closed with force. More glass breaking.

"Daddy?" Beth asked in a frightened tone before Stan shushed her.

"Where is she?" the short Russian asked Stan with a heavy accent, the English barely recognizable.

Stan shook his head, his heart pounding in his chest like a sledgehammer. "Who?"

"Where is she?" the soldier asked again, a dollop of spittle flying from his lips in anger.

"I don't know who you're talking about. It's just us. There's nobody else here."

The short man waved at the two soldiers on his right, both sporting a shadow of stubble across their chins. The camo-covered men sprang into action, slinging their rifles before grabbing Stan by the arms. He tried to resist, but they were too strong, dragging him to the center of the kitchen.

"Stop hurting my daddy!" Barb screeched before her tears took over.

Beth held her sister close, both girls crying uncontrollably.

The short man dropped a hand from his rifle and sucker punched Stan in the gut. The force of the impact doubled him over, sending him to his knees in a search for air. A foot came at him next, barely missing his face, but catching his shoulder. He flopped sideways and landed on his back.

Stan fought through the pain as he turned over and pushed himself to all fours. It was difficult to steady himself with his chest heaving in gasping thrusts.

When he brought his eyes up in search of his daughters, he found them in the corner, holding each other in a cradle of fear, their adorable faces drowning in tears.

Stan continued to fight for oxygen as more footsteps found his ears. They were outside the kitchen. The stairs, he figured, based on the creaks and groans of the wooden steps.

Seconds later, a fifth soldier entered the kitchen with a bloody uniform in his hand. He said something in Russian to the short man before delivering the clothing.

Short man brought his rifle down and let it hang on the sling across his chest to accept the garments. His hands turned red from the transfer of blood as he separated the blouse from the pants. The shirt had a tear across the front, looking as though someone sliced it open with a knife.

Short man's eyes grew wild with fire. He turned to Stan and held the uniform in front of his face. "This was in the attic."

"I don't know how that got there. I've never seen it before in my life."

"Where is she? What did you do to her?"

"I don't know who you're talking about! We didn't do anything. You have to believe me. Please. Just let us go. Please."

Short man looked at goatee man and sent him a signal with his eyes.

A moment later, the boots of goatee man tore across the kitchen floor in a straight line toward the girls. Stan put out an arm to stop the marauder's advance, but another punch from the short man reached him first. The blow penetrated his cheekbone with a crack, slamming him to the floor on his chest.

Stan's mind blinked out for a second, then found its traction as an army of specks filled his vision. The pain was relentless too, shooting across his body.

He could hear the twins pleading with the Russians to stop, their high-pitched shrieks amplified by desperation. He needed to get up and protect his children.

After he opened his eyes, he told his body to move, but it refused. He tried again, but his limbs didn't respond. They were limp, devoid of energy, hanging on his body.

All that remained were the waves of dizziness, pounding at his skull with the force of an ocean current. Then the room started to spin, slowly at first, before it went wild, whirling with ever-increasing speed.

Stan slammed his eyes shut, trying to keep a lock on reality. His mind latched onto the most powerful emotion remaining in his thoughts—his love for his daughters. He prayed it would be enough to keep him in the here and now. But it wasn't.

The darkness came a heartbeat later, taking his consciousness away.

CHAPTER 102

Two hours later . . .

Allison Rainey plopped into the chair by the kitchen table, her leg and back muscles aching. Her mom was in the seat across from her, her hands locked together like she'd been praying. "Misty's finally asleep, thank God."

Martha seemed pleased. "That poor woman's been through a lot today. I don't know how she keeps it together."

Allison's mind flashed a scene of the men digging up Angus' naked body, his skin covered in dirt and bugs. The imagery tugged at her insides, making her want to throw up. "Me either. Finding out that you've lost your father and your fiancé on the same day is more than I could ever deal with."

"I doubt that. You're a lot tougher than you think."

"Thanks, Mom. But I'm really not. I just pretend to be. For Victor's sake." She shrugged after a quick exhale. "Not that it's done any good."

Martha put a hand on Allison's forearm, squeezing it gently. "He'll be all right, sweetheart. The Sheriff will find him."

"I hope so, but it's been two hours. It's getting chilly out there."

"He's a strong boy. You just gotta have faith the Good Lord will protect him."

Allison shook her head, wondering what she'd done wrong. God was obviously punishing her for something. "I wish I knew why he took off like that."

"It wasn't anything you did, if that's what you're thinking. I'm sure it's just the stress of everything that's happening right now. It's a lot for a young man to handle."

"You're probably right, Mom, but I never know with him. I swear, he's moodier than his father."

"We all have that trait, honey. It's just human nature."

Allison nodded, feeling a trickle of comfort ease into her soul. Mom always seemed to know exactly what words to say.

Martha rubbed her arm again, using those tender, side-to-side thumb strokes that only moms know how to do. "You need to get some sleep, too. If the Sheriff comes back, I'll wake you up."

"Okay," Allison said, realizing that she had a tendency to take her mom for granted. Her arms came up on their own and wrapped around Martha in a firm embrace. "I know I've been difficult over the years, but I want you to know how much I appreciate you always supporting me. No matter what."

"No need to thank me, darling. It's what a mother does. Just like you do for Victor. Just gotta give it time. He'll come around. He's a good boy."

Allison let go of the hug and stood up with newfound energy in her legs. "I'm just glad the Sheriff is out there looking for him. Victor's gotta be scared to death in those woods."

"Gus is a good man. He won't stop until he finds him," Martha said, her tone genuine. "You need to go and get some sleep. I'll keep an eye on things down here."

Allison nodded, then turned for the door that led into the living room. The stairs to the second floor were waiting beyond the table, assuming her legs had sufficient strength to ferry her up the fourteen steps.

Just one more time, she thought.

If her legs failed her request, she might have to stretch out on the dining room table and call it a night. It wouldn't do her back any good, but at this point, she really didn't care.

Exhaustion has a habit of changing your way of thinking, even if it leads to a crippling wake-up in the morning.

* * *

Rusty ran through the front door of Martha Rainey's place, his lungs feeling the strain from the sprint down Old Mill Road. The news he carried had supercharged his muscles, allowing him to run faster than ever before.

A blur of movement caught his eye from the left. It was Allison Rainey with her hand on the guardrail, heading up the stairs, her feet on the fourth step from the bottom.

Allison stopped her ascent and locked eyes with him, but didn't say anything.

"They're back!" Rusty told her.

"The Sheriff and Dicky?"

"Yeah, just now. Coming up the road."

"My son?"

Rusty couldn't wait to tell her. "He's with them."

"Is he okay?"

Rusty waved at her. "You gotta see this!"

She turned and flew down the stairs, her feet pounding at the steps like a woodpecker.

Rusty held the door open as the woman zipped past him in a breeze of air. For an old lady, she could run, probably feeling an adrenaline rush like him.

They tore across the front yard in seconds, then turned left onto the dirt road. About fifty feet ahead were three males and seven horses, all of them on a path to the Rainey homestead.

The Sheriff and Dicky were to the left, sitting proudly on their mounts with backs straight and heads high.

Victor was to the right, his face covered in a wide grin as he worked the reins with his left hand.

"Oh my God, Victor!" Allison screamed, somehow accelerating her pace.

Rusty pushed his legs even harder to keep up as the Sheriff waved a hello at him. Rusty sent a signal back with his arm, timing it between his widening strides so he wouldn't lose speed, or his balance.

Victor's upper body had a slight twist to it, one hand trailing behind. Rusty could see a rope in the kid's grasp, linking together four saddled horses in single file formation.

The last animal in the procession had something strapped to its saddle. It was a bicycle—his racing bike—in two pieces—the front wheel strapped to the left side. The rest of his ride was on the opposite side, lashed down and bobbing in concert with the stride of the horse.

When Allison arrived, Victor swung his leg over the saddle and hopped to the ground.

Rusty took position next to the Sheriff's horse, about ten feet from the mother-son reunion.

"I thought I was never going to see you again!" Allison cried as she wrapped him in a powerful two-armed embrace. She picked him up from the ground and swung him around with his feet dangling. The hug continued for another twenty seconds before she put him on the ground and let go.

She grabbed his cheeks in her hands. "Why did you take off like that? We were all worried sick."

"We needed horses, Mom. So I took responsibility like the Sheriff told me to do."

She turned to Apollo and sent him a penetrating stare. "This was your idea?"

"No. It wasn't like that. Not at all," the Sheriff stammered, climbing off his horse in a plop of feet. "He misunderstood what I told him. I was talking about taking responsibility for his actions. I never said to go find the horses."

She paused for a second, then looked at Victor. "Where did you go?"

"Franklin's stables. I knew the horses were around there somewhere, so I went to get them. I thought if I could find Megan's horse, it might cheer her up."

"By yourself? Do you know how dangerous that was?"

"Yeah, but I knew a secret way there. It was easy, Mom. Until it got dark."

"We found him two miles out. I think he'd been wandering around in circles," the Sheriff said, his tone somber and to the point.

Allison hugged Victor again, this time lingering for a good minute.

Martha appeared on Rusty's left, her face covered with delight. She brought her hands up like a preacher, leaned back to the heavens, and said, "Praise the Lord Almighty."

Allison turned to her mom with tears streaming down her cheeks. "He's back, Mom. Safe and sound. Just like you said."

"I told you not to worry," she said, sending a smile to the Sheriff. "Thank you, Gus, for bringing my grandson home. You too, Dicky."

"My pleasure," the Sheriff said, looking proud.

"Just doing our job, ma'am," Dicky said, still seated in the saddle.

Apollo gave Dicky the lead to his horse, nodding for him to continue down the road. Dicky did as he was told, escorting the Sheriff's horse toward Tuttle's place.

"Allison?" Martha said, hesitating until Allison looked her way. "Aren't you forgetting something?"

Allison pinched her nose, but didn't respond. She looked confused.

Martha leaned her head in the direction of the Sheriff.

"Oh, right," Allison snapped, her face blushing red. She sauntered to the Sheriff with a huge smile leading the way. "I'm sorry. I got so excited when I saw my son that I almost forgot to thank you."

When she brought her arms up for an embrace, Apollo stopped her with his hands. "That's really not necessary, Allison."

"The hell it isn't," she answered with attitude, pushing his hands away. "You risked your life to save my son. I'm giving you a hug, whether you like it or not."

Her arms found his shoulders a second later, leaving him looking mortified, his arms hanging down at his side.

Rusty held back a chuckle. It was obvious the Sheriff wasn't comfortable with her sudden affection. Rusty didn't understand why. It was just a hug, after all. The man had earned it.

Right on cue, as if Apollo had been reading Rusty's thoughts, he brought his hands up and put them on her back. He wasn't giving her a hug, exactly. It was more of an awkward double pat on the back, but at least he responded.

Rusty was close enough to feel the heat from their bodies pressing together. It felt weird to be standing so close. He took a step back to give them room. You never knew when a thankful mom might pick up a hefty Sheriff and swing him around.

A few seconds later, she leaned back from the hug and stared into his eyes, her lower half still pressed into his.

Apollo must not have expected it, pulling his hands free from her back. He held them in mid-air, about six inches away.

Rusty figured the hug was just about over.

Then, out of nowhere, Allison closed her eyes and tilted her head, kissing him full on the lips. It wasn't a quick peck, either. It was an open mouth, vise-like smooch.

Apollo brought his hands up and wrapped them around her back, as if he had given in to all of his most secret desires.

It looked like one of those kissing scenes from the movies—their lips, hands, and bodies reacting to each other like some kind of choreographed play bursting with moans.

Rusty looked at Martha to see what she thought of the kiss.

The old woman's eyes were a mile wide, with a smile showing all of her teeth.

CHAPTER 103

Early the next morning . . .

Bunker pulled back on the reins to slow Tango to a stop, then unfolded the area map. The sun had just cracked the eastern horizon, showering his back with elongated rays of mostly yellow light. He turned sideways to give his eyes a better view of the path outlined in red marker ink.

So far, it appeared Apollo and Burt's waypoints had been spot-on, taking him exactly where he needed to go. He hadn't seen any sign of the Russians, or anyone else for that matter. Only the occasional critter lurking in the bush.

Tuttle's night vision goggles had been a godsend, lessening his fear of relying on Tango's ability to see in the dark. In retrospect, he probably could've saved the batteries since the amazing creature seemed to know exactly what to avoid and where to step to keep its rider safe.

Bunker checked his location on the map to confirm what he already suspected—Patterson's Meadow was only minutes away. All that remained was a hundred-foot climb over the rise ahead.

After an extended yawn and an arm stretch, he tucked the map away, wishing he'd gotten more shuteye. The problem wasn't the campsite he'd chosen on the ridge overlooking a stream. Nor was it the time he'd spent inside the lightweight sleeping bag.

It was the endless deep-throated croaks and ribbits from the frogs. There must have been a thousand of them within thirty yards of his makeshift camp. They were everywhere, never stopping their vocal calls once the sun went down. He finally fell asleep sometime around midnight, but then Tango's unexpected whinny at 4 AM put an end to his slumber.

Yet, despite the final interruption, he wasn't upset with the beast. In fact, he was thankful. If Tango hadn't decided to be a twelve-hundred-pound alarm clock, he might still be asleep and behind schedule.

Then again, he wouldn't have complained if he was able to enjoy another hour or two in dreamland, where curvy women and cold beer were served in abundant supply.

There's something soothing about the constant trickle of water over rock. It pampers one's senses, keeping your mind from dwelling on the shit you forgot to do the previous day. Or in his case, thoughts of all the crap he had to accomplish the following day, including scouting the town of Clearwater.

Bunker continued on, conquering the hill ahead thanks to Tango's steady feet and boundless energy. Each stride of the four-legged taxi sent a rocking motion into Bunker's hips, gently stressing the muscles in his back. At least the saddle wasn't as painful as it had been, meaning his skills as a rider were improving.

Daisy would be proud, he thought to himself after an image of her beautiful face flashed in his mind. Stephanie might have been put together better in the figure department, but Daisy oozed her own brand of sex appeal.

He smirked, thinking about the differences between the two women. They were polar opposites in almost every respect, but he knew deep down that either of them would make a weekend in Vegas memorable. The kind of memorable that would reinforce the adage: *What Happens in Vegas, Stays in Vegas.*

The old Bunker would have entertained the idea of a three-way, taking both of them to bed together. Sure, it would have been an easy solution to the dilemma ahead, but it wasn't who he was anymore.

Stephanie was more about the here and now, while Daisy invested in the long game. He figured either of them could tame a wild man with nothing more than look, or a stroke of their hand.

He'd sensed a growing connection with both of them, but he'd purposely avoided anything romantic. Not because of their history of torrid love triangles. It was more about his own sanity. He was still a work in progress—a reclamation project—trying to figure out who he was and what kind of man he wanted to be.

The last thing he needed was to worry about the emotional needs of another person. Plus, he still hadn't come completely clean with either of them, keeping the darkest of details hidden from those who cared about him.

Chances were, once they learned of his culpability in the Kandahar Incident, they'd want nothing more to do with him. That day in his past was the single most important reason why he needed to keep his distance from everyone, and not get attached. Otherwise, it would make their impending hatred for him just that much harder, once his dark secret sent him packing.

Bunker tugged the reins to have Tango bypass a thicket of scorched trees and protruding rock, all of it covered in the black of carbon. Lightning, he figured, searing off vertical streaks of bark, killing a good portion of the limbs.

He craned his neck to the southern sky and noticed a massive thunderhead forming in the distance. The billowing cumulonimbus cloud rose to the heavens and flattened out like a mushroom of white, towering over the mountain peaks below it.

Daisy would be pleased if the drought came to an end, as would the other residents in the area. Assuming, of course, anyone still occupied their homestead after the Russians marched across the county. He shook his head, realizing that he might be the only person dumb enough to be wandering through the area alone. With minimal supplies and firepower, no less.

He took Tango thirty degrees to the left, guiding him down a natural path that led to an impressive string of mature pine trees bordering the clearing. Based on the straight-line nature of their position along the edge of the meadow, Bunker knew this clearing was manmade. Nature didn't feature straight lines or many right-angled corners, both of which were present in the pasture before him.

The thick trunks of the pines matched their soaring heights; lofty enough to reach the middle of the pasture, he calculated, if someone were to drop them accurately with a chainsaw from either side. That chore had Dicky's name written all over it.

Pine trees were perfect for what he had in mind—narrow and tall, making them easy to rig after a climb. He nodded, storing the information in his memory, with the names of Rusty and Dallas attached.

He hoped Albert was busy working through the items on the list he'd given him, with speed and efficiency. There wouldn't be a lot of time to catch up once he returned from this scout.

Bunker brought Tuttle's high-end binoculars to his eyes to study the sightlines from his position. The scan started at one end of the clearing and finished with the other, carefully checking the tree line that stood beyond.

No threats detected. Time to advance.

The grass in the pasture rose up in a streaky mix of green and brown, its tips reaching above Tango's knee joints. The horse stepped gingerly after a nudge of Bunker's heels, taking them forward to the center of the expanse.

All four corners of this rectangular-shaped meadow were now in view, as were the soaring mountains and endless trees swarming its exterior. He took out the map and studied it again, making sure the printed topography matched what his eyes were reporting.

"Only one way in or out," he mumbled in affirmation, noting the landscape and elevations on all sides. He took another minute to run through several tactical scenarios in his mind, deciding what would go where, and who would be assigned to the various stations.

He smiled as the blueprint came together, visualizing himself running with socks in his hands, each covered in axle grease. "Just might work. But they'll have to over-commit."

Bunker spun Tango around before sending him into a trot toward the closed end of the clearing. He swung his leg over the saddle and dropped to the ground once they arrived.

"Stay here, boy. I'll be back in a flash."

Tango flicked his head and snorted, then resumed his tail-flapping, fly-swatting duties with his head buried in the grass. Tango would soon need water to wash down the feast he'd just started. With any luck, the waterholes on the map hadn't dried up, or else the rest of today's trip might be shorter than anticipated.

Bunker paced the width of the clearing from one edge to the other, counting the strides required. The final tally was more than he expected, leading him to wonder if his crew could complete the critical task he had in mind.

The lack of rain in recent weeks meant the ground was harder than normal, and would slow the process. However, if the rising storm over the mountaintop did its job, then they'd have a chance to complete what he needed in time.

A chance was all they needed. Something that would galvanize hope and lead them to victory. Yet it would take everyone, including Burt and his mechanical magic. Even the little ones would have to pitch in.

It was obvious the strategy evolving in his brain needed a bit of luck to succeed, but that was all he had at the moment. Well, luck and a few friends who believed in him. Some of those same friends had a deep connection to God, or so they claimed.

He smirked, realizing their faith had started to rub off on him and affect his decisions. God or luck, they were the same thing, he decided. After all, if God wanted to step in and lend a hand with a downpour, who was he to complain? He'd take it and any other help that came his way. Divine or not, he wasn't picky.

He went back to Tango and climbed into the saddle. "You ready, boy? It's time to take care of a few errands, then head into the lion's den."

Bunker leaned forward to rub Tango's neck, sending the four hooves under him into a prance, almost as if a veterinarian had just shot a dose of adrenaline into Tango's body.

He tapped his hand twice before leaning back in the saddle with a squeak of leather. "Oh yeah. You're ready. So am I. Let's ride!"

CHAPTER 104

Dustin put a stack of boxes containing steel wool onto a portable table he'd just set up outside of Tuttle's barn. Albert placed a dozen glass jars on its surface and Rusty delivered a few other household items they'd scavenged from Tuttle's inventory.

"Why can't we do this inside, out of the sun?" Dustin asked, wiping a bead of sweat from his brow. "It's frickin' hot out here."

"We could, but this reaction will create toxic gas that I'm betting your lungs will hate. We'll need proper ventilation."

"Okay, that makes sense. Good safety tip."

Albert gave him a handful of magnets he'd acquired from Martha Rainey's fridge. "Put the steel wool into the jars, then secure it to the bottom with these."

"On the outside, right?"

"Yeah. They'll keep the steel wool from floating once we add the chems."

Dustin dropped the first piece of steel wool into the container, then lifted the jar to gain access to the bottom. He put the magnet to the underside of the glass, then set the assembly back on the table. He completed the same process with the other jars. "Now what?"

"Pour in enough vinegar to cover the steel wool completely. But don't go crazy."

Dustin took off the twist cap from a bottle of white vinegar and poured in enough liquid to soak the steel wool and cover it. "Like that?"

"Perfect. Now the others."

Dustin filled the remaining jars with vinegar, then put the bottle down and secured its cap.

"Now the bleach."

Dustin grabbed the plastic container of bleach. He removed the cap and held it near the opening of the first jar. "How much?"

Albert pointed at the glass, aiming at a point about two inches above the steel wool. "Fill it to here, but hold your breath. The gas will start almost immediately."

Dustin took a deep breath before pouring the bleach, using a thin stream for control. He stopped when the level inside the jar reached the height Albert had indicated. He backed away, took another breath, then went back in to fill the rest of the jars. Once done, he put the bleach down, closed its container and stood next to Albert.

He exhaled, using an exaggerated lip pucker for effect. "How long will this take?"

"Couple of hours. Then we drain, filter, and repeat until we have the supply Bunker asked for in his notes."

"That's all there is to it?" Dustin asked, watching the chemical reaction turn the steel wool a red color.

"Yeah, simple, if you know what you're doing."

"Huh. I never knew you could make rust this way. I suppose we could've used some old nails, too."

"They'd work, but this method is faster. Steel wool has much more surface area, accelerating the process a thousand-fold."

"I take it you've done this before?"

Albert didn't answer, turning his focus to the Mayor's grandson. "Let's get the aluminum ready."

Rusty nodded, opening a cardboard box that he'd hauled from Martha Rainey's house. He unfolded its flaps and pulled out a black-colored device about the size of a lunch thermos.

Dustin recognized it. "A coffee grinder?"

"I hope she doesn't mind," Albert said, taking the lid off the machine.

"You didn't ask her?"

"Nah. This was too important to waste time on politeness. Though we could've melted down a bunch of Tuttle's empty beer cans and put them on a spindle for the lathe, to create the shavings. But then we'd also need to make a ball mill to grind them into powder."

"That's a lot more work," Dustin said after visualizing Albert's alternative.

"Absolutely. The coffee grinder is a lot faster," Albert said, turning to Rusty. "Just need the foil."

Rusty took out a box of aluminum foil. "How much?"

"Tear off a couple of six-foot pieces. One for both of you."

Rusty drew out two runs of foil and tore them from the roll, giving one to Dustin.

"Now we need strips, gentlemen. Lots of them," Albert said.

"How small?" Dustin asked.

"As small as you can make them."

The two men started building a pile of foil strips, while Albert grabbed two handfuls and stuffed them into the coffee grinder.

He put the lid on and secured it, then plugged the unit into an exterior electrical outlet near the barn's entrance. The power light illuminated, thanks to Tuttle's backup power.

"First we grind them with the coarse setting." Albert pressed the power switch and held the lid as the aluminum foil was ground into tiny flecks by the whirling blades inside. The high-pitched squeal of the motor was annoying, but it appeared the device could handle the process easily.

Albert turned the unit off and opened the lid to add more strips. He repeated the process until all of the foil strips had been processed with the coarse setting.

"Now, we run it all through on fine." He flipped the setting, sending the flakes whirling a second time.

Albert turned off the motor after another ten minutes of grinding. "Time for the moment of truth." He removed the lid from the container, his eyes darting about the area. "Where's that strainer?"

Rusty went back into the box and pulled out an extra fine strainer they'd found in Martha's baking cabinet.

Albert held the wire mesh over the worktable and poured the aluminum shavings through it. The smaller fragments slipped through and landed on the table. When he was done, almost eighty percent of the powder he'd made with the grinder had passed the size test.

"Is that enough?" Dustin asked, his eyes locked onto the modest pile of aluminum powder.

"Not even close. We'll need several more batches of everything. Once that steel wool is done cooking, we'll filter it as well, then we're good to go."

"That's it? Just mix them together and we're done?" Rusty asked.

"Basically, though the mixture has to be in the proper proportions, depending on who you ask."

"What does that mean?" Dustin asked.

"It means there is more than one answer to the mixture question. It depends on the purity of the components and some other goodies that we could add to the recipe."

"Like what?"

"Plaster, for one. Bunker didn't ask for any, so I'm assuming he's planning to make some kind grenade with TH3, based on the components on his list."

Rusty took out four coffee cans, the eight-ounce variety. Each of them carried labels that said *Folgers* on the side. "I'm guessing that's what these are for?"

Albert nodded, his eyes tight with focus. "We just need to be careful once it's mixed."

Daisy showed up after Dicky relieved her at the roadblock. "What are you guys doing?"

"Making thermite charges," Albert said, sounding as though he was trying to impress her.

"For Bunker," Dustin added.

Albert shot him a glare while Daisy's head was turned.

Daisy bent forward and studied the jars on the table. "What's in there?"

"Steel wool," Dustin answered.

"We're making iron oxide," Albert added. "One of the core components."

Dustin pointed at the mound of gray powder on the table. "That used to be aluminum foil."

"Bunker asked you to make this?" she asked, her tone hesitant.

Albert held up the list of items. "Among other things."

"Are you sure?"

"Positive. Just need to get it done before he gets back."

Daisy seemed to accept Albert's statement.

Albert continued. "But there is one problem. Unless we find a supply of magnesium tape around here, we'll need to figure out a way to light it. Something that will burn with a sufficient temperature."

Her eyes went round. "What about the pocket torch Dallas found?"

"Good idea," Albert responded in a flash. "But we still need sulfur and some barium nitrate to complete the TH3."

Daisy cleared her throat, looking proud of herself. "I know where the sulfur is, gentlemen."

Albert sent a suspicious look her way, but didn't speak.

She didn't seem to care. "It's under the chicken coop. Bunker and I found a bunch of explosives and chemicals down there."

Albert's expression remained unchanged.

Daisy shot Albert a sidelong glance, her eyes scanning his midsection. "But you'll never fit down the hatch."

"Yeah, well, being a gopher really isn't my thing."

"I'll go," Dustin said.

"Me too," Rusty added.

Daisy continued, with one eyebrow raised, "I think there's aluminum power, too. And maybe the barium nitrate."

Albert's face scrunched like he'd just sucked on a lemon.

Daisy let out a short chuckle. "Tuttle has all kinds of chemicals and explosives down there."

"What about iron oxide?" Albert asked, his tone indicating he didn't want to know the answer.

"Is it a red powder?"

"Yep."

"Saw that, too."

Albert's tone turned harsh. "You've got to be kidding me."

She shrugged. "Like I was trying to tell you before, I don't think you guys had to make all this stuff from scratch."

Albert exhaled, shaking his head. He looked at Dustin. "Why didn't Bunker tell us?"

Dustin paused, sifting through his memory of the conversation with Bunker about the list. Then it hit him. "Well, technically he did. He said to ask Daisy if we needed help finding anything."

"I guess I missed that part," Albert said, sounding defeated.

She put her hand out, palm up. "Maybe I should take a look at that list."

Albert gave her the paper.

She scanned it for a short minute and then nodded as if she had reached a conclusion. "Follow me, boys."

CHAPTER 105

Bunker crawled forward on the hilltop rise outside of town, keeping his profile low to avoid detection. He'd left Tango behind after tying him to a tree two hundred yards to the rear.

The storm clouds had doubled in size, painting a section of the distant horizon black. He wasn't sure if the build-up meant the storm was heading his way, or only building in size. Either way, the inclement weather might come into play soon.

Storms look closer than they truly are when you're in an elevated area with sparkling clean air and tremendous visibility. The rain might arrive in minutes, or hours, or not at all. There was no way to be sure, not without active radar.

He brought the binoculars up and began his surveillance. To the right was the main road leading into Clearwater. It was the same swatch of pavement he'd used to lead the kids into town after their rescue from the bus accident.

A Russian checkpoint sat on the pavement, blocking access to town.

It featured all the usual trimmings: Russian flags, razor wire security fence, sawhorse-style barricades with white and black stripes, sandbags protecting a machine gunner's nest, single-man guard shack, squad of heavily armed soldiers milling about, two armored vehicles sitting at intersecting angles behind the barricades, and a red and white colored pedestal sign that he assumed said STOP.

There were also guards walking a pair of German Shepherds on a leash.

He watched a convoy depart in a slow crawl after approaching the checkpoint from somewhere in town. The two lead vehicles were military issue: all-terrain Russian GAZ Tigrs. As were the pair of chase vehicles holding up the rear.

Three American-made flatbed trucks were sandwiched between the infantry carriers, ferrying a load of civilians wearing bright orange coveralls. He could see the grille on the lead truck—its emblem said GMC and it appeared to be an older model.

Wooden boards surrounded the truck beds, reminding Bunker of three-rail cattle fencing. Each civilian had their wrist attached to the plank closest to them. All looked to be adults, their heads hanging and bobbing with the movement of the transport.

A few minutes after they drove off, another convoy came into view—this one arriving at the checkpoint. Like the first, it featured two lead vehicles and two chase vehicles. However, this procession only carried a single truck of civilians. They, too, had their wrists secured to the rails.

When the middle truck stopped, he was able to get a better view of the prisoners. Their coveralls were dirty, noticeably so, the orange color covered in black splotches and not as bright.

Some of the captives looked young and fit, mid-twenties if he had to guess. Both male and female. Others were heavyset with gray hair, looking as though they should have been enjoying retirement in an assisted living facility somewhere.

"Slave labor for the mine. Or the fields. Maybe both," Bunker said in a mumble, working through the facts as the vehicles drove inside and disappeared. The Russians weren't concerned about age, but at least he didn't see any children.

Bunker brought the glasses down and let his eyes take in a view of the city below. He figured razor wire had been installed around the access points of the perimeter. It also seemed likely that other checkpoints had been erected, somewhere beyond his vision.

He was even more confident that the insurgents were watching everything with the helium-filled Aerostat balloon floating fifteen hundred feet above the center of town. He'd seen that type of surveillance blimp in Afghanistan many times. In fact, almost every base he visited back then had one deployed.

The tethered, 117-foot dirigible resembled a giant all-white fish, except this floater came complete with infrared and high definition cameras. During his tour in Afghanistan, they were part of the Pentagon's Persistent Threat Detection System, though it looked like the Russians had adopted a similar program.

The locals hated them, but the commanders loved them. So did the bean counters in Washington—saving the cost of multi-million dollar drones flying overhead 24x7.

Bunker still remembered his shock when a maintenance team brought one of the blimps down to repair the bullet holes in its skin. He counted twenty-two, but there may have been more. Apparently, the Aerostats were almost impervious to target practice, able to withstand several hundred hits before they could no longer fly. They were also safe against incendiary rounds since Helium is a noble gas and noncombustible.

Weather was usually the flight technician's biggest headache. Most notably, the frequent sand storms. Climate concerns weren't the only drawback. Blind spots were also an issue, depending on how the cameras were mounted and deployed.

Bunker brought the binoculars back into position when a black Land Rover approached the roadblock from his right. He couldn't get a count of its occupants, not with its windows tinted dark.

The truck slowed to a stop about twenty feet from the barricades as the guards spread out to cover it with their rifles held high.

He imagined one of the guards yelling something along the lines of "Halt and be recognized."

The driver's door swung open. A man stepped out with his hands up. He was dressed in dark-colored attire, including long pants, long-sleeved shirt, and shoes.

"The men in black," Bunker muttered, remembering his painful encounters with the Pokémon men in the miner's camp.

The driver pulled up his shirt and spun around, showing the guards he had nothing strapped to his torso. Nothing that might go boom.

Three additional men slid out of the vehicle in a controlled manner, one from behind the driver and two on the passenger side—all of them with their hands over their heads.

They too, completed the bomb vest security spin before three guards escorted them to the driver's position, herding the group together like cattle.

Finally, the fourth soldier checked the inside of the Land Rover, starting with the open door on the driver's side. His rifle went in, then his head, looking for threats.

A few moments later, he swung around to the other side of the truck and completed the same maneuver through the rear passenger door. As Bunker expected, he climbed out and signaled for the canine units to approach.

The dogs began to sniff the exterior, following the finger pointing commands of their handlers.

The search for weapons and explosives was a slow and dangerous process, for both man and beast, but these units showed little fear.

Once the outside of the truck was secure, the handlers led their dogs inside with a tug on the leash. One handler cleared the front seat, while the other focused on the back.

When the search was over, one of the guards retrieved two duffle bags, one suitcase, and a black backpack from the vehicle. He stood them together, leaning their weight into each other like a rudimentary teepee.

A tall, slender man appeared in the doorway of the guard shack, then made his way to the SUV with a clipboard in hand. He looked to be unarmed, though his beltline did feature some kind of device attached to the leather. The tall man stood in front of the driver, checking the paperwork with a flip of his hand.

Russians love their lists, Bunker thought to himself.

The tall man took a step back and brought the device up from his belt. He aimed it at the man's crotch for a ten-count before motioning to the driver to step forward.

The driver did as he was told, bringing his arms down in the process. Tall man turned his attention to the second visitor and went through the same scenario with the clipboard and scanner, before moving onto detainee number three.

Right then, a new idea hatched in Bunker's thoughts. He dug into his pocket and pulled out the Pokémon card Jeffrey had given him, holding it in front of his eyes.

"Holy shit. That's what these are for," he said in a whisper, more facts lining up in his brain. "A covert ID."

The men in black didn't carry identification, so the Russians would need a reliable method to clear them for entry.

He knew from experience that checkpoint verification was a common problem at most military bases, given the sheer number of troops under command. Especially when you're under standing orders not to wear insignias, nametags, or ID badges in a red zone, where snipers are a constant threat.

The same would be true for those who went out on patrol. Or in this case, hauling civilians outside the wire for some kind of work duty.

Usually the guard at the gate would need to know one or more of the troops leaving the compound. Otherwise, they could never be sure if a returning squad was a threat or not.

In this case, though, these were unknown operatives joining their base, and probably doing so for the first time. They'd need a method to identify covert personnel.

He smirked. It was brilliant. The cards would look harmless to the uninformed.

Bunker took a minute to run through the Russians' check-in protocols in his mind. He realized the visitors must have supplied a codename to the clipboard guard first, which was then confirmed with a scan of the hidden card. He nodded, appreciating the simplicity of their double-verification system.

If his theory were correct, it would also explain something else. Something that had been nagging at him ever since he first set foot in the miner's camp. The men in black spoke perfect English. Not a hint of Russian.

"Wouldn't need to speak Russian," he muttered, thinking about the reasons behind a double-verification entry system. Especially while in-country and welcoming unknown operatives who may have only spoken English.

Bunker held the card up to the sunlight like Jeffrey had done the day before. That was when he noticed it—a tiny dark spot in the corner—something embedded between the layers of paper. He guessed it was metallic, with micro-encoded circuits. Something a scanner could read.

"Clever boy," he said, thinking about Jeffrey. The inquisitive youngster wasn't fooled, not for a second, noticing the difference immediately.

After more consideration, Bunker decided the men in black must have been either Russian sleeper agents who'd just been activated, or Americans conspiring with the enemy. Nothing else fit what he'd learned thus far.

"Guess this is useless," he said, putting the card in his pocket. If he had the codename, he could have used it to gain entry to Clearwater and gather valuable onsite intel regarding troop placement and strength.

Part of him was tempted to tear the paper apart to expose the technology, but he'd made a promise to keep the card safe. The tech was useless anyway, so no need to break a kid's heart.

Bunker opened his rucksack and fished out the baggie of red crystals. "I guess this is all that's left." He sifted through a number of approach scenarios, trying to find one that wouldn't get him shot before he could deliver the drugs to a corruptible addict.

Albert's idea had merit, but he decided it was too dangerous. The plan would work better if he were traveling with a non-threatening visitor. Someone distracting in all ways. Someone like Stephanie. Her curves would be far more effective than a missing codename. Assuming, of course, she was wearing the proper outfit.

He flushed the idea, chastising himself in the process. She'd never go for it. She had Jeffrey to think about, not to mention her own wellbeing. If he put her in that situation and she got hurt, how could he live with himself?

No. If he was going inside, it needed to be his risk and his alone. Codename or not.

Out of nowhere, an image of the demon-looking squirrel creature on the Pokémon card danced in his mind. The vision called to him, begging him to refocus and dissect. He yanked the card out of his pocket and stared at it.

Jeffrey's voice rose up from his memories in an echo. "His name is Charmeleon."

Bunker's jaw dropped open, thinking about the other odd but unique names the kid had mentioned: Metapod, Arcanine, and Parasect.

"Could it be that simple?"

His logic dug through the cloud of clutter surrounding the cards and their origin, the facts lining up one at a time.

Each card a different character.

Each card sewn inside the pants.

Each card scanned for verification.

Just then, the data points coalesced like the perfect storm, leading him to a new conclusion: each undercover operative carried a unique Pokémon card and knew the name of the character.

"That has to be it," he stated. "Simple and efficient."

Bunker dug into his pack, pulling the microscope out first. He gently put it aside, standing it upright on its base. When he found it in Albert's house, it was bigger than he expected but located exactly where Albert had indicated.

A red-colored pet collar came out next. Unfortunately, Daisy's cat was a stiff lump of fur when he'd arrived at her trailer. He buried the lifeless feline near Daisy's withering flower garden out back, but kept the collar as a memento. He wasn't looking forward to delivering the news to her when he got back to camp.

He found his civilian clothes near the bottom and began to change his attire, his mind churning with more theories.

Jeffrey had told him there were over eight hundred characters in the Pokémon world. Bunker wasn't sure if they all had their own card or not, but it seemed likely. The organization behind the game never would have invented all those characters if they weren't going to take advantage with trading cards and other collectibles.

Regardless of the count, he figured it was more than enough to cover a few dozen operatives. Possibly a lot more. In fact, the higher the number, the better his chances of getting past the checkpoint unscathed.

The Russians had their choice of codes and could have chosen anything. Hell, old baseball cards would have worked. Yet they went with Pokémon. He figured it was due to the sheer number of characters and their unique names. They needed both.

It saved them from having to devise a system of codenames and do so on a large scale. Especially if the number needed was in the hundreds, as he suspected. Plus, the cards were available everywhere in society and easy to obtain. Both in the US and elsewhere.

Sure, he was guessing at this point, but the odds favored his conclusions. Even more so if the Russian invasion had been launched in a rush, like his gut was telling him. He couldn't explain why, but the feeling of Russian urgency was clear and consistent, ever since he'd witnessed the Area 51 jet crash site.

If he was correct about the high number of cards needed, it also meant the soldiers on guard duty had their hands full. Operators would arrive at all hours and in different modes of transportation. Some might even be walking, if their rides broke down.

"Or crashed," he mumbled, looking at the bandage around his left arm. Then he remembered the scars on his neck.

A new idea came unbidden to his mind—one that might increase his chance of success. He couldn't do much about his missing all-black attire, or the fact that he was arriving alone. However, if he could distract the guards long enough to get close, he might be able to provide the codename and be scanned.

Bunker took out his knife and drew it across the palm of his hand. The blade opened a gash about a half-inch long. He held the wound over the bandage, letting the blood drip onto the cloth and down his arm. A quick smear of the blood hastened the process, then he painted his neck and shirt collar red, making it appear he'd been injured in a car wreck. His forehead and cheeks were next, taking only seconds to help conceal his face from any cameras that might be active at the checkpoint.

The final item needed was a limp—something that would be noticeable from a distance. The guards would be curious and let him approach for inspection, where the blood prep would take over to complete the backstory.

The problem with a fake limp is remembering it when you're under duress. Consistency is critical; otherwise, you'll find yourself under arrest, or worse.

The best way to sell a limp is to actually give yourself one. Pain is an effective reminder.

A pebble with jagged edges caught his eye in the dirt. It was the perfect size and shape. He put it into his pocket, planning to stuff it into his sock and walk on it as he advanced on the checkpoint.

CHAPTER 106

Allison took a deep breath and let it out, hoping to rid her body of its anxiety as she continued her trek down the hallway in Tuttle's place. For a moment, she thought about turning around to avoid the encounter, but Misty needed her to deliver a message to the man Allison knew was in the master bedroom.

She found Sheriff Apollo sitting on the foot of the bed, his head tilted back at an angle and facing a wall covered in newspapers. He looked lost in the visuals before him, his eyes pinched and scanning the articles.

"Excuse me, Sheriff. Do you have a minute? Misty would like to talk to you."

Apollo nodded, never looking her way. "Sure, just send her in."

"Not here, Gus. She won't leave Martha's bedroom."

He brought his eyes around and let out a gentle smile. "Okay. I'll head over as soon as I finish up here."

His sudden gaze brought a tidal wave of pressure to her heart. It felt like a bulldozer had just smashed into her chest, making her want to run for the exit. Yet somehow, she found the courage to hold her position, even though she wasn't prepared for any of the newfound feelings.

He scooted over on the bed in a single lift and shift of his rear end, obviously making room for her to sit down.

Allison gulped, standing there like a mute statue. She needed to move or say something, but her body wasn't reacting to commands. All she could do was blink at him like a zombie. It was embarrassing.

"Please. Sit. I have something I want to show you," Apollo said in a gentle tone. He tapped the bed next to him, then nodded as if he'd just issued a direct order to one of his deputies.

Her feet finally responded. She sat down, with her breath growing shorter by the second, keeping several inches of space between them. "Is something wrong?"

"No, it's not that," he said, pointing at the newspapers hanging on the wall. "Tell me, what do you see?"

She peered at the newsprint, seeing headlines highlighted in yellow. Other articles had sections outlined in black ink. Next to them were handwritten phrases in the margins. Most of the notes were messy and unreadable.

Allison shrugged, wanting to answer intelligently, but her thoughts flickered in disarray. "I see a bunch of crazy."

"I thought that at first, too. Then I got to thinking. Why would a high-strung recluse like Tuttle mark up the maps the way he did? It was almost as if he knew exactly what we were going to need and left them for us."

She peered at the newspapers again, this time pushing aside the emotional thoughts bubbling inside. The Sheriff needed her to understand the point of this exercise and she wanted to oblige. "He must have known something was coming."

"That's exactly what I thought after I sat down and took a long, hard look at this little project of his."

She took a look around the room, hoping her intellect would rise to the top. It was time to contribute to the conversation. Otherwise, she'd continue to come across as a blithering idiot. Or more accurately, a middle-aged woman caught in an emotional snare, all because of a single unexpected kiss.

The newspapers were everywhere, covering most of the walls in front of her and behind. Some were on the adjacent walls, near the door and around the window. "He must have been at this a while."

"Trying to put the pieces together."

She pointed at the folded papers, stacked up on the floor. "Looks like he wasn't done yet, either."

Apollo stood and walked to the left. He pointed at a headline that read, *Uranium One Purchases 20% of US Reserves.*

"Okay, so?"

"Wait, just read them all and let it soak in like I did."

She nodded as his finger moved from headline to headline, her eyes taking them in one at a time:

Russia / China Purchase More US Debt

China on Massive Gold Buying Spree

The Holy Grail of High-Pressure Physics

New Super Fuel on the Horizon

Miracle Material Disappears from Lab

Discovery of Miracle Element Debunked

Secret Russian Land Grab Inside USA

China Buying US Stocks by the Truckload

Canadian Firm Sells Out for Billions

Cash Flows into Foundations after Approval

Uranium Production Falls to Record Lows

Defense Cuts Leaves USA Vulnerable

Border Crossings Surge

Record Debt Cripples States

Law Enforcement Cutbacks Planned

Jade Helm 15 Rollout Commences

Washington Ignores Cyberthreat Study

Power Grid Upgrades Stall in Senate

Apollo continued with the headlines for another minute or so before resuming his seat on the bed. "What do you think?"

"I know you're trying to make a point, I'm just not sure what I looking at here."

His tone turned serious and deliberate. "It's the greatest conspiracy of all time, Allison. This is all about our government's systematic sale of assets, technology, and territory to foreign countries, just to save its own ass."

She looked at the articles again, her mind in stutter mode. "You got all that from this?"

He nodded. "It took me a while to connect the dots, but it's all here. Tuttle must have figured it out. That's why he went off the grid and built the underground bunkers."

"So he wasn't crazy?"

"Crazy like a fox. But nobody would listen to him, including me. That's why he spent his wife's inheritance to stock up on everything. He knew this was coming."

Her throat ran dry in an instant. It took a full minute to find her voice again. "If what you say is true, we need to tell somebody."

"Who would we tell? They're all in on it."

She couldn't believe what she just heard. "No, that can't be. It just can't."

"You need to open your mind," he said, aiming his hand at the papers around the room. "The proof is all right here. You just gotta be willing to see it."

She didn't respond. There were no words.

He continued, pointing to headlines as he spoke, "Here, let me walk you through it . . . It all starts with our country being buried up to its eyeballs in debt, with more piling on every minute of every day. We're talking about an imminent, massive bankruptcy, the likes of which the world has never seen."

"Yeah, I've seen the numbers before. Everybody has."

"Then you also know there's no chance in hell that we'll ever pay any of it back."

She smirked. "Not with the way our government spends."

"Yet our enemies are lining up to buy our toxic debt at record levels, even though they know we can barely afford the interest as it is."

"Which gets a lot worse if interest rates rise."

"Exactly. Investors don't pour trillions into something they know will fail, not unless there's another way to profit."

"I see your point."

"This all centers around Cowie's new super element," Apollo said, looking sure of himself. "Something that will change the energy industry forever, but then it suddenly disappears from a lab. Unfortunately, nobody cares or pays much attention because the scientific community comes out and claims that it never existed in the first place."

"I remember something about that on the news."

"It's all just a little too convenient, wouldn't you say? First, we have Metallic Hydrogen being discovered. Something that will get us off fossil fuels forever and make trillions in profits for whoever controls it. Then it just disappears and nobody seems to care because some scientist says it never existed in the first place."

"Okay, I get that. Oil companies made it go away. Not the first time, right?"

"Actually, I don't think Big Oil was involved this time. It looks like Washington sold the discovery to the Russians for a huge payday. Or a ransom, if you believe what Misty said about the stolen formula."

She nodded, the theory coming together as he explained it. "A ransom payment is a sellout, depending on how you look at it."

"True, and it's not the first time our leaders have done it, either. Remember in January 2016 when the State Department paid Iran four hundred million dollars in return for those hostages?"

"Yeah, vaguely."

"That's how it starts. Once they know you can be manipulated like that, our adversaries will never stop. They'll hold a gun to your head for all kinds of reasons, like foreclosing on all your debt."

"Those bastards."

"But there's more. In recent years, foreign investment in our country has exploded, with trillions of dollars pouring in to buy stocks, land, and businesses all across our country. And it doesn't stop there. A huge chunk of our uranium deposits were sold to Russia, without anyone blinking an eye. Think about that for a minute. Uranium, the stuff nuclear bombs are made from, sold to our biggest enemy. And you wanna know why?"

She flared her eyes but didn't respond.

"Because politicians on all sides were paid off in the hundreds of millions to look the other way. And I'm talking Republicans, Democrats, and Independents. All that money funneled through backdoor projects and charitable donations, then paid out as needed to keep the swamp creatures happy. It's unbelievable, Allison. It's all here, on these walls, in black and white."

"Unreal," she said, unable to utter anything more intelligent.

"Now here's where it all starts to come together. First, US production of uranium falls unexpectedly, which I assume is to make room for Russian dominance in the marketplace. And again, nobody gives a crap. Then we see border crossings surge to get their troops and operatives in place while nobody is looking. Defense spending is slashed to the bone, leaving us weak and vulnerable. Debt spirals out of control across all fifty states, leading to local law enforcement cutbacks," he said, pausing. "There's a pattern forming here."

"Like chess pieces being positioned."

"For the kill. But what really sticks out is Jade Helm 15—an unprecedented military readiness exercise that's conducted inside our own borders."

"To move equipment into place," she added.

"Yep. Right under our noses," Apollo said. "And the media never bats an eye."

"God, how could we have been so stupid?"

"Because we've all been brainwashed by the news media and the Deep State who control them. We're supposed to believe everything they tell us, like good little slaves who are too stupid to think for themselves."

"You're right. Nobody pays attention anymore. We're all too busy trying to keep food on the table."

"Or trying not to kill each other."

She nodded. "It seems like every other day, another riot breaks out and the news goes nuts over it."

"That's all by design."

"To keep us divided."

"And distracted. If we're too busy fighting with each other, we don't have time to notice how we're being sold down the river."

"Unbelievable."

"But it gets worse. Despite all the research studies and the dire warnings, our leaders decide to leave our computer networks wide open to cyberattack and never upgrade our power grid. Does that make any sense to you?"

"No. Why would they do that?"

"Because the decision makers were paid to look the other way. They knew the attack was coming and agreed to let it happen."

"My God."

"Let's face it, when there's no way out, those in power will sell their souls to the devil if that means saving themselves. Especially if that devil is holding all the cards."

"You're talking about blackmail, right?"

"You're damn right I am. Russia and China must have gotten together and threatened to foreclose on all our debt," Apollo answered. "That's why there's been no resistance. Our enemies held a financial gun to our head. We either surrender to their demands, or they destroy us by flatlining our economy. We're talking about massive bank failures, starvation, and social anarchy. That's why we turned over technology, leaving ourselves ripe for takeover. This has all been planned from the start. Step by step."

She shook her head, not wanting to believe what he was saying.

He threw up his hands. "They just let them march right in and take over. It was easy once all the equipment was positioned a few years ago as part of that huge military exercise."

Her heart ached, for her country and her son. "Okay, let's assume what you say is true. It would mean Tuttle knew they'd invade Clearwater County, specifically."

"There's no doubt. Just look around."

"That's why he created those maps—" she said.

Apollo continued her thought before she could finish. "—to show where the roadblocks would be and to mark possible escape routes. He knew this was coming."

"But how exactly?"

He shook his head, looking tired. "I haven't figured that part out yet, but the clues must be here somewhere. All I know for sure is that this was meant to be kept quiet until it was too late."

"How do you figure that?"

"It's why we haven't seen any Russian jets or helicopters. They'd be too noticeable in our skies. A secret ground invasion could be kept quiet, especially in the backcountry, as long as communications and transportation are taken out first."

"By the EMP."

"Once the Russians got everything into place, it would be too late for anyone to do anything about it."

"So . . . what you're saying is that the EMP and cyberattack were done to cover it all up."

"Bingo. Nobody would ever expect that our own government was in on it from the start. Not after the EMP and computer hacks took everything down. It's the perfect excuse, Allison. Think about it. Our guilty leaders can claim the attacks caught them off guard. They can use them as the reason why the Russians were able to waltz right in. They can say they tried to stop it, but weren't able to. In fact, it wouldn't surprise me if the EMP and cyberattacks were done by us, not Russia, to make sure it all went as planned. Who else would know exactly what to do and where?"

"To save their own asses."

"And get rich in the process."

"Do you think the President is in on it?"

"I don't think so. The Deep State doesn't need the President to pull off any of this. We all know that presidents come and go. So does his staff. They only exist to give the citizens the illusion that this is a democracy, and that we have some say in what happens. But it's all a lie, Allison. The Deep State runs the show. Always has. Always will. They are always there, decade after decade, lurking in the background with their fingers into everything. They have the real power. Not the elected officials."

"It's always about the money and power," she said.

"It's just like with the UFO conspiracy," Apollo said, pointing across the room. "There's an article over there that talks about how Bill Clinton and his CIA director tried to dig into the truth about Roswell and Area 51. But they were stonewalled by those who are really in power. Nothing was ever revealed to the President of the United States, if you can believe that nonsense, because the

Deep State knows he'll be gone in a few years. All they have to do is stall long enough and it goes away on its own, without having to answer a single question."

"You're right. He's just a figurehead to keep us in line."

"Tuttle highlighted another article that proves Marilyn Monroe didn't commit suicide, either. She was murdered by the Deep State because she was getting ready to go public and tell all. Remember, she was sleeping with both of the Kennedy brothers in the White House, and we all know what happened to them. Men in power like to brag when they're in those types of situations with a sexy woman. Imagine the secrets she learned."

"Okay, I get all that, but why invade now? Why this week?"

He shrugged. "Something must have triggered it."

"What about that Area 51 jet? The one Bunker and Stephanie saw crash. Could that have been the reason?"

"Sure, anything's possible. Word might have leaked out about the sellout of our country, and someone on our side decided to take action with some kind of new tech to stop it. That could be why the Russians launched their plan now, before Area 51 got everything in place."

"Or someone on that plane was headed to NORAD to spill the beans."

"That, too. I'm afraid we'll never know. This might have been scheduled to happen this week, or it was a last-second thing."

Allison paused to search her memory. "Misty did mention she had a meeting planned with an old friend in NORAD. Maybe that's how word leaked out?"

"Or at least raised the question in someone's mind. The truth has a habit of working itself free, no matter how much money has been used to bury it."

"You know, something just occurred to me. Back when Angus spent that first summer here when he met Misty, Angus and Tuttle might have started talking about conspiracy theories. What if that's when Tuttle got the idea about the sellout?"

"Sure, that's as good a starting place as any. Something had to trigger all this research."

Allison pointed at the article with China in the headline. "What about China? Why haven't we seen anything from them yet? They're part of this, right?"

"I was thinking about that very thing before you walked in. Assuming this is happening elsewhere, then some of the other cities might be under Chinese control. Not Russian."

"It's like they're carving up a pie."

He sucked in a lip and nodded. "A red, white, and blue pie, and we're the cream filling."

CHAPTER 107

Bunker tossed his pack to the side, then sat on the embankment with his eyes glued to the road. The Russian guards protecting access to the town's main entrance couldn't see him from this position, but his paranoia wouldn't let him accept that proposition blindly.

He took off the sneaker on his right foot, then pried the sock away from his ankle so he could tuck the small rock he'd brought along inside. Bunker worked it to the bottom, positioning it under his arch, before putting his shoe back on.

If he had to do it over, he would have come prepared with all-black attire—assuming, of course, he had access to it. The charcoal-colored, flat panel pants would have to do. So, too, would the long-sleeved turquoise dress shirt he'd squeezed his frame into before smearing on the blood.

Both were snug, but he figured he looked like your everyday undercover Russian operator trying to blend in as an American civilian.

He finished his outfit with a baseball cap, the brim facing forward and curved with a firm cup of his hand. He pulled it down tight around his ears to keep it in place against the breeze in his face.

With any luck, the guards on duty would see him as a casual thirty-year-old having a bad day—a very bad, very bloody day. If he'd applied the blood properly across his shirt, neck, and face, they should buy his act.

Bunker stood and took a few strides to test the limp maker in his shoe. The pain registered as a level five injury. Not completely debilitating, he decided, but certainly enough of a reminder to keep his injury consistent and believable.

"That should work," he muttered, knowing the line between believability and mobility requires a delicate balance. Too much believability would destroy mobility.

After a quick double-check to make sure the Pokémon card from Jeffrey was in his right front pocket, he pushed the covert ID to the left as far as it would go. He thought the scanner should read it and confirm his identity, as long as the chip embedded within the card hadn't been damaged.

He grabbed his pack, walked to the bend in the road ahead and continued, bringing his eyes to the spread of armed guards two hundred feet away. They must have seen him too, snapping to attention with their rifles at the ready.

It's never easy to keep your shit wired tight when you're walking into overlapping fields of fire, but the sting in his arch helped keep him focused and in character. Selling his ruse was the only goal at the moment. Well, that and not getting himself killed during his unscheduled arrival.

His Marine Corps training had taught him a great many things, one of which is that it's always best to act like you belong when you're approaching any form of challenging post. Especially if it's manned by a team of itchy trigger-fingers from a hostile country. Anything else will get you carved up with a chest-full of lead.

To that end, he angled the brim of the cap down slightly to conceal his eyes, then gave the men a friendly hand wave—the kind you'd send to your neighbor as you drive by so you don't have to stop and have a chat with the nosy bastard.

"Halt and identify yourself," the center guard said when Bunker drew closer. As expected, the words were in English, with a heavy underpinning of a Russian accent.

Bunker stopped his feet, put his pack down, and raised his hands. If his theory about the Pokémon cards was wrong, the situation would spin sideways in the next ten seconds.

He took a deep, relaxing breath, then let the words out with conviction, using the character's name on the card as his ID. "Charmeleon, requesting entry."

"Raise your shirt and turn around," the guard commanded.

Bunker lifted his shirt, pulling it up to his chest. He spun slowly, having seen this same security exercise performed at US checkpoints in Afghanistan, where suicide bombers are a constant threat.

Those threats would arrive on foot with explosives strapped to their chests, hoping to get close enough for the detonation to kill scores of troops. The Russians were obviously wary of the same tactic.

"Approach and be recognized," the Russian responded.

One of the guard dogs took action next, trotting to Bunker's backpack under the control of his handler. The German Shepherd kept its snout in active search and detect mode, sniffing the air particles for the hint of explosives or weapons.

Once cleared, the dog and his partner disengaged, while a tall man from the guard shack arrived, clipboard in hand. Three guards came with him, covering Bunker with a trio of guns, each man about ten feet apart.

The tall man checked his list, scanning to page three before he spoke again. "You're late."

Bunker paused for effect. "Would have been here sooner, but my Land Rover hit an elk and rolled off the highway. Was starting to think I'd never find this place."

"The rest of your team?"

"Dead. I was lucky to crawl out of that wreck alive."

Tall man's face held its suspicious look for a few beats, then he brought the device up from his belt. He flipped a switch along the side, then aimed the unit at Bunker's crotch.

After a distinctive ping, the scanner's red LED display changed to show a new set of words in Russian.

Tall man locked eyes with Bunker for a moment, then he spoke to his men without taking his eyes away. Unfortunately, the words were in Russian.

Bunker held his tongue, while time seemed to tick by in super-slo-mo, as he wondered what was being said. The troops closed in on his position, making his heart skip a beat. Clear or detain? That was the only question on his mind.

When one of the guards removed the barricade and waved him clear for entry, Bunker didn't hesitate. He limped back to his pack, grabbed it, and slung it over his shoulder before turning and taking a direct line for the center of town. It only took seconds to pass the tall man and his team.

"Medical, two streets down on right, report to command after," tall man said in his version of English.

Slow is smooth and smooth is fast, he told himself, modifying the meaning behind one of his fire team leader's favorite sayings. He raised a hand and sent a blind acknowledgement signal to the guard station, never looking back or stopping his feet.

Fifty yards ahead was a Honda Pilot SUV. Most likely abandoned, he surmised. Its sky-blue paint made it look new. Its perfectly aligned position next to the sidewalk told him it had already been parked there when the EMP hit. He figured it belonged to one of the employees who worked in the two-story museum across the street.

The museum's front porch held signs for the tourists, inviting them inside for a look-see. The three old-style water barrels were a nice touch, evenly spaced apart to make room for a wooden rocker and a bronze spittoon between each of them.

The roofline featured the top half of a wagon wheel built into the facade, completing the obvious western theme. He guessed the red color along its spokes was for emphasis, offsetting the tan-colored paint used on everything else.

The windows on the first floor provided a clear view of the antique items stored within, making the establishment look more like a secondhand store than a historical repository. "Tourists love that shit," he murmured, convincing himself he was reading the situation correctly.

A half a mile away, at the far end of the main street, was another guard station, this one beyond the overhead sign for the Ye Old Bike Shop. He remembered that corner well, having led the kids he'd rescued from the bus accident past it a few days prior. To the right of the interior checkpoint was the town square, where he hoped to find Mayor Buckley in his office.

Bunker continued, passing two roving patrols who didn't seem interested in him. They must have been on the lookout for someone else, he decided, counting his blessings. They didn't seem alarmed by the blood, or his limp.

He took out the photo of Dallas' family and studied the faces as a handful of residents came his way. The ten-year-old had told Bunker the photo was recent, except his mom's hair color was now black instead of blonde.

The snapshot showed her in the middle of the back row, with her arms wrapped around her husband and her son. Her daughters were in the front, crouched down like an umpire behind home plate, their smiles big and bright. A happy day, to be sure.

Some of residents stopped to stare as he and his bloody clothing passed them on the sidewalk. Others ignored him, keeping their eyes low, no doubt due to the heavy presence of soldiers watching their every move. None of the locals matched the kid's mom or sisters. He put the photo away.

A faint hum purred in the background. It sounded like a machine running. Possibly an engine or generator, but he couldn't determine its position. The noise seemed to change direction as he traveled, no doubt due to the buildings acting as an ever-changing echo chamber.

He made a right at the second street and began a slow walk toward the Russian medical tent thirty yards ahead. This wasn't the course he had in mind, but it was necessary. He could feel the weight of the tall man's eyes monitoring his activity from the main entrance he'd just cleared.

The soldiers standing in front of the tent were busy chatting to each other in a makeshift circle. He didn't think any of the four had noticed his arrival, so he took the opportunity to slip into a nearby alleyway.

He ran a quick calculation and determined that the close proximity and height of the buildings would provide effective cover from the hovering Aerostat. His eyes went up to confirm with a crane of his neck. He couldn't see the mini-blimp and its surveillance array. Just like in Afghanistan, Aerostats are an effective tool, but not foolproof.

The dumpster behind the first establishment was full of trash, so much so, the mound of refuse had crested several feet above its sides. Some of the garbage had spilled onto the ground, leaving it to bake in the morning sun.

Despite the incredible stench, Bunker ducked behind the far end of the trash bin to use it as a shield. If anyone walked past the entrance to the alley, he needed to remain hidden. His arrival sent a scurry of rats heading for cover, their tiny squadron of feet churning a trail of trash into the air.

He leaned his backside against the wall and brought up his right shoe. The sneaker came off first, then the sock, giving him access to the pebble hiding inside. He grabbed the rock and tossed it aside before unleashing his fingers on his arch. Ten seconds into the rubdown, he discovered a bruise that had formed, making him wince.

Next up on the to-do list, the water spigot on the wall. He put his sock and shoe on, then spun and bent down to reach the handle. After a quarter turn, the faucet sent an unexpected spray of water shooting out. It splashed into his pant leg like a torpedo hitting its mark. He slid to the side to avoid any more fluid, then adjusted the stream to a trickle.

The background hum he'd heard must have been a generator, he decided. Otherwise, the pipes wouldn't have pressure. He didn't know if the Russians had brought along their own power station, or if the citizens had made other arrangements.

Either way, he was thankful, taking a few minutes to clean off the blood on his face, neck, and bandaged arm. He needed it, not only to remove the evidence of his ruse, but to invigorate his body.

He gulped down a few swigs, its coolness quenching his thirst. Yet replenishing his fluids wasn't the only benefit—it also made quick work of the sweat covering his skin.

There's something stimulating about cleaning up after a long trip. It restores not only your mood, but your energy levels. Unfortunately, the blood on his shirt wasn't going anywhere. He needed to score a new shirt.

Bunker planned to avoid the secondary checkpoint he'd seen at the end of the main street. Getting through one challenge post with false credentials was difficult enough. Pressing his luck with a second was not worth the risk, unless he acquired additional intel first. To so do, he would need to study the procedure of the interior station, then devise a plan that wouldn't get him arrested. Or killed.

Additional intel would take time—time he didn't have. Hopefully, there was an alternative access point to the square. Otherwise, he'd have to abandon his search for the Mayor in his office.

He took a left at the end of the alley, where it dumped onto a sidewalk that ran parallel to a city street lined with greenery. The street sign said Caribe Avenue, but the name meant nothing to him. Direction was all that mattered; he figured the town square was another two blocks ahead.

The tethered Aerostat was in full view, its nose pointed in the same direction he was traveling. Like everyone else in town, he needed to assume his actions were being monitored on one of its many cameras.

Speaking of actions, he had no way of knowing if his shooting spree in the miner's camp had been caught on video by the hovering drone. If it had, he was glad he'd decided to wear the baseball cap. They might have his face on file and could be actively looking for him. Then again, maybe they'd already scoured the city and come up empty.

His side of the street was free of people, but the two cars ahead of him would require a change of course, not because they were mangled together in a crumpled heap but rather, because they were blocking his path on the sidewalk.

The broken glass near the center stripe of the asphalt indicated where the two sedans had collided, but there were no skid marks to the sidewalk. It didn't make sense, unless someone moved the wreck out of the way. Someone like the Russians, he figured. They would want the streets free of obstacles to move their infantry and equipment. It would also keep the sightlines clear during convoy travel, avoiding a blockade that could lead to an ambush.

Shortly after Bunker made his way around the crash, two soldiers on foot patrol turned onto the same street. Their path would intersect his on the sidewalk in mere seconds.

He thought about crossing the street to avoid the encounter, but a sudden redirect might appear suspicious after the car wreck didn't chase him to the opposing sidewalk. There were several manicured hedges and bushes along the street. Some of them would have made effective cover, if he'd seen the patrol sooner.

He kept his eyes low and marched ahead. The clatter of boots and equipment went past him without incident, bringing the air back to his lungs. He took the next right and found himself in another alley—this one much narrower than the last.

Dead ahead, maybe three hundred feet away, was a group of five men wearing civilian clothes. They were approaching in a triangle formation. The man in the center led the pack in a business suit and tie. The others were dressed in casual attire, though one of them did have a pair of jean shorts covering his thighs.

Bunker slowed his pace when two of the men pulled out what looked like baseball bats from under their shirts. One of the others brandished a knife with an imposing blade.

At first, Bunker thought they might be after him, but he soon realized their attention was on the sky above. Probably to keep an eye on the location of the surveillance blimp.

He ducked behind an electrical service box to see what would happen next. The men continued their advance for another hundred feet or so before stopping at a white service door on the alley's left. They huddled for a short minute, then the door flung open and they went inside, with weapons raised.

CHAPTER 108

Mayor Buckley led the charge through the back door of Charmer's Market. The throbbing sting across the back of his hand was getting worse, dripping blood from the handkerchief wrapped around the wound.

If only he'd been more careful a few minutes earlier, the bent piece of sheet metal never would have sliced open his skin. He'd been around long enough to know that most accidents happen when you're distracted. Even more so when you're tired, or in this case, when you're in a rush to have a chat with a pair of brothers like Bill and Kenny King.

The four men he'd commandeered as reinforcements kept pace as they scrambled through the stock room and into the employee break room. Buckley released the latch under the wall cabinet, allowing him to pull the fridge open on its hidden mount.

Buckley entered the secret hallway behind the refrigerator. The others joined him a few seconds later. Buckley turned to the last man. "Close it. We don't want anyone wandering in here uninvited."

The man in the jean shorts did as he told.

The door ahead wasn't open, giving Buckley time to rally his men. He was sure Kenny King had framed Stan Fielding for the disappearance of the Russian interpreter, Valentina. Stan's execution was scheduled in a little over an hour. Buckley and company were here to confront Kenny about what he'd done.

"We go on three," Buckley whispered, receiving four head nods in return.

When they burst into the room, they found the Russia interpreter lying on her side, still strapped to the chair, eyes closed. Valentina was completely naked, with dozens of cuts across her body. Blood seemed to be everywhere on the floor, pooling in spots.

Kenny King stood over her, with his hunched back to the door. Bill King was also in the room, but there was no sign of Rico or the other deputies who had been in this panic room earlier.

"What the hell did you do?" Buckley screamed at Kenny.

The blond man brought his head around, peering over his wide shoulder, his eyes filled with venom. "Doing what needs to be done."

Buckley flashed a look at his men, then charged the escaped convict with fury in his heart. He knew Kenny was bigger and stronger, but he couldn't stop himself.

Kenny stood upright and spun on his heels only a moment before Buckley arrived. That's when the Mayor saw it—a ten-inch knife in Kenny's right hand, pointed his way.

Buckley tried to halt his attack, but it was too late to stop his momentum. He gasped when the tip of the blade impaled his abdomen, penetrating his skin with ease. The cold steel sliced its way deeper, burrowing a path to his organs.

Kenny was now nose-to-nose with Buckley, close enough for the man's bitter rage to wash over Buckley in a huff of breath. The criminal clenched his jaw and held a maniacal stare as he twisted the knife in a steady fashion.

Buckley watched a grin take over Kenny's lips, while bolts of pain radiated outward from the knife's damage path, ripping at the tissue holding Buckley's insides together.

When the twisting blade reached a vertical ninety degrees, numbness crept into Buckley's body. It started at the tips of his toes and continued to spread, seeming to match the amount of life force gushing out in a spray of red.

"It's time to finish this, Mayor, once and for all," Kenny said in a growl, holding his pinched eyes in a glare.

Buckley steeled himself, figuring Kenny was about to draw the knife up to put a violent end to this ordeal.

"Come on, Kenny. Do it," Bill King demanded from a few feet away, breaking his silence.

If this was going to be his last minute on Earth, Buckley needed it to count for something. He summoned all of his remaining strength and sent it to his right arm in one final push.

His hand responded, rising up in a tremble to Kenny's face. He aimed his thumb and jammed it into Kenny's eye, burying it up to the knuckle.

Kenny let out a painful howl, only moments before a shadowy blur came into view from the right. Buckley felt a massive weight slam into his right shoulder, separating him from the knife. He sprawled airborne, landing next to Valentina's body in a tumble of arms and legs. He rolled onto his left side.

The impact was from Jack Bunker. Somehow, the mysterious drifter had found his way here. He stood across from Kenny King in a ready position, much like a wrestler starting a match—his shoulders hunched and arms extended. A few feet behind him was a backpack, sitting on the floor in a lean.

Even though Kenny's left eye had suffered significant trauma, he remained on his feet and still held the knife. His breath was short and powerful, like an angry bear preparing to attack.

"Kill him," Bill King yelled to his brother. "Kill him now!"

Kenny charged Bunker and swiped with the tip of the blade. Bunker reacted in a flash, completing a series of moves in an instant.

First, he dodged the blade with a twist of his hips, then he brought his left arm under the inside of Kenny's right elbow. Bunker closed the gap between them, then wedged his weight against the attacker's outstretched arm. His right hand came down to latch onto Kenny's wrist with heavy force.

Kenny lunged as Bunker tugged the man forward, bringing the blade safely past his right leg, then using his kneecap as a fulcrum to snap Kenny's wrist. The knife fell to the floor as Kenny screamed in pain, grabbing at his wrist.

Buckley heard the hollow pings of aluminum baseball bats hitting the floor before a scamper of feet headed toward the exit. The Mayor's posse had just taken off, leaving him bleeding in spurts on the floor.

Bill King took a run at Bunker, driving him backward and away from his brother with a shoulder to the gut.

The two men staggered across the room in tandem, until Bunker's back smashed into the wall with a sudden thud. Bunker brought his arms up and made a double fist, driving them down in a swift chopping motion.

King grunted when the impact slammed into his upper back, but he didn't release his grip.

Bunker landed three more lightning-fast blows, driving his fists down with successive force.

King let go of Bunker's waist and dropped to the floor, face down.

Bunker spun and dropped a knee into the man's spine, then threw a firm right, smashing his knuckles into the back of King's skull. Buckley heard a horrendous crack when King's nose flattened against the floor.

Bunker was about to land another blow when a foot came around from the one-eyed Kenny, catching Bunker in the face.

Bunker toppled backward, with blood flying from his mouth. He landed on his back and didn't move. Neither did Bill King. Both men were bleeding from their head wounds; however, the amount of blood pouring out of Bill's face was much more noticeable.

Buckley wasn't sure if the younger King was still alive, but his older brother Kenny was, stumbling to the abandoned knife. He bent over and picked it up with his left hand, then went at Bunker.

Buckley wished he had the strength to call out to Bunker, but his air was thin. All he could do was watch, straining to keep his eyes open.

Kenny dropped next to Bunker on his knees, keeping his injured wrist against his body. He positioned the tip of the blade over Bunker's chest and drew the knife up to shoulder level.

Just as Kenny brought the blade down in a stabbing motion, Bunker's eyes snapped open. Bunker's hands came up to catch Kenny's wrist in a two-handed grab, stopping the knife just short of his chest.

Kenny let out a commando yell, leaning forward to add more weight behind the blade.

Bunker pushed back, groaning to summon additional strength as the struggle continued.

A few seconds later, the dagger began to rise. Bunker released one of his hands, then sent three sharp jabs at Kenny's throat, all of them hitting the mark. The final blow cracked the man's windpipe.

Kenny let go of the weapon and fell back to the floor, his voice a jumble of gasps, gurgles, and grunts.

Bunker didn't hesitate, crawling to Kenny with the knife in his hand. He aimed the tip of the blade at the bottom of Kenny's throat, pushing it deep with both hands wrapped around the handle.

Buckley watched the last shallow breath escape from Kenny King's lungs. The lawbreaker's life came to end a moment later, his head tilting toward Buckley with eyes open.

* * *

Bunker rolled off the man he'd just stabbed to death. He crawled to the naked woman to see if she was still alive. The volume of blood on the floor around her body gave him little hope, but he still needed to check.

Most of the cuts and bruises on her body didn't look life-threatening. There was one injury, however, that did—a wide gash between her breasts. The size and shape of the wound appeared to match the blade Bunker had just driven into the one-eyed man's throat.

He put two fingers to her neck and held it there for a ten-count. No pulse. Her chest wasn't processing air, either. There was only one conclusion. She was dead. Probably slain by the same man who'd stabbed the Mayor just before he arrived.

The other attacker hadn't moved since Bunker knocked him out with a blow to the back of the head. The loud crack from the man's nose smashing into the floor was fresh in his mind. Bunker wasn't sure if he was alive or dead, but, like the woman, the sheer amount of blood on the floor wasn't a good sign.

Three possible dead, two by his hands, and Bunker didn't recognize any of them. It wasn't surprising; he hadn't spent much time in this town after arriving with the kids from the bus crash. They could all be locals. Or outsiders. He didn't know. But Buckley did.

He slid over to the Mayor, wishing he'd arrived a minute earlier. Buckley's gut was bleeding in spurts. Bunker put his hand on the wound, adding pressure to slow the blood loss.

Buckley opened his eyes, showing only a sliver of white. "Bunker? How?" he asked in a weak, thready voice.

"Snuck in through the main gate. Saw your crew in the alley, then followed the blood trail in here."

"The Russians," he grunted. "They're—"

"I know, Mayor. Save your breath." Bunker scooped his arms under Buckley. He pressed to his feet and turned for the door.

"Desperate—" Buckley said in a grunt, his tone barely audible. "She's important. To him."

Bunker didn't understand the words Buckley had just uttered. He wanted to ask more about it, but the Mayor needed to save his strength.

The door to the hidden room swung open. An elderly woman with gray streaks in her hair stood in the entrance, her eyes wide. The smock across her front said *Charmer's Market*. The garment looked as old and frazzled as she did.

"What are you doing?" she shrieked.

"Getting him to a doctor," Bunker answered, searching his memories for the location of Doc Marino's clinic. "Hold the door."

She nodded, standing aside with her arm outstretched, wedging the door open.

Bunker kicked two baseball bats out of the way, sending them to the corner of the room, then nudged his backpack to the right on the floor with his foot. After he slipped through the door with the Mayor in his arms, the woman ran ahead and pushed open the refrigerator.

Bunker stepped outside into what he assumed was the break room in the back of Charmer's Market. Buckley put his hand out and grabbed onto the woman's sleeve as she closed the fridge. "Help him, Grace. Help Bunker."

"Help him what?"

"Stop the execution," Buckley said, letting go of her.

She looked at Bunker, the shock evident.

"You can trust him, Grace," Buckley said, before looking at Bunker. "Daisy? The Sheriff?"

"They're safe, Mayor. So are Steph and her son."

"Rusty?"

"Yes. And Dicky. Burt's there, too," Bunker answered, deciding not to waste time mentioning Franklin's death or the others in camp.

"Where?"

Bunker didn't want to divulge too much information. "That's not important right now. We need to get you to a doctor."

Grace took Buckley's hand in hers. "Who did this to you, Mayor?"

"Kenny King," Buckley said, his eyes weak. A moment later, they closed and his arm fell limp.

"Is he dead?" she asked.

Bunker could see the Mayor's chest moving air in short, shallow breaths. "No, but he will be if we don't get him medical attention."

"Doc Marino's clinic is just across the square." She put out her hands. "I'll help you."

"No, I got him," Bunker said, adjusting the weight in his arms to better center the Mayor's body. The man was in good shape; otherwise, his weight would have been impossible to carry in his arms. A heavier man would have forced him to use an over-the-shoulder firefighter's lift, putting extra pressure on the Mayor's belly wound.

Bunker motioned with his head for Grace to lead the way. "What execution is he talking about?"

"Stan Fielding's." She turned and hurried to a different door. It wasn't the entrance Bunker had used to follow Buckley and his gang inside.

Bunker followed, running the condemned man's name through his mind. An image flashed of two bubbly young girls he'd rescued from the bus. "Stan Fielding is the twins' father, right?"

"Beth and Barb. The redheads."

"Nice kids," he said, remembering their playful nature during the walk back to town. Their banter never took a break, wearing out Deputy Daisy in the process. "What happened with Stan?"

"The Russians want revenge for the disappearance of their interpreter. They found a bloody uniform in his house," she answered, shooting a troubled look back at the fridge.

Bunker stopped his feet. "The woman back there?"

Grace nodded, tugging him forward with a grab on his arm. "She's the interpreter. Her name is Valentina. They've been looking all over town for her ever since I . . . ah . . . well . . . knocked her out."

"You did this?"

"I didn't mean to; it just happened. One minute she was nosing around the back of my store with that Russian attitude of hers, and the next I'm hitting her over the head with my broomstick. I don't know what came over me."

Bunker angled the Mayor sideways to fit through the door, following Grace out of the back room and into the retail area of the store. "Who were those other guys?"

"Bill King and his brother."

"Stephanie's ex?"

"Yeah, I went to him for help," Grace answered, leading him through the maze of display racks and counters. "But I didn't know Kenny was there. He just escaped from prison. Had I known—"

"Which one was he?"

"The bigger one, with blond hair. Did he stab the Mayor?"

"I'm afraid so."

A few turns later, they were in the center aisle, heading for the front of the store. When they reached the halfway point, two men in civilian clothes flew through the entrance and took a path straight for them.

Bunker stopped, flashing a look of concern at Grace.

Grace shook her head. "It's okay. That's Rico and Zeke. They work for the Sheriff."

When the men arrived, Grace stopped. So did Bunker.

She looked at the man on the left. "Rico, take the Mayor to Doc's."

"What happened?" Rico asked, putting his arms out.

"Kenny stabbed him," Grace said as Bunker slid the body into Rico's hands. "Better hurry. He's lost a lot of blood."

Rico carried the Mayor to the front door and went outside.

The other man grabbed Grace's arm, then motioned to Bunker. "Who is *this* guy, Grace?"

"Jack Bunker."

"The drifter who saved all those kids?"

"Yes, and he's a friend of the Mayor's, Zeke."

Zeke turned his attention to Bunker, looking him over from head to toe. His eyes spent the most time on the blood covering Bunker's shirt. "You're taller than I thought."

Bunker held back a comment about the man's shorter stature.

Zeke looked at Grace. "Why would Kenny stab the Mayor?"

"I don't know," she said, pulling her arm free from his grip. "I wasn't there."

Zeke pointed at Bunker. "Then how do you know this guy didn't do it?"

"Because the Mayor just told me."

Bunker was out of patience. "Look, you don't have to take my word for it. Just hunt down the men Buckley brought with him; they'll confirm what happened."

"What men?" Zeke asked.

"I only caught a glimpse of them, but they didn't look familiar. Then again, I haven't met many of you people. Buckley obviously knew them. All I can tell you is there were four of them and they took off running as soon as the shit went sideways."

Zeke ran quiet, his eyes turning to the side in a long stare. After a short pause, he asked, "Where's Kenny now?"

Grace pointed to the back of the store. "In the panic room. On the floor."

"He's dead," Bunker added.

"What?" Zeke asked, pausing for a two-count before he took off running, his feet pounding the floor.

Bunker and Grace followed him to the break room.

Zeke opened the secret hatch and went inside, making a beeline through the secondary door and straight for the bloody pile of meat in the center of the room. He stood over the one-eyed corpse with his jaw hanging open. "What the hell happened?"

"I arrived just after he stuck a knife into the Mayor, so I took action."

"You did this?"

"Didn't have a choice. He came at me next," Bunker said, pointing at the other body. "So did his brother."

Zeke ran to Bill King and checked the body for vitals. "Jesus Christ! Both of them?" Zeke got to his feet and charged Bunker with his jaw firm.

Grace stepped in front, stopping him with a grab of her hands. "It was self-defense, Zeke."

Zeke flared his eyes at Grace, then brought them to Bunker, his chest heaving.

Grace latched onto Zeke by the shoulders and brought his attention back to her. "Kenny did this, not Bunker. The Mayor would be dead by now if Bunker hadn't stopped Kenny when he did."

Zeke tucked in a lip and shook his head, looking defiant.

Bunker could feel the heat from the man's rage. It was palpable, bolstered by the fury within.

Grace leaned her head to the left, blocking his view of Bunker. "What else was he supposed to do, Zeke? They'd already killed the woman. He couldn't let them kill the Mayor."

Zeke's rapid breaths continued for another minute as the three of them stood there, nobody moving.

Grace let go and took a step back when Zeke's eyes finally softened. "It was self-defense, Zeke. You know Kenny and his temper."

Zeke nodded, his breath slowing.

"We need to deal with these bodies," Bunker said, wanting to move the situation along.

Zeke walked to Valentina's corpse, his hands on his hips. "Was this you, too?"

Bunker shook his head. "She was dead before I got here. I'm guessing that's why Buckley and his posse showed up. To stop the torture."

"Dammit, I was afraid this would happen," the man snapped, his eyes focused on the floor.

Bunker took his statement as a confession, confirming what he already suspected after Zeke led them straight to the panic room without any direction from Grace. Zeke had obviously been inside this space before, probably after they'd taken the Russian interpreter hostage. "I was wondering if you were in on this."

"We all were. Me, Rico, and Russell."

Grace raised her hand. "So was I. Oh, and Billy Jack. Almost forgot about him."

Bunker pinched his eyes but didn't respond. He'd heard the name Billy Jack, but wasn't sure until now that the man actually existed.

"I guess you haven't met him yet," Zeke said. "He owns the Pump and Munch and the café."

A new thought burrowed into Bunker's brain. "Just curious—why isn't he here?"

Zeke paused, looking at Grace before bringing his eyes back to Bunker. "Good question. He was all gung-ho to start, but I haven't seen him since we first agreed to interrogate her."

"Maybe he changed his mind," Grace said.

"Do you trust him?" Bunker asked.

Grace answered. "I didn't like him much after he opened that convenience store across the street, but I think he's trustworthy. Why do you ask?"

"Because it comes down to one simple premise. The more people who know about this room and what happened to Valentina, the higher the risk. For all of us. If he changed his mind and mentioned Valentina's death to someone in a Russian uniform, then—"

"We're fucked," Zeke said, finishing Bunker's sentence.

"What about the Mayor? Was he okay with interrogating the woman?" Bunker asked, even though he was sure of the answer.

"No, he was against it from the start," Zeke said before an extended exhale passed over his lips. "Kenny was just supposed to get information from her. Nobody was supposed to die."

Bunker nodded, but kept his thoughts to himself. He knew torture was never the answer. Usually, you end up with bad intel because the prisoner is desperate and will tell you whatever you want to hear. Or else the captive ends up dead. Like in this case.

"What's done is done," Grace said, her tone somber.

Zeke's eyes indicated he agreed, but he didn't respond.

"Was Fielding involved?" Bunker asked.

"No. Stan had nothing to do with this," Grace said. "It was just us."

"Then how did the uniform end up in his place?"

"Kenny must have planted it," Zeke said after a beat. "Now that I think about, he did say something about getting some payback when the Mayor first tried to stop him."

"Payback for what?" Bunker asked.

"Testifying. Stan's the reason he went to prison. So was the Mayor."

"Which is why he stabbed Buckley," Bunker added.

"Shit," Zeke said in a sharp tone. "None of this should have ever happened."

"What do we do now?" Grace asked.

"We get rid of the bodies," Zeke answered, sending a single head nod to Bunker. "If anyone sees them, then—"

"I was talking about the execution," Grace said, interrupting. "We have to stop it."

Zeke shook his head. "I don't think we can. There are too many of them."

"We could, if we still had guns," she said.

Bunker took her comment to mean the insurgents had confiscated their weapons. He wasn't surprised. It was step one in the Russian Occupation Playbook.

Zeke nodded, looking dejected. "Though Bill and Kenny did mention they had a stockpile the Russians didn't know about."

"Where?" she asked.

"They didn't say," he said, looking at Kenny's body. "Now I guess we'll never know."

The volume of Grace's voice shot up a level. "Then that's it? We just give up and let them murder Stan?"

"There may be a way," Bunker said, using his most confident tone, "but it's risky."

"If it stops the killing, we have to try," Grace said. "Stan's innocent. His girls can't grow up without a father."

Bunker wasn't sure if these two were ready for what he had in mind. "If we do this, it means doing some things none of us wants to do as civilized human beings. Are you ready for that? Because this is war and there's no turning back once we go down this road."

Grace gulped down a bulge in her throat. It looked painful. "Yes."

Zeke nodded, though it wasn't convincing.

A flash of words stormed Bunker's thoughts, taking him back to something the Mayor said a few minutes ago. He replayed them in his mind.

The Russians were desperate.

The woman was important.

To him.

Bunker figured Buckley's clues meant the woman was close to the General. Made sense if she was part of his personal staff. Perhaps there was more to her assignment than simply being an interpreter. Maybe they had a relationship. Romantic in nature.

In the US military, that type of relationship would violate the Uniform Code of Military Justice, specifically, the rules against fraternization that would compromise the chain of command. Then again, these were Russians. They might have different rules about getting involved romantically with a junior officer.

Regardless, her corpse presented a unique opportunity. Assuming, of course, the "him" in Buckley's statement was referring to the General. Right then, a slew of new ideas percolated in his mind, causing him to re-evaluate his plan.

Bunker looked at Zeke. "You were right when you said there are too many of them, plus they'll be well armed. We can't go head to head in a straight-up fight. Not with untrained civilians."

"It would be a slaughter," Zeke said.

"Even with guns."

"Then what are we gonna do?" Grace asked.

"We use asymmetrical warfare techniques," Bunker said without hesitation, delivering the words with the intensity they deserved.

Grace threw up her hands. "What does that even mean?"

Bunker slowed his tempo as he answered. "Normally it means we go blood simple with small unit tactics, hitting them hard and fast to create chaos. In this case, we're going to need something a little more clever. Something with a specific goal in mind. If we can get them off their game, we might just have a chance. But the timing has to be perfect. We'll only get one shot at this."

Grace pointed to the three of them with a circular sweep of her hand. "Us?"

Bunker nodded. "We could use a couple more reinforcements. People you trust."

"How many?" Zeke asked.

Before Bunker could answer, three men appeared in the doorway. One of them was Rico, the man who had hauled the Mayor to Doc Marino's clinic.

The second man was one of the deserters who had bailed from Buckley's posse—the young man wore jean shorts and was extra thin. Bunker doubted if he was strong enough to complete a single pull-up.

The third man was an unknown, but looked physically capable. He stood several inches taller than the others, almost matching Bunker's height.

"Ask and ye shall receive," Grace quipped.

Rico pointed at the body Bunker had stabbed. "Is that Kenny?"

Zeke nodded, then aimed a finger at the other male victim. "And Bill."

Rico looked dumbfounded. He turned his eyes to Valentina's blood-covered carcass, shaking his head.

Bunker picked up his rucksack and slung it over his shoulder.

"How's the Mayor doing, Rico?" Grace asked, her tone genuine. Her concern was obvious, exaggerating the wrinkles across her face.

Rico looked unsure when he answered. "Doc said it's sketchy. He's lost a lot of blood, but they're working on him now."

Grace gasped, tears welling in her eyes. "It's too bad FEMA isn't still here. Their medical teams would have helped."

Zeke fired back, "You know that was all bullshit, right?"

Bunker wasn't sure he heard Zeke correctly. "FEMA was here? Already?"

"Yeah, *some blokes from down under*," Zeke said in an entertaining Australian accent. He returned to his normal voice. "Just showed up out of the blue with trucks and medical supplies."

Grace nodded. "Right before the Wal-Mart semis brought all the food."

A torrent of thoughts slammed into Bunker's mind, one of which was a vision of the now-dead Angus Cowie. He, too, was from Australia. "And none of that raised any red flags?"

Rico shrugged. "From what the Mayor told me, they were in Denver for a multi-national first responder training exercise when the EMP hit. FEMA needed help, so they volunteered."

Bunker couldn't believe what he was hearing. "Please tell me someone checked their credentials?"

"I think the Mayor did," Grace said, turning to Rico.

Rico looked puzzled. "It's possible he didn't. Everyone was pretty stressed at that point." Rico looked at the third man who'd arrived with him. "What about you, Russell? Did the Mayor mention anything about asking for IDs?"

"I don't think so. Everyone was in panic mode and worried for their lives."

Zeke pointed to the side of his neck. "When FEMA told us that an airborne virus was on its way here, we all lined up for the inoculations without a second thought."

"Well, almost everyone," Grace said, challenging Zeke's answer.

Rico spoke next. "Grace is right. There were a couple of families who resisted, but FEMA convinced them to get inoculated. I think Fielding and his daughters were skeptical at first, if I remember right. Anyway, at that point, everyone was thankful for FEMA's help."

"Of course, later we found out that the virus never existed and they supposedly shot Russian tracking devices into our necks," Zeke said.

"And explosives," Russell added.

Zeke pointed at the dead female prisoner. "That's why Kenny wanted to interrogate her. He didn't buy any of it, which, as it turned out, was correct. Valentina eventually told us the injections were fake. They were done to keep us under control so we'd work the mine and not cause trouble. They've been drafting people to work ever since."

"I had one couple come into my store earlier and tell me that some of those workers never returned from their shifts in the mine," Grace said.

"It's dangerous work," Zeke said. "That's probably why they're holding back on dragging everyone to the mine all at once."

"Or it's a space issue," Grace said, the words sounding more like a question than a statement of fact.

Bunker shook his head. "It was done as a security measure. When I first arrived, they were hauling small groups in the backs of trucks under heavy guard."

"At least they're keeping us fed," Grace said.

"It's more like they're keeping their inventory of slaves fat and happy," Zeke added.

"Wal-Mart was obviously in on this, too," Russell said.

"He's right," Rico said. "They don't just show up in force like that right after a disaster."

"Unless the Russians stole their trucks," Zeke answered. "Hell, it wouldn't take much to paint some trucks to look like the real thing. Wouldn't surprise me a bit. They knew we wouldn't question a fleet of Wal-Mart trucks showing up."

"When's the execution?" Bunker asked Grace.

She grabbed his wrist and looked at the watch. "At the top of the hour."

"Are you sure?"

"That's what Colonel Orlov said in his morning announcement. But General Zhukov could have changed it with the storms in the area."

Bunker knew the Russians would never break their schedule. Everything they did was part of a plan. They'd never deviate once it was set. It was a pride thing. Or arrogance. Those two terms being blood cousins.

"Those poor girls," Russell said, shaking his head.

Bunker retrieved the photo from his pocket and gave it to Grace. "Before I forget, have you seen any of these people in town? Specifically, the women."

She took the photo and studied it. "Sorry. Haven't." She gave the photo back to Bunker.

Zeke shot Bunker an inquisitive look.

Bunker stowed it in his pocket, deciding to keep the answer to Zeke short. "Part of a family who's missing." He looked at Rico, remembering the changes occurring in the sky on his way into town. "What's the weather like outside?"

"There's a storm rolling in. Gonna be a big one, too. At least the drought will finally be over."

"Then it's now or never, gentlemen," Bunker said, using a commander's tone. He thought he had more time to set up his plan, but the change in weather and the availability of the female's body provided a better opportunity. He'd have to adjust on his feet and advance the timetable. Hopefully, Albert had his shit together and wasn't sloughing off.

"What's the plan?" Zeke asked.

Bunker scanned the gray-haired woman's figure. "We start with Grace getting naked."

"I'm sorry, what was that?" she asked, her eyes as big as softballs.

"We need you to take off your clothes, Grace. Now, please."

CHAPTER 109

"Any word from Bunker?" Albert asked Daisy after she delivered the final two boxes of Tide laundry detergent.

"No. All quiet."

It was all Albert could do not to stare at her whenever she was around. It wasn't just her incredibly sexy walk, her hips swaying from left to right like a stripper working the stage. It was all of her—how she carried herself—how she filled out the uniform. Even her smile was mesmerizing. He knew she wasn't interested in him, but it still didn't stop his desire. Or his eyes.

"No news is good news," Rusty quipped as he emptied the last of the potable containers, splashing water onto the outside of the barn. The liquid pooled under the back leg of the portable table Albert had just set up.

Daisy furrowed her brow, nodding gently. "As long as his radio is still working."

"Maybe you should call him?" Dustin asked.

Rusty put the empty five-gallon jug on the rolling cart in front of Dustin. It was next to a handful of others he'd already prepped.

Daisy shook her head with vigor. "Bunker was explicit about maintaining radio silence unless it's an emergency."

Albert sniggered. "Wouldn't want our Russian friends getting a fix on our location."

"At this point, all we can do is wait and listen." Daisy looked at her watch. "Speaking of which, I gotta go." She scampered away, with two of the three men watching her from behind.

"Damn," Dustin said, craning his neck to watch her progress. Albert flared an eyebrow in agreement.

Rusty seemed oblivious to the sexual overtones. "Wouldn't the fifty-gallon drums out back work better?"

Albert picked up one of the heavy-duty water jugs from the cart and shook it. "On paper, yeah. But there's a reason Bunker put these on his list. We can move them a lot easier once they're filled with diesel. Those drums would weigh over four hundred pounds. Dicky's strong, but he's not that strong."

Dustin grabbed the handle on the front of the cart and began to push. "Now for the fun part."

"I love the smell of napalm in the morning," Albert said, his tone deep and purposeful.

"*Apocalypse Now*, right?"

"Great flick, especially that intense scene with the ox."

Rusty marched alongside Albert, both following Dustin's lead to the pasture behind the barn. They made the first corner and headed to the elevated, 300-gallon, gravity-fed diesel supply.

When they arrived at the overhead tank, Dustin stood on the bottom rail of the metal platform and grabbed the fuel hose hanging above. He hopped down, then removed the cap on the first water container. "Here, you're in charge of these," he said, tossing the cap to Rusty without warning. "Put them on after I finish filling each one."

Rusty nodded, then looked at Albert. "Do we fill them all the way?"

Albert pointed to the side of the blue container, his finger several inches below the top. "No, we stop about here to leave air space for combustion."

Dustin removed the rest of the caps and gave them to Rusty. He put the fuel hose into the first spout and began to fill it. "After we make the pressure plate detonators, we should test one of these. Just to be sure it works."

Albert let out a snort, the corner of his mouth raised on one side. "Sure, we could do that. But first we'll need to decide who's gonna be the guinea pig."

"For what?

"To step on the board and test the switch. If you want to volunteer, I'm good with it. What do you think, Rusty?"

"Sure. Dustin can be the trigger man," Rusty said with a smile, his tone playful and exaggerated.

Dustin rolled his eyes. "I'm sure there's another way to test it, without me having to step on the board and get cooked to a crisp."

Albert laughed. "You need to relax, bro. It's gonna work. No need to waste all that fuel. As long as we have good batteries and some wire, these things will blow, no problem."

Rusty looked at Albert. "I get the diesel part, but what's all the Tide detergent for?"

"Soap flakes. We mix it in to turn the fuel into a sludge, like jelly. That way, when it blows, the fire sticks to whoever is standing near it."

Dustin moved the hose to the next container. "Basically, it's homemade napalm."

Albert continued. "When someone steps on a board buried in the dirt, the wire leads will make contact and send a spark to these containers. Then it's Russian barbecue time."

* * *

"Wait for my signal," Bunker told Rico and Zeke in a whisper, while the three of them kept low behind a set of bushes lining Caribe Avenue.

Bunker knew this path well, having walked it earlier that day. His training had taught him to scout locations as he traveled, memorizing details he might need later. Intel is key when you're in a combat zone. Even when that combat zone is a sleepy community in Colorado, where nothing happens.

Bunker peered through a gap in the greenery to confirm the timing, then brought his eyes back to his new friends. "We go on three. Be sure to immobilize like I showed you. Be decisive. Don't hesitate. I'll take care of the rest."

Zeke nodded, putting the green-colored towel Grace had given him on the ground. He tucked the cloth out of sight, near the base of the hedge. Rico did the same with his.

Zeke flexed his fingers, his eyes like steel. Rico took deep, slow breaths, his chest expanding to double its normal size.

Both men were noticeably nervous, but they looked ready. As ready as two small-town deputy sheriffs could be, given the situation.

Few train for this situation, but Bunker had confidence they would see it through. He needed them to perform on cue; otherwise, their failure would bring a swift halt to his plan. He'd put a significant amount of thought into the steps to come, but mission success relied on a slew of others to do their part.

The best opportunity to strike was now. The winds had picked up in advance of the rumbling storm clouds. The gusts were giving the Aerostat and its cameras fits, its tethers failing to maintain a fixed position. The squall also provided background noise and natural terrain movement. Both would help conceal their location from the approaching soldiers.

Bunker readied a weapon in his right hand as the targets arrived, only a foot beyond the far side of the hedge. He waited for them to reach the midpoint of the blind, then started a finger count in one-second increments.

3 . . . 2 . . . 1 . . .

When the count hit zero, Rico and Zeke stood to attack the two-man patrol who had just passed their location. They approached the men, grabbing their elbows from behind in a pinning, locked-arm maneuver.

Bunker brought the baseball bat around and landed a swift, full swing on the first Russian's head. The man fell limp in Rico's arms.

Before the other soldier could react, Bunker spun in one continuous motion, using his inertia as a catapult to deliver the bat in a second strike. Like the first, the Russian took the blow in the head, sending his consciousness into the black.

Zeke and Rico dragged their men behind the bush, covering the wounds with towels to contain the blood.

"Get dressed, quick," Bunker told the men, keeping watch through the gaps in the greenery.

The sidewalks were clear of activity; so was the street, giving him hope that nobody saw the ambush. He could have taken the Russians down solo with a knife to their throats, but the uniforms would have been useless if covered in blood.

Zeke removed the rifle sling from his man and detached the AK-47 assault rifle. Rico did the same.

Next up, removal of the tactical vests. Each chest rig had four lower pockets designed to hold magazines in pairs—7.62 caliber. The soldiers had loaded heavy with mags. They'd also stuffed the upper pouches with grenades, and one of them carried a radio.

Each Russian also had an eleven-inch, fixed-blade tactical knife and a holstered pistol. Bunker took the semi-auto from Zeke's man, checked its magazine, then made sure the chamber held a round. The handgun was a GSh-18, fully loaded with 9x19mm Parabellum rounds.

He took the sidearm from Rico's man as well, stuffing both pistols inside the back of his pants for quick access. He covered the guns with the tail of his shirt for concealment. The remainder of the gear would transfer to Zeke and Rico, completing their transformation from Deputy Sheriffs into Russian soldiers.

Neither of the men carried ID or personal effects. None of that was a surprise. The mythical Russian Occupation Playbook, at least Bunker's interpretation of it, wouldn't allow for it.

Their anonymity was Clearwater's advantage, assuming all went according to plan. The key would be executing the plan quickly, while the occupiers' belief in their superiority held steady at one hundred percent.

Confidence and arrogance are blood brothers, the line between them thin and exploitable. Too much of either becomes a tactical weakness, leading to what Bunker hoped would transpire next.

CHAPTER 110

Stan Fielding stumbled forward with limp noodles for legs as two men dragged him by his arms. Their boots hit the hard surface with a distinctive, repetitive patter, meticulously tracking time with the precision of a grandfather clock. Or perhaps the taps represented the uniformity of a countdown—his countdown, winding down to the ultimate end.

He could only see black with the hood over his head, but knew he was still inside a building somewhere. Probably heading down a hallway, he figured, based on the echoes of travel landing on his ears.

The blood dripping from his face had slowed, but the swelling hadn't. Most of the pressure centered around his eyes and nose. Even if the hood wasn't present, his vision wouldn't have been much more than a thin strip of light.

The guard who'd inflicted the damage promised Stan a quick, painless death, but only if he'd cooperate and tell them where he'd hidden the female interpreter. The Russians assumed she was dead, beating him even more fiercely with revenge on their minds.

Of course, Stan couldn't give them the answers they sought. He had nothing to do with her disappearance. Someone had set him up. That much was clear. And now the gallows were calling his name.

His demise would come after they cleared the last door and found the fresh air outside. Then the grass would comfort his bare feet only moments before he was dragged up a series of metal steps to a stage built for intimidation. He'd seen their brutality before, but that was as a spectator. Now he would be the star of the show.

He worried his girls might be in attendance. They were already scared after seeing him led away at gunpoint from the house in which they were born. Witnessing his last breath would traumatize them beyond imagination.

Then again, maybe General Zhukov wasn't the heartless butcher that seemed to fuel his reputation. It also was possible the guard's English was in error, misusing the words to describe the Russian commander.

Either way, the beating had left Stan defenseless. He had nothing left. It was time for it to be over, even though he knew what the execution would mean for his girls. He prayed they would forgive him.

There are times when a person welcomes death, even when it's the worst possible outcome for those he cherishes above all others.

Once you're broken beyond repair, even the love of family can't save you from the despair that breeds within.

It consumes you, taking you deeper inside the blackest of shadows inhabiting your heart. Eventually, the malignancy swallows you whole, draining every ounce of humanity remaining.

Stan turned all his thoughts to Beth and Barb, hoping to etch their faces into his memory. He didn't know if his consciousness would transcend time and space, traveling with him on his journey to the next plane of existence. But he had to try. Otherwise, what was the point of struggling for one last breath?

He wished he were a stronger man like his longtime pal, Burt Lowenstein, mechanic by day, stubborn asshole by night. A man who knew how to take the pain and fight back, even when all hope was lost.

That's what he needed right now, to be like Burt.

But who was he kidding? He was a complete phony. A coward. He only associated with men like Burt to raise his standing on the streets.

Stan's one regret would be giving up when his girls needed him most. Soon, they'd become orphans. If only his wife Ambrosia hadn't fallen asleep at the wheel. Then she wouldn't have driven off the Mason Bridge in the dead of winter.

* * *

Bunker gave the encrypted radio from Tuttle's place to Zeke before hoisting the female corpse over his shoulder. He centered her weight before testing the stability of his carry hold with a bounce of his legs.

Grace's clothes were a close match to Valentina's size, leading him to believe they would effectively conceal the Russian's injuries. Of course, he was assuming the bandages underneath would contain the blood.

He wished they had a black-colored wig to conceal the interpreter's blond hair. It was the lone piece of the costume missing. Hopefully the makeshift ensemble would keep the curious unaware, giving him a chance to get into position.

"You guys ready?" Bunker asked Zeke and Rico.

They both nodded, looking officially Russian in their stolen uniforms and gear.

"What if someone asks us a question?" Zeke asked, stuffing the radio into one of the empty pockets on his chest rig.

"Yeah, it's not like either of us speaks Russian," Rico added.

"Just nod and keep walking."

That directive didn't seem to sit well with Zeke, his forehead pinching. "What if that's the wrong answer?"

Bunker didn't have time for sudden doubt. "Trust me, just act like you're too busy to interact. If it escalates, then follow my lead."

"You mean kill them."

"If that's what it takes, then yes. But I doubt it's going to come to that. Not with this body over my shoulder. Anyone who approaches would be focused on her and assume you are escorting me under armed guard. Just keep your rifles on me and it'll all work out."

"I hope you're right."

"Relax; this is why we're taking the back way around. Most of their manpower should focused on the proceedings in the square. All we need to do is get this body to the back of the church. I'll do the rest."

Zeke nodded. "I wish I could be there to see the looks on their faces."

"Me too," Rico quipped.

"Well, boys, we've all got our jobs to do," Bunker said, turning his focus to Grace. Jean shorts man was standing with her, looking like a male version of Daisy Duke. "And ladies."

Grace smiled.

Paulo didn't, answering in a less than manly voice. "Sure, take a shot. Everyone else does."

"Just trying to lighten the mood. Don't take it personally," Bunker said.

"How else am I supposed to take it?"

"Just . . . forget it," Bunker said with a stammer. "It's not important."

Paulo turned to the side and struck a pose. "I don't know about you, but I like these shorts. They look good on me."

Bunker ignored the man, locking eyes with Grace. "When you see my ugly mug, that's the signal. Make sure you get everyone's attention."

Grace wrapped an arm around Paulo. "We'll be ready."

"Are you sure Russell is up to the task?" Bunker asked Zeke.

"Yep. He used to play minor league ball, so his aim should be right on target."

"It better be, or else this will be the shortest uprising in the history of the world."

* * *

Bunker waited in the rain for Zeke to open the back door of the church, then followed Rico inside with the dead Russian draped over his shoulder. Water dripped from his clothes and from hers, landing on the marble floor. "Like I said, nothing to worry about. They can't be everywhere all the time, especially in a working city like this. That's why they used the neck injections to elevate their perceived control."

"Glad you were right," Zeke said, stepping in last. He, too, was soaking wet from the rainstorm passing through the area. "Though I did think that last patrol was going to change direction. Made my heart skip a few beats."

"That's the beauty of small unit tactics. It's a lot easier to blend in than most people think, as long as you keep your cool and never lose your shit. Most low-level soldiers are conditioned to look for the obvious signs of trouble. And by that, I mean big ticket items. Tanks, armed insurgents, weapons fire, RPGs, suspicious vehicles, and of course, the expected face and movements of the enemy. You guys looked the part, so they never questioned it."

"Just doing our *thang*," Rico said with attitude.

"I'm sure the rain helped convince them to keep walking, too," Zeke said.

"Exactly. You two are just part of one big happy Russian Army."

"Yeah, a wet army," Rico said, shaking water off his clothes.

Zeke looked pleased, taking Tuttle's radio from the pocket on his vest and giving it to Bunker. "It's brilliant, actually. Hiding in plain sight like that."

Bunker appreciated the compliment but chose not to respond with a customary "thank you." He adjusted Valentina's body to reduce the pressure on his lower back. There wasn't much to her, but carrying weight over distance has a cumulative effect, especially when it's sopping wet. "Where's the staircase?"

Rico pointed. "Near the end of the hall. Second door past the drinking fountain. Can't miss it. Just look for the rope hanging down."

Bunker gave him a silent look that questioned the facts.

Rico nodded with confidence. "When I was younger, I spent a lot of time helping the pastor during Mass. My favorite job was ringing the bell before service."

"Who are you kidding?" Zeke asked Rico, flashing him a sarcastic look.

"What do you mean?"

"You were never an altar boy."

"Yes, I was. Right after grade school."

"Maybe for a weekend, that's it."

"Still."

Zeke looked at Bunker, shaking his head. "The only reason he knows about the stairs is because we used to climb them on Friday nights after football. It was the perfect place to get high. The only other person who ever went up was the maintenance guy. But that was rare."

Bunker didn't care why they knew what they knew, just that they did. "I'll take it from here, gentlemen. You guys get into position. Make sure Russell has a clean approach."

Rico put out his wet hand and held it. "It's been a pleasure working with you, Bunker."

Bunker took his hand and shook it, sending water into the air. "Likewise. I know we got off on the wrong foot earlier, but I appreciate you guys keeping the faith."

"Not a problem. Just doing our job."

"As Americans," Zeke added, shaking Bunker's hand as well.

"If all goes according to plan, I'll be back sometime tomorrow. Make sure you're ready like we talked about."

"How will we know if it's you?"

"You'll know. I'll either be driving one of their vehicles or hanging from a noose."

CHAPTER 111

Bunker finished the climb, then slid the body from his shoulder. He put Valentina at the base of the four-foot-tall safety wall that surrounded the highest point in the bell tower. He propped up the corpse in a modified sitting position, with the woman's wet hair hanging loose to one side.

The church bell was quiet, waiting for the next Sunday, when it would ring into service at the hands of some overly attentive altar boy. Thank goodness Mass was a few days off; otherwise, he'd probably lose his hearing when the dangling rope was assigned to active duty.

Bunker checked his watch to confirm the time—he was right on schedule. He peered over the wooden railing, keeping his profile low.

The buzz of the crowd was louder than he expected, given the steady pound of rain. Most of the town folk were facing the stage in silence, though a few were grouped together and chatting away as if nothing was wrong.

He'd seen it all before—everyday people becoming immune to the horrors of occupation. Even a bloody, senseless execution can harden one's soul. Usually after it becomes a regular occurrence.

From what Zeke and Grace had told him, Stan Fielding's death wouldn't be the first. Nor would it be the last, unless he could put an end to the occupation.

Bunker had hoped for more time to perfect his plan, but time wasn't cooperating. Neither were the circumstances. Valentina's body presented a unique and sudden opportunity, one which he needed to take advantage of. To do so, his inner beast would have to be summoned, exposing all that he was to those around him.

He estimated there were at least two hundred civilians in the square below. However, there was room for more. None of them had umbrellas. He wasn't surprised. The Russians wouldn't allow them for security reasons.

A high percentage of the crowd was men, yet at least a dozen women were in attendance as well. The only children he could see were on the stage—two redheaded girls—under guard and drenched. He couldn't see their faces, but he assumed they were Stan Fielding's twins, Barb and Beth.

As expected, several hundred troops had been deployed, most of them covering the perimeter of the square. The soldiers were well-armed and standing with purpose, their heads on a swivel. Some wore rain gear, others not; all of them certainly miserable, given the weather conditions.

A Russian-made T-72 tank had been positioned to his left, not far from the secondary checkpoint he'd avoided earlier. It wasn't surrounded by infantry for support, nor would it be much use in the tight quarters of an urban setting. Bunker figured it was on display simply as a show of force. In fact, he'd lay odds the tank was without its customary three-man crew.

Four squads of soldiers stood in a tight skirmish line across the front of the sprawling stage. Yet they were not his primary concern. The four-man security team covering the center of the platform was his focal point. Their rifles were aimed at a kneeling prisoner who wore a black hood.

Bunker assumed it was Fielding. The condemned man appeared calm, but it was impossible to know for sure from this distance. Bunker could only imagine what the Russians had done to Stan in order to extract information about the missing interpreter—the same female whose lifeless body was lying in the bell tower next to him.

If Fielding was innocent as Grace had claimed, then he couldn't have told the Russians what they wanted to know. It also meant Fielding was in rough shape under that hood, lucky to be alive.

Since the scheduled time of the execution hadn't arrived, nor had Fielding been shot, Bunker figured the men on the stage weren't the executioners. This rain-filled pageantry was simply a preamble to the main event. Something to increase the tension.

Bunker checked his watch once more. It was time to get in character and prep the body. He started with Valentina's borrowed smock and shirt, then took off her pants and shoes, leaving her naked, except for a smattering of bandages.

Grace had done a masterful job of patching the wounds. The extra gauze would keep the last remnants of blood from leaking into her clothes.

Bunker paused for a second, studying Valentina's body. He realized a tortured prisoner never receives medical treatment. Thus, the presence of bandages would give away his scam. They had to be removed before he showed the world who he was.

Once the bandages were removed, Bunker took off his shoes, but only long enough to remove his socks and put them aside. Next, he slipped off his shirt to expose the artwork across his chest, back, and arms.

If he had a choice, he would have preferred to keep his tattoos hidden from the throng of civilians below. However, the artwork he hated also made him unique and identifiable—something the Russians would remember when the next phase of the plan began.

Bunker shook his head, remembering the day when he tried to burn off some of his tats with a blowtorch. He'd now come full circle, thankful the rest of them were still a part of his skin.

Time to make contact and deliver a little shock and awe. It would start with the radio he'd brought from Tuttle's place. The power switch was on top of the unit, next to the volume and frequency dials. He lowered the volume and double-checked the channel before turning on the device.

After a momentary crackle of static, a background hiss came out of the speaker. He pressed the transmit button. "Base, this is Bulldog, do you read me? Come in, Base. This is Bulldog. Over."

Twenty seconds went by without a response. He transmitted the same message again. Nobody answered.

"Come on, girl, be there," he mumbled before pressing the transmit button again. "Base, this is Bulldog, do you read me? Come in, Base. This is Bulldog. Over."

A crackling squelch replaced the hiss. Then a male's voice called out. "Ah. Hello. This is Tin Man. I read you loud and clear."

"Tin Man? What are you doing on this frequency?" Bunker asked, dropping the formality of radio procedure once he knew an untrained civilian was on the air. A lazy one at that.

"Well . . . Miss you-know-who had to pee. She asked me to walk up here and wait for your call."

"She asked *you*?"

"Sure, why not? You know me; I'm always willing to lend a hand."

Bunker knew Albert would never do anything that didn't help him in some fashion. But there wasn't time to worry about it. "All right, fine. But keep the conversation general. No names or specifics. This could be a party line."

"Of course it is, dude. Only a moron would think it wasn't."

Bunker held back the curse words lining up on his tongue. "What's the status of those items on the list?"

"Working on the last one now. Why? What's the rush? I said I'd have them ready by the time you got back."

"I've had to accelerate the timetable. I need everyone to be ready. Now."

"Almost there. Would've been done sooner, but some of this shit is rather potent and my helpers bailed on me. Even with the masks. At least the kids helped with those damn frogs, so that saved some time."

"I understand. Just get it done and packed so you and the others can meet me."

"All of it? How?"

"Use the vehicles out back. You'll need to get creative for it all to fit."

"Hey, there's something you should probably know. Junior asshole is back from his little bike ride and he brought a few more Tangos with him, if you know what I mean. Seven more, to be exact."

Bunker couldn't believe it. Victor actually contributed to the cause. Good for him. Maybe the Sheriff's talk did some good. "Excellent. Use them, too. Just don't overload."

"You got it."

"Did your former boss and Goliath make it back in one piece?"

"Yeah, they found little asshole wandering around in the dark. Kid got lucky. Where do you wanna meet?"

"Wrench will know. Just tell him it's the same spot where the man with all the newspapers was planning to build a hunting cabin."

"Cool. I remember."

"The girls can stay behind with the little ones, but I need you to bring the rest. Be there in three hours."

"Okay, but is it safe to travel?"

"Just stick to the same route I used. Wrench can show you. Should be able to four-wheel it without resistance. I'll also need you to bring stuff for cutting, digging, and rigging, in addition to the items on the list. Talk to Goliath. He'll know what I need."

"Will do."

"One last thing. Make sure you bring the extra handset with you, but leave it off. I repeat, leave it off. We go radio silent from here on out."

"What if you don't show?"

"I'll be there."

"I know, but there's always a chance, right?"

"If I'm not there by sunrise, then return to camp and dig in. Just stay the hell off the radio. Am I making myself clear?"

"Copy that."

"Bulldog out."

"Wait. There's one more thing," Albert said.

"Go ahead."

"Since we're coming to you, what about that thing we dug up behind the house? It's starting to stink, big time."

"Toss it back in the hole. We'll deal with it later, assuming there is a later."

"Wow, dude. You're not exactly giving me a warm fuzzy right about now."

Bunker needed the conversation to end. "Is there anything else, Tin Man?"

"Nah, that's it."

"Bulldog out."

CHAPTER 112

Colonel Sergei Orlov timed his steps to remain precisely three paces behind his commanding officer, General Yuri Zhukov, as his boots found the cement sidewalk outside of the Town Hall's main entrance.

The crowd gathered in the square had an air of desperation about it. He could feel it washing over his skin, crawling like a centipede on the hunt, looking for a soft target to burrow into for shelter.

Some of locals' collective anxiety was due to his battalion's presence, taking armed positions in and around the area to maintain control. However, the rest of it was a result of the proceedings about to start. All of it had been orchestrated to perfection by his boss—a seasoned General who planned to handle the execution personally.

Orlov had served under Zhukov long enough to know when his commander was simply bending protocols to maintain order or walking the path of revenge. Today was the latter.

Vengeance is a powerful instigator. It can transform even the most honorable soldier into something less than human—someone who's willing to commit deeds that would make a bloodthirsty drug lord cringe.

Orlov's heart ached for the residents of this American city. They had no idea who they were dealing with, nor did they understand what Valentina Zakharova meant to the General. He'd handpicked her from scores of candidates, bringing her along slowly under his tutelage the past seven years.

Orlov had witnessed it firsthand, watching the General dedicate significant time and energy to groom her career on a personal, one-on-one basis.

Yet it didn't end there.

The General had also protected her more times than Orlov could count. Not just from bullets on the battlefield, but from the Kremlin and the jealousy swirling inside its chain of command.

The military is full of type-A personalities, all of them competing for accolades and for the limited resources available. Resources come in all shapes and sizes, not just in terms of equipment, but staff as well.

Thus far, the General had been victorious, keeping Valentina assigned to his command after others of similar rank had tried to poach her away. It had cost the General plenty, cashing in a slew of markers to keep her at his side.

Valentina was more than just the General's star recruit. Orlov was sure of it. This young beauty had fostered feelings inside the prideful man. Whether those feelings were romantic in nature, Orlov couldn't be sure. But it didn't matter now that she was missing and presumed dead.

Sure, a certain level of casualties is expected any time you engage in active combat. Yet, of all the troops under the General's command, Valentina was the one officer that Stan Fielding never should have touched. Whether she was still alive mattered not. The General's retaliation was just getting started.

Orlov scanned the residents for additional threats as he followed the General and his protective detail around the security perimeter. Orlov had no idea if Valentina's disappearance was due to the lone actor kneeling on stage, or if a group was responsible. There could be more of the guilty hiding in the crowd, just waiting to strike.

A minute later, they arrived on stage. Orlov held back as the General continued his trek to the prisoner. The guilty American was on his knees with his hands bound behind his back.

The General had ordered the man's daughters to witness the execution. He wanted them close, with eyes wide, to serve as a reminder for everyone in town. When the rules are broken, no one will be spared, not even the children.

The General put his hand on the prisoner's hood and yanked it off with the flare of a magician beginning his show.

The twin girls screamed as the crowd gasped.

The General held the mask high, letting everyone get a look at the swollen, bloody mess on stage. The beatings had twisted Fielding's appearance, making him look like a bloated clown who'd been run over by a Russian semi.

The redheads turned away, crying into each other's shoulders. So did a small portion of the crowd—women mainly—though there were a few men showing the same emotional distress.

The General tossed the hood aside, then walked to the girls with his pistol drawn. He grabbed the girl on the left and dragged her to the center of the stage, her arms and legs kicking.

The skinnier of the two girls remained behind, calling out to her sister in a wail of tears. The girl struggled to break free, but her rail-thin body was no match for the strength of the guard holding her captive.

The General finished dragging the redhead by the wrist and stood her behind her father. He put his pistol in her hands and cocked the hammer.

"Shoot him!" he commanded in English, his Russian accent thick.

"No! Please! Don't make me do it!" she screamed, shaking her head.

"Shoot him! Now! Or I shoot sister."

The girl's tears exploded with the force of a monsoon when she turned her eyes to her identical twin. "Beth! Help me! Please!"

Just then, a female's voice screamed from the crowd. "Look! Up there! That man! He's got Valentina!"

The General pulled the gun from the girl's hand and spun on the stage.

"He's gonna kill her!" a male's voice said, his tone high-pitched and tinny, as if his balls were stuck in a powerful vise.

Orlov peered into the crowd and followed the voices. They belonged to a couple near the back, both of them pointing at the church's bell tower.

When Orlov looked up, he saw a hulk of a man standing behind the safety wall, directly in front of the church bell.

Tattoos covered his powerful chest and arms, making him look like a member of the Chechen Mafia. His left arm was above his shoulder and it appeared he was holding something in his gloved hand. Possibly a field radio. Orlov couldn't be sure.

The man's other hand was also gloved, but it held the wrist of another person—a naked female—dangling precariously beyond the safety wall. Oddly, the slender female wasn't kicking or screaming.

The troops on stage brought their rifles up and aimed them at the man in the tower.

"Don't shoot!" the General yelled in Russian.

The soldiers lowered their weapons without hesitation.

The skinny redhead broke free from her guard and ran to the center of the stage. She wrapped her arms around both her plump sister and her bleeding father.

"General Zhukov," the tattooed man bellowed from the church steeple, his voice booming across the square. "By order of General Apollo of the National Resistance Army, you and your interpreter are hereby found guilty of war crimes against the citizens of Clearwater."

The crowd roared, cheering in unison, their fists pumping in the air.

The man with slicked back hair continued once the volume eased, emphasizing each word. "The sentence for both of you is death!" He let go of the woman a moment later, raising his arm in celebration as the blonde plummeted to the cement.

"Open fire!" the General commanded, pointing at the man in the tower.

Then the inconceivable happened—the General took off in a sprint, without an armed escort, heading toward the church after giving the order to shoot.

Orlov flew across the stage to follow his commander downrange as the General plowed into the crowd.

* * *

When the troops on stage raised their weapons in Bunker's direction, that was his cue to retreat. He spun around and put the radio on the ledge, then tossed the backpack down the shaft. He lunged at the rope with his sock-covered hands, feeling the twisted braids of nylon land in his palms. His legs swung in below, the weight shift taking him forward like a pendulum, making the heavy clapper inside the bell smash against the side.

CLAAAANG!

The incredible noise shook apart his eardrums. It took all his strength to hang on until his legs were able to wrap around the rope using a brake and squat technique.

CLAAAANG!

He released his grip to start the fast rope process, using the friction around his feet to control his descent speed. The bell continued to ring as bullets tore up the tower, some of them plinking against the side of the bell. Other rounds obliterated the building, sending chunks of wood down the shaft and on top of Bunker.

Bunker ignored the chaos, focusing only on the whine of the nylon as it zipped through his hands and past his shoes. It only took seconds to make a soft landing at the bottom of the shaft.

He let go of the rope, grabbed his pack and tore down the rear hallway of the church. Thirty feet later, he made a high-speed corner to the left, retracing the same path he'd used on the way in.

The troops continued to spray the church with lead as the back door came into view. Bunker increased his speed, pushing his legs even harder. Seven strides later, he bolted through the door and found the alley outside.

* * *

The firestorm stopped the moment Orlov arrived at the church. Bits and pieces of the wooden structure continued to rain down from the steeple, landing on the sidewalk in a clatter of plinks and thuds.

His eyes confirmed what he already suspected—the body belonged to Valentina. She was lying face up on the sidewalk with her left arm bent at an impossible angle behind her back.

For the briefest of moments, Orlov thought Valentina might have survived the fall. Then he saw it—the back of her head caved in, brain matter hanging loose in clumps. But that wasn't the end of the damage. One of her legs had a pair of fractures, each showing a jagged bone penetrating the skin.

The bruises were mostly on her face, centered on her swollen eyes. In addition, there were at least a dozen cuts across her body. Some of them were wide, with the skin gaping open. Probably attacked by a knife, he decided. Yet, there was no blood. Not a drop anywhere, despite the horrific fall.

General Zhukov stood next to him, frozen, his face twisted into a snarl as he looked at the twisted body. His eyes burned with fury, showing an excess of white.

"Orders, sir?" Orlov asked in Russian.

The General huffed an angry breath, never taking his eyes from Valentina. "Find him, Colonel! I don't care what you have to do, but I want that tattooed son of a bitch in my office on his knees before this day is over. Tear apart this town if you have to, but get it done!"

"Yes, General," Orlov said before a proper salute. He turned and marched back to the stage with far less resistance than before. The crowd was a tenth of the size it had been, no doubt dispersing when the shooting started.

When the platform came into view, he noticed the redheads were gone. So was their father, yet the contingent of troops remained the same.

Orlov trotted to the men standing in the center of the platform. He spoke to them in Russian, the beat of his chest fueling his words. "Where's the prisoner?"

A solider to the right responded, his tone downbeat. "Escaped, sir. Slipped out during the firefight."

"And the two girls?"

"Unknown, Colonel."

Orlov couldn't believe it. They had one job to do and they'd failed. "Find them! Now!"

"Yes sir," the soldier replied, his team breaking into a sprint off the stage.

CHAPTER 113

Bunker kept to the shadows along the alley wall, mixing in a combination of short sprints as he advanced toward his destination. Visibility was poor, maybe twenty yards at best, with the storm's vengeance smacking him in the face.

The combination of rain and wind chilled his skin with a shivering sting. He considered pulling a shirt from his pack for warmth, but knew the solution wouldn't last. Eventually, the garment would be soaked like the rest of his outfit. A wet shirt would lead to hypothermia five times faster than going without, especially around his core.

Yet avoiding wet clothing wasn't the only reason. He didn't want to give his final ensemble away. Right now, the Russians were looking for a shirtless, tattooed man with slicked-back hair. He needed their attention focused on that description. Otherwise, they'd turn their retaliation against the town, and that was something he couldn't let happen. He needed them to stay locked and loaded on him—the lone perpetrator.

Despite the cold, he was thankful for the squall because it gave him cover against his eventual pursuers. It would also challenge the skills of the Aerostat operators, making the high-definition cameras difficult to use.

When he made it to the end of the second alley and peered around the corner, he saw the first sign of resistance: two squads of troops, maybe fifty yards away, locked in a dead sprint— headed his way.

He kept his profile thin, his mind crunching the facts in an instant. Not only was their direction of travel on an intercept course to his position, they were also following the shortest path to the center of town—the latter being the most likely destination, he decided.

The General must have called in reinforcements, Bunker thought. He figured their attention was still on the church, working to contain the scene.

The fast rope allowed him to escape quickly before they could surround the building. He knew it wouldn't be long before the General ordered a search of its interior, only to realize their containment plan had failed.

Bunker dropped back from the corner and ducked behind the same dumpster he'd used earlier. He didn't see any rats this time, but the pebble he'd removed from his sock was still where he'd tossed it. Only now it was swimming in a puddle of water.

The unmistakable sound of boots pounding at the pavement grew louder. So did the rattle of gear. He kept his shoulder against the wall, giving him a thin, vertical view behind the dumpster.

In truth, hearing the stampede race past the entrance would have been sufficient, but something inside needed to witness it. He wasn't sure why, but the feeling was there nonetheless, keeping his eyes glued and heart thumping.

Bunker waited, counting the seconds. He figured if the number ten arrived before he saw a blur of movement fly past, then the troops knew his location and had slowed their approach in advance of an ambush.

Eight seconds later, the throng of soldiers zoomed past the alley with feet churning. When the parade was over, Bunker slipped out from his hiding place.

"Zeke and Rico better be in position," he mumbled, continuing his stealthy trek to the main entrance.

* * *

Colonel Orlov used his hands to separate the thicket of soldiers blocking his path in the hallway of the church.

"Make a hole," he said in Russian, working his way through the men and gear. They parted, albeit slower than he would have preferred.

Orlov was impressed with the building's stout architecture, its walls holding firm despite the damage unleashed by his men. He'd seen his share of structures crumble after similar assaults, but this building had been designed with longevity in mind.

When he arrived at the drinking fountain, one of his men appeared, standing at attention in the rear hallway.

Orlov didn't have time for formalities, not with the General demanding results. "Report, Sergeant."

"We searched the building, Colonel, but we didn't locate the target," the man said, his words crisp and assertive, not wasting a second. "But we found this on the catwalk." The Sergeant gave him a handheld radio. "Must have dropped it when we opened fire."

"Then he wasn't working alone," Orlov said, turning the unit on. It was still functional, with a generous amount of battery life remaining. He inspected the other settings. "Looks like someone was kind enough to enter the encryption code for us."

Orlov flipped the power switch off and gave it back to the Sergeant. "Get this to communications. I want viable intel by sundown. Make it happen."

"Yes sir."

Orlov turned to the rest of the men standing near. "Let's move out. Search the area. I want him found!"

* * *

Bunker crept forward in the rain, keeping his eyes locked on the main checkpoint fifty yards away. He settled in behind the hood of the Honda Pilot he'd passed earlier on his way into town. It was still parked next to the sidewalk. Another useless relic of civilization before the EMP.

The guards at the gate looked miserable, even in their rain gear. He didn't blame them. Guard duty was grunt work, literally. Nobody wanted it, at least not any of the men he'd ever served with. With everything happening in town, he was sure the soldiers were itching to go join the search for him, each soldier wanting to get some.

Bunker was happy to see that their pair of all-terrain Russian GAZ Tigrs hadn't moved. They were adjacent to each other and sitting at slightly opposing angles, their hoods pointing the way to the main gate.

He turned his attention to the right, scanning the second story of the town's museum. Something in the center window caught his eye—the front sight of a rifle barrel. It was aimed at the checkpoint. The sheer, green-colored drapes around the window kept most of the weapon and its shooter hidden. If Bunker didn't know exactly what he was looking for, it would have been difficult to spot.

A moment later, the top half of a head appeared. It was Zeke. He sent a subtle head nod Bunker's way, then pointed to the roof.

Bunker let his eyes drift up, where he noticed another rifle, this one sticking through the spokes of the wagon wheel built into the roofline. Rico finally showed himself, though it was only a sliver of his head peering through the wood.

Thank God architects love their Western themes, Bunker thought. Plenty of cover.

It appeared Rico had a tarp of some kind draped over his head and his rifle. It looked to be dark-colored and probably made of vinyl.

"Must have found it in the museum," Bunker mumbled, holding up a closed fist to tell his snipers to hold fire until he gave them the signal.

He took a minute to study every aspect of the scene in front of him, looking for anything unexpected on the ground or in the air. All was as expected—except, of course, for the rainwater forming tiny rivers across the pavement.

Thus far, the deputies had followed the script to the letter, using their stolen Russian uniforms to get into position. He assumed Russell was hiding nearby with the grenades—the final piece of the escape plan.

Bunker checked his six, looking for threats approaching from behind. All he saw was the downpour from the sky. However, it wouldn't be long before this area was crawling with search teams.

At least the Aerostat was no longer floating above the city. Its handlers must have finally decided to stow it until the storm passed, a wise safety precaution given the tremendous cost of the onboard equipment.

It's now or never, Bunker thought, preparing his legs for the sprint that would come next. He made eye contact with Zeke and Rico, then gave them the signal he was about to move.

Bunker ran for the Russian trucks.

Zeke and Rico opened fire on the main gate from the museum.

Bunker didn't need them to be accurate, just to keep the guards busy with cover fire.

While the firefight continued, Bunker found the door handle on the driver's side of the closest truck, its front wheels aimed at the main gate. He opened the door, tossed in his pack, and crawled in, keeping low as he slinked his ass into the seat.

After his feet found the pedals, his hand went for the ignition button. Just like with American-made military Humvees, the Russian transports didn't require a key.

Bunker pressed it, firing the engine into a roar. He put the truck into drive and jammed on the gas. The tires spun on the wet payment, but finally gained traction and sent him forward in a lurch.

Right on cue, Rico and Zeke disengaged their triggers. Hopefully they bugged out as planned, not waiting around to see if he was successful. Russell would need their protection now, if the next phase of the escape was going to succeed.

When Bunker made it to the guard shack, all he could see through the raindrops were boots and legs diving out of the way. He let out an invigorating scream as the front grille smashed into the one-man building. Wood and metal blew apart, pieces bouncing off the windshield. He didn't know if the tall man was inside the shack or not, but he didn't give a fuck.

"Die motherfucker!" he screamed as the vehicle continued its rampage, plowing through the rest of the guard station. When the hood smashed into the security arm protecting the entrance, it disintegrated, splinters of red and white colored wood shooting everywhere.

Bunker continued with the gas pedal floored, mowing down the rest of the wooden barricades. Seconds later, he was outside the wire and speeding down the center of the two-lane highway with a fist pump in the air.

An explosion rocked the guard station behind him, bringing his eyes to the rearview mirror. The second GAZ Tigr was now airborne, flipping end over end in a tumble of billowing fire.

"Attaboy, Russell. Right down the pipe," he said, thinking about the man's minor league baseball career. Sure, baseballs didn't weigh nearly as much as a grenade, but having an accurate throwing arm was still a huge asset.

Two more explosions hit the checkpoint, only they didn't include flames. One after another, the shrapnel from the fragmentation grenades tore up more of the station.

"That should get their attention," Bunker said, regripping the steering wheel. If his friends stuck to the plan, all three of them were now in the wind. They had better be, since the General would be redirecting his troops to the front gate.

All that remained was to finish baiting the trap.

CHAPTER 114

Bunker turned the windshield wipers off and enjoyed the sun as it broke through the storm clouds. The rain had finished its purification, giving everyone and everything a sudden, welcoming reprieve. It was a strange sensation, but he felt as though he'd just been reborn, his sins washed away with the dust across the land.

There's something uniquely special about the minutes following a heavy downpour. The crispness of the clean mountain air invades your senses with a sense of awe, demonstrating once and for all that Mother Nature is all-powerful and in complete control. She is a fickle, unstoppable mistress who takes her job seriously, cleansing some while punishing others, depending on where you stand.

Despite the magnificence of her power, he questioned if the sudden storm was more than that, the rain appearing just when it was needed most. Maybe none of it was random. Maybe there was intelligent thought behind it. Maybe, just maybe, Mother Nature had stepped in and helped the innocents of Clearwater.

After more thought, Bunker decided the answer was yes. Mother Nature had come to the rescue because of the good people in Clearwater. Not because of him. She would certainly never go out of her way to help his sorry ass.

But then again, maybe that's exactly what happened. Almost as if she had taken notice of him, directing her purity of spirit in his direction.

He blinked a few times, trying to focus the swirling inconsistencies in his brain. The paradox was difficult to unravel, but there was meaning in it all. Somewhere. He was certain of it.

Sure, he was being sentimental, almost spiritual, but it didn't change the splendor of the moment, filling his heart with a sense of wonder.

Or was it relief?

Shit. He couldn't decide.

"Come on, Jack, get a grip," he mumbled, washing the conflicting emotions from his heart. "This is far from over."

He took his foot off the accelerator and turned the wheel to the right, taking the truck off the highway in a downhill pitch. The uneven terrain hit the tires hard, but it was softer than it would have been if the rain hadn't thundered through the area. Even so, the suspension on the Russian vehicle wasn't any better than the US Humvees. Neither was built with the comfort of the occupants in mind.

"Almost done, Jack. Just see it through," he muttered after a bump sent his head smashing into the top of the cab.

He'd taken a beating, much like the truck he was piloting across the uneven countryside, but a righteous man ignores the pain and presses on. There was no other choice. Time was precious and it had to be dead-nuts perfect.

The Russians were now primed for the hunt. Hopefully, they'd come in full force because of the brutality he'd shown in public. It was a savage, embellished act to be sure, but dropping the woman's body from the bell tower was a necessity. His identity was now cemented into their minds, turning their hearts black with revenge. Exactly what he wanted.

Bunker figured the troops were now swarming the main gate to investigate his fiery escape. If they bought the evidence, then they should follow the trail he'd left, hopefully calling in the tanks from the roadblock Burt had spoken about.

The tracks in the mud would help them follow his lead. The trail was clear and identifiable, carving a path that a monkey could follow. Even a bloodthirsty Russian commander couldn't miss them, keeping the focus solely on Bunker and away from the town.

So far, so good, he thought, but he needed to keep enflaming the General's rage. The best way to do that was to build frustration, and nothing accomplishes that goal better than a dead-end trip into the forest.

Little did the Russians know, Bunker's secret weapons were not advanced weapons or explosives. They were a four-legged creature named Tango, a little boy with freckles, an obnoxious meth cook who produced more sweat than work, a smelly mechanic, and a beautiful Deputy Sheriff whose cat had just starved to death.

Bunker laughed, thinking of the tactical books he'd read over the years. None of them had those types of secret weapons listed. He was in new, uncharted territory, making it up as he went, pulling from every minute of every fight he'd ever been in—both in the military and on the streets.

Somehow, over the years, he'd gotten away from his love of reading. It first started after he enlisted for the Marine Corps. Each year he was required to read three books from the Commandant's Reading List. Most of the titles had something to do with military history or life as a grunt, but a few were more science fiction in nature.

His favorite was a novel called *Starship Troopers,* by Robert A. Heinlein. The 1959 masterpiece laid the groundwork for what space warriors would have to do to claim their rightful place as *citizens*. He remembered how that futuristic theory hit home and reinforced the teachings of his deceased father.

Bunker was certain that in all of recorded history, there was no previous reference to such an odd combination as Tango, Jeffrey, Albert, Burt, and Daisy.

But those same pages might soon need to be amended with their names added, if he could somehow pull this off.

* * *

Stephanie opened the side door of the Land Rover she'd driven and got out, wishing Burt hadn't added the extra steel. Bunker wanted the protection, but it seemed unnecessary. In fact, if the weight hadn't been added to both vehicles, they would have arrived at the clearing much sooner.

She'd never been to Patterson's Meadow before. Deep down, she wished that fact had continued, questioning her recent decision to volunteer.

There was something about this place that gave her the creeps. She wasn't sure what it was, but she knew what it wasn't—the endless trees surrounding the horseshoe-shaped field. Nor was it the muddy grass that sat in the middle.

Everyone knew that low spots collect water when it rains. They turn into a swampy mush, swallowing nearly everything that crosses their path. Nothing new about that, especially in Colorado. God knew Jeffrey had brought plenty of mud into the house over the years, making laundry day twice as hard as it used to be.

At least the truck she'd driven was able to plow through the muck without much issue, though the engine did whine in protest when the mud swarmed its tires.

Right then, out of nowhere, the skin across her neck tingled with a crackling static. It felt like danger was closing in. The strange sensation made her look up. That's when she saw them—a flock of vultures, circling overhead in silence. The scavengers were huge and black, with wing spans that seemed to stretch out for miles.

Their instincts must have led them here, banking high above, knowing that death was coming. She could sense their ravenous thoughts as they studied the stupid humans below.

That's what she and her friends were—stupid humans, brought here by another stupid human who claimed to have a plan. A plan that reminded her of the parable *David versus Goliath*, except this wasn't some religious fable from the Book of Samuel, detailing an impossible battle from days long past. This was real and happening in her own backyard.

It had started with an alluring drifter named Jack Bunker. A man with serious flaws wrapped inside a hypnotic personality. A man with skills that had been inextricably fused with his own obvious defects. A man who believed in doing the right thing, yet he had no connection to God—or anyone, for that matter.

None of it was logical, yet somehow it made perfect sense. His presence here was meant to be, as if fate, or perhaps a higher power, had stepped in and brought him to a town in need.

At first, she thought he'd been sent to Clearwater just for her—a woman in desperate need of saving—but she'd come to realize that was blatantly narrow-minded. And flat-out wrong.

This was more than a selfish rescue. More than some quest for personal salvation. This was about redemption. For him, for her, for her town, and possibly for her country, if she chose to believe what Allison and Apollo had explained to their group.

Often times, even the most righteous person wanders off course, taking them down a path that leads them into the flames of hell. Only when fate steps in and shows them the path of virtue will they claw their way out of the blackness and back into the light.

Sure, Bunker was hiding something. Something big. Everyone could feel it, if they chose to pay attention. It was written all over him, not just in the artwork she'd seen across his skin. His troubles covered his aura, smothering it in a blanket of misery.

Yet she didn't care what he'd done in the past. She knew he was a good man. A man who'd made mistakes like most everyone else on the planet. All he needed was a second chance, given by people who believed in him. God knows she needed a do-over, so why should he be any different?

Even though Stephanie disagreed with Bunker's plan, something had pulled her here. It was a draw she couldn't describe. She'd volunteered, sensing she didn't have a choice, even with a little boy back at camp who relied on her for everything.

She had to join the team. Not for the blood, but to keep an eye on Bunker—to keep him safe, both from his own demons and from the enemy. Someone had to, because these other cretins wouldn't. They didn't understand him. They didn't have her same connection to his soul.

At least Jeffrey was safe. Daisy, Martha, Allison, Misty, and Megan were with him. Others might question her presence here, but her heart had convinced her to join the operation. Then again, maybe it wasn't her heart. Or her logic.

It may have been her guilt making the choice for her. Guilt for never having the guts to take a stand against anything insurmountable, or remotely dangerous. Either way, the decision was made and she had penetrated the sanctity of the all-man wilderness assault team.

"He's late," Stephanie said to Albert, forcing her mind to shift gears to something more productive than self-reflection.

Albert had his hands full with one of the blue water containers they'd brought along. "So are we," he said after a grunt, leaning his body to the left as he carried the container to the others he'd already stacked.

Dustin was helping him with the chore, though his rail-thin arms looked like they were about to snap each time he took on the weight of the diesel inside.

"What if he was already here and left?" she asked, hating the fact that they were late for the rendezvous.

"He would have waited," Burt said, carrying a chainsaw with a coil of rope around his shoulders. "Nah, we got here first."

"He'll be here. Gotta have faith," Sheriff Apollo said from twenty feet away. The box in his hands was from the other truck. It had the letters TNT on the side.

She didn't think they understood the severity of Bunker's lateness. "What if he never shows? What if he's dead?"

"Relax, Steph," Apollo said. "We don't know anything at this point. Give the man a chance. He's never let us down yet. There's no reason to think he'll start now."

"Where do you want this, Sheriff?" Rusty asked, his hands pushing the wooden spindle that formerly dispensed cable for the phone company. The kid had turned it on its side, rolling it like a wheel.

"Stand it up next to the tracer wire. Same with the other one. We'll get them set up as soon as we finish unloading the trucks and horses."

Dicky was customarily quiet, standing thirty yards away on a raised outcrop of rock with the futuristic-looking rifle in his hands. The man always seemed eager to sign up for guard duty, probably to get away from the smell of Burt, she mused.

Burt's stockiness had a fragrance all its own. None of it good and all of it ripe, requiring those around him to become proficient at breathing through their mouths.

It reminded her of the time when she was at the employee appreciation picnic with her then-husband. Some of the men had just finished their shift in the Silver King Mine and had come straight to the festivities. She put on a fake smile and ignored the stench, welcoming the staff as the owner's dutiful wife.

It worked then. It'll work now, she decided, realizing she'd exchanged one asshole for another. Stephanie smiled, then gave the mechanic a wide berth as he carried a cardboard box with the word *Bleach* scribbled across its sides in black magic marker ink.

Burt stood it next to a plastic carton of roughly the same size—a carton her nose knew contained several bottles of ammonia. But the ammonia wasn't half as bad as the carton of chlorine she was carrying.

Dallas and Victor were also onsite and inseparable as usual. They worked together as the little man team, doing their best to stay busy and contribute—a far cry from a few days ago when both of them were focused only on themselves. They had been tasked with the picks and shovels, hauling the equipment in multiple trips.

She was still amazed that Victor had run off on his own to get the extra horses. Horses they desperately needed for this mission to nowhere.

Allison's son was evolving before her very eyes; at least that's how it appeared. She knew the game all too well. Men or boys, it didn't matter. Sometimes, they do or say exactly what they think you want, just to shut your ass up. However, this situation felt different.

The boys' enthusiasm for the plan was infectious, giving her hope that the events of the day would turn out how everyone hoped. Well, everyone except the Russians.

The mere thought of those men, guns, and tanks made her heart skip a beat. So far, she hadn't seen any of them up close and was thankful.

However, everyone in clearing at the moment knew that was probably going to change.

And soon.

CHAPTER 115

Colonel Orlov followed General Zhukov down the last thirty feet of wilderness trail. They'd been following the fresh tire tracks set wide in the mud. It had been a simple task thus far, but now the trail had run thin, bringing newfound worries to the surface.

Under normal circumstances, Orlov would have raised concern about how deep they'd traveled into the countryside. However, he knew the look of vengeance consuming the General's face. His commander would never stop. This mission wasn't about tracking down a member of the resistance. It had become deeply personal, inflamed by the fact that Valentina's death occurred in front of everyone, including the General.

The crawl, as Orlov called it, had been slow and methodical, taking careful plotting to traverse the randomness of the uneven terrain. Rocks, dirt, and deadfall had challenged everyone, but the convoy found a way through. At least until the tracks came to a halt in front of a steep rise in terrain.

The stolen infantry vehicle was dead ahead. The GAZ Tigr sat abandoned, with its driver door open and engine running. He figured the driver ran off in haste after failing miserably to cover his tracks. Orlov didn't think it would take long to find the target, given the assailant's tactics thus far.

The oak trees ahead were thick and interspersed with a dense stand of pines and some other foliage Orlov didn't recognize. The kind of trees didn't matter—they were effectively blocking vehicle travel forward, including the tanks that were following a half-mile behind their position.

Despite what's portrayed in the movies, tanks and trees don't mix. In fact, tanks are typically useless in a mountain setting, unless you brought along almost endless ammo and planned to level the forest with a few hundred rounds from the main cannon. Other than that, firing a shell at a target buried within the trees was a fruitless endeavor. The round would rarely reach its target, getting detonated by one of a hundred tree trunks blocking its path.

Orlov had raised concerns about the T-72s with his CO before the start of this hunt, but the man with the stars refused to listen, ordering a trio of vulnerable relics to join the pursuit.

Newer tanks rolled off the assembly line with reactive armor and upgraded weapons systems. The older T-72s were effectively naked, with only factory hulls to protect their crews.

Every commander desires the latest and greatest, not just in terms of manpower, but equipment as well. Unfortunately, that is simply an empty dream. No matter how big or powerful or determined an Army or its commanding officer truly is, they still fall under the control of the bean counters and their wallets. Every mission is about cost, which drives the choices for deployment. The numbers get even worse with occupations, since logistics become far more expensive.

Regardless of the aging T-72s, it was clear the General wasn't processing objectives logically. Even so, Orlov's duty was to carry out orders, no matter what the danger. Luckily, they were dealing with a rank amateur, a man who was now running for his life without much in the way of a plan.

Mortars could have been used to level the mountainside in front of them, driving the target into the open. Unfortunately, they were not an option. The General's orders were clear: the tattooed man was to be taken alive and brought before him on his knees. That single directive was the driving force behind the operation.

The General bent down and inspected the footprints leading into the dense brush. His finger tested the freshness of the track with a light touch. Its edges held together. "These are fresh," he said in Russian.

"Must have continued on foot, General. Up that hillside, I suspect," Orlov said, knowing how ridiculous his comments sounded. Of course the target went up the hill, but he still chose to utter those words, regardless.

He'd come to realize over the years that when you disagree with a superior officer, whether it be on tactics or logistics, the best course of action is to state the obvious as long as it gives the appearance of loyalty. Not only can you sleep at night if the mission fails, you won't have to worry about subsequent disciplinary action when the Kremlin reviews the mission report. "Orders, General?"

"Send in three squads. He's up there somewhere. Find him! Bring him to me! Alive!"

"Roger that," Orlov said, sifting through the choices of manpower in his mind.

* * *

Ninety minutes later . . .

Bunker slowed Tango's trot when he reached the crest of the third mountain beyond Patterson's Meadow. An hour ago, the horse, bag of drugs, and the microscope were right where he had left them, making his pickup clean. Thus far, his egress had gone smoothly, teasing the Russians with just the right amount of stupidity.

He figured they were scratching their collective heads right about now, wondering what to do with the steep terrain in front of the GAZ Tigr he'd left for them. Bunker imagined three to four search teams were combing the mountainside, following the initial tracks he'd made for them. He couldn't help but snigger, knowing the trail would run inexplicably dry for them about halfway up the mountain, after his long walk upstream. They'd have to spend hours and even then, unless they followed his tiptoe jaunt over the nearly endless rock bed, they'd never find his trail again.

Bunker was thankful to be out of the wet civilian clothes, preferring the comfort of his camo-greens. They felt like home—a home he'd been missing for the better part of the last decade. A home that had welcomed him back without a second thought, ignoring all that happened only days before his tour ended.

He could have decided to hang around and watch their reaction when they found the GAZ Tigr with its engine running, but tactically, it would have been a mistake. All he could do now was bask in the theory that they should've come to the conclusion that they were chasing an untrained civilian who had run off in panic.

General Zhukov didn't know he was dealing with a trained operator. Someone with the balls and the skills to make his enemy believe that he, a local tattooed miscreant, was leading them unwittingly to the secret hideout occupied by whoever was on the other end of the radio he'd left in the tower. Of course, nothing could be further from the truth.

Warriors are taught never to give the enemy time to rest or the opportunity to consolidate their forces and hit back in force. However, that's exactly what Bunker needed—the Russians to consolidate and hit back hard. In fact, he was counting on it.

The beginnings of a grin took over his lips, turning the corner of his mouth up slightly with one of the seven deadly sins—pride. "Misdirection is key," he mumbled.

Well, that and tapping into a man's primal need for revenge. Specifically, a General's need. When done properly, it fosters the deepest level of hate that consumes his soul with an evil that's difficult to control. It also makes him blind to the obvious. And predictable.

Bunker stopped at a small creek to let Tango take a drink before they headed deeper into the woods. He let the horse finish, then nudged Tango in the ribs with his heels, sending his trusted comrade forward to what he hoped would be a reunion with a few more friends.

Friends with a number of items that could be classified as *exotic and deliberate*—a phrase Tin Man had coined before Bunker departed camp.

CHAPTER 116

Bunker led Tango down the mountainside, weaving his way through the terrain that had kept him alive thus far. He needed the woodland's protection to continue for another twenty-four hours. Not only for himself, but for the others that should be waiting for him when he arrived. If his navigational skills were accurate, then a swarm of smiles and gear should greet him after a few more bends in the trail.

The wind had picked up in the last hour, working its way across the countryside with a determined steadiness. It wasn't a gale, nor was it a breeze. It was something less, barely more than noticeable, yet sufficient to provide a much-needed cooling effect on his sweat-soaked skin. As good as it felt, he needed the wind speed not to increase; otherwise, it would put his plan in jeopardy.

The lingering humidity had left the air unstable after the storm. The heavy scent of dampness from the oak leaves and pine needles was unmistakable, bringing a warm solace to his heart. The sensation sparked a recent memory, one from the night he spent in the sleeping bag on the ridge overlooking the river. The frogs had kept him up for hours, despite his complete exhaustion. He remembered complaining initially, but it was pointless. Nature's splendor wasn't going to adjust its schedule or its cadence simply for his personal comfort.

After Tango stepped over a rotten log, his legs came to a sudden stop without any direction from Bunker. The steed's ears began to twitch, twisting like spastic radar dishes attempting to lock onto an incoming missile.

"What is it, boy?" Bunker asked, leaning forward to run his hand along his friend's neck.

That's when Bunker heard it. A faint voice to the left, drifting through the trees in an intermittent mumble. The person's tone was light and airy, almost high-pitched. Even though he couldn't make out the words, he thought the speech pattern was familiar.

Bunker didn't want Tango to worry because a confident horse is much more reliable than a frightened one. He gave his friend a double pat on the neck. "It's okay, buddy. Those are our friends. It means we're almost there."

He assumed the voice belonged to one of the younger boys, based on the pitch. However, there was a chance it wasn't a friend. It could have been a foe, laying a lethal trap for his arrival.

If the sudden rise of paranoia was justified, it meant Albert didn't follow his directions, allowing the Russians to beat him to the rally point.

Bunker ran it through his head again and came up with the same conclusion. Albert was a man who followed his own agenda, even when he agreed to do otherwise. The meth cook may have only been pretending, uttering the words he wanted Bunker to hear.

Let's face it, saying he was part of the team was much different than actually delivering, especially after their heated face-to-face in the barn. When you're dealing with a career criminal who's adept at surviving in the shadows of anonymity, you never really know where he stands. Words are cheap and meaningless for those with a secret agenda.

Bunker had met his share of sociopaths over the years. Most of them were easy to read, with their emotions leading the charge. But not Tin Man. Albert was clearly brilliant and carried a unique skillset, allowing him to use his intelligence to manipulate, all the while hiding his true self.

Albert reminded Bunker of many of his old riding partners in The Kindred. At first blush, everyone appeared to be working together toward a common goal. Yet under the surface, personal agendas were actually in control.

To the uninformed, being a member of The Kindred might appear to be very much the same as being a member of the Marine Corps. Both outfits were tight-knit brotherhoods who wore the same colors, battled the same enemies, rode together, ate together, fought together, and bled together, everyone striving to win the day.

Nevertheless, at the core, they were vastly different in the one area that mattered most: *integrity*. Personal agendas destroy integrity, eroding the foundational belief in one another. If you don't have integrity, then you can't carry yourself with honor, courage, and commitment. They are intertwined and mutually dependent.

He'd lived in both worlds, sacrificing parts of himself for those who stood alongside him in the heat of combat. His past gave him a unique perspective—one few could match. Riding with The Kindred was the polar opposite of his days humping the dusty trails of Afghanistan.

Bunker stopped the mighty steed with pressure on the reins, then dismounted in one smooth lift of his leg. He stood nose to nose with his mammoth ride. "You hang back, Tango, while I do a little recon. Don't want to put you in harm's way, if I'm wrong about this."

Tango twisted his head and let out a blow from his muzzle. He shook his head, then sent his tail into an all-out offensive against a regiment of flies that had been tracking him for miles.

Bunker wished he could help conquer the relentless, buzzing creatures. Animal or human, it didn't matter—everyone has their own swarm of demons that seem to follow them everywhere.

He tied Tango to a nearby tree and crept ahead, blending into the greenery with his camo for cover.

Just then, he heard the snap of a twig. The sound wasn't from his movement. It was ahead, somewhere beyond a pair of pine trees surrounded by bushes reaching shoulder height. One of the trees had a broad-leafed vine spiraling up its trunk, resembling the stripe on a barber pole, only this stripe was lime green instead of the customary red and white.

Bunker moved silently to investigate. When he peered through the bush, he saw Stephanie squatting with her pants down.

She looked at him and screamed.

He stood up in a flash, his hands out to the side. "Wait! Steph, it's me! I'm sorry!"

She spun away in a sudden flash of legs, crotch, and butt. "Oh my God! Bunker! Quit looking!" she said in a harsh tone, tugging at her pants in a panic.

He turned his head, slamming his eyes shut.

"What the hell are you doing?" she asked, grabbing his arm after a dash around the bushes.

He brought his head forward and locked eyes with her. "I didn't know it was you, Steph. It was an accident. There weren't supposed to be any females on this mission."

"Well there is one—me. So quit sneaking around like some kind of perv."

"I said I was sorry. I heard a twig snap, so I came to check it out."

"What did you see?"

"Nothing. Really. I swear," he said, not wanting to admit he saw everything.

She paused, her eyes digging deep into his soul. "All right, don't do it again."

"Trust me, the last thing I ever wanted to do was see you naked."

"What the hell does that mean?" she asked with attitude.

"Shit. That came out wrong. I'm sure you look fabulous naked. I just, well, ah . . . never mind," he said in a blundering stammer.

She snickered, shaking her head. After a short pause, she waved a hand forward. "Come on, everybody's waiting."

He followed with gratitude in his heart. Not for the free peep show, but for the fact that someone he knew was here and walking around freely. That meant no Russians. Unfortunately, he couldn't un-see what he had just witnessed. The embarrassment would haunt both of them to no end.

CHAPTER 117

Bunker pulled Sheriff Apollo aside, walking him twenty yards from the others in Patterson's Meadow. Dallas, Rusty, Victor, Dicky, Burt, and stickman Dustin remained behind with Stephanie King, the only female from Tuttle's camp. "What's Stephanie doing here?"

Apollo shrugged. "I tried to talk her out of it, but she insisted."

"Well then, I guess you didn't try hard enough. She should be back at camp with her son."

"I agree, but I don't think she's totally onboard with your plan."

"Ah, shit. She's gonna try to talk me out of this, isn't she?"

"Or she wants to keep an eye on you. I hate to say it, but I think she's here as more than just a friend."

"Great, just what I needed."

"Daisy wanted to join the fight as well, but at least I could order her to stay. Someone with training had to stand guard. Hope it's enough."

"Should be. She's capable. Plus I'm betting we'll keep the Russians focused on us for a while," Bunker said, thinking about his promise to Daisy. He'd agreed to come clean about his past when he returned. However, since she wasn't here, he figured he wasn't breaking his word if he waited until they all got back to camp.

Bunker's eyes found Stephanie on their own, specifically her shapely backside as she bent over to adjust the position of one of the boxes next to her. "I still can't believe she's here."

Gus seemed amused when he said, "Steph never listens to anyone, anyway, so why should we be surprised?"

"That's true, but Jesus, Sheriff. This is the last place she should be. It's gonna be beyond dangerous."

"That's what I told her, but I think that just made her want to come even more. Not sure what else we can do at this point. She's a free person and can do what she wants."

"You're right. The harder we push, the more she's gonna want to stay."

A sly grin arrived on Apollo's lips. "I could be wrong, but I'm pretty sure Stephanie King has her eye on a little Bunker meat."

"Don't even go there," Bunker said in a sarcastic tone. He'd have to find a subtle way to convince her to head back to camp. Something that she thought was her idea.

"What did you find out in town?" Apollo asked.

"About what you'd expect. It's pretty intense. The Russians showed up in force."

"Everyone okay?"

Bunker shook his head. "Some are starting to fight back. There've been some casualties."

"My God, I should have been there."

"There's nothing you could have done, Sheriff. Casualties are inevitable. No way around it. But what we do here, right now, in this meadow, can put an end to all of it. So we have to stay focused and not dwell on the shit we can't control. Agreed?"

Apollo nodded. "Who's been hurt?"

"The Mayor for one. Stabbed by Kenny King."

Apollo sucked in a quick breath. "He's out of prison?"

"Apparently. But he's been dealt with."

"What do you mean, dealt with?"

"He came at me and I took him out."

"Well, I can't say that's a bad thing," the Sheriff said, looking almost relieved. "Is Buckley dead?"

"Not as far as I know, but he was losing a lot of blood when Rico rushed him to Doc's."

"Anyone else?"

"Yeah, but I don't know who. There were some executions before I got there."

"Shit."

"That's why we need to get this right. It's the only way we can help everyone in town. There isn't time to waste on anything else."

"Agreed. But we'll need to talk later, though. I discovered a few things after studying Tuttle's obsession."

"The newspapers?"

Apollo nodded. "They tell an interesting story."

"Does it affect what we need to do here?"

"No."

"Then it can wait."

"My thinking exactly."

Bunker walked back to the group.

Dallas and Rusty stopped his approach, working together as the junior varsity team to block his path. He could see the apprehension smothering their faces, looking as though it was about to explode from their eyes.

"What's up, boys?"

"Did you see my grandpa?" Rusty asked. "What did he say? Did he ask about me?"

Bunker didn't have the heart to tell the kid the truth about the stabbing. The youngster had a right to know, but Buckley's condition was an unknown. The Mayor could be dead or recovering nicely.

That left two options, one of which would break the kid's heart. If Bunker could somehow soften the information to avoid what little he actually knew, it technically wouldn't be lying. It would be more along the lines of protection, until they actually knew more.

Bunker cleared his throat, buying a few more seconds to formulate his response. "As a matter of fact, I did. One of the first things we talked about was you. I told him you were safe and helping all of us deal with this crisis. I know he's proud of you."

Rusty smiled, sending the concern in his eyes screaming for the exit.

"What about my mom and sisters?" Dallas asked. "Were they there?"

Bunker took the photo from his pocket and gave it to the boy. "I'm sorry, I looked and asked around, but I didn't see them."

The boy's eyes started to tear.

Bunker didn't let a second pass. "But that doesn't mean anything bad has happened to them. The town is a big place with lots of hiding places. I probably just missed them. So let's not worry about something we don't know."

Dallas sniffed before he wiped his eyes with the sleeve of his shirt.

"Bunker?" Apollo said, nudging his arm. He pointed at the items stacked together. "We need to get this stuff into position."

Bunker was thankful for Apollo's save. Had he been pressed for more information, he would have run out of spin to sling at the boys. The last thing the kids needed right now was the harshness of truth.

Bunker took a quick visual survey of the load the gang had brought with them. They'd stacked everything in neat, ordered piles. Boxes of explosives, including Tannerite, were waiting to the left with spools of detonation cord and blasting caps.

They'd also brought several handguns, a half-dozen rifles, a stack of tactical vests, and a healthy reserve of ammo. They even remembered the camouflage netting and gas masks.

Bunker looked at the oversized meth cook, reminding himself not to call him Tin Man. "I'm guessing it's all here?"

Albert pulled a folded wad of paper from his pocket and gave it to Bunker. "Yep, plus a few items. Go ahead and check the list, if you don't believe me."

Bunker opened the papers and scanned the items he'd written, then visually checked the inventory they'd stacked. He didn't have time to review everything, but Albert's thoroughness was evident. "Impressive work."

"Thanks, but I had a little help," Albert said, moving his eyes from person to person in acknowledgment.

"Don't believe him, Bunker," Dustin said. "Albert did most of it. We just helped where we could."

"Speak for yourself, Slim," Burt snapped, holding out his arms. Several new burn scars were present, no doubt from all the welding the man had been doing. "Those hides were a bitch. But they're done. So is the drawbridge. So you better come through with your end of the deal."

Bunker had no plans to break the agreement he'd made with the sweaty mechanic. "The gun's yours, Burt. As soon as we're done here."

"I'll hold you to that," Burt said, pausing for a ten-count before he spoke again. "Looking at all the shit we hauled here, did we really need me to do all that fabricating? We got enough to start World War III."

"We'll need them if this plan doesn't work," Bunker answered, turning to Albert. "Did you bring the handheld?"

"It's in the glove compartment of the truck Stephanie drove. Kept it off like you asked."

"Excellent," he answered, noticing an item that looked out of place. It was a large duffle bag. It was black with long straps draped over the middle. He pointed to it. "What's in the duffle?"

"Punji sticks," Albert said. "Thought they might come in handy."

"Actually, it was my idea," Burt said, sounding a little miffed that Albert tried to take credit. "Turned them on that old lathe Tuttle had. They're all exactly the same length and fucking sharp."

"Not sure there's time for them," Bunker said, wishing Burt hadn't wasted the effort on something he didn't need. Punji sticks are best used in massive numbers with poisoned tips or feces, either buried in a drop pit or to booby trap trails against foot patrols. There wasn't time for any of that. Plus, his team of untrained civilians would lose track of where they were located.

"Well, use them if you want. They're here. I don't really give a shit."

"I gotta tell you ya, Bunker," Stephanie said, breaking the tension. She pointed at the stockpile. "It took some creative packing to get all that stuff here. Especially on the horses. Good thing I took charge, otherwise it wouldn't have fit. Not with all of us tagging along."

"Yeah, all of you," Bunker said, holding back what he truly wanted to say. If she'd stayed at Tuttle's place, there would've been more room available. Not to mention, there would be one less person he'd be responsible for—a single mother, no less. A mother with no tactical skills whatsoever.

"What do you want us to do first?" Burt asked, cracking his knuckles. "The sooner we get this over with, the sooner I get what's coming to me."

"We start at the center and work our way out. It's safer that way. I'll need the blasting caps, det cord, and TNT first. Once that's done, we'll move one of the Land Rovers into position, then focus on the rest of the perimeter."

"Not both trucks?" Albert asked. "I'm sure we have enough trinitrotoluene."

"One is all we need," Bunker said, adjusting his plan on the fly. They'd need to hold back one vehicle for Stephanie to use when she decided it was time to head back to camp. He still wasn't sure how he was going to accomplish that feat, but he figured it would come to him. "Bring the shovels and auger, too."

He turned to Dicky, pointing at Tango's position. "Tango's half a click up that ridge. Grab him and the rest of the horses and take them to the top so they don't get spooked."

"Consider it done."

"But I'll need them back down here when we're done."

Dicky nodded, the expression on his face indicating he'd come to a conclusion. "In case we need to make a fast getaway."

"That, and other things."

"Easy enough," Dicky said, moving the TrackingPoint rifle away from his chest. "Should I leave this here?"

"Yes, you should, cuz that's mine," Burt said, trying to grab the rifle from the big man.

Dicky spun away, keeping the precision guided firearm out of the mechanic's reach. Dicky locked eyes on Bunker, waiting for orders.

"Take it with you. It needs to be up on that ridge at all times. If you see anyone, fire a warning shot."

"I'll go with him," Burt said in a matter-of-fact way, turning to follow Dicky.

Bunker grabbed Burt's arm. "Look, I know you're anxious, but I need you to be patient until this is over."

Burt ripped himself free. "Get your fucking hands off me!"

"Easy now, Burt. We're all on the same side here."

Burt's temper fumed with a clench of his teeth, his face flushing a deep shade of red. "I know you think you're hot shit around here, but don't ever try to manhandle me. Otherwise, you and me are gonna go. And trust me, I can throw with the best of 'em."

"Didn't mean anything by it," Bunker said, searching for the proper words to calm the situation. "There's a lot of work to do and I need your steady hands down here, with me. Otherwise, none of us makes it through this alive. So it's in everyone's best interest, including yours, that we work together."

Burt paused until the heave in his chest waned. He looked exhausted. "You know, I've been quiet and gone along to get this done, but there are limits. And getting grabby is one of them."

"I understand. I overstepped my bounds."

"You're damn right you did."

"Just need you to see this through, as agreed. I know you're a man of your word. So am I."

Burt exhaled a slow breath, nodding. "Fine, but as soon I get done killing me some Russians, I'm outta here. With that rifle. Don't get in my way, Bunker. I'm not bullshitting here."

"Fair enough."

* * *

An hour later, Bunker, Apollo, and Burt had all but one of the blocks of TNT buried in a straight line across the head of the clearing. Blue detonation cord connected each one in a series, precisely how Bunker had envisioned. Albert and Dustin were on hand as well, though their primary duty was that of observers during the rigging process.

The calculations Bunker had made earlier by pacing the width of the meadow were right on the mark. He might have been a little rusty, but his math about the number of charges and length of detonation cord needed was dead-on.

The fence-post auger had made quick work of the digging requirements, manually corkscrewing the earth loose to make deep, six-inch wide holes. It would've taken them ten times longer with a pick and shovel, and not been nearly as precise. Apollo and Burt had done most of the auger work, though Bunker had taken his turn as well.

Blasting caps had also been buried with each charge after being inserted into their respective brick of TNT. The process was simple and repetitive—so much so, a monkey could do it. Well, a trained monkey, that is. One who chewed dirt for a living in the wasteland known as Afghanistan.

Rusty, Victor, and Dallas stood a hundred yards away with anxious feet, the tree line at their backs. Stephanie was in front of them, playing chaperone, her arms extended like a member of security protecting the band on stage. A high-energy blasting machine sat a few yards from her feet, its hand crank waiting to be engaged.

Bunker looked at Apollo, then nodded in the direction of the boys. "What do you think, Sheriff? Should we teach them a little something about explosives? The world's a much more dangerous place than it used to be a week ago."

Apollo nodded. "That's true. We all need to learn new skills. Even young men."

"My old man taught me when I was about their age," Burt said, his skin glistening in the overhead sun. "You know they're chomping at the bit to be part of this."

Bunker chuckled. "What member of the male species doesn't want to blow shit up? That's why I became a Sapper in the Marine Corps."

"That must have been a total gas," Burt said.

"Most of the time, as long as you didn't find yourself at the end of a sniper's scope." Bunker waved at the young men to come forward.

Stephanie shook her head no, keeping her arm block in place.

"It's okay, Steph. Trust me. I used to do this for a living," he yelled across the clearing.

She still didn't move.

Bunker assured her again. Same words. Firmer tone.

After a short pause, she dropped her arms, though she didn't look happy about it.

The boys didn't hesitate, sprinting to Bunker's position. They arrived short on breath but long on enthusiasm.

"It's time to earn your stripes," Bunker told them.

"Awesome," Victor answered, standing between Rusty and Dallas. All three of them had mile-wide grins, showing nothing but teeth.

Bunker grabbed the last block of explosive. It was a yellowish cream color and slightly bigger than a double deck of playing cards. He peeled off the protective paper and held it up for the boys to get a clear view.

"Looks like C-4," Victor said, sounding confident.

"Actually, this is trinitrotoluene, also known as TNT."

"Oh, like dynamite," Dallas said.

"Not exactly," Bunker answered, not wanting to dampen the kid's interest with a hard no. "But a lot of people get them mixed up. Even a few Marines I once knew. It all comes down to chemistry."

"It always does," Albert said with pride in his voice. "Gotta love the symmetry of formulas."

Bunker continued, "Dynamite is nitroglycerin and diatomaceous earth wrapped together in paper, with a little sodium carbonate mixed in for good measure. I'm sure you've seen sticks of dynamite used on TV and in video games."

The boys nodded in unison.

"The white powder inside dynamite is extremely sensitive to shock, which makes it very dangerous to handle. TNT, on the other hand, is a yellow crystalline aromatic hydrocarbon and it's much more stable. It doesn't sweat or deteriorate over time like dynamite does. In fact, we could store this brick underground for sixty years and it wouldn't change its molecular properties at all."

"You know what else is really cool?" Albert asked the boys. "We could melt the TNT and pour it into shell castings to make any shape we want. Like a rabbit or a keychain. For booby traps."

"Exactly," Bunker said. He was glad Stephanie wasn't standing close. There was zero chance she'd approve of the conversation. But these kids needed to learn and the best way to do that was to make the class fun and interactive. "Now, if we added a little ammonium nitrate, which is basically fertilizer, it would serve as an oxidizer and feed high amounts of oxygen into the explosion."

"Like a turbocharger on a car," Victor said.

Bunker nodded, even though the kid's answer was wrong. "We'd end up with a hyper-explosive called Amatol. Something I got to use a few times when I was stationed overseas."

"How do you light it?" Rusty asked.

"Not with a fuse, if that's what you're thinking." Bunker held up the detonation cord in one hand and a thin, pencil-shaped blasting cap in the other. He assembled the pieces together. "We send an electrical charge through this wire, which in turn sets off the blasting cap. That's the proper way to detonate TNT."

"Oh, so that's what the hand crank thing over there is for," Dallas said, shooting a quick glance at Stephanie and the device sitting close to her. "I was wondering."

Bunker was pleased with their understanding so far. "Okay boys, time for a pop quiz. Do you know why they used to call a brick of TNT a *canary*?"

Victor shook his head and held quiet. So did Rusty and Dallas.

"Because if you handle it a lot, it turns your skin a yellow color. In fact, I should be using gloves right now, because technically, this stuff is toxic."

"Shit, didn't think about gloves," Albert said.

"There's like ten pairs of them on Tuttle's workbench," Victor said.

Bunker smirked. "At this point, it really doesn't matter." He pointed at a spot in the dirt. "Would you do the honors, Burt?"

The man's biceps came alive as he grabbed the blue handle of the auger and put the tip of the blade into the dirt. He cranked the T-shaped handlebar in a circle, screwing the blade into the dirt until it was buried completely. He pulled the corkscrew blade from the earth and shook off the soil before repeating the process several more times.

When the hole was deep enough, Bunker pushed the blasting cap into the center of the TNT block. "All we have to do is insert the cap like this. Then position it where we want it." He let the block slip from his fingers, accidental like. "Whoops!"

When the explosive hit the bottom of the hole, Victor and Dallas scampered back about ten feet. Rusty never moved.

Bunker laughed; he'd hoped to get a rise out of the boys. "Remember, it won't explode until we send a charge through the cord. That's when you need to make sure you're behind cover."

"That wasn't funny, dude," Victor said, retracing his steps.

"Now you understand why we don't use dynamite, especially old dynamite, because dropping it into a hole like that might have sent some body parts flying, depending on its condition. You never know with that stuff. TNT or C-4 is always my first choice."

When Bunker sent his gaze at Stephanie, he found that she hadn't moved from the tree line, though her arms were now crossed over her chest. He imaged her lips were pressed together in a thin line, with her eyes shooting daggers at him.

Burt filled the hole with dirt and packed the soil, keeping the detonation cord near the center.

"How big is the explosion?" Rusty asked.

"Let's find out," Bunker quipped, pointing at Stephanie. "Time to get in a safety position. I need all three of you over there, pronto. Get down behind that dead oak tree up on the hill. Stephanie will show you."

"What about you guys?" Rusty asked Bunker.

"We'll be right behind you. Now, get moving before Stephanie has my ass."

Victor laughed as he turned his heels and ambled with a hurried step. Dallas followed second, with Rusty holding up the rear.

"Just so you know, you made my heart skip a few beats, too," Apollo said.

"Yeah, thought the kids would get a kick out of it," Bunker answered, gathering the detonation cord in his hands.

"Didn't look like Stephanie thought it was funny," Burt said. "She could probably chew nails right about now."

CHAPTER 118

Apollo knelt down on the right side of Stephanie King, who had the three boys to her immediate left. Burt was on the far side of her, next to Rusty, Dustin and Albert.

Everyone was cowering behind the massive oak tree lying on its side, waiting for Bunker to finish attaching the detonation cord to the terminal block on the side of a high-energy blasting machine. The manufacturer's label said it was a BART-2.

The all-black unit looked like a carrying case for a cordless drill, except for the hand crank on the side. The crank was positioned above a pair of red-colored buttons that were recessed below the surface of the plastic housing.

The Sheriff assumed the design kept the buttons from being pressed accidentally. Immediately below the buttons was the word FIRE stenciled in red.

Bunker cranked the handle like a madman to charge the capacitor inside. Then he turned to the group and asked, "Is everyone ready?"

Apollo ducked his head and covered his ears.

So did the rest of the crew.

"Fire in the hole!" Bunker yelled before detonating the charges.

The ground shook with the force of an earthquake, rattling everything in the vicinity. Apollo kept low as the compression wave hit his skin, arriving at almost the exact same moment as the sound tore past his hands and landed on his eardrums.

The deep resonating thunder was impressive, waking up every cell in his body, almost as if a bolt of lightning had just missed his head. Even though he knew the blast was coming, he couldn't stop his heartbeat from surging ahead at an even greater rate than before.

"Holy shit," he said, not able to contain the words. When it was over, Apollo brought his head up and uncovered his ears.

The boys were already on their feet and cheering with raised hands, high-fiving each other as if they were in the stands at the Super Bowl. So were Burt and Dustin, looking as juvenile as the kids next to them.

Bunker stood with them; however, he wasn't celebrating or acting foolish like the others. Though he did have a noticeable grin on his lips.

Albert's head remained buried behind the log. So did Stephanie's. Neither of them moved.

"Is it over?" Stephanie asked in a muffled tone.

"You can get up now," Bunker said, his voice calm and reassuring.

"Damn, that was loud," Apollo said, pressing to his feet. "I hope they didn't hear that in town."

"I doubt it," Bunker said. "Sound doesn't travel that far, especially with all the mountains and trees around us."

Apollo wasn't so sure. "What about the vibration?"

"It'll stay localized. Trust me, I've done this more times than I can count. Let's go see how we did."

With those words, the boys took off in a dash, tearing down the hillside with arms waving, dodging trees as they went.

* * *

Twenty minutes later, Bunker straightened the steering wheel of the Land Rover and stepped on the brake pedal after easing the truck into a position parallel with the trench. "How's that looking?"

"That's about it, I wouldn't get any closer," Apollo answered, his face filling the passenger side mirror.

Bunker peered out the driver's window, locking eyes with Stephanie standing fifty yards away. "Am I centered?"

She gave him a thumbs-up. "Close enough. You're good."

Bunker turned off the motor, ending the purr of the engine. He opened the door and hopped out, walking to Apollo.

The Sheriff's toes were dangerously close to the edge of the twenty-foot deep trench that ran from one side of the meadow to the other, its width almost as wide as its depth. "I thought for a moment the edge was going to collapse. That's a lot of weight."

"Wouldn't this be better if we parked it on the other side of the trench?" Stephanie asked, looking over her shoulder at the entrance to the clearing. "Where the Russians couldn't get their hands on it so easily. All they have to do is march right here to this spot, assuming they can get past all the mud in the middle."

Bunker opened the rear hatch and fished out the detonation cord he'd already prepped for the ten bricks of TNT inside. He held it up to her. "That's why we have this."

"Oh, I see. You want them to get close."

"Yep. By the time they figure it out, it'll be too late."

She nodded, her eyes locked onto the trench. "So the trench is a barrier to keep them from getting to the trees."

"Among other things," he said, not wanting to waste time explaining every detail. "We need them to run where we want them to." He looked at Apollo. "Is the BART-2 in position?"

"Rusty hauled it over there for you. It's by the first tree on the right. Hope that's where you wanted it."

"That's perfect. Just gotta run this det cord and we'll be ready for the next phase."

"Then I better go relieve Dicky," Apollo said. "It's best if he runs the chainsaw."

"You can wait a bit on that. Let's get the other stuff done first. We'll finish with the trees."

* * *

Burt wrapped the last of the tracer wire around the middle of the two-foot-tall cable spindle, tucking the end of the wire under the previous revolution to hold it in place. "That's it for these."

"Too bad we didn't have room for a few more," Dustin said, standing next to the other three Burt had already set-up.

"We would have if Miss Sugar Tits over there hadn't come along," Burt said, lifting the bottom of the spindle and turning it onto its side. He gave it a shove. The makeshift wheel rolled a few feet on its own, then stopped. "Excellent. Not too heavy. Just need to get them into position and finish prepping."

"You should probably let Bunker handle that," Albert said in a snarky tone. "Unless you want us to start calling you Stumpy."

"I plan to, Jumbo. Don't get your panties in a bunch."

"So we're back to that now?"

"Like I care. This is almost over, so you can drop the whole 'let's be friends' act."

"Works for me, dipshit."

"Yeah, fuck you, too."

Dustin cleared his throat. "Come on guys, not now."

Burt bent down and put his hand into what he'd call the axle, if it had one, running through the steps in his own head. He visualized the outcome, bringing a smile to his lips.

"Won't the Russians see them and wonder what's up?" Dustin asked.

Burt scoffed. "Not with all that tall grass out there. It's frickin' brilliant, if you ask me."

"I better go get the pressure boards we made," Albert said, walking toward the stockpile of gear they'd brought from Tuttle's.

"Don't forget the batteries," Dustin said to his back.

Albert gave him quick hand wave but didn't turn around before speaking again. "If you guys want to roll them to Bunker, I'll meet you there."

Burt added volume and attitude to his voice, making sure Albert got the message. "Might as well bring enough for the diesel containers too, assuming you're not too tired yet from all your *observing*."

Albert flipped him the bird, never looking back.

* * *

Rusty waited for the big kid, Victor, to grab the five-hundred-round box of .223 caliber rifle ammo before he snatched the box of three-inch framing nails.

His container had twice the number of nails they needed, but it seemed silly to empty half before carrying them to the spot Bunker had indicated. It would have been much lighter, but he thought it best not to waste time.

"What did Bunker say about your grandpa?" Victor asked as the two of them marched toward the far side of the tree line, their eyes almost level with each other.

Rusty didn't want to sound concerned around his new friend, but he couldn't help himself. Victor might have been a lot younger, but the kid didn't act like it. "He's okay, I guess."

"What does that mean?"

"Bunker really didn't say. I kinda get the feeling there's more."

"You think he's lying?"

"Could be, but he said he talked to my grandpa. So I don't know."

"You should've asked more questions. I would have."

"I wanted to, but we need to get this place ready. At least Grandpa knows we're all safe."

"Well, not everyone."

A video of Franklin's dead body rolling into the grave flashed in Rusty's mind. "Yeah, poor Megan. I can only imagine."

Victor leaned in close as they walked side by side, his voice a purr. "What about Dallas' family?"

Rusty answered in a whisper. "Bunker said he didn't see them."

"You think they're dead?"

Rusty shrugged. "Maybe, I don't know. I get this feeling that something bad happened."

"Yeah, me too. They're probably dead. I'm sure the Russians killed them and dumped their bodies into a hole somewhere. It's what they do, from what I hear. Dump people into a hole."

Rusty wasn't sure how to respond to those comments, so he didn't. Right then, a new thought stormed his mind. "Hey, did you bring the screwdrivers?"

"Shit, I forgot," Victor said, stopping his feet. He turned. "Hey Dallas, grab those fat screwdrivers! All three."

"I was just looking for them," Dallas shouted back, his feet only a foot from the stockpile. "Where did you put 'em? And those stick things with the orange tape?"

"In the red toolbox. Under the top drawer. They might be buried, so dig a little," Victor said, turning his attention to Rusty. "I wonder if Bunker will let us help this time?"

"Probably not. They'll say it's too dangerous."

"It's more like we're just slave labor," Victor said with attitude. "But they should at least let you. You're way older than us."

Rusty agreed, but didn't want to admit it. "I think they're just trying to protect everyone."

"Yeah, but Bunker can't do it all himself. He's gonna need help."

"He has the Sheriff and Burt. They're not afraid to get their hands dirty."

"Yeah, but not Albert and the other guy. They're pretty useless."

"Don't forget, they did their part back at Tuttle's. Now it's up to the rest of us."

"Except Miss Sugar Tits," Victor said, laughing.

Rusty couldn't hold back a grin. "She doesn't seem too enthused."

Victor's tone turned sour. "Always sticking her nose in and asking questions. And Dicky, just sitting up there on that ridge, looking all tough with that gun."

"Somebody's got to do it," Rusty said. "At least they showed us some stuff about explosives. That was pretty cool."

"Yeah, totally intense. I can't believe how big that explosion was. Holy shit."

CHAPTER 119

Dallas watched Bunker jam a screwdriver into the soil, pushing it lower until the full length of the blade disappeared. Then he twisted it with his fingers like he was putting a cap on a bottle. Victor stood at attention next to Dallas, with Rusty on the other side, all three sets of their eyes locked on Bunker's demonstration.

"Once you have the hole made, check the depth like this," Bunker said, pulling the screwdriver from the dirt and sliding in a wooden dowel to replace it. The diameter of the dowel matched that of the hole—a perfect fit.

Bunker pointed at the orange tape wrapped around the dowel, bringing extra attention to the line of black ink drawn across it. "Use this mark to know exactly how deep you need to go."

"What if it's too deep?" Victor asked.

"Simple," Bunker said, removing the wooden rod and pushing some loose dirt into the empty hole. "Just be sure to tamp it down flat with the end of the dowel." He demonstrated the packing procedure, then pointed at the black line again after inserting the dowel. "Once you have it perfect, then put a nail in with the head down. It's important that the tip be sticking up and centered."

Bunker took the dowel out and put it aside, then held out his hand. Rusty gave him a framing nail from the box. Bunker put it into the hole with the head down. Like the dowel, it fit snugly down the shaft. "If you made the hole properly, the size of the head should just fit inside."

"Here's the bullet," Victor said, holding out a .223 round.

Bunker took it and held it above the hole with the tip of the bullet pointing to the sky. "They go in with the nose up like this, but I'm going to wait until later to take care of these. You three focus on the making the five hundred holes we need and putting the nails in. Be sure to check the depth carefully with each one. There's a screwdriver and dowel for each of you."

"What does the nail do exactly? I'm confused," Dallas said.

Bunker turned the .223 round horizontal, with the back facing Dallas. He aimed his finger at the rear of the bullet. "This is what's called a centerfire cartridge. When you pull the trigger, the firing pin on the rifle makes contact with the primer right here, in the middle, which sets off the propellant inside. That's how a bullet gets fired. In this case, the tip of the nail takes the place of the firing pin. It's what sets off the primer."

"Oh, I see, when someone steps on it," Dallas said, nodding his head.

"Exactly. That's why the depth has to be perfect. Otherwise, when the enemy steps on it, his boot won't press the round into the nail. We could have used a .762 round for more firepower, but the diameter of the .223 is closer to the size of the head on the nail. It fits the hole tighter. Fewer misfires."

Rusty nodded. "Makes sense."

"In the Vietnam War, the NVA made life hell for US troops with this booby trap. It's their version of what we called toe-poppers. The Russians will never expect these. Not from a bunch of civilians in Colorado. They think we're nothing but fat, lazy Americans who don't know anything about booby traps."

Rusty smiled. So did Dallas.

Victor pointed across the clearing, in the direction of the stockpile. "Why are we only putting them on this side? Don't we need them on both?"

"Can't all be the same. I've got something else planned for the other side. It's important to keep the enemy guessing. Plus, I'll need a safe path to the middle when the time is right, and that's not easy to do with a minefield of toe-poppers."

"I can do it," Rusty said.

Bunker hesitated before he spoke. "Do what?"

"Install the bullets. Just show me how."

Bunker shook his head. "It's too dangerous, Rusty. If you drop one in too hard, it'll take your hand off."

"I'll be careful," Rusty said. "You gotta let us do something."

"You will. I promise. Just be patient."

"When?" Victor snapped before looking around the meadow. He pointed at Albert, Dustin, and Burt across the way, setting up one of the cable wheels. Apollo was close to them with a shovel, digging in the dirt. Stephanie was holding one of the pressure boards they'd made at Tuttle's. "Everyone else has something to do. Even Miss Sugar Tits."

"Hey, let's not use that kind of language," Bunker snapped. "You need to show some respect, young man. Or haven't you learned anything since your talk with the Sheriff?"

"When are we gonna get a turn?" Dallas asked before Victor could answer.

Bunker looked at him, his face red from scolding Victor. "When we rig the trees. I'll need you three for climbing. There'll be plenty to do then."

"That's something, I guess," Victor said in a defeated tone.

"I can do this, Jack. I really can," Rusty said. "I'm not some kid, you know. I'm old enough to vote and join the Marines, like you did."

Bunker paused, but didn't say anything.

Rusty continued. "You can't do all this by yourself. You really need to trust me. My grandfather called it delegation. Something a good leader does."

Bunker exhaled an extended breath, his eyes lowering to the ground for a few seconds before they came back up. "Okay, let's assume I let you do this. How would you do it without blowing your foot off?"

"By carefully putting the bullets in the holes, like you said. Just don't drop 'em in, right? Seems easy enough."

"Not what I meant. What about the order? You can't walk around here without a plan. Otherwise, you'll forget where you're at and step on one you've already primed."

Rusty shrugged, looking smug. "I start at one end and work my way across. How hard is that?"

"It's not that simple, Rusty. I've seen trained Marines forget where they left off and get hauled away on a stretcher."

"Couldn't we just create two or three long rows spaced like twenty feet apart? Then set the toe-poppers one at a time from left to right so we know where we're at. Like mowing the grass."

Victor broke his recent silence. "What about using rocks to mark the rows? That way we know exactly where they are. The tall grass will cover them up so the Russians won't see them until they're right on top of them."

"Hey, that's a good idea, isn't it?" Dallas asked in a confident tone, seeing the pinch in Bunker's eyes loosen. "Yeah, I can see it in your face. That is a good idea."

"As a matter of fact, yes. But it's still very dangerous. I'm not sure I'm comfortable making the decision here. Maybe we should go ask the Sheriff and Mrs. King for their input."

"Shit, she'll never go for that," Victor said. "Everyone knows she's afraid of her own shadow."

"I thought *you* were the man in charge?" Rusty asked.

"Yeah, Bunker. Grow a pair," Victor added, sounding amused.

"Well, technically, the Sheriff's in charge," Bunker answered.

Victor laughed, shaking his head. "Come on, dude. Everyone listens to whatever you say. Even Burt. If you say it's okay, they will, too."

"Please, Bunker. You gotta let us help," Dallas said.

CHAPTER 120

Several hours later, Bunker picked up one end of a rotting log, while Burt took the other. They could have used a third pair of hands to support the weight in the middle, but Bunker thought they could manage on their own.

Burt walked backwards through the forest, looking over his shoulder as the distant sound of a chainsaw buzzed the air. Dicky was hard at work near the entrance to the meadow, cutting down a handful of selected trees. Apollo was up on the ridge with the TrackingPoint rifle, keeping watch on the valley below.

Hopefully, the three boys were paying attention to what Dicky was doing. Bunker needed them engaged in something new. Not just to learn from the former lumberjack, but to keep busy until it was time for the trio to start climbing trees.

Despite Stephanie's strong objection, Rusty had done a masterful job with the toe-poppers, adding confidence to his budding manhood. Bunker figured Mayor Buckley would be proud of his grandson's bravery, assuming the man survived the stabbing by Kenny King. Bunker still hadn't told Rusty about the incident, deciding to wait until the time was right. It was a conversation he didn't want to have. But eventually, he'd need to sit Rusty down and go through it all.

"Where do you want it?" Burt asked as they hauled the dead tree into the clearing.

Bunker peered to the left, drawing a visual line from Stephanie King's position to an intersecting point where they were headed. She was standing in the grass thirty yards away, with one of the cable spindles hidden at her feet. Her position marked the interior edge of the booby traps. "Keep going. I'll let you know when we're there."

"The booby zone," Burt said, laughing after glancing at Stephanie with an amused look on his face. "In more ways than one."

Bunker couldn't help himself, letting out a snort as they continued another twenty feet. "Right there. That's good."

Burt stopped his feet and dropped his end of the log. "Looks like we'll need a few more if we want two on each side."

"Actually, that'll be too obvious for a trained eye. We don't want it to look like a marker, so we'll just use two more. One positioned on the end of this log, and another sitting perpendicular near the entrance. That way I'll know which side of the logs is safe."

"Good idea. No perfectly straight lines," Burt said, pointing at the tree line. He traced an imaginary line with his hand from the edge of the meadow to his feet. "Maybe we should remove the sunflowers through here as well."

Bunker was impressed with the man's quick thinking. "I like that idea. Their absence will be a marker of sorts."

"And it won't look too obvious to a trained eye, like you said."

Bunker decided to educate the bulging mechanic. Not only to share knowledge, but to help pass the time. "We called them Combat Hunters in the Corps. Their job was to survey the area ahead and look for anything that didn't belong, or looked out of place. Those guys saved a lot of lives, especially in urban settings where Haji liked to plant IEDs. Whether it was a mailbox out of place, some discoloration in the cement of a sidewalk, a bicycle that didn't belong, cars riding low on their suspension, or whatever, you had to be alert. Those booger-eaters were damn clever."

"I can't imagine walking into an area like that where everyone wants you dead."

"It got the blood pumping, that's for sure. After a while, you get addicted to the adrenaline high."

"Probably changes a man, too."

"Roger that. Though sometimes not for the better."

"Well, just so you know, we all appreciate your service," Burt said, walking next to Bunker as they headed back to the trees. "I would have signed up outta high school, but my old man needed me at the shop. So that's what I did. Been there ever since."

"Good choice," Bunker said, thinking about the man's short temper and lack of physical fortitude. "You're obviously good at it."

"Thanks. But still, there are times I think I should have done my part."

"We all have our callings, Burt."

"Did you ever have second thoughts? You know, when the bullets started whizzing past your head."

"Sure. But honor and duty kept me moving forward, right until I was due to rotate out. Then I knew I was done. It wasn't even a question at that point," Bunker said, avoiding the details about the shit storm that happened after being assigned on special mission for an unscrupulous Army major.

"Can you imagine if Albert had tried to join?" Burt said, laughing through the words. "Especially the Navy."

"Probably wouldn't have gotten very far. The recruiters I know are always trying to make quota and would lie through their teeth to get grunts to sign up. But even they would have turned him away at the door."

"If he could even get through the door," Burt quipped. "I'm guessing Dustin would have been rejected, too. My right leg weighs more than that guy."

"It's possible he could've made weight. It all depends on which branch of service we're talking about. They each have their own physical standards, so he might have squeaked by."

Burt grabbed his midsection with both hands, squeezing at the roll. "I guess I'd have to lose a few pounds myself." He let go of his flab, then brought his arm up and made an impressive curl with his bicep. "At least these guns can still bring a little thunder."

Bunker held back a snicker. He could've matched the man's display and then some, but didn't want to embarrass his only helper available for this part of the operation.

Burt's abdominal core looked like a squishy donut. His attempt to show off his powerful arms looked ridiculous—and lazy. "I know I'm new in town, but don't remember seeing a fitness gym."

"Because there isn't one. Besides, I prefer the dumbbells in my office anyway. Can pump out a few sets when it's slow in the shop. Don't need all that other shit," Burt answered, starting the trek up the hillside. "Seems like a total waste of money to me. We all know people don't go there to work out. They just wanna stand around and gossip. I'd probably end up punching somebody."

* * *

Albert made his way through the brush to Bunker's position, carrying the camo-colored backpack he'd put together back at Tuttle's place. He kept his hands on the carrying strap, purposely avoiding the smear of axle grease that had transferred to the zipper pouch along the top.

"Is that what I think it is?" Bunker asked, taking the pack in one hand.

"Yep. Was able to get four of them done."

"The list only called for three."

"I know, but I had enough aluminum powder for make a fourth. Figured having a spare might just come in handy. Explosives are easy."

"But discretion is hard," Bunker said, his tone sounding rehearsed. "I've got that microscope you wanted. Remind me later. It's in my pack."

"Awesome. Thanks. I'm sure everyone is anxious to get Cowie back in the ground where he belongs. Talk about ripe."

"I thought we talked about that on the radio?"

"Yeah, we did. But some of the females got upset. Wasn't my place to argue."

Bunker held quiet, opening the pouch and looking inside. His focus lingered longer than Albert expected.

"Not enough axle grease?" Albert asked him, wondering if the numb expression on Bunker's face indicated a problem. "The specs didn't indicate how much."

"Actually, it looks perfect," Bunker answered, pausing for a beat. "Tube socks?"

"It's all Tuttle had. Found them in his hamper. I looked, but there weren't any clean ones in his dresser."

The corner of Bunker's mouth turned up in a smirk, stopping just short of a smile. "They'll do. I'm sure the Russians won't mind."

"I also made a few adjustments to the mix."

"What kind of adjustments?"

"I juiced up the temperature a bit. Something with a little more sizzle, if you know what I mean."

"TH3?"

"Yep. Tuttle had the material on hand, so I thought, what the fuck? Might as well."

"Looks like I picked the right man for the job. It's good to see you use those chemistry skills for the greater good."

Albert ignored the fake compliment. It was actually a carefully worded slam. He decided not to address it, keeping his tone light and friendly, as if he didn't notice the insult. Keeping Bunker in a good mood would help with a question he needed to ask, but first a little setup was needed. Something smooth and transitional. "Say what you want about the old coot, but he took prepping seriously. If you need something, I'm sure he has it."

Bunker snorted a half-laugh. "That man really should've written a book. He had it covered, that's for sure."

"No doubt," Albert said. It was time to ask the question he'd been saving. "Speaking of material, I was wondering if the baggie I gave you came in handy?"

"Actually, I was able to get past the checkpoint without it," Bunker said, locking eyes with Albert. "But I'm not giving the shit back, if that's where you're going with this."

Albert hesitated, needing to spin Bunker's accurate guess. He did want his pound of Clearwater Red returned, but upsetting the infamous Bulldog wouldn't help. He decided to wait for a better time to ask for his ice back. Maybe even steal it when Bunker wasn't looking, assuming the man lived through what was coming next. "Nah, keep it. Not much of a market left for it anyway."

Bunker leaned in close, his eyes coming to an even tighter focus. He spoke in a charged whisper, spittle flying from his mouth. "Just so you know, Tin Man, I buried it deep in the forest where nobody will ever find it. I don't want that crap falling into the hands of the kids around here. Now or in the future. Am I making myself clear?"

Albert held up his hands, keeping them out to the side in total surrender. "Perfectly. It's cool, dude. What I gave you is all there is. Wasn't time to make any more. I swear."

"Because if I see so much as a single red crystal within fifty miles of town, I'll gut you from your balls to your neck, and feed your fat ass to the buzzards."

CHAPTER 121

Apollo stood at the base of a towering pine with his head craned, keeping an eye on Dallas as the kid shimmied up the trunk. The boy could climb, working his way up the tree with ease.

"Monkeys got nothing on him," Dustin said from Apollo's right. "Damn, he's good."

The widest part of a triangle-shaped red, white, and blue bandana slid around the boy's neck. It landed on the front of his chest when he angled his body up and around the next branch.

Apollo wondered if the scarf from Tuttle's place would work itself loose before Dallas would need it at the top. If it did, they would need a way to get it back up there to protect his lungs.

Dallas stopped his ascent to fiddle with the string of plastic quart-sized bottles hanging on a short rope from his waist. His hands worked the homemade cargo around a troublesome limb before he continued the climb, his face showing no sign of fear.

"He's getting awfully high," Stephanie said, holding her hands out as if she was planning on catching the young man if he fell.

"He'll be all right, Steph. Just needs to take his time and plan his route," Apollo said. "It's obvious he's spent a lot of time in trees. I know I did when I was young. Of course, that was long before my investment in bagels and pancakes."

"Among other things," she quipped, glancing down at his gut. "But we all have our vices, now don't we, Sheriff?"

Apollo didn't take offense at her callous remark. It was just her stress talking. It's not every day you find yourself part of an advance team preparing a meadow for a deadly battle against an overwhelming enemy—one with enough manpower and weaponry to wipe you out in a heartbeat.

Nobody had said the words since they arrived, but they were all thinking it: Bunker had better know exactly what he was doing. Their lives depended on it, and so did the lives of everyone in town. One miscalculation and they'd all draw their last breaths.

Bunker and Albert stood at the base of another pine twenty yards away. Apollo estimated their tree was the tallest one in the area, which was probably why Bunker had selected it first when he scouted trees.

Height was a key. So was clearing a path between it and the ambush area, which is exactly what Dicky had done with the chainsaw earlier. The lumberjack made quick work of the felled trees, chopping them into manageable segments for Burt and Bunker to carry away. Luckily, the other pines they'd targeted didn't require as much prep work, keeping the hauling requirements down to a minimum.

Victor wasn't as agile as Dallas, but he showed the same lack of fear, his hands and feet working in concert to carry him higher in the taller tree.

"What about this one?" Victor asked Bunker, pointing above his shoulder. He, too, had a dangle of plastic bottles hanging from his beltline.

"Keep going, I'll let you know."

Rusty had been assigned to the stockpile where the lone remaining Land Rover was parked. Most of the horses were secured there as well, their reins lashed to a triple-wrapped band of paracord that had been strung between two stout trees.

Rusty was busy readying the next payload, his capable fingers threading the paracord through the handles of each bottle before wrapping them around. He'd need to string ten more sets before the trees on both sides of the clearing were prepped and ready.

Dustin brought a hand up to his nose and sniffed it. "Jesus," the skinny former deputy snorted, turning his head away.

"What's wrong?" Apollo asked.

"Can't believe I can still smell those frogs. I've washed my hands a bunch of times and they still stink."

"Trust me, that's not the worst smell around here," Apollo said, rolling his eyes.

"That's for sure," Stephanie added, shooting a glance in Burt's direction. "Thanks for giving him something to do, far away from here."

"My pleasure," Apollo said, lauding his own decision to assign Burt to help Rusty, not as a foreman to oversee the process, but to get the mechanic's stench as far as way as possible. All the manual work of the day had sent the man's body odor into orbit.

In all fairness to the short-tempered jerk, Apollo figured he smelled almost as bad as Burt. The hours of shovel work to bury the diesel-filled water containers had challenged his back and his old bones. The thirty-plus years of flying a desk as an architect had taken its toll, long before Mayor Buckley drafted his sagging butt for Sheriff's duty.

Either way, Apollo's nose needed a break. So did everyone else's, except maybe Dicky. The former offensive lineman was back on the ridge, standing watch with the precision rifle, far beyond the waft of Burt. The big man had taken one of the horses with him in case he needed to make a hasty retreat. As long as their group didn't hear the sudden echo of a gunshot, everyone knew to keep working.

They weren't expecting company yet, but Bunker didn't want to take any chances. Apollo agreed, deferring to the former military man, who possessed far more tactical training than he did.

Thus far, the entire process had gone smoothly, thanks to Albert's skills as a chemist and Bunker's planning. The former Marine must have been working on this strategy for a while, Apollo decided, watching the pieces come together like a chess master preparing for checkmate.

There was still plenty of work to do rigging trees and running detonation cord. But soon, they'd be ready.

Apollo gulped, pushing down a fleshy bulge of mucus.

* * *

"That should do it," Bunker said to Apollo after finishing the last run of detonation cord. The two of them stood in the elevated position Bunker had for the blasting machine. It was a straight shot downhill to the end of the trench and provided the best vantage point to initiate.

A sharp, shrieking whistle broke through the serenity of the mountainside from below.

"Sounds like Dicky is finished with the final cuts on the trees," Apollo said.

"Excellent. Just need them to hold until we're ready."

"I'm sure they will. He knows what he's doing."

"Are the Tannerite charges in place?"

"Ready to go, boss," the Sheriff said, smiling, his tone sarcastic. He pointed at the TrackingPoint rifle sitting next to Bunker. "You might want to double-check their placement with the scope. Make sure they're right."

Bunker took the rifle and brought his eye behind the long-range optics. He scanned the near side of the clearing, locating the charges Apollo had rigged at the base of each pine tree the boys had climbed. He confirmed their placement. "Nice work."

Apollo picked up the empty spool of detonation cord. "Are you going to bury the det cord in the trench?"

"Would take too long. I tucked it along the wall instead. Shouldn't be an issue."

"Pretty clever to use the trench."

"Figured we might as well use what we've already made. No reason to duplicate work."

"Or take the chance it's spotted in the grass."

"Exactly. The element of surprise only works once," Bunker said.

Apollo tossed the spool next to the others. "I can't believe how much of this stuff Tuttle had. He must have been stockpiling for years."

Bunker agreed, but needed to shift their focus to something more pressing. His thoughts turned to Stephanie. "We should probably talk about the thousand-pound elephant in the room."

"Who? Steph?"

"It's probably time for her to take the truck and get the boys back to camp."

"I agree. I'll go have a chat with her," Apollo said, turning to walk away.

Bunker grabbed the man's arm, spinning him around. "Better let me do it, Sheriff. If what you said earlier is true, she's here because of me. This is my problem."

"What are you gonna say?"

"Not sure yet. But I'll think of something."

"You know she's going to resist."

"Trust me, I'd rather walk into a hornet's nest—naked."

"You and me both," Apollo said after a quick chortle. "Except maybe the naked part."

Bunker smirked, his mind conjuring a visual of Apollo doing that very thing. "Yeah, I might have to rethink that last statement."

Apollo flared an eyebrow, looking amused. His tone turned serious a moment later. "We also need to decide on long gun placement. I'm assuming your preference is Dicky on the TrackingPoint."

"Actually, Sheriff, I was thinking about you," Bunker said, aiming both hands at his feet. "I need someone I trust right here, on overwatch. It's too important. Especially the first shot."

"Dicky's trustworthy."

"Not what I meant. I need to know the shooter will do what needs to be done. You have the training. He doesn't. This will turn into a shit storm damn quick."

"I may have the training, but not in a live combat situation."

"You'll do fine. I can see it in your eyes."

"I appreciate the confidence, but—"

Bunker didn't wait for the man to finish. "I hear what you're saying, Sheriff, but trust me. You can do this. I've spent enough time in combat to develop a keen sense for these things."

"You do realize that I used to be an architect. Not that long ago, either."

"And Dicky used to be a lumberjack. So what's your point?"

Apollo cleared his throat. "I don't think you get my meaning."

"Sure I do, Sheriff," Bunker said, not wanting to show an ounce of apprehension. "As far as I'm concerned, you're the one and only man for the job. I'm not worried in the least."

"That makes one of us. I hope you realize Burt's not going to like me on the TrackingPoint. I get the feeling he wants to be behind the scope."

"Yes, he does. And that's the problem. He's much too eager. I don't think he fully understands what taking the shot means."

"You're worried he might freeze."

"Or just take off with the rifle, when it all gets a little too real. I've seen it before," Bunker said, putting a hand on Apollo's shoulder. "So, we all need to know, Sheriff. Are you up to the task?"

Apollo paused, his eyes indicating he was unsure. Then he nodded. "Let's do this."

Bunker knew the man would step up, despite his obvious trepidation. Some men have it, while others don't. Even so, Apollo looked like he could use more encouragement. "Look, I know you have your doubts; that's normal. We all do. But the TrackingPoint will do most of the work. All you need to do is breathe and wait for the green dot to light up the targets. I will take care of the up close and personal stuff."

"Sounds simple enough, but I'm gonna need a complete run-through on the rifle."

Bunker checked the position of the sun, calculating the time remaining until it set behind the mountain range. It was imperative that he have the sun at his back, plus he needed to pad some leeway for delays. It was going to be close, especially if he wasted time appeasing Stephanie and Burt, but he thought there was time for everything.

Apollo must have sensed Bunker's concern, because he didn't wait for an answer. "I know we have a schedule to keep, but I don't want to take any chances. It's too important."

"I'll get you up to speed. Just remember, it's them or us, Sheriff. No different than an armed standoff with criminals. It's all about the mindset. You need to act, don't react."

"I'll do my best."

"First and foremost, wait for my signal before you set those charges off. Then all you need to do is not let any of the stragglers get to cover.'"

"With all we've set up, how likely is that?"

"Some will inevitably get lucky and stumble through, so you need to be ready. Gotta keep them in the kill zone until it's over. We can't count on the others to hit Jack-shit."

CHAPTER 122

"Hey, gotta minute?" Bunker asked Stephanie in a whisper.

"Sure, what's up?" she asked with eager eyes.

He pulled her away from the rest of the team, who were busy with Apollo divvying up the weapons and ammo.

Bunker's mind went into whirl mode, sifting through a dozen possible approach scenarios, searching for something that would achieve his objective with her. "I need your expert advice about something."

"Expert advice? Really?" Stephanie quipped, flaring her eyes. She smirked. "Okay, that's a first."

Bunker ignored her reaction, pretending he didn't notice. Feigning ignorance is one of the key advantages to being a man. So is selective hearing. You can play oblivious when it suits you, allowing you to push an agenda with delicacy. "It has to do with the boys."

"Is something wrong?"

"Yes and no," he said, pointing in the direction of Victor and Dallas, both of whom looked like they were about to burst out of their skin in anticipation of receiving a weapon from the Sheriff. "I'm not sure how I'm going to tell them that they can't stay. It's too dangerous."

"Just sit them down and have a talk. That's what I do with Jeffrey, when it's really important."

"On paper, I would agree. Except I'm not their parent. It's really not my place."

"I'm sure they'll listen, if you explain it properly. Just be calm and rational. That usually works best."

"Maybe, but I think I screwed up big time when I got them involved and showed them how everything was going to work. They feel like they're part of this operation now, and it's going to be hard to send them packing."

"It's all about being firm but fair. They'll try to guilt you into caving, but you can't."

"They'll hate me for it."

"Probably, but that's how it goes sometimes. Kids can't always get what they want. Somebody needs to look out for their best interests."

Bunker didn't respond, wanting his phony anguish to hang in the air until it soaked into her skin. She'd come around; he just needed to plant the seed and let it grow into her own idea.

She held his hand, squeezing it gently. "Everything will be fine, Jack. They look up to you."

"Yes, they do. But that's because of my confidence in them. I'm not sure either of them have had that before from a father figure. If I take that away now, it'll crush who they are trying to become as young men. It's a rite-of-passage type thing."

She let go. "You can't be their guardian and their friend, Jack. That never works. It's one or the other. Someone has to be the grownup."

"I hear you, but they're just now starting to get their footing and feel like they belong to something important. I don't want to wreck that."

"You won't."

"You don't know that, Steph."

"Yes, I do. You're a good man. You care what happens to them. Like you do with the rest of us."

"That's what makes this so hard. If I screw this up, I'll lose the ability to keep them safe down the road. And I can't let that happen."

She put her hands on her hips, tilting her head to the side as her tone turned sarcastic. "What you really mean is that you'll lose the ability to keep them under control. Like a prisoner."

Shit. He needed to backpedal. He was pushing too hard. "That's not what I meant."

"It's not about control. It's about respect. For them and for you. You gotta treat them like adults. Otherwise, they'll resist and never listen to anything you have to say. They're at that age, Jack. The slightest thing will set them off."

He nodded, letting a cloud of doubt take over his face. "Is that what you do with Jeffrey? Treat him like an adult?"

"He's not like these boys. He actually listens to his momma."

Bunker threw up his hands. "God, I wish I had more experience at this. If I choose the wrong words, they'll revolt and take off on their own. That's how they'll get themselves killed. Especially Victor. He's done it before. How would I ever explain that to Allison? She's counting on me to keep him safe."

Stephanie gave him a tender hug, then squeezed him tight before she pulled back. Her tone turned soft. So did her eyes, peering deep into his soul where the guilt was hiding. "You have to find a way, Jack. They can't stay here."

"Even if I manage to somehow convince them to leave, how do I get them back to camp in one piece? We can't send them alone."

"The answer's obvious, silly. Somebody needs to drive them," she said before hesitating with her mouth open. When her eyes tightened on him, Bunker knew she was deep in thought, processing the facts he'd just floated. Then again, she may have been churning through the details he'd glossed over in his rush to manipulate.

Stephanie let go of her expression, looking confident, as if she'd just landed on an answer. "That's why you used only one of the Land Rovers by the trench."

A stab of pain in his gut told him she may have been on to him. She was smart and capable, but he decided to move forward as if her comments meant nothing. Otherwise, if he switched focus now, she'd know something wasn't right.

"See, that's just it. I can't spare anybody right now," Bunker said, pointing at the ridgeline where the BART-2 blasting machine was waiting to be connected to the detonation cord. "I'm going to need everyone who can shoot up there, on that ridge, when the bullets start flying. It's going to be hard enough to pull this off as it is. I can't spare even a single shooter."

"Bullets, huh?"

"And there's gonna be blood. Lots of it. And that's not counting if the Russians bring a few tanks along. I'm not sure if the rest of them understand what's about to happen."

"No, I suppose not," she mumbled.

"I've been down this road before. It's not something you can un-see or forget easily. It'll leave scars for the rest of their lives, assuming they don't catch a bullet first."

Her gaze fell to the grass as her neck turned slightly to one side.

Bunker didn't think she was looking at anything in particular when her breathing changed, slowing to a deep, exaggerated rhythm.

Stephanie's empty stare continued until she brought her head up in slow motion, almost as if her neck had run stiff and was filled with pain. "I'll tell you what, Jack. How about I go talk with the boys and convince them to head back to camp with me? That way, you don't have to be the bad guy or lose any of your shooters."

"Would you? That would be amazing, Steph. Thank you!" Bunker said, feeling damn good about his success. He didn't like having to manipulate her that way, but it was necessary for the good of everyone involved.

* * *

Twenty minutes later, Stephanie stood by the open door of the Land Rover, waiting for the group's tattooed leader to make his way over to her. All that remained was to say goodbye, then slide her rear end into the driver's seat. Once she fired the engine and put the shifter into first gear, this part of the ordeal would be over. She wasn't looking forward to it, but it needed to be done.

Apollo, Rusty, Albert, and Dustin stood in a huddle twenty yards up the path, waiting for the next phase of the mission to begin. Dicky was still on guard duty, watching over the valley from his perch on the ridge.

She was thankful Dallas and Victor didn't put up much of a fight about returning to camp once she'd put her foot down. She only had to raise her voice once after their initial objections, ending the debate. Sometimes it pays to have a reputation as a vengeful bitch.

Bunker was busy chatting with Burt about something, looking as though he'd rather be somewhere else.

Stephanie felt the same way, wishing none of this was happening. It was all a little too surreal for anyone to process, let alone a recently divorced single mother who didn't want to say goodbye to the man she couldn't stop thinking about. Her heart wanted her to stay, but her logic had other ideas.

She'd dragged herself to the meadow with her own mission in mind. Now she was abandoning her desire for the needs of others, a strange twist of fate. It felt both wonderful and nauseating at the same time. She wondered if she was asleep somewhere, lost in dreamland after passing out from an all-night drinking binge with the girls.

If only, she thought as Bunker turned away from Burt and started a slow walk to her position. Deep down she knew Bunker had talked her into this, even though she distinctly remembered it being her idea. A strange paradox, indeed.

Maybe her heart was the culprit, letting him maneuver her to do his bidding. She was usually on her game around men, but that was more of a necessity around her ex. Bunker was different in so many ways. Granted, his charm wasn't always obvious. Neither was his guile, but his true colors always shined the brightest.

Victor got into the backseat through the passenger door on the far side of the truck and slammed the door shut.

Stephanie made eye contact with Dallas, who was standing next to her. "Time to go."

"Hang on a sec," he said, never taking his eyes from Bunker.

When Bunker arrived, Dallas said, "I've got something for you."

Bunker looked intrigued as the youngster climbed into the truck on his knees, facing the backseat. His arm went over the bench.

"I found this hidden in Tuttle's barn," Dallas said after climbing out of the truck, giving Bunker a curved tube with a cloth-wrapped handle sticking out of one end. "I thought you should have it."

Bunker took it and pulled on the handle, sliding a long, curved sword out of the scabbard. He twisted it in the air, moving it from one side of his body to the other, much like Stephanie had seen Samurai Masters do in the movies.

"Is that what I think it is?" she asked as the sun reflected off its polished surface.

"It's a Samurai sword," Dallas answered, wearing an ear-to-ear smile.

A vision flashed in Stephanie's mind, showing her a severed head lying next to its lifeless body. "Is it real?"

"I don't know, but it's well made, that's for sure," Bunker said before stopping his side-to-side motion. "The balance is amazing." He brought a hand to the blade, sampling its honed edge with a light touch of his finger. "And razor sharp."

"Do you like it?" Dallas asked, his boyish tone bleeding through the syllables.

"I love it." Bunker slid the sword back into its guard. He shook Dallas' hand. "Appreciate it, little buddy."

"We need to go, Dallas. Get in the truck, please," Stephanie said, nudging the kid on the shoulder.

Dallas waved goodbye to everyone before climbing into the Land Rover.

Stephanie closed his door. "Well, I guess that's about it," she said, bringing her eyes to Bunker.

"Do you know the way back?"

"I think so."

"I do," Victor said, leaning forward from his seat to make eye contact.

"Me too," Dallas said.

Stephanie let out a phony smile, trying to hide the sadness swelling in her heart. "There you have it. One pilot and two navigators. This should be interesting."

When Bunker leaned forward, she thought he was going to kiss her. The thought of his affection sent lightning bolts shooting across her body. However, his advance stopped a moment later when he put his arm behind his back. When his hand returned, a pistol was in his grasp. "Here, take this in case you run into trouble."

She shook her head, keeping her hands away from the weapon. "You know guns are not my thing."

"I understand, but you should have it just in case."

"I'll take it, if she doesn't want it," Victor said, holding his palm out like a panhandler on the street.

Before Bunker could respond, Albert breezed in and stood next to Stephanie, his hand extended. "I'll take it from here, Bunker."

"What are you doing, Albert?" Stephanie asked.

"Riding shotgun."

"You're going with us?"

"Apparently," he said, shooting a look at Apollo.

"It was my idea," Apollo said, looking at Stephanie first, then Bunker. "I think we'll all feel better if at least one of us goes along."

"Agreed," Bunker said without a moment of pause.

"What about your shooters?" Stephanie asked Bunker in a charged voice. "I thought you needed every one of them."

Apollo put a soft hand on her shoulder. "It's best if he goes with you, Steph. We can't send you out there without an escort."

Albert was a lot of things, but he wasn't anywhere close to what she'd consider an escort. A pervert, yes. Escort no. "Don't I get a say in the matter?"

Apollo shook his head. "I'm sorry, the decision's been made."

She looked at Albert, catching the heavy man's eyes drooling over her chest. She snapped her fingers in front of him before pointing at her face. "Eyes are up here, Albert."

"Right, sorry," he said in a stammer, his face flushing red.

Stephanie sneered at Bunker. "You can't be serious about this."

He didn't respond. Neither did Apollo when she turned her scorn his way.

"Have a fun trip," Bunker said, looking amused.

Stephanie had planned to say goodbye to Jack with one last hug and perhaps a kiss, but not now. Not with that twisted grin on his mug.

She spun in the dirt and got into the driver's seat, then closed the door with extra force to make a point.

Albert ambled around to the other side of the vehicle and hoisted his huge backside onto the open seat. The truck leaned to the right, then back again as his size settled in for the ride to Martha's.

Stephanie didn't have to look over at him to know he was checking her out again. She could feel the weight of his eyes pressing on her body. Sure, she was proud of her figure and dressed in such a way that men would notice. But not this man. Albert's gaze felt like a violation of decency, even though there was nothing she could do about it. He had a right to look—no law against that.

She put her forehead on the steering wheel and sighed, knowing the ride would seem twice as long with Albert sitting across from her—with a loaded weapon, no less. Both in his hand and in his pants. It made her want to throw up.

A triple tap came at her window.

She sat up in the seat and rolled the window down with the hand crank. When she peered up, Bunker's chiseled face filled the frame. Even though she was very upset with him, she couldn't stop her heart from puttering.

"Stick to the back roads. You should be fine," he said as if nothing was wrong.

She nodded, knowing this might be the last time she ever saw him. She needed to say something—anything—but couldn't convince her lips to speak. Her mouth felt like someone had dumped a truckload of cotton inside, then covered it with cement.

He stepped back, resuming his previous position next to the Sheriff.

She held back a torrent of tears as her hand cranked the window closed. Her mind filled with a flash of memories, each one involving the man who'd protected her on the train. Jeffrey was in those scenes as well, the three of them somehow finding their way to each other with the help of fate.

They say that your life flashes before your eyes right before you die. But what about when someone you love is about to meet their end?

How does that work?

Do your friends and loved ones witness the flashes, too, seeing those same memories from their own perspective?

Is that what she was experiencing?

It was the strangest feeling, one that she hadn't felt before. She looked at the boys in the back seat for inspiration. They were chatting with Albert, not realizing what was happening in the driver's seat.

She brought her focus forward, gripping the steering wheel with extra force. Her mind went into self-reflection mode, trying to unravel the puzzle filling her thoughts.

Torment is a lonely punisher, consuming a person from the inside out, she decided. Despite the nearly endless attempts by millions on Facebook, intense loss is something that can't be shared. Nor can it be part of some social experiment. Not in any meaningful way.

Loss was a solo act. She was sure of it. So were guilt and loneliness, affecting each person differently. Each of them splays your heart open with a jagged edge, exposing all that you are as it tunnels its way to your very core.

Even though the Land Rover was full of people, she was alone. More so than ever before.

She didn't want to start the engine, but that's exactly what she did. The grind of the starter motor tore at her emotions, preparing her for the journey that would soon begin, taking her down the darkest of trails. A trail that would most likely be without the new man in her life.

She put the clutch in and moved the shifter into first gear, taking one last look at Bunker.

He gave her a tentative smile, looking vulnerable for the first time since she'd met him. He must have known it, too.

When Bunker sent her a half-wave, she released the clutch and stepped on the gas. His face disappeared from view a second later, sending a single tear rolling down her cheek. The burning inside her chest was profound, igniting an emptiness she knew would never be extinguished.

Despite everything she was feeling, her foot never came off the accelerator. Nor did she turn the truck around. Her job was simple and all-important—get the boys back to camp. To do that, she knew she must forget all that had come before, erasing that which was bubbling inside.

CHAPTER 123

"Well, you did it," Apollo said to Bunker, patting him on the back. He studied the former Marine's reaction, wondering if Bunker had seen Stephanie's torment about leaving.

"Wasn't sure there for a moment," Bunker said, walking with Apollo. Their pace was slow, heading to the others, who were waiting by the items yet to be deployed.

"That look on her face said it all."

"Yeah, I felt it, too," Bunker said. "God, I hate goodbyes. I totally suck at them."

"She'll be okay. Steph's a lot stronger than anyone gives her credit for."

"I hope you're right. She deserves to be happy."

"We all do."

"Hey, I need you to do me a favor, Sheriff."

"Name it."

Bunker stopped his feet and turned to face Apollo. "If for some reason today doesn't go as planned, I need you to tell Daisy something."

"Let's not go there, Jack. Positive thoughts."

"Yes, we've done all we can, but—"

Apollo wouldn't let him finish his sentence. Doubt was the last thing the group needed to see on his face. "Your plan is sound, Jack. We will win this thing. I'm sure of it. We have God on our side."

"That may be true, but there are a number of variables we can't control, no matter how well we've prepared. The Russians are no different than we are when it comes to the biological imperative to survive. It's not going to be easy, Gus, no matter what side God is on. So I need you to listen. Please."

"Sure, what do you need me to do?"

"For one, tell Daisy that I did go to her trailer and check on her cat. Unfortunately, the fur ball didn't make it. I buried Vonda out back by the garden. Wasn't sure what else to do."

The look on Bunker's face indicated there was more he needed to say. "Is there anything else?"

Bunker nodded, looking petrified about the words yet to arrive. "There's something I've been carrying for a long time. Daisy's been waiting patiently for me to say it. In fact, I promised her I'd come clean when I got back. But since there's a chance I won't—"

"I understand," Apollo said, cutting off the confession on purpose. "You don't need to say it. We all know you love her. She's a very special young woman."

Bunker's eyes lit up in shock. "That's not what I'm referring to."

"So you don't love her?"

"I didn't say that. I was talking about something else."

"Oh, my mistake. Go ahead, shoot."

Bunker lifted his shirt to expose the tattoos across his chest. He was covered with them. The most prominent was up near his shoulder. It was an emblem of an infamous group known as The Kindred.

Apollo had to force his lips to speak. "The white supremacist biker gang?"

"Yeah, it's something I'm not proud of," Bunker said, turning to expose the artwork across his back.

Apollo instantly understood the symbols and numbers.

Bunker continued after turning forward, letting his shirt drop. "I was on the run after going AWOL from the brotherhood when I met Steph and Jeffrey on the train."

"Jesus, I had no idea," Apollo said, his mind reeling from the revelation. The man he'd come to know and trust was a drug-dealing, law-breaking thug. He'd heard the words clearly and seen the evidence across the man's body, but he still didn't want to believe it. "So, let me get this straight. You weren't in the Marines?"

"Yes, I was. But that was before I decided to join The Kindred. When I left the Corps, I was broken and desperate, trying to find meaning to my life. Everything I believed in had been shattered by something that happened right before my tour ended. I was in full-on revolt mode when I joined the brotherhood. I guess I thought riding with them would somehow fill the emptiness I couldn't seem to shake. I know it doesn't make any sense, but that's what happened. I went from one end of the spectrum to the other. Of course, the misery inside continued to grow until I finally walked away after they started selling meth to kids."

Apollo shook his head. "This is going to break Daisy's heart."

"Actually, she already knows. It all came out in the miner's camp when we ran into one of my former riding partners. His name was Grinder."

"Was?"

"I had to put a bullet in his head before he let my former boss, Conner Watts, know where I was."

"I've heard of Watts."

"I'm sure you have. He's on the FBI's top ten most wanted list. If I had let Grinder live, it would have put everyone in danger. They're never going to stop looking for me. So I had no choice but to take him out. He was holding Megan hostage at the time. Stephanie was there. So was Jeffrey."

"They know, too?"

"Not exactly. Though I suspect Stephanie has put some of the pieces together on her own. Daisy's the one I'm worried about the most. She's been carrying my secret around and it's killing her inside."

Apollo couldn't believe that Daisy didn't share this information with him. It wasn't like her to lie to his face like that.

"She's a good deputy, Gus. Don't judge her for agreeing to keep my secret. I made her do that. For the greater good. But she'd come to the end of her rope yesterday. That's why she made me promise to come clean when I got back from my recon mission. That was our deal. Otherwise, she was going to do the right thing and turn me in. To you."

"So this is you coming clean?"

"My version of it. My name is not Jack Bunker. It's Jack Terrier and I have a rap sheet. But I don't want the others to know. Not yet. Not until we finish what we've started here. It's too important."

"Yes, it is."

"Just a few more hours, that's all I ask. I don't want what I've done or who I am to shake their confidence in our plan. It'll put everyone in danger."

"I see," Apollo muttered in a condescending tone. Part of him wanted to pardon Bunker on the spot. However, the lawman inside was on a different path altogether. His heart ran cold, wondering how he could have been fooled this long by a criminal deviant.

"Look, I get it, Sheriff. You have no reason to trust me right now, and frankly, I don't blame you. Sometimes, I don't trust myself. But I'm being honest when I say I'm not that guy anymore. I know I've made plenty of mistakes and some God-awful decisions, but I'm trying to make amends and start over."

Apollo shook his head, but didn't answer.

"I hope you can find it in your heart to forgive me long enough to finish this. If, after that, you want to toss my sorry ass in jail, I'll go willingly and take the punishment I have coming. Just let me do the right thing now. I need to pay back all of those who've given me their trust. We've got exactly one shot here, Sheriff, and we have to do this together. Right here. Right now."

Apollo understood the man's words, though he still had a long list of questions. First up, motive. It's the key to understanding why a criminal makes the choices they do. "What happened in the military?"

Bunker hesitated, his eyes darting left and right, probably in search mode. "I think I've told you that I was a Marine Corps Sapper. My job was to make sure the infantry had a clear path into combat. That usually meant identifying and clearing any IEDs or other booby traps the enemy may have deployed. If I didn't do my job, men got hauled out on a stretcher, or worse."

"I can imagine."

"I also did the usual combat engineer stuff. Sweeps with metal detectors, fortifying perimeters with explosives and wire obstacles—you name it. It's a hybrid position, one involving both offensive and defensive techniques, depending on the mission objectives. I even provided fire team support on occasion, once the assault began. So I got to do a little bit of everything. The perfect mix for me."

"That still doesn't answer my question."

"I'm getting to it, Sheriff. Right before I was due to rotate out, I was offered the chance to join a special operations unit tasked with eliminating terrorist cells who were also deeply entrenched within the drug cartels of Afghanistan. A two-for-one deal. Obviously a high-value target. We're talking the blackest of black bag operations, whose primary mission was to eliminate the bad guys and destroy their source of financing."

"Sounds honorable."

"That's exactly what I thought. When I was told the orders came direct from the Commander-in-Chief, I signed up, eager to score a few more high-profile wins for our country. I figured it would be a good test of my skills and something new and different. When you're a combat engineer, it's important to keep the juices flowing, which was something I needed at the time. It's easy to become complacent, which gets people killed, including yourself. I also figured it would help me decide if I was going to ship-over again or not. Otherwise, my tour was getting rather tedious and it was time to find something else to do with my life."

Apollo nodded, listening carefully.

"Anyway, I was the lone Sapper assigned to this special unit and my job was to establish a defensible escape plan for the assault team after they breached the target. They were to get in, gather intel on the cell's finances and drug supply lines, then destroy the place before heading to the extraction point. A no-witnesses type thing."

"What do you mean establish a defensible escape plan?"

"If the op went sideways, which they often do when intelligence gets the resistance levels wrong, then my skills would come into play. Instead of clearing a path to the enemy, my job was to use explosives and other techniques to help get our team to extraction if they came out hot. Simple enough. I'd be on the other side of the equation for a change and get to take out a few terrorists by using their own ingenuity against them."

"I can see why the mission drew you in."

"Yeah, again, it was the perfect fit for me. Who wouldn't want to take out a few more terrorists masquerading as drug lords? Now, it turns out that the CIA was actually running this op with the help of an Army major, who shall remain nameless. I was anxious to get to work, so I never stopped to think about the unique relationship between the Army and the CIA."

"Wait, are you saying the CIA and military don't usually work together?"

"From what I know, it's rare but I could be wrong. Then again, if it does happen, it's usually a top-secret mission, which I'd never know about anyway. The CIA has their Special Activities Division, which is a covert paramilitary operations unit made up of ex-military superstars like Green Berets, Delta Force, and SEALs. I'm sure there are a few Force Recon Marines and pilots mixed in, too. But the mission I was on was not part of the S. A. D."

"So I take it, something went wrong?"

"You could say that. This CIA spook, who went by the name of Flapper, shows up and takes charge from the Major. We all fall in line under the new chain of command and wait for the order to deploy. Everything's good at this point. I had my fallback plan all worked out, so I was ready to do my part for brother and country. While the breach team went in, I went to work getting the explosives set up, with Flapper overseeing everything. That should have been my first clue, but of course, I was a good Marine who kept his head down and focused on his job. Too well, as it turned out."

"Jesus, what the hell happened?"

"Flapper happened. Apparently, the mission objectives weren't exactly what I was told. We were there to negotiate a major drug deal with the local cartel. Millions in cash type thing. However, the warlord decided to keep the money and the drugs, then opened fire. It was a shit storm of biblical proportions. Our team came out hot and I covered their egress, setting off charges and killing everyone in pursuit. And I mean everyone. Total devastation."

"So the drug deal aspect . . . is why you left the military?"

"That's part of it, but let me finish. When the smoke cleared, we went in to identify some of the bodies to verify if any of them were on the Terrorist Most Wanted List. Of course, none of them were. At least the parts we could find. That's when reality smacked me in the face. The chase vehicles were filled with kids. Dozens of them. We're talking six, seven, eight years old. There were bits and pieces of them everywhere. All because of me."

Apollo was stunned, yet he said nothing. He didn't have the words. His mind filled with a string of bloody visuals as Bunker continued.

"Turns out, that warlord wasn't a terrorist at all. He was just some lowlife motherfucker who was famous for using kids as human shields. And Flapper knew it, which is why he ordered me to detonate heavy. He expected it and wanted me to send a message that he'd kill everyone, even kids, if you double-crossed him. When I confronted him about it, he just laughed, like it was no big deal."

"My God," Apollo said, feeling the guilt oozing out of Bunker's pores.

"All those children, Sheriff! Dead because of me! Then Flapper had the nerve to thank me for a job well done. Are you fucking kidding me?"

"I can't even imagine."

"Had I known there was even the slightest chance of kids being in those chase vehicles, I never would've agreed to the mission."

"I take it that's when you walked away?"

"Well, not exactly. A few days later, when my tour was up, I hopped a ride on a C-130 out of Kabul to Bagram, then got stuffed into a chartered 747 with a few hundred jarheads heading in the same direction."

"A few hundred? That had to be an interesting flight."

"I'm not sure *interesting* is the right term, but trust me, every Marine remembers their final trip home. Unfortunately, I would remember mine for a completely different reason," Bunker said, pausing. "Anyway, we left Bagram and landed in Munich, where we needed to change crews and refuel. So there were a few hours to kill. As I'm sure you can guess, most of us headed to one of the dozen bars in the area. Now keep in mind, I was still trying to figure out what I was going to do, if anything, about the massacre. I had to be careful, though, because if the orders had come directly from the President, like I was told, then I was totally fucked if I said anything."

"What did you decide to do?"

"The only thing I could do at that point—drown my sorrows in a case of beer. A group of us swarmed this hole in the wall and I took a seat at the end of the bar, planning to sit there and numb the pain. About an hour later, it all changed when Flapper came wandering in to meet up with some of his friends."

"Did he see you?"

"Nah. The place was packed. He was too busy with his buds to notice me. Since none of his pals were in uniform, I figured they must have been more undercover spooks like him. I sat there and watched him for over an hour as he pounded shots with the some of the local talent, trying to get his dick wet."

"I'll bet you were fuming."

"That's an understatement. When Flapper stumbled out back to take a leak in the alley, that's when I decided to get off my ass and go have a chat with the asshole."

"In the alley?"

Bunker nodded before more words arrived. "Like I said, the place was a total dive. Only one of the urinals worked, so the line for the head was a mile long. Some of the guys didn't want to wait and went out back to piss, like Flapper, which turned out to be my opportunity. His pals were busy getting hammered, so they didn't notice me following him outside. After I made sure we were alone, I approached him."

Apollo figured Bunker pummeled the guy, just like he would've done. "And?"

"He was still tapping a kidney when I took my knife and gutted him like a fish. I started with his balls and ended with his neck, enjoying every second of it. While he was bleeding out, I laughed in his face just like he did when I confronted him about the kids. At that moment, I thought I'd finally found peace, but of course it didn't last. Not when the ghosts have a key to your soul."

"Holy shit," Apollo mumbled, wondering what he would have done in the same situation. He didn't want to judge Bunker, as a civilian or as a lawman. Not when he didn't have a frame of reference to understand what it was like over there. Everyone knows war is far from perfect. Those who serve do what they need to do to survive, even in the back alley of a Munich bar. "Well, all I can say is Flapper had it coming. End of story. Those deaths were on his hands, not yours. I don't think anyone would blame you."

Bunker shrugged, not looking convinced.

"What about the investigation?" Apollo asked. "Someone had to notice the body."

"I'm sure they did, but we were long gone by then. You gotta remember, when they ship us stateside like that, it's basically a cattle car service. They don't track who's on what plane or hand out tickets. It's as close to anonymous air travel as you can get."

Apollo nodded. "Not much of a trail to follow."

"Roger that. Hell, they don't even bother with a head count before they take off again, because they know there isn't a grunt alive who would ever miss that connecting flight home. Plus, everyone's drunk off their ass, so it's a cluster-fuck anyway. But the brass doesn't care. There's plenty of time to sober up before landing in New York."

"So, that was the end of it?"

"Yeah, I sat in my seat and didn't say another word until I made it all the way back to Camp Pendleton. Then I was done."

"At least justice was served for those kids."

"Except for one problem. I was still alive—the butcher of children—walking around free. In the end, Sheriff, I killed those kids. No two ways about it. I couldn't sleep. I couldn't hold down a job. I hated myself and everything this country stood for. That's when I found The Kindred. They took me in and gave me an outlet for my rage."

Apollo exhaled, his mind taking in all the new facts. He wasn't sure what to say, so he turned to the first question that popped into his brain. "What ever happened with the Army Major?"

"Never saw him again. He's still out there. Somewhere. Probably a General by now."

CHAPTER 124

Sometime later . . .

Bunker gave the AR-10 rifle to Rusty after engaging the safety. "Are you sure you want to do this? It's not too late to head back to camp."

"I am. I'm ready."

Bunker wasn't keen on the idea, but he needed to let Rusty make his own decisions, even though he was the Mayor's grandson. When it comes to combat, who you are doesn't matter. It's what you're made of inside that counts.

Young men his age enlist every day, looking to find their place in the world. Some join up as a challenge or to pay for college; others do so out of a sense of duty. Regardless of the reason, Rusty had to be the one to make the call.

"I can do this," Rusty said, sounding as though he were trying to convince Bunker of his manhood.

"All right, then. Rule number one: you follow orders. And by that, I mean you do whatever Dicky and Burt tell you. Without question. They have more experience than you. They'll help keep you safe."

"I thought *you* were in charge?"

Bunker pointed at the trench. "I'll be busy down there, so you need to follow the chain of command. Otherwise, you need to head back to camp. So what's it going to be, Rusty?"

"I'll do what they say. I promise."

Bunker was both pleased and disappointed by the answer. Pleased that this kid had the stones to join the fight, but disappointed Rusty wasn't already in the saddle, heading for safety. "Pay attention closely. I've sighted this in for you based on the center of the clearing."

Rusty took the weapon in his hands. The excitement in his eyes was only matched by the nervousness oozing from his pores.

Bunker remembered the feeling well, his brain scrambling to maintain control of his body the first time he prepared for combat. "When you're ready to fire, be sure to disengage the safety and adjust for distance. And to do that—"

"—I use the marks on the crosshairs," Rusty said before Bunker could finish his sentence. "Just like when Grandpa and I were out hunting. He showed me how to do it when I was like twelve."

"Those are called mils. But yes, just like when you're hunting. If the target is beyond the center, you aim higher with the reticle. If it's closer, you aim lower. I'd suggest keeping it simple with two aim points: the enemy's forehead or his nuts. Then you'll hit somewhere near center mass, depending on which distance adjustment you need."

"Okay, I can do that."

"Most of them will be along the front to start, so aim for their balls. Remember to breathe and control your fire. This isn't like a bolt-action 30-06. This is a semi-automatic, so that means—"

"One round each time I pull the trigger."

"Exactly. With twenty rounds in the magazine," Bunker said, realizing Rusty wasn't as green as he first thought. He didn't want to insult the kid's intelligence, but needed to make sure the new recruit was prepared. Better to oversimplify than to leave something out. That's how young men find themselves on the 'X'.

"You know how to change these, right?" Bunker asked, holding up one of the eleven magazines sitting next to Rusty on a small, flat rock. He wanted to give the kid a bigger stack, but he needed to split the rest of the 7.62 magazines equally with the other snipers.

Rusty pointed at the side of the weapon. "Just press this release and then pop in a new one."

"That's correct. There'll be a lot going on, but if you keep your shit together and focus on each target, you'll be okay. Just remember which one is me, okay?"

Rusty nodded. "You'll be the man without a uniform."

"Roger that. If you see me, aim somewhere else. Just wait for the targets to wander out of the smoke cloud."

"What if they try to come up here?"

"They won't. It'll be complete chaos down there after Albert's Bufotoxin takes away their eyesight."

"That's the milky white stuff he took from all those toads, right?"

"Part of it. The rest is a little magic known as chemistry."

"Albert really seems to get off on all that chemistry stuff."

"Lucky for us, he's damn good at it. Otherwise, I don't where we'd be right now."

Rusty turned his focus lower, staring at his shoes. "Maybe I should have done more studying in high school. I'd be more use right now."

Bunker realized he'd played right into the pity party taking control of Rusty. Negative thoughts were that last thing the kid needed, especially when they were wrapped inside a cocoon of self-doubt. A redirect was needed. Something a little more uplifting. "We all have our gifts, Rusty. From what I hear, yours is that racing bike. I don't know how you do it. That takes a lot of dedication and some long, hard hours on the road."

Rusty shrugged, his tone turning cynical. "Like that's worth anything anymore. It's not like there's ever going to be another Olympics. Talk about a waste of time."

"We don't know that, Rusty. Things could be a lot different out there, versus here."

"Still, my gifts, as you call them, are pretty useless."

Bunker could see the pain oozing from the kid's pores. He figured the pity patrol had just showed up to cover up his nervousness—a smoke screen, if you will. Bunker had seen it before. Countless times. Everyone reacts differently when preparing for a deadly showdown. Panic and fear are never easy to control, but it is possible to smooth out the rough spots and remain focused. It starts with leadership—Bunker's leadership. Those in charge must figure out what motivates each person under their command, then use it to help them find their confidence.

Confidence alone can keep a person alive, even more so than a loaded assault rifle. In fact, all the weapons and all the training are useless without confidence. "You did a fabulous job today with those toe-poppers. It took a lot of guts and smarts. Most men would have walked away, but you stepped up. That shows me what you're made of. You should be proud of yourself. I know I am."

Rusty didn't respond, looking as though the pep talk was failing to rally his spirits.

Bunker decided to try a different strategy. "Rusty, you may not believe this now. But as you get older, you'll learn that everyone second-guesses themselves. It's human nature, especially after the fact. Like they say, hindsight is 20/20. Everyone wishes they could go back and do things differently."

"Yeah, but you know how to fight and do all that bomb stuff. All I know is how to take a corner in a race so you don't get tangled with the racer next to you."

"Look, I may not be the smartest man. Hell, I may not even be a good man. But one thing I do know is that you can't choose your destiny. It chooses you. I'm living proof of that. All you can do is go along for the ride and make the best decisions possible. It's about trying to become the best version of yourself you can. Everything else is a guess."

Rusty brought his eyes up. "Everyone looks up to you and does what you say. Me, I'm just a nobody."

"Hey, that's not true. You're an extremely valuable member of this team. You always watch out for the boys and Megan, plus you take on the tasks nobody else will. Every squad needs a man like you. I, for one, know we wouldn't have gotten this far without you."

"Thanks," Rusty said, his tone sounding less depressed.

"Right now, we work as a team and take care of business. Nothing else matters. But we have to do it together, and we do it one step at a time. Then we'll worry about the rest later. Can you do that?"

"Okay."

"Because success is only achieved through teamwork and dedication."

"And hard work."

"Yes, hard work brings it all together."

Rusty hesitated for a short minute, his face looking numb. "Can I ask you a question, Jack?"

"Sure. Anything."

"Do you ever get scared?"

"Yeah. Sure. Everyone does."

"Really? You?"

"Fear is your friend, Rusty. We need it. It's what keeps us alive. But you can't let it take over. It'll paralyze you. That's what I meant earlier when I said you gotta keep your shit together. When you start to feel it get out of control, take some long breaths and focus on the next thing you need to do. I won't lie. It's not gonna be easy, but if you don't panic, you'll get through this. Do you understand what I'm saying?"

"Yeah. I think so. I get those same feelings right before every race."

"And you do fine, right?"

"Usually."

"This is no different," Bunker said, glossing over the truth—at least the part of it that might get Rusty killed.

"What if they bring tanks?" he asked, leaning over the log in front of them. He pointed at the bottom of the hillside leading to their position. "Wouldn't take much to get up here."

Bunker knew they would bring tanks, but didn't want to scare the kid. He aimed a finger at the trench they'd dug with the TNT charges. "That's what the ditch is for." The twenty-yard-wide channel sat a good fifty yards in front of them, running left to right across the head of the meadow. "They'll be focused on me and the truck down there. They won't even know you're here until it's too late. That's why you guys don't shoot until after Apollo detonates. It's critical that you keep your head down until the charges are finished."

"Got it. No shooting until the charges go off," Rusty said, his tone purposeful, almost as if he were trying to convince himself he could do it.

"Then pick off whoever stumbles out of the smoke cloud. That's all you need to do." Bunker peered at the opening to the clearing, across the expanse. It was straight ahead, several hundred yards away. "The Sheriff won't set them off until everyone is inside."

Rusty locked his eyes on the entrance. "Past the choke point, like you said earlier."

Bunker realized he was preaching a bit, much like his old man used to do. He decided to tone it down. "Exactly. The terrain in the meadow is perfect. The minute I saw it, I knew what we were going to do. As long as the enemy is focused on me and we block their retreat, it'll be a slaughter."

"You really think they'll go for it?"

"If I were a betting man, I'd lay 10 to 1 odds that they will. When you're luring somebody into a trap, the key is to make sure you pushed all the right buttons first. If you can blind them with emotion, they'll take the bait. Every time. I made sure they got a good look at me in town, so I know they'll be coming. In full force, with any luck."

"And that's a good thing?"

"If they assume they are dealing with untrained civilians, then yes. Just like when the Soviets invaded Afghanistan. They thought they were taking on a bunch of helpless sheepherders," Bunker said, snickering. "You know, it used to piss me off that the rest of the world viewed America as nothing more than a bunch of fat, lazy people. I never thought that perception would come in handy, until today. The Russians will never expect any of this. But the timing has to be spot-on. And it all starts with the Sheriff," he said, pointing at the far side of the meadow, "and that entrance."

"Where is he from here?" Rusty asked, his eyes in search mode.

Bunker pointed to the left. "Straight up from end of the trench. See that thick green bush by that oak tree? To the right about ten yards."

Rusty took a second before he answered. "Oh yeah. I see him."

Bunker picked up the gas mask at his feet. "One last thing. If the wind shifts, use this and get the hell out of here. Keep low until you get to the horses."

"What about you?"

"I'll be okay. Just worry about yourself. Your number one job is to get back to camp safely. Understood?"

Rusty nodded but didn't say anything, his eyes in full attention mode.

CHAPTER 125

Bunker made his way to the left, working across the hillside to the next sniper. Burt was manning the second station, his hands inspecting the stack of reserve magazines. He, too, had one of the AR-10 rifles from Tuttle's place. "Any questions, Burt?"

"Just one," he said, striking a Wyatt Earp pose with the butt of the rifle on his right hip, barrel pointing toward the sky. His eyes, face, and chin looked ready, but Bunker knew from experience that appearances could be deceiving. Usually when the mayhem starts. "When do I get to kill me some of them Russians?"

"Soon. I just need to make sure everyone is ready up here, then I'll get this party started. It's imperative that you keep your position hidden until Apollo sets off the charges."

"Easy pickin's," Burt said, turning his eyes to Apollo's position. "The Sheriff better take good care of my rifle over there. I'm gonna expect it back in one piece."

"He will. Thanks for working with me on this. I know it's not what you wanted, but we all have a job to do."

"I hope you realize, Bunker, I could've done Apollo's job without breaking a sweat. It ain't rocket science, you know. Just push them red buttons, then aim and shoot at whatever comes out of the smoke."

Bunker went into spin mode, needing the brute to remain committed to the mission. False praise is almost as powerful as fake confidence when you're manipulating a short-tempered man with severe ego issues. "I never had a doubt, Burt. Not for a second. But I need you here, to keep an eye on the Mayor's grandson." He swung his attention to Rusty's position, twenty yards to their right. "You're a lot more mobile than Apollo."

Burt laughed. "That's an understatement. Has he ever heard of a salad?"

Bunker ignored the comment. "If this shit goes sideways, I need you to make sure Rusty gets back to camp in one piece. We'll figure out a Plan B later. You with me?"

Burt straightened his posture with his shoulders back, almost looking the part of an honorable recruit. "Sure, I can do that," he said. "But what if the kid don't listen to me?"

"He will. I made sure he knows you're in charge."

"He'd damn well better," Burt said, bending down to pick up the gas mask he'd been assigned. "What if they have these as well?"

"They won't. Troops hate to lug them around unless they're expecting a gas attack. Which they won't. They think they're dealing with a bunch of backwoods farmers."

"I hope you're right," Burt said, putting the mask down. He adjusted the rifle in his grip. "But either way, I'm taking out my share of Russians. Fuck 'em."

* * *

Dicky was next. The burly man was busy digging into sniper's nest number three when Bunker arrived. He, too, was armed with an assault rifle, only his was an AR-15 chambered with 5.56 rounds stuffed into a thirty-round magazine. His reserve stack of ammo stood taller than Rusty's. Smaller rounds meant less damage with each shot, but Bunker was sure his friend could handle it. The quietest of men are usually the most focused and, by extension, the most dangerous. For the enemy, that is.

"Any questions, Dicky?"

"Just one. What if the charges fail?"

"Then this is over before it starts."

"I can probably shoot some of the Tannerite from here," he said, holding the rifle in a shooting position with his right eye behind the scope. "As backup."

"You could, but that won't help with the entrance. The TNT along the front must blow first; otherwise, the rest of our plan is useless."

"In that case, what about the others?" he asked in a terse tone, looking at Burt, then Rusty.

"I think you already know."

Dicky flared an eyebrow, looking sure of himself. "Focus on the Mayor's kid first."

"Copy that. I told him to do whatever you said, so get him outta here and keep him safe. The Sheriff and Burt can fend for themselves. We'll rally back at Tuttle's place."

"What about Dustin?" Dicky said, looking in the opposite direction. Dustin had been assigned to sniper position four, halfway between Dicky and Apollo. "Ten bucks says he's outta here the moment the Russians show."

"I'll go see where he's at. But I needed to check in here first."

"I'm good. Thanks."

"Never had a doubt, my friend," Bunker said, letting a thin smile take over. It vanished as soon as his thoughts turned to Dustin. "Now scarecrow on the other hand…"

"I've been watching him. He looks a little nervous. I think he misses his boy Albert."

"Probably," Bunker said, letting out a short chuckle. Dicky was the quietest man in the group, but when he did speak, it was always memorable. "That's why I'm chatting with him last. He's the weakest link."

"Which is why you gave him the 30-06," Dicky said in a matter-of-fact tone, his expression indicating he agreed with the decision.

"He's not gonna hit much, anyway. No reason to waste one of the true assault weapons."

Dicky nodded, his voice turning to a whisper. "Anything he takes out will be a bonus."

Bunker slapped the big man on the back, friendly like. "Great minds think alike, brother."

Dicky hesitated, his face indicating there was another question coming.

"I know that look," Bunker said. "Come on, out with it."

"You said before about them wanting to take you alive, but how will you know for sure?"

"Well, the obvious clue will be if they start shooting as soon as they see me."

"That's what I'm worried about. We packed the Land Rover pretty full."

"I doubt that'll happen."

"But what if it does?"

"Then I won't feel a thing."

"How can you be so callous about all of this?"

"It comes with the job. You get used to it," Bunker quipped. "But in all seriousness, our strategy is sound if everyone does their job. If something goes wrong, you know what to do."

"Get Rusty back to Tuttle's."

"There's plenty of food and supplies there, plus we fortified the place."

Dicky stood frozen. Still unsure.

"Look, I know you have your doubts, Dicky, but that's normal. I've got my share, too. Even though military strategy is rarely sound, it's always predictable. To a fault. First, they'll send the tanks in, then the infantry, then command will arrive once the area is secure. The key will be how the tanks approach. If they slow about halfway and spread out wide, that'll indicate I'm right. They'll send the infantry ahead next to cover me on multiple fronts, with the tanks hanging back on overwatch. Then it's hook, line, and sinker, my friend."

"What if the tanks don't spread out?"

"Then they'll stay in triangle formation and take the offensive. At that point, I'll have to make some adjustments before Apollo does his thing. I can't let them fall back into a hedgehog."

"Hedgehog?"

"It's a three-sided defensive formation where the tanks back up to each other like a pinwheel, with their cannons pointing out in three directions. It's done to protect their six and give them 360 degrees of coverage. If that happens, we probably lose. I'll surrender at that point."

Dicky nodded slowly. "Okay. Got it. Thanks."

Bunker realized the big man wanted it straight, not sugar-coated. Full disclosure was obviously important to him. "Are we good?"

"We're good."

"Then I'd better get moving. Daylight's burning."

Dicky held out his hand for a shake. "Been a pleasure, Jack."

"Likewise." Bunker took the man's enormous palm in his. "I don't say this often, but I want you to know, you would have made one hell of a Marine."

* * *

"How you doing?" Bunker asked Dustin when he reached the skinny man's position behind an eight-foot-tall rock.

"I'm not so sure about this," Dustin answered with shortness in his breath. His left shoulder was leaning against the turquoise-colored boulder, whose size and shape was roughly that of an outhouse.

Its surface was pitted, as though someone had used it for target practice—a few thousand rounds' worth. It also had a recessed groove running north and south, probably from centuries of erosion. It reminded Bunker of the edge along an almond shell—one that's cracked and ripe enough for picking.

If he were a fictional giant, he could finally end that dreaded Almond Duty once and for all by wrapping his arms around the boulder and squeezing it. It would split in half down the middle, freeing the bounty inside. The bounty being the end of his nightmares.

The giant rock was the best cover in the area—large enough for stickman and a few friends to hide behind during a firefight. It was also the most logical place for a sniper to hide, which is why he didn't want Rusty assigned to it. The Russians might blindly target the rock, assuming any of them could see well enough to do so. It wasn't that Dustin was expendable, just older. Old enough to stay low or bug out if the Russians targeted his location. Plus, his skinny frame would give the enemy less to shoot at. An unlikely bonus, but a bonus nonetheless.

"I hope you know, I totally suck at shooting," Dustin said, with the bolt-action rifle slung in front of his nonexistent chest. His hands were holding the weapon with a light touch, almost as if it were toxic.

Bunker waited for the man's eyes to find his before he spoke. "You'll be okay. If it gets too intense, this boulder will protect you."

"What if I miss?"

"Then you miss. It happens. More than most people think. That's why we call it spraying and praying. But remember, we have four snipers, plus Apollo on the TrackingPoint. I'll be down below doing my thing, so all you need to do is keep firing until every target you see has been neutralized. We have plenty of ammo."

Dustin kept his lips silent, his eyes bursting with terror.

"But please, verify what you're shooting at before you pull the trigger. If it doesn't have a Russian uniform, then aim somewhere else."

"Don't worry, I won't shoot you. I'm not that stupid."

Bunker was a little surprised the man caught his meaning so quickly. Maybe Dustin's mind wasn't as crippled with fear as Bunker assumed. "I appreciate that. You've got your mask and you know where the horses are, right?"

Dustin shot a glance at the top of the hill behind him. "Yep. One for each of us."

"Don't be a hero, Dustin. If my plan falls apart, get the hell outta here and head back to camp. That's where we're all gonna meet."

Dustin nodded. "The rally point."

Bunker put a hand on the skeleton's shoulder. He squeezed it twice. "You'll do fine. Control your fire and verify your targets. If we all do our job, we'll get through this."

"Thanks," he said, his tone still unsure.

"You know you could've left with Albert?"

"I thought about it, but I wanna help. I really do. I just can't keep my hands from shaking."

"Just hit what you can. The scope's all set."

"Head shots, I assume. Like in *Call of Duty* on the Xbox."

"Actually, I'd suggest you aim for their stomachs. That way you should hit something, whether you're a little high or low."

"That makes sense. Stomachs, not heads."

"Remember, those 180 grain bullets go out at 2,700 feet per second. They'll deliver a truckload of force when they reach the target."

"What if I only hit part of them or something?"

"It won't matter. These rounds can take down a seven-hundred-pound elk, so they'll handle a pudgy Russian, no problem. Wherever you hit them, they're gonna feel it."

"Elk, huh?"

Bunker let out a fake grin, needing to stoke the man's confidence a bit more. "Oh, yeah. I'm pretty sure the 30-06 has killed more elk than any other cartridge on the planet. It'll do the job, if you do yours."

"I'll do my best."

"I'm sure you will. We all have the utmost confidence in you. By the time we're done today, all the vodka in the world won't help the assholes who come marching in here. They'll wish they never set foot in our neck of woods."

"Focus. Do my job. Control my fire," Dustin said in a mumble, nodding with each phrase.

"I need to get into position. Any questions before I go?"

"No, not really. But that towel you wanted is in the truck. It's behind the driver's seat on the floor. Almost forgot to tell you."

"Good, I'll grab it with the radio. Anything else?"

"No. I'm good, I think."

CHAPTER 126

Stephanie King couldn't steady her breathing as she navigated the Land Rover over the uneven terrain. Air flowed in and out of her chest in short, rapid spurts, making her lightheaded in the process. The disorientation was getting worse with each roll of the tires, the blobs and flecks popping up in and out of her vision. She blinked rapidly, trying to clear them.

She wasn't sure what was happening, but didn't think it was the anxiety from driving the truck over the dangerous back roads. No, it was something else. Something inside her gut, twisting her intestines into a knot. It felt like she'd swallowed a grapefruit whole. The constriction was intense, making her want to throw up.

A half a mile later, Stephanie decided she couldn't take it anymore. She jammed on the brake and brought the ride to a stop on a steep incline.

"What are you doing?" Albert asked from the front passenger seat.

Stephanie kept her foot on the pedal to keep the vehicle from rolling backward. "Do you know the rest of the way?"

"You want *me* to drive?" Albert said, pointing a sausage finger at his chest.

"I'll do it," Victor said, his voice energized. "I'm an excellent driver." His butt was forward in his seat, with his hands pressing on the back of Albert's seat.

Stephanie ignored Victor's comment. She put the shifter into neutral and engaged the parking brake. Her vision cleared an instant later, but the shortness of breath continued. She cracked the driver's door open, hoping the fresh air would help.

"You're not getting out *here*, are you?" Albert asked in a sarcastic tone, his eyes locked onto the steep angle of the hood.

Stephanie slid out of the truck and set a course around the back of the truck. She carefully landed each step on the rocks lining her path to Albert. The soles of her shoes slipped twice, but she made it to her destination safely.

The fat man rolled down his window. "What are you doing, Steph?"

Her respiration calmed a bit, reinforcing her will to do what was in her heart. "I gotta go back. I need you to drive the boys the rest of the way."

"And how am I supposed to do that without breaking an ankle?" he asked in that obnoxious voice of his.

"Improvise, Albert. That's what I've been doing."

"I see that," he said, sticking his wide cheeks through the open window, peering down at her feet.

"It's a little slippery around back. Just take it slow."

Albert didn't say anything.

"Or you could try sliding across the seats. Either way, I need you to get the boys back to camp."

"Nah, I'll walk around," he said, using the handle on the inside of the door.

Stephanie took a step back as the door swung open.

Albert stepped out, locking eyes with her. This was the first time he looked at her and didn't make her skin crawl.

"Are you sure about this, Steph?"

She didn't hesitate. "Absolutely. If I don't make it back to Tuttle's, tell my son I love him. And I'm sorry."

"Okay," Albert said in a tentative, condescending tone. "If that's what you need me to do, I'll do it. But I gotta ask, Steph. If this is that dangerous, why the hell are you going back?"

"Because I have to. I've got this feeling in my stomach that the guys need me. Like their lives depend on it or something. It's hard to explain, but I'm sure of it. In fact, I've never been more sure of anything in my life," she said, planting a kiss on the Albert's overly round cheek. She wasn't planning to ever touch the man, but her heart made the decision and her lips obliged.

Albert froze for a second, looking stunned. When his expression cleared, he said, "You can't do this. He's not worth it."

"Yes, he is."

"No, he's not. I knew Bunker back in LA. He's not who you think he is. He's a stone-cold liar."

"I know he has a past, Albert. We all do. But sometimes, all someone needs is a second chance. Or someone to believe in them."

With that, she turned and headed down the hill, hoping to make it back to the meadow in time.

* * *

Bunker leaned the sword Dallas had given him against a tree at the entrance of the trench. He took off the backpack Albert had prepared for him and put it next to the sword. A lot was riding on Albert's skills, not just inside the pack, but across the trees and in the grass.

If Bunker had the time, he would have tested everything first. Since that wasn't an option, he needed to have faith in the brilliant man who was known for pushing his own agenda—even at the expense of others. Tin Man was a wild card to be sure, but Bunker didn't have a choice.

He picked up the pair of 1911s sitting to the right, ejecting their magazines for inspection. They were fully loaded with .45 ACP rounds. He shoved the mags back in and racked the slides before stuffing the semi-auto handguns inside the back of his pants. They needed to stay hidden. So did the reserve mags he'd already loaded into his pockets.

Tango neighed, snapping Bunker's attention to the saddle. Bunker made sure his gas mask was secure around the saddle horn before mounting the steed. The leather welcomed his underside as he nestled in for the short ride. Two clicks of his heels sent the animal forward, taking a direct path along the freshly exposed dirt of the trench.

Tango appeared to be ready, not showing any signs of fear. Of course, the four-legged freight train didn't know what was actually coming. But then again, maybe Tango could sense it. It wouldn't be the first time the two of them had connected on a psychological basis. Or maybe it was telepathy. He wasn't sure which term to use, not that it mattered.

There were other horses Bunker could have chosen to avoid putting Tango in mortal danger. On paper, it would have been the logical choice, one he figured most would make. But this wasn't about logic.

This was about friendship and, more importantly, trust. Specifically, trust in combat, something he never thought would happen with a horse. They'd come a long way together, forming a bond that only warriors know.

If this was to be their collective end, it seemed fitting they go out together. As a team. There's honor in a hero's death. Whether that hero walks with two legs or four, the sacrifice is just as profound. A warrior's death certainly beats the alternative—living until you're so old that nothing works anymore.

Just then, a vision flashed in his brain. Bunker saw himself lying on a semi-clean gurney in some run-down, government-sponsored nursing home in Florida, long after his tattoos had faded into one extended blob of history. His muscles were nothing more than a mush of skin, keeping him a prisoner on the soiled sheet below his spine.

He could almost feel the dryness of the plastic feeding tube that someone had crammed down his throat. He imagined his mind was a muddy blur, desperately trying to hold onto a single thought—*don't shit yourself today.*

Old age might be the goal of some, but not him. An honorable death was what he preferred. Today, or in the future, it was the only path he could see for himself. It's how his firefighter of an old man left this world—doing the right thing for others.

Bunker knew his death would never come close to balancing out all the wrong he'd done. Nor would it bring back the innocents who died tragically because of his decisions.

Even so, it might be enough to erase some of the evil deeds he'd done. Even if it only wiped out one of those horrendous acts, he could live with it. Or die with, if he chose to be technically correct.

He pulled back on the reins when they made it to the middle of the trench. The Land Rover was parked above his left shoulder, waiting for him to climb aboard.

"You ready, buddy? I know it's a big ask, but I need you to cover my six," he said, running his hand over Tango's neck, paying close attention to the time spent. He didn't want to waste a second, but some preemptive goodbyes must take place. It's never easy preparing for a worst-case scenario, but only a fool doesn't take advantage when the opportunity is there.

Tango didn't respond like he'd done many times before. Bunker was okay with it. He dismounted, then tied the leather reins to a stake he'd driven into the ground a few hours before.

He took a step forward and stood at attention. For some reason, he felt like a Drill Instructor addressing the platoon one last time before graduation. All that was missing was the form-fitting uniform and the brown campaign hat—a flat, broad-brimmed cover known as a Smokey.

Bunker found his deepest, most sincere voice before addressing Tango. "Listen up, Marine. No Houdini acts this time. Once we deploy, I need you to stand fast until the time comes."

Tango flipped his head to the side, nudging Bunker in the ribs. When the horse did it a second time, a warm sensation washed over Bunker, sending the nerve endings across his skin into a tingle.

Before his next breath, a deluge of new thoughts entered his brain, igniting a wave of clarity he'd never felt before. It brought tranquility to his heart. "Right back at ya, pal. It's been a pleasure."

Bunker turned and latched onto the knotted paracord he'd tied to the rear bumper of the Land Rover earlier. After a few arm pulls, he was out of the ditch and standing next to the truck.

He opened the door and grabbed the encrypted field radio and the white towel Dustin had left for him. He ambled to the front bumper, then used it to climb aboard the hood, then the cab, where he ripped off his shirt to get into character.

Bunker was sure the Russians were monitoring radio signals, trying to gather intel about Valentina's tattooed assassin. He'd purposely left the radio behind, with its frequency and encryption code already primed. All part of spoon-feeding the enemy.

Zero Hour had arrived. Time to make the call.

He found the power switch on the handheld and turned it on. Normally, he'd follow proper radio procedure while in the field, but he needed to toss protocol away and sound like an untrained civilian answering a distress call from a friend.

After a deep, cleansing breath, he was ready to season the appetizer with just the right amount of spice. He pressed the transmit button, hesitating a full second before speaking with urgency in his voice. "Bulldog, I hear you but you're breaking up. It must be that damn backup radio. I told you to take the other one."

Bunker let static-filled silence fill the airwaves before continuing the fake conversation. There are times when only one side of a communication is heard by the monitoring team. When it happens, they usually assume the unheard signal is too weak to pick up on their end.

Bunker continued his deception, planning to keep his follow-up transmissions short to avoid triangulation.

Direction is easy.

Distance takes time.

The first broadcast caught them by surprise, sending them into scramble mode. He wouldn't have that luxury again, not now that he had their full attention. He engaged the talk button. "Did you say Patterson's Meadow?"

He waited a few more seconds, then pressed transmit one last time. "Okay. Patterson's Meadow. Got it. Keep pressure on that wound until—" he said, releasing the button in mid-sentence. He shut off the radio a second later, hoping his unfinished communiqué would linger in their minds. If it did, then their imaginations would complete the sentence.

Whoever was listening should now report the details to the General, who in turn, would deploy his men. If dropping the interpreter from the church tower didn't get their attention, then leading them to the dead-end trail at the base of the mountain did.

There's nothing quite like a frustrated, frothing-at-the-mouth General, when you're baiting a trap for a ruthless warmonger.

CHAPTER 127

When a faint rumble landed on Apollo's ears, his pulse rate shot up to DEFCON ONE. His senses went on full alert, honing in on the sound, attempting to use the differences in timing, volume, and frequency to determine its direction.

The soundwaves carried an echo while they traveled across the expanse, confusing his brain for a moment. However, the answer found him a moment later—the low-pitched rumble was coming from the entrance to the clearing.

Bunker must not have heard it yet. He was still lounging on the hood of the Land Rover with his back against the windshield—the same position he'd been in ever since the phantom radio call.

Apollo put two fingers into his mouth and sent a shrieking whistle blast at the Land Rover below.

Bunker sat up in a hurry.

Apollo pointed at the entrance, jutting his arm forward several times to show urgency.

Bunker scrambled to his feet and stood on the cab, with the white towel in his hand.

The rookie snipers on the hill to the right must have gotten the message, too. Each of the four was busy with their rifles, disengaging the safety switches. They were elevated slightly from Apollo's position, with Rusty at the far end, but he could see them well enough to know each was ready.

Apollo brought the TrackingPoint scope to his eye and reviewed the targets on his side of the meadow. The Tannerite charges hadn't moved from the bases of their assigned trees. He didn't expect them to, but he needed to verify, nonetheless. He wasn't sure if the compulsion to check was some sort of deep-rooted anxiety response, but he felt better knowing that everything was where it was supposed to be, including him.

The long run of detonation cord had already been attached to the BART-2 blasting machine. It connected to the line of TNT charges mounted on the trees bordering the far side of the expanse. It also ran to the set of trees acting as sentry guards on both sides of the entrance. Dicky had prepped them to fall across the opening. If all went according to plan, they'd pin the Russians inside the kill zone.

Apollo cranked the handle on the BART-2 until the unit was fully charged, then settled in behind his cover and waited for the Russians to show themselves.

Now it was up to Bunker—the quarterback of this mission. Apollo's job was to wait for the former Marine to give him the signal, then detonate the charges. Until then, everyone needed to show patience.

"Stay hidden and stay frosty" were Bunker's exact words. Words from a man whose past was a jumbled mess of honor and criminality. Apollo wasn't sure what he was going to do about Bunker's unexpected confession, but it needed to wait until this operation was over.

A handful of troops were the first to appear at the mouth of the clearing, moving into view. They looked like a swarm of determined ants descending on discarded food. They spread into small fire teams, each taking successive positions along the trees lining the entrance.

Bunker began to wave the towel, indicating he would surrender to them. The sun was low and at his back, but Apollo figured the enemy could still see the white flag.

"This better work," Apollo mumbled, wondering if the advance teams would fire on Bunker or move forward. Bunker was betting his life on the latter, continuing to wave the flag as the rumble of man and machine grew progressively louder.

More and more Russians scrambled into view, leapfrogging their comrades in front of them.

"So far, so good," Apollo muttered, checking for activity on the hillside to his right. He didn't see anyone, which meant his friends were following orders until it was time to strike.

A handful of seconds later, Apollo identified the source of the rumble: tanks—three of them, their tracks tearing up the soil lining the entrance. They approached in a staggered diamond formation, each surrounded by a wall of well-armed infantry.

Apollo estimated at least five hundred troops were flooding the area. If it weren't for the tank engines, he figured he'd hear the clatter of the tactical gear and boots from a thousand legs pounding the dirt.

The visual was both impressive and frightening. Bunker never gave Apollo a force estimate, but the man did say to be prepared—a significant number would be arriving. In fact, Bunker was counting on it.

Bunker slid two steps back on the Land Rover's cab, while continuing the white flag signal. His subtle retreat meant that it was almost time.

Apollo moved his hand to the side of the blasting machine, positioning his fingers a half-inch away from the recessed fire buttons. He forced down a gulp, then began to take long, slow breaths to keep his hand steady. He knew once his fingers touched the plastic, the war would start. Only God could stop it then.

A convoy of six low-profile vehicles arrived in a single file behind the throng of foot soldiers, crawling through the entrance. Apollo didn't recognize the make or model of the four-door trucks. Each had tinted windows and looked like a personnel carrier, but they certainly weren't Humvees.

Two of them had suites of antennas rising up from their hulls. He figured the extra technology meant they were the command vehicles—the kind of rides that ferried a soldier of significant rank. Hopefully, one with a few stars on the collar.

The tanks broke formation and began to spread out wide into a single line, just as Bunker had predicted. Apollo worried that if the tanks continued to widen their spacing, they would hit some of the toe-poppers or run into the pressure plates he'd helped bury in the dirt.

Just then, the tanks stopped churning mud with their tracks, coming to a halt just past the midpoint of the grass, where the muck was thickest. The rain-infused mud may have been why they chose to stop their advance, instead of rolling closer to Bunker.

The infantry continued their deliberate march toward the tattooed man, passing between the wide gaps in the tank formation.

Apollo checked the entrance. The flow of troops arriving had dwindled to a trickle. He brought his eyes back to the man waving the white flag from atop his perch.

"Come on, Bunker. What are you waiting for?" Apollo said to the air around him.

Before the Apollo's next breath, Bunker tossed the flag into the air and dropped into a backwards roll as planned, disappearing from the Russians' view.

Apollo drove his fingers into the detonator. He felt them land squarely on the twin buttons as he ducked for cover, keeping his eyes on the tallest of the trees guarding the area.

The TNT charges at the bases of the trees exploded simultaneously, both on the far side of the meadow and along the entrance. Dicky's pre-cuts guided their height into position, felling them toward the middle. The trees across the front landed together in a crisscrossing heap, blocking the Russians only part-way out of the kill zone.

The other pines carried the toxic chemicals in their upper limbs, rigged in plastic bottles by the tree-climbing boys. When the tall spires hit the surface, the bottles split apart, spraying their deadly mixture of ammonia, bleach, and chlorine across the army of invaders. Bottles of the amplified Bufotoxin gas were also among the chemical delivery, something Albert had cooked up.

Two of the homemade napalm bombs went off from the tree limbs hitting their pressure pads, spraying the area with flaming dollops of diesel gas. The brown grass caught fire and quickly spread, while the patches of green grass smoldered with fury, filling the area with a thick wall of black smoke.

Apollo put on his gas mask after the first wave of screams hit his ears. The bloodcurdling yelps meant soldiers were being cooked alive by the gelatinous napalm. Others around them choked in panic, blindly stumbling along in the cloud of chemicals.

When Apollo locked eyes on the trench, he saw Tango's long nose coming his way. The horse was at top speed, with Bunker riding low in the saddle. The combination of smoke, tall grass, and the deep trench provided the perfect escape, keeping both man and beast below the threat line.

Above the trench, Burt, Rusty, and Dicky were now visible with weapons in hand, waiting for the first targets to emerge from the gas cloud. Apollo couldn't see Dustin behind the oversized boulder, but that wasn't surprising. He was only a sliver of a man.

Apollo heard a multitude of toe-poppers detonate. He brought the TrackingPoint rifle to his shoulder, visualizing hundreds of soldiers in a blind panic, unwittingly running into more of the improvised anti-personnel mines Rusty had set.

The Sheriff aimed the precision-guided scope on the Tannerite charge farthest away from him. He tapped the weapon's Tag button to paint the intended target, then pressed and held the trigger. The moment the center of the reticle found the container of Tannerite once again, the fire control system sent the round spinning down the barrel at supersonic speed.

It reached the target in milliseconds, causing an explosion that tore a chunk out of the tree's base. The pine tree toppled over, delivering yet another round of gaseous hell onto the troops. The Sheriff repeated the process again and again, each time bringing yet another tree down under the guidance of Dicky's lumberjack skills.

More of the napalm bombs exploded as tree limbs and Russian boots found their respective pressure plates. The soap flakes carried the sticky diesel onto more victims. Gas, fire, and smoke were now covering most of the clearing as more toe-poppers went off.

On the left, Apollo heard an even louder explosion. It came from the front corner of the meadow. Russian boots must have triggered one of the cable spindle bombs, sending out a barrage of copper shards from its center. The homemade claymore mine was a work of genius, its shrapnel tearing through bone and flesh.

One Tannerite charge remained—the one closest to Apollo's position. He brought the scope to the base of the tree and tagged the center of the bomb with the laser-guided optics. However, before he could bring the reticle to bear, something slammed into his shoulder.

A splash of red hit his face, just as a searing pain tore through his body. He twisted backwards, letting out a grunt-filled scream before landing on his back in a thud.

When he turned his head, he saw the impact point. His right shoulder. Only runny chunks of meat remained. It was mostly muscle and tendon hanging loose in meaty strands, looking like something out of a Clive Barker movie.

Three feet away was an arm lying in the grass—his arm, with the bicep torn apart. That's when the pain skyrocketed, his eyes registering what had happened.

Before his next thought arrived, dirt and grass exploded within inches of his feet. He flipped over and crawled on his belly, dragging himself with one arm into a natural recess in the terrain.

The pain never took a second off as he fell into the hole head-first to escape the gunshots. The speed and number of bullets increased, pelting the area from what he could only assume was an automatic weapon.

The gunfire must have been coming from the clearing, since the Clearwater crew only had semi-autos. It meant at least one enemy soldier had survived the gas cloud—a straggler, as Bunker put it—and was able to see, despite the blinding Bufotoxin and other chemicals.

Apollo knew there could be more. He had to stop them before more Americans got hurt. He felt around the dirt with his left hand, but the TrackingPoint rifle wasn't there.

Shit! He must have dropped it when the bullet tore him apart. He didn't remember seeing it by his severed arm, but it couldn't have flown far.

Apollo turned to his side and pushed one-handed to raise his body. He crawled to his knees, planning to slink out of the hole and recover the rifle. All it would take was one good arm to aim the weapon. The precision firearm would do the rest.

A smarter man would have stopped to put a tourniquet around his wound, but Apollo's mind was focused on something else—his friends. If the enemy was able to find him with their rifles, then Rusty and the rest of the gang would soon suffer the same fate.

Apollo made it about two yards before his strength vanished. His face slammed into the dirt, trapping his one good arm underneath.

He could feel the thump of his heart across his body, its pace ever-decreasing, setting his life-force free from the wound in spurts. The Reaper was near, waiting in the shadows, ready to pounce after the final moment of life departed.

Apollo wanted to take in the beauty of the sky one last time. He tried to turn over, but couldn't find the strength. All he had left was his imagination. Well, that and the memory of a single, magical kiss.

Allison's face appeared in his thoughts a split-second later. In his vision, she tilted her head and brought her lips to his. Her touch sparked a blissful sensation—one he needed to hold onto forever.

When the air in his lungs withered to a stop, death came, filling his vision with permanent black.

CHAPTER 128

Bunker slid down the saddle to the side of Tango, keeping his profile thin as his ride tore up the incline extending from the trench. When Bunker's feet landed in the grass along the slope, he took the gas mask from the saddle horn.

"Yaw!" he yelled, slapping the horse on the hindquarters to initiate a gallop. Tango flew up the hill in a flail of hooves, passing Apollo's sniper hide before he disappeared into the trees at the top.

Bunker slipped the backpack over his left shoulder, then put on the gas mask, with its virgin filter ready to go to work. Not only would it protect him from Albert's toxic gas, but it would also *smoke the smoke*, as his DI used to say. Gas masks can be used in a fire, but the filter would clog sooner than normal. He'd have to work quickly, especially now that the gunshots had started.

The sword was of little use. He left it behind, preferring the lethality of the twin 1911s stuffed inside the back of his waistband.

He pulled out one of .45s and took off in a crouched-over sprint, aiming for the path Burt and he had lined with the logs. If he chose the wrong entry point, he'd most certainly land a foot on one of the pressure plates they'd buried beneath the surface.

Bunker figured the rounds tearing up the countryside were coming from his crew. There wasn't time to verify, not with the tanks on standby. He figured their three-man crews had buttoned up by now, eliminating their exposure to the gas. It would decrease their lateral visibility, but not enough to stop them from bringing the main cannon online. Its infamous autoloader would then take over, prepping the breach with the first round of death and destruction.

He remembered most of the details from training videos. If he recalled them correctly, the carousel held twenty-two rounds of powder and projectile, with a maximum fire rate of eight per minute. The autoloader would spin the roundabout to deliver the next ordnance into position. The 125mm projectile would then be raised level to the breach and rammed inside. The powder charge would follow next, shoved in behind the shell before the breach was closed.

The autoloader is fast and merciless, much like its tank commander, who selects each target for annihilation. Bunker figured the tank boss would wait until the smoke cleared before he gave his Gunner the order to fire. Each time that happened, one of the Clearwater crew would meet their end.

A dead soldier lay at the midpoint of the entry path with a large chunk of his head missing. Someone on the ridge must have taken the man down. Bunker figured the shot came from Dicky or possibly Burt, the others less reliable due to age or other factors.

If it was Rusty, then the young man just popped his cherry and was no doubt dealing with the emotional aftermath.

Bunker picked up the pace, dodging flames along the trail.

When a tall, camo-wearing shadow presented itself, he pulled the trigger on the 1911. The .45 blew half of the soldier's face apart, sending his body flopping sideways. The Russian's size eleven boots were the last items to disappear into the veil of smoke.

Another hostile came into view directly ahead, its eyes swollen into a thin, horizontal line. They were bleeding, just like Albert had predicted.

The enemy's incapacitation didn't stop Bunker's trigger finger, or the next bullet from leaving the pistol, tearing apart the enemy's throat in a swash of red.

Another round sent, another KIA, just as it should be, Bunker thought. *Kill or be killed. The math doesn't get any simpler than that.*

He continued his assault, picking off targets left and right—all of them in distress. Everywhere he looked, it was more of the same: Russian blood, burns, blisters, blindness, and body parts missing. All of it due to the manmade booby traps they'd encountered.

When the first magazine ran out of ammo, Bunker changed pistols, working his way to the last known location of the tank platoon. Exchanging weapons was faster than replacing mags, the latter of which he would do once the backup gun was empty.

The exact position of the tank platoon was a guess at this point. The smoke provided the cover he needed, as long as the tank crews hadn't retreated into a hedgehog formation. If they had, the battle was already over.

Bunker needed them running solo, hopefully in a panic, giving him access to the most vulnerable part of the armored vehicle—the rear grille.

A climb up the tracks was possible, too, but you never knew if or when the driver might spin the tank, turning your ass into what the Marines called a "crunchie." He'd seen his share of bodies driven into the dirt. Usually only a sponge or mop bucket was needed to clean up the pieces, if they could be found at all.

Bunker would never forget the aftermath of a new recruit who thought sleeping in the recess under the tracks was a good idea. All the kid wanted was some peace and quiet. That he got, until a member of the maintenance crew decided to take it out on an early morning fueling run. The resultant mess was beyond description.

Whether a tank crew panicked or the infantry failed to give them the right of way, the men inside the metal beast didn't care. All four directions belonged to them—an unwritten rule—and everyone else needed to get the hell out of the way.

Bunker took down three more Russians who wandered into the kill zone. It took four shots instead of three because one of the bodies didn't go down as quickly as the others.

He pressed on, keeping his eyes scanning for targets. A few feet of visibility were all he had, but it was enough, as long as the filter on the gas mask held up until the effects of Albert's chemical warfare faded.

Others might have had trouble with the endless screams or the bloody smears of death, but he hardly noticed. For him, self-preservation took care of his mental state—and his focus. Everything else was secondary. Act, don't think was the mission objective now. If it moves, kill it.

He figured by now the airwaves were jammed with panic calls in Russian. The tank commanders, like everyone else, were blind from the smoke, hoping to receive orders from Command.

The Command personnel had their own issues, hunkered down in the less than airtight GAZ Tigr trucks. The gas cloud had most certainly engulfed them, meaning the staff inside was battling for fresh air.

Some of the officers may have fled on foot, while others tried to back the vehicle up, only to run into the trees blocking the entrance. Dicky's precision cuts were a thing of a beauty, dropping the soaring pine trees exactly where they were needed.

Combine the trees with Albert's prowess for cooking up something wicked, and you had yourself the makings of an ambush—a term few veterans got to use, even after years of service.

It isn't often that assault plans run perfectly. When they do, it's called an ambush. They are rare, but they do happen, usually when the adversary is caught ill-prepared or they over-commit. In this case, it had been both.

Bunker figured he had run far enough to be inside the minefield's perimeter. He changed course, turning five degrees to hunt down the first tank.

The smoke lessened with each step toward the middle of the clearing. What had begun as a heavy black cloud was now a fading mist of gray. The mud from the rainstorm must have been the reason why, collecting near the low spot of the meadow.

Mud would temper the brushfire's advance, decreasing the smoke accordingly. Less smoke meant a dwindling advantage. Bunker needed to complete his objectives before the enemy adjusted.

He continued another ten strides before he spotted the first tank. It was parked perpendicular to his direction of travel, with its main gun low. He figured the Land Rover was its target, its location the Russians' only known fact. However, the gas cloud may have changed their priorities, shifting from offense to defense.

The other tanks weren't visible from his position, eliminating his worry about the hedgehog maneuver. The odds of success had just gone up in his favor, he estimated, climbing north of fifty percent.

Bunker ended his jog and brought the backpack around to his chest, with the upper pouch facing forward. He was about to put his hand inside to grab one of the socks covered in axle grease, but stopped when another troop wandered into his field of fire.

The solider stumbled like a drunken zombie, shifting from side to side as if the Earth was spinning too fast to keep his balance. The man's face had been deeply burned. It looked as though a flame thrower had melted the skin on one side—a gruesome sight to be sure, one Bunker could relate to. His neck scars had mostly healed, but his memory of the pain hadn't.

Bunker aimed the pistol and fired at the zombie man just as the Russian staggered to the left. The soldier never flinched, nor did he go down. The bullet must have missed, whistling into the forest beyond.

He fired again, this time taking out the soldier's eye in a spray of red, his camo-covered body hitting the ground hard. His legs flopped to one side, his boots twisting over themselves.

Bunker scanned the area again. This time it was clear. Time to take out the tank.

He knelt down in the mud for cover, putting the pack on the ground. He opened the zipper on the side compartment to liberate the pocket torch Dallas had found in Tuttle's kitchen.

The tube sock was next.

His fingers went in and wrapped around a glob of axle grease. The ooze covered his hand in slippage, but he was able to lock on and pull the thermite charge free from the pouch. After a quick press to his feet, he slung the pack around his shoulders and ran to the T-72.

When engaging a tank, a rear approach is the preferred angle of assault. The troops have view ports, like a periscope, but they are operated manually and are fraught with blind spots.

In order to stop Bunker's approach, their eyes would have to be looking directly at him when he broke through the smoke cloud. The odds were slim, he calculated, thanks to the chaos his friends had created across the expanse.

If it weren't for the blinding chemicals and toxic fumes, the tank commander would have popped the hatch above his seat and jumped on the machine gun, mowing down everything in sight. Including Bunker.

Instead, the commander was likely too busy attempting to break through the overlapping radio chatter. When troops panic, the airwaves congest, just as Bunker needed. Tank platoons are only effective when they can share information and work as a team. That can't happen if pandemonium takes over.

A single tank is a sitting duck, especially without infantry support to protect its six. Three tanks are only marginally better if they're spread out and unable to communicate, or locate targets.

Scratch my back is the term used when a tank commander needs assistance from another crew. The coaxial machine gun makes quick work of any would-be hitchhikers, assuming the support tank can range the targets clearly.

Bunker was tempted to plant the greasy sock on the rear-mounted exterior fuel drums. It would have been quicker and made one hell of a fireball, but it wouldn't be nearly as effective as what he had planned.

The autoloader's carousel was his intended target, located directly below the turret. Its inventory of explosives would destroy the tank from the inside out, including its unsuspecting crew.

He climbed onboard using the metal rails of the rear protection grille, passing between the two auxiliary fuel drums. He scampered to the main cannon and planted the sticky bomb near the center of the turret.

The mini-torch he carried fired on the first pull of its trigger, sending out a brilliant flame. It glowed orange, fighting for its life against a gust of wind that came out of nowhere, smacking Bunker in the face.

He figured the late afternoon thermals were the reason for the sudden burst, a typical change in the mountains. More flurries would be coming, hopefully in the same direction.

Bunker brought the flame to the sock, aiming for the center as the wind took a short respite. The intense heat burned through the layers of greasy cotton almost instantly, igniting the thermite inside.

He slid back a few feet as the white-hot reaction began to melt its way through the hull. He hopped off the tank and hit the ground running. A good amount of distance was needed before the thermite reached the—

BOOOOOM!

The pressure wave threw him forward, his legs somersaulting in front of his head. He landed in a twisted, uncontrolled dive, sliding end over end until he came to rest against one of the dead soldiers. It was the same man he'd shot in the eye.

"Holy fuck!" Bunker said in an uneven grumble, crawling to his knees. It felt like someone had smashed a baseball bat into his spine. He ran a quick body check, but found no blood or holes. Only the lingering ache from the impact.

He coughed as smoke entered his lungs for the first time. It was at that moment he realized the gas mask had been thrown clear. He scanned the area, but couldn't see it. At least the pocket torch was still in his possession. So were both of the pistols in the back of his waistband.

The slight burning in his throat was due to Albert's toxic chemicals drifting his way. Distance, time, and wind had weakened their effects, failing to incapacitate his eyes or lungs completely. Even so, prolonged exposure would be an issue going forward. He needed a solution— something to slow it down— even if it was only temporary.

Random echoes of gunfire continued as he searched the one-eyed corpse for something he could use as a mask. There was nothing in the man's uniform pockets except lint, a picture of a huge, round woman with frizzy hair, and a half stick of gum.

Bunker removed the man's tactical vest, then took his canteen. That's when he noticed a pair of holes in the man's shirt, just under the armpit. One was on the front of the shirt, and the other on the back, clearly an entrance and exit point. The damage must have been made by Bunker's first shot—the bullet that missed when the man stumbled.

He stuck his finger inside the hole and tore off a long strip of cloth. He poured water on it from the canteen before tying it around his head, making sure it was snug over his nose and mouth. Then he stole the man's combat goggles and slipped them over his eyes. The thievery wasn't the best solution, but it would buy extra time.

Before he got up, a pair of soldiers broke through the thinning smoke and came at him from the left. Bunker dropped the pocket torch and grabbed both pistols from his waistband, firing numerous rounds at the attackers. The targets went down like cannon fodder, his rounds landing with precision.

It was only at that moment, the moment after he pulled the triggers, that he realized both men were unarmed and suffering the effects of the Bufotoxin. Their eyes were red and puffy, looking as though they'd taken blasts of tear gas to the face for hours.

Bunker pushed to his feet, still feeling the effects of the explosion. When he looked up, he saw the tank burning uncontrollably, its hull a mangled wreck of steel.

Somewhere inside those flames were the remains of the crew. Their violent deaths came without warning, but when you invade a proud country of what you assume are fat, lazy people, that's the fate you risk.

Sometimes, the softest of targets fight back with a vengeance, he said, mimicking something his fire team leader once told him.

He ran ahead to pick up his pack, then changed course for the next tank. It was possible the second tank commander may have given the order to move ahead, driving blindly to find better visibility. If they traveled too far, they'd end up nose down in the trench and useless.

If they reversed course, not only would they create a host of crunchies in their wake, they'd run into the felled trees blocking the entrance. Another option for them was swinging wide, but again, they'd run the risk of painting the meadow red with the blood of their comrades, or they'd find more of the IEDs Bunker and company had buried for them.

A brilliant flash went off at Bunker's eleven o'clock position. It was immediately followed by a booming blast, tearing into Bunker's eardrums. Instantly, an explosion broke through the haze of smoke on the right.

Bunker hit the deck, watching the billowing flames tunnel into the smoke-filled sky. He realized one of the tanks had just taken out the Land Rover parked by the trench. The charges Apollo had stuffed into the rear of the truck added to the explosion, hopefully taking out any Russians standing close.

The tank commander's decision to fire gave Bunker a fix on their location. He got up, set a course, and brought his vengeance to bear, sweeping a few degrees to the left to allow a rear approach.

He killed a few more soldiers along the way, most of them only half-alive. In reality, he was doing them a favor, saving them from a life of horrible disfigurement, or a painful death by asphyxiation.

The second tank was still buttoned up when he arrived. The tank commander hadn't popped the hatch to man the machine gun, nor were its tracks moving. He figured they were covering the area ahead for signs of resistance—resistance being the tattooed man who dropped the General's interpreter from the church tower.

Once again, he climbed onboard and planted the TH3-filled sock. He held the flame above the sticky bomb for a two-count, preparing himself for a quicker retreat. When he was ready, he lit the thermite and took off. By the time the intense chemical reaction melted its way through the hull, he was far enough away not to feel its explosive effects when the thermite ignited the rounds sitting in the autoloader.

"Two down, one to go," he mumbled as the wind picked up again. Only this wasn't a momentary gust like before. The change was sustained, roughly a moderate breeze, strong enough to push gas and smoke toward the entrance of the clearing.

Mother Nature had stepped up and was now protecting his team on the ridge. Unfortunately, there was a down side—he was exposed and without the cover of hovering smoke.

CHAPTER 129

Burt Lowenstein ejected a spent magazine, then grabbed another from the reserve stack of ammo. He jammed it into the lower receiver, pulled the charging handle back and let it snap loose to prime the chamber with a round.

This was the third magazine he'd loaded. Out of the dozens of rounds he'd fired thus far, he hadn't missed many, easily leading the scoreboard in kills—assuming, of course, anyone was keeping track, other than him.

He did miss one Russian early on when the gun jammed. It only took a few seconds to clear the misfire, but it did cost him the chance at claiming the first kill of the day. Dicky won that award, sending the Russian to an instant death when the bullet tore a gaping hole in the side of his head.

Up to this point, that first kill had been the most important death on the books. It kept the soldier from unleashing any more rounds at Apollo's position. Burt feared the Sheriff might have taken a bullet in that exchange. He hadn't seen any sign of the lawman since.

Just then, another Russian appeared from the smoke cloud, looking dazed and confused like the others. Burt brought the rifle into position and fired, hitting the target in the neck. Blood and tissue shot out in a wide pattern, adding to the run of blood around the trench.

It was almost too easy, feeling as though he was locked inside a massive video game where the good guys got to do all the shooting, while the bad guys did all the dying.

His first kill had sent a charge of adrenaline into his body, the likes of which he'd never experienced before. It was even more intense than the rush he'd felt after his one and only skydive at the age of twenty-three. He was sure both of those firsts would stick in his memory until the end of time.

Burt peered to the left to check on Dicky. Even though the big man had racked up the first kill, Burt figured he'd taken down at least twice as many. Granted, he was burning through three times as much ammo, but in the end, all that mattered was how many bodies he piled up in the record book.

Rusty wasn't much of a threat to the leaderboard. The Mayor's grandson had fired a few sporadic shots, but Burt wasn't sure the kid had hit anything. At least the boy was still dug in and trying.

Dustin bugged out shortly after the bullets started to fly, running away like the pencil-thin coward he was. Albert would have done the same, if he hadn't chosen to hitch a ride back to camp with Miss Sugar Tits and the annoying kids.

When another flurry of wind roared past him, not only did it whistle through the trees, but it pushed the leading edge of the smoke cloud away from the front of the clearing. The Land Rover was still engulfed in fire, though only its melted tires and a section of the drivetrain remained.

Two of the three tanks were now visible from Burt's elevated position. Their mangled hulls were ablaze, no doubt due to Bunker's tactical skills and Albert's prowess as a bomb maker.

Burt had felt the explosions and seen the flashes, but this was his first view of the actual results. Both Albert and Bunker knew what they were doing. Impressive to say the least.

He couldn't see the third tank. Not yet, but the wind hadn't finished its purge. The smoke's rollback revealed wave after wave of Russian bodies, almost as if a curtain was being pulled back at the start of a show.

Not a single victim had a gas mask, leaving the troops to suffer the wrath of Jumbo and his bag of tricks. Some were nothing more than a pile of lifeless, bloody meat, while others writhed in pain. A few were missing legs. Others were without arms after discovering the toe-poppers and homemade bombs buried around the perimeter.

Burt raised the rifle and began to pick off the injured soldiers on the ground. There were dozens of them to finish off, but he was up to the task. Each round brought satisfaction to his heart, driving the pressure in his chest a level higher.

His new rule was if it moves, shoot it, and that's exactly what he was doing. Each trigger pull sent more blood and guts into the air. Each subsequent death would add to the overall tally, earning him the title of lead badass.

Payback is a bitch when it's served up by a mechanic who's had enough of life's relentless disappointments. Today was his coming out party, one that would earn him the right to carry the TrackingPoint rifle with distinction.

He was tired of being the sweaty jerk that nobody liked. If he stayed true and completed the mission, he'd walk the streets of Clearwater as a legend. Something he knew would make his deceased father proud.

When this ambush was over, the next step would be to rally a posse of his old buds from high school. Someone needed to take on whatever troops were left in town. Bunker told him earlier that he didn't think it would be many, and judging by the bloodbath below, the man was right.

If the Sheriff had indeed taken a bullet, then the town would soon be in search of someone new to take charge. Granted, he didn't know Apollo's condition, but his gut was telling him the man was down. Permanently.

He'd still have to contend with Mayor Buckley, assuming the pressed suit was still alive after the stabbing. Burt had overhead Bunker and Apollo chatting earlier about the incident with Kenny King.

Even if Mayor Buckley pulled through, the man was a pussy and would never get his hands dirty. Not with the physical stuff. It wasn't his style. Buckley preferred to sit in his office and pretend he mattered, spying on everyone through the plate glass window.

That left Dicky, Jumbo, Rusty, or Dustin.

Burt ran through an imaginary checklist, realizing none of them were worthy candidates. They each had at least one deficiency that would disqualify them from consideration by the townspeople.

Dicky was built like a supertanker but preferred to stand in the shadows, not lead the masses. He was too reserved—the people would never respect him. So no worry there.

Jumbo was—well, let's face it, Jumbo. Nobody would ever take the fat-ass seriously. Sure, he had some smarts, even though he didn't always show it. But in the end, he was a pacifist. A coward. A man who could barely climb a set of stairs without having a heart attack. Nobody would ever choose him for anything, other than as a favorite in a donut-eating contest.

Dustin would snap under the pressure, both figuratively and literally. Burt had crapped bigger than him. It wouldn't take much to back down the scarecrow, so he was out.

The Mayor's grandson had promise, but the relentless athlete was much too young. If Rusty couldn't grow a beard, then he couldn't lead a town. Simple enough, Burt thought. In fact, that rule should be added to the town charter. Burt smiled after deciding that idea would be his first order of business when this was over.

A grin invaded Burt's mouth as his trigger finger continued to send rounds downrange, making tissue pop, guts fly, and heartbeats vanish. Once he was in charge, there'd be nobody to stop him. Not after what he'd done today.

The only person who could match him was Bunker—a man whose eyes gave away his soul. Burt could see it bubbling just below the surface every time he looked at him.

Bunker had one desire—to wander off into the woods and never be seen again. Sure, Bunker was more than capable and a worthy competitor, but the man was nothing more than a down on his luck drifter who preferred solitude.

That's what he was doing when he hooked up with Sugar Tits and her obnoxious kid— drifting, trying to stay off the radar.

Burt snickered while thinking about Bunker and Stephanie. Two prime examples of the kind of assholes who take fucking Amtrak. People who want to stay off the radar. Well, them and old geezers who hate to fly.

A better choice would have been the bus. Sure, it's slower and less comfortable, but effective. Something a true drifter would do.

Well, that and hitchhike.

Shit. His reasoning kept unspooling the more he dwelled on it. In the end, it doesn't matter how you disappear, just that you do.

Bunker was clearly running from something. Burt could sense it. That's all that mattered. There was zero chance Bunker would stick around. Zero. Nothing to worry about, he decided. Bunker was gone the second this was over. End of story.

Bang! Bang! Bang!

Burt continued firing at the wounded in the dirt, moving the scope from target to target with ease. The gas had devastated the troops, leaving Burt with only slow-moving targets to aim at. He kept his focus sharp, looking for a few more notches on his side of the ledger.

Something inside of him craved the next kill. He wasn't sure if it was becoming an instant addiction or some kind of new compulsion. Either way, it felt glorious and he needed more— something to fill the deep emptiness in his gut.

Before the next shot, a new thought tore into his mind. It was a vision of Stephanie rubbing Bunker's back while the group huddled together, reviewing the maps in Martha Rainey's house.

Stephanie's body language, eyes, and voice signaled her intentions—she was dripping wet, just aching to bed the man.

Burt knew that look. Her every thought was focused on one thing—Bunker slipping her the high, hard one—over and over—like some kind of street whore in heat.

He figured location didn't matter, either. She'd do it anywhere and at any time. Just the kind of woman a man like Bunker would like. Sure, her reputation as a freaky slut may have been part of Burt's assumptions, but it seemed likely, given all the clues.

Then there was Daisy. Serious, attentive, and easily engaged. The deputy seemed to go out of her way to spend time with Bunker. She was always standing close to the man with her eyes locked onto his, as if he was God personified.

It was disgusting to watch, but Burt didn't give a shit. She wasn't his type, either, but that didn't change the fact that the Deputy was enthralled with Bunker. It wasn't as obvious as Stephanie's sexual overtones, but it was there, in every subtle gesture.

Burt's conviction about Bunker taking off started to wane. He couldn't discount the sensual allure of Stephanie and Daisy. Both were attractive in their own way, sending out vibes that would snare most men. Even a troubled drifter, like Bunker. A man who'd probably tapped more ass than a professional basketball player.

"Shit, he might just stay because of them," Burt muttered between shots, realizing Bunker could be a threat to his plan after all.

He moved the scope up and to the right, bringing the reticle onto Bunker's back. The man was heading away from the trench, moving toward the entrance as he sidestepped the fallen.

Burt watched Bunker wait for the smoke to pull back before he advanced again, taking down more of the targets as they came into view. Bunker held a rifle now, not the pistols, undoubtedly picking one up from the abundant supply lying about.

"What are you doing?" Rusty asked from his perch to the right.

Burt pulled his attention from the scope and peered at Rusty. "Giving Bunker cover. Why don't you go ahead and head out? I've got this."

"No, I'm not leaving until this is over."

"Look, kid, Bunker told me to keep you safe. It's time to bug out. I'll finish up here. Take a horse and head back to camp. Dicky will go with you and make sure you get there in one piece."

Rusty shook his head in defiance, his eyes cautious.

Burt shot him a look that said *Go now, punk!*

Rusty must have finally gotten the message. He slinked away from his position and began the crawl up the hillside, taking a direct path toward the horses waiting on the other side of the rise.

The wind increased again, doubling its speed. Its direction remained constant, aiming its force at Bunker's position, pushing the gas cloud farther away.

Burt brought his eyes to Dicky. The big man must have sensed it, dropping the barrel of the rifle and looking back at Burt.

Burt pointed at Rusty. "Keep him safe. I got this."

Dicky nodded before a quick spin and climb up the hill.

Burt laughed, watching Dicky disappear over the rise.

Gotta love a Neanderthal who takes orders without question.

Burt got back on the scope, locating Bunker in the bedlam below. The smoke peeled back another twenty yards, revealing Russian vehicles parked parallel to each other. The antennas on the two center trucks swayed erratically in counterpoint to each other.

Bunker dropped to a knee with the rifle in a ready position, the barrel swinging from side to side in search and destroy mode.

The doors on the vehicles were open, but Burt couldn't see anyone inside. His direct line of sight was through the windshield, but the seats were empty. He couldn't see much else.

If a head popped up, he would fire, aiming a few mils higher with the scope. He figured the 7.62 rounds would easily penetrate the glass. Even if his adjustment for distance was off, anyone hiding behind the seats would still take one in the chest.

Bunker crept closer to the truck, weaving his way around the bodies, the rifle tight against his shoulder. His steps were deliberate. Predator-like.

Bunker made it to the lead vehicle unharmed, then moved to the open door on the driver's side. He moved with caution around the perimeter of the vehicle, looking for targets hiding inside.

Burt thought Bunker should shut the doors as he went, marking his progress. Closed doors would make a surprise assault from inside the vehicle that much harder. Then again, Bunker may have decided to leave the vehicle as-is, fearing a bomb inside—one that might be triggered by movement.

Bunker aimed the sights of his rifle to the second vehicle—the truck sporting all the antennas. The twenty-yard trek was filled with an assortment of corpses, some stacked three high, as if they were in the middle of a group hug when their last breaths were taken. He pressed on, adjusting his path to avoid the dead, with the rifle sweeping from point to point. His strides were short, taking a slower, more deliberate route than before, as if he sensed a nearby threat.

Just then, a portion of Burt's scope blurred out with a shadow. He lowered the rifle to adjust the focal point, allowing the image to render clear. When he brought the optics back into position, he saw a soldier running at Bunker wearing a gas mask. He must have been playing possum under some of the bodies.

Before Burt could blink, the camo-covered Russian flew in the air and landed on Bunker's back.

The attacker's gas mask flew one way and Bunker's rifle the other as the combatants tumbled together in a heap.

CHAPTER 130

Bunker spit out a mouthful of dirt, then crawled to his knees with a heavy weight on his back. It must have been a Russian, pounding at his skull from behind. The impacts were sharp, but not rapid-fire, giving Bunker an opportunity to react between blows.

He twisted a shoulder and threw a series of elbows at his attacker. The first two hit muscle, but the third blow found something solid, making a loud crack.

The attacker's clutch weakened, allowing Bunker to work himself free. He got to his feet and turned with hands fisted, ready to fight.

The gray-haired man across from him stood quickly. He was slender but appeared to be in good shape, his forearms the size of Popeye's. His face ran red with blood, as did his uniform.

A gas mask sat in the dirt a few feet away, which explained the pressure crease across the man's forehead. He must have been lying in wait, probably covered by the bodies of his fallen comrades.

Bunker looked for a name and rank, but the man's greens offered neither. The very next instant, his mind tapped into a recent memory from the church tower, when he was observing the activity on the stage.

The vision was of an older man about to shoot Stan Fielding. Bunker's vantage point wasn't the best at the time, but it did offer additional data he could use. Given the man's gas mask, obvious age, and the details from the memory flash, Bunker guessed at the soldier's identity. "General Zhukov, I presume."

He waited for Zhukov to respond or pull the holstered pistol from his hip. Zhukov did neither, growling something in Russian after his face pushed into an angry snarl. The man raced forward with his arms extended.

Bunker ducked the attack, then wrapped his arms around Zhukov's waist. He kept his shoulder centered in the groin area for leverage, driving the General back.

The blaze of the sun pelted Bunker's eyes, making him squint. He couldn't see the path ahead, or the collection of bodies he knew were there. They'd trip him if he continued, so he stopped the tackle and sent all his strength to his biceps.

He swung the aging Russian up and around, driving Zhukov into the dirt with his dominant side. A rush of wind left the General's chest when the soil smacked his spine with a thump.

Bunker climbed on his opponent's chest and drew back a coiled fist. He let it loose, delivering a sharp right, snapping the officer's head to the side. Blood sprayed from Zhukov's lip before he bought his eyes back, the intensity locked in.

Zhukov's right hand shot up to grab Bunker by the throat, focusing his grip around the larynx. His fingers tore at the skin with the force of a hydraulic press, catching Bunker off guard.

Bunker landed a pair of rights on Zhukov's chin, but the old man took the beating, looking as though he enjoyed the pain. Bunker felt his air supply slipping. He tore at the officer's thumb in distress, attempting to pry it free from his skin. Zhukov's grip was beyond anything he'd ever dealt with before, and that included his old pal Grinder, the most feared pugilist he'd ever met.

Grinder was a three hundred pound human tank, able to chew glass and crap thunder, neither of which he thought would pry Zhukov's hand free at the moment.

Bunker sent another barrage of jabs at Zhukov's face. They had little effect, except to raise more blood and liberate a tooth from the old man's mouth.

The battle against the fingers tearing into his neck continued with his left hand, while his right found its way to Zhukov's eyes. Bunker aimed a thumb for the nearest pupil and pressed hard, adding every ounce of force he could muster.

Zhukov's grunts turned into a bellowing howl as Bunker's nail broke the surface. Yet the General's claw of death never faded.

Bunker pulled his thumb free from the socket and landed another flurry of punches, pounding at Zhukov's face, arms, and chest. The assault wasn't working. He needed to change tactics before his windpipe succumbed to the pressure.

Right then, a voice from his past broke through the pain in an instant. It belonged to his grizzled Drill Instructor, a persistent actor in many of his most vivid memories. The brick of a man was preaching safety tips about chokehold training to Bunker's platoon of bleary-eyed recruits. The DI warned against applying too much pressure around the neck, especially when sparring with someone over forty. It might shake loose the natural plaque buildup that occurs with age in the arteries.

Blood clots are common in the elderly and the General certainly qualified as such, despite his Herculean grip. Bunker knew it was a long shot, but worth a try.

He adjusted his aim, landing alternating blows on the sides of Zhukov's neck. The mounting desperation in his chest added more and more force behind each strike, but his accuracy suffered as a result, missing the mark with the first four punches.

The fifth salvo landed on target, sending the old man's good eye rolling upward, showing only white after the pupil disappeared into the top of his skull.

Zhukov's hand dropped away and his body fell limp.

Bunker landed two more thumps as insurance, then rolled to the left, his energy reserves spent. He landed on his back in an awkward flop, his lungs gasping for air.

Spotty confusion filled his head as he wheezed, making it difficult to marshal his thoughts. They spun and flickered, showing disconnected flashes from his past. Most of the visions were linked to one of his many regrets, yet all of them were bloody, completing a red-colored mosaic in his mind.

The throb across his neck ran deep, but Bunker was able to resume breathing. Air came slowly at first, then the full force of his lungs kicked in, making him cough in response. The oxygen energized his body in one massive rush, bringing clarity to his mind a moment later.

He wasn't prepared for the incredible strength of the gray-haired commander. Yet he should have been after pushing the man's buttons. Valentina's brutal death had done its job, driving Zhukov's blood-fueled rage into the super-soldier category, almost killing Bunker in the process.

Only the effects of Father Time had saved Bunker, with a little help from his Drill Instructor's constant teachings—the neck punches. Were they a stroke of genius, or some kind of miracle?

He scoffed, deciding the arterial assault was nothing more than sheer luck. Even so, he'd gladly take it, stopping Zhukov with a plaque-induced blood clot.

When your last breath is only a heartbeat away, you'll try anything to survive, even a crazy stunt like that.

Bunker turned on his side, taking in a few more breaths in recovery. He surveyed the area for threats.

The third tank sat motionless forty yards away. The rear of its engine compartment had been pushed against the felled trees, blocking its retreat. The main cannon was aimed his way, though turned slightly to starboard and elevated by the same amount.

The driver's hatch was open along the front. So, too, were the hatches up top. They belonged to the tank commander and the gunner, neither of which was manning the machine gun. The tank crew must have bailed out. It was the only explanation.

Bunker crawled to his feet, feeling both relieved and proud. Their ambush had worked, yet the mission wasn't complete. Some of the Russians still clung to the last moments of life. An arm movement here. A leg twitch there.

Bunker took the semi-auto handgun from the General's holster, his thumb releasing the safety in a flick. He snatched a reserve magazine from a pouch attached to Zhukov's belt, then racked the slide to make sure the weapon was ready to fire. A round ejected in the process, landing in a spin as it caromed atop the flattened grass.

A soldier sat up in a sudden twist, dead ahead, twenty yards away, his hands grabbing at his throat. Before Bunker could raise the pistol and fire, the Russian's brain matter blew apart in a spray of chunks.

Bunker brought his eyes to the hillside beyond the trench, following the sound of the gunshot. The sun's late afternoon brilliance made it difficult to see more than a centralized glare. He put a hand up to shield his eyes, gaining more visibility as he continued the search for the shooter.

He was able to zero in on a low-lying dark spot. It was entrenched in one of the sniper hides. The location belonged to Burt, who held up a thumbs-up signal right on cue.

Rusty's position to the left looked abandoned, as did Dicky's on the right. Either they'd retreated or they'd been hit. Same with Dustin. His phone booth of a boulder stood alone in its own shadow.

Bunker worried for them all, but he couldn't stop his immediate mission to check on them. He moved ahead, aiming the pistol from body to body. If something moved, he shot it, leaving no survivors.

He kept his search restricted to the center of the meadow, avoiding any active booby traps near the tree line. He changed magazines when the pistol ran empty, but continued to fire on the survivors, making sure to end every invader.

Burt's job was to cover the perimeter, plinking skin and bone like target practice as Bunker moved. One by one, those who were still alive became dead, finishing the ambush in a hail of lead.

When it was over, Burt stood in celebration, his rifle held high with both hands. Bunker nodded at the mechanic, the thrill of victory finding his chest as well.

When Bunker's thoughts turned to Apollo, he realized the Sheriff's position had been quiet. He couldn't see the portly man or his rifle, even after the wind had cleared much of the area of smoke.

One of the trees holding a Tannerite charge was still upright, its upper limbs covered with an adornment of plastic bottles, ready to deliver another volley of deadly chemicals. It meant only one thing—the Sheriff failed to complete his most important task. Something went wrong.

Bunker motioned to Burt that he was heading to Apollo's position on the ridge. He changed course, planning to retrace the safety trail next to the log markers.

He sidestepped a pile of seven Russians, stacked up like cordwood, three deep and two wide, with one lying diagonally on top. Every soldier was face down—odd to say the least. If he didn't know better, he would have guessed someone arranged them that way.

Three strides later, Bunker felt an impact along his right side, just below his armpit. The force spun him sideways only moments before the sound of a gunshot tore into his ears. The grass cradled his fall, his focus finding its way to the gunshot's originating position an instant later.

The mechanic was still on his feet, holding the rifle near his right hip. It was loosely aimed at Bunker, with a wisp of smoke rising from the end of the barrel.

CHAPTER 131

Bunker kept watch on Burt as the wound under his arm leaked red through the press of his hand. His fingers told him the bullet went through and through, damaging mostly skin, he hoped. Even though he didn't think it hit anything vital, it didn't lessen the pain. Or the shock.

Did the mechanic just shoot him on purpose?

Or was it an accident?

Bunker's mind went into instant analysis mode, scrambling for answers before his next breath finished its run through his lungs.

He knew none of the bodies around him were alive, so it didn't seem likely Burt had a Russian target in mind when he fired. If he had, then the shot was an accident, catching Bunker's torso by mistake.

Perhaps it was a misfire. When your finger is resting on a trigger, it doesn't take much pressure to push it past the sear point in error. Even less force is needed when trigger work has been done on the rifle to lessen the pressure required to fire. Many seasoned shooters prefer lighter, more sensitive trigger pulls, increasing their precision.

It was also possible Burt could have been using the scope to glass the area, covering Bunker's movement against sudden threats. Overwatch mistakes are an unfortunate part of the job, though they are usually caused by the unexpected movement of an ally.

Bunker's path had been true and consistent. No sudden moves. Burt knew where he was going—on a direct track to Apollo's elevated position.

Anyone who's served knows that blunders with firearms happen, whether in combat or not. More so when the weapon is in the hands of an untrained civilian. Hell, even highly-skilled Marines miss their target on occasion.

After-Action Reports do include occasional incidents of friendly fire. In truth, it happens more often than most Commanders dare admit. Yet, despite every precaution, accidents are part of the battlefield.

Whether from errors in position, identification, or communication, they add to the victim toll. Some are a result of faulty intel or collateral damage. Others are from the mishandling of weapons. A rare few are intentional.

Weather, terrain, and navigation can also play a role in the untimely death of a fellow patriot. Human or machine as the cause, it didn't matter. The percentages stayed true across the statistics. Troops get wounded by their own. Some die. It can't be avoided in a red zone.

Bunker didn't know why, but his mind flashed a series of incidents from his past: a mud-driven crunchie from a tank's sudden turn—a high-powered sniper round finding its way to an allied troop who was in the wrong place at the wrong time—a premature pistol discharge by a squad mate cleaning his firearm.

He wished his heart didn't carry the haunting images, but they were part of who he was, having been etched into his long-term memory years ago.

Bunker lay in the grass, his eyes locked with Burt's, waiting for a reaction. Something that would answer the question burning a hole into his soul. Something that would keep him from raising his pistol to return fire. All it would take would be the slightest of body movements. A facial expression. An apologetic hand wave. A shoulder shrug. Anything to de-escalate the nagging feeling in Bunker's throat.

The answer came when Burt brought the rifle up to his shoulder, then slid his eye behind the scope with its barrel aimed at Bunker.

Shit. Intentional.

Bunker sent his body into a fast roll, completing several revolutions in retreat. Each time his injured side made contact with the ground, the pain sent a searing jolt through his abdomen.

Burt fired three more shots, none of them hitting their mark.

Bunker continued his whirl in the dirt, catching a glimpse of Burt ejecting a magazine from the AR-10.

Bunker got to his feet during the lapse in fire. He took two steps and dove over the double stack of corpses he'd passed earlier, using them as cover. He landed on his right side, aggravating the bullet wound.

Burt continued his flurry of rounds, firing one shot after another with little time in between. When he stopped to change magazines, Bunker brought the pistol up and fired several rounds, keeping his profile low. Each of the rounds missed, hitting only dirt and grass beyond the target.

Pistol accuracy decreases with range, especially when you're injured and under duress. Bunker was a decent shot but didn't possess the marksmanship needed. He needed to get lucky. Not just with his aim, but against Burt's elevated position.

Burt's location gave him the clear advantage. As did the scoped rifle in his hands. Oh, and the stack of reserve mags.

Bunker pulled the trigger two more times. The first bullet traveled down the barrel, but the second didn't. The pistol's slide had locked open.

Shit. Out of ammo.

He didn't have another magazine, either. He tossed the empty gun away as Burt sent another firestorm his way.

Pop! Pop! Pop! Pop! Pop!

The dead soldiers in front of him carried rifles, but Bunker didn't think he could get to them. The weapons were tucked under their respective bodies, all of which were lying face down on each other. He'd have to rise up to dig for them, exposing himself in the process.

There were weapons available on his flanks, but again, he'd have to leave cover to retrieve them. His only option would be to wait until Burt changed magazines again, then make a stab for them. He'd only have seconds to get there and back. Not an easy feat, but he was out of choices. Eventually Burt would figure out a solution to Bunker's cover and advance to change the angle of fire.

Burt fired another seven rounds, bringing the total to twelve. When the count reached twenty, Bunker would go for the rifle on his left.

Pop! Pop!

Fourteen.

Bunker focused on his breathing, taking long, slow breaths. He held them for a two-count before exhaling. It should lower his heart rate, lessening the amount of blood pushing out from his wound.

Pop! Pop! Pop!

Seventeen. Three more. Almost time.

Just then, another gunshot rang out, only this discharge was louder. Immediately after, he heard a man's grunt. It was a sharp, painful grunt.

Was it Burt? Or someone else?

Bunker waited for more gunfire, but it never came. He brought his eyes up to peer over the mound. Burt wasn't visible.

Bunker leaned higher, surveying the landscape in front of him. The mechanic wasn't charging his way. The path to the right was clear as well. No sign of Burt advancing on his position.

Right then, movement caught his attention. It was on the right and elevated—Apollo's sniper position.

Bunker's heart energized. "It's about time, Sheriff," he said to the air around him, focusing his eyes on Apollo's position.

A handful of seconds later, a head came up, exposing the eyes and nose. He'd expected the face of an elderly lawman, but that wasn't what he saw. The face and hair belonged to Stephanie King, and she was behind the scope of the TrackingPoint rifle.

"What the hell are you doing, Steph?" Bunker mumbled. She was supposed to take the boys back to camp, not join the fight. She hated guns.

Another groan came from Burt's position. Bunker turned his eyes to the left in a flash. Bunker couldn't see the mechanic, but the facts seemed clear. Stephanie had just put a bullet into Burt. Since Burt was moaning, it wasn't a fatal shot. At least not yet.

Bunker thought about the rifle lying in the grass next to the dead soldier on his left. It was now or never, he decided. He took off for the Russian long gun, running in a hunched-over style. The wound in his side howled after the sprint, but it didn't stop him from snatching the gun from the corpse.

Bunker checked Burt's position. Still no sign of the shooter. He ran back, taking only seconds to return to cover.

A quick check of the AK-47 confirmed it was ready to fire. He plopped the weapon on top of the bodies to line up the sights. "Come on, Burt, just show me something."

CHAPTER 132

"That fucking bitch," Burt groaned through the pain as he wrapped his hand with a strip of cloth he'd torn from his shirt with his teeth. The log in front of him was covered in a spray of blood. Blood that belonged to him.

Somehow Stephanie King had landed a lucky shot—with his soon-to-be rifle, no less. He couldn't believe it. The dumb broad figured it out and pulled the trigger, tearing his right hand apart.

He scanned the dirt, hoping to recover the two missing fingers. All he saw was more blood. No skin. No bone. No fingers. "Fuck!" They'd been blown apart.

The thumping throb across his hand was intense, making it hard to focus his thoughts. He needed to bring the rifle up and fire back at her. He still had a couple of fingers he could use, if he could reach the trigger.

Burt closed his eyes, visualizing how glorious it would feel to see her annoying head fly apart when he took her down. Her big mouth would finally be silent. Permanently.

After he killed Stephanie, he planned to climb down the hill and take out Bunker, a man he knew was wounded and probably bleeding out. Bunker hadn't fired in a while, meaning he was either out of ammo, unconscious, or dead. Any of those would work. Burt decided it was time to finish off the witnesses before the sun completed its day.

"Just need to get up," he moaned in a thready voice, his breath short due to the pain. "Come on, it's only a flesh wound, you pussy. Get the fuck up."

A crunch came from the left. It was uphill from his position. A moment later, a male's voice said, "Yeah, just try to get up. I dare you."

Burt brought his eyes around in a squint, following the sounds he'd just heard. When the tone and inflection of the voice registered in his mind, a face appeared from his memory.

"Jumbo?" Burt asked as his vision cleared. He found a pistol aimed at his head from three feet away.

"Looks like your welding days are over, asshole," Albert said as two more sets of legs appeared behind him. They belonged to Victor and Dallas, their eyes wide.

Burt held up his injured hand. "What, this? Ah, this ain't nothing. I can still whoop your sorry ass."

"Those are tough words coming from a man about to die," Albert said as his hands shook, sending the end of the pistol into a bobble.

"Who're you kidding, Albert? You don't have the stones to pull the trigger. Hell, my ninety-year-old grandmother has more guts than you and she's been worm food for ten years."

Burt sat up and put his back against the log, feeling emboldened. It was obvious. Albert was scared, unable to keep the gun still in his hands. He wasn't going to fire. Neither would Bunker, not with Albert and the boys standing close, assuming the man was still alive.

Burt wasn't so sure about the wildcat behind the TrackingPoint. He flashed a hand in Stephanie's direction. "Someone might wanna tell Miss Big Mouth over there to hold her fire. I'd hate for one of you fine, upstanding citizens to end up down here with me."

Albert turned to Victor. "Go tell her I got this."

"Why me? Why don't you send Dallas?"

"Both of you go. I'll finish up here."

The boys didn't move.

"I said go! Make sure she's okay."

The boys turned and cut across the hill, heading for Stephanie's position.

"Okay, lard-ass. Let's finish this," Burt said, his eyes glancing at the rifle lying next to him.

"Don't do it, Burt. I'm warning you," Albert said, the shake in his hands double what it was before.

"Hell, you'll miss. Even from there. Look at your hands. You're shitting in your pants right about now."

Albert looked down at his pistol. "This isn't nervousness, Burt. It's excitement. I've been waiting a long time for this."

"Ah, go fuck yourself, Jumbo. You ain't gonna—"

Boom!

Burt choked back the last word he was going say, feeling the impact of the bullet Albert had just fired. He looked down. His stomach was bleeding, just below the diaphragm. "Fuck . . . you shot me," he said, fighting for air. "I can't believe you sh—"

Boom!

Burt felt the impact above his left eye. He took one massive breath, trying to hang onto the last trickle of thought fading from his mind, but it vanished when his heart gave out, turning everything black.

* * *

Stephanie King couldn't seem to convince her body to move after watching Albert shoot a man—twice. Her limbs were frozen, much like Albert's arm at the moment, his hand holding the gun on its lifeless target.

She never thought Albert would pull the trigger. Not in cold blood, but he did. Almost like it was nothing. But who was she to judge? She'd just shot a man, too. The same man, adding her name to the list of the guilty.

The vision of Burt's head blowing apart kept replaying in her mind. Each time the bullet hit, the blood spatter grew in intensity and color, like some kind of malignant cancer set free from hell.

The world went into a sudden spin, sending her to her backside. She couldn't convince her eyes to focus. Nor could she catch her breath, not with the jackhammer pounding inside her chest. It felt as though someone was trapped below her ribcage, trying to break free.

"Focus, Steph. Focus. You can do this," she mumbled with her eyes closed. The shake in her hands had spread to her knees, making her want to throw up. But somehow, she held it down, even with the severed arm lying near her feet.

The gruesome sight must have belonged to the Sheriff. A thick trail of blood indicated he'd crawled to the left—somewhere—and probably died. Nobody could lose that much blood and survive.

She choked back tears, trying not to see his kind face in her thoughts. At least Apollo was able to share one kiss with the woman he'd been chasing.

Stephanie wasn't sure how she was going to relay the news to Allison. The middle-aged woman put up a good front when it came to her feelings about Apollo, but Stephanie could sense there was more there than just the excitement of a first kiss.

Sometimes a woman convinces herself that she's not interested, even though her emotions tell a different story. Preconceived ideas of the perfect guy never come true, catching a woman off guard when a different kind of man enters her life.

Whether the new mate seems against her acceptable age range, body type, or even occupation, the feelings creep in and take residence, growing against every effort to stop them. They persist no matter how hard she tries to bury them. They can't be faked or denied, waiting just below the surface. And now, after all the chasing and flirting, their budding love affair was probably over.

Stephanie flushed the depressing thoughts and turned her attention to the boys. Thank God they were headed in her direction when Albert killed Burt. They didn't need to witness someone's last moment on Earth.

Hell, she wished she hadn't seen it. The mechanic was already wounded from the shot she'd taken a minute earlier. Albert could have let the man live. He didn't need to shoot him.

Stephanie opened her eyes and sent a charge of energy to her legs. She got up in a sideways stumble, barely able to hold her balance. The boys had started their climb to her position. She needed to intercept, before they saw the bloody arm lying in the dirt.

Stephanie turned sideways and short-stepped a slow, methodical path down the steep-angled terrain.

"Did you see it?" Dallas asked when she arrived. "Did you see the shot? What did it look like? Was there a lot of blood?"

She ignored the boy's dig for information. "Let's not worry about that now. We need to find Jack. Burt shot him."

"What about the Sheriff?" Victor asked, peering up the rise.

"I haven't seen him, but I'm sure he's around here somewhere," she said, spinning the truth to diffuse Victor's curiosity.

CHAPTER 133

Bunker kept pressure on the through-and-through wound in his side. He was fortunate Burt wasn't a better shot; otherwise, the bullet would have shredded his heart, sending his consciousness to the realm of the afterlife, assuming he chose to believe in such things.

Right now. Right here. He needed to focus on one task—finishing the job. There was still plenty to do, but first he needed to control the pain.

A focused mind is a Marine's greatest weapon, not only for pain management, but in the relentless pursuit of victory. Unlike his body, his mind was locked and loaded. That's all he needed. Well, that and the abandoned tank sitting behind him.

Bunker swung his head, locking his eyes on the multi-ton death machine. Its hatches sat open, much like a hostess extending an open arm, greeting patrons for dinner at the entrance to a five-star establishment. The invitation was obvious; so were the issues that still remained.

The last few days had been brutal, but at least he was still alive and breathing. That was the minimum required. As long as one breath remained, a Marine could still deliver hell.

Right then, a phrase from his past rose up and landed in his thoughts. It was something his Drill Instructor had said—more than once—usually when a member of the platoon was down and ready to quit.

"Get up; otherwise I will haunt your dreams like a ghost! And I'm not talking about Casper, either. Think Freddy Krueger, motherfucker."

A vengeful spirit was a term that fit the situation, Bunker decided. So did unstoppable demon. He was sure the Russian occupiers in town were on full alert, waiting for news from their commander about the tattooed man who'd started his own little war against them.

He figured the sudden swell of lingering radio silence would only ramp up their apprehension, adding to the legend that was surely growing by now about the Clearwater demon. But it wouldn't last. The time to strike was now.

"Come on, Jack. Get the fuck up," he mumbled, pressing to his feet only moments before Stephanie, Victor, and Dallas arrived in a rush. They were unharmed after their collective jaunt, remembering to follow the marker logs near the entrance to the trench.

Albert wasn't far behind, his legs pumping in an uneven, pegged-legged running style. He was holding the pistol that ended Burt—a shot Bunker thought would never happen. Not from Tin Man.

If Bunker had to choose one characterization for Albert, he'd pick the Cowardly Lion. Someone who preferred to hide rather than fight. Intellect can do that to a man, taking him down the road of self-preservation, thinking it's the smart move, despite the danger.

Yet, when facing a force as lethal as the Great Red Menace, intellect rarely protects you from a bullet with your name on it. The right move was to act. With speed, force, and intent. Anything short of that would get everyone killed.

Stephanie wrapped her hand under Bunker's armpit. "Oh my God, Jack. You're bleeding."

Bunker turned to face the trees blocking the entrance, Stephanie's grasp never waning. "I don't have time to bleed. We've got to finish this, while we still can."

"Finish what?" Albert said, his eyes scanning the area. "Dude, you killed them all. It's like something out of a video game around here."

"Time to take care of the troops in town. Right now, we have the element of surprise on our side."

Albert shook his head, throwing his arms up in confusion. "How?"

Bunker pointed at the tank. "First we need to clear a path. Someone get me Dicky's chainsaw. Hurry."

"I will," Victor said, taking off an instant later.

Bunker peered at Dallas. "I need you to bring me that sword. It's by the tree, next to the trench."

"Sure," Dallas said, his feet spinning in the dirt before he, too, began a full-on sprint toward the marker logs.

"Sword?" Albert asked.

"I'll explain later," Bunker said to the fat man, shooting a subtle head nod at Stephanie. He hoped Albert would understand his cryptic gesture, because explaining the gruesome details with Steph present was something he wanted to avoid.

She wasn't going to like what came next and he was too tired to debate the merits of the medieval Vikings and their preferred method of intimidating the enemy.

Those ancient seafarers had been extinct for centuries, but their ruthless reputation still struck fear in the hearts and minds of those familiar with their tactics. Or their lore.

"Where's Dicky?" Stephanie asked. "We could really use his help."

There were a number of answers Bunker could give, most involving blood and guts. However, he was dealing with an emotionally-charged Stephanie. Caution was needed if he had any hope to keep her calm and cooperative. He chose the explanation with the most positive spin. "I told him to make sure Rusty was safe. He must have bugged out."

"Leaving Burt alone, with an assault rifle," Albert said in a matter-of-fact way, his tone even and slow.

"Thanks for that, by the way," Bunker said, giving the man a nod out of respect. He turned to Stephanie. "You, too. Didn't think either of you had it in you."

"We couldn't let him kill you, now could we?" Stephanie answered.

"Yeah, but how? I never showed you how to shoot."

"Men," Stephanie scoffed in a quick retort, rolling her eyes. "You always think women are clueless when it comes to guns, or tools, or whatever. Just because I don't carry a machine gun and get all decked out in camouflage doesn't mean I can't pick up a rifle and pull the trigger. Don't forget, I'm a country girl. We all know how to shoot. It's sort of required around here."

Bunker looked at Albert, whose eyes were locked onto the cleavage she was sporting—at least until Stephanie brought her head around. Albert's eyes came up only an instant before she caught him gawking.

Stephanie's tone turned sharp as she addressed Albert. "And you—I told you to take the boys back to camp. What the hell are you doing here?"

Albert cleared his throat, stalling. "We were almost there, but Dallas convinced me to turn around. Well, actually, it was both of them. A vote type thing. They didn't want you to go alone."

"The boys, huh?" she said in a sarcastic tone. "I find that hard to believe."

Bunker got the impression she knew Albert had just been staring at her boobs. Then again, maybe her odd look meant she sensed Albert was lying about why he came back; his body language and tone were off, even for him.

"It took a little convincing, but I caved. Not sure what else I could have done. They're not my kids."

Time to change the subject, Bunker decided. "I'm going to need a huge favor, Steph."

"What kind of favor?"

"I need you to drive."

"Drive what?"

"The tank."

"You can't be serious!"

"It's cramped quarters and you're the only adult small enough to fit," Bunker said, thinking of the height restrictions. The T-72's low profile was an efficient design, though it required the tank crew to be no more than about five-foot-five inches tall.

"What makes you think I can drive a tank?" she asked, her tone one of shock.

"Relax, it's easy. In fact, they're designed to be monkey simple. It's only a couple of levers and a gas pedal. Anyone can do it. I'll show you everything you need to know."

"So now you're calling me a monkey?"

"You know what I mean. There really isn't any choice. I'll never fit."

She looked at Albert, lingering on his rotund middle before nodding. "I guess the boys are too young."

Bunker was pleased she agreed. A rare event, indeed. "I'll be in the tank commander's seat, working the override controls."

"What do they do?"

"They control the main cannon and the autoloader."

"No. No. No. Please tell me you're not planning to fire that thing at our town?"

"If we play this right, we won't have to."

"What does that mean?"

"Please Steph, just trust me on this. For once. I've got it covered."

"Fine," she said, her lips pinched. "But we'd better think about patching up that wound. You're no good to us if you're dead."

Bunker nodded. Not out of agreement, but rather one of surrender, to save time. He aimed the next statement at Albert. "You'll be driving one of the transports."

"Ah, no. I don't think so. Getting involved really isn't my thing."

"And yet here you are. Standing there with a smoking gun."

"That was different."

"So is this."

"Well, that's your opinion, dude. Not mine."

"Look Albert, I don't have time to debate everything. So you might as well get used to the idea. You *will* be driving the GAZ Tigr. End of story."

Albert didn't respond, taking a step back. Every muscle in the man's face was screaming two words: *hell no.*

Bunker realized he'd come on too strong. He knew Albert didn't like to be pushed. Or volunteered. Pressing the issue was a tactical mistake, one he should have avoided. An effective leader must understand his men, knowing what motivates and what antagonizes. It's all about which buttons to push, and when. Albert was no different. Neither was Stephanie.

"Look, we all gotta pitch in, Albert," Stephanie said in that pushy tone of hers. "You included."

Bunker thought he was seeing things when she leaned forward, giving Albert a prime view down her shirt. Her tone turned coy, surprising Bunker even more when she turned on the charm in a full court press. "Can I count on you, Albert? I can't do this alone. I really need you."

Albert didn't respond, his gaze finding its way to the glorious sight being presented. He must have suddenly realized what his eyes were doing, because he turned them away in a lurch.

Bunker held back a chuckle, watching Albert scramble to cover his embarrassment, pretending to search for something in the dirt around his feet. It was comical but not entirely unexpected. Bunker couldn't help but take a peek as well. Few women were put together like Stephanie and she obviously knew it. She was a master manipulator, working the meth cook with the assets available.

A ten-count ticked by before Albert brought his attention back. His face was calm, almost serene, as if he'd flushed all of his humiliation and done a hard reboot. "Sure, I'll help, Steph. Someone has to babysit the boys."

"Hey, wait a minute," she said, firing her eyes at Bunker. "They're not coming along, are they?"

"No. They'll be heading back to camp. Just have to work out a few more details in my head, first."

"Good, because there's no chance that was happening. Not if I have anything to say about it."

"What about the Land Rover? I parked it just over the ridge," Albert said.

"Okay, genius. Who's gonna drive?" Stephanie asked.

"I was thinking Victor could. He kept asking to take the wheel. Maybe we should let him?"

"I don't know. Those roads are pretty rough," Stephanie said.

"I've got a better idea," Bunker said, putting two fingers into his mouth. He let loose with a series of sharp whistles, sending the hail toward the rise beyond the trench.

A short minute later, Tango appeared atop the hill, standing proudly like a general overseeing his troops.

Bunker whistled again, sending Tango into a trot, his hooves working against the steep angle of the slope.

"Hey Dallas?" Bunker yelled.

The eager kid stopped near the entrance to the trench and turned.

Bunker added volume to his request, pointing at the horse. "Bring Tango with you."

"Okay!" Dallas responded, changing course.

Stephanie cleared her throat. "Before the boys get back, there's something I should probably tell you, Jack."

"The Sheriff?"

She nodded, forcing down a gulp. "I think he's dead. I found his severed arm by the gun and there's a lot of blood. It's everywhere. He crawled off, but I couldn't see him."

Bunker exhaled, his chest growing heavy. "I figured as much. There's no chance he would have failed to detonate all of the charges."

"I'm pretty sure I know who killed him," Albert said. "There's a totally messed-up Russian by the entrance to the trench. Half his head is missing."

Bunker nodded. "I saw him, too. Must have come out of the gas cloud and fired on the Sheriff before Dicky or Burt could take him out."

"We should go find him," Stephanie said.

"Normally, I'd agree, but there isn't time. We need to stay on mission and finish this. The clock's ticking, Steph. We'll deal with the casualties later. They're not going anywhere."

"What if he isn't dead?" she asked. "Shouldn't we be sure?"

"If he's not, he will be soon. A wound like that requires immediate medical attention. Without a trauma doc, he'll bleed out in minutes. There's really nothing we can do for him way out here. We'd need a helo to medivac him somewhere in time."

"How can you be so unfeeling about all of this?"

"Because people die in war, Steph. Just look around. It's inevitable. The Sheriff was a brave man and we'll have time to mourn him later. Right now, we need to make sure his sacrifice counts for something."

She didn't answer, only blinking.

"You knew him a lot better than I did, but I'm betting he would have wanted us to continue and finish this."

She nodded.

* * *

Bunker tied off the bloody artwork he'd just created with the glistening edge of the sword, dangling the severed head from the barrel of the 125mm cannon of the Russian tank. It was front and center, positioned for maximum visibility.

Stephanie had made him wait to do the deed until after Victor and Dallas were on Tango and out of sight. Then she crawled through the hatch and into the driver's seat of the T-72, refusing to witness Bunker's decapitation of the General.

Albert wasn't present either, stuffing his waistline behind the steering wheel of the GAZ Tigr, with his head turned away. At least the fat man had found the stones to shoot a murderous Burt, but Bunker figured that act of heroism was a one-off event. Albert's true self was back in the driver's seat, so to speak.

Bunker wasn't surprised by either of their reactions. A cold, ruthless heart takes years to develop. Even then, emotions are hard to bury, bubbling to the surface at the most inopportune time.

However, a true warrior must do what's needed. A warrior doesn't have time to second-guess, nor does a warrior have time to heal. The wrap around his middle was snug, but he figured it would do the job until he could complete the final phase of his plan.

Severed heads had been used throughout history for mostly the same reason—fear and intimidation, none done more perfectly than the ancient Vikings. They would hang severed heads from the hulls of their ships when they cruised into a new harbor.

That's what Bunker was doing, selling the legend. Only his transport of choice was a main battle tank, not a wooden ship full of bloodthirsty killers.

Either way, displaying the head of your enemy is an effective tool, more so when your reputation precedes you, reinforcing the notion that you are a ruthless adversary who will stop at nothing to achieve victory.

Bunker hoped the remaining Russians in Clearwater were of the same mindset, fearing the man who'd escaped after dropping the female officer from the bell tower. And now, that same man had brutally killed their commanding officer.

It was more than likely that someone in uniform had made contact with the troops in town before they died from the toxic gas, or were taken out by a member of the Clearwater Resistance Movement.

Bunker liked that term and its abbreviation: CRM. He couldn't hold back a grin, knowing how the military loves its acronyms. It's a religion for the brass, always going out of their way to find something that fit. Much like he just did.

Bottom line, it didn't matter whether the Russian situation report had been initiated by the General or by one of his tank crews, as long as word of the massacre had found its way to those Russians still on their feet.

Fear of an unstoppable opponent is a powerful tool for those who oppose. You can kill a man, but you can't kill an idea. That's what the severed head was for, to sell the myth he'd been forging ever since he'd dropped Valentina in front of everyone.

CHAPTER 134

Colonel Orlov finished his sprint to the main gate at the entrance to town. His communications officer and security detail were right on his heels when he stopped, each soldier's chest pumping hard from the run.

The sentry in charge pointed, leading the Colonel's eyes to the pavement beyond the gate. Two vehicles approached—about half a mile out and closing. One was a tank and the other a truck.

Two of the other station guards had binoculars glued to their eyes, keeping watch on the road. One of them reported in Russian, "They're ours, Colonel."

"What happened to our infantry?" the second guard asked.

A pause hung in the air until the first guard spoke again. "Do you see that? Hanging from the barrel."

"Looks like a . . . head," the second guard responded, his voice tentative.

"Must have gotten the son of a bitch," Orlov said, the tension in his chest disappearing in a flash of relief.

"Wait a minute," the first guard said with urgency. "That looks like it belongs to—"

"General Zhukov!" the second guard snapped.

Orlov grabbed the binoculars from the guard and took a look. Sure enough, the report was accurate. The General's severed head was hanging from the main cannon, cut off at the base of the neck. He checked the left side of the tank, where he saw a man with slicked back hair and tattoos sticking out of the open hatch—his upper chest, shoulders, and face visible. "There he is! In the commander's seat."

"Who the hell is this man?" the first guard asked.

"His name is Jack Bunker," someone said in perfect English—the voice originating directly behind them.

Orlov spun, his eyes landing on the muzzle of a rifle pointed at his face. It was in the hands of a man wearing a Russian uniform. Even though the person's face was badly swollen, Orlov recognized the would-be shooter.

It was the American, Stan Fielding. The prisoner who'd escaped from the execution stage with his twin daughters during the chaos with Valentina. Fielding wasn't alone, either. There were three others, each dressed and armed like him.

A heartbeat later, all four men pulled their triggers, shooting Orlov and the guards in the face.

* * *

"Zeke, get out there quick, before Bunker fires that thing!" Rico said, pointing at the tank rolling toward them.

Zeke stepped over the body of the Colonel and ran, waving his arms over his head. "Bunker! It's us! Don't shoot!"

Rico turned to the third member of their assault team. "Russell, get on that machine gun and watch the street in case we missed any."

Russell sprinted to the sandbag fortress. He stood behind the automatic weapon, with his hands on the stock.

"I'm surprised they got that gunner's nest rebuilt so quickly," Rico said to Stan Fielding, who stood with a mangled face next to him.

"I wish I could have seen that," Fielding said, one of his eyes barely open beyond a thin horizontal slit.

Rico could have made light of the comment, given its dual meaning, but he chose not to. Fielding deserved his respect for facing death like a man, with his little girls watching. "Oh yeah. Shit flew everywhere, Stan, just like Bunker wanted. I'll tell you what, that man had this all figured out, which is pretty damn amazing when you think about it. Kudos to the Marine Corps."

"Our tax dollars at work."

"Thank God for that," Rico added, the pride in his heart swelling.

The tank continued in a slow crawl, its tracks plowing forward, sending a thunderous vibration into the blacktop. Rico was sure the roadway was failing under the immense weight. He imagined deep, irregular cracks forming in its wake, with random chunks of asphalt working themselves free.

He didn't think there were many civil engineers who would have had the presence of mind to plan ahead and design a roadway for a vehicle such as this. Certainly not in Clearwater County, or anywhere else for that matter.

The severed head swung from left to right as the crosswinds rocked the remains of General Zhukov. Rico wasn't sure how Bunker had managed that all-important kill, but he was grateful the former Marine was on Clearwater's side, not the other way around.

He didn't know Bunker very well, but one thing was clear: some men are born to fight. Men like Bunker. They eat it. They breathe it. It's who they are at the core.

* * *

When Rico drew a finger across his throat, Bunker bent his knees to peer into the open hatch below him as he spoke into the communications headset. "Go ahead and shut it down, Steph."

She gave him a quick hand flash in response, then the great metal beast came to a full stop in front of the main gate, the engine roar turning silent. Bunker removed his headset and exhaled, his body weak from exhaustion.

In truth, there wasn't much remaining of the Russian checkpoint after his escape earlier, but *main gate* was still the correct term. Russell was on the machine gun, apparently watching their six with an eye on the street heading into the center of town.

Bunker's elevated position gave him a decent view of the secondary checkpoint at the far end of the road. He couldn't see any activity, not like before when he snuck into town after posing as an injured collaborator. In fact, the checkpoint looked abandoned.

Zeke and Rico stood in wait, just beyond the tracks to Bunker's right, their smiles evident. A third man with a twisted face was next to Rico.

Bunker assumed it was Stan Fielding, the condemned man he'd saved with the fake execution of the Russian interpreter.

Stan nodded in respect, his lips quiet. No words were needed. Bunker understood and returned the gesture with a half-smile that said, "You're welcome."

Stephanie climbed out of the driver's hatch, her mouth taking in a full gasp of air when her feet hit the pavement. The hair on the back of her neck stuck to her skin as if it had been glued down. Again, not surprising. Cramped quarters and rising tensions would always bring about the most sweat, even for seasoned tank operators. She was obviously not immune.

The tank's movement hadn't been smooth or even in a straight line, but the first-time tank operator got them here with minimal training.

The term *Monkey Simple* flashed in Bunker's mind, ridding the remaining stress from his chest. Stephanie didn't like the term, but it fit—not as a slam against her. More as a general operations term, precisely what the Russian engineers intended when they designed the controls.

Albert pulled alongside the tank in the GAZ Tigr. He got out of the driver's seat and walked in his customary slow stride to Stephanie's position, his hands in his pockets.

"You coming?" Stephanie asked, waving for Bunker to join her.

"Not yet," he said, nodding in the direction of the secondary checkpoint. "Need to make sure the rest of them got the message. I might still have to unload a round or two."

"We took care of it," Rico said, shaking his head.

"All of them?" Bunker asked, needing confirmation.

"Zhukov only left a skeleton force when he went after you. Wasn't hard, once we found that stash of weapons that you-know-who was bragging about."

Bunker nodded, not wanting to reveal the subject of Rico's comment. Stephanie didn't know her ex was dead and he thought it best to keep it that way for a while longer. He still needed to figure out a way to tell her what happened.

Stephanie wrapped her arms around Fielding and gave him one of her patented kisses on the cheek, much like a beloved sister does when you show up late for Thanksgiving dinner at her house. "I'm so glad you're alive, Stan. How are Barb and Beth? Are they okay?"

"They're a little traumatized, but Doc Marino says they'll be fine. Eventually," he answered, his voice sour and unsteady.

None of Stan's demeanor was a surprise given the beating he'd taken. It was a miracle he was standing, let alone joining the last segment of the operation. Most men would have been in the hospital, suffering from some level of brain damage.

Rico turned to Russell in the gunner's nest. "Go ahead, call 'em out. I think it's safe."

Russell whistled at the empty street and waved with both arms over his head.

Seconds later, citizens began to spill out onto the street from the buildings on either side. Some of them were armed with rifles, others held knives or pistols, filling the pavement with shoes and smiles.

Rico gave his rifle to Zeke, then climbed onto the track, moving to Bunker's position. He put his hand out for a shake. "Nice work, Jack."

Bunker took his hand in a firm grip. "You too. Thanks for covering my ass."

"No, thank you. Otherwise, we're all slaves forever."

CHAPTER 135

Sometime later . . .

Bunker felt a sharp pain erupt along his right side, rousing him from a slumbering, dream-filled state.

His thoughts were slow to arrive, forming as a cloud of hazy memory shards—a speck here—a flicker there—taking more than a minute to run clear. Once it did, the pieces coalesced into something his mind could process, bringing conscious thought to the surface.

Reality swarmed his senses as he opened his eyes. He was on his back in a ten-foot by ten-foot space, lying on a bed with soreness across his body. The sun was beaming in through the window to his right, casting short, intense shadows across the floor.

The room featured mostly white, antiseptic-looking walls, which matched the chemical odor floating about. The coolness of the room felt stale, almost artificial. He searched the area under his nose, but an oxygen supply line wasn't there, as expected.

He studied the two rolling carts hovering nearby. Each held a bank of equipment, but the lights were off and he didn't hear the whirring steadiness of white noise emanating from their cooling fans. Each had a tangle of wires connecting the technology together, but they were nonfunctional, much like he felt at the moment.

Then it hit him, the facts lining up in an instant: The EMP and cyber-attack. No power or electronics. The bus rescue. The Russian invasion. Mortar shells. His carefully plotted ambush. The hand-to-hand battle with the General. Burt shooting him. Stephanie driving the tank with the severed head as decoration.

His mind finally snapped awake, assembling his memories into the proper order. He remembered what transpired after he shook Rico's hand. It happened all at once, his knees buckling when the energy vanished from his body. The collapse sent him down the hatch in a heap.

Bunker felt the back of his head to find a bandage. It was rectangular, several inches in width. Probably stitches underneath, he figured. He must have cracked his head against the steel framework inside the tank.

A plastic IV bag hung on a pole opposite from the carts, dripping a clear liquid with the consistency of a metronome. He watched the medicine enter the clear tube hanging from it, snaking down the line and disappearing into the central vein of his arm. In some odd way, it reminded him of detonation cord feeding into a blasting cap. If that analogy fit, then he was a brick of TNT. An old and tired brick of TNT.

He wasn't sure how many men would characterize themselves as a plastic explosive, but his past was filled with dozens of women who had, always complaining that he would go off without warning. When you answer to no one, even yourself, your temper tends to take over.

That's the old me, he thought to himself, taking the time to convince himself it was the truth. Accountability is important for most men. It keeps them flying straight and in check.

Bunker's vision was still spotty, but improving with each passing minute. There was someone in a white lab coat, standing at an angle, facing away, about three feet beyond the foot of the bed.

It was a man, the heavy stubble on the side of his face evident between the flecks and blobs floating in Bunker's sightlines. The stranger was short, dark-complected, with mostly black hair. His eyes appeared to be focused on a clipboard, reviewing a thin stack of paperwork.

Bunker peered down, feeling the squeeze of another bandage. This one was along his right side, just under his armpit, covering a swatch that extended down to his waistline. The skin under the cotton wrap ached with each breath he took, stressing the stitches that he assumed were hiding beneath.

His left forearm had been wrapped with a fresh dressing as well. More stitches, he assumed.

Damn, he wasn't sure if he resembled the laces on a football or an old lady's Christmas quilt, the embroidery everywhere. Either way, he was happy to be resting for a change.

"Well, well. Good of you to join us," the man in the lab coat said, his Italian accent clear and evident.

At that moment, more clues came together. Bunker knew he was at the clinic in Clearwater. That meant the man in front of him was Doc Marino.

Bunker tried to sit up, but pain in his side wouldn't allow it. He winced, flopping back to the sheet. "What the hell happened? My head is killing me."

"You just had surgery, Jack. What you're feeling is the aftereffects of the makeshift anesthesia I used. Sorry about that, but the supplies are limited around here. I had to improvise a little, using a combination of techniques. It took me a while to clean out the infections and remove the dead tissue from your wounds. You're pretty damn lucky, my friend. A lesser man would never have remained on his feet as long as you did. It's a miracle you're still with us after the blood loss and dehydration."

Bunker was shocked to hear those words. He didn't think he was injured that badly. Maybe it was a cumulative effect of the last few days.

The Doc handed him four pills. Tiny, yellow, and round. "Here, take these. It will help."

Bunker held his palm out. "What are they?"

Marino gave him the meds and a small cup. "At this point, does it matter?"

"No, not really, as long as it helps."

"It will, just give it a few minutes. Between the concussion, blood loss, infections, exhaustion, and the modified Propofol cocktail I used, it might take a bit for the cobwebs to clear. Normally, procedural sedation requires a fifteen-minute recovery period, but in your case, it will probably require more time. I had to exceed the maximum dosage in order to keep you out. Big men like you usually require a heavier mix. Plus, I had to administer the dosage in increments, keeping close watch so that I did not stop your heart."

"I appreciate that, Doc. Though there've been more than a few women back in the day that said I didn't have a heart anyway."

Marino laughed.

Bunker popped the pills into his mouth and chased them down with the small amount of water in the cup. It wasn't until that very moment that he realized he was thirsty, almost as if he'd been asleep for weeks. "How long have I been out?"

"Thirty-two hours."

"Damn, Doc. That must have been some cocktail."

"Actually, that was all you, Jack. My guess is your adrenaline system was keeping you alive and moving. When was the last time you ate? Or slept?"

"Not sure. It's all a blur right now."

"You're lucky I had a few reserve units of blood available. Otherwise, I'm not sure we'd be chatting right now."

Bunker blinked a few more times. Right on cue, the specks disappeared from his vision. The pounding in his head had lessened as well. What had started as a twelve on the ten-scale was now around a seven. He exhaled after a long, exaggerated breath, allowing his chest to expand with air.

Doc let out a thin grin, looking confident. "I take it the meds are starting to kick in."

"Yes, thank you. For a while there, I thought someone had cracked me over the head with a pipe. Been there, done that, if you know what I mean."

"Yes, I do. The Kindred?"

Bunker didn't want to admit it, but the secret was out. "Not my finest hour."

"Sorry, but I couldn't help notice the tattoos. There's a story there, I take it."

"Yeah, you could say that. But that's the old me, Doc. I'm not that man anymore."

"What about those scars on your neck?"

Bunker chuckled. "My version of tattoo removal."

"You did that yourself? Those look like serious third-degree burns, if I'm not mistaken."

"You're right. Hurt like a bitch, but that's what happens when you use a blowtorch. I was a little desperate at the time. Again, not my finest hour."

Doc hesitated, obviously shocked by the confession. "I'm surprised sepsis didn't set in as a result."

"Nah, I cleaned and dressed the skin. All part of our field medic training."

"You served?"

"Marine Corps. I was a Sapper, which is basically a combat engineer. Explosives were my specialty."

"Well, thank you for your service."

Bunker nodded, but didn't respond. The conflicting emotions in his heart about his time in the military wouldn't allow him to answer. Not with honor or conviction. Sometimes, it's better to just keep your mouth shut.

"I will be back in a few minutes to check on you," Doc Marino said, turning for the door. He was in the hallway and out of sight ten steps later.

Bunker put his head back on the pillow and shut his eyes.

Sleep found him again.

CHAPTER 136

When Bunker opened his eyes again, he found himself still on his back in the hospital bed, only this time his head was turned to the right, facing the window. Beyond the glass was total darkness, the sun long since missing. He wasn't sure how long he'd been out, but at least his headache was gone.

He grunted out of habit before correcting his head position on the pillow. The artificial lights across the ceiling seemed brighter than before, making him blink rapidly to clear the sudden wave of spots.

Wait a minute, he thought quietly. *How could the lights be on?*

He looked at the rolling carts next to the bed. Their lights were blinking. The power was back on. He didn't understand how, but he was happy to see it.

"Hey there, sunshine," a familiar voice said, the words delivered in perfect English.

Bunker brought his eyes to the left. Mayor Buckley was arriving in a wheelchair, wearing a hospital gown. He looked a thousand years old, the bags under his eyes puffy, with heavy shadows beneath.

Rusty was behind the chair handles, steering his grandfather on an intercept course. A grin took over Bunker's lips as the words arrived. "Damn good to see you, Mayor. You too, Rusty."

"I could say the same thing about you," Buckley said in a steady tone, glancing back over his shoulder at Rusty, before bringing his attention back to Bunker. "From what my grandson told me, you've had quite the adventure the past few days."

"You could say that, but I'm afraid I won't be dancing a jig anytime soon."

"Yeah, you and me both, brother. But at least we're still alive and kicking. Rico and Zeke filled me in on the rest a little while ago. This town owes you a debt of gratitude, Jack, one I'm afraid we will never be able to repay."

"Well, it wasn't just me out there. Rusty was a big part of what happened. Without his help, I doubt any of us would have survived. You should be proud, Mayor. I know I am. He really stepped in when it mattered most."

Buckley smiled, looking honored.

"I never had kids, but if I did, I'd want a son just like Rusty. You did well raising him, sir."

"Thank you. It's not been easy over the years, but we're getting through it," Buckley said, turning his head. "Right, Rusty?"

"Yes, Grandpa. I'm just glad you both are going to be okay."

Buckley nodded. "Doc Marino is a miracle worker, I tell ya. I don't know what we'd do without him. Looks like he spent a little time on you, too, Jack."

Bunker couldn't hold back a laugh, aggravating the patchwork along his side. He winced before answering. "I feel like I've been run over by a tank."

"Curious choice of words, from what I've heard. A tank, huh? With Stephanie at the controls?"

Bunker raised an eyebrow, thinking about the severed head hanging from the cannon. "We had to improvise, but she did a great job. Only complained a couple of times the whole way."

"That must be a record for her," Buckley said as a full grin took over his lips.

Stephanie's beautiful face flashed in Bunker's mind, her eyes fierce and lips pinched. "The more I get to know her, the more I appreciate how rare that is."

"And that terrible business with Burt?"

Bunker shrugged, tucking in a lip before he spoke. "Yeah, who knew?"

"It's a shame, really."

"What about the Sheriff?"

Buckley shook his head, his lips silent. He didn't have to say anything; his eyes gave away the answer.

"He was a brave man," Bunker said, feeling a stab of pain slam into his chest.

"He will be missed by all those who were lucky enough to have known him," Buckley said, using that tone that politicians turn to when they're addressing a tragedy. He flashed a hand signal to Rusty. "Why don't you get Jack a little water? He looks thirsty."

Bunker licked his lips. "That's an understatement."

Rusty grabbed a pink water pitcher from the rolling tray a few feet away. He gave it to Bunker after adjusting the direction of the straw protruding from it.

Four sips later, Bunker gave the small jug to Rusty. The water was beyond refreshing, invigorating his body. He pointed at the ceiling. "The power's back?"

"Just here, unfortunately. A bunch of the guys pitched in an hour ago and moved the only working generator to the clinic. Everyone wants to see you get better, Jack."

"Wow, I don't know what to say. Thank you."

A long silence hung in the room, before Buckley spoke again. "Okay then, we should probably get going. There are some other people outside who want to say hi. Are you up for it?"

Bunker was tired and wished he could say no, but he felt obligated after what the town had just done for him. "Sure. Not a problem."

"You take care now. We'll stop back in a little later to check on you." With that, Rusty spun the chair and rolled Buckley out of the room.

A few seconds later a pair of crutches came through the door. So did Megan, her face lighting up in an ear-to-ear smile.

"Jack!" she shrieked, working the crutches with lightning speed.

Bunker's heart nearly leapt out of his chest. He pushed himself into a sitting position, powering through the pain.

The ebony child wrapped her arms around him the instant she arrived, her crutches falling to the floor in a loud crack. She had to stand on her toes and lean over the edge of the bed to reach him.

Bunker wanted to say something as she squeezed him tight, but he couldn't find the words. He was content to just hang on in silence.

She let go a minute later, standing with more weight on her good leg. "I brought you a present!"

"You did?"

"Uh-huh. It's a special present," she said, pulling an energy bar from her pocket. She held it up. "I wanted to get you something else, but they wouldn't let me. They said you can't eat it until later, when you're all better."

"Thank you, Megan," Bunker said, taking it from her, his heart filling with joy.

The video player in his mind replayed a scene of him with Megan before he left Tuttle's homestead. They were sitting together on the horse feeding station when he peeled open the wrapper on the treat he'd brought to cheer her up.

Now she was doing the same for him.

He was touched. Again, there were no words to express what he was feeling.

Stephanie and Jeffrey walked into the room next. Their pace was slow until Jeffrey broke free from his mom's hand in a sudden tug, then took off in a full sprint, his tiny feet pounding at the linoleum floor.

Jeffrey stood next to Megan with anxious feet, looking as if he was about to pee his pants. "Hi Jack!"

"Hey sport. It's good to see you."

Stephanie flashed Bunker a tentative smile, standing a few feet back, while the kids took the lead at the side of the bed.

Bunker pointed across the room. "Jeffrey, why don't you fetch my pants from the closet over there."

"Okay," the boy said, flying to the closet and returning a few moments later.

Bunker put his hand into the pocket and took out the Pokémon card. He gave it to Jeffrey. "Thanks for loaning this to me. It probably saved everyone's life. Especially mine."

Jeffrey grinned, snatching the card. It looked like he was about to ask a question, but he stopped when Stephanie stepped forward, corralling the little ones with her hands. "Come on, kids. Mr. Bunker needs his rest."

"Bye Jack," Jeffrey said before picking up Megan's crutches and giving them to her. He walked next to her as she navigated the room, hobbling through the door a few strides later.

Stephanie remained behind, her eyes locked on her son and Megan. As soon as the kids were out of sight, she turned and leaned forward, kissing Bunker full on the lips. It was closed mouth, but she held contact for a good five seconds.

After she released her lip lock and stood upright, Bunker said, "Well, hello to you, too. What was that for?"

"A thank you. From everyone," she said, turning her eyes to the door as if she expected something to happen.

Just outside, Allison Rainey and her mother Martha came into view. Victor appeared as well, and so did Dicky, towering behind the family. He stood tall with arms folded across his chest, looking both the part of sentry and that of warrior.

Bunker raised a hand to his forehead and sent the goliath a momentary salute.

Dicky stuck out his chin and nodded once in return.

All four of them turned ninety degrees and walked away, as if their task were complete.

"That poor girl," Stephanie said, shaking her head.

"Who, Allison?"

Stephanie twisted her mouth to the side. "You weren't there when she and Gus finally kissed. It was like something outta the movies. She's just gotta be heartbroken."

"If she is, she's not showing it."

"I'm afraid she's keeping it all inside at the moment. I'm not sure if that's for her sake or for her son's, but eventually she's gonna need to deal with what she's feeling."

"And Misty?"

"She disappeared as soon as we got back to town. So did Albert and his sidekick."

"Can't say I'm surprised."

"But Dallas found his mom and sisters. That's something at least. I'm sure they'll be in tomorrow to say hi."

"I look forward to meeting them."

Stephanie leaned forward again, coming right at him. Bunker thought she was going for another smooch, but that was not what happened. Stephanie brought her lips next to his ear and whispered, "I know what you did, Jack."

Bunker paused, working through the words she'd just used. His gut was telling him she was referring to Bill King's death. Her ex.

Stephanie continued, her lips only an inch from his ear. "Grace filled me in. You should have told me yourself."

"I'm sorry. I wanted to, but I didn't know how to tell you that I'd killed your son's father."

"From what Grace said, you didn't have a choice."

"I didn't. I hope you can forgive me. But the Mayor's life was at stake and I had to do something."

"I know, but please don't say anything to Jeffrey. Let me tell him when the time is right."

Stephanie pulled back and stood with her trademark piercing eyes locked onto his. She was clearly waiting to see what he was going to say next.

"You got it. My lips are sealed. I won't say a word."

Stephanie picked up his hand and held it softly. She rubbed her thumb across the skin, her eyes welling with tears. One dripped down her cheek after her lips started trembling. She spread his fingers apart and laced hers with his, holding on tight.

Bunker didn't know what to make of the gesture. "What's wrong, Steph?"

"I don't want to say goodbye." Her voice cracked as she stammered through the sentence.

Her words took him by surprise. "You're leaving?"

She nodded, her lips sealed in a thin line until she spoke again. "Dicky's going to take me and Jeffrey to Denver in the morning. I need to go find my mom and the rest of my family."

"Are you coming back?"

"I don't think so."

Bunker didn't want her to leave, but he wasn't going to stop her. Family had to come first. "Dicky will keep you safe. He's a good man, Steph."

"Yes, he is," she said as more tears flooded her cheeks. She stood there in silence for another thirty seconds before she let go of his hand. "There's one more person waiting to see you."

Bunker nodded in silence, wishing he could formulate his feelings into words. She was obviously waiting for him to say something meaningful. But he came up dry.

Stephanie looked disappointed when she turned away, putting a hand over her mouth in an emotional gasp. She left the room in a fast shuffle, crying.

A moment later, a new person appeared in the doorway wearing a uniform and a Sheriff's badge. It was Daisy, her hair pulled up and back, looking amazing.

Her tender eyes met his, holding his stare for what seemed like forever. Then she walked in, taking a direct course to him.

Bunker drew in a sudden breath, never taking his eyes from her. The new Sheriff knew his darkest secrets. He wondered how her new role would play out, both for her and for him.

Bunker didn't wait for Daisy to speak when she stood next to the bed. "Sorry about Gus. That was my fault. I never should have put him—"

Daisy touched a finger to his lips, stopping the rest of his words. When the tears filled her eyes, she crawled onto the edge of the hospital bed, then stretched out and nestled in close. She never said a word, laying her arm across his mid-section as her head found its way to the soft of his shoulder.

She'd made physical contact with him before, but somehow this was different.

Her intimacy ignited a calm that washed over Bunker, spreading from cell to cell until it tunneled its way into the marrow of his bones.

He knew what the sensation meant. It was something he'd been looking for ever since his father died.

He was home.

Finally.

In the arms of Daisy.

THE END

From the Author:

Thank you for reading through to the end of this saga. It's been a wonderful journey of discovery for me and I hope you've enjoyed the saga as well.

In case you weren't aware, I'm an independent author who relies on star ratings and reviews to help get the word out about my books. Reviews are very important to me and I truly need your help. Leaving a review, no matter how short would be greatly appreciated. Thank you for your assistance!

Want an all-new Jack Bunker story for free?

All you need to do is sign-up for my VIP Newsletter on my website at www.JayFalconer.com and you'll receive a free copy of the prequel *Bunker: Origins of Honor*.

Find out what happened in the days just before Bunker got on the train.

There's plenty of action in this exclusive story, so be sure to visit www.JayFalconer.com and join my VIP Newsletter, while this free book is still available.

About the Ambush Scene, IEDs, and Tactics
It took months of planning, setup, and execution to create the epic battle scene. I hope it hit the mark.

Of course, none of it would have come together without the invaluable guidance of two highly respected Marines, each of whom spent countless hours assisting me with military tactics, operations, weapons, munitions, IEDs, and booby-traps. Thank you, Ret. Sergeant Major Dennis R. and former sniper Rocket H. I am more than honored to be your friend.

Books by Jay J. Falconer

Frozen World Series
Silo: Summer's End
Silo: Hope's Return
Silo: Nomad's Revenge

American Prepper Series
Lethal Rain Book 1
Lethal Rain Book 2
Lethal Rain Book 3 (Coming Soon)
(previously published as *REDFALL*)

Mission Critical Series
Bunker: Born to Fight
Bunker: Dogs of War
Bunker: Code of Honor
Bunker: Lock and Load
Bunker: Zero Hour

Narrows of Time Series
Linkage
Incursion
Reversion

Time Jumper Series

Shadow Games

Shadow Prey

Shadow Justice

(previously published as *GLASSFORD GIRL*)

ABOUT THE AUTHOR

Jay J. Falconer is an award-winning screenwriter and USA Today Bestselling author whose books have hit #1 on Amazon in Action & Adventure, Military Sci-Fi, Post-Apocalyptic, Dystopian, Terrorism Thrillers, Technothrillers, Military Thrillers, Young Adult, and Men's Adventure fiction. He lives in the high mountains of northern Arizona where the brisk, clean air and stunning views inspire his day. When he's not busy working on his next project, he's out training, shooting, hunting, or preparing for whatever comes next. You can find more information about this author and his books at www.JayFalconer.com.

Awards and Accolades:

2020 USA Today Bestselling Book

2018 Winner: Best Sci-Fi Screenplay, Los Angeles Film Awards

2018 Winner: Best Feature Screenplay, New York Film Awards

2018 Winner: Best Screenplay, Skyline Indie Film Festival

2018 Winner: Best Feature Screenplay, Top Indie Film Awards

2018 Winner: Best Feature Screenplay, Festigious International Film Festival - Los Angeles

2018 Winner: Best Sci-Fi Screenplay, Filmmatic Screenplay Awards

2018 Finalist: Best Screenplay, Action on Film Awards in Las Vegas

2018 Third Place: First Time Screenwriters Competition, Barcelona International Film Festival

2019 Bronze Medal: Best Feature Script, Global Independent Film Awards

2017 Gold Medalist: Best YA Action Book, Readers' Favorite International Book Awards

2016 Gold Medalist: Best Dystopia Book, Readers' Favorite International Book Awards

Amazon Kindle Scout Winning Author

Dedication

This novel is dedicated to the loving memory of John, Dorothy, and Dana. We miss you more than you know.

Made in United States
Orlando, FL
29 August 2023

36501589R30407